THE DUKAYS

Zia – Betrayed in love, clinging to her aging father while embracing the new era and her blossoming womanhood, she follows her dream to become a photographer.

Kristina – Her sister, she lives on the edge of intrigue during the tumultuous changes in Europe before WWII.

Count István Dukay – Their father, one of the richest landowners in Europe. He refuses to see his centuries-old traditions crumbling all around him, even as his daughters leap into a drastically different world.

Filippo – He seduced Zia into marriage, only to scorn her love while he used her wealth.

Mihály – Zia's lover, a scientist who risked it all to bring equality to his country by attacking the Dukays and their way of life.

Rere – Count Dukay's "idiot" son, whose keen eye sees things for what they really are.

Mussolini, Hitler, King Charles and actual historical events share the stage in this story about a family and a time that are both changed forever.

The Dukays

The Dukays

Lajos Zilahy

Translated from the Hungarian
by John Pauker

Warwick, NY

ISBN 10: 1-933698-18-7
ISBN 13: 978-1-933698-18-2

To the memory of my sister Ica

Contents

Publisher's Note

Lajos Zilahy was famous throughout Europe, and ultimately the US, as a playwright and novelist. He was wounded on the Eastern front in WWI and was forced to hide from the Nazis during WWII. It was during this time that he wrote *The Dukays*, which was later inserted as the second book of a trilogy about the Dukay family. However, it was written before the other two books, and *The Dukays* stands alone as the author's masterpiece.

The Dukays was published in English shortly after the author fled to America after WWII. Two of the author's plays had Broadway productions and two were Hollywood films. Zilahy, 1891-1974, a pacifist during a time of international war, was a keen observer of the decay of the social order.

Born in Budapest and educated in the United States, John Pauker, translator, was managing editor of the quarterly *Furioso* and author of poetry, fiction and articles for *Story* magazine, *Town and Country*, *The Kenyon Review* and other periodicals and anthologies.

This edition marks the first publication of *The Dukays* in paperback in the US.

1. Ararat Castle

Chapter One

THE bells of the stubby, hexagonal medieval steeple were ringing eight o'clock of the evening in the village called Willensdorf. The summer evening was bright. The ringing of the chimes mingled with the hum of an unseen waterfall. Seated on the railway station's single bench a young footman in hunting livery, one Tobias, dozed while waiting for the incoming train. Half asleep, he felt that the chimes were stripes of burnished gold drawn across the murmur of the waterfall. Below the village the Inn River hurried along its cliff-bound channel, swinging its blue-green train like an agitated dowager who is swollen with anger and bursting to pour out all the things that have long been ready on her tongue. The scandal exploded at the watermill, white waves foaming indignantly. The mill protested, beating its paddles and querulously trying to explain an aspect of the great quarrel, but the Inn would not listen as she argued ahead, pulling at the hair of the bushes alongside and occasionally ducking them completely under in her rage.

The scream of a train whistle split the summer evening, as if someone had driven a dagger into the stomach of the Allenberg. At the foot of the mountain the train, like an escaping assassin, dodged sharply into the valley. It was the end of July, 1919.

Only one passenger descended at the station, an elderly woman who, after casting importunate glances at her fellow travelers to beg assurance that the stop was really Willensdorf, painstakingly lowered her large, knotty feet in their shapeless, high-laced shoes from the coach oblivious to the conductor's call of "Schnell, schnell, bitt'schön" because she understood not a word of German. At the moment when she and her baggage were finally disembarked and she stood a little dizzily on dry land, that very land itself began to retreat, moving her backward at a gradually increasing tempo. As the train vanished from her side, the ground beneath her feet suddenly came to a smooth and noiseless stop. Madame Couteaux looked around. The black and yellow postbox, the trainman in his red cap, the lachrymose water tank, the mountains imprisoning the sharp mountain air with their great blue pillars...Grand Dieu, comme tout cela est étrange—this was written on her face. How different, after the flat expanse of warm, glistening seashores along the Midi!

Madame wore a black dress, as if she were in mourning. Her meager hair, yellowish-blue with age, was covered by a simple felt hat, now askew. Her gray, bony face was the face of a peasant woman, the face so favored by painters and sculptors because it is expressive of an entire people. The eyebrows are scanty but the jaw and the mouth are that much stronger, liberally and honestly furnished for eating and for as much talking as possible. Such a face has plenty of room to display the greater and more common human emotions. Above Madame Couteaux's left upper lip there was a substantial mole out of which three strong, crescent-shaped hairs grew, like modest flowers in a pot, albeit flowers which were never watered.

The train departed and Madame's face still wore the terror of having been cast away on a desert island unfrequented by man. Furthermore, she was in the land of the Boche, and the inferno of Verdun had been glowing just one year ago. Ah, que tout m'est étrange! It had all come about so quickly. On Wednesday M. Pellissier...yes, on Wednesday he wired from Paris to ask if she was willing to undertake the French instruction of an eight-year-old little girl in Austria. Certainly, certainly, if Monsieur Pellissier requested it, though she had never acted as a language instructor before. Came the next telegram: she was to take the train and notify Stephan Dukay, Willensdorf, of the time of her arrival. She would be met at the station. Half the population of her village helped her to compose an itinerary, and then she wrote ahead her exact time of arrival and even sent a photograph.

Tobias was already at her side, smiling sheepishly as he took her baggage, a large checkered English suitcase, reminiscent of the previous century, and a battered handbag.

"Merci, merci, mon cher ami," Madame Couteaux said, her somewhat hoarse voice expressing friendship and the recognition of mutual servitude. They started to move along but exchanged no further words, for Tobias did not know a syllable of French. Leaving the station, they did not go toward the village but in the opposite direction. Madame Couteaux had to exert herself a little to keep up with the footman's athletic stride. Bent over, she hurried after him with the gestures of someone leaning on the air as if it were a railing. As she walked, the outline of the black dress betrayed her sagging breasts and sagging belly. At the edge of the white highway, which was bordered with red fruit trees, an ancient yellow house stood on the hillside, enveloped by a small park and with several outbuildings at the end of a garden. All this revealed nothing about the inhabitants of the house or the significance of the name: Stephan Dukay—told nothing of his function or his fortune. The old house merely attended with wrinkled, quizzical brows and made no answer to the mute questions of the newcomer.

Madame Couteaux, who in the course of her journey had already abandoned herself to an unknown fate, was the widow of a Frenchman, sometime master chef of the Berkeley Hotel in London. She had often seen corpulent Queen Victoria hold aloft her famous salmon-colored umbrella while riding along Piccadilly. Out of the sheer arrogance which often occurs in adherents of some of the greater languages, the master chef and his wife lived in London for twenty years without learning to speak English. Although London is like a thick-skinned beast whose armor repels every foreign phrase, not only the directors and waiters of the hotel but even its kitchen-boys persisted in speaking French, for the simple reason that the majority of them came from France or from Switzerland.

At the turn of the century Monsieur Couteaux and his goatee could no longer withstand their incurable homesickness, so he decided to retire to the village of his birth and there, at the edge of the Mediterranean, to realize, out of his careful hoard of English pounds, an old ambition. He wanted to breed lobsters, on the theory that whereas the Midland Bank paid only one and a half percent interest on the pound, a single lobster laid three hundred thousand eggs or, if in an ill humor, only three thousand—but even in the case of the latter caprice its rate of interest was still considerably larger. The sunny little meridional village was one of the many centers of France's remunerative fireside industry; every household for blocks and blocks around was devoted to the production of carved briar pipes which bore the imprint "Made in England"—the neighboring villagers specialized in the production of umbrella handles—and every smoky hearth was jammed with the shiny copper pots and earthenware pans in which, with judicious admixtures of white wine and cognac and thyme and pepper, simmered that most glorious of delicacies, tripe, notably *tripe à la Cannes*. However, the little French village did not live up to its imagined promise, for native lands generally do not in reality possess the excellences imputed to them from afar by an aching nostalgia. Lobster breeding was a failure. In fact, it ended in a series of ugly lawsuits, of which one was so vehement that a fist-fight broke out at its close and during the fight the plaintiff knocked out Monsieur Couteaux's left eye, something which would never have happened in the enormous white kitchen of the Berkeley Hotel, although even there the master chef once came to blows with a waiter in a matter of feminine honor that had nothing to do with Madame

Couteaux. After the failure of lobster breeding the former chef took to drink on the remnants of his accumulated pounds. All day long he could be seen sipping his apéritif on the narrow terrace of the Café du Grand Monde, where the four tiny metal tables were hardly larger than fairly substantial Stetson hats. Here the retired master chef, his single eye all bloodshot, spent the day casting insults at the passers-by. He died a few years later, leaving a widow and daughter in utter poverty. Heroic struggles followed: threadbare years of want, a grocery store, a sewing course, and as the years went by nothing more momentous happened than that little Louise grew up and one year ago, when she was already at work as a certified teacher, she died in a few days during the influenza epidemic, forgetful of the debt owed to a weary mother. But mourning and dark hopelessness lasted only a few months. Monsieur Pellissier's wire came from Paris, and now here was the liveried footman leading her somewhere. Here, and even carrying her luggage, was the shape and objectification of all heavenly care and concern.

Meanwhile the eight-year-old little girl, having awaited this moment in great excitement and listened anxiously for the whistle of the train, was darting from window to window like a caged bird. Was the Frenchwoman here yet?

Tobias rang the doorbell. The little girl darted to open the door. In the intervening seconds Madame Couteaux stood outside with a bad conscience, for the photograph she had sent by way of introduction had been taken in the good London days and on it the mole above her lip was carefully retouched. She was red with the excitement of an anxiety to overcome the probable disappointment of this first meeting. All of a sudden the door swung wide and there before her stood the little girl, just as flushed with excitement. Her ash-blonde hair fluttered about her thin shoulders. The clear green eyes in the delicately freckled face were wide with expectancy and joy. Her narrow, pale little arms flew open for Madame Couteaux with such a sweet and thirsty gesture that the widow cried out, an inimitably French guttural cry encompassing the several incoherent words with which she instantly locked the image of the child into her heart and locked her physically, too, into her ancient body, pressing and holding the little girl interminably.

"Aaah...te voici...tu sera la mienne...ah, ma petite...here you are...you're going to be all mine...dear little thing..."

She held the little girl at arms' length and then embraced her again, her face red, murmuring all the while in a voice that seemed to scold or quarrel. Madame Couteaux had imagined that the meeting would be cold and polite, and she had supposed that the child would be distrustful and suspicious, but something completely different imbued her when the door flew open so suddenly. The two of them embraced stormily, laughing and stammering like two souls that have finally managed to find one another. The child's joyous outbreak seemed almost incomprehensible.

"Elle n'est pas heureuse," she muttered to herself as they went into the corridor. This child is not happy. The child has no mother. Or if she has one, then the mother plays no part in her life. This child simply thirsts for affection.

There was a good deal of truth in her supposition, but it was supplemented by something that Madame Couteaux did not discover until later. A German governess had attended the girl so far, nagging and torturing her out of a sense of duty. Only the day before had she been liberated from Fräulein Elsa. Up to this point the child did not know a word of French. During the war it was impossible to secure French governesses; had it been possible, it would have been considered unpatriotic.

They stood in the corridor, still clinging to each other. Tobias disappeared with the baggage, and no one else in the household appeared. Madame Couteaux's face was tearful as she held the girl:

"Quel est ton nom? What is your name?"

The child did not understand her question. Madame pointed to herself.

"Je…suis…Marianne!"

Speaking the name again, she pointed to herself each time.

"Marianne! Marianne! Marianne!"

Then she quickly pointed to the little girl and poked her chest as if trying to elicit sound from a key on a mute little piano.

"Tu es? Tu es?"

The child finally understood and cried out, beaming:

"Zia!"

"Ah, Zia!"

Laughing, they embraced like two people who have definitely established a relationship and as if their first outpourings had been based on some ridiculous mistake.

"Ah, tu es Zia! Nom charmant…Terézia?"

"Ja."

"Nicht ja!" Madame Couteaux cried sharply, for this constituted her entire knowledge of German. She drew her brows into a furious frown—only a playful exaggeration, of course, and intended to amuse Zia. And she gave the child, like a bit of sweetness passed from mouth to mouth, the French for yes:

"Oui, oui, oui..."

And then she laughed aloud again.

It was in these moments, preceding both Versailles and Trianon, that Madame Couteaux and Zia signed the armistice and re-established the peace of the world.

In Madame, Zia discovered anew the velvet Teddy bear of her early childhood, now grown up and alive but still the mother bear of old; so she snuggled up to her and, embracing her awkwardly, said with a tearful and tight little laugh: "Dear sweet..." but the rest of the words remained unspoken, expressed only by her shining eyes. Perhaps she wanted to say: "Dear sweet Madame, dear sweet Marianne, dear sweet Nanny," but after a few seconds she added just one word, "...Berili," and this with a frightened giggle. It was the name she had given the Teddy bear that only a few years ago she used to take to bed with her, used to squeeze and play with in outbreaks of her desire to give and receive affection. In that one word she found the right name for the person she had so ardently awaited, the person who was different from what she had imagined, uglier, older, but one who radiated good humor and fiery maternal warmth. And in Madame Couteaux's soul Louise had come back to life, her little lost Louise with the prominent ears and the thin long nose inherited from her father, with her delicately traced dark eyebrows and her sad, velvety glance. She could be a mother once more, overwhelmingly, exuberantly, like the meridional peasant woman, the Carcassonne cheesemaker's daughter that she was.

At the end of the corridor—thickly studded with Alpine ibex antlers—there was a guest room, and Zia pushed Berili into it, mutely showed her the washstand and left her there. Berili looked about the old-fashioned, simply furnished room; its walls too were decorated with different varieties of antlers and stuffed birds, and there were some framed pictures which showed the effects of the dampness of the wall. The pictures, relics of the past century, represented hunting scenes. Berili concluded from all this that she had happened into the home of a well-to-do forester or a forestry superintendent.

A half hour later Tobias knocked on her door and led her to the dining room. The room had an odd, sweet fragrance, for it was paneled to shoulder height with branches of yellow *cirbolya* pine. Only three people sat at the large table: Zia and two men. One of the men was a broad-shouldered athletic type, with a completely shaven head revealing the bony structure of his skull. His piercing black eyes seemed too small for the large face. He stood up and introduced himself. Berili clung to the man's muscular hand and flooded him with questions, but Mr. Badar answered her only with an apologetic gesture and a yellow-toothed grin, for he did not speak French.

The other man, who remained seated, presented a frightening and horrible aspect. His fish-eyes looked in two directions, one at the ceiling and the other at the center of the table. It was at once apparent that this young man was an idiot. A high winged collar enclosed his thick bull's neck like a manacle. There was something in him of an animal's touching sadness, and something laughable as well. Giggling, Zia squirmed on her chair, for at this moment Berili's face was like a blackboard on which, inscribed in chalk, two words appear: Fright and Horror.

During dinner Berili was condemned to silence. The language spoken around her was full of short *e*'s and similar to the croaking of frogs. She knew it was not German, for on the train she had spent half a day listening to spoken German. The German tongue is full of short *i*'s as if one had a mouthful of thorns: ich, mich, nicht, wir, dir, Sie…Ah, c'est horrible! She had once observed the English language in this way, noting the ubiquitous long *i*'s: I, why, my, right, like…and then the crazy Italians, with nothing but *i*'s!

Not a thing happened in the house for four days: it was like a haunted house. Had Zia not been constantly at her side, like a nestling kitten, she would have gone mad. The routine of meals was exactly like dinner on the first night, and the young idiot's eyes kept pointing in two directions, one at the ceiling and the other at the center of the table. The fifth day came, and she was still unable to exchange an intelligible word with anyone. She felt as if she had fallen into a deep well and would never be able to climb out. And the eternal croaking around her! Where was the family? The large table, the numerous rooms, the many hats and overcoats hung in the hall, the toilet articles in the bathroom—the whole climate of the house spoke of men and women who belonged there but were absent for some unknown reason.

On the sixth day, as nightfall approached, the situation changed completely. Three automobiles slid to an almost noiseless stop at the entrance and ten people jumped out to storm into the house, filling it with raucous clamor, populating the quiet rooms with the noise and excitement of what must have been a great event or significant political turn.

The door of Zia's room popped open and a tall gentleman stepped in. He swung Zia off the floor, kissed her on both cheeks and laughingly cradled her in his arms like an overgrown infant. Beneath his black Turkish mustache his lips were red and his teeth still white. He might have been fifty years old. At first he laughed and croaked at Zia in his incomprehensible tongue, without even a glance for Berili. There was something oriental in his manner, and something unusually distinguished. When he put Zia down, he turned to Berili and offered his hand with a kind, warm smile:

"–Dukay."

And with his warm, murmuring voice he began to talk in French. In French, in French! Madame Couteaux felt that this tall, sympathetic man had snatched her up out of the well. Bursting with joy, she stretched out her hand and almost embraced him, although Dukay had merely asked a few questions about her trip, her arrival, about messages from Monsieur Pellissier and whether she liked the little cricket—meaning Zia.

The little girl's mamma entered the room too, with a silk cape about her and on her hat the sort of veil—this one was lilac-colored—that ladies then wore for traveling in open cars. She seemed about forty-five, with very delicate lines, but ice-cold. She spoke excellent French, although with a harsh accent. And then came the others, twenty-three-year-old Kristina with her unbelievably slim waist and large, blue, sleepy eyes; György, a short-necked, stocky young man who resembled none of his brothers or sisters; and János, a young scamp of thirteen whose gawky arms and legs made him look like a paddle-bird. Berili learned that the idiot was Zia's eldest brother.

The rooms were filled with trunks and everyone began to pack feverishly. The mistress of the house stood talking in the corridor to an Austrian whose hat was decorated with a brush made of goat's beard; he stood before her meekly, hat in hand.

Next morning the caravan departed, back to Hungary: three passenger cars and a trailer truck jammed with luggage. The Willensdorf hunting lodge was to be shut down and the keys were handed to the brush-hatted Austrian with whom Madame Dukay had been talking in the corridor the day before; who now continued to bow low even after the last automobile had swept away in a cloud of dust.

The passengers were noisy and good-humored, as if merely returning from an extended but extremely jolly excursion. The grownups, to tell the truth, had spent most of the excursion in Vienna's larger hotels.

The first closed car carried the master and mistress, Zia and Madame Couteaux, known as Berili to the entire family by now.

"What is your real name?" Dukay asked Madame Couteaux.

"Marianne."

"Marianne!" cried Dukay, as if he knew something special about that name. Then, closing his left eye and giving every syllable the emphasis of a secret password, he asked:

"Connaissez-vous Marianne? Do you know Marianne?"

Madame Couteaux, surprised at Dukay's broad knowledge of French history, answered with a swift gesture. Raising her left hand in front of her, she quickly tapped her thumb three times with the tip of her forefinger. Then she brought her thumb to her forehead and, lowering it, ran her thumb from her heart to her stomach.

"Très bien!" Dukay cried, laughing.

"What is that?" Madame Dukay asked in her low, pleasant voice that was always somewhat distant, far removed from mundane things. Not a single muscle of her face moved even as she put her question.

Dukay—they generally spoke French to each other—explained that during the reign of Napoleon III in the Fifties a secret society was formed in Paris for the re-establishment of the Republic. The conspirators used the "Do you know Marianne?" query and the gesture as sign and countersign. That was how red-capped Marianne became the symbol of the Republic.

Then he started to talk of other things. He had said all this merely by way of historical anecdote, to parade his learning a bit.

During the journey Berili learned little more about the cause and purpose of the trip than that the Hungarian Commune had collapsed two days ago and the Dukay family was now in a position to return to its estate on the farther side of the Danube. In March, when the Communists seized power, Dukay and his wife had crossed the Austrian border in disguise, one dressed as a chimneysweep and the other as a peasant woman. The fleeing family assembled at the Willensdorf hunting lodge, a property of Madame Dukay, who was of Austrian extraction.

Eyeing the undulate landscape from the automobile, Berili was beset by a feeling that these regions, gradually and slyly, were bent on tricking her. But what seemed to be treachery was, perhaps, no more than tenderness: the East was reluctant to launch too sudden an assault upon this daughter of a Carcassonne cheesemaker. As the autos descended from the Austrian mountains the black pine forests made a change of costume as if in slow motion, became oaks and poplars. And soon afterward tall green cedars appeared, mighty grenadiers—never before had Berili seen such giant trees. The narrow, cobblestoned and winding streets of diminutive Austrian hamlets, the compact little houses of medieval German design with iron grillwork at their windows, the Gasthäuser trimmed with gaudy signboards, the diligent little shops, the great wide peasant courtyards, the weighty, quivering-thighed draught horses in their ornate trappings, the tiny flower gardens—all these gradually disappeared, and in the course of a brief hour the hues of the West gave way to the vast Eastern plains onto which summer sunshine poured endlessly, yellow and well-nigh shadeless. Bicycles went wheeling along the roadside less and less frequently, as though civilization were taking leave of the travelers. Huge hay-wagons hobbled toward them, their tremendous loads sweeping either edge of the highway, and the teams of four oxen which drew these wagons, immense white behemoths with sooty thick necks, boasted forked horns so large that they attracted particular wonder from Berili. They lumbered ahead with their heavy loads as slowly as if they meant to make an especial show of the dignified calm of the East for the edification of the loquacious, gesticulating old Frenchwoman. The aspect of the villages changed too: dissolving, the roads flowed in broad swathes among tiny reed- and straw-thatched houses which seemed almost to hug the earth, as if for centuries they had existed under a constant threat. The flocks of geese multiplied until their patches of white appeared to be splashes of whitewash along the side of the road; and the automobiles were periodically forced to slow down when they happened into the midst of great flocks of sheep which bleated with boundless melancholy while the vehicles swam among them as if on a sea of greasy fleece. And to the right and left of the roadside stood hordes of cattle, grubbing the bleak pastures to a motley of blackness. Berili felt as though she had found her way into some larder of legendary dimensions, and she was not mistaken, for this fat Hungarian soil, like an enormous breast, had ever nourished the lean ribs of the Austrian mountains. The ploughed fields, unmarked, without boundaries, stretched into infinity about them, giving the impression that they were in the realm of giants. Modestly, almost apologetically, an occasional small farm came into sight, with curious mosquito-shaped wells and, invariably, a round-headed, fleecy-furred white dog that broke from beside the hedge, barked at the passing automobiles in ardent rage and pursued them with leaps and bounds until the halter about his neck sent him tumbling.

Around noon they reached a village called Ararat; it lay on the topmost plateau in the midst of a range of gently sloping hills. Just below the village they turned to drive along an apparently endless stone fence and stopped at a gigantic iron gate whose pillars supported a pair of granite angels. The gate opened at the sound of honking horns, and they began the last leg of the journey: through the park, along the yellow-sanded roads, over bridges which spanned running brooks and under the shade of century-old trees drove the cars. To the left a giant fishpool glistened, its smooth gold and silver mirror furrowed by swans as they raced shoreward at the din of the approaching vehicles. On the opposite bank a Chinese pagoda gleamed in the tumid sunlight, coruscating through the mournful willows with vermilion, blue, yellow and black tints. Then, after the red clay rectangles of tennis courts, they reached a wide, level lawn on which the castle stood, its wings outspread, the ancient tower of the chapel at its center, as tremendous as an ocean liner, with countless windows.

In front of the main entrance, in the middle of a pool lined with tinted stones, stood a fountain which cast its rainbowed and glowing rays and pearls as high as the second floor. A peacock trailed the exquisite train of its long tail at the edge of the pool, while acrobatic green parrots on brass perches broke into a raucous chorus and a black and tan great Dane with cropped ears stood in petrified scrutiny of the newcomers, as if unwilling to believe the evidence of his eyes, unable to grasp the fact that his long-lost masters had truly returned. Flower beds in front of the castle veritably flamed with color in the noonday sunshine, and the air was full of sweet, heavy fragrances. Everything seemed so very amazing, so very improbable. The huge three-story castle, nobly compact and ponderous in the style of the Empire, stood forth proudly in the brilliant light, the monotony of its ocher-yellow walls relieved by the sun-faded Pompeian red of the shutters. The automobiles came to a halt at the main entrance, where four Grecian pillars supported a lofty balcony. Madame Couteaux looked about her and said only: "Oh, là là."

Men and women both, obviously the castle staff, thronged around the dusty cars. But it seemed to Berili that the signs of welcome manifested by these people were merely imposed on their faces, mutely, soundlessly. And she was further struck by the fact that elderly men kissed not only the hand of their mistress but that of their master. This affected her like that greeting whereby the Chinese are said to rub noses, something she had heard of but never seen.

The family referred to the castle—baroque in the extreme, with ninety-two rooms—as "the house." There was, in this term, not only a sense of inheritance but also a seeming protest against the word "castle," for in the past fifty years every three-room Hungarian villa with tin turrets and a grape arbor at its side had been called a castle by the lawyer or greengrocer who built it.

Some of the walls of the Ararat house had truly ancient histories. The Gothic vaults of the so-called "old dining room" were remnants of a Benedictine monastery which had been the only stone edifice in the Pannonian swamps and marshes of the tenth century, standing like a lonely torch in the barbarian darkness. Five hundred years later King Sigismund gave license to Demeter Zoskay, who in 1414 had accompanied him to the Council of Constance, to erect an armored fortress on an appropriate site: *unum castellum seu fortalitium aedificare,*—as the original warrant read. In November of that same year a royal decree granted Demeter Zoskay the juridical right to build, and in the spring of the following year he began the construction of his fortified castle. There was no trace of the original drawing and estimates for the castle, although its walls guarded a great number and variety of relics of the Hungarian Renaissance. Historic love affairs had been concluded and destinies decided in its bedchambers and buildings, most notable among them the decapitation of old Kelemen Dukay in the former onion storehouse, in 1670. At that time the castle had already been in the hands of the Dukay family for two hundred years. At the beginning of the eighteenth century it became vacant and for more than sixty years only owls and bats used it for a roost. In 1759 Lászlo Dukay tore down the castle and began construction of the present baroque palace. But the old fortress did not disappear completely. The Old Tower, as it was called, became the western buttress of the new castle—either out of sentiment or from shortage of funds—and similarly the quondam bootmaker's lodge, adjoining the Old Tower, and the halberdiers' cottage were spared; the latter's mantelpieces are still in evidence, for it has since been remodeled into a garage. According to family tradition, in 1758 Maria Theresa said to Lászlo Dukay at the annual court ball, "Next year's maneuvers will be held beyond the Danube and I shall stay at your castle...." Lászlo Dukay replied: "I shall expect you, Majesty!" although at that time he had no castle, merely the ancient uninhabitable owl's nest and belfry. Nevertheless he careened and panted home from Vienna, and a year later the new baroque edifice stood ready; the empress occupied one of its mezzanine bedchambers for three days, and ever since then it had been called the Maria Theresa Room.

During the nineteenth century they continued to patch and renovate the castle, and finally a few years before the war, in 1910, the present proprietor, Stephan Dukay, installed electricity, running water and nineteen modern bathrooms.

The village, an ancient settlement which dated back to the first conquest, was originally called Hemlice. But in those days it did not lie here, on the plateau below the castle, but three miles away, in the depths of the valley, where the white ribbon of the county highway can now be seen. The devastating Danubian floodwaters of 1625 raged even as far as this valley, and a prodigious inundation it must have been, for the Danube is at a great remove from here. In a matter of hours the torrential waves reduced the tiny clay huts of the seisin to mud. Bundling up their goods and chattels, the inhabitants took refuge under the walls of the Dukay fortress on the plateau. In the course of the years they built a new village, to which the Biblical fancy of the people gave the name Ararat. From that time forth Hemlice existed only in old records.

The Ararat estate included fifty-two thousand acres of arable land; from his mother's side, in addition, Stephan Dukay inherited an eighteen-thousand-acre property at Gere, and from his uncle Mihály forty thousand acres of woodland in the county of Csík; among Dukay's other holdings there was the palace on Septemvir Utca in Buda, and nine apartment houses in Pest, and the Dukay Palace on Bösendorferstrasse in Vienna, and a more modest three-story mansion on the Rue Général Ferreyolles in Paris, not to mention two steam mills in Hungary, a large sugar refinery at Gere, the sawmills in Transylvania, the copper mines in Hovad and the eight thousand five hundred sixty-two head of cattle, three thousand one hundred forty horses (including the famed stud at Ararat), more than twenty thousand sheep, five thousand six hundred and twelve swine all told (sucklings included), and poultry to the approximate number of twenty-five thousand.

The above statistics were assembled by Sir Lawrence Gomma out of sheer boredom once when he spent a period of months hunting mouflon in the game preserves of the castle. Sir Lawrence set out for a long walk one afternoon, but soon he came running back breathlessly and, upsetting the chairs about him in his haste to grab a rifle of the highest caliber, dashed away again oblivious to the warnings shouted after him. It was later discovered that he spent the next half hour flat on his stomach stalking the two oxen of an Ararat peasant, having mistaken them for wild Cape buffaloes. He bagged them both. One of the sources of the nobleman's error was his failure to realize the considerable difference between Hungary and Africa; he even referred to the peasants in the field, having seen their baggy trousers, as "natives." The foolish arrogance of the clubs along Pall Mall lurked in all this, of course, but he managed to hint, nevertheless, at a somewhat embarrassing essence of reality.

At that time, having also catalogued the art treasures of the Septemvir Utca palace—chief among an abundant sampling of Courbet, Delacroix, Renoir, Greco and Munkácsy was the *Woman in Purple* of Corot and a unique fragment of Ispahan tapestry, the only one in the world of its kind—and the family jewels as well, the same Sir Lawrence Gomma estimated the value of Stephan Dukay's fortune at fifty-six million dollars.

This fortune suffered some reverses as a result of the Communist revolution. Although it took the police only a few days to restore the furniture which had been looted from the house at Ararat, a dark and greasy sickle-shaped spot was found on the silk upholstery of one of the light green sofas, for Comrade Ibrik had taken his afternoon naps on it during the delightful summer season of the Commune; and so the upholsterer had to be summoned to spread more pure silk on that noble piece of furniture. Otherwise the Dukay fortune reverted to its own without substantial loss, and after the return of the family—on August 2nd, 1919—life was resumed at the point where it had been abandoned in the days of Franz Joseph.

The household staff of the castle totaled fifty-eight persons. Only five of them failed to return—Miss Wenlock and Mr. John, son the stablemaster, British subjects who had left for home when war was declared; Mam'selle Barbier and Monsieur Cavaignac, loyal citizens of France; and Józsi Simon, a footman who lost his left arm in 1915 during the battle of Chlebowitz, near Lemberg. It was rumored that he later became a Communist agitator.

✝

Encyclopedias write of the Dukay family as follows:

THE DUKAY FAMILY (of Duka and Hemlice, duchy and county), one of the most ancient lines of Magyar nobility; springing, according to the patents, from the Ordony family which, in the days of Árpád and the Hungarian national incursion to the crescent valley, established itself by the right of prime tenure on land—namely, Hemlice and Duka—that today still constitutes a part of the entire estate, taking the name of the latter holding. The Ordony clan, having participated in the original allocation of national land, settled in the county of Bihar and became the root of various family branches, some of which have died out. Among these families were: Ozy, Zoskay, Néma, Alacsy, etc. The Dukay line, gradually outstripping the others in wealth and position, assumed a place of prime importance over the centuries and is still flourishing. The authenticity of the family origin is based on genealogies presented in the course of family lawsuits and accepted by the Curia. According to these genealogies, Pál (de genere Ordony), a descendant of the paternal ancestor István, bore the name of Dukay as early as the fifteenth century. Among his progeny was Endre (died 1593), whose daughter Julia became the second wife of King Omello of Naples. Mihály Dukay (died 1645), the first Lord Lieutenant in the family, was granted new patents for his estates and elevated to the county by Ferdinand II. In 1791 György, a descendant of Pál, was elevated to an hereditary dukedom by King Leopold II. In 1796 György married Princess Maria Josephine of Hesse. He died without issue in 1829, whereupon the István branch of the family assumed succession. The family crest is as follows: black millstone on a cordiform escutcheon with double bars dexter and cerulean with argent, below a green woodpecker ensconced on a heptangular stelliform or coronet in a field of vermilion.

The encyclopedias go on to list at length the more prominent members of the family, among whom there was one short-lived palatine, one cardinal, two bishops, three diplomats, two lords chamberlain, one renowned cattle breeder, one famous lion hunter, one less famous lyric poet, one Costa Rican brothel keeper and an Ohio taxi driver. The last two are not mentioned in any encyclopedia although these two Dukays added more romance to the family history than any of the bishops or lords chamberlain. Similarly, the encyclopedias maintain a

17

discreet silence on the subject of Irma Dukay, the eternally good-humored "mad countess" who at the age of sixty served a suburban lawyer as chambermaid and cook, and spent her free half-Sundays competing in the clay-pigeon tourneys on St. Margaret's Island, where she won occasional prizes.

According to Prinsault, the French genealogist, the vermilion blazon of the family crest symbolizes, in virtues, heroism and bravery; in sanguine humors, passion; in planets, Saturn; in signs of the zodiac, the Ram; in precious stones, the ruby; in days of the week, Saturday.

Therefore it is understandable that there was an overwhelming number of rubies among the Dukay jewels and, according to the family chronicles, that every major Dukay enterprise had been undertaken on a Saturday. This was the reason, then, for the breathless haste with which they packed until dawn at Willensdorf—in order to leave on the following day, for that was Saturday and they did not want to wait another whole week. Thus they regained their native land on a Saturday, and occupied their castle and vast estates once again on that extremely significant turning point in history.

According to the interpretation of Spanberg, the German expert in heraldry, the green woodpecker represents human life and the inconstancy of circumstance, a warning lest one become overconfident of wealth and fortune.

Chapter Two

ISTVÁN—or Stephan—Dukay was born in 1868 in the Maria Theresa room of the Ararat castle with two prominent gynecologists from Vienna and Prague in attendance, as well as the county practitioner and Mrs. Puttony, the ninety-year-old local midwife. The gynecologists received a daily fee of fifty gold crowns apiece; Dr. Birkássy, the bearded general practitioner, five florins; and Mrs. Puttony, one florin twenty kreutzers.

The child, Peter Dukay's first-born son, entered the world with two whole teeth at four o'clock in the morning. Next morning the famous specialists took their places in a jingle-belled sledge-and-six, with their enormous fur capes bundled about them and their pockets stuffed with a thousand-crown bonus, and they left the castle with the air of men who have truly done their duty. Dr. Birkássy and Mrs. Puttony remained at the bedside, but they received no bonus at all because the young countess died of puerperal fever three days later.

The young countess was buried with great pomp in the family mausoleum at Ararat. The entire nation went into mourning, for the newspapers of the capital reported that the young countess, née Baroness Adrienne Zoskay, "went to her untimely grave as the last female representative of the ancient Zoskay line, *de genere* Ordony." Discreet telegrams of condolence arrived from the specialists in Vienna and Prague—the telegraph was a big thing in those days—but they did not return their thousand crowns apiece.

The newcomer, whom fate had deposited—one year after the Alliance of 1867—on the threshold of the Austro-Hungarian Monarchy and of the great age of Franz Joseph, was baptized István and given over to governesses and tutors in his early youth. He already rode excellently at the age of six; at the age of thirteen, despite his father's every remonstrance, he entered a gentlemen's steeplechase. The famous yellow mare "Go On," however, tripped over the water jump. Except for a broken leg the young count suffered no injury, for the mare had plunged into the water. His face was covered with two inches of mud when they pulled him out. In the following year the first knuckle of his left index finger fell a victim of carelessness. The local newspaper's account of the unfortunate accident was headlined "Playing with Firearms." But this did not discourage the young count in his further career as a hunter. At the district hunt in the fall of the same year he accidentally shot one of the grooms, János Kalap, in the stomach, and although Dr. Birkássy painstakingly picked sixty-three pieces of shot out of his belly old Kalap kept to his bed for six months and would cheerfully have remained bedridden for another six months, since the estate gave him ten acres of land and a breeding cow as compensation.

Young István Dukay shot his first stag at the age of fifteen, and a year later, at the Görgeny hunt in which Archduke Rudolf also took part, he shot his first bear.

At the age of eighteen he simultaneously contracted the two venereal diseases, gonorrhea and syphilis, from a Budapest streetwalker named Angela with whom he nevertheless fell madly in love. But he was successfully cured of all three ailments, although he lost considerable weight as a result of the strenuous quicksilver treatment He was in any case a slim, tall boy, with gleaming silken hair the color of toasted bread-crust. His warm eyes, too, were dark brown and constantly ready for laughter, while his nose was delicately thin and slightly bent. In those days he had begun to wear a narrow Turkish mustache and it became a habit of his to scratch the narrow mustache with the crippled forefinger of his left hand whenever it was necessary to concentrate, something he did not care to do at all. He availed himself of even the most insignificant opportunity for a hearty laugh. He had a rather large mouth, and on those occasions his sensitive, fleshy lips first opened soundlessly, revealing strong, stubby teeth, and then the laughter issued from his throat with the dry, hoarse sound of a thick-voiced rasp. His face was rather handsome, his glance sincere and full of a kindly curiosity. Measured by the strictest standards, his forehead could have been somewhat higher and his well formed ears somewhat larger. His small ears gave the impression that István Dukay, in the hustle and bustle of the great storehouse through which customers thronged to collect their human particulars, had accidentally been issued a set of ears just one size too small. But this, though noticeable, was not disturbing.

By that time he was known as Dupi everywhere. Even the footmen called him Count Dupi. In general, none of the members of Austrian or Hungarian aristocracy managed to outlive the nicknames of childhood. Historical figures, who had already been cast—most often on horseback—in bronze, answered at home to names that are usually given to lapdogs. A former prime minister, for example, was known to his family and in the Casino as Hunyi, not to mention the many Sityis, Butyis, Pipis and Popos, diplomats and lords chamberlain of manly and dignified mien whose life-sized oil portraits with the then fashionable short-trimmed Henry IV beard glared down from the mighty and forbidden heights of society in various halls of state. Possibly some determined historian will be able to detect the decadence of aristocracy lurking, as far back as the final quarter of the past century, in the overripe sweetness of these nicknames, but at the same time the scholar will have to record that noblewomen guarded the original historical beauty of their names to the very end; the Elizabeths, Juliannas and Susannes never permitted themselves to be demoted to Bebis, Jucis or Zizis when the disease of diminutives began to plague the entire civilized world.

Upon finishing military school Count Dupi became a lieutenant in the Viennese Dragoons. It would have been difficult to obtain an exact estimate of his intellectual capacities, for his good-natured instructors never harped on that problem to any extent. Generally Dupi was a good-hearted lad. He gave early proof of this when, while still a lieutenant in Vienna, having endorsed a twenty-thousand-florin note for one of his fellow officers Dupi, being still under age, eased his friend's financial difficulties further by endorsing the note with his father's name as well, at the advice of the "broker." When the note was presented to Peter Dukay, the State Counselor—the jurist Dr. Rainer—rushed to Vienna and after explaining to Dupi that such acts were contrary to certain legal statutes warned him to refrain from these acts in the future, particularly because His Excellency the old count did not approve. Dupi thoughtfully scratched his mustache with his crippled finger. He had acted with true unselfishness in the interest of a friend, without receiving a penny of the money himself. Of course there was no reason for him to take any of it, since his father kept him liberally supplied with funds.

Around Christmas time he wrote a letter to his father explaining that after considerable deliberation he had decided to marry his first and only true love, Sacy Klein, who was so popular at that time in Vienna that even her age could be precisely established. The soubrette, a singer of incredibly filthy little songs which were only somewhat mitigated by Viennese slang, performed on the stage of the tiny old Apollo Theater and was known to be at least twenty years older than Dupi, who had just reached his twenty-first birthday.

The paternal reply was late. It was effectively preceded by an order of the War Ministry forthwith transferring István Dukay from the Viennese Dragoons to the Lebovice Uhlans.

Lebovice was the most distant and most obscure garrison in Galicia.

Dupi had to leave the Viennese Dukay Palace, its French mantelpieces and the liveried footmen who had hardly been able to cope with his numerous houseguests. Lebovice had a population of three thousand, but it would have been impossible to find as much soap and as many towels in the whole town as there were in the Dukay Palace on Bösendorferstrasse. The officers lived in barracks, where it was customary to give the corporal of the day an hour of extra duty for every bedbug found in the officers' rooms. In the entire military history of the Austro-Hungarian Monarchy there was not a single unit which assigned so many extra duty hours as the Lebovice garrison. The officers managed to survive these hardships only by riding into Lemberg, thirty kilometers away, every day.

In his sorrow, Dupi took to drink. The word sorrow must be understood to mean that degree of melancholy which could affect a twenty-two-year-old lieutenant of Uhlans who had unlimited funds at his disposal in 1890. There was something decidedly light-hearted in his sorrowful palliatives. The above-mentioned historian would sort these palliatives into three categories: ribald palliatives, romantic palliatives and social palliatives.

It was a ribald palliative, for instance, to organize the Officers' Reading Union. This was the result of an Offiziersbesprechung delivered in a high, thin voice by Baron Born-Hedwitz, lieutenant colonel and unit commandant, a biting philippic which sharply inveighed against the unprecedented lack of culture among the younger officers, who were said never to have read a single book. He made them promise solemnly to spend at least a half hour a day reading the books which he distributed among them.

"Versprechen das die Herren? Is that clear, gentlemen?"

"Jawohl, Herr Oberstleutnant!" came the chorus from beneath the narrow little mustaches.

The books were military histories, principally the memoirs of Austrian generals. The colonel could not imagine any other kind of reading matter.

The Officers' Reading Union began its proceedings by the candlelight of one of Lemberg's bordellos. So far there could have been no objection; for candlesticks, however, the members of the Union used live female bodies. The naked nymphs stretched out on large tables and did not hold the candles in their hands. Elbows on the table, chins in hand, the members of the Union seated themselves around the ladies and read the memoirs of illustrious Austrian generals. All conversation and laughter were forbidden during the study period. Drinking was permitted. Meanwhile the gypsy fiddler, stationed behind a curtain in the adjoining room—

they were very careful to observe the proprieties—softly played melancholy Hungarian tunes.

The fame of the Reading Union spread throughout the Monarchy, and was said to have reached even the ear of Franz Joseph himself by way of Katalin Schratt. The emperor's gloomy dignity, however, overrode whatever sense of humor he had, especially where his illustrious army was concerned. An investigation was ordered and Dupi, as founder and president of the Union, was sentenced to thirty days of room arrest, although everything had been denied.

The case of Fanny Nathanovics belonged in the category of romantic palliatives. Fanny was the sixteen-year-old daughter of the only lumber dealer in Lebovice. Her fiery red hair recalled to Dupi the finish of the antique cherry-wood furniture in the Vienna palace. Fanny was as freckled as a turkey egg, a feature which heightened the effect of her two sleepy, large, violet-blue eyes. She was a chubby, attractive little girl who chewed her nails to the quick when daydreaming. She met Dupi while ice-skating, and arm-in-arm—as in the Lajos Goro cartoons in the *Sunday News* of those days—they pivoted and turned on the frozen Lebov Brook, Fanny outfitted in muff and fur cap, Dupi in his ice-gray officer's jacket with the tiny gold tassel of the Uhlans. The entrance fee at the brook was ten kreutzers, and this paid for the services of a local band which was even more unbearable than the cold, subzero weather. In the course of the afternoon, while attempting figure eights, Fanny disclosed that her birthday was in the following week and that her favorite flower was the lily of the valley.

Next day Dupi's agents were on the way to Vienna by express train, commissioned to purchase all the lilies of the valley in the flowershops along the Graben. At night stealthy figures appeared on Myhliczky Alley and noiselessly measured the windows, fence and gate of the Nathanovics house. On the eve of her birthday Dupi hired a gypsy band to serenade Fanny, and while the primás played that well known song which begins "Csak egy kislány van a világon," a song without which no serenade was possible or even imaginable in the Nineties, the stealthy confederates silently nailed previously prepared frames on the windows, fence and gate. Every morning at six o'clock Moses Nathanovics hurried to his lumber yard, and when he stepped out of the door the next morning he shook his head in disbelief to see his whole house banked with lilies of the valley. Nearly weeping with emotion, he hastily attempted to compute the probable cost of so many lilies of the valley in the middle of February. Many of the passers-by did not even notice the elaborate display. The whiteness of snow overwhelmed it all, for snow was falling hard and it was bitter cold. Even the bell-pull and the black branches were covered with exquisite icicles of finger thickness. All this, including the delicate foliage etched in frost on the windowpanes, was definitely more beautiful than the cold-bitten, wilting lilies of the valley. When the officers came to make a personal inspection around noontime—casually, as if they merely happened to be passing—and stood on the street corner craning their necks at the Nathanovics home, they came to the conclusion that violets or red roses would have made a more satisfactory arrangement. Dupi looked at them with mute disdain, as at uninitiates ignorant of the secret: that the lily of the valley was the favorite flower of the lady in question.

The wholesale purchase of the Lower Market Place in Lemberg belonged in the category of social palliatives. This happened at dawn after a night-long drinking bout during which Dupi and three of his friends invaded Lemberg's Grand Caffée Kazmer on horseback and mounted to the first floor where, under the influence of their researches in literature, they carried out military maneuvers among the billiard tables, swords drawn and Uhlan képis tightly strapped under their chins—still on horseback, of course. The three billiard tables, whose occupants fled, cues and all, into an adjoining room, were readily subdued in the first charge and captured by the attackers. Wide, weighty cavalry sabers cut the green felt covers to ribbons. The café's large windows and mirrors met the same fate during the second cavalry charge. Meanwhile the gypsies were incessantly playing the Radetzky March, with metal trays inserted between the strings of the cimbalom for greater sonority. In the course of the engagement all the patrons of the café retreated, leaving only a few battle-scarred damsels behind. As a result of assiduous application to the literature of military strategy, the young officers emerged from their operations brilliantly victorious, which is to say that not a single piece of china or glassware remained intact and even the spoons, one by one, were carefully bent out of shape. By way of triumphant conclusion the double-bass player was compelled to hold his bull fiddle over his head while the officers made a sieve of it with their pistol fire. At that the gypsies decamped; fearing that it would next be the turn of their violins, and aware of the similarity in shade between their swarthy faces and their fiddles, they flew off like sparrows. The sudden silence which ensued upon the departure of the musicians was accompanied by the first awakenings of sobriety, which made it clear that the broken glass and chinaware would have to be swept away. Charwomen were summoned, and in the interest of order and cleanliness the officers had the entire café scrubbed with French champagne. The golden-green royal liquor foamed dirtily under the scrubbing brushes.

None of this can yet be called social action, except in the sense that the activities of the evening did contribute to an upswing of business for certain trades and industries within the Monarchy. The palliative of that memorable May 9th can be included in the social category because of what happened subsequently.

Descending from the first floor, the horses struck sparks out of the stone steps as the hoofs on their delicate, trembling legs groped nervously down the steep incline. The minuscule troop galloped toward the Lower Market Place of Lemberg in the clear light of dawn. Dupi himself summoned the market supervisor and informed him that everything offered for sale was purchased by the officers. Next he ordered the distribution of all the products and produce to the populace. In the space of seconds a tumultuous confusion broke out. People poured toward the market from near-by streets. Gingerbread cakes, earthenware and ironware, hats, shoes, boots, sausages, linens, cackling geese, screaming pigs, fish both dead and alive flew above the heads of the crowd and a thousand hands reached for them all. That hour-long and noisy mob scene at dawn was a fitting climax to a truly eventful night. The members of the police force, called out to restore order, stuck round cheeses on the tips of their swords to avoid inflicting any injury.

The press maintained a discreet silence concerning this affair. Only the Warsaw *Kleine Zeitung* mentioned it. A lead article devoted many words of high praise to the generous and noble deed of the young Hungarian count and even established, on the evidence of the affair having occurred at dawn, that the count was an early riser. The secret police in Warsaw had long been under orders from above to watch the editors of the *Kleine Zeitung* on suspicion of Socialist sympathies. At that time the word Socialist sounded as if someone today were to call himself a technocrat or a eugenist. It meant little more than a new and dangerous kind of thought which, although it offered no threat to the perpetual security of the Monarchy, was nevertheless intolerable. A few weeks later, as a consequence of the laudatory article in the *Kleine Zeitung*, Dupi was expelled from the army, a solution which clearly could be disadvantageous only to the army itself.

The Galician palliatives, and especially the card-fests with Lemberg horse traders and Polish adventurers, had proved a great strain on the resources of the Dukay estate, wherefore Peter Dukay gave the new development, despite the disgrace attached to it, his heartfelt approval. A Dukay, finally, remains a

Dukay. Dupi himself was weary of duels, quicksilver treatments, liquor and gambling. The attorneys collected and paid all the notes circulating among the moneylenders throughout the Monarchy, and this concluded the first phase of Count Dupi's life.

✚

He stayed at Ararat at his father's wish and began to occupy himself with agricultural matters, which consisted principally of day-long hunting. The following year he journeyed to India with appropriate letters of introduction and participated in the tiger hunt of the Maharajah of Gehuzaz. He brought a month-and-a-half-old tiger cub back from the East and it was raised on fresh cow's milk at Ararat. He spent eight months of the subsequent year hunting in Africa—in Abyssinia, in Kenya and points south. He was in Cairo before he noticed he had forgotten to take his binoculars along. He wired his valet to start for Cairo at once with the binoculars. He returned from the African trek with great quantities of trophies, and the high vaulted corridors of the Ararat castle, which up to that time had been decorated merely with the antlers of roebucks and stags, the hooks of ibex, the horns of wild goats, the heads of boars and the pelts of bears and wolves, were now enriched with mounted giraffe and antelope-heads, cusps of wild Cape buffaloes, lion, panther and hyena skins as well as some elephant tusks of considerable size. He spent 1893 in Paris and 1894 in London, where he became an intimate of Edward Prince of Wales.

In London he met the eighteen-year-old Princess Klementina Schäyenheim-Elkburg, who was his second cousin on his mother's side and who possessed a pedigree which satisfied the unusually rigorous demands of the Dukays, whose entailment required a consort with at least sixteen ancestral members of the nobility on both the paternal and maternal branches. By that time Count Dupi was thinking seriously of marriage. His first choice, a tall and slightly creole Countess Hannah from Transylvania, was out of the question because her ancestry exceeded by two the number of inferior titularies permitted by the statutes of entailment. Before the year was out Count Dupi married Klementina Schäyenheim-Elkburg.

The young princess was blue and white, with sharp shoulders, sharp fingers, sharp elbows and a sharp nose. Even the expression of her blue porcelain eyes was sharp. She was an icicle out of heaven, holding a lily in one hand and in her other hand holding an enormous inheritance which derived partly from her father, who was Master of the Equerry in Franz Joseph's Austrian domains, and partly from her mother, daughter of the Earl of Padkinson and the Midland Bank. The marriage poured gold into the deep cracks which Count Dupi had made in the Dukay fortune during the past years. The art treasures in the palace on Septemvir Utca, in Buda, were also augmented.

In the following year he stood for Parliament as a candidate of the National Party. The election contest was watched by the whole nation with bated breath, like a medieval tourney or a trial by ordeal of the Divine Will. It was the battle of David and Goliath, the role of Goliath being played by the Bánffy administration which in the preceding year had defeated its opponents by every device of power politics, money and corruption. "A Dukay will show them!" the embittered Nationalists told each other on their croquet courts in the country, and in truth Count Dupi, as David, loaded his sling with such a large sum of money that the lawyer Hunszky, candidate of the administration, was defeated with nine votes to his credit, something which under the given circumstances was tantamount to a victory for him.

In his maiden speech in Parliament István Dukay referred to Franz Joseph as an executioner, and this was the very least the nation expected of a Dukay in those days. Count Dukay had manifested his anti-Habsburg sentiments even earlier, when he refused to accept the key symbolic of his position as chamberlain.

During the first twelve years of their marriage Princess Klementina presented her husband with four children. Apparently he was not completely satisfied with the results, for during those twelve years he engendered countless illegitimate offspring. Among his natural progeny there were some who, in later decades and regardless of sex or social rank, became valuable individuals in their own right; who inherited not only biological advantages, such as harmonious physical proportions, a slightly bent Turkish nose and the large brown eyes of the Dukays from their father, but also a tenacious thirst for life which swept them—depending on their fate—either into prison or to the heights of society. These children enjoyed various relations with their father and society. There were some among them whom Count Dupi acknowledged as his own, and these were entered by public understanding in the registries of turn-of-the-century romance. At times when his wife was sojourning at a foreign spa, a reception for the mothers was held in the palace on Septemvir Utca and the butler, like the receptionist in a pediatrician's office, announced the ladies to the count one at a time, in the order of their arrival, while those waiting in the anteroom looked daggers at each other. The mothers, with sweet maternal smiles on their lips, urged their little boys and girls through the wide gilt-covered baroque doors; the little tots were all especially dressed for this occasion. Especially dressed for the occasion meant, in this instance, that the children were dressed as shabbily as was compatible with cleanliness and neatness, dressed in neat and clean patched hand-me-downs, the patches sometimes sewn prominently in places where they were not necessary. The little boots, too, were cracked at the toe if possible, in mute and modest evidence of material want. Count Dupi greeted all his children with the same "Hello Zizi!" or "Hello Pali!" and, seizing them under the armpits, tossed each of them with the same gesture nearly to the ceiling, snatched the howling Zizis and Palis out of the air in masterly fashion, tweaked their noses and distributed money to their mothers, larger or smaller sums depending on his mood or on the rush of affection which flooded him when the mother entered the room. And then he was already pushing them out the door, for there were many others waiting. The children slowly grew up as the years went by until, finally, it was no longer practicable to toss them ceiling-high, and thus the prime ingredient of a show of fatherly affection was rendered impossible. Some grew mustaches, some got married, some stayed away or disappeared altogether, while the obstinate ones, the persistent and obtrusive ones continued to apply to his secretary for the varying sums consonant with appendicitis operations, evictions and public auctions. And it was his secretary, too, who answered the letters requesting urgent assistance, or influence, or protection, letters which were usually limited to a statement of bald fact by the young men and women who, no longer permitted access to their progenitor, were not quite sure how to address themselves to him. Obviously, the salutation "To His Excellency the Count" implied an abdication of certain blood ties and their concomitant privileges, while a cheery "Dear Dad" might have provoked unfavorable reactions. And only the slightest shadings of difference were available between those two extremes.

The first-born son arrived in the fall of 1895, in that same Maria Theresa room with which newcomers into the Dukay family circle were becoming quite familiar during the second half-century. The child was named Imre at baptism, but the name of Rere stuck to him from his earliest childhood, for at the age of ten he was still unable to speak any intelligible tongue. His responses, his desires, his moods, his queries, his joys and sorrows were expressed in a short, somewhat whinnying laugh which sounded like "rere." Kalt, the well known Viennese specialist, established during the young count's infancy that his was a case of a not uncommon form of idiocy, the luetic, marked by the alternating symptoms of dull passivity and restlessness.

When Professor Kalt delivered his diagnosis of the infant's incurable ailment, Count Dupi's decision—accompanied by the specialist's approving nod—was to send the child abroad to a sanatorium. But the countess, who was then nineteen years old, protested tearfully at the thought of separation from her first-born. Human experience teaches us that not only the flesh but the maternal soul, too, is torn during the first childbirth, and the wound goes on bleeding for an entire lifetime. Mothers generally are fondest of their first-born, and the more imperfect the child the more vehemently is mother love lavished upon it. For years the countess steadfastly refused all pleas, every persuasion and countless medical advices, the mute, determined toss of her head suggestive of a disturbing hidden threat. Count Dupi eventually gave in, if only after some solitary gnashing of teeth; and in the meantime he had become accustomed to Rere. Familiarity is the single remedy for this as for every sort of horror.

While still a child Rere occasionally gave touching signs of his human sentiments. When Miss Wenlock, the English governess, made his smaller sisters or brothers kneel in a corner or sent them to bed without supper, Rere would smuggle the most variegated objects to the culprit by way of consolation: leaves, dead mice, empty cartridges or dried little dog-turds which he found, bleached to whiteness, in the park. On these occasions he placed the objects at their side with a trembling hand, his large, bulging eyes brimming with tears, and then he tiptoed away quickly and surreptitiously, upsetting the chairs before him as he went. After the death of his maternal grandmother he spent days weeping in her room, as if he had some secret and personal knowledge of what happened after death. Day and night he wept, not knowing that the old dowager princess had always turned her head away in horror at the sight of her idiot grandson, and at family councils had been the most persistent advocate of the view that the child should be placed in an institution. Once, in the flush of controversy she had

29

cried—with fitting refinement of innuendo—that the wisest thing would be to destroy the child altogether.

Rere also knew the transcendental joys of giving. Once he carried a priceless Ming vase, which was five feet high, from the ballroom to the park, where he presented it to the gardener's three-year-old daughter. Unfortunately he suffered from occasional fits, and the duty of restraining him fell upon Mr. Badar, who played the part of "tutor" in the castle. He had in fact been a schoolmaster, but lost his position because of certain irregularities which were not entirely moral. He had been, in addition, a middleweight wrestling and boxing champion, with a thorough understanding of jujitsu. He was selected for the job principally because the adolescent Rere had the strength of a bull. Once, during a picnic in the pasture below the woods, they stretched out on the grass. The tutor yawned, produced a paper-bound novel from his pocket and began to read. From time to time he cast a dutiful side-glance at Rere, who was squatting like a Turk and staring blankly forward. Soon he noticed that the count had begun to nibble at a dried cake of cow-dung, daintily breaking it into small pieces. He gently informed the lad that this activity was not worthy of a gentleman. Rere began to mutter fearfully; at a further warning he threw away the cake and an unfriendly light crept into the corner of his eye as his curved fingers groped for the tutor's neck. The latter instantly sprang to his feet and knocked the count flat with a rabbit punch. This did not in the least deter Rere from giggling amicably at his mentor when he regained consciousness, or from inquiring, as the sun declined on the horizon somewhat later, about the approximate distance of the sun from the earth. The tutor answered this surprising question with the offhand reply that it was two million kilometers away. He was quite safe in his extemporization, for besides the grazing cows there were no astronomers in the vicinity.

Count Rere was given to extremely remarkable decisions. At the age of twenty-three he decided to get married. In whispers he confided to his brothers and sisters that he had become the affianced bride of Lojzi, otherwise known as Alajos Galovics, the chaplain of the castle whose laced boots always trotted so quickly beneath his short surplice and whose swollen face was in a constant flush. The young reverend's external appearance did not qualify him as a suitable bridegroom, but Rere in all sincerity found him as attractive as he found everything, person or object, connected with religion. He never missed Mass. Rere was the only one in the whole great castle—where even the servants had to be Catholic—who knew how to pray truly, sincerely and fervidly. Occasionally, while kneeling among the

30

beautifully carved ancient benches of the chapel, he emitted a short, barking laugh during the most solemn and silent moments of Mass, or made loud, unmistakably intestinal noises, but this did not detract from the fact that Rere belonged among the most faithful sheep of the Mother Church. One time, after services, he asked the Reverend Lojzi with embarrassed zeal and fervent secretiveness to tell him his birth date and his favorite flower, and on the basis of information given he began to knit a light blue necktie, for his fingers were as intelligent as they were nimble. He had nagged Viktoria, his mother's elderly chambermaid, until she taught him how to knit. All the castle roared with laughter when his light blue necktie reached a length of two yards, but Rere kept knitting ceaselessly, in the solitude of a corner or on a bench under a tree, with the facial movements of complete and determined absorption or with angry grimaces when he dropped a stitch. He wound yarn with furrowed brow and arms violently waving.

Summer and winter, Count Rere was dressed in jackets of excellent cut, striped trousers and a derby, as if he were constantly on the way to or from the racetrack. His cheerful horseface protruded beneath the derby, his eyes were forever wide with wonder and joy, and the corners of his half open, thick, fleshy mouth were continually shiny with spittle. His mustache was narrow and crescent shaped, like that worn by Chinese mandarins. Binoculars in a large leather case were slung over his shoulder, and in addition Rere carried a monocle, a magnifying glass, sunglasses, a pince-nez and horn-rimmed spectacles in his several pockets, using none of them except the sunglasses which he put on when he had to go through a dark room. This indicates that certain associational capacities were not absent from his make-up. He had a vast number of rings, of which he wore one, a fat emerald, on the thumb of his left hand. He carried a bunch of keys in his trousers pocket, suspended at the end of a gold key-chain in the fashion of the early Nineteen Hundreds. The chain was fastened to the top trousers button underneath his vest and fell in a graceful arc to his pocket. The bunch of keys weighed at least four pounds, for it included large, rusty storeroom keys as well as small, finely wrought antiques which opened century-old wardrobes, flat, cunning Wertheim keys—in fact, all the keys which incomprehensibly disappeared from time to time and reposed uselessly in Rere's trousers pocket. He also demonstrated the collector's urge by composing his sentences of Hungarian, French, German and English words. He spoke through his nose, and the constant "rere" washed away the meaning of his words just as the ground bass of a 'cello in a string quartet drowns out all other sounds.

31

Rere did not smoke and never touched liquor of any kind. He had made the attempt, but the smoke of tobacco gave him a coughing fit and when he accidentally tasted wine one day he started to sneeze like a dog whose nose has touched a slimy toad.

His intellectual abilities were evidenced in various ways. Sometimes he spent long hours in the library, reading the memoirs of Chateaubriand with complete abandon. Unfortunately, he often besmirched the tall, chamois-bound folios with his dirty hands, even the most moving passages in those marvels of French book-bindery. But he read incessantly and with fervor.

Rere naturally took his meals with the family. He only ate apart with Mr. Badar the tutor when foreign dignitaries were invited or on the occasion of large banquets. In the immediate circle of family and friends, when there were no more than twenty or twenty-five settings, it often happened in the course of conversation that someone asked for a name or a historical date. At such times, during the cautious silence which followed, Rere would suddenly blurt out the answer, whether it was the date of the Council of Trent or the successor to the throne of Károly Robert. His remarks were infallibly greeted with shrill laughter. Even the shoulders of the footmen shook and the wide silver trays danced in their hands, although Rere never missed a single name or date. This was not because he knew them all; he simply happened to know the ones required. At these times, under the spell of his success, he would giggle with modest satisfaction.

Given such an intellectual capacity, his difficulties with a derby are all the more inexplicable. He possessed countless derbies, because it was his habit, at unexpected times and in unexpected places, to put a derby on the ground, roll down his trousers and relieve himself into it. As if acquainted with the tenets of social behavior, he did this only when alone. No threat or persuasion could break him of the habit. His preoccupation with derbies was referred to Professor Kalt in Vienna, but the noted specialist did not know what advice to give. "In dieser That des hochgeborenen Herrn Grafen—in this activity of His Excellency the Count," began his exhaustive reply, "there is an atavistic element of the primitive, the relic of a mysterious religious ceremony the traces of which are still manifest among the natives of the Andaman Islands. Aside from this, a closer examination of this activity of His Excellency the Count—in der That des hochgeborenen Herrn Grafen—reveals the mark of a considered wisdom. Certain human matters, viewed in a broad perspective, have a meaning different from that given them by the conventional interpretation. Let us return to the Andaman Islands and consider a native who has never in his life seen a derby. What does he think of when he turns this bowl-shaped object in his hands? Certainly he cannot imagine that intelligent human beings put it on their heads, but rather that they keep something in it, and it follows that this something must first be *deposited in its interior.*"

In those days the venerable Professor Kalt enjoyed such international fame that the family council, though with some misgivings, had to take the matter of the derbies out of his hands, if only because his expert opinions were more expensive than five hundred new, silk-lined derbies from Locke, on St. James Street in London.

Unquestionably the problem of Rere weighed upon the whole household, in that climate of aristocratic tradition where the refinement of manners had filtered down through the centuries to regulate life, social intercourse, meals, dress and the most insignificant activities—manners, and principally the English manners, which dictated that even the servants maintain an air of quiet religious devotion in the performance of their duties, whether announcing callers, passing the roast leg of lamb or the box of Havanas, or in the holy ritual of running a bath. To tolerate Rere, the half-witted terror whose very presence blasphemed everything that was held sacred in a house and atmosphere where no effort or sacrifice was spared for the extirpation of the unseemly smells, sounds and savors of life—this was not a great thing only, it was a thing worthy of respect.

But it is also true that Rere performed inestimable services for the household. Souls cast in the armor of discipline, manners and good breeding tend to break out in galls and sores, like feet and armpits which are unventilated. The arrogance with which these people enclose their society in a charmed circle and by means of which they isolate themselves from all contact with their fellows on a basis of equality finally ends only by wounding them, like the rusty barb of a wire fence. The aristocratic castle-dwellers, swooning with mutual disdain and choking with boredom, tried to remedy this obvious malady by inviting the more presentable writers, actors or musicians into their midst—a kind of quackish panacea. These gatherings regularly turned out to be awkward failures. Upon arrival, the noted artistic personalities nearly collapsed, as if struck by hammer blows, at the totally unexpected honor of being addressed with the familiar thou by the master of the house, and for the remaining days of their sojourn they strained what wits were left to them in a mighty effort to behave, move, smile, pronounce the word *yacht* as "yot" and generally to modulate their diction as if they too stemmed from the Kürt family or the Ordony clan and had come visiting from a neighboring castle. They hastily concealed all their refreshing individualities, their attractive impertinences, like people who are uncomfortably aware of having dirty underclothes on. However, if the lord of the manor did not give them the thou of familiarity they were stung to the core and, smarting, were often moved at the end of such a visit to contemplate membership in the Socialist Party. In both cases the castle-dwellers heaved sighs of relief when they finally managed to rid themselves of the whole deadly, dull gang.

Rere relieved this malady as only the forces of nature—the wind, the sunshine, the salt air of the ocean—can do: imperceptibly. His remedy was not parceled out and packaged, nor was there a label on it which read: "before meals," or "after meals." Medicine serves only when we do not know it for medicine, otherwise it always has a slight taste of death. Medical men claim there is refreshment in a frenzy of weeping or a paroxysm of fury. An inner commotion brings into play the muscles of the diaphragm which because of their anatomical position draw no benefit from external blows and batterings. Only psychological forces are capable of reaching into the chest and the intestinal cavities. From time to time Rere gave these interior muscles a vigorous pummeling. The footmen ran breathlessly to tell the kitchen staff that "Rere has let go in his derby again—" and in the space of seconds the outer gateman had been informed of the event. Rere served as an oxygen tank for this castle, this park, this tightly closed high-flown compartment of society. To the staff, Rere represented an outlet for shrill liberation, for exultant finger-pointing, for a malicious settling of accounts, for light-hearted forgiveness, for a mysterious leveling strength, for latent hatred—half-wits are always dear to the hearts of servants. By virtue of this one quality—by keeping Rere among them, seating him at their table, tolerating him, forgiving him and surrounding him with warm mirth—the counts and countesses themselves became human in the eyes of the staff. But Rere meant even more, perhaps, to the members of the family. He was the loathsome and horrible absurdity of life. The cheerful horseface bore a slight resemblance to everyone—the forehead was his father's, the eyes his mother's, the nostrils Kristina's, the thick-fleshed lips György's—he was a Dukay too, but mysteriously and maliciously. And this was reflected as well in his actions as in his grotesque lineaments—actions of Rere by means of

34

which the others were liberated from the self-consciousness of their own petrified and drowned condition. Rere was the twisted mirror in front of which thronged laughing, grimacing faces, all telling themselves: I might be like that too, but I'm not. Oh, how very much not! And Rere was the phenomenon, the jacket-wearing derby-hatted human-shaped phenomenon who made no mental reservations, who was as transparent as glass. In a house where the glance behind the eyelid so painfully, achingly closed sometimes turns inward with startling suddenness and savagery, where the reticent politeness of silence is often a spear beating at another's heart—in such a house, despite the emerald on his thumb, the keys and the optical devices, despite the derbies and Chateaubriand and the cake of cow-dung and the two-yard-long necktie, Rere was the clumsy but continuous presence of wisdom, of goodness, of gentleness, of innocence and love.

Chapter Three

KRISTINA: born in 1896, in the year of the Millennium, during the intoxication of Hungary celebrating its own first thousand years. And this intoxication characterized not Hungary alone but all of Europe. In the last years of the century there seemed to be no doubt that the material and spiritual power which had accrued to the white race as a result of the early achievements of technology—Andrée's airship floated away in the direction of the unexplored North Pole in the summer of that year, and that year Henri Becquerel, by absent-mindedly leaving a slice of bread-and-butter and a photographic plate in the neighborhood of a uranium particle, accidentally discovered radioactivity—this power would place European man in rightful and perpetual ascendancy over all the peoples of the world. Indeed, European culture and enlightenment seemed to stand at an unbelievable and exclusive height. It was commonly supposed that in the east the vast hordes of Russians, Hindus and Chinese were as static as Asiatic mountain ranges and as incapable of further development, while America was thought to be nothing but a spacious European hunting ground where, in place of buffaloes, beavers, endless flights of great stock doves and Indians, the dollar had become fair game. Whatever remained to call itself human beyond this, in Africa and on the far-swept ocean islands, was merely the "native." It went without saying that all the regions of the whole round world shipped their raw materials for the use of the ruling classes in Europe. To eat and drink all the coffee, chocolate, cocoa, rice, oranges and bananas, to smoke the fragrant black Havanas, to wear out the cottons of Turkestan and the silks of China, to display the emeralds of India and the diamonds of South Africa: this was the onerous responsibility of imperial rule, or what Rudyard Kipling called the white man's burden, although he meant it in the large idealistic and visionary sense, by which he betrayed himself to be as prone to belief in the magical powers of certain words and concepts as the savages of the Fiji Islands. And perhaps he was right, for the magic worked magnificently. Nothing was beyond European self-confidence and bank deposits. Ambergris-laden sperm whales of the arctic oceans struggled at the end of a harpoon in order to provide the ladies of Lyon or Warsaw with scented hand lotions, and Amboina trees flourished in the East Indies solely to enable cabinetmakers to outdo themselves on the curly-grained furniture of several thousand European clubs and salons. No one seemed to notice that Tsarist Russia was already rustling and shaking like a brown wilderness of reeds, which can be seen to move in the mysterious breeze during the most motionless calm. The English did not care that, while they galloped about in pith sun helmets on the polo fields of Bombay and Calcutta, more and more Hindus were attending Cambridge and absorbing, in a single day, more of the mysteries of European life than the youths of Mayfair could do in an entire lifetime. They took phrases and ideas home with them, these Hindus, ideas which struck at the foundation stones of high suffering with the heat of the glass blower's intense flame. At the peak of a Germany which was forged of railroad tracks sat Wilhelm II, too busy with his mustache curlers to notice the Chinese with felt-soled shoes and a frozen smile who for days had been noiselessly padding in the wake of the German envoy in order to shoot him and to deposit his body on the threshold of the new century, opening mankind's bloodiest age in the summer of 1900 with the Boxer Rebellion. No, no one in Europe thought that a billion human beings in the East, among them men comparable in understanding and intellect with Lao-Tse and Buddha, were waiting and preparing for something. The reason for all these preparations was simple: the other peoples of the world had begun to wonder whether it was absolutely imperative for them to tolerate the yoke of European domination, a rule which they already suspected to be the contrivance of a handful of sovereign courts, military cliques, industrialists, merchants and their hangers-on who, like tight-rope walkers, cast winning smiles at life. At the end of the century Europe, or as much of Europe as met the eye, glittered and pirouetted to the music of her own enchantment, like a Christmas tree overweighted with decorations, revolving on a base in which a music box played "God Save the King," or "Deutschland, Deutschland über Alles," or the soothing chords of the "Gotterhalte." In a rocking chair alongside the Christmas tree sat the white-haired departing century, once the toast of Metternich, Disraeli and Bismarck, now the very image of Securitas, matron of security so revered by the Romans; but in place of a lance her right hand held Queen Victoria's knitting needle and on the index finger of her left hand rested her chubby face as, lost in admiration for her grandsons, she often dozed away.

The Christmas tree went round and round, the women in Parisian cabarets were completely nude, the stout burghers of little Holland accumulated the gold of distant island kingdoms, Italy merely kept on clearing its fine baritone voice, and in Berlin even the policemen turned homosexual out of a sense of conformity and propriety. Firmly established in that Europe stood the Austro-Hungarian Monarchy, and firmly established in that monarchy stood the castle at Ararat, not as a peculiarly Hungarian exoticism but as the very index and coordinate of Europe's ruling class, for the strains of Italian, German, Spanish, Polish and English aristocrats, of Swedish and Greek industrialists and of Levantine merchants had long been mingling with the blood of the half-Austrian nobility. At one and the same time the halls of Ararat resounded with German words, Viennese accents, French and English phrases and Hungarian slang from across the Danube. The furnishings came from Paris, and the marvels of English industry filled every corner. Miss Wenlock once had to poke her head into a chamber pot because she could not otherwise decipher the dark blue stamp which read "SANITAS NEW REAL FAYENCE" and "Manufactured in Oxford," a discovery which understandably made her English heart beat faster; but often, when seated on that convenience, she wondered whether it was proper for a manufacturer who dealt with her sovereign "by appointment" to stamp his royal crest, with its two British lions, inside the receptacle, thereby exposing the holy symbol of Imperial dominion to disconcertingly close and frequent contact with brute metabolism, although it is true that even in this unworthy position the crest bore its original motto: "Honi soit qui mal y pense," which is to say: "Evil to him who evil thinks."

The outward condition of the fashionable world naturally had no physical effect on the newborn girl, but her date of birth cannot be recorded without noting that it marked the glorious zenith of Hungarian nobility, which thereafter began a gentle downward decline until one generation later, in 1919, it turned a complete somersault and precipitously plunged into the same European abyss that had engulfed three emperors and four kings by the end of the first World War.

When Dr. Birkássy, whose beard had turned quite gray, announced the happy outcome of the childbirth, István Dukay wrinkled his brows. He had hoped for a son. The estate could not continue without a male heir, and the year-old Rere was already known to be incompetent. The wearisome travail of reproduction had to be undertaken anew at the side of a woman whose heavy, cloying perfumes he hated and whose feet remained ice-cold even under the thickest down-filled comforters; whereas the world, notably Paris and Vienna where his houses were constantly open, was filled with bright stars of the theater, women of every rank and condition, who competed feverishly for the wealthy thirty-year-old Hungarian nobleman's favor, for in those years his handsome oriental visage and his winning personality were so well known that the comic weeklies in Paris frequently ran cartoons on "le charmant comte Dupi."

As a child Kristina was not pretty, since a child's prettiness depends on the single ingredient of health and she was from birth the constant victim of intestinal catarrh, tonsillitis, whooping cough and especially severe eczema. Her childhood was almost uninterruptedly spent in bed. Her delicate skin was as lifeless and pale as an Alpine edelweiss. In the lonely, sorrowful eyes of such children there is always something suggestive of a desire for revenge, whether dark or cheerful, revenge on people, on life, on the bed, the pillows, the medicine bottles and the strong-scented ointments. Kristina had inherited her mother's large, sensitive blue-green eyes and the light frame which even in childhood betrayed a perfection of form. She developed the symptoms of adolescence somewhat prematurely, in her thirteenth year, and from that time on she began to shed her illnesses like a snake its outworn skin. Thereafter the long-legged, unbelievably slim-waisted countess could be seen in the park all day long, casting her diabolo top high in the air—for in 1910 this fad and hobby had so enthralled the whole leisure class that elderly ladies in their gardens and dignified, corpulent statesmen in the privacy of their rooms spent hours spinning the devilish little toy on its taut string.

In those years Kristina consumed large quantities of cod-liver oil, a potation which at that time was as compulsory for the offspring of country gentlemen as the smallpox vaccination; for it was by the ingestion of such nauseating emulsions that the white race tried to cure itself of a weakness of which neither the causes nor the consequences were clearly understood.

By then Kristina spoke German, English and French excellently, or better at least than she spoke Hungarian. Five years of Miss Wenlock's ministrations were followed by the tutelage of Mam'selle Jacqueline Barbier. These French and English governesses went from family to family and from castle to castle, like cast-off but imperishable leather breeches, as the children outgrew them, and often reverted to the same castle when new little tots appeared. The mam'selle was a tall, bony woman of forty who wore long lentil-colored skirts and blouses with masculine cuffs and high stiff collars. Her jet-black hair was enriched in front with a false braid which she could never find in the mornings and occasionally had to rescue from the chambermaid's dustpan. Her face was dry and angular, and two gold caps stood out among her bluish gray teeth like gold lettering on a marble tombstone. She knew the modern methods of child training, and the melody of the French language was in her veins, climbing the steep staircase and then suddenly sliding down the banister of her sentences. She devoured one French novel a day, played *The Afternoon of a Faun* without score and, according to Count Dupi, smelled like a mouse. She professed conservative principles in all matters, but the chambermaids noted that she furtively smoked a cigarette from time to time, and they were also aware of her affair with Mr. Johnson, the English stablemaster. Jacqueline was at once a mother and a friend to Kristina, but there was nothing soft about her training methods. Often she chased Kristina, who wore short white socks, into the nettlefields of the park in order to acquaint her naked white legs and tender thighs with the aching, if transient, pains of life. And for interminable minutes she made Kristina hold a green frog, no matter how much the child dreaded it, in her shivering hand. Kristina's smallest mistake was severely punished. At those times Rere brought pebbles, dead bugs and other offerings to the kneeling little Madonna.

Kristina learned to play tennis, to play the piano, to swim and to ride. Horses cautiously nibbled at the lumps of sugar in her upraised, outstretched hand, for they liked her and considered her a friend, as if especially grateful for the feathery weight of her when she rode; in the company of the French governess Kristina often watched the whole great copulative storm of a stallion covering a mare with no more understanding of the sight than what her restless twitching nerves told her, for the mam'selle, who tried not to miss a single one of these occasions, gave only nervous and incomprehensible replies to her eager questions.

The development of her frail body began in the swimming pool principally, as if water were the ancestral element to which the child had to return for urgent compensation of everything she missed during the years of illness, like a body left back in school and forced to repeat class after class but finally passing a number of examinations successfully all at once. The sand and air of the swimming pool bathed her in vitality, burned her sensitive white skin, like a green coffee bean in the roaster, to the color of dark gold, and drew mysterious and fragrant oils to the surface of the youthful but developing feminine body, a body which was at the cautious, diffident stage of development when the outlines of the bosom are still in hiding. They had built the swimming pool in the previous year, right next to the fishpool, surrounded it with a high fence and encircled the spacious cement cavity with sifted white sand; it was fed by the brook. The Chinese pagoda at the edge of the fishpool served as bathhouse and boathouse. The brook was not a native of the expansive park. It had been captured during the past century, like a beast, lurking in the woods and thickets. They trapped it, subdued it, manacled it and led it, confined between artificial banks, through the park. They tamed it and it became a source for the giant fishpool and later for the swimming pool. But the brook never forgot what they had done to it, and wept quietly, wiping its copious tears on wide plantain leaves and the lace fringe of green ferns.

The dressing rooms of the bathhouse were furnished with canvas covered couches, mirrors, combs, straw slippers and sunglasses; the many signatures in the leather-bound guest book often stuttered as cold water was dripped won them.

Sometimes, on warm summer days, the Chinese pagoda and the pool rang with the noise of guests invited to the castle; but this happened rarely, since István Dukay and his wife regularly spent the summer months at Reichenau, outside of Vienna, taking the French chef and the more important servants with them to the countess's villa. At such times Ararat was for the children, for Rere, Kristina, and the brothers György and János, who were her juniors by several years. In those summer months the bathhouse became the children's El Dorado, and the rhythmic count of Swimming Laci's voice could be heard from afar, "One…and…twooooo!" as he gave the children their swimming lessons, dangling them in the water at the end of a long line and pole. Swimming Laci, whose real name no one knew, wore abbreviated sun-faded bathing trunks while performing his duties, which included the responsibility of sticking the children's wet feet into straw slippers as they left the pool and drying them off with large shaggy bath towels—only the young men, of course. Swimming Laci was an importation from the village, and was reputed to have been chosen as bathhouse supervisor because he had eyes of a Chinese cut which matched the pagoda. He had originally been destined for the shoemaker's trade, but soon abandoned his apprenticeship. In winter his zither supported him, supplying accompaniment at weddings, shearings and harvests. Hand-carved zither under his arm, he spent the winter months wandering far afield over snow-covered highways, but by late spring he was always back at the bathhouse, like a bird of passage. He knew other ways of making music. A willow leaf at the tip of his tongue turned him into a nightingale, and from a blade of grass pressed between his thumbs Laci could entice mellow ocarina-like sounds. This eighteen-year-old peasant might have been a native of Easter Island. His muscle-packed flexible body was almost as black as his bathing trunks. When he had nothing to do he sat cross-legged at the edge of the pool and moved only to slap at flies on his person with lightning speed and apelike cunning. Sometimes, to relieve the heat, he hit the blue surface of the pool in a graceful dive and scurried on under water like a seal. In the summer, wearing only skin and muscle, he was a gleaming, beautiful beast; in winter, dressed in his peasant clothes, he was nothing but a respectable shoemaker's apprentice.

The children's bathing hours customarily came to an end before lunchtime. But Kristina did not care for the shrill racket of her juniors; it was almost as if her skin were sensitive to harsh sound. She swam in the mornings, when the sunshine was still yellow and the shadows still long and black, and in the afternoons until twilight, when the stillness was as soft as the wind, the sand and the water. Mam'selle Jacqueline, who never bathed in front of others and gave the impression that she kept her lentil-colored skirt and her starched cuffs on even at night, read her yellow-backed novels in the protection of the shade. Her eyes closed, her arms outstretched, Kristina would lie in the silken sifted sand like a weightless gold crucifix. As five o'clock approached, Mam'selle Jacqueline began peering impatiently at her watch, for she was jealous of Mr. Johnson. A little later she rose out of her apparent calm like a whirlwind and, calling "Je viens tout de suite," flounced off. These "I'll-be-right-back" moments regularly stretched into long hours.

Only the plantain trees, whose early flowering leaves seemed to descend out of sheer curiosity onto the mirror of the water and the warm sand, could tell what passed between Swimming Laci and fourteen-year-old Kristina in those long hours. And the thrushes, too, could tell, as with sweet flutelike calls they cruised easily above the bathhouse. And the trees, looking thirstily down from the heights in the red-and-lilac August twilight, could tell.

Mam'selle Jacqueline spent the next few months in a frenzy of near-madness because Mr. Johnson had broken with her. It is understandable, therefore, how she failed to notice until November that the girl entrusted to her care was three months with child. Seizing Kristina by her slender shoulders, mam'selle began to interrogate her; the girl regarded mam'selle's desperate agitation with wide eyes of wonder, and proceeded to give a completely innocent account of all the games she had played with Swimming Laci. Mam'selle Jacqueline, in the first throes of her distraction, ran to the village to find the boy, but both Swimming Laci and his zither had long been gone by that time, as if swallowed up in the earth.

She struggled her way home from the village around midnight and, embattled as she was, muddy and bedraggled, she burst into her mistress's boudoir. The princess was still awake, playing patience in the light of a blue-shaded lamp. When Jacqueline, weeping and quaking and wringing her hands, told her the unhappy news, her sensitive blue eyes lit up and, leaning forward, her body stiffened in the armchair while her hands unconsciously swept the cards from the table before her. But all this lasted no more than an instant. Then the discipline of Schäyenheim-Elkburg breeding mastered her, and the ice-cold sobriety of her race, and the sad wisdom which, since Rere's birth, had accompanied her lonely games of patience, her endless Masses and the exertions of her acts of charity. She knew all about her husband's affairs and adventures, not only by means of her surreptitious spies but by inadvertent expressions of his secretive face, by occasional preoccupied, vigorous head rubbings, or by the way he scratched the bristles of the thickening mustache with his crippled index finger. She could interpret his muteness and his motionless reveries, and was as sensitive to his intangible feelings as some plants are to the invisible rays of the sun. She was rendered finer, wiser, more mature, more humble by the knowledge that in Rere she had produced a horror and besmirched, with the product of her own body, the life around her and her husband; and often, when her self-discipline flagged and the forced and perpetually frozen little smile on her lips faded, her glance became the glance of a dog that sits in a corner and looks so boundlessly miserable because, though already housebroken, it has committed a nuisance once more. This glance was filled with the sorrow of her impotence to remedy the fault; to clean the filth off the rug and make it good; it was a glance which eternally begged pardon and was eternally resigned to the lash. In her case the lash was Dupi's extracurricular love-life, which settled into the depths of her soul, where we are all animals, as a recompense for the entire matter of Rere. But all this had an element of divine pride in it, for Princess Klementina never forgot that she had descended from the heights of the house of Elkburg to marry a Dukay, and the memories of her childhood survived in her like large, mystical, religious murals. Hungary, Ararat, and the whole Dukay tribe were in some respects still barbaric and inferior, for the blood of a Hohenstaufen and a Barbarossa flowed in the veins of the Elkburgs, and Uncle Otto—present inhabitant of the Elkhard castle which, together with its Traumitz fortress, had been built in the thirteenth century during the reign of Emperor Frederick II, with walls whose Gothic mosaic windows stared down a steep cliff side into the foaming depths of the Drau—yes, Uncle Otto still set a table with towering dining chairs along one side only, under the windows and facing the platter-burdened footmen, very much like medieval tapestries, a custom which made meals and social intercourse somewhat stiff but preserved the beautiful smoke-colored legacy of the past even as did the Old German carving on the chairs; and when guests arrived the great rusty chains of the iron drawbridge still creaked long and weightily.

There are people whom such a situation would turn sour and cruel. It made her humble with wisdom and proud with humility. These qualities were outwardly manifested in a manner that made people call her "the good Menti." "Mit csinál a jo Menti? Was macht die gute Menti? How is the good Menti?" his companions asked Dupi at the National Casino or the Jockey Club, companions who, like him, were profligates and faithless. But everyone loved her; affection for her was, after all, comfortable and inexpensive. The staff loved her too, with an embarrassed adoration, as if she were the picture of a saint come alive. In the servants' quarters she was "the good Countess Menti, die gute Gräfin Menti," for in those houses it was customary to give a woman her husband's rank no matter how much of a princess she was by birth. It would have been strange indeed if the footman referred to the wife of a Dukay as Her Grace the Princess and at the same time called her husband nothing more than His Excellency the Count. The attitude which held this usage to be natural was undoubtedly a result of the higher perspective. Among ordinary gentry, lawyers or such, when a man married the impoverished widow of a knight or baronet his servants were instructed to put all their vocal strength into "The Honorable Justice is out, and only Her Excellency the Baroness is at home," in order to let the neighbors hear it too.

Countess Menti, whose pretty name of Klementina was pruned at both ends, like the ears and tail of a Doberman pinscher, to produce her nickname, spoke Hungarian badly. A language can be imperfectly spoken with a variety of effects; and in general a poverty-stricken and misapplied vocabulary is revelatory of the soul in the same way that a torn bathing suit exposes the body. The effect of a language badly spoken can be antagonistic, or irritating, or becoming and cheerful. Countess Menti's accent and intonation elicited cheerfulness. She was a living example of the theory held by the then fashionable French philosopher, Henri Bergson, that humor is nothing if not mechanical. The countess's spirit dwelt perpetually on the heights of religion, and she addressed her seamstresses in precisely the tone that a cardinal employs in greeting strangers; nevertheless, seated at the head of the table or conversing in the salon, she often and innocently sprinkled her sentences with the most devastating obscenities. The most sophisticated lyric-writer of cabaret songs would have been incapable of the charm and humor which Countess Menti's unwitting talent produced, for her unconscious creations bore the mark of spontaneity. Yes, they were creations, for great art is not couched in odes and epodes alone; a single slip of the tongue can be a masterpiece. Countess Menti was the author of remarkable and at times immortal masterpieces in this genre. What aggravated the situation, however, was her fondness for public speechmaking, as if she herself took pleasure in the gentle and distinguished melodies of her own careful and somewhat hesitant sentences. The Reverend Lojzi, the chaplain, wrote the speeches she made as president of the Catholic Women's Union, and the countess read them aloud with the aid of a lorgnette. But even his conscientious printing, each letter capitalized to the size of a sparrow's head, could not prevent the gay little devils of mispronunciation and malapropism from doing their work. At a convention of the Women's Union, for instance, the opening of her speech originally read as follows: I *wish to extend a welcome to My Lord Bishop and to all the Canons.* Instead, Countess Menti stood at the center of the platform, her face suffused with spirituality, the very figure of a princess, and said: "I wish to extend a welcome to My Lord Bishop and to all the Cans." The bishop himself bit his lips until they were ruddy, while the substantial stomachs of the dignified canons shook silently throughout the meeting and the strain of maintaining a serious mien made them look as if they were crying.

When Mam'selle Jacqueline stuttered out the fact of Kristina's condition, the good Countess Menti's eyes flashed and her first gesture seemed to suggest an impulse to spring up and scratch the French slut's eyes out. But this was a momentary impulse and was occasioned by a depth of maternal concern. Then the scarlet flush left her face and her ears, and she resumed her usual pallor as quickly and imperceptibly as only polyps change color. And in the ensuing quietude of nerve and mind the rapid association of cool thought began. It occurred to her first of all that the responsibility belonged to her, not to the servant hired from abroad. Why had she never loved Kristina? Perhaps because she was ill during so much of her childhood. And perhaps because she would have preferred a boy. A boy, a boy, a healthy, rugged boy, fat enough to be hefted like a bag of salt, a rosy-cheeked little creature, as wild as peasant children or Hortense's son; a boy like that, to show in defense, or proof, after Rere. Her second thought encompassed the extent of the catastrophe, since she realized from the words of the governess that it was too late for medical intervention. At the same time she decided that she would not throw Jacqueline out; in fact, she determined to bind the woman to her side for the rest of her life. If she threw her out, the affair would be all over Hungary in a day. Mutual awareness of guilt is the best means of winning people over and silencing them.

"Who else knows of this?"

"Nobody," Mam'selle panted, her face puckered, her fingers wringing a little batiste handkerchief—with care, it is true, lest it be torn.

Countess Menti nodded quietly. She made her plans with clarity, speed and decision. She would tell her husband that the child was in need of a prolonged change of climate. She would take her daughter to Switzerland, or to some little village in the French mountains. But she did not communicate these plans to Jacqueline at once. Her French cards around her, she merely sat back in the large silken armchair, majestic and tragic but not theatrical, the signs of inner concentration on her face. Some time later she looked at Jacqueline and whispered:

"Well talk about it in the morning."

There was friendship and encouragement in her voice. Jacqueline wept.

"Poor Kristina," the countess sighed.

Jacqueline stretched out her long arms, as if reciting poetry, and said:

"A flower opened, and its stigma caught the pollen out of the air!"

…l'étamine d'atmosphère! It could not have been more prettily said. The pomp of the words was suited to the milieu of the circumstance. Mam'selle Jacqueline was well satisfied with herself at that moment. The countess nodded coldly, the interrogation came to an end and the lentil-colored skirt rustled out of the room.

Next day the countess went to Budapest and summoned the Minister of the Interior to the palace on Septemvir Utca around noon. This was nothing remarkable, for the Dukay name had magic in Hungary at that time. When a member of the family wanted something from one of the ministries, he summoned the minister. It was only natural. Countess Menti told the minister she wanted to send abroad a village girl whose worthless father was in prison for various crimes, so the child should not have to go without a husband in later life because of her father's misdemeanors. She therefore needed a new name, an identity card and a passport for a fourteen-year-old girl. The minister nodded understandingly. Knowing the countess to be a patroness of many charities, he found her request natural. He even admired the extent of her kindness, and at the same time he rejoiced to have survived the interview so inexpensively.

A week later Countess Menti, together with Kristina and Jacqueline, was on a train. It was her plan to place the prospective child in an orphan home somewhere abroad, and to take Kristina home unpunished and cured, as if she had undergone an operation for appendicitis or the minor surgery necessitated by an acccident But fate decided otherwise, and the child was stillborn, a circumstance which afforded the countess immeasurable relief in her ordeal.

György: born in 1898 in a room of the Park Hotel in Nice, because the countess was indisposed and spent that winter on the Riviera. The infant, when he had shed his swaddling clothes, soon proved to have inherited the physical and spiritual characteristics of his father's maternal side, the extinct Zoskay branch. He became a short-necked, thick, muscle-bound youngster, a red-cheeked moss-eyed rascal who resembled neither his parents nor his brothers and sisters. Whenever he saw the child his father snatched him up and tossed him to the ceiling several times. The family and the household staff treated him like an heir apparent, for he was to inherit the whole entailed wealth and estate.

At the age of eleven he took his tutor and a friend called Helmut to spend the summer on one of the estate's lumber tracts, because in that year the entire castle was overrun with workmen installing bathrooms, painting and papering the walls.

Helmut had come from remote Austrian relatives to spend his vacation in Hungary. He was two years older than György, a somewhat rabbit-mouthed and jag-toothed boy whose two front incisors had been knocked out with a hard object during a fight. Helmut did not like to talk about the incident. But he continually whistled through his jagged teeth, unconsciously and absent-mindedly emitting an unpleasant shrill devoid of melody, jauntily swinging the sound like a cane given in recompense for the broken teeth. He was an ugly, freckled whelp, the son of a debt-ridden officer, brought up by hard-fisted sergeants in the barracks of the Seventh Dragoons. The game warden had to chase Helmut off with a spade when the muscular daredevil tried to violate a little goose-girl. Had the warden caught him, he would have cut the boy in two, but Helmut was not to be overtaken once he started running. György experienced the sort of awe, joy, excitement and terror in Helmut's presence that he would have felt if someone had given him the wolf pup or the well-developed bear cub he had always yearned for in secret. Helmut once bit György on the neck, and it frequently happened that György emerged from an altercation with a swollen mouth or a black eye. The tutor and the two boys settled in the hunting lodge, with the forester's family to serve them and to give them meals. The tutor was a third-year student of liberal arts, a bespectacled, quiet, preoccupied individual; before he entered a room he took care to test the door handle with his forefinger, for he had good reason to expect it to be smeared with jam or heated with matches; or if the door was partly open, he kicked it sharply and jumped back lest the bucket of water fall on his head. The tutor wore stockings to bed constantly, for it sometimes happened during the night that his charges placed slips of paper between his toes and lit them, a practice commonly known as the kick-off or the hot-foot. At mealtimes he had to be wary of the sugar bowl, the contents of which were regularly mixed with salt. The eternal vigilance gradually exhausted his sense of tutorial responsibility and he was overjoyed when the boys stormed away from his side and left him alone, although even then he had to be on his guard, for Helmut was willing to spend half the night sewing up all the pockets of the tutor's suit. The tutor smiled philosophically at it all and revenged himself thenceforth by ignoring the youngsters completely. He was a poverty-stricken university student, a former scholarship boy who luxuriated in windows which opened on a pine forest, in his peaceful room, clean sheets and the excellent food; he had brought a suitcase full of source material along and considered the vacation a splendid opportunity to write his first novel, which was placed in the period of the Angevins. At all events, a few years later the tutor emerged as a bright young star on the horizon of Hungarian literature.

The two boys, wearing nothing but bathing trunks, scampered in the forests and along the river banks all day. Helmut swam like an otter. Once, crawling crablike under water, his eyes open and inspecting the rocky wall of the riverbed, he happened upon an underwater canal. He retreated from the dark hole, shot to the surface, filled his strong lungs with air and ventured once more on his daring submarine exploration. After swimming a few yards he felt the canal widen, and he rose to the surface. A roaring darkness met him, the air heavy and stuffy. It was clear that he had found a subterranean cave, its entrance opening some yards below the surface of the river. He could not even guess at the dimensions of the cave because the darkness was complete—there was only the mysterious roar, and the slapping of water. The cave evidently breathed through the cracks in the cliff wall, for there was sufficient air. Full of his discovery, Helmut regained the river and the canoe. Chest heaving, he told György, who had been terrified by his long disappearance and believed him lost, of the result of his underwater travels. The two boys, dripping wet, scurried back to the hunting lodge and returned with a flashlight, which Helmut carefully wrapped in a waterproof bathing cap. Once more he dived in and headed for the cave. György did not dare to follow him. Teeth chattering with excitement, he awaited the return of the intrepid explorer. Meanwhile Helmut was flashing his light about the interior of the cave. It was a void of formidable size, as large as a modest peasant cottage. The beam of the flashlight could not penetrate the zigzags of the high, stalactitic ceiling, from the heights of which a fractured waterfall limped along with the uneven stone parapet for a crutch, its querulous voice complaining like an old crone as it came, the white foam a fichu of lace on a black dress—it all suggested the eternal monotony of life imprisonment.

Helmut emerged again with a recital of what he had seen. He exaggerated the dimensions of the cave and described a series of wonderful animal statues which were, perhaps, of gold. He declared himself sole proprietor of the entire cave. György protested vehemently, maintaining that the lumber tract belonged to his father. By way of answer, Helmut punched him in the chest so hard that György fell out of the canoe. The treacherous current had almost swept him away before Helmut jumped in and dragged him ashore. There they continued to debate their property rights and finally agreed on mutual ownership. Still György lacked courage to venture into the submarine passage, for the idea of going below the surface and disappearing into a black hole frightened him.

"Three strokes and you're inside...then you come up for air..."

György did not answer; his teeth were chattering. A cruel desire to see the cave possessed him, and even more than drowning he feared that Helmut would remain sole owner of the cave in the end. After long consultation they agreed that Helmut would go first with one end of a long rope and György would follow him at the other end of the rope, to be pulled out of the cavernous tomb by Helmut in case he lost consciousness. György was already a resourceful man who anticipated every exigency.

After careful preparations Helmut disappeared under water with the flashlight and the rope. Soon a tug on the rope told György he was to start. The lad slipped into the water with the expression of a person hurtling into his grave. His passage, however, was accomplished without incident. Helmut, grinning at the edge of the subterranean pool, pulled him out of its black depths. The boy's chest heaved wildly for a time, more from fear and terror than from weariness. The flashlight filled the cave with its eerie and intermittent yellow glow. In that strange light Helmut's silent, self-satisfied grin seemed diabolical. Still panting, György kept staring about the interior of the cave. He was on the verge of tears.

A few minutes later the two boys undertook a further exploration of the cavern, insofar as that was possible in the relatively small area above water. In places the rock formations which ringed the pool made admirable bench-like resting points, but elsewhere the damp black cliffside gleamed unbroken in sheer and forbidding ascent and towered above them threateningly.

A quarter of an hour had passed when the flashlight suddenly began to fail. Either water had seeped into it or the batteries had simply given out. The Cyclops-eyed yellow beam faded to a dull red, flickered and then died altogether, to György's immeasurable dismay.

"Don't be afraid," Helmut grumbled, feeling György's ice-cold hand bite into his arm. But he shivered too, for the darkness was dreadful, thicker and different from darkness on the earth above. All at once the air seemed to have been exhausted. Moreover, Helmut had no idea at this point where the exit was located.

"Is the rope around your waist? You get into the water too!" He had to shout to be heard above the noise of the waterfall.

The water reached almost to their chests.

"I'll go ahead," said Helmut, and he submerged to look for the exit. Soon he came to the surface, sneezing like a walrus.

"I found it!" he shouted, and the stalactitic pipe organ returned his voice with a curious echo.

"Look out—I'm going under!"

But György waited in vain for the tugging signal of the rope. Terrified to death, he began to imagine that his friend had simply been swallowed up by some enormous sea monster, tenant of the underwater cave. Helmut soon reappeared at his side.

"That wasn't it!" he panted when he had caught his breath. His lungs kept heaving with exhaustion. György began to weep loudly.

"Don't cry!" Helmut yelled, and attempted to punch György's head but only hit his shoulder in the darkness. This gesture was his defense against the terror which had begun to possess him as well. The canal that he had taken for an exit had turned out to be nothing but a sack-shaped hollow in the side of the cliff. Now he realized that there might be more canals beneath the surface, some of them leading into the interior of the cliff, and if he swam along one of these at any length he might use up all his breath and be unable to return.

He circled the pool, feeling the bottom with his feet.

"Look out—I'm going under again!" he called, having found another hole. György heard a second submersion and soon felt the tug of the rope once more. He was half unconscious during the entire retreat. When he reached the surface Helmut was already in the canoe, and as he pulled György toward him like a lifeless corpse he grinned good-naturedly, although his face was green with fright. Outside everything seemed unusual: the sunshine, the savor of the air, the willows murmuring in the breeze, the incredibly high and distant sky. For a few moments the boys were absorbed in the great wonders of life, which always set a heart to beating faster when they are thought to have been forever lost. The noonday sun scalded their shivering bodies and burdened them with its hot invisible weight.

"Listen to me!" Helmut said finally. He pointed to the wall of the cliff. "We'll make a hole a yard and a half high here, so that we can enter the cave with a canoe. Well wall up the entrance with stones and camouflage it so that nobody else will know…"

He was so pleased with his own engineering schemes that he unexpectedly began to revile himself for not thinking of them before.

Later their hunger drove them homeward.

"At the entrance—" he continued the elaboration of his plans while walking "—we'll leave an air vent, which will serve as a source of light too."

György was set on fire by the plans. He looked at Helmut as if the boy were a god in human form.

It seemed odd to the tutor that the two boys stayed at home that afternoon. Fearing the worst, he took precautionary measures. Through the keyhole of their room he saw that the boys were engrossed in composition with many whispered consultations.

They put the terms of mutual ownership into writing, and sealed the document with promises, blood, oaths and a handshake under the table. Helmut had elaborate plans for the cave. He decided to furnish it with a stove, cooking utensils, shotguns, a grandfather clock and a woman as well. He thought one woman should suffice the two of them. With all these objects assembled, he planned to move into the cave permanently, bidding farewell to the outer world forever, to the world of report cards, haircuts, compulsory washing of hands, church attendance and the other horrors of civilization. They would leave the cave only on the occasion of pirate expeditions in search of sustenance.

Early the next morning, armed with hammer and chisel, they returned to the cliff. A few hours later their hands were bloody with endeavor, but the steel-like andesite resisted all their efforts.

"We need some dynamite," Helmut concluded finally, rubbing his aching palms. Their arduous operations had succeeded only in marking the site of the cave entrance on the cliffside.

They postponed the final accomplishment of their plan until the following year because there were only a few days left of their vacation.

The following year, however, Helmut did not show up, since he had fallen victim of a motorcycle accident in the meantime. In his case this does not mean that a motorcycle ran him down. No, it would never have happened that way with him. During a family quarrel, after his father had slapped him roundly, he stole his brother's motorcycle and drove off at a speed of eighty miles an hour on the Semmering highway, resolved never to return home. And he carried out his resolution, for the next day he was found dead at a crossroad, his body stretched alongside the mangled motorcycle.

Thus György became the sole proprietor of the secret of the cave. In those days he did not imagine that the cave, during the inferno of a frightful epoch in the distant future, would play an important part in his life.

Chapter Four

IN THE course of the years two more children were born to the Dukays: János and Terézia. János was born in 1906, Terézia in 1910. The children played and laughed as they grew up; the rooms and the long, vaulted corridors of the castle resounded with them. The Ararat castle was in use all the year around, each of its tremendous fireplaces consuming a modest forest of firewood during the winter months, although every September after the deer-run the parents generally moved to the palace on Septemvir Utca in Buda. They shortened the winter with several excursions to St. Moritz or the Tátra, and at the beginning of February they ran impatiently to greet the spring on the Riviera, whence Count Dupi was always called home by a telegram from his game warden:

THE SNIPE HAVE ARRIVED. KRCSMEK.

Sniffing the air along the seashore, Count Dupi waited for the telegram with bags packed, and often hopped on a train even without a telegram, having sniffed the wind like the Alaskan caribou hunters or the nomads of the Asiatic desert who follow the migrations of wild game, and so the passenger entrenched in an entire first-class compartment of the Nice-Vienna Express, with his odd-shaped and outsized heavy pigskin suitcases, buried in French newspapers and the smoke of Havanas, had something of primordial man about him as he adjusted his life in the midst of civilization's distractions and implements and burdens to the mating seasons of the birds and the beasts.

Having met all the members of the Dukay family so far, if only briefly, we owe it to ourselves to make the acquaintance of the rest of the household. The household staff at Ararat consisted of fifty-eight members.

The staff members were graduated on a hierarchical scale in accordance with their rank and influence. Next to Count Dupi there was Mr. Gruber, the confidential secretary who—despite a mute expression—was fluent in six languages; and Miss Malvin, his typist and stenographer, of whose tendency to imitate Countess Menti in gesture, intonation, dress and coiffure neither she nor anyone else was aware; and Herr Jordan, the major-domo who once served Archduke Charles Leopold and was said by some people to be the very image of the life-size portrait of Emperor Ferdinand V. His appearance suggested that there might be Habsburg blood in his veins, but no one knew this for certain and no one mentioned it. Nevertheless, Herr Jordan's carriage implicitly commanded respect, so much so that Professor Schön, the librarian of the castle, often raised his hat to him in the park by mistake. Count Dupi too used him gently as if in acknowledgment of the fact that in Jordan he had an emperor *manqué* supervising the personal valet who laid out his shirt and tie every morning and ran his bath. The major-domo stood motionless, hands locked behind his back, when he carried out this important responsibility of his position. The respect in which Count Dupi held Herr Jordan is evidenced by the fact that in the course of fifteen years he only slapped the major-domo's face once, when the major-domo spoke back to him one morning right after he awoke, and considering the fact that the count's temper on awaking was that of a wounded lion, it is obvious that Herr Jordan chose the worst possible moment to forget the respect due his master. Later, seated in his warm bath, Count Dupi regretted his hasty gesture, a gesture he did not habitually employ toward servants, and regretted it especially because the major-domo was privy to a number of family secrets. Therefore he pressed the button beside the taps and ordered the valet to summon Herr Jordan.

"Ich verzeihe Ihnen, Johann...I forgive you," and the count, seated in the tub, offered his hand to the major-domo.

Herr Jordan, shaking the outstretched hand with a deep bow, was aware of the gesture's momentous import, for he knew that never before in the centuried history of the family had a Dukay been known to shake hands with his major-domo. The break with tradition was somewhat mitigated by the fact that Count Dupi's hand was soapy and wet.

At the peak of the hierarchy of servants around Countess Menti was the housekeeper, whom even the members of the family called Fräulein Hilda. Miss Hilda was a thin, lopshouldered old maid of the sort found only in convents, whose sense of heavy responsibility kept her nostrils forever quivering as rodents quiver even when they are at rest. Her left eyelid, paralyzed from infancy, half covered one of her eyes and gave her a sarcastic, superior and suspicious look. In the realm of household affairs her authority was so great that Count Dupi called her the One-Eyed Regent. Not even Countess Menti could make a decision without her; she had to be consulted on every detail, and woe betide the person who dared to act without her knowledge. There were constant border incidents and frontier clashes between her and the governesses and the chatelaine, for the governesses reigned in the children's apartments and the chatelaine had charge of the guest rooms.

The One-Eyed Regent gave the impression that she was willing to die at any moment for the ideal that she served. Her ideal was the house, the house at Ararat with its endless rows of linen closets, Countess Menti's bath salts, the machines in the sewing room, everything in the house whether alive or inert, from the children's imported English suits to the dog brush, from the most obscure dustcloth to the countess's jewel box. To superintend all these, to keep the objects in motion among people who were often ill-humored, or lazy, or sick, or drunk, required a talent for administration that Fräulein Hilda did not lack. But she still could be swayed with small gifts. For years Balázs, one of the footmen, was undisturbed in his open raids on the cigars, the imported wines and the ammunition stores because he occasionally gave bouquets of violets, lilies, carnations and roses to the Regent, who thirsted for such little tendernesses and protected the rabbit-mouthed footman from all suspicion. Human nature being what it is, unfortunately, Balázs extended his operations beyond the limits of his protection and was caught on a Budapest trolley with his hand in a gentleman's pocket, very much like the elephant hunter who cannot restrain his passion and fires on a squirrel in a residential zone. A ray of sunshine was extinguished in Fräulein Hilda's life with his departure.

The Regent always wore a black dress with a black apron, and she was of course entitled to wear a hat, unlike the chambermaids who wore light blue uniforms with lace-fringed white aprons while on duty in the castle and covered their heads with kerchiefs when in civilian clothes.

Before the war, according to the compilation of the aforementioned Sir Lawrence Gomma, the Ararat household included the following employees: the master's personal staff comprised a librarian, a secretary, a stenographer, the major-domo, a personal valet, a bootman, a chauffeur and a permanent game warden, eight persons in all. The countess had in her personal service a companion, the housekeeper, a senior chambermaid and a younger one, and the second chauffeur. A castellan and his staff of three footmen looked after gentlemen guests, while visiting ladies were cared for by the chatelaine and three chambermaids. These footmen and chambermaids wore a distinctive livery. The lowest rank of house servants was made up of two sturdy charwomen and three porters, who scrubbed the corridors and bathrooms, tended the furnaces and carried wood.

The kitchen was ruled by the French master chef, with an assistant to cook for the staff. Two kitchen boys assisted the chef and two scullery maids assisted the assistant. In terms of command three dishwashers belonged to this division, but they were not allowed to enter the kitchen.

The laundry was permanently staffed by a laundress, a presser and four washerwomen.

Peripheral positions were held by the two gatekeepers, who still wore the livery made fashionable in Maria Theresa's time, one at the south gate and the other at the north gate of the far-flung grounds. They lived, with their families, in little cottages adjacent to the iron gates. The park itself was tended by a flower gardener, who supplied centerpieces for the dining table, a vegetable gardener and two caretakers.

A large force manned the stables, headed by the English stable-master and the chief groom, who commanded two Hungarian coachmen, one English coachman and six grooms. There were frequent horse shows. This meant that large armchairs were set up and visitors were served after-dinner coffee and brandy in the stables. On the day of a show the splendid horses of the Ararat stud were curried to such a high polish that they outshone the sun, and their manes were adorned with ribbons; the grooms strewed fine sand on the floor of the stables and traced the names of the horses in the sand with broom handles. Visitors spent hours there, mingling the fragrance of their excellent Havanas and of the fresh coffee with the strong ammoniacal smell of the stables while they debated the important problems which inevitably arise in connection with horses.

The tutors and governesses who hovered around the children constituted a special caste, the membership of which fluctuated with the number and age of the youngsters. In Sir Lawrence Gomma's time the castle was served by four governesses—two German, one French and one English—and a tutor.

God was served by the Reverend Lojzi, the chaplain.

Altogether fifty-eight persons were in the permanent employ of the castle. Naturally, there were additional day-laborers: extra men to cut the lawns, nuns from the village to operate the sewing machines, nurses, doctors, swimming instructors, music teachers and tennis coaches. The house was never without visitors, and thus meals had to be provided for approximately one hundred mouths a day.

The hierarchical scale of the staff required four separate tables in four separate dining rooms. Professor Schön the librarian, Mr. Gruber the secretary, Miss Malvin the stenographer and the Reverend Lojzi ate in the small dining room off the billiard room. These individuals were also exceptionally privileged in that they were invited, more or less frequently in accordance with their rank or occupation, to take an occasional meal at the main table, where even sports shirts were permitted during dinner but at supper the ladies wore evening dress and smoking jackets were *de rigueur* for the men. At noon the tutors and governesses ate at the family table, but in the evening, except on special occasions, they took their meals with the children.

At the main table in another wing of the castle sat the major-domo Herr Jordan, the One-Eyed Regent, the English stablemaster, the chief groom, the castellan and his wife the chatelaine. Their refectory was furnished like the dining room of a contemporary undersecretary, a provincial chief surgeon, or a substantial landlord. The service and the silver were in the same style. Platters were passed by chambermaids.

At the third table, in another and more simply furnished dining room, sat the chambermaids, the gardeners, the footmen and chauffeurs, with the assistant cook at the head. They were served by the scullery maids.

The fourth and most populous dining room housed plain pine tables for the porters, charwomen, kitchen boys, grooms, laundresses and scullery maids. They waited on themselves. Although wine was only served on the principal feastdays here, this table was the loudest and most cheerful.

The household staff entered the chapel in the same order every Sunday morning and on holidays. Attendance at services was compulsory. Entrances and exits took place in strict accordance with rank. First came Fräulein Hilda, on her head a fantastic hat and in her hand the ivory-bound breviary once given her by Countess Menti for Christmas. At her side, full of importance, marched the major-domo Herr Jordan. They walked beside each other like Philemon and Baucis, as if they were a married couple, sailing along like the exemplars of marital fidelity in Phrygian mythology; whereas in truth they despised one another, and in the course of the weekday bustle of work they muttered all the Carinthian and Bavarian idioms in the German language at each other, baring their gums and showing their teeth as they passed like two dogs. They were accompanied by the stablemaster Mr. Johnson, the castellan and his wife, all appropriately dressed in Sunday black. Only after they had settled into their separate pew did the chambermaids, footmen and chauffeurs troop into the chapel, and after them came porters, kitchen boys, scullery maids. The count and countess sat in their own oratorium, while the children and their governesses took seats on the mezzanine of the chapel.

From infancy the children were known to the staff as Countess Kristina, or Countess Zia, Count Rere or Count Gyuri or Count Jani. But this style was dropped when they reached the age of eighteen and the girls became Her Excellency the Countess Kristina and Her Excellency the Countess Terézia, while the boys turned into His Excellency the Count Imre, His Excellency the Count György and His Excellency the Count János. The tutors and governesses had the right to call the children by their Christian names in private conversations, and on entering a room the children gave them precedence, and walked to their left on the street, whereas the other servants were required to open doors for the children and to permit them to walk on the right, a rule from which not even the Regent was excepted.

The major-domo accompanied the count on trips, handled the mail and supervised the serving of meals. He poured wine at table, but did not touch the serving platters. During meals, his hands locked behind his back, he stood watching the glasses at a few paces from the table and directed the footmen and waitresses with the mute whiplash of his eyes. The senior footman polished the silver, the castellan greeted arriving guests at the main entrance of the castle, the second footman carried the countess's breakfast to a certain point in the corridor where it was taken from him by the countess's senior chambermaid, but it was the Regent who actually carried it to her lady's bed. The footmen wore livery, the major-domo wore a smooth black tail coat with a black tie. The scullery maids had special uniforms to distinguish them from the light blue of the chambermaids. Mr. Johnson and the English coachman wore top hats, unlike the Hungarian coachmen in their cherry-red dolmans and ostrich-plumed hats.

Monsieur Cavaignac, the French master chef, arrayed in white and with a tall duckcloth cap on his head, entered the countess's salon promptly at eight o'clock every evening when the first footman announced him. Book in hand, he read off the menus for the coming day. Count Dupi usually assisted at these conferences too, for he was familiar with the most subtle nuances of French cuisine and sometimes found it difficult to decide whether to have *esturgeon sauce verte* or cold venison for the next day's dinner.

2. Kristina and the King

Chapter One

IN 1911 *The Aristocratic World*, a weekly publication printed on sumptuous rag paper, issued a richly illustrated Easter edition in the columns of which the firms whose letterheads boasted the phrase "by appointment" vied with each other in advertising their cognacs, harnesses, flea powders and lingerie. *The Aristocratic World*, a masterpiece of the Hungarian printing industry, regularly appeared in only one thousand copies. One might well ask: Can a weekly paper exist on a circulation of a thousand copies? It can. No more than half the columns of *The Aristocratic World* were allotted to the news of the aristocracy, if only because a true aristocrat would not pay for space unless it contained an article of his own composition. There were, it is true, some aristocrats of literary pretension who shocked Mr. Lusics the editor by actually expecting payment for their endeavors, but such people were as few and far between as white crows, and one took care to avoid them. The remaining columns were devoted to the nieces of drug manufacturers, to the marriageable daughters of boondoggling contractors and to *arriviste* state councilors, who were always ready to make a sacrifice in the interest of literature and art. During that time a great Hungarian writer died in dire poverty, with nothing more than a candle to his name because the electricity had been disconnected—but it served him right, for he had not learned to recognize the secret signposts which lead terrestrial tourists to the top of Parnassus. Mr. Lusics, who was not only editor but owner of *The Aristocratic World*, set his rates for the middle class by the distance in inches between the picture of a commoner and the portrait of the champion fox terrier of a real count. And he shuffled his coverage of banquets, christenings, births and deaths until the reader no longer knew who was count and who was brick manufacturer. For example, a photograph captioned "Wife of Dr. Elmer Trock de Lebernye Sunbathing on the Terrace of her Villa at Leányfalu" netted a small fortune, since Mr. Lusics exacted an extra tariff for the use of pseudo-titles like *de Lebernye*. And when we consider that the Trocks merely rented the villa at Leányfalu for the summer months, we may well suppose that the scale of rates was equitable.

The following poem appeared in the Easter edition of *The Aristocratic World:*

A goose-girl stood at the edge of the wood,
　　Pasturing her little white geese.
Oh so happy were she and her brood!
　　And her hair reached to her knees.

But lo! A hunter skirts the mead,
　　And lo! A rabbit on the run!
Here is a sorry tale indeed:
　　He shot the goose-girl with his gun.

The poem recounts the misadventure of the goose-girl with the uttermost succinctness of noble balladry. Editor Lusics made only one revision in the whole manuscript. Originally the last line of the poem had read: "He banged the goose-girl with his gun." Mr. Lusics was right to make the revision, for in the course of the development of language certain innocent words, especially in metropolitan usage, had taken on a suggestive meaning which the poet—whose manuscript came from Vienna—could not know. Such improper usages serve to emphasize the gulf between the higher spheres of society and the living language itself, between aristocratic heights and the everyday world. In German the word *Dreck* is as acceptable in polite use as the word *muck* in English, for "dirt" and "filth" are among its subsidiary meanings. This often leads multilingual noblewomen to assume, erroneously, that the colloquial terms for excrement lend themselves to polite discourse in other languages as well, and they casually introduce them into social conversation, thereby sending cold shivers down the backs of prelates or lord lieutenants. Nor do languages allow a free interchange of words without a corresponding change in meaning. In French the word *aborder* means: to approach, to address someone. In view of her German pronunciation, Countess Menti was well known for the statement that she frequently "aborted" her acquaintances on the street.

The poem, entitled "The Goose-Girl," meant a sum of one thousand nine hundred and ninety crowns to its author. This was, in truth, a substantial sum, when we recall that the greatest lyric poets of the time—poets for whom the history of literature was already conning its paeans of praise—received payments of thirty or forty crowns for verses which have since become immortal. This large sum, however, should be credited not so much to Mr. Lusic's liberality as to his editorial talent. *The Aristocratic World* charged the author of the poem one thousand crowns for "printing expenses" upon publication of "The Goose-Girl." Another thousand crowns went to the young Viennese journalist-poet who was despicable enough to translate the poem into German. In return for the high fee, however, he provided a German version of not two but four stanzas, and his rendition bore a greater resemblance to one of Schiller's lyrics than to the original. The Viennese *Die hohe Gesellschaft* sent the poet a check for ten crowns, which goes to show that Viennese editors were much less resourceful in such matters than their Budapest counterparts. Various stern critics, who considered the poem clumsy in composition and callow in content, could not have known that its author was extremely youthful. The poem appeared under the signature of Countess Kristina Dukay. The expenses of publication were handled with utmost discretion by Mr. Gruber, lest the little countess be disillusioned by the cruder economic aspects of literature; the ten-crown check from Vienna, however, went straight to Kristina, and its intoxication unfortunately provoked further onslaughts on literature.

Kristina's poetical proclivities betrayed only a faint glimmer of the fire which burned inside of her. She was beset by unbridled, soaring dreams of achievement, and by a certain sense of dedication. Her intelligence was well above average, and she held independent, disparaging opinions of Italian policy in Tripolitania, of Debussy and of Bernard Shaw.

It was in these years that a certain revolution of world-wide proportions came to a head—a revolution, originally conceived in an American colony at the end of the seventeenth century, which gradually transformed the world with its perseverance. Its influence still cannot be readily estimated. At the turn of the century the women of Vienna and Budapest, too, were swept away by the revolution, two fiery apostles of which had already broken countless umbrellas on masculine heads. The two ladies in question were Emmeline and Christabel Pankhurst, mother and daughter. American servant girls and European princesses found themselves on common ground in the struggle for women's suffrage. This revolution, as we know, ended in complete victory for the women, and from that point on the state of the world began to deteriorate breathlessly. A certain school of historical thought contends that the fanaticism and hysteria which beset our contemporary world are largely the result of the success of the Suffragette Movement, but so biased and bigoted a theory is clearly incapable of proof.

The emancipation of women was completed in the first years of the century, whereupon the middle-class and even more eminent apartments of Europe began to resound with feminine coughing fits as women succumbed to the cigarette habit; Countess Isabella, in fact, took to smoking long Havanas. This was when women began to free themselves from coiffures of three and four pounds in weight, for since time immemorial they had nursed a grudge against the proverb which ran: "Long on hair, short on brains." Kristina was among the first to wear a boyish bob. This was a constant topic of lively debate in the salons of the time, and Count Dupi steadfastly maintained that women's brains would not increase in direct ratio with the shortness of their hair.

Kristina took an active part in the Suffragette Movement, and even addressed one of their meetings. Since women reached biological maturity at an earlier age than men, she reasoned, they should be given the vote, too, at an earlier age. This argument was greeted with applause, but when she declared for the right of women to wear trousers even the most extremely radical contingent hissed her down.

The emancipation of women had an important effect on their sexual activities. Some of the younger daughters of the nobility arrogated a favorable balance of the new freedom to themselves by claiming the right to greater leeway than the virgins of the middle class or of the gentry. In the masculine circles of Viennese society it was rumored that Kristina could be had. Kristina was sixteen in January, but she seemed more mature. Women generally achieve their true beauty only after the birth of their first child; but, apart from Countess Menti and Mam'selle Barbier, only Dr. Freyberger, the family physician, knew the secret of Kristina's ripening beauty. Count Joachim the painter, who "did" Kristina in a slate-blue dress at Christmastime, considered his niece a Caucasian type, dark haired, white-skinned, blue-eyed, brachycephalic and leptoprosopic—or short-headed but long-faced—and of medium height. This much is certain: Kristina was beautiful.

✠

A solitary walk from Septemvir Utca on an afternoon in the early spring led her to the Lajoshegy, where she made a strange discovery. Tilemakers of old had once mined white clay from the side of the hill, and at the opening of one of these abandoned mines she espied a subterranean hut, barely visible because its roof of rusty tin and broken planks and dried weeds was only a few inches above the surface of the ground. On a tree trunk outside the hut sat a gigantic old woman, wearing a black dress and an old-fashioned black lace kerchief. Both lenses of her large spectacles were broken, and there was dirt and dust in the cracks of the glass. She held a club between her knees and stared fixedly into space, but her eyeballs, grown large beneath the thick lenses, could be seen darting from side to side as one drew near. About twenty varicolored cats idled beside her; at Kristina's approach they took flight and vanished, which was something that cats do not generally do. Repulsive scraps of food littered the neighborhood of the hut, and several dented kettles stood on the ground. The tattered dress and dirty hands of the old woman, together with her haughty carriage and the lace kerchief on her head, bespoke a strange combination of misery and majesty. She presented a bloodcurdling appearance. Kristina eyed her with consternation for a moment or two, and then asked timidly:

"Do you live here?"

The beldame did not turn her head at the sound of the Hungarian words, and when Kristina repeated her question in German the apparition replied in perfect English, clutching her club:

"Go to hell."

The sound of English speech was rare indeed on the Lajoshegy in those days. Before returning home Kristina went to the Buda Home for the Aged, where she knew the director because Countess Menti was one of the trustees and often brought gifts—knitted goods, sacred images or discarded rocking-horses—for the elderly inmates. Kristina reported her discovery on the Lajoshegy and asked the director to have the unfortunate old woman removed to the Home at once. The director began to search through the drawers of his desk and finally produced a pictorial magazine.

"Is this the woman you mean?"

The photograph showed the old lady amid her cats, seated in front of her hut; but the picture was clearly taken from a distance —the photographer had not dared to brave the menace of the club.

"Countess, please be reasonable," the director said. "Every month somebody or other discovers this old woman and wants to place her in the Home. It's hopeless."

"I'll pay all the expenses."

"Others have made the same offer. In the course of the past few years we've brought her in twice, with the assistance of the police, for this magazine used her as an excuse for an attack on the mayor. The second time we assigned her to a room on the second floor and locked her in. The next morning there was no sign of her. She escaped through the window. She's nearly six feet tall, of course, but it was quite a stunt nevertheless, for our medical examiner says she's well over eighty. Her health is excellent, and she spends the whole winter in that hut. She speaks perfect French, German and English, and so we think she may have been a language teacher or a governess. She must have experienced some sort of emotional shock, for she's not entirely sane. She makes the rounds of the villas in the neighborhood and collects scraps of food for her cats in those kettles of hers. She's incredibly proud, and will accept money from no one. People have named her Frau Katz, but nothing is known of her past. It's rumored that she tells fortunes."

A fortuneteller! This was all Kristina needed. The fortunetellers and graphologists of Buda and Vienna knew no more assiduous client than Kristina. Her every penny and even her smaller pieces of jewelry had already fallen into the hands of soothsayers whose anterooms were still more crowded than the most exclusive beauty salons, and Kristina was beginning to lose her faith in them. But a certain fascination emanated from the old woman on the Lajoshegy, and it had cast a spell over Kristina from the very first moment.

The next day she visited Frau Katz on the Lajoshegy once again. Knowing the old sorceress's rude temper, she approached the hut with circumspection, humming to herself absent-mindedly and pretending to pick flowers. This ruse finally brought her to the side of Frau Katz's tree trunk, but the old woman did not budge. The thick, broken lenses of her spectacles were fixed on the southern sky, above the Buda Fortress. The broken glasses formed a barrier that split the world in two, and if there was any truth in the statement that Frau Katz was mentally deficient, then one might say that the spectacles were outward symptoms of her schizophrenia. Kristina kept on humming, as if she were alone, and only spoke after a long while:

"Gnädige Frau, would you have a look at my hand?"

"Let me see it."

Kristina extended her rosy palm. Frau Katz spat into the hand with extreme cunning and fixed her eyes on the southern sky again.

"Palm!" she remarked finally. "You think I'm a palmist? Your palm doesn't say a thing. Be here before dawn tomorrow, and bring a handful of dried lentils."

"I'll be here," Kristina said obediently, and she was off for home, wiping her palm. She recalled the story about old Schoolmaster Karika at Ararat, who used to tell his students: "We're going to discuss the chicken in tomorrow's science class, so I want each of you to bring an egg." When she reached the palace she directed Monsieur Cavaignac to prepare a five-pound package of the best dried lentils. By this time Kristina's habits of life were such that it was more natural for her to retire at dawn than to rise at that hour. Everyone from Herr Jordan the major-domo to Margaret the chambermaid was instructed to wake her before dawn. The palace on Septemvir Utca was equipped with an automobile by then, the third such privately owned vehicle in Hungary, but it was in constant disrepair because no one knew how to cope with its intricacies. A faint, pleasant smell of ammonia still filled the courtyard, for the famous Dukay four-in-hand grays stood in the stables, rattling their silver bridles.

It was still dark when the young countess mounted one of the closed carriages and set out for the Lajoshegy the next morning. Kristina halted the carriage by the tall pear tree at the foot of the hill, took the five pounds of lentils in hand and headed for the hut on foot. Dawn was breaking by then, but the hut was hard to find—it was much farther away than she had thought. The cold dew soaked through her shoes, and the unaccustomed hour made her teeth chatter. Her bag of lentils grew heavier at every step. Frau Katz was sitting outside the hut, as always, with the club between her knees, as black and motionless as if she were a wisp torn from the departing night by a sharp edge on her tree trunk. Roosters called to each other on the distant hills, and the brightness of the morning star pierced the early dawn with a pang that was like an incipient toothache. Kristina began to hum absent-mindedly again, and sat down beside Frau Katz but offered no greeting. A long while later, without taking her bifurcated eyes from the southern sky, Frau Katz spoke:

"Did you bring the lentils?"

"Yes, I did."

Another long period of silence followed, during which the air took on a dull sheen of light. When it was light enough, Frau Katz stood up from the tree trunk. Her great height was apparent for the first time. She was like a black tower beside Kristina. She started for the hut, toward the steps which were cut into the ground.

"Follow me."

Frau Katz negotiated the door only by bending double at the waist. Dreadful stench and dirt greeted Kristina inside the hut. There was a table of bare boards, a single chair, several shelves, and in the corner a straw sack covered with a sinister horse blanket. On the shelves and on the ground stood more kettles which exuded the stench of food scraps. When Frau Katz sat down on the single chair, the black lace kerchief on her head almost touched the boarded ceiling of the hut. Her deep voice said:

"Give me a strand of hair from beside your right ear."

Kristina did as she was told. Frau Katz took the strand of hair, examined it with care, then gave it back angrily:

"No good. Pull one out by the roots."

It was amazing how sharp her sight was through the thick, dirty spectacles, even in the dimness of the hut. From one of the shelves she brought a little wooden box full of blue, yellow, red, brown and white medicine bottles. Selecting a small, empty white bottle, she tied the strand of hair around its neck. The hair barely supported the weight.

"Hold this!" she commanded, and Kristina's hand trembled as she gripped the strand of hair. Frau Katz took a handful of lentils from the bag and began to count slowly. Each time she spoke she dropped a lentil into the bottle, and her pauses were so long that the auroral light increased at every count. Kristina could hardly hold her arm outstretched any longer, and the bottle was beginning to dance wildly at the end of the strand of hair. The eighty-seventh lentil broke the strand. Frau Katz put her hands in her lap and was lost in thought for a long time. Then she said:

"Let me see your breast."

Kristina unbuttoned her dress and bared a shivering little breast.

"Not this one. Your right breast."

She took the nipple, completely blue with twilight cold and with fright, between two fingers, and examined it at great length. First one and then the other lens of her broken spectacles hovered over the little nipple, so close that the warmth of her wheezing breath touched Kristina's skin. With a wave of her hand she directed the girl to button up her dress, and clambered out of the hut. Outside she resumed her seat on the tree trunk, and the sievelike stare of her spectacles studied the southern sky anew, as impassive as if she were contemplating all eternity. The fringes of the clouds began to gleam with violet light as the sun neared the horizon. Kristina cowered beside Frau Katz on the tree trunk, but she did not dare to speak.

"The number eighty-seven means a mist and a mountain," Frau Katz said finally. "At the moment there is not much I can tell you. But a mountain is always full of great things. Life has great things in store for you—some very great, important role."

Now she turned toward Kristina and studied the girl from head to foot through the thick spectacles, as if seeing her for the first time.

"Who are you? The daughter of Herz the lawyer, on Kruspér Utca?"

"No," Kristina answered faintly.

Frau Katz questioned her no further. Another long silence ensued. Only the song of the awakening birds could be heard.

"Can't you tell me some more?" Kristina asked.

"Not a thing. Isn't that enough for you, dirty-face?"

Kristina thanked her and began to walk away.

"Hey!" Frau Katz called after her. "The lentils—you forgot the lentils!"

And when Kristina stopped, nonplused, the old woman shouted rudely:

"Come along now, take them, take them! One-two-three..."

Kristina had to carry the heavy bag away with her. She eased her burden by making a hole in the bottom of the bag and strewing the contents along the way. By this time the round globe of the sun was floating in the clouds of smoke that issued from the chimneys of distant factories. The famous Dukay grays were restlessly shaking their silver bridles at the foot of the hill, beside the pear tree. The coachman did not trouble to wonder where the young countess had been and what she had been about at this hour, for he was accustomed to every sort of oddity.

Returning to Septemvir Utca, Kristina crept back into bed. A mist and a mountain! These two words held her in thrall with their mystery and their might. The prophecy did not say a great deal, but it sufficed to fill her with immoderate and vainglorious dreams. Frau Katz and the strange dawn seemed wholly otherworldly.

✢

A few days later the two Dukay parents and Kristina transferred their residence to Vienna. The other children were too young to go: György was thirteen, János five, and Zia was only a one-year-old armful. Rere, half-witted and nearly seventeen years old, never accompanied his parents to Vienna.

Every year since their marriage István Dukay and his wife had given an elaborate garden party in their palace on Bösendorferstrasse, and this reception was always attended by the elite of the aristocracy in the Monarchy. This season Countess Menti made her preparations with especial care. The long list of invited guests included the names of six young aristocrats, one of whom—so Countess Menti hoped—would surely fall in love with Kristina and ask for her hand in marriage. Rather than being too much to hope for, surely, this represented a willful compromise with fate; but Countess Menti longed to see Kristina wed as soon as possible. Her daughter's activities as a suffragette were a source of grave concern to the countess, and she lived in constant fear that Kristina, in the exuberance of feminine emancipation, might conceive another illegitimate child, a circumstance which would now be more difficult to keep secret.

These garden parties usually began in the early hours of the afternoon and continued until dawn. The trees were decked with lanterns, to furnish illumination in the evening. Stags, roebucks and wild boars had arrived on the preceding day, shipped from the Dukay estates for Monsieur Cavaignac's magnificent meat pies. Dukay wines of far-flung fame, from Tokay and the shores of the Balaton, came by the case. The gypsies from Budapest arrived in the morning, and by the time the first guests began to appear the blossoming chestnut trees were ringing with Magyar tunes and popular Viennese waltzes. In keeping with the fashion of the day, the women wore hats as large as millstones and gloves that reached to their elbows, while the men wore frock coats and top hats; and there were many glittering uniforms, of course. The various armed services of the Monarchy were represented by the cavalry, principally. In those years the ugliest military headgear in the world was worn by the armies of the Austro-Hungarian Monarchy. They wore tall, trumpet-shaped shakos, the inner wire supports of which were generally out of kilter. At this time a bearded Jewish doctor, a certain Sigmund Freud, was already working on his "Symptoms, Inhibition and Anxiety," in which strange new words like *Unbewust* and *Minderwertigkeitskomplex* appeared—thus the unconscious and the inferiority complex were invented. The tall officers' hats served to elongate their wearers' heads.

Everyone was in high spirits. The sound of French and German speech bubbled beneath the music like the beer and champagne in glasses which nimble, liveried lackeys were distributing. The Monarchy was on as sound a footing as it had ever been since the days of Metternich, and the minor conflagration of Italy's Tripolitanian campaign gave no one cause for concern.

The number of guests did not diminish after the cold buffet, for elderly dignitaries who left early were replaced by an influx of newcomers. At five o'clock in the afternoon there was a concert in the great salon, with several members of the Vienna Opera taking part. The famous Hardt-Schlesinger Quartet filled the gold and white hall with Mozart's most exquisite melodies, but the principal attraction on the program was Miss Gertrud Lingel, *tragédienne* of the Burgtheater: after a poem by Goethe and two by Heine, she proceeded to recite a poem called "The Goose-Girl." Mr. Gruber had spent entire days battling over the *artiste*'s fee to bring this about. But the actress had been wrong to object; the recital of Kristina's poem was greeted by a storm of applause. Officers from the rank of captain down stamped their feet, in fact, until Kristina appeared on the platform. Handclasps of speechless emotion pressed Countess Menti's hand as she sat beside Archduchess Clarisse on a large fauteuil.

There were many who left after the concert, but new guests continued to arrive. The younger people began to play parlor games. The games, relics of their grandmothers' times, were remarkably foolish, in the opinion of Count Dupi; but Count Dupi, who was accustomed to another sort of parlor game, was not a qualified judge in this case. There was old-fashioned charm in these games, and an undercurrent of arch flirtation.

The young people formed a circle of chairs in the great salon. Their elders took part only to lend courage to the more timid youths, or perhaps because they were still young in spirit. At the instigation of Countess Julia, who was sixty years old and had a deep, metallic voice, they began to play *Apfelstrudel*. The countess threw a ball into the lap of General Baron Neuwirth-Pölz and called: "Apfelstrudel!" The one who received the ball had to ask: "Do you like it?" In reply to the general's query Countess Julia replied: "I like it because it has a cute mustache." Now Apfelstrudel is well known for the fact that it does not sport a mustache, but the rules of the game decreed that any answer at all was acceptable. A player who did not answer with alacrity, however, had to pay a forfeit. A special committee set the penalties; to redeem a gold cigarette case, for example, Captain Stolz-Heinburg was required to crawl the length of the room on hands and knees, thus exposing his enormous bottom to the view of Archduchess Clarisse and the entire company. Young Countess Ersperg-Hegwitz redeemed her bracelet by standing on a chair and crowing three times. The drawback of this penalty was that it advertised her thick legs, which were like mammoth sausages.

Kristina, still under the spell of her literary triumph, had learned only a few minutes previously that the inordinately youthful captain in the uniform of the Brandeis Dragoons with the modest ribbon of the Order of the Golden Fleece in his buttonhole was Archduke Charles, the heir presumptive, whose eyelids were visibly weary with much brandy as he sat twiddling his thumbs. The archduke was twenty-four years old, but seemed much younger. The lips beneath his trim little mustache were pursed like the lips of a three-year-old boy after finishing a glass of milk. Charles was the son of the "handsome archduke," of Otto, and he fortunately took after his father, for his mother—the daughter of the King of Saxony—was a stout, heavy-footed creature with large freckles and carrot-tinted hair who strutted like a Prussian general in hip boots.

Kristina threw the ball into the lap of the young archduke.

"Apfelstrudel!"

"Do you like it?" asked the little archduke, bobbing his head forward politely.

At this point, if someone answered, "I don't like it," or "I like chocolate mousse better," the game passed on to other players.

"Y-y-yes," Kristina replied uncertainly, scrutinizing the young man with care for the first time, but feeling that the moment had come for the mountain to fill and the mist to shimmer,

"Why?"

"Because…because…"

"Forfeit!" the company chorused.

Standing in the center of the circle, Kristina brushed her black hair back over her ear, where it glistened with the warmth of burnt bread-crust as she fumbled with a bad grace for the catch of one of her pearl earrings, an operation which took some time. Countess Julia had the feeling that there was a certain ostentation in her slow movements, that it was all designed to display her pink ear, which was truly beautiful, to the world. With a gesture of majestic melancholy she handed the earring to the archduke. The committee returned with a verdict which Prince Fini, Countess Menti's brother, announced. They had chosen the most severe penalty for Kristina: she was commanded to jump in the well. A shocked murmur ran through the assembled company. Kristina hung her head as she walked out of the room. It was with such an expression that Aztec virgins mounted to their immolation before the Corn Goddess of Ixtapalapa. Prince Fini turned to the heir presumptive and directed him to fulfill his knightly obligations by pulling the young lady from the well before she drowned. The archduke was perplexed and looked around somewhat foolishly, for he did not know the rules of the game and was taken aback by the complexities which had grown out of *Apfelstrudel*. But three other players jumped to his side and enlightened him in whispers. The dip in the well was purely symbolic: it meant that the young lady had to retrieve her forfeit with a kiss. Relieved, the archduke nodded in quick comprehension.

Kristina was waiting behind a wing of the great carved oaken doors for the knight to pull her from the well. And then the archduke appeared, and stiffened to attention with a slight click of his spurs. He wore a confused smile, as if he had unwittingly stumbled into a situation that was fraught with danger. In such cases a girl generally throws a kiss toward the boy's cheek and runs away amid noisy giggles. But Kristina was of a different stamp. She closed her blue-green eyes halfway, and her lips slowly approached the cognac- and cigarette-scented Habsburg lips. After the kiss Charles clicked his spurs again and gave Kristina his arm. The company acknowledged the successful rescue with a loud ovation, which was principally directed at the high color of the archduke's cheeks. This all goes to show that the grandmothers were not so very foolish when they invented the game called *Apfelstrudel*.

The game continued, others threw the ball and others caught it, but no one paid attention. The news of Kristina's dip in the well quickly overran the palace and the garden. The incident was discussed with more gravity than a reliable report, just furnished by the Minister of War, that the Italians had advanced in Tripoli. Prince Andrew considered the entire affair to be in the worst taste, while Countess Julia retired from the game and angrily muttered suspicions into her husband's ear: Prince Fini's innocence was called into question, and the dip in the well was viewed as a sinister plan to advance the interests of the Dukay family.

The lanterns were already glowing in the garden. The pleasant weather remained unchanged, and the balmy May air of Vienna came from all sides, even from the direction of the Eisberg. Since it was time for supper, the hungry guests attacked the abundant buffet tables once more; only the occupants of the upstairs game rooms did not budge, for by this time the cards were dealt to high stakes. Count Charles the lion hunter had just lost his two-thousand-acre estate at Iper—acacia forests, prize roosters, oxcarts and all—to the monocled, heron-necked Count of Innsbruck. The archduke had already left, and there was no sequel to the dip in the well that evening.

The six young aristocrats, invited for the secret purposes of Countess Menti, were hardly favored with a tango or a boston or a waltz apiece, for men were trampling one another in Kristina's neighborhood. Her literary triumph, but more particularly her dip in the well, had enhanced the value of a dance with Kristina—who was, in any case, completely entrancing in a sky-blue dress trimmed with golden bees, and her bare white shoulders, her slender waist, her magnificent youthfulness, her ill repute flashed audaciously as she floated in the arms of her partners. But she was overwhelmed by all that had taken place in the course of the day. Soon after midnight she vanished, but she spent sleepless hours listening to the gypsy music that filtered into her room from the garden. She put cold applications on her heart, and took sleeping pills, but neither were of any help. Frau Katz, the gigantic, sinister sorceress, hovered behind her closed eyelids, and the mysterious prophecy began to fill with meaning. The mountain symbolized by the number eighty-seven could be nothing but the throne, somewhere far away in a mist. Still she was not completely convinced. The great literary triumph which had preceded her dip in the well was confusing. Perhaps the mountain augured sudden and tumultuous success for the novel she was writing. She consigned all literature to the deepest circle of hell, and decided to return to Budapest the next day and, before dawn on the following morning, to visit the Lajoshegy once more.

Her parents knew Kristina was working on a vast historical novel that dealt with the original occupation of Hungary and was entitled "The Ordony Chieftain." Consequently they raised no objection when Kristina explained her urgent Budapest trip with the statement that she lacked certain facts which were available only in Hungarian libraries. A trip of this nature must not be postponed, lest the miraculous creative fervor that gives birth to literary masterpieces cool and evaporate away. Ever since Miss Gertrud Lingel's truly moving recital of the poem about the goose-girl, Countess Menti had regarded her daughter with a sense of holy terror which was akin to the expression on an Umbrian cloth merchant's face when he contemplated his son, who was to become St. Francis of Assisi; for Countess Menti did not realize that writers, in most cases, indulge their fits of inspiration simply to terrorize the members of their family and put their credulous votaries on the defensive.

Wracked with exhaustion, not only because of the early hour this time but as a result of two restless, sleepless nights, Kristina appeared on the Lajoshegy well before dawn. Her face was pinched and her eyelids swollen when she dismounted from the carriage alongside the tall pear tree. She started up the hill, but soon lost her way. An abyss blocked her progress, and there were thick woods to the left; it was clearly the wrong path, and she was forced to turn back although already staggering with weariness. She was afraid of being late, too, for daybreak was perilously close. There was not a single living soul near by of whom she could ask the way to Frau Katz's hut, and she was ready to weep with exasperation when, instead, she gave a cry of surprise and joy. A light green and circuitous footpath led the way along the hillside, like a mute sign from heaven. The lentils had taken root since she had strewn them away.

Frau Katz was sitting on the tree trunk in front of her hut, with the club between her knees as always, tremendous and black, like a fearful Neanderthal figure, studying the southern sky through her broken spectacles. One would not have been surprised to find a heap of infant bones in her hut. She was alone, for her cats had not yet returned from their nocturnal wandering, their frenzied love affairs.

Kristina settled on the tree trunk beside Frau Katz without a word of greeting. With her blue-green face and her blue-green coat, she looked like a tiny anthropomorphic patch torn from the blue-green cloud mass that began to glow in the east soon after the roosters, scattered among the gardens of little houses on distant hills, had given the dawn their permission to come out of hiding.

A few minutes later Frau Katz turned her head toward Kristina but said nothing, merely acknowledged through her thick, owlish glasses that the so-called human society of beasts had once again appeared on the threshold of her palace in the shape of an apparently fugitive young girl. There was nothing inimical about the curt turn of her head.

"Liebe Gnädige Frau," Kristina said finally, "I should like you to give me another examination, please."

Frau Katz did not look at Kristina as she answered in her strange, masculine voice:

"No more examinations. Anyway, I know what's wrong with you. You're in love."

Kristina's heart filled with dread and bliss at the sound of that Word. We all feel something like this when somebody pronounces the secret of our happiness.

Frau Katz's broken spectacles were fixed in space as impassively as the lens of a telescope in an empty, locked room. She must have seen something in her binary world, for after some time she spoke again:

"A king has entered your life…."

And a moment later she added:

"And someday you will hold the king's heart in your hand…."

Kristina closed her eyes and almost fainted. Her whole body quivered. The prophecy suffused her being like the most ecstatic pitch of sensuality. She sat thus, with her eyes closed and her back bent, for a long time, two shivering fists clenched to her mouth, looking like an embryo in the maternal womb. Right now the entire universe was, to her, the warm darkness of the amniotic fluid, where great things were in preparation, awash in secrecy. She only opened her eyes when a peculiar, warm, red radiance filtered through her eyelids. The sun had risen.

Kristina said in a tortured, timid voice:

"Liebe Gnädige Frau…can you tell me how long Franz Joseph and the crown prince Francis Ferdinand will live?"

Frau Katz nodded.

"Yes, I can. Bring them here so I can examine their toes."

Kristina realized that Frau Katz could not be expected to concoct prophecies out of empty air; but the examination she proposed was clearly out of the question. She descended the Lajoshegy with a soulful smile on her lips, trusting herself to the lentil path. A morning wind was gathering on the hill, a wind which broadcast the clear meaning of the prophecy to the world: "And someday you will hold the king's heart in your hand…."

She closed her eyes in the carriage, hardly able to bear the nervous throbbing of her heart. When they entered the city she directed the coachman to a fashionable suburb in the Városliget, giving him the number of one of the villas. The dancing hoofs of the Dukay grays played an exhilarating melody on the wooden pavement of the deserted Andrássy Ut, which was aglow with the violet tints of early morning.

Kristina rang the bell of a bachelor flat on the first floor of a rented villa. The old cleaning woman who opened the door already knew the young lady by sight.

"Is your master in?" Kristina asked while she unhesitatingly crossed the hall, the walls of which were covered with silken oriental draperies.

"He's probably still asleep," came the whispered reply.

Kristina opened one of the doors, beyond which she was greeted with the warm, heavy perfume of a masculine room, carefully darkened with curtains. Kristina evidently knew the way, for despite the darkness she found the bed from which the quiet wheezing breath of the sleeper could be heard. The bed was low and extravagantly wide, large enough to contain an entire family. Seated on the edge of the bed, Kristina began to take her clothes off, and her cold, quivering little body slipped beneath the warm comforter without waking the sleeping man. No one can blame her, upset as she was by the ultramundane things she had heard, stricken half dead by the dazzling lightning bolt of the prophecy, for taking refuge here. There are beds in which one cannot sleep. The lonely bed at home in Septemvir Utca was padded with insomnia. Here, however, she was sound asleep in a matter of minutes.

At about ten o'clock the man began to stir, and yawned loudly. He stretched out his left hand and rested it on the hip of the woman sleeping at his side. Then he stretched out his right hand, but drew it back with a start. He sat up in bed, terrified: at his right side, too, there was a woman, although he distinctly remembered bringing only one woman home with him at dawn. They had had a good deal to drink, true, but he was unable to recall the second woman. The situation promised to be perilous; to avoid further complications, therefore, he climbed from bed with the cautious agility of an acrobat and ascertained, in the light which shimmered through the crack in the curtains, that there were really two women asleep in his bed, a dark-haired feminine head sprawling on the pillows to the left and a blonde head on the right. He dressed with the stealth of wild animals when they sense danger in the forest. Then he vanished from the room.

It was nearly noon when the blonde head stirred, yawned, stretched, and looked beside her. She too sat bolt upright, terror-stricken and unwilling to believe her eyes, when she sighted the black tresses of the woman on the adjacent pillows, for she clearly recalled coming home with a man. Kristina also woke up at the creak of the bed, and she in turn was brought to her hands and knees by the surprise that met her: for a long time they exchanged lupine glances. Then, in sudden anger, they turned their backs on one another and went back to sleep, for both of them were still very sleepy.

When Kristina finally awoke in the late afternoon, she was alone in the wide bed. Everything that happened to her nowadays had assumed a dreamlike quality.

She took the midnight train back to Vienna. Her first visit was to Madame T., the most famous fortuneteller in Vienna, whose name it was forbidden to pronounce. By dint of persistence and the unusually large sum which she gave the receptionist, Kristina effected an entrance, and Madame T. answered her questions with the unqualified assertion that Franz Joseph would die in 1931, at the age of one hundred and one, while Crown Prince Francis Ferdinand, in view of his lingering consumption, would die three years later, in 1934. Kristina estimated that under those circumstances she would be forty years old when Archduke Charles succeeded to the throne. This second prophecy disheartened her, but she comforted herself in part with Balzac, who placed the highest valuation on the fortieth year of a woman's life, and in part with the thought that a fortuneteller like Madame T. did not seem entirely reliable after the experience with Frau Katz.

The next day the housekeeper, nicknamed the One-Eyed Regent by Count Dupi because of the cast in her eye, appeared in Kristina's room and announced that Countess Menti was waiting for her daughter in the downstairs salon. There was an ominous solemnity about the message. Kristina found her father in the salon too, resting his elbow on the white mantelpiece and staring into the smoke of his cigar.

"Sit down, Kristina—" and Countess Menti waved her daughter to a chair.

The silence of the next few moments was so great that one could almost hear the smoke curling from Count Dupi's cigar.

"This morning," Countess Menti began, "I received a very sweet letter from my dear old friend Charlotte. You probably know that Charlotte is the mother of Erich."

She paused momentarily to observe the effect of her pronouncement on Kristina's face. Count Dupi did not turn to look. Kristina's face showed no emotion whatever.

"The letter said," continued Countess Menti, "that she was pleased to hear Erich express an interest in you, and that she herself would be very happy if Erich were to marry you. I have talked the matter over with your father, and we feel that the project must be given the most careful consideration."

Erich was one of the six young men whom Countess Menti, for reasons of her own, had invited to the garden party. He was a youth of twenty-two, long-necked, narrow-chested, with the delicate, reserved manner with which only Austrian aristocrats were endowed, a manner which gave the impression that he was constantly half asleep. Their castle was one of the smaller and more ancient fortresses in the Inn Valley, high on a cliff—one of those medieval citadels which leave a fleeting image of the romantic age of knight-errantry in the memories of passengers on the Innsbruck Express. Rheumatism had afflicted every inhabitant of the castle in the past four centuries, for it was exposed to the constant pounding of violent windstorms on the heights of the cliff.

In lieu of reply, Kristina slowly raised her eyes toward her father, who was still reluctant to look anywhere but at the billowing smoke of his cigar. His thoughts nevertheless assumed almost palpable shape in the air. A fourth person in the room, very much present though invisible, was Archduke Charles. When Kristina entered, in a white muslin dress trimmed with tiny red and blue flowers, Count Dupi had found his daughter truly beautiful. The fine forehead beneath the warm, black highlights of her lustrous silken hair, the marvelously expressive blue eyes, the straight little nose, the sweet, sensuous beauty of the lips, the perfect lines of the neck, the masterly shoulders and bosom and wrists, the astonishing self-possession of the entire girl, the mysterious spiritual depths which were most vividly expressed in the fluttering arch of her eyebrows—all this, in Count Dupi's view, was much more than such a mere Erich deserved.

The thought that pervaded the room was inexpressible. This thought was more than a simple family matter. Prince Andrew or Countess Julia were lost in thoughts like this when they looked at their daughters nowadays, although they unquestionably had fewer grounds for hope. The aristocracy of Hungary had been gravely offended, ten years ago, when Francis Ferdinand married a plain Czech countess. It was, of course, an offense which did not permit open complaint, but offenses of this nature are the most heartfelt. Hungarian aristocracy could assuredly have supplied the heir apparent with prettier girls and more venerable families. Those thick-nosed Czechs, every mother's son of them, seemed to have been born on the bass drum of a military band. One faction of Hungarian aristocracy made a political grievance of the Czech marriage, for they were incredibly practiced at interpreting all matters of family or class in terms of national interest. And in the present case there was a certain logic in the eloquence of their arguments: if Charles were to marry a Hungarian girl, Hungary—that most refractory constituent of the Monarchy—would be thoroughly appeased. Were Metternich still alive, his splendid high forehead and his long, sharp nose would undoubtedly nod approval of this secret thought. A hundred or a hundred and fifty years before, such an alliance would have been out of the question.

But the male branch of the Habsburgs became extinct shortly thereafter, and if Francis of Lorraine—green in the memory of history as the prize breeding bull of Europe—had not put in an appearance at Maria Theresa's side, even the Pragmatic Sanction would have been of little help to the Habsburg law of succession. But Francis of Lorraine (and, according to gossip, the handsome pigtailed officers of the Palace Guard as well) attended to duty, and the House of Habsburg-Lorraine multiplied like the two Angora rabbits for whose progeny Countess Menti, ever since she received them as a present from England, had hardly been able to provide sufficient warrens. The strict laws of marriage which governed the House of Habsburg were rendered null and void by the indomitable forces of excessive proliferation, which generally bring catastrophe to regions and races both. At the turn of the century the situation in the courts of Europe was such that only the Wittelsbachs of Bavaria and the Bourbons of Italy could possibly come into consideration when a Habsburg contemplated union with a consort of equal rank. Other houses of comparable rank had no marriageable daughters. First to break the fetters of the overpopulated Habsburg cage was Archduke Johann Nepomuck Salvator, who resigned his titles to become the captain of a sailing vessel and perished mysteriously, ship and all, off the coasts of South America. After that one Habsburg mésalliance succeeded another, and newspapers the world over were dumbfounded to note that sensations of this nature were gradually losing all news value. "So what!" the Jewish wine merchants remarked in their Budapest cafés, when banner headlines proclaimed that Archduke Rudolf's daughter had snared nothing more than a certain Prince W—.

Kristina's silence was eloquent.

"I am afraid, Kristina—" began Countess Menti, but she did not finish the sentence. What she left unsaid was: "—that some delusion of grandeur has turned your head." But she did not say even as much as this.

Count Dupi turned and left the room without a word. On his way out he cleared his throat thoughtfully, as if in support of Kristina's silence. Immediately upon reaching his own room he began to compose an invitation to Archduke Charles, mentioning the plentiful stock of mouflon in the Ararat game preserves and calling attention to the impatience with which the horned rams were awaiting the forthcoming four-day hunt.

Kristina, learning of the invitation from a casual remark of Count Dupi on the following day, abandoned herself to a pitch of anticipation which has its equal only in the birds and smaller insects when they await the dawn after the air has filled with ultraviolet rays. Countess Menti, with solitary sighs, took cognizance of the fact that Kristina would not marry Erich, and she wrote to Charlotte: "…For Kristina is such an inexperienced child as yet…she was sixteen only last January, and she still pays more attention to her dolls than to thoughts of marriage." And Countess Menti continued to live in fear.

At that time Franz Joseph was beset with similar concern for Archduke Charles. He would have liked to see the young heir presumptive face the altar as soon as humanly possible, for the archduke was reputed to spend his Sundays picnicking with daughters of the Viennese middle class, and one such secret report asserted that a young lady in Tyrolean dress was giving him harmonica lessons in the Wienerwald. According to this report, the music lessons were administered behind a hazelnut tree, and long, frequent silences of the harmonica indicated that the instruction included theory as well as practice. It was from these days that one of the elderly emperor's famous remarks stemmed: "Spannt's a Plachen über Wien, da habt's a ganz grossen Puff!" which was his way of saying that an awning stretched over all of Vienna would cover nothing but a tremendous brothel.

The reply of Archduke Charles's aide-de-camp to the invitation to hunt at Ararat soon reached the Dukay palace on Bösendorferstrasse. The aide-de-camp declared that His Highness was eternally grateful for the kind invitation which the exigencies of a trip abroad made it impossible for him to accept.

But no one besides Franz Joseph and Princess Maria Antonia of Bourbon-Parma knew the real significance of the trip abroad. The emperor had summoned the heir presumptive into his presence and asked him with paternal solicitude whether he would care to go abroad for a few weeks. He mentioned only incidentally that a warm welcome awaited him in the Pianore house of Maria Antonia, in the Po Valley, and he completely neglected to say that the house was full of marriageable daughters. Charles seized at the opportunity, for so far he had seen nothing of the outer world besides some garrisons in Galicia.

The rest we know. On June 14th, 1911, he became engaged to Zita Maria Adelgunde, daughter of Prince Robert of Parma and Princess Maria Antonia of Braganza. Count Dupi heard of this momentous event in the Jockey Club of Vienna a few hours before it was announced to the press.

Kristina learned of the engagement from the front page of the *Wiener Tageblatt* the next morning. When the chambermaid returned to remove the breakfast tray she found the young countess unconscious on the bed, with soft-boiled egg all over her lips, for the spoon had fallen from her mouth. Tea and honey, trickling from the overturned dishes, stained the blanket.

She lay in a coma for days. No detailed reports were available of the prostration from which other young noblewomen suffered, in the neighborhood of Prince Andrew and Countess Julia.

Kristina returned to Budapest as soon as she was well enough to travel. She arrived on the noon train, and was too impatient to wait until the following morning. She went to the Lajoshegy that very afternoon. The summer heat had withered the lentil path, but its traces were still in evidence. There was disenchantment in the sobriety of the sunshine, of the heat, of the squeaking trolleys and other noises which resounded from the city. She met with a calamitous disappointment at the end of the lentil path. Frau Katz's hut was gone and the spot where it had stood was hardly recognizable. A sign read: SÁNDOR VRABEK, BUILDING CONTRACTOR. Construction of a new villa was progressing by leaps and bounds—the foundation had already been poured.

Here and elsewhere in the vicinity her search for Frau Katz proved fruitless, although she walked the suburban streets of Buda until late at night and addressed her questions to everyone she met.

A starless, black night had swept away Frau Katz's black dress, her black lace kerchief and her black chimpanzee hands. Nothing remained of her but the few words which were engraved on Kristina's heart with the blue flame of a blowtorch: "And someday you will hold the king's heart in your hand...."

Chapter Two

YEARS later, young György Dukay—who was in many ways a rebel against the standards of his own kind—inclined to the opinion that the Dukay family was responsible for the catastrophe of the first World War. But, in view of the state of the world as it existed then, his sense of justice impelled him to modify this position somewhat, however true it was that he could discern, in the castle at Ararat and the palaces on Septemvir Utca and Bösendorferstrasse, every symptom of the prevalent moral temper. Certain historians, unable to express themselves except in large, vague terms, called this moral temper "imperialism," a designation which hardly epitomizes the movement of Countess Menti's hand as she rang for her chambermaid, hardly describes the silver-knobbed riding crop with which Count Dupi struck the face of one of the grooms when Kristine horse was ineptly saddled.

The historians were right, at best, in that the organization of the world at the turn of the century was particularly conducive to the unfettered gratification of man's desire to dominate his fellows. Karika, the schoolmaster at Ararat, lived in dread of the inspector of schools, and addressed himself to his classes in a manner designed to make the children live in dread of him, although he was a gentle, good sort at heart. Egry-Toth, the estate agent, quaked at Count Dupi's every word, and the overseers quaked at every flash of Egry-Toth's eye, while the peasantry had reason to live in terror of the overseers' slaps and kicks. The established order of things, whether in barracks or bureaus, came simply to this: who lived in fear of whom, and why.

In this sense men were truly imperialists the whole world over, but especially in Europe. Occasionally there were poets, like Tennyson in England or Petőfi in Hungary, who clamored for universal freedoms, but they themselves were not quite clear as to the meaning of the term. Every nation taught its children that if the world was the cap of God then their native land was the feather in the cap, while the others did not count. Every public oration or military anthem explained how inconceivably mighty and masterful a nation was the English, or the French, or the German, or that the whole world would fall flat on its face once a Hungarian hussar or a Rumanian guardsman drew his sword. The smaller the nation, the greater the lies it told about itself, from kindergarten upwards; this educational system succeeded in making the citizens of every country stupid enough to believe that if war ever broke out their national consciousness and courage would suffice, like a pick-handle, to smash the entire world. The concepts of universal freedom and world federation were never so far from the minds of men as during the second half of the nineteenth century.

This question deserves a more searching scrutiny, however. It has been beyond the powers of human knowledge, even unto the present day, to investigate the *psychology* of peoples or of political systems. Education for nationalism has claimed many lives, without question, and there have been hundreds of thousands of mothers throughout the world who relinquished their sons to the battlefield with the thought that they were making a sacrifice to some great, obscure deity; but it would be an exaggeration to assert that all men were of this mind. Any historian, speaking of England or Germany or Russia as separate psychological entities in this epoch, is as open to suspicion as if he were discussing the constellation of Andromeda, where he has never been. The races and nations of mankind consist of many, many millions of human beings whose individual examination and tabulation is impossible of accomplishment if only because men do not reveal themselves completely even in their conjugal beds; and without the benefit of complete revelation any inference whatsoever would be sheer conjecture. It is a fatal fault of our perspective, in appraising races and states, that we take into consideration only such as have actually fallen victim to a certain system of education, a certain propaganda line. It is much likelier that there is no distinct psychology of races and states. This is suggested by the fact that burglars the world over bear a remarkable resemblance to each other, not only physically but in terms of their tools as well; and at the same time a respectable Englishman— however incredible it may sound—betrays a surprising similarity to a respectable Hungarian, for example, in relation to the really important things in life. And so it is with all peoples. Reliable statistics in this regard are obtainable only from men like Dickens, Dostoyevsky, Flaubert or Henry James, because they studied *man* and were wise enough to assign historians the completely hopeless task of studying the psychology of peoples or political systems.

In every age there have been men, individuals or groups, foolhardy enough to propagate the falsehood that they spoke in the name of an entire nation—a fiction made possible for them by a remarkable absence of social communion which persists even in our own time. Thus, when Prince Andrew or Count Cini used phrases like "We Hungarians" or "We Austrians" in the downstairs salon of the palace on Septemvir Utca, it was an indulgence in the height of insolence, fundamentally, since Prince Andrew had absolutely nothing in common with— for instance—János Puska, the elderly chief shepherd of the Veresk estate, although there was only one such Prince Andrew for every one hundred twenty thousand János Puskas, whether in Hungary or anywhere else in the world. Herr Heller, who manufactured excellent eyeglasses on the Alte Kirche Strasse in Frankfurt, was completely unlike Emperor Wilhelm, while Mr. Farthing, wielding his tailor's shears in Manchester, was filled with thoughts utterly unlike those of Sir Edward Grey; and when Ivan Sylvestrovich Garinin fell to his knees before the tsar's portrait somewhere in Irkutsk, this was no proof that he was thinking with the Little Father's head, an achievement which would have been difficult if only because the Little Father did not confide his secret purposes to Ivan Sylvestrovich Garinin.

Under these circumstances, when we study the antecedents and causes of the first World War, we must not forget that we are dealing with the activities of only certain groups of men, in respect to whom, however, we can accept the designation of imperialist without reservation.

At that time the world consisted of six states: England, Russia, France, Germany, Italy and the Habsburg Monarchy. The rest did not count. There may have been some kind of India and China somewhere to the east, but these were of no interest. The Japanese were more to be reckoned with. The diplomatic staff of the Japanese Embassy was invited to one of the larger banquets at the Septemvir Utca Palace, and Herr Jordan the major-domo saw one of the ambassadorial gentlemen—full of smiles, bows and gold-rimmed spectacles—produce a little scissor when he was alone in the smoking room for a moment and quickly snip off a piece of wallpaper, which he thereupon slipped into his pocket. Throughout the western world the Japanese were passionately pillaging European civilization, and allegedly had built a great, gallant nation for themselves. Furthermore, on the yonder shores of the Atlantic Ocean stood the United States, which could not be taken into account if only because its president, a round-headed individual, one Theodore Roosevelt, wore a pince-nez. We have only to recall that at the same time Emperor Wilhelm, clad in a silver cuirass and a snow-white cape, visited the Holy Land on horseback and had the ancient wall of Jerusalem torn down at one point because he would otherwise have been forced to dismount from his horse in order to enter the Old Gate. America was far inferior to Europe in style and thought. In one of his speeches, for instance, Roosevelt said that inhabitants of the Philippine Islands must be trained for self-government and then allowed to determine their own destiny. And when the western world quelled the Boxer Rebellion in China, the United States was the only nation which refused reparations and sent teachers and doctors to China instead. All this demonstrates how little feeling America had for European thought; and when mention was made of this nation in the Casino a man like Prince Fini, who had traveled throughout America, spoke from personal experience in predicting that the gum-chewers would come to nothing.

Thus the fate of the world was in the hands of six European states. England hated Germany, because English merchants noticed that Germans were beginning to manufacture the better dyes. Emperor Wilhelm hated King Edward, despite their avuncular relationship, because England had more oceans and colonies. France, whose degrading peace treaty of 1871 had been dictated by the walrus-headed Bismarck, panted for revanche. Italy, only lately unified, gnashed her young, white teeth at the aged Monarchy, which had made excessive inroads on her northern frontiers. Tsar Nicholas quaked ever more violently at the thought of Emperor Wilhelm's forked mustache since Germany had bound the Monarchy to her leash.

The rulers, ministers, diplomats and generals—three hundred eleven in all—of these six states decided that it was about time to hurl their millions of troops at one another, for it was obvious to each that only he could win. But as men of conscience and deliberation, aware of their responsibilities toward their fellow men, they summoned a convention of the representatives of all the sovereign nations in the world as far back as 1899, at which convention they promulgated a set of articles outlawing the use of certain improper holds, grips, twists and turns in the coming struggle. The convention, which met in the Hague, was called a "peace conference." From that time on they stood in readiness for war, but without revealing their intentions to the people. Neither the Italo-Turkish quarrel of 1911 in Tripolitania nor the two dwarfish Balkan wars that followed were considered a suitable pretext for the major bout to begin, if only because they all wanted to see what effect the new secret weapon would have—on someone else, of course. The new weapon was really marvelous. By means of a certain intricate mechanism a single barrel could spit out a thousand rounds of ammunition in a stream; consequently it was named the machine-gun. Reports of its use in Balkan and Tripolitanian rehearsals convinced military experts that the new weapon was truly capable of reaping a rich harvest of blood and bodies.

Finally a Serbian student by the name of Gavrilo Princip fired the starting gun. In Frankfurt, in Manchester, in Irkutsk, Herr Heller and Mr. Farthing and Ivan Garinin privately discussed the matter with their wives and came to the conclusion that the murder of the Austrian heir apparent and his consort was a shocking thing—but, after all, it had little to do with them. They did not dare, however, to say as much before their neighbors, who sought to behave as befitted Englishmen, Germans or Russians, although it was not impossible that they also had had similar discussions with their wives.

The death of the archduke and archduchess touched Kristina's inner life above all others. It was in those days that she started to keep her diary. Aside from its wealth of hitherto unrecorded historical data, the diary illustrates the development of Kristina's style since the days of "The Goose-Girl," although one must not overrate this document in a literary sense, for when a woman begins to keep a secret diary it is, to some extent, interesting in itself, whereas a man's diary, penned by however important an author, is almost always deadly dull.

The very first entry in the diary makes mention of the mysterious Juan Hwang, of whose nationality, occupation, age, appearance and weight Kristina says nothing, as if purposely intending to becloud the person of this curiously named Juan Hwang.

28 June 1914—Budapest

I have decided to keep a diary, for great things have begun to happen. My nerves are not in the best condition, but it is no delusion of the senses that everything—Sarajevo, Belgrade, Vienna—seems to be happening to *me*.

I spent two weeks at Ararat this summer. The family bores me: Mamma's quiet tenderness toward me, the sort of tenderness one usually reserves for people with cancer—Papa's loud joviality,—György, who has just graduated, and pursues me all day with explanations of the concept of the cosine or the events leading up to the Peace of Westphalia,—János, who shoots his shotgun all over the park until it's worth one's life to go out there,— Zia, who hangs on my neck affectionately simply because Mamma doesn't pay any attention to her and she very properly hates Fraulein Elsa,—but it's Rere whom I can stand least of all, for his very presence gets on my nerves. I despise everything at Ararat, the guests and the excursions, everything except an old oak tree that stands at the very end of the park, where the noise of the castle cannot be heard. Unfortunately I couldn't bring the oak tree with me; but since I fled back to Septemvir Utca I do seem to have changed. Besides the doorman and the chambermaid, I'm the only one in the house. Behind the lowered blinds there is darkness and quiet, quiet, quiet, which is what I need most of all right now.

Today is Sunday, so I went to Mass in the chapel of the Fortress in the morning, and then spent a long time in the library reading Fugger de Babenhusen's *The Glory of the Habsburgs*. After dinner, as usual, I lay down on the couch. There is a little white pillow which I cradle in my arms during my afternoon naps. The little pillow is cool, its fragrance of clean linen mingles with the good scent of laundry soap. I don't know why, but I always imagine the skin of the man I love must have a fragrance like this. I abhor all perfumes; some of them give me gooseflesh.

It must have been about half past one in the afternoon, and the room was filled with a blue-green dimness which came from the brocade wallpaper. The nickel rim of one of the ashtrays, only one side of which was struck by the faint light from the window, glittered like the half moon I once saw before daybreak above the Lajoshegy. Beyond the cool obscurity of the room the summer afternoon flooded the world with warm and yellow silence, and I could almost hear a distant bubbling, as if the asphalt were melting in the street and the old shingles cracking with heat on the rooftops. Occasionally the gentle, sonorous steeple clock of the Garrison church struck the quarter hour, a sound I dearly love. I lay in the arms of a sweet, clear melancholy. I thought—and this was not unusual, for every afternoon, every night I fall asleep with these thoughts—I thought of the swift, dangerous passage of time, and that I was already closer to nineteen than to eighteen. If I were to tell someone about this he might laugh at me, but in my life the passage of time is different. There was, for one thing, the bloody, mucous piece of flesh, about the size of a bowling pin, that tore from me amid incredible pains when I was fourteen—only months later did I discover that it was a baby. I blame Mamma for all that, and if I ever have a daughter I shan't bring her up in such dark, stupid ignorance. That incident alone shows that I am destined for entirely extraordinary things. I know that youth is leaving me more quickly than it leaves others. I listen to a string quartet differently, and taste a *caille Cavaignac* differently, and feel differently when I slip on a warm pair of gloves, than Agnes or Franciska or any of my other friends. As for men, and love, their touch is, to me, as if I were seated motionless in the quietude of a forest, and a young, wild

90

bird flew to my shoulder or my hand, and I felt the tender, somewhat painful but still beautiful and mysterious touch of its claws. In the past three years I have lost fourteen pounds, and this does not suit me at all. My shoulders, my waist, the lines of my thighs are not so soft as they were at sixteen; Juan Hwang says so himself when he tries to make me go on a milk diet. But I hate milk, I would rather drink a glass of dilute whiting. I have become the prey of some great inner fire, and I am afraid it will soon go out. What is in store for me? If I did not know that Great Things were ahead I'd kill myself, for the life which surrounds me is like a slow death by thirst or torture. Things move slowly, and when I consider them objectively they seem hopeless. I last saw Archduke Charles in October of the past year, at Uncle Andrew's reception in Vienna. A great many people were present, and the archduke and his wife barely put in an appearance—a half hour, and they were gone. During that half hour they shook hands with as many of the guests as they could. I stood in the right corner of the large salon, talking with Uncle Cini, when the archduke reached us. For an instant I thought I would faint; it was the first time I had been so close to him since the dip in the well. I saw him at his wedding, yes, but only from a distance, and I don't even like to think of those moments. He stretched out his hand to Uncle Cini as if it were a block of wood for which he no longer had any use. His eyes were tired, like eyes that have had to swallow a vast number of faces whole, undigested, lest he offend someone. A friendly little smile was pasted on his lips, a charming, attractive smile poured of lead in some secret workshop of the Habsburg court especially for this occasion. When he gave me his hand, his cloudy gaze had not yet recognized who I was. I was one among the many, the fiftieth or the sixtieth evening gown and a handful of jewels, nothing more, but when my glance met his glance he caught his head to one side ever so slightly, as if I had touched his eyeballs with the fine point of a needle. Yet there was no effort in my glance, no desire to make him notice me and remember me, rather a light, apologetic melancholy,—I did it wonderfully, I think. The fraction of a second when he should have released my hand was over, and then a sudden, gay little light of complicity flashed in his tired eyes, he pressed his other hand on mine and said… the way he spoke was as if the words, hidden in the silent depths of his heart for three years, had come back to him all at once…he spoke the words as if they were all-encompassing, all-meaningful…one could tell from his voice that his every nerve was shaking with the majesty of the words as he pronounced them. He said:

"Ah, Kristina."

And then he walked on, extended his hand to someone else, and once again the artificial, lifeless little smile appeared on his lips. What was beautiful and wonderful about it was that nobody so much as noticed what had happened in the impact, the ardency of those few seconds. But the moment when the words issued from his lips was, to me, as if the *Mountain* were opening, as if the *Mist* were suddenly pierced with light. I don't recall who stood beside me later, or what I said. For the rest of the evening this phrase alone sang inside of me: *Ah, Kristina*—as if I had never heard that word before, as if I had just learned who I was, as if I had been given a new, strange name, with magic and mystery in its meaning: *Ah, Kristina*. The word sang with ecstasy inside of me: *Kri-i-istina, Kristina-a*...and later, when the dancing began, this was what the violins played. I have no idea whom I danced with. The phrase—*Ah, Kristina*—took form and danced before me like a naked nymph on a lonely woodland clearing, tossing its head back during its leaps and swimming in air as no one but Cerdoux or Nijinsky can do.

Only Uncle Fini knows that I am in love, but the ultimate secret of my life, the final aim of my destiny—this is something he doesn't know. This is something only Juan Hwang knows. Did I say I was in love? That word belongs to my friends, and to shopgirls, and I'll gladly let them keep it. There are things that human speech cannot accommodate, simply because they are rare, spectacular even in the history of a thousand-year-old nation. I must prepare for the fate to which the destiny of my people calls me. Sometimes, when I am all alone, I am so full of pity for myself that I break into tears. I should like to be a simple, happy, ordinary little woman like everyone else. The destiny of my people calls me? Juan Hwang puts it this way, for he is the only one who can express the things that make my heart tremble with their greatness. Have I gone mad? Archduke Charles already has three children; and everyone says that his married life is blissful. Franz Joseph is still alive, and if Madame T.'s prophecy does not come true then Francis Ferdinand may live to be eighty. And by then I shall be at the brink of fifty and the grave. But Francis Ferdinand's consumption may return... the *galoppierende* may take him away in a matter of months, and Charles too may be widowed, for the world is full of accidents and illnesses. We are all mortal, sadly enough.

These were my thoughts, when the News Telephone—which we call the Nuisance Telephone—sounded overhead. The buzzing was unusually strong and insistent, and after it had buzzed repeatedly I picked up the earphones. I thought

I misunderstood what was said—I thought the words that issued from the stubby, black earphones were merely a sequel to my own vague reveries, for the voice was faint and blurred. Francis Ferdinand and his wife had been assassinated in Sarajevo an hour and a half ago. The details were confused...a bomb...Slavic street-names...and then a series of revolver shots. I threw the earphones down, and my head fell back on the pillow in a daze. I still did not know whether it was true or a dream. The buzzer signaled again, like a groan from the depths of the earth, tearful and ghostly. New details...the bullet had severed the crown prince's jugular vein, and he was dead by the time they reached the hospital. He expired with his head resting in Sophia's lap. More details continued to arrive, but I still felt I was imagining things. The peculiar buzzing and the odd half-light in the room completely deranged my senses. Then the telephone rang, a clear, silvery, sober sound. Juan Hwang was calling: "Did you hear what happened?" So it was true. Before he put the receiver down he shouted into the telephone, and it was as if he were on a tall mountaintop, a vast distance away, and I on another mountaintop, and his voice was beckoning, urging, rousing me, a triumphant voice of transcendental strength—as if Time and History had made a funnel of their hands and were calling: "*Kristi-i-i-na...!*"

I staggered back to the couch. Now the crowing of a faraway rooster pierced the silence, and a winding lentil path led toward the heights, and the crepuscular light of dawn shimmered in the darkened room. The *Mountain* opened once again, slowly, and revealed a dark, tremendous stage in its depths. In the strange light of the stage, on a monumental throne, sat Franz Joseph, so old and bent that his wrinkled head almost hung in his lap. Behind the throne stood Frau Katz, motionless and black, so huge that by comparison Franz Joseph looked like the petrified babe in the lap of a gigantic statue of St. Christopher. The thick, broken spectacles of Frau Katz were still staring into nothingness, and her immobility was appalling. Two bloody corpses sprawled at the foot of the throne, their arms outstretched, like discarded dolls. Then, in the uniform of the Brandeis Dragoons, Archduke Charles suddenly appeared from the left, hurried up the steps of the throne, stiffened to attention and announced himself to Franz Joseph, in a clear, ringing voice: "Apfelstrudel!"

My head has begun to ache dreadfully.

6 August

I've learned a new term, which I first heard from Juan Hwang's lips: *World*

93

War. I like the term. It has a lovely sound, like the two deepest tones of the organ in the Garrison church. I like everything that is of an incalculable greatness. How shall I write his name? Charles? The new crown prince? Sometimes, to myself, I call him *Il Seul*—the Only One. He has been ordered to Supreme Headquarters at Teschen. Juan Hwang says I must become a volunteer nurse in the Red Cross at once. It won't be difficult to get an assignment to the military hospital at the Teschen Headquarters. Juan Hwang says I must do everything possible, without losing a single day, to be near the crown prince, near him always. I shall be glad to go to Teschen from here. My retreat on Septemvir Utca has come to an end. All Ararat has arrived, boisterous, excited—I can't imagine why—and they seem happy, as if preparing for a great and entirely new sort of hunt, as if hordes of dinosaurs and behemoths had broken into the game preserve. Papa unpacked his old uniforms, and the house is filled with the cloying smell of camphor.

20 August—Ararat

> It was a strange, strange summer even:
> An angry angel beat a drum in heaven.

These lovely lines are the beginning of a poem by Ady which appeared yesterday—the poem is about the evening of the outbreak of war.

Once again Ararat is packed with guests. Hussar, Uhlan and Dragoon uniforms glitter in the salons. Yesterday they played cards till dawn.

During the night I went for a solitary walk in the park. I stood beside the old oak tree and listened.

I could hear, quite clearly, the drumming of the angry angel in the sky. A curiously formed mass of clouds even described his shape. I couldn't see his face—that terrifying visage—for the snail-curled flowing ringlets of his thick, metallic, glistening hair dangled down to his mouth as he leaned over the drum with bent back. The ghostly, hollow drumbeat flowed over the starry firmament like some repulsive fluid, and it was like blood bubbling from an enormous corpse.

A strange, strange summer even. From the open windows of the castle the loud racket of the guests, tinted with the tinkle of a piano, wove its way through the branches of the slumbering trees, like the glow of light through closed eyelids. It was always Papa's rumbling voice that carried farthest, like the croaking of the bull fiddle in a distant gypsy band. I'm afraid everyone had had a great deal to drink by that time.

10 September—Teschen

Headquarters is now officially within the combat zone, although Teschen is more than six hundred miles from the front. It is strange how all the uniforms have changed, and everyone is in olive-gray. I've never seen such battle dress before. I asked one of the majors on the staff why they were all wearing olive-gray, and he said it was to keep the enemy from seeing them. In other wars they didn't pay attention to this sort of thing.

The commander-in-chief is old Archduke F., who wears side-whiskers in order to look like Franz Joseph. Here at Teschen they see everything that happens at the front, for motion pictures of the fighting are shown every evening at seven. It's exactly as it was in Sweden, where I went to see Psylander in person last year. I watched the films being made, and the material prepared during the course of a day was projected without any continuity whatever in the evening. These battle scenes have no continuity either. We are admitted to the screenings, and I sit in the back rows with the army doctors and the nurses. Because old Archduke F. is extremely nearsighted, he and his staff sit in the front row; consequently the generals who are farsighted also have to sit there, and they cannot see a thing. The pictures show charges into battle, artillery, cavalry and then the infantry, in long broken lines, setting out over the stubble fields and the potato patches, exactly like beaters at a hunt. The difference is that here they are the hunted. Occasionally one of them trips and remains behind. All you can see of the war itself is the occasional explosion of a grenade, sometimes in front of them and sometimes behind, kicking up a great black tower of dirt. At such times old Archduke F. knocks on the floor with his marshal's baton, which is always between his knees, and shouts: "Boom!" The old gentleman is vastly entertained by the war, and he wouldn't miss a single screening for the world.

I look at the screen only rarely. In the front row on the right there is the outline of a head which the light of the projector frames in a bluish-white halo. I watch that head constantly. Here in the theater I am hardly more than fifteen yards from the crown prince, but in the first five days I didn't have a single chance to talk to him.

The hospital here is small, too small to hold serious casualties, and it shares a courtyard with the headquarters buildings. Yesterday morning I met the crown prince, in the company of a tall general, at the main entrance. They were deep in conversation, and he only looked at me with half an eye, but when I was a step or two beyond them he stopped and stretched both his hands toward me:

"Kristina—you here?"

"Yes, Your Highness. I work here in the hospital."

"That's very nice. Truly, very nice."

He pressed my hand once more and passed on. This would not have meant anything, in itself, but this afternoon Sister Anna, the head nurse, leaned over to me and whispered excitedly:

"Do you know who's in Number Seven? The crown prince!"

"Sick?"

"A slight cold."

I was on night duty tonight. At nine o'clock I took over from Sister Grete, who gave me the archduke's fever chart with the comment that his temperature would not have to be taken any more tonight, he had no fever at all, His Highness wanted to be left in undisturbed quiet. I felt that these instructions applied to everyone but me. At about half past nine I entered his room. The crown prince was lying on his back in bed, with his eyes closed, as if he were dead. I moved quietly, trying to behave as I had seen professional nurses do. I straightened the carpet and moved a glass to one side on the table. The crown prince opened his eyes and said softly:

"Ah, Kristina."

The way he said it was wonderful. I asked him whether he wanted to use the bedpan. He said no. I turned off the light, and now only the little blue hospital lamp over the door lit the room. The room filled with a marvelous blue mist. I stepped to the bed, smoothed the blankets, then slowly bent over and kissed his lips.

When I left the room I saw someone hastily disappear at the end of the corridor.

12 September

I have been ordered back to Budapest, to serve in the Garrison hospital. I can't understand this sudden transfer, but there's a war on and I suppose one must get used to such things.

At this point there is a long silence in Kristina's diary.

The war made rude inroads on everyone's life, even disrupting the precise and delicate mechanism of the castle at Ararat, the palaces on Bösendorferstrasse and on Septemvir Utca. From one day to the next Monsieur Cavaignac the master chef, Mr. Johnson the English stablemaster, Mam'selle Barbier and Miss Wenlock became enemy aliens and had to leave the Monarchy. Mobilization laid waste the ranks of footmen, grooms, kitchen boys and porters, snatched the silver platters, corkscrews, checkreins and mixing spoons out of their hands. The first draft reduced the staff of fifty-eight by twenty-three members, and the castle at Ararat could not be maintained, even on the most modest scale, with the remaining thirty-five, most of whom were women. Count Dupi and Countess Menti moved to Vienna, but the rest of the family returned to Ararat because Count Dupi was reliably informed by the War Ministry that the war could not last more than four or five weeks. Thus the declarations of war caused no great upheaval; at most Count Dupi felt the discomfort which often filled him when a white-gloved policeman peremptorily waved him away from a detour and made him feel like an ordinary pedestrian, a sensation which in part irritated him and in part struck him unexpectedly, as if he had bumped his head into an invisible wall, with a dim half-recognition of the existence in the world of an unknown and enormous power through the confines of which even he could not go— unaccustomed to obstacles, he found this, at the very least, unusual. It occurred to him, for instance, that the stupid World War would prevent him from going to Paris in September, though he had decided just that season to have his Paris mansion repaired and to replace the wine-red brocade tapestries in the upstairs salon with a mallow-colored wallpaper. He was fond of his little study in that house, and liked the way the subdued hum of Paris came through the windows, a sound so infinitely human and so metropolitan, mingling the rattle of carriage wheels, the cries of newsboys, the bell of a near-by workshop and the rustle of women with their many perfumes. Always his tailored suits and overcoats from London first saw the light of day along the sun-drenched Champs Élysées, and on these occasions the tradesmen, café proprietors, restaurateurs and seasoned headwaiters ran out on the street to shake his hand with deep bows of greeting and to laugh with him like cheerful fellow members of a special, mysterious and improbable world, to walk bareheaded at his side as far as the next corner while reciting, with the loquacity of the Parisian idiom, the latest fiery chapters in the torrid lives of the many Amélies, Charlottes and Loulous; and although he had long forgotten the names and faces of the women it all moved him like warm and spicy music at the climax of which his obtrusive and enchanting friends handed him, like a farewell gift of flowers, the latest and smuttiest French jokes. He considered this Paris to be as much his own property as the oily whirr of the tiny lift in his house on the Rue Général Ferreyolles, or as the inimitable voice and visage of his doorman Emanuel, than whom there was no greater rascal on the face of the earth, when he ushered his foreign master into the house with "Bonjour, Monsieur le comte!" and a sweep of his gold-braided cap to the ground. Count Dupi frequently received well-intentioned anonymous letters from Paris which nevertheless hissed with unrestrained envy as they informed him that Emanuel had put his mansion at the disposition of adventurers in their casual hours, had in fact established a regular clientele on the proceeds of which he had purchased a villa outside of Houlgat; this was indubitably the height of insolence and an affront to one's property rights, but Count Dupi still tore the letters up fretfully when they arrived because he had a certain sense of social justice which often made him feel like a culprit when newspapers informed him that there were people who lived in tenements or caves, bringing images to his mind of the innumerable unoccupied rooms in his empty, padlocked castles and palaces at home and abroad. He sometimes let two or three years pass without visiting the Dukay establishments in Vienna or Paris, not to mention the villas in Reichenau and Nice, the hunting lodges in Willensdorf and Hungary, the tremendous castle at Ararat and the palace on Septemvir Utca. Therefore, if Emanuel occasionally permitted a vestige of life to enter the house in Paris, it was an unparalleled insolence which must nevertheless go unnoticed. Count Dupi, in his wisdom, had realized long ago that furniture and rooms existed, finally, for certain definite purposes. So far did his social awareness go that he always sent Emanuel a brief telegram heralding his arrival, to avert the possibility of finding a naked French nymph in his bed with a Cuban tobacco salesman snoring at her side. All this was the result of his sense of ownership, his liberality, his desire to give pleasure, or perhaps of his cynicism, but now the war had blocked the frontiers and cut him off from his properties, reached into the wardrobes of his rooms, ransacked the unopened letters and the toothbrushes waiting for him in Nice and Paris—it smacked of insult, both physical and spiritual.

Twenty years earlier, when he was a lieutenant in the Lebovice Uhlans, several bottles of good French champagne under his belt and under his nerve would have made the war seem as much an exultantly savage and deadly adventure to him as it was to the mounted hussars and dragoons who made the cavalry charge at Satanov, bent over their horses with their broad, weighty sabers drawn and their plumes waving and their capes fluttering as they stormed into the woods in the face of concealed Russian machine-gun fire that cut them down in droves—but forty-six-year-old István Dukay was content to serve in the Kriegsministerium in Vienna, where, when one of the orderlies placed an enormous pile of *strengst reserviert* documents on his desk, his duties required him to direct the sergeant to take the documents into the adjoining room and put them on the desk of Hauptmann Schlössel, who in civilian life was a registrar of deeds in Linz. Nobody could blame István Dukay for his abhorrence of documents in their every form.

In connection with the outbreak of the first World War, we must mention young Joseph Dukay, who, although not a member of Count Dupi's immediate family, was still a Dukay.

Young Joseph Dukay put in his year of military service with one of the Hussar regiments directly before the war. The regimental commander himself, Baron Herbert von Plitz-Sieburg, was on hand when it came time to take the examination for an officer's commission. Under the direction of an awesome examining board, the cadets rode to the outskirts of town and came to a halt on the open highway, which was flanked on both sides by fields of corn.

"Cadet Dukay!" Colonel Plitz-Sieburg's rumbling voice summoned the youthful Joseph Dukay.

"What would you do," asked Baron Herbert von Plitz-Sieburg, "if you unexpectedly met with strong machine-gun fire from both cornfields while riding along this road at the head of a cavalry column?"

Joseph Dukay answered without pause for reflection:

"Colonel, sir, I would fall from my horse and drop dead!"

The colonel's horse reared at the insolence of this prompt reply, so heatedly did he dig his sharp spurs into the ribs of his mount. His neck turned blue and he began to shout so incoherently that at most only two recurrent words were comprehensible: "*Verfluchter Kerl! Damned fool!*" Joseph Dukay's reply won him two weeks of room arrest, not to mention the fact that he flunked his examination, although it was obvious that Joseph Dukay had made the only acceptable reply to the question. But he would have done better to answer in prescribed military style, thus:

"I would call the column to a halt, sir, order the men to dismount, form along the highway in defilade and open fire on the enemy from the prone position."

Had this been the answer, Baron Herbert von Plitz-Sieburg would have nodded his head in approval and shouted: "Bravo!"—neglecting to consider that the hussars, if they dismounted and formed in defilade amid strong crossfire from machine-guns, might well assume the prone position but would surely never rise again, for neither horse nor rider could possibly survive in such a situation.

This is precisely what happened at the battle of Satanov, where young Joseph Dukay, demoted to private, fell from the saddle with a bullet through his heart, positive proof that his answer at the examination had been the right one. This was the beginning of the process known to history as the first World War, when sober minds were thrown into discard and the inconceivably stupid were made generals. Baron Herbert von Plitz-Sieburg took part in the battle of Satanov as divisional commander.

But it would be grossly unfair to place the whole blame on him. The Austrian generals met with strong competition from the English, German, Russian and especially the French military leaders. The French debacle in the first few weeks of the war was the result of the very same stubbornly conservative strategy which flunked Joseph Dukay on his examination.

The French opposed the stormy German attack through Belgium with the methods of open defense which had become as obsolete since the Napoleonic Wars as the muzzle-loader had become antiquated through the invention of the machine-gun. But they considered themselves secure, for they thought the fortifications of the Belgian frontier would prove impregnable to the Germans. They completely forgot that the armored towers of Luttre or Brussels had been manufactured by German firms, and that Ingenieur Herr Hoch, micrometer in hand, had handed the precise measurements of these steel plates to Ingenieur Herr Weissmüller in another department, whose German thoroughness at once impelled him to devise cannon which would easily pierce the aforesaid armor. That is exactly what took place. Under the fire of the German 30.5's, the proud steel towers split like watermelons dropped on the floor. The German forces broke into France, swept the French left wing to the north with irresistible strength and bottled up the remaining British troops at Ypres.

Recalling the beginnings of the first World War, we are reminded that it was the taxi drivers of Paris, transporting French troops to the front with the indefatigable industry of ants, who stopped the marvelous military machine of the Germans when it was headed toward the French capital. This came as a great surprise to the German generals, for never in the history of warfare had they known taxicabs to play a part in engagements of that nature. The German soldiers on the Marne, having already sighted the narrow silhouette of the Eiffel Tower on the southwestern horizon, were forced to retreat with broken heads which were the more painful because they had been led to believe that all of France was the produce of German culture and civilization, for the Eiffel Tower itself was the work of German engineers—they did not realize that the idiotic iron tower was the greatest eyesore in all Paris. The German generals, *von* This and *zu* That, were as surprised by the taxi-borne French counterattack as an enormous wolfhound is flabbergasted at the sight of a long-tailed monkey, smaller than a cat, which stands on its hind legs and begins to slap him with such violence that the fang-toothed wolfhound can only slide back on its haunches in astonishment, never having experienced the like before.

After the success of the French counterattack the western front, as we know, became static for a long time. The same thing happened on the eastern front. Behind the fronts, meanwhile, life went on gaily, for the civilian populations were threatened with no danger. As far as they were concerned the war was taking place somewhere at a great remove, almost in secret, like the overnight cleaning that is given public lavatories in small towns. In general, the war proved to be a much messier matter than people had imagined at first. But the mourning of parents and sisters was greatly assuaged by the knowledge that their soldiers had died in the interest of an exalted, glorious cause, known everywhere—through some egregious error, perhaps—as "love of country"; while the sovereigns and statesmen of embattled countries constantly declared their wish to save Europe, though what they wished to save Europe from was not quite clear in their declarations.

In February of 1915 a great ball for the benefit of disabled soldiers was held in the Vigadó of Budapest. These balls were famous for the fact that they had more chief patrons, associate patrons, chairmen, vice chairmen, directors-in-chief and entertainment committeemen than could possibly be accommodated in the banquet hall, which had been built to house two thousand persons. The notabilities, with an archducal pair in the van, sat on red plush seats along a separate platform; Countess Menti was there too, of course, wearing her most formidable jewels, and at her left sat Kristina, who was already nineteen. Now and then a hussar pelisse asked her to dance, but Kristina's face swam so far above the melee in the ballroom, and her cold beauty was so aloof, that Countess Menti, watching them through her lorgnette, suddenly dropped the lorgnette and turned her head away, having noticed that after a few turns the partners invariably escorted Kristina back to her place, probably with the thought that there was little to be gained by dancing with a statue.

Count Dupi stood beside a pillar at the edge of the dance floor and watched, through the smoke of his cigar, the white shoulders of the women, naked to the uttermost limits of propriety, as they dipped and swayed in the waltz and the boston. Count Joachim, passing by with the little mouse-headed Princess Karola, did not fail to observe:

"Dupi's expert eye is picking out a woman to invite to his bachelor flat after midnight..."

Right now there was no basis whatever for this remark. Count Dupi was dispassionately admiring a young couple on the dance floor, for the very sight of youth and love can delight a man on the verge of fifty. And the two young people in question were truly happy to the point of ecstasy. The boy wore the uniform of a cadet, and his arm was in a sling. Count Dupi recognized him—he was Feri Kontyos, the son of the estate blacksmith at Ararat, a young soldier who had proudly paid the count a visit with the little silver badge of bravery on his breast after the wounded arm had healed sufficiently to allow him to leave the hospital. Even now he held his partner with only one hand, but the glow of his eyes was an ample compensation. Count Dupi was in tails; he had wearied of the Kriegsministerium in Vienna, and in any case he felt that the several months behind a desk had been an adequate service to his country. All at once he noted that an infantry captain, standing like a detective beside one of the pillars and obviously an inspector from the municipal garrison, had beckoned to the disabled ensign at the end of the dance. He saw the young man stand at rigid attention before the captain and raise a frightened hand to the collar of his cadet's uniform, which had come undone while dancing—unquestionably a serious infraction of regulations. Count Dupi heard only this much of the captains spluttering reprimand: "Gehen Sie sofort nach Hause! Morgen um neun Uhr zum Raport! Get yourself home at once! Report to the orderly room at nine in the morning!"

Seeing the cadet head toward the exit in compliance with the captain's order, Count Dupi hastened after him and put a hand on his shoulder in the cloakroom:

"Wait for me here—I'll be back in a moment!"

He turned on his heel and returned to the ballroom, where he approached the platform reserved for notabilities and sought out General Baron Herbert von

Plitz-Sieburg, a former comrade-in-arms whose appointment as commandant of the municipal garrison was affording him a well-earned rest after the battle of Satanov.

"Come here a moment..."

Strolling with his hand on the general's arm, he explained something to him quietly, and when they came within range of the captain he said:

"There's the dirty dog."

And he left the general to himself. The scene which followed was like the onslaught of a tiger upon a hound that has just torn a rabbit in two. The general summoned the captain:

"Have you been in combat yet, Captain?" His voice was as friendly as if he were offering an invitation to dinner.

"Not yet, sir," the captain replied, and his face went pale as he stood at attention, for he surmised the worst.

"Come and see me in my office tomorrow morning at nine."

He nodded his head curtly and went to the cloakroom. Finding the perplexed cadet, he shouted:

"Herr Fähnrich! Gehen Sie zurück und tanzen! Weiter tanzen, eins zwei...Get back on the dance floor at once! On the double!"

All this was in the hearing of the captain, who was hastily putting on his cape in order to rush home and take leave of his wife and children, for he knew quite well that the morning appointment meant his immediate assignment to the front.

Without this little story—as full of generosity as of meanness—we could scarcely fathom the psychology of the first World War. Men in uniform spent most of their time "zeroing in" their subordinates. Under the influence of the domineering spirit of imperialism, man's most sordid impulse, the impulse to crush his fellows, was given free rein. When two fishwives had a misunderstanding in the market place, their frothing lips mouthed things like this: "Just you wait— I'll teach you a thing or two—I'll have you know my son-in-law is a sergeant, and he'll cook your son's goose, that dirty Zugsführer!" Life, honor, human dignity were measured in terms of cloth stars and gold braid; a new caste system overspread the entire world as a result of the mobilization of more than two hundred million men.

Meanwhile the war diligently collected its dead and disabled, its frozen feet, and condemned its prisoners of war by the million to a fate which civilized men would have thought inconceivable only a few years earlier. Thus the first two years of the war went by, and nothing more happened at the end of 1916 than that Madam T's prophecy, according to which Franz Joseph would die in 1931 at the age of one hundred and one, proved to be as groundless as the longevity she had augured for Francis Ferdinand.

One November morning several rooks alighted on the trees, already bald, in the park at Schönbrunn, an event about which there was nothing odd or unusual; nevertheless the Lord Chamberlain the Duke de Montenuovo, standing at the window and gazing out into the foggy gardens, looked at the rooks thoughtfully. The two physicians were still in the emperor's study.

"Well...?" the duke asked softly, when the door opened and the two doctors appeared.

"The fever has abated, but the general condition is worse. His Majesty should be in bed, but he is stubborn—"

The duke nodded sadly.

"His Majesty believes that if he took to his bed now he would never leave it."

The aide-de-camp on duty noted that the emperor had been sitting at his desk since four o'clock that morning, though he was so tired that his head nodded until his chin was resting on his chest. This wrinkled, ruddy, bald, gray-bearded head was the head of Franz Joseph. It was the hoary head of Europe.

By now the whole world knew that the eighty-seven-year-old emperor was dying. The emperor himself knew it too, for he nodded briefly when the Lord Chamberlain announced a caller and he appeared to be in readiness when the court chaplain entered with the sacristan. The aged emperor, clad in an olive-gray military cape, took a faltering step forward.

The pale prelate came to announce that he bore the blessing of the Pope, and added in a trembling voice:

"Your Majesty, it is a commandment of the Church that the final sacrament must precede the blessing of His Holiness..."

"Bitte schön." Cool and courteous, a tart smile in his broken eyes, the sick man raised his two hands slightly, as if in encouragement of the prelate and the sacristan to whip forth their weapons from beneath the fringed vestments and execute him on the spot by the right of a law which even he could not countermand.

The priest draped the violet stole about his shoulders and heard the half kneeling, half sitting emperor's confession. A lackey placed the crucifix and two lighted candles on the desk. The sacristan rang his bell, and the emperor crossed himself.

"Per sacrosancta humanae reparationis mysteria remittat tibi omnipotens Deus..." the prelate's chill voice rapped.

In the vestibule Archduke Charles and Archduchess Zita inquired about the emperor's condition in choked tones.

When the visitors were announced, the emperor summoned his major-domo and insisted on having his clothes changed, for he refused to receive a woman while wearing his house-coat.

In the Dukay Palace on Bösendorferstrasse, as the early afternoon darkened, Countess Menti sat in the great green armchair near the fireplace, resting her cheek on her forefinger, while Count Dupi, cigar in hand, walked mutely up and down. The door kept opening to admit men and women who did not even sit down before they delivered, panting and whispering, the latest news. They were relatives and friends—from the Paar, Bolfras and Montenuovo families—with the most minute details of what was happening at Schönbrunn, the privileged few to whom reports leaked through the closed doors every quarter hour.

The door between the A.D.C's anteroom and the study is open, and the colonel on duty watches the emperor by means of a large mirror on the wall. The old gentleman sits at his desk in the dim north light of the room. His two hands rest on the arms of the chair, and his head is bent over his chest, his breathing is heavy. From time to time he lifts his head slightly, and his eyes open in a jellied stare. Shortly before five o'clock the emperor reached under the pile of documents to his right, pulled out a little brush and carefully brushed off the wine-red felt top of his desk, leaving not a single speck of dust. This habitual gesture was the last one he made at the desk where for sixty-nine years he had done his imperial work.

By eight o'clock in the evening it was known even in the Dukay Palace that Maria Valéria, the emperor's only daughter, had already been kneeling for an hour at the foot of the field cot on which the emperor rested. The restless heir apparent Charles, and his wife Zita, with her stony composure, also knelt at its side. A few steps away, near the tin washstand, stood the two elderly adjutants: Paar and Bolfras. Montenuovo, biting his lower lip, tiptoed in and out of the room like someone with a pressing amount of work to do. The two veteran aides sometimes cast long and weary glances at the face of the dying emperor and at the head of the kneeling heir apparent.

A violent windstorm raged in Vienna during those hours. István Dukay still walked to and fro in the room, chewing a cigar. Countess Menti still sat motionlessly in the green armchair. Both of them sensed that something of great moment was taking place in the window-rattling hurricane. Something was passing, something was changing, but they had no clear conception of what it was or how, and merely felt its weight and its shadow.

Pacing among the black coppices and the rain-streaked Greek deities of the Schönbrunn park in the wild wind, a group of newspapermen were discussing the emperor as if he were no longer among the living. There were about ten of them, including three Hungarians and two Germans from Berlin. They were the sort of journalists who are devoted to their craft, and even on such a dark, windy November night they lurked about a source of news. Yet it was not so much news as human interest they were after. One of the young reporters seems hardly more than twenty-five years old. His name is Paul Fogoly. His companion is of the same age but much more corpulent. He is called Imre Pognár, and he is another who will appear again in the course of the years. So violent was the wind that they retired to the refuge of the palace walls. It was about eight o'clock in the evening.

They were discussing the five bloodstained family corpses which sprawled in the memory of the dying old man, now that his past was coming back to take final leave of him. First of all there was his younger brother with the two-tufted blond beard, Maximilian, shot to death while Emperor of Mexico. Then his son, Archduke Rudolf, and the mysterious tragedy of Mayerling. Then his wife Elizabeth—the older newspapermen were well informed about her tremendous, beautiful crown of hair, and the tiny black fan with which she never parted, and her love affairs with Hungarian aristocrats. She was never without the little black fan because her teeth were poor and when she laughed she opened the fan and held it in front of her face. In 1898, as she was about to board ship in the company of her ladies-in-waiting, an Italian anarchist stabbed her through the heart. According to old Bunz, this happened on the 6th of September; according to Özessy, who parted his blond beard in the middle exactly as Emperor Maximilian had done, the assassination took place on the 10th of September. They made a bet of one hundred Virginias, those long, thin, strong, black cigars rolled on a straw—the favorite smoke of the dying Franz Joseph. Then there was

Sarajevo: the murder of the crown prince and princess, which set off the World War. The old gentleman's life had not been exactly enviable.

The bearded Özessy carried his camera slung over his shoulder on a strap, in a case as large as a foot-locker, for he was a representative of the prehistoric age of press photography.

One of the newspapermen asserted that Katalin Schratt, former Viennese actress and mistress of the emperor, was kneeling at the bedside of the dying man. The others rather doubted this. Lame Karai told the story of another of the emperor's amorous idyls with a famous and celebrated Hungarian actress, and maintained that he had the story from Madame Sisa herself. It was in the late Seventies that Madame Sisa, still a raving beauty, was summoned to the Viennese Chancellery, where one of the higher officials, a Hungarian aristocrat, delicately invited the *artiste* to make a certain sacrifice for her Hungarian fatherland. He asked her, in the name of His Majesty, to appear at the palace at six o'clock in the afternoon. The lovely woman was led to one of the smaller French salons in the Burg and left alone. Sitting with her back erect on a squat and uncomfortable Louis Seize sofa, laced in an elaborate whalebone corset that was then fashionable and surrounded by a labyrinth of lacy petticoats, with an ostrich-plumed hat on her head, she had hardly more than a minute or two to wait before the great gold and white door swung open and the forty-seven-year-old emperor stepped in, wearing the uniform of a general with all his decorations on his chest and a sword at his side. He clicked his heels and nodded his head ever so slightly, but said nothing. His cerulean trousers were made of heavy flannel, on which it was difficult to manipulate the buttons. Therefore the emperor proceeded to unbutton himself only where absolutely necessary. The narrow, short little French sofa did not prove a comfortable resting place, but this did not disturb the emperor. According to Madame Sisa's account, the whole thing lasted no longer than it takes to countersign a parliamentary bill. The emperor was famous for the fact that he sometimes attended to affairs of state in a matter of minutes. Afterward he turned to the wall and carefully buttoned his heavy cerulean flannels. But he still did not favor the *artiste* with a word, which was understandable enough, since it would have been difficult for an emperor to find the appropriate word in the given situation. Before leaving he clicked his heels again and inclined his head. Later the chief of the Chancellery kissed the actress's hand and bade her farewell with a mysterious smile of gratitude, quoting the Gospel: "Render unto Caesar the things which are Caesar's, and unto God the things that are God's."

Everything was satisfactory up to that point, as Madame Sisa said, but several days later she received a crested envelope from the Chancellery with five one-hundred-florin notes inside. This aroused her wrath. She returned the money to the Chancellery at once with the following message: "Tell His Majesty that I am not a prostitute but a patriot."

The newspapermen mused over the story, the very bluntness of which made it believable. The idyl bore a resemblance to the military terseness of the emperor's speech. According to old Bunz, who also knew Madame Sisa, the incident was credible to the last punctuation mark. In his expert opinion, however, it was impossible to conceive of five hundred florins which Madame Sisa would return under any circumstances. At most she might think the sum too little.

While the reporters leaned against the wall and discussed the dying man in this fashion, the eighty-seven-year-old emperor opened his eyes again and said only:

"Some water..."

The hands of both Maria Valéria and Ketterle, the old major-domo, simultaneously reached for the glass of iced lemonade, and they succeeded in upsetting it. But there was enough left in the glass for the emperor, raising his head slightly, to slake his thirst, although very little of the liquid found its way to his dark blue lips, for he spilled most of it on the camel's-hair robe. Montenuovo entered the room in a panic and looked at the physicians. The commotion had led him to believe that death had come. When the situation became clear, he returned to the adjoining chamber, where the court chaplain stood motionlessly behind a long black marble table that was surrounded by Gobelin chairs embroidered with brownish-red and green stalks of wheat. He seemed an actor in the wings, waiting for the climactic scene of the play. A candelabrum stood ready on the black mirror top of the large table, and beside it a box of matches and a silver cruse of holy oil. The somnolent pastoral of one of the rococo clocks sounded in a near-by room. It was nine o'clock in the evening.

Outside the reporters were discussing the number of times—if at all—each of them had seen the emperor at close quarters, spoken to him or shaken his hand. Old Bunz declared that Franz Joseph had once shaken hands with him. A skeptical silence greeted this declaration, for it was common knowledge that the emperor had an abiding hatred for newspapermen, so much so that the representatives of the press were never allowed to cross the military cordon when their sovereign was on parade.

"It was at the horticultural exhibit in Graz," old Bunz began to explain. "I was standing near the entrance, beyond the cordon, when the senior A.D.C. suddenly appeared, opened the cordon, led me straight to His Majesty and introduced me."

Pognár cleared his throat noisily to indicate his conviction that Bunz was lying. Old Bunz continued placidly:

"His Majesty shook my hand and said, 'Ich gratuliere Ihnen...you're the only man in the world of whom there are two exemplars.' The senior A.D.C. turned as red as a poppy. Herr Meyerhoffer, the mayor of Graz, stood behind His Majesty. The A.D.C. had mistaken me for the mayor, for we were really very much alike."

This way the incident seemed more believable. Then Özessy—the photographer who parted his blond beard in the middle like Maximilian, sometime emperor of Mexico—straightened up from the wall. There was pride and disdain in the wave of his hand as he said:

"Gentlemen, His Majesty once pissed on me!"

The glowing cigarettes turned toward him in the darkness.

"It happened in 1904," began Özessy's recital, "during the Veszprém maneuvers. You gentlemen may know that His Majesty could not bear to have reporters within a mile of him—and we must concede, as we look at ourselves, that he was entirely right. Nevertheless, I succeeded in concealing myself and my camera in a blackthorn bush, about twenty paces from a little round hillock where I knew the meeting of the general staff would be held. The photograph promised to be wonderful, with a cloudy sky in the background—a beautiful group picture. My camera was so well hidden that only the lens showed through the branches. The generals were already assembled, with the emperor in their midst, but before the meeting began I clearly heard the emperor say: 'Verzeihen die Herren....Excuse me, gentlemen'—and he turned on his heel and headed for my blackthorn bush. A moment later a warm, yellow liquid was sprinkling my beard, about as much as would fill a pitcher of beer. Naturally I didn't dare move."

The reporters gave credence to this story without comment. Paul Fogoly looked at old Bunz and said, in the tone of an umpire:

"That's more than a handshake."

Pognár approached the photographer and took one of the tufts of the long blond beard in hand. He sniffed at it and said to Özessy:

"It's true, you know. How many years ago did it happen, pop?"

It was with stories and crude jokes like this that the newspapermen, who never respect the grandeur of an epochal moment, lightened the boredom of the dark, windy night. In the black coppices of the park the statues of Mars, Minerva, Bellona and Aeneas cast scandalized looks at each other, their faces glistening with long streaks of rain. The captive Prince of Reichstadt once walked among these statues, and when he asked about his father, Napoleon, his guards answered with a sardonic smile. He died of consumption here in Schönbrunn Palace, at the age of twenty-four.

Upstairs in the dying man's room Maria Valéria brought her tearful face closer to the emperor's large-lobed, wrinkled ear, once brick-red but now the color of spoiled meat.

"Would you like some more water, Papa?"

The emperor did not answer his daughter's question, nor did he open his eyes. The court physician leaned over the bed and felt for the pulse on the emperor's left hand, which lay motionlessly on the camel's-hair robe. A few seconds later his eyes swept above the kneeling group and sought the Duke de Montenuovo. Someone passed his glance along into the adjoining room, and the Lord Chamberlain entered with the court chaplain, who immediately leaned over the emperor and administered extreme unction. A warm fragrance of melting wax emanated from the candles. All the people from the anteroom came in, lackeys and archdukes, and the room filled with kneelers. The chaplain began the prayer for the dead, in a voice which seemed to come from the depths of bygone centuries, and the kneelers echoed him with a murmur that was like the intermittent patter of rain:

"Subvenite sanctos…"

Now and then a woman's sobbing rose above the monotonous murmur. The physician had still not taken the tip of his thumb from the emperor's artery, nor his glance from the white face of his watch. At the close of the prayer he cautiously returned the emperor's hand to the camel's-hair robe, slid his watch into a waistcoat pocket and turned toward Crown Prince Charles with a salutation which no human voice had ever addressed to the archduke before:

"Your Majesty! I beg to report that His Imperial Majesty has quietly mounted to the bosom of the Lord."

The newspapermen sensed something from the shadows darting behind the lighted windows, and they hurried to the main entrance of the palace. In less than a minute a young colonel appeared on the uppermost steps, the wind tossing his blond hair:

"Gentlemen, His Majesty died at five and a half minutes past nine."

In a matter of moments the news filled the imperial city, like an explosion in a hollow cave. Everyone knew it was coming, everyone had expected the report for days, but it still rang sharp and clear, solemn and frightening, like an incredibly long, subdued cannonade, which is very similar to the pervasive rumble of an earthquake. It took but a few minutes for the sound to pass along the sky, through forests and mountains, over battlefields and oceans. Everyone felt that only a rusty, vast iron gate could make such a thunderous noise, at the mouth of some huge, timeless tomb.

In the court stables Hans Karg, the lead coachman of the imperial hearse, opened a drawer to see whether moths had eaten his white wig and his peaked cap of black silk.

On this day Kristina entered only a few confused lines in her diary:

21 November 1916—Vienna

Today the *Mountain* opened again, and the frightful depths of its blinding interior lay exposed for a long time. I was on my knees in prayer until three o'clock this morning. And someday you will hold the king's heart in your hand. Amen.

Five days later a company of twenty people left the Vienna train at Enns to change to the local which was leaving for Steyrdorf. All the members of the group were in deep mourning, black ties on the men and heavy black veils on the women. Most of them were quite young, and they caused a sensation as they poured off the train, some holding their sides with mirth, jostling each other, the young women's long mourning veils floating behind them as they ran laughing for the local train. The red-capped station master and a few kerchiefed Styrian peasant women were scandalized at the sight of this rollicking company, which seemed to be on the way to a wedding rather than a funeral.

And that was the case. The young aristocracy was on the way to the wedding of a kinsman at Steyrdorf. The deep mourning was for the emperor; the nobility of the entire Monarchy was in official mourning for him. Kristina Dukay made one of the group. She was the only one who was not laughing. The signs of transcendent love were on her cold, strained face.

The change in monarchs affected István Dukay very much as did the brisk, stinging hot- and cold-water hoses with which the attendants at the Karlsbad baths simultaneously drenched the naked bodies of their guests. Franz Joseph was dead; one realized this with something of a shudder. They knew from Juliette, Montenuovo's cousin, that the army medicos had used a new process in embalming his body, and the experiment had not succeeded. The emperor's face had twisted into grotesquerie and his body had begun to decompose in the course of the week-long obsequies. There was dark foreboding in this.

Kristina's diary contains the following account of Franz Joseph's funeral:

30 November 1916—Vienna

We had a splendid view of the funeral from a second-story window in Uncle Andrew's house. The entire procession was to pass below. Beneath the gray sky a gray mass of soldiery flooded the streets of Vienna, and flooded the square below our window, too, like a thick stream. The walls of the houses are plastered with placards advertising the sale of war bonds—they are straining every nerve to make this mob of hundreds of thousands of people believe that war is the most profitable investment in the world. But as I looked out into the square I had the feeling that the entire population of Vienna constituted the employees of a bankrupt funeral home.

Mamma and Aunt Julia and I sat by the same window. Finally the cortège neared. A team of eight horses pulled the hearse, topped by a black crown, that carried the emperor's body. Behind the hearse walked Emperor Charles—an emperor to the Austrians, but a king to us Hungarians. He is my king. It was almost impossible to recognize the queen, so completely did her heavy, long black veils shield not only her face but her figure as well. Between the two of them, in a white silk cape, the new little heir apparent quickened his steps lest he be left behind. In the crowd the four-year-old child, who was clearly asking a stream of questions, looked like a white mouse among black antediluvian beasts—a white mouse capable of pulling, with its teeth, one of the slips of varicolored paper with fortunes printed on them from a rectangular tin box. But there was no occasion for such a display of skill right then.

Our binoculars kept the long procession under constant fire—only with difficulty could we make out the shapes of Papa and Uncle Fini, for everyone was uniformly clothed in black. Aunt Julia remarked that if Franz Joseph had died three years ago, his hearse would have been followed by the King of England, the Tsar of Russia, the President of the French Republic, the King of Spain, the King of Italy, the monarchs of Sweden, Norway, Denmark, Holland, Belgium, Rumania, Greece, Serbia—all the kings in the world. But now there was but one king in the funeral procession,— Ferdinand, King of the Bulgarians; and, according to Aunt Julia, he looked like a subaltern. Of course the King of Bavaria and the King of Saxony were there, but for a long time now they have not been considered real kings, merely the discarded trimmings of the old German Empire, like the rain-swept statues of ancient Hellas in the park at Schönbrunn.

Mamma and Aunt Julia were constantly scanning the neighborhood of the funeral coach for some sign of Katalin Schratt, former favorite of the Burgtheater and an old love of the emperor. Aunt Julia says the actress appeared at the emperor's deathbed after all. Emperor Charles himself escorted the elderly woman, past sixty and veiled in black from head to foot, into the room. In Mamma's opinion this was in extremely poor taste, but I think it was a beautiful, human gesture. The archdukes and duchesses shrank back with revulsion when they entered the room. The actress placed a bouquet of violets on the camel-hair robe and knelt by the bedside. She noted that the seal ring which bore the head of an ibex in miniature was no longer on the corpse's hand. Ketterle, the aged major-domo, muttered as he watched her, for he was the person who knew most about the emperor's secrets. This scene was described to Aunt Julia by Uncle Cini, who was present.

Not for a moment did King Charles escape the view of my binoculars as he paced behind the coffin. His stride was indifferent. Occasionally he cast his eyes around at the crowded windows of the houses, and for an instant I felt his glance meet mine. The procession moved very slowly and in great silence.

Then a dreadful thing happened. I distinctly heard a revolver-shot in the silence, like a tiny click in the great square. The king did not notice it, but the heavy mass of black veils which was the queen seemed to falter. All at once someone stepped to her side and took her arm. I screamed softly.

"What happened? Did something happen?" Mamma asked impatiently.

I didn't answer, and the binoculars danced in my hands. Neither she nor Aunt Julia had noticed anything. Nor had the crowd, apparently. The attempt at assassination had failed, and the procession went calmly on.

I saw Juan Hwang this afternoon. A mute nod indicated his knowledge of the matter. But he put a finger on his lips, signaling that we were not to discuss it. The affair has been kept in strict secrecy, even from the press.

Chapter Three

IT WAS four o'clock in the morning. The grimy dark of night covered the winter sky. A thick fog engulfed the tolling of the steeple clock on the Garrison church as it struck the hour. It was a curious sort of dawn. Light was already filtering into the fog from the windows of every house in Buda, and at that unusual hour the light beneath the darkly impending heavens was like gold embroidery on an endless bolt of black cloth trailing in the black mire.

The fog was preparing for a great occasion, the like of which was seen no more than once or twice in a century. Police detachments in parade dress marched the streets, and hussar platoons hastened toward the Royal Fortress, the heavy, damply glistening brown and black masses of their mounts melting into fog at every few steps. The only sound was the brisk metallic ring of the horses' hoofs on the pavement, and even this sound was as faint as if it were seeping through the thin wall of the past century while every ancient little house in Buda pressed an ear against the wall to listen. Something in the fog made the entire Buda hilltop, roofs and towers and all, seem on the verge of flying off somewhere; the two great bronze eagles atop the stone pillars of the golden-spiked iron fence around the royal palace almost seemed to move, ruffling their feathers. Men and women scurried from one arched gateway to another, an army of domestics who had risen betimes to carry mysterious messages or borrow curling irons for their mistresses. Had advertising pillar posts not stood along the narrow streets, the medieval illusion would have been complete, for there was hardly a point in Europe which better preserved the mood of bygone centuries than this section, high on the hilltop above the Danube, of the Buda Fortress, with its lovely little palaces whose bent backs, tiny windows and thick walls reminded one of the creased, kindly eyes and hunched necks of very old great-aunts. At the moment they were blinking with excitement: what would the great-grandsons of their former baroque-garbed masters wear, how would they behave on the great occasion?

Could they possibly have known that this was the last such festival? Did they know that death, their own death, too, was lurking in the black fog, not too far off, only three decades away? Their old, vaulted cellars did not terminate where the wine-barrels stood in a fusty, cold air beside the cobwebbed walls. Pebbled tunnels, dripping with damp, led from narrow, secret doors into the depths, to meet in a common cave somewhere in the belly of the hill, a hundred and fifty feet down, to meet and then disperse again. These ancient cellars branched into the deep like the subterranean labyrinths of beetles and beavers, hamsters and moles. And these deep cellar passages, the relics of Turkish domination, were displayed to tourists from abroad, too, who shuddered in the torchlight as they looked into the face of the middle ages while the guides rattled off an account of the way the hapless populace of past centuries had taken refuge from murderous Turkish hordes in these underground dens. These tumbledown caverns sometimes pulled the ground from under the foundation of one of the modern apartment houses, particularly on the western slope, playfully, like earth sprites vexed because there was no longer any use for them, and the town council had begun to debate the ways and means of filling in these deep tunnels and caves. Fortunately the decisions of a town council never keep pace with history. The gentlemen councilors could not have foreseen the future; but did the four-and five-hundred-year-old matrons, with the lacy stone ruffs of antique balconies about their necks, know that these deep cellars would save thousands upon thousands of lives when the tempest came?—the tempest of which no Hungarian scholiast or Turkish caliph had ever dreamt, when the sky would open in flame and thunder from thirteen sides (as the old soldier's song says), when hundreds and thousands of bombs would make a heap of rubble and ash and blighted beams of the lovely little palaces, the slumbering old streets. On their temples it was written, now, that they knew, for houses can sometimes seem ineffably sad. But they did not reveal this secret of theirs to the interminable troops of policemen and hussars marching into the Fortress.

Pastry shops exuded a warm smell of vanilla into the cold black fog. Workmen were still feverishly laboring on the scaffolding of the rich crimson draperies in the great Gothic nave of the Matthias church, and the strong floodlights poured into the dirty fog through the main entrance like the heavenly contents of an overturned golden pail.

It was the dawn of December 30th, 1916, the day of the coronation of Charles Habsburg and Zita Bourbon in the Hungarian capital.

Flocks of newspapermen stood at the church entrance and watched the decorators at work, for there was nothing else to look at in these early hours of dawn. There were about thirty of them, including not only photographers but noted illustrators and painters with sketchbooks and easels under their arms. All the newspapermen who had been in the park at Schönbrunn were there: hobbling Karai, young Paul Fogoly, Pognár, and Özessy, the photographer with the two-tufted blond beard of historical renown. They stood smoking cigarettes, with the collars of their winter overcoats turned up, sleepless and shivering in the cold fog. This time their ranks were augmented not only by Austrians and Germans but by Bulgarian and Turkish reporters as well.

Suddenly Paul Fogoly tugged at Pognár's arm and whispered in his ear:

"Come with me!"

And he was off, running into the fog, which was so thick that Pognár could hardly keep him in sight. Ahead of them, in the light that filtered from the windows, a tall, slender figure was hurrying toward the near-by Dukay Palace on Septemvir Utca. He wore a costume of the Angevin period, a knee-length choga which took its motif from the capes of the wandering Huns and was later worn even by Venetian noblemen. The heavy cherry-colored silk frothed with spangles; it was cut diagonally in front, and at the left its hem was split to accommodate the lower half of a long sword. The slits were trimmed with sable, which in turn showed the influence of the Byzantine style. The long, straight sword, sheathed in velvet, dangled on a silver chain pulled through the hilt, in French fashion, and the chain was slung over the right shoulder. The buskins were long and cambered at the tips; the soft, lemon-yellow leather was folded double at the ankles to a breadth of four fingers, and the fold was adorned in slate-blue. The cavalier wore a rounded, fur-trimmed velvet cap with an upturned brim, like the one worn by Prince Andrew at the Synod of Cividale del Friuli. Only the falcon was missing from his gloved hand.

In these dark hours of dawn he seemed like a ghost who had spent the past six centuries in the attic of one of the ancient houses of Buda, in the form of a spider or a bat.

Paul Fogoly was evidently in pursuit of this figure. But before the reporters could catch him, the Angevin nobleman had disappeared through the arched gate of the Septemvir Utca Palace.

"Who was it?" asked Pognár, panting.

"Didn't you recognize him? Prince Schäyenheim!"

The name told a good deal. Everyone knew that Prince Ferdinand Schäyenheim-Elkburg belonged to King Charles's most intimate circle. His appearance at this early hour, in full regalia, suggested nothing but a secret and important conference in the Dukay Palace, which could only be concerned with the question of a separate peace.

"Go back to the church and tell Karai, but don't tell anyone else," Paul Fogoly whispered.

Pognár galloped away, and a few moments later old Karai, hobbling on his walking stick at his colleague's side, issued from the fog a limb at a time. They took cover in dark corners, lest someone see them, for they wanted to score a beat over the foreign reporters in the matter of the secret conference, so unexpectedly discovered, and of the prospective interview. Old Karai, too, was of the opinion that Prince Schäyenheim's appearance at the Dukay Palace at this hour was linked with some momentous development in foreign policy. For the new king came bearing the olive branch of peace. One of the queen's brothers served in the Belgian Army, and the other in the French Army. Rumor had it that Prince Xavier had already conferred with Cambon, the French Foreign Minister's deputy, informing him that his brother-in-law was unwilling to sacrifice the Monarchy to the cause of German conquest. Charles had already dispersed the Germanophile general staff at the Teschen Headquarters.

The three journalists felt they had happened upon a most secret synapse in the nervous system of history, and this propinquity almost made them shudder. Old Karai took up a post at the front of the palace, with Paul Fogoly and Pognár respectively to the left and right of the entrance, in order to prevent Prince Schäyenheim's escape from the interview, whichever way he might turn upon leaving.

Meanwhile the Angevin nobleman—otherwise the brother of Countess Menti and known to friends and acquaintances as Fini—had mounted the steps of the Dukay Palace after the porter, already awake at this unusual hour, greeted him with a mute bow to which Fini paid no attention. The heavy, pea-green carpet absorbed the sound of his buskins as he ascended the staircase, and this soundlessness made his progress seem even more spectral, as if he were floating. There was a light, springy elegance in his walk, combined with a hint of exhaustion—he was the sort of man who could be anywhere between thirty-five and sixty years old. His thin ears were somewhat prominent, his two eyes were noticeably far apart, the nostrils of his nose were sharply defined, and his large lips were curved in a pleasant bow, exceptionally suitable for sipping at oysters, champagne, women's lips or other parts, as a result of the same evolutionary process which gave the elephant a trunk or the giraffe a neck long enough to reach the highest branches. There was a certain perfection in Prince Fini's appearance, in the fragrance of his physical cleanliness, as if it were all framed for the enjoyment of the highest savors of life, and particularly for the pursuits of love in the most artistic sense. A degenerate shell of a man—this is what people guided by the hiss of prejudice might call him. The prince's diminutive chin ran into his neck abruptly. This might have been the face of a circus clown, after he had wiped off the livid lines and the clashing colors. But Fini's face expressed more than that: tender, laughable, sympathetic, it was at the same time cruel and aloof.

A few light bulbs were already glowing along the staircase, and voices could be heard from the servants' quarters. Fini floated to the second floor, turned right and walked down a long corridor one side of which was lined with closets. Several chambermaids, passing him in their flannel-soled morning shoes, whispered a respectful greeting to the costumed visitor. Every bedroom was filled with guests who had come to town for this day. Fini floated ahead with head held high and back erect, like a household ghost who knew his way about these halls. He turned to the left at a fork in the corridor, and although the passage was completely dark he readily found the knob of the third door, and entered without knocking. Warm darkness greeted him inside the room, its air somewhat oxygenless and mingled with soft little scents. He reached for the switch on the wall and turned on the light. The Venetian chandelier lit a paneled room, with wide, dark green silk curtains which completely covered the outside wall. The dark mass of curtains would have suggested a mortuary to anyone visiting the room for the first time. Large paintings hung on the other walls, a Courbet, a Delacroix, a Renoir, a Greco. By the right wall, on a low, capacious studio couch, slept Kristina. Only a few unruly locks of her black hair peeped from beneath the comforter, fascinating in their promise. The down-filled comforter suggested the outlines of the sleeper's body, as she lay on her side, her back bent, her knees drawn up, her ten fingers curled beside her nose. It was the position of an embryo dreaming its wonderful dreams in the maternal womb. People who sleep this way after reaching maturity retain something of the bloom of infancy until the end of their lives. On the floor below, in a similar room and on a similar bed, slept Countess Menti, similarly curled up like an embryo—two weeks ago she had been named a lady-in-waiting to the new queen. The billions of cells which constitute the human organism are incessantly and feverishly at work in their lymphatic prisons, carrying on an incredible commerce known to modern science as inner secretion. In the swarming laboratory of the cells, too, are produced substances which are not expelled with the waste but return to the circulatory system to help or hinder the digestion, to inhibit or stimulate the sexual life. These elements are known to science as hormones, but the world at large obdurately persists in referring to these effectives as feminine virtues, deep religiosity, criminal impulses or creative abilities, whereas it is obvious that the timeless and mysterious laboratory would brook little interference in its work on the part of man-made laws, guileless books of prayer or provincial rules of etiquette.

Fini approached the bed, and his tobacco-bitten voice rasped:

"Giddap yore old neck!"

Fini had picked up this expression well before the war in America, where he spent a year and a half after telling the entire Casino that he was going on a puma hunt. Fini was a well-nigh professional cardplayer, habitually risking stakes so large that he floated on the waves of financial ruin or unexpected affluence every evening, like a canoe with its bow upstream or down. He arrived at the decision to go abroad on a morning when his canoe stood somewhere in midstream, which made possible a trip to America of the duration and in the style to which he was accustomed. Prince Fini was a member of the Hungarian nobility too, for he owned an enormous estate beyond the Danube, an estate which had melted to a mere eight thousand acres in the course of time and was hidden under mortgages, tax arrears and bootmakers' bills, as copious as ice floes about the pillar of a bridge during the spring thaw. Fini knew approximately eight Hungarian words. The impoverishment of his vocabulary was redeemed by the circumstances that his eight words sprang from the innermost gold mines of the popular idiom, flavorsome and fiery words normally used to designate sexual intercourse and organs. Fini sometimes pronounced these unkempt and potentially explosive words in the pauses between conversations in German, English or French, while sitting at dinner in feminine salons or at diplomatic functions, unexpectedly and without premeditation, and on those who understood them—the footmen waiting on table, principally—these words had an effect which could otherwise only have been achieved by releasing live rats on the tablecloth and letting them scamper among the crystal glasses and the gold tableware. Fini would fling these words—or brief but baneful oaths composed of these words—into conversational pauses, with the same intonation and expression which he might use in saying *Michelangelo*, or *Society for the Prevention of Cruelty to Children*, or *Liberty, Fraternity, and Equality;* and in the utterance of these scabrous words there was something of the human spirit's revolt against the bleak emptiness of formality, against deadly boredom. The occasional surprising splash and spatter of these unlooked-for words also indicated that a Schäyenheim prince could permit himself anything at all. Fini's trip to America, when he announced it, was considered a normal thing by everyone, for even on an international scale the prince was accounted a formidable huntsman, and his most recent triumph had been at the clay-pigeon finals in Nice. After a few months of stalking he managed to find, in Iowa, the spoor of a puma who wore thick glasses and was the richest girl in the city of Des Moines. Her father wore shirtsleeves to the dinner table, and at his office he leaned back in his chair, stacked his snub-nosed shoes on the desk and linked his thumbs under his suspender straps at the armpit, meanwhile gripping a cigar in the extreme left corner of his mouth as tightly as a dog grips a bone when in fear that someone will snatch it away. Instead of speech, Mr. Horndike emitted throaty grunts from beside his cigar, which were comprehensible to Iowans, according to Prince Fini, because they also used this language instead of human speech. Mr. Horndike controlled the entire hog industry in Iowa, in addition to which he owned a coal mine outside of Dubuque. It did not bother Fini that all the members of the Horndike family—father, mother, daughter and fourteen-year-old son—looked like overfed hogs, since Patricia, who was on the brink of thirty, came with a dowry of several million dollars. Fini, a good hunter, approached his prey against the wind by engaging papa in business negotiations. He knew exactly how close to lure the beast, and knew that he must fire at a point exactly between the eye and the ear. This point was the European cultivation of Patricia, who spoke a tolerable French and had read Dumas's *Count of Monte Cristo* in the original. Fini had faith in his firearm, and waited for the opportune moment. The season was good for hunting, for it was in those years that a number of European aristocrats bagged their first big game on Wall Street and along the virgin slopes of American industry. But Mr. Horndike proved to be a remarkably thick-skinned beast, for after the reverberation of the opening shot (which was the prince's request for his daughter's hand in marriage) had died away, he exiled Patricia to relatives in Mount Vernon and broke off his business negotiations with Fini. Mr. Horndike did not know what he was doing, did not realize how he was depriving his daughter of an opportunity to dip into the wondrous color and savor of life, for Prince Fini would have swung that kindly, spectacled, pink female in a waltz of *savoir vivre* and high style the like of which the Iowan girl, accustomed to the consumption of putty-flavored apple pies, had never conceived, not to mention the fact that in Fini's hands her dowry would have wrought agricultural and industrial miracles in his poor but glittering little European homeland, since Fini was not only a gambler but a thoroughly grounded agriculturalist and a tender husband as well, a gentleman from head to foot. Fini did not pursue his prey, but veered in another direction and produced another fine weapon: his skill at cards. The notabilities of Iowa, however, with Mr. Horndike at their head, stripped him of his last dollar at poker in the Black Hawk Club, an achievement which may possibly be attributed to the fact that those mossback Lutheran hog magnates were the exemplars of sobriety at a time when Iowa was one of the few states where the sale of intoxicating beverages was prohibited. Having fired all his ammunition, Fini transferred his seat of residence to a smaller town, Ames, and, in view of the fact that his cabled requests for help seemed to have fallen into the ocean on their way to Budapest, he accepted temporary employment as a teamster, for in addition to his other skills he was very good at handling horses. Being a well balanced and cheerful soul, he derived considerable amusement from this adventure. Several months later, when he resumed his seat at the card tables of the Casino, eager questions provoked only the answer—muttered from beside his long cigarette holder—that there were no more pumas in America.

Now, as he stood in the costume of an Angevin cavalier by Kristina's bedside, with a fantastic array of ribbons on his chest and the fist-sized gold emblem of a chamberlain dangling at his left hip, his "Giddap yore old neck!"—a phrase he had picked up from the teamsters of Iowa—seemed rather out of place in these surroundings, directed at a swan-necked countess sleeping under a lighted chandelier.

Kristina's head stirred and, blinking an eye toward the door, she spoke in a bird-voice which was like the first chirp of a bird at daybreak.

"Fini?"

"Yes, darling."

He answered in English. It was a matter of mood with him whether to start the conversation in German, English or French, for their spirit was, after all, above mere nationalism.

"What time is it?"

"Four o'clock. Don't you remember I was supposed to wake you up?"

Kristina sat up in bed and yawned, forming a lopsided O with her lips. Then she blinked her sensitive blue eyes:

"Turn off the chandelier."

At the same time she lit the little shaded lamp on her bedside table. Kristina had already enjoyed a romantic liaison with her uncle. She was now twenty, while Fini was fifty. It goes without saying that no flame of passion leapt in their affair, Kristina took the demands of her body as a matter of course, in all simplicity, and saved her ardor for more transcendental things, like an evening of Wagner at the Opera or a quiet little Mass in the Garrison church.

Fini settled in the low-slung, cushioned armchair beside the bed. Kristina yawned several times, sniffed, rubbed her eyes with her fists and then poked her feet from beneath the comforter, to slip them into a pair of Caucasian slippers with upturned toes. The heels of her white legs were still bright red from sleeping, as if daubed with paint.

"Did you bring the invitations?"

"Yes, darling."

Kristina left the bed, and as she stood stretching for a moment the lamp at her back shone through her light mallow-covered batiste nightgown. She started toward the bathroom, but Fini suddenly interposed his long buskin-shod Angevin legs. For a moment Kristina stood scratching the nape of her neck thoughtfully at the sight of the unexpected obstacle, and there was both charm and humor in her gesture. Then, resting an arm on Fini's shoulder, she carefully proceeded to step over the dangerous barrier. Under the circumstances it was fairly simple to upset her spiritual and physical equilibrium. With a single motion Fini pulled her into his lap. Kristina stretched out her hand to switch off the lamp, and the room was pitch black once again. Later, from the sounds which ensued, it was possible to conclude only that Fini was unstrapping his velvet-sheathed sword, and that the ancient sword, which had played a similar role on countless occasions in past centuries, rattled faintly when it was placed on one of the little glass-topped tables. They did not think to lock the door, for it was entirely unnecessary. During most hours of the day it was customary for servants in great houses such as this to enter only upon the ring of a bell, and the discipline of the staff secured the ponderous oak doors more surely than any lock. When the light went on again, Fini was alone in the room, straightening his fur-trimmed cap before a mirror. Upon Kristina's return from the bathroom Fini reached for his wallet with a movement well known to the exclusive brothels of Paris.

"Here are the invitations. One is for the church, the other for dinner. Look for me in church; I'll sneak you in among the ladies-in-waiting, where you'll have the best view. By the way, yesterday His Majesty asked me, 'How's that pretty little Countess Dukay, der tulli Katz?'"

He waved farewell with a white-gloved hand and vanished through the oaken doorway. His stride, as he passed through the long corridors, was as buoyant as when he came, and he descended the carpeted stone staircase with the same dignified carriage, his head held high and a somewhat cloudy, sleepy expression on his face, like the chancellors of old. He had not slept a wink that night, having left the Casino at three o'clock in the morning, where a host of Austrian aristocrats, down from Vienna for the coronation, had played for high stakes against the lords of the puszta.

✝

When he stepped through the arched gate of the Dukay Palace the newspapermen who were lying in wait rushed him from three sides. Old Karai addressed him first, for he alone of the three of them spoke a good German. It was not sheer unselfishness which had prompted his younger colleagues to share their secret with him.

"Your Grace, would you be good enough to give the Hungarian press a few words on the reason for…"

He had not finished his sentence before Pognár, standing behind him, interrupted in atrocious German:

"Was ist geschehen in die Dukay Palast?"

But he regretted his interruption at once, sensing that *Palast* deserved not *die* but *der.*

Fini was surprised by the onslaught of the reporters, but at the same time it fed his vanity. He raised his chin slightly and said, with inimitable elegance, with the inflexible courtesy of which only an Angevin nobleman was capable:

"Gentlemen, I'm terribly sorry, but—no comment."

Under the circumstances it must be admitted that there was really nothing else to say. He nodded and disappeared into the fog of Septemvir Utca. Fini was an important member of the Committee on Arrangements, which was keeping a sleepless vigil all night. Right now he was on his way to committee headquarters.

Disappointed, the three journalists drifted back towards the church. But human interest is as important as fact to the profession of journalism. Pognár lagged behind the others, and in the light of a pastry shop he made the following entry in his notebook:

"4:12 A.M. The neighborhood around the coronation church is still asleep. Prince Ferdinand Schäyenheim-Elkburg just entered the baroque gate of the Dukay Palace on Septemvir Utca, dressed in a gorgeous Angevin costume. Your correspondent sensed that history was panting behind the shutters of the upstairs windows of the palace at this moment. Quietly, but with decision, the fate of the Monarchy took a new turn. Millions upon millions of men are suffering in damp, black trenches in this dark, wintry hour, all of them at a rendezvous with death. At nine minutes after five Prince Schäyenheim-Elkburg left the Dukay Palace. There was relief on the prince's face. He is known to be in close friendship with King Charles. Not only the Hungarian nation and all the peoples of the Monarchy but the whole suffering world as well owes a debt of gratitude to the noble prince for the influence he exercised on important questions of foreign policy during those fifty-seven minutes in the Dukay Palace."

In the meantime Kristina was sitting on the edge of her bed, her somewhat nearsighted eyes in a squint as she studied the two invitations, engraved with the golden crest of the crown of Hungary. Fini had kept his promise. She did not believe a word of the king's alleged inquiry concerning herself, for she knew Fini well and knew he would not balk at a little white lie in order to give pleasure to someone. And Uncle Fini was a wise man, for his words had really pleased her, however transparent the lie. "Der tulli Katz"—this Viennese phrase, applied to pretty girls, was so typical of Fini, as much his own as his watch-chain or his seal ring. But was it impossible, after all, for two men to happen upon the same expression out of the whole bottomless sea of words? Perhaps it was true. The king, too, used Viennese idioms in his speech.

Kristina's shoulders twitched, nervously and spasmodically, for she was beguiled by the sweetness of the lie, like a bird trapped in lime. She closed her eyes, and her clenched, somewhat irregular teeth glistened whitely behind her lips, as when someone is in great pain or mutters a fearful curse. She fell back on the bed with arms widespread.

Not once had Kristina spoken of her love for the king to anyone except Uncle Fini, who—as we may recall—stage-managed her dip in the well. This happened one night when they chanced to be alone with several bottles of champagne. So

125

moved was Fini by the celestial beauty and purity of her unrequited love that he began an affair with Kristina that very night, employing the utmost tenderness and one of the prophylactics which he always carried in his wallet. He meant the affair to be both consolation and cure, the gift of a good-hearted uncle.

✛

It was six o'clock. Chambermaids and valets appeared at the stroke of the hour, by prearrangement, to light the chandeliers in the rooms of Count Dupi, Countess Menti, the children and all the guests. György, eighteen years old and a cadet in the Hussars, was to be one of the scepter-bearers. The costume of a page awaited ten-year-old János. And Zia, who was only six years old, had been assigned, together with her governess, to a window in the right wing of the palace which opened on the line of march and would give a good view of the procession. The adjacent window was reserved for Rere, with special instructions for Mr. Badar to keep him under constant surveillance, for the excitement of so large a crowd might be expected to provoke unpredictable responses from half-wits.

Eyewitnesses who had attended the coronation of Franz Joseph and Queen Elizabeth in 1867 and, after the death of Victoria, were present at the coronations of Edward VII and George V, asserted that the coronation of Charles IV and Zita Bourbon surpassed all the others in pomp and splendor. And there was no exaggeration in this claim. Of eastern ancestry, the Hungarian people—and more precisely the members of its topmost stratum, of ancient Turkish blood, whose Asiatic forebears levied tribute on tribes from Korea to the Black Sea for thousands of years, and collected their taxes in horses, furs and gold—these people knew more about oriental pomp than any other nation in Europe. Furthermore, this coronation took place in the third year of a World War, when the young royal pair and the aged aristocracy were filled with gloomy forebodings; it was a valedictory, an elaborate dance of death to the solemn shrill of hymns and carillons, to the rumble of organs at Mass, while the thunder of cannon on the hilltops of Buda sounded as if wild sobs were shaking the crests of the hills. Against this dark background the display of color was even more brilliant. Flags, stately coaches, gala costumes, guardsmen, shield-bearers, harnesses and ancestral jewels twinkled from the depths of the past like the iridescent tints of deep-sea fish—incomparable indigos, ineffable carmines, glittering greens and yellows, blacks and whites, marvelous hues of the deep which last as long as the hooked game still pants and works its gills but take flight from the mucous scales in a matter of seconds and leave nothing but a gray, dead fish in the bottom of the boat. The antique pomp of the coronation ceremonies on this foggy and cold December day, the barbaric and virginal loveliness of the thousand-year-old klenodies, resurrected from the glass catafalque of time, rose from the waves of the World War like a Gorgon's head which the Perseus-sword of the Entente had already severed from the ancient nation; but of this severed head, of the baleful grin on its lips, the dire curse on its blue and dangling tongue, the serpents writhing in its hair—of this head the several skilled artists in the service of the Committee on Arrangements made an image which assumed the features of ideal beauty even in the extreme agonies of death, as Leonardo's brush and Daujon's chisel did for the frightful countenance of Medusa. The idealization was a success, and the coronation was beautiful. The people? The people were represented by a handful of young and enthusiastic newspapermen, half of whom were lost in the enchantment of the sound of their own words after having been roused from sleep in the dead of night by the bleak summons of professional duty, while the other half were gruff and surly, shivering with cold after a sleepless night at the Press Club. Distribution of the invitations was carefully restricted to prominent and trustworthy elements, cabinet ministers, generals and the relatives, valets and mistresses of lord lieutenants. The people were nowhere to be found behind the military cordons which guarded the Fortress; the crowd along the patrolled line of march was sparse and full of holes, like an unsuccessful apple pie; and the reviewing stands, too, were gap-toothed. The people—many of whose simple sons had plodded from distant farms toward the great recruiting centers on the day war broke out, with their earthly possessions dangling from a stick over their shoulders, had gathered like the children of Rákóczi and Kossuth, with the notion that they were going into battle against the Austrians and the Habsburgs (for who else could offer a threat to Magyar freedom?)—the people, as a result of sage and tactful arrangements made by the Committee, did not take part in the coronation. When one of the artists, for example, suggested that the most beautiful scene of the ritual, the coronation oath, be staged on the Fisher's Bastion, where the crowds along the Danube shore could see the sight and where the symbolism of the ceremony would be significantly aimed at the plains to the east, the Committee flatly rejected his proposal, fearing that the king would be an easy mark for an assassin's bullet on the open bastion. It was best to keep His Majesty and the prominent socialites behind the thick walls of the Buda fortress, as in a padlocked box.

Nevertheless, the war was also present at the coronation, in the persons of fifty warriors. Their group of field uniforms constituted the only olive-gray patch in the motley of color, a patch from out the purblind firmament of war. They were the golden-spurred gallants kneeling at the foot of the throne, waiting for the king to knight them with St. Stephen's sword. The Committee on Arrangements deserved the highest praise for not forgetting those who had spilled their blood on distant battlefields for king and country. It is true, of course, that a historian of the future, reading the list of fifty heroic names—which included twenty-four aristocrats and, by some miraculous accident, twenty-two whose names were very like those of certain generals and cabinet ministers—reading this list, the historian might be led to conclude that the trenches, hospitals, prisoner-of-war camps and lime-pits were exclusively occupied by princes, counts and ministers' sons, while the people sat smoking their pipes beside the stove. But aside from this slight and seeming disproportion the knights-to-be were truly seasoned veterans, some of them with only one leg or otherwise crippled; and still, somehow, they looked like a triumph of German chemical science, which knew how to make edible butter of the surface grease on dirty dishwater.

The Committee, in its wisdom, went even further. An entire platoon of disabled soldiers was ordered from an army hospital and stationed on one of the side streets. The disabled veterans sang gay and humorous army tunes without pause, and the street veritably rang with "Fanny Schneider," with the marching rhythms of "Örmester ur fekete subája" or "Vékony héja van a piros almának" —as if to prove that those who had already lost a leg were still singing cheerily and, had a number of policemen not been on hand to restrain them, that every last one of them would have rushed away to beat the enemy's brains out with their crutches.

At half past six in the morning it was still dark, but the Upper and Lower Houses of Parliament were already sitting in joint session, giving the coronation their legislative sanction in accord with the ancient laws of the land. After the brief meeting, fifteen hundred carriages headed for the Fortress, for at that time the horse-drawn carriage was considered more elegant even if one owned an automobile. The rain was drizzling quietly. It was still dark at seven, when two crown guards broke the seals on the iron grill of the Loretto chapel and opened the iron chest inside. They placed the crown, the scepter, the mantle and the apple of gold on cushions of red velvet, in reverent silence, as if exposing real sacraments to the mundane air. A detachment of costumed crown guards stood watch over the proceedings.

Meanwhile the Matthias church began to fill with spectators, like a vast theater. The marvels of antique goldsmitheries fell into artistic groups, gentlemen and ladies adorned with precious stones, foreign diplomats in gold-braided full dress, prelates in wintry vestments and generals in the plumage of parrots. The walls and pillars of the church were covered with crimson velvet, which gave added brilliance to the coruscation of colors beneath the bright chandeliers. Archdukes and archduchesses took their places in the sanctuary and, even aside from the fact that the queen was carrying her fourth offspring beneath her heart, it was comforting to see that the House of Habsburg was far from extinction.

At half past eight the organ began to peal, and the choir broke into the "Ecce Sacerdos Magnus." The officiating prelacy entered in a rainbow of purple, red, white, black, gold and silver colors. Each member of the group had a special part to play in the liturgy. A special bishop, the *infulistus,* carried the Prince Primate's miter. A special canon, the *bugifer,* bore the episcopal taper. The pastoral staff was carried in gingerly fashion by a *pastoralistus* who was as anxious of countenance as if the ornate staff had been baked of gingerbread. The censers and the frankincense were carried by *thuriferi.* A *librifer* conveyed the enormous prayer book, and behind him came the candle bearers, or *acolythi,* and the *lotores,* or band washers. The service of the Lord proceeded without a flaw, harmoniously. The discord in the disposition of the spectators was correspondingly greater. A large-nosed, heavy-set oldster with a neck as red as a turkey scolded the Committee on Arrangements loudly because he, *he,* the sole royal guest at the coronation, had been seated in the same box as a four-year-old child. This gentleman, wearing the crimson uniform of a Hungarian general, was Ferdinand Koburg, King of Bulgaria. They vainly sought to explain that the child was Crown Prince Otto, heir apparent to the throne of the Austro-Hungarian Monarchy; his eyes flashed as he turned his back on them and he waved his hand angrily, as if he knew from some mysterious source of information exactly what that throne was worth.

In general, everybody was offended at being placed where they were placed, because they had studied their gala dresses in a mirror before leaving home and each one had decided that his or her costume—and more particularly the person inside the gorgeous costume—achieved a height of perfection and beauty which it would have been difficult to surpass. Each and every spectator accordingly felt that the others were blocking the view of his own splendor, which is why icicles of insulted haughtiness decked the noses and lips of them all.

✝

Kristina searched for Prince Fini in the crowd, standing on tiptoe and attempting to see over the golden epaulettes. Finally she succeeded in catching his eye through the closely packed mass of heads. Fini signaled to her with a friendly wink of his left eye. A few seconds later he was wriggling toward Kristina in the mob, and he exclaimed nervously, reproachfully, almost rudely: "What do you mean by coming so late?" and having dispersed all suspicion of special privilege by this rudeness, he took Kristina by the wrist and stood her among the ladies-in-waiting, only a few yards from the sanctuary and the throne, a position which afforded the best view.

Kristina stood beside a pillar, holding the palm of her left hand on her neck as if in fear that her jugular vein would burst into a flow of blood. On the point of collapse, she closed her eyes for seconds at a time. She was waiting for the king, waiting for the introit. The rumble of the choir and the piping of the organ made her body feel weightless, almost seemed to raise the entire audience, exalted by its own raiment and jewelry, off the floor.

And the king was on his way. The royal state coach, which had once conveyed Maria Theresa, had already left the Fortress, drawn by eight cream-white horses. Bewigged coachmen sat on the backs of the foremost and hindmost horses; shield-bearers trotted about the gold-mounted, plate-glassed coach; courtiers and guardsmen rode behind. The foot guard preceded the coach, while an entire squadron of hussars took up the rear. Handkerchiefs waved from the reviewing stands and windows; the populace was cold but it cheered nonetheless. At the church the scepter-bearers held a baldachin above the heads of the royal couple as they entered.

Fanfares rang out in the church, and kettledrums began to roll. Count Charles the lion hunter remarked to Countess Marie at his side that the whole affair bore a certain resemblance to the huli-huli ceremonials of the natives of Uganda, and would be even more similar if all present took off their clothes. The countess turned her delicate little bird-head away in vexation. Every soul was moved to its depths by the historical grandeur of the moment. Kristina could hardly see a thing through her tears. The little four-year-old heir apparent, wearing a costume of snow-white satin, whipped off his egret-plumed cap and waved it in every direction while he hastened to keep up with the adults, pumping his tiny legs. The cheers mounted when the royal couple approached the double throne on the altar, exactly as they had rehearsed it the day before, like conscientious actors, clad in raincoats, declaiming the historical tragedies of Shakespeare on a bare stage and to a deserted pit.

The ceremony began. The prelates questioned and answered each other in Latin, intoning the archaic poetry of traditional texts whose simplicity stemmed from distant centuries; for all its bleak splendor, their performance was not devoid of the rustic charm of a Passion play. "Is it your wish to elevate the most excellent knight here present to the heights of royal rank?" asked one of the prelates, while another intoned: "Is it known to you that he is deserving of such dignity?" And a singsong voice replied: "Yes, I do know and so believe!" Whereupon the Prince Primate declared with relief: "Deo gratias!" Thank God, then there's nothing wrong, let's go ahead and crown this most excellent knight. Yes, decidedly there was something of the charm of folk plays about the ancient ritual, something of the refreshing sweetness of storyland about the make-believe of the prelates as they chorused at each other and tried to pretend that everything depended on the response of the Archbishop of Kalocsa; that things would go otherwise if the archbishop, for example, began to scratch the nape of his neck with the forefinger that bore the pontifical ring and replied: "Don't take it ill of me, Reverend Father, but to tell the truth I'm not entirely sure that the most excellent knight here present, well-mannered enough but not averse to an occasional spot of wine, is truly suited to the throne in these terribly trying times"—that if the archbishop should answer thus, the Prince Primate would say: "Then what are you blabbering about, my dear son, take this young man home and let's wait until we find a man suitable for the throne of St. Stephen. As for you ladies and gentlemen, about face, off with you, the coronation is temporarily postponed." Fortunately no such danger threatened the traditional drama, for its author was history itself, of that stubborn breed of playwrights who brook no change in the script; but when the play is over, when it is too late, the playwright himself will demonstrate that this young man of twenty-nine, who has just knelt on the steps of the purple throne and taken an oath on the constitution, is truly unfit for his task and would have been wiser to apply for a pension as a captain in the dragoons while there was still time, to open a shoe-store or poultry shop along one of the lesser streets of Vienna, or to become a tobacco planter in South America, the better to raise his prospective seven children in decency. But who can foresee the future? Only the Palatine, perhaps, the first gentleman of the land, the bearded, thickly spectacled, lean Protestant nobleman who placed the crown on the king's head and whose fate is already written on his face—for only two years from now the rifles of the revolution will lay him low in the hallway of his apartment.

But now, in the high excitement of the pomp and splendor, no one thought of the future; even among the newspapermen there was not a soul so cynical as to remain unmoved when—much to the surprise of them all—the young king touched his forehead to the steps that led to the throne, in deep Christian humility, guided at this moment not by the stage directions of his role but by the dictates of his own soul. Now, in this obeisance of his, the drama reached its peak, a drama which transcended the walls of the church and was the drama of millions and millions of men in the damp trenches of distant battlefields.

Suddenly, unexpectedly, a woman's sobbing broke the profound silence from the direction of the pillar where Kristina stood. It was as if she, and her sensitivity, constituted a single nerve which suffered the unbelievable spiritual strain that prevailed in the crowded church. Elsewhere, too, women could be heard sobbing more quietly, as if at a funeral.

"Accipe gladium!" came the Primate's voice, when the Master of Ceremonies, the Lord Steward and the Lord Chamberlain, assisted by the bishops, girded the thousand-year-old sword of the first holy king about their sovereign's waist as he rose from his knees. The king drew the heavy blade from its scabbard, turned toward the congregation and brandished the sword three times, then wiped the blade on his sleeve three times and returned it to the scabbard with the expression of an egg-juggling conjuror on his face, careful not to make a wrong move. At this moment he seemed a lifeless puppet once more.

Upon the conclusion of the coronation ceremony the king left the church at the side of his gold-braided Minister of Foreign Affairs, and was handed into the saddle at the main entrance by an ensign-bearer who was pale with excitement because he had come too late for the performance. While dressing he had noticed that the jeweled studs of his gorgeous Magyar regalia were missing. Hectic inquiry revealed that his eighteen-year-old son had pawned the studs a few days before to pay some gambling debts. The pawnshop was closed in the early hours of dawn, and St. Stephen's crown had already graced the forehead of Charles IV by the time the studs were recovered.

Now the procession was led by a squadron of mounted militiamen, behind whom rode the mayor and the deputies of the municipality, followed by the representatives of the judiciary, of the counties and townships with their traditional banners. Next came the members of the Upper and Lower Houses, stepping with great dignity. At their backs the eleven flags of the nation, held by cavaliers in full dress, fluttered in the breeze—that is, they would have fluttered if there had been a breeze, but only tiny drops of rain drizzled from the overcast sky. The eleven flags were the standards of Bulgaria, Kumania, Ladomeria, Halics, Serbia, Rama, Croatia, Dalmatia, Slavonia, Transylvania and, finally, of Hungary itself, again—and for the last time—unfurled before the half empty reviewing stands, funereal relics of the might of King Matthias and the Angevins. Behind the massed colors rode the Royal Herald, the Lord Usher and the ensign-bearers, holding their symbolic cushions of office. Then came the Palatine, with the scroll of the coronation oath in hand, and back of him rode the archdukes. About ten yards behind them pranced the king's charger. The crown was on the king's head, the mantle of St. Stephen about his shoulders and the sword of the holy king at his side. Evidently the king's charger was livelier than necessary, for the king suddenly caught a hand to his head and seized the heavy crown as it slipped to his temple. Everyone's blood ran cold at this sight. A bishop, with the apostolic cross in his right hand, rode at the right of the king, mounted on the horse that was not only the gentlest and oldest horse in the kingdom but had also been fed sleeping pills with its morning oats for the occasion. The Prince Primate, the nuncio and the Archbishop of Kalocsa eschewed the example of bygone centuries, considering it the better part of wisdom to ride in a coach. The pedestrian spectators followed the privy councilors, chamberlains and other dignitaries, and a mixed squadron of hussars closed the procession.

One of the walls of the Dukay Palace on Septemvir Utca faced the line of march. The windows were crowded with the heads of the stay-at-home staff and the two Dukay children, Zia and the half-witted Rere. As the procession passed by an unfortunate thing happened, interrupting the solemn exaltation of the marchers for a moment or two. In their excitement everyone, even Mr. Badar, had forgotten all about Rere; left alone in the room where the tall Christmas tree still stood, the half-wit began to nibble at the Christmas decorations in his boredom. One after another, not only the gilt walnuts and the chocolates but the sparkling trimmings as well and even the colored wax candles, seasoned with a few sprigs of pine, disappeared into the bottomless pit of his stomach. Rere truly had the stomach of an ostrich, but when he heard the loud cheering and rushed to lean out of the window he pressed this stomach against the sill, with the result that the entire decoration of the denuded Christmas tree shot from his lips amid a series of groans at the very moment when the representatives of the Upper House passed below. The heads immediately vanished from the windows, and two footmen helped Mr. Badar to pull Rere out of sight of the scandalized glances outside, which was not a simple matter because Rere opposed their endeavors with every ounce of his bullish strength.

After the coronation oath came the "flourish of the sword" on a mound that had been raised for this purpose near the Royal Fortress. The mound was composed of ten pounds of earth from the soil of every county, mixed with a similar quantity from every famous battlefield throughout the kingdom. The king rode to the top of the mound, drew the sword of state from its scabbard and flourished it toward the four points of the compass. At coronations of yore, when there was peace on earth, the flourish of the sword meant that the king would defend his land against attacks from every side. It was a symbolic scene, and the sword merely cut the empty air. Now, however, the sword pointed at Russia to the north, Rumania to the east, Serbia and Italy to the south, France and England to the west; and for a moment the spectators were brought back to reality, reminded that the ancient sword had never in the course of history had so much to do. From a window in the Royal Palace the queen and the little heir apparent watched the flourish of the sword, the ill-omened gestures of which were mitigated only by the fact that everyone looked for a speedy peace under the new monarch, even at the cost of facing up to Germany.

By now it was getting late, and the ceremony of the coronation dinner was still in store. A horseshoe-shaped table, set for six persons in all, stood beneath a gold-trimmed red velvet baldachin on a staircased dais in the throne-room. There were six plates of gold on the table, and a golden bowl in the center held a large bouquet of flowers. First came the ritual laving of the hands. After the royal pair had taken off their gloves, the Palatine sprinkled a few drops of water on their hands from a golden pitcher, while the Prince Primate offered towels. Pages of noble blood assisted them. Before they sat down to table the Prince Primate said grace, and when the king took his place at the head of the table the Lord Steward lifted the crown from his head, for it was not, after all, proper to dine with one's hat on. He put the crown on a golden tray on a special little table, and two crown guards stood beside it throughout the meal. The dinner consisted of nineteen courses, including every marvel of French and Hungarian gastronomy (for Austrians know nothing about cooking). The meal began with an "Homage" roast and continued with broiled chicken "à la Reine," which was followed by "Coronation" ham. Then came a loin of pork from the Hortobágy, mountain trout from the Tátra, and a series of cold dainties, desserts and fruity sweets which only lunatic chefs can prepare when they soar to the heights of poesy with a bloody kitchen knife in hand. One might suppose that the nineteen-course dinner lasted for hours. This was not so, of course, for the pages merely marched in with their platters in hand, bowed and departed, as if they meant to tantalize the diners, who were almost ready to fall from their chairs with hunger. But they all sat rigidly in place, obedient puppets of an ancient show. During the brief symbolic meal the throne-room was packed with selected notabilities who had received special invitations to the royal "dinner." They stood watching the rapid ebb and flow of the platters. Only two speeches were made, and there was no cause to complain of their length. The king stood up, raised his glass and made the following speech in faultless Hungarian, not even transposing the word-order: "Long live our land!" He was answered by a resounding cheer from every corner of the room. The second speech was made by the Prince Primate, and Hungarian after-dinner speakers could have learned a lesson in brevity from him as well. He said merely: "Long live the King!" Again the speech was answered by a resounding cheer.

After dinner the royal couple retired to their apartments and quickly had dinner, excitedly discussing the events of the morning, the roaring successes and the minor mishaps, like exhausted and exuberant actors after a momentous opening night. But the program was still not over. The devoted deputations of the two Houses of Parliament awaited them in the throne-room, after which more than four hundred privileged ladies were presented to the queen in the ceremonial hall of the palace. Pale and weary, the queen stood stiffly on the platform and moved only her head, as if performing prescribed neck exercises. She nodded at each of the women as they approached the platform and sank in a laboriously practiced curtsey, so low that their legs and knees seemed to disappear beneath the skirts. They came in single file from a door on the left and disappeared in single file through a door on the right. The master of ceremonies was in a frenzy, because the queen had given him strict instructions to conclude the presentations in a half hour, and the ladies were moving altogether too slowly. Every one of them wanted to make an impression, every one of them was convinced that her name and her bewitching personality alone would stick in the queen's memory, and not a single woman there but hoped against hope that the queen would engage her in conversation. The minutes flew at an alarming pace, and the master of ceremonies drove the ladies toward the platform at an ever-increasing clip, until they were actually running. As a consequence the queen's nods quickened, like a machine gone haywire. By now they were flinging women at the queen's feet as mailmen throw bundles of letters when pressed for time; and since the time was too short to pronounce the names, one of the Countesses Eszterházy was introduced as *Cntss Sztrhzy*. Panting after the race, the older and more corpulent ladies collapsed into chairs upon reaching the anteroom.

The reason for this great haste was that the train stood ready and the royal couple wanted to leave for Vienna that very evening. They had no idea how deep a scar this haste of theirs would leave on the heart of a pro-monarchist nation, a nation which considered that they had accepted the coronation gift of ten thousand gold pieces, accepted the ringing bells of the ancient churches, accepted the salutes of the cannon when the Prince Primate exclaimed, "Long live the King," accepted the truly dazzling homage of the entire land, but had stood with watch in hand the meanwhile lest they miss the train to Vienna. To Vienna!—that was the catch. The disillusionment would not have been so great had they been on the way to Istanbul or Berlin, but in nearly four hundred years of Habsburg rule Vienna was always the city in whose favor the king of Hungary had constantly deceived his Royal Palace in Buda. And now, too, they had hardly sworn eternal allegiance before they were striking their tents and dashing to Vienna, which was very like the scandalous behavior of a newlywed husband who goes straight to his mistress from the altar, not giving a moment's thought to whatever might be in his young bride's heart beneath the veils of her wedding dress.

Hardly had they left before the offended whisperings began. The next day, in fact, the newspapers launched an attack on the Committee on Arrangements for its shortcomings, since it would have been libelous to express their frank opinions of the royal couple. The reviews of the gala performance were definitely disparaging. The Finance Minister had not played his part well, he had not mounted a horse in accord with ancient custom; and the critics took especial exception to the fact that he had not strewn money to the people. As far as the strewing of money was concerned, the Finance Minister really left no room for complaint in his military expenditures; as for straddling a horse, it must be considered that the worthy fellow had never been on horseback in his life and was even afraid to approach a hack horse. It was said, in complaint, that the Committee had completely ignored the House of Deputies, pushing the Upper House to the fore instead. Public opinion in general viewed the entire coronation as a personal affair of the aristocracy.

In the afternoon the dismantling of the crimson draperies began in the Matthias church. One of the cleaning women found an enormous topaz, fallen from the crown, near the altar. This, too, was taken as an ill omen. But those who had been present at the coronation were struck to the depths of their hearts with the brilliance of the pomp and the physical propinquity of living history.

Kristina's diary contains the following entry for the coronation day:

30 December 1916—Budapest

A dull, empty day. I had a headache, and took three of the pills which Dr. Freyberger recommended. The doctor is in love with me. He always holds my pulse somewhat longer than necessary. Sometimes his silent glance is quite beautiful. He's an ugly, stoop-shouldered man. A bachelor.

The entry for the following day has rather more to say:

New Year's Eve

Black, dripping, wintry rain. Life seems so much bleaker to everyone today. At nine o'clock precisely I was on duty at the Garrison hospital, where a young artillery lieutenant and a one-armed captain in the reserves are both madly in love with me. Counting Freyberger and the new interne, this makes seventeen. I'm doing well, oh so very well. Lieutenant Hüvelyes, who talked the chief surgeon into diagnosing a deviated septum for him just because he wanted to spend another few weeks in the hospital, wrote me a long letter saying that his father was a chamberlain at the Imperial court; that an aunt of his had married a baron; that he would inherit five hundred acres of land; that he was preparing for the diplomatic service; that I had been right in saying that Puccini wrote *Cavalleria*

Rusticana, and that he wanted to marry me. I prescribed cold poultices for him.

I put on my white smock and took the daily list of assignments from Tessa. I was to begin by bathing No. 7. Tessa is the daughter of a rich paste manufacturer, and looks as if she were made of paste herself. She tried to be familiar with me at first, but I soon broke her of that and now we're on good terms. We stretched a rubber sheet under the patient, who could hardly sit up in bed because of his stomach wound. We took off his pajama top, and then the pants, and when he was completely naked on the rubber sheet I started to soap his body with a sponge and hot water. Tessa held the bowl; her hands always tremble slightly when she sees a naked man. I worked the soap bubbles over his pitiful body, washing his back, his chest, armpits, abdomen, then the genitals and the rectum, in the course of which a desire to be closer to the king struck me with such force that I suddenly stopped what I was doing and turned to Tessa: "Take over, please."

I washed my hands, took off the smock and left the hospital as if I were walking in my sleep.

I took the afternoon train to Vienna.

Chapter Four

THE accession of Charles Habsburg and the collapse of the Russian throne in the spring of 1917 gave a new and eddying impetus to world affairs and shook up the comatose battle-fronts. These events have completely lost their significance for present generations, as the stuff of human history generally does. Although there are historical studies, and even schoolbooks, which do not hesitate to pronounce final judgment, they present such a contradictory picture of events that the credulous reader is left in complete confusion. The state of the world decidedly indicates that even today mankind is still unable to comprehend its past or to give an intelligible account of its plans for the future.

As its tone shows, Kristina's diary does not pretend to historiographical authority, although the claim would be entirely justified by the circumstance that she belonged to the king's most intimate circle in those dramatic days. It is true that this young Hungarian noblewoman, who soared to dreams of becoming a queen on the wings of a subterranean soothsayer's words and of her own beauty, saw events through the eyes of her dream; but it is equally true that Kristina unpacked her fashionable suitcases, striped with the Dukay colors, and her silver toilet set, embellished with the woodpecker crest, in the most exclusive cabins and compartments of history. Therefore it is worth one's while to devote attention to her notes.

18 January 1917—Geneva

Although there is no danger that this diary might fall into anyone's hands, I hardly dare describe the commission which has brought me to Switzerland. I have been entrusted with the delivery of the king's secret peace proposals, in the form of a letter, to his brothers-in-law, the two Bourbon princes, who serve in the enemy's forces and are expected here in a few days. Switzerland is veritably swarming with spies, counterspies, secret agents, political adventurers and foolhardy fanatics of every nationality. I have only German agents to fear.

I brought two kinds of poison with me. If I get into great trouble I'll have the means of killing myself.

My credentials were obtained with the confidential help of King Alfonso of Spain, whose mother is an Austrian archduchess. Even the king realized I couldn't undertake the assignment alone. I chose Juan Hwang to come with me. Our passports are made out to Juan Vango, wine dealer from Barcelona, and his wife, Donna Kristina Caldera. The Spanish passport and my Red Cross uniform give me a feeling of security. I like the nurse's uniform. The king himself says the blue veil suits me very well.

I had to share my secret with Juan Hwang. No one can really understand our relationship. Juan Hwang is like my own brain. His hand, when he drops a letter in the mailbox, or when he turns on the light, is my hand, but much steadier. The eyes through which he looks at things, the ears with which he hears for me, are like my own eyes and ears. According to an old oriental tale, Nishra cut the first created beings in half with his sword; one half turned into women, the other into men. Thus divided, they have been roaming the world ever since, dripping with blood, hopeless and unhappy, seeking their other halves without success. Sometimes I feel that Juan Hwang and I are the exceptions, the only ones who managed to find each other and become one again, truly, physically.

And our spiritual unity is even more important. I'd be completely lost without him. I'd be no more than a few suitcases and several dresses, and the splitting headaches that go with them, especially during my menstrual periods. The effect of Juan Hwang's dazzling cultivation is to make me feel constantly surrounded by all the volumes of the Encyclopedia Britannica in the form of his deep, clear voice. He is wonderfully quick and acute at appraising people and things. He is the only one who can give clear, succinct expression to the great interconnections of this bewildered world. He is lightning-swift to act, but never rash.

Juan Hwang arrived in Geneva two days ahead of me. He looted a three-room furnished apartment, an achievement which verges on the impossible in Geneva right now. Our apartment is on the Rue Chantpoulet—the "Street of the Chanting Chicken," as Juan Hwang jokingly translates it—and there is a great French bed in the bedroom, wide enough to hold us both comfortably. Paul Klee's *La fuite du fantôme* hangs above the bed—an ultramodern nightmare, but beautiful all the same. A friendly fire was blazing in the fireplace when I arrived, and the fragrance of Flowersmoke, the incense I like so much, was in the air. Unfortunately the tiles in the bathroom are sky-blue, a color which makes me shiver no matter how hot the water is. Otherwise the apartment is furnished more like that of a philanderer called Juan Hwang than of a respectable wine dealer from Barcelona known as Juan Vango. But I'll manage to put up with it. Our only servant is a fiftyish woman by the name of Madame Astade, who has an incredibly, ridiculously tiny stub of a nose and is said to be a good cook; but her chief advantage is that she believes every word of our Barcelona story.

I crept into bed immediately after dinner. The exhausting trip, and particularly the unheated Austrian trains, sealed the ice-cold Alpine air into my bones. Of course we stayed up late, talking. I told Juan Hwang about the slip of paper the king gave me before I left, with the address of a Swiss, Monsieur Robert de Varaillet, who lives on the Rue Pradier here in Geneva. I must look him up tomorrow. Juan Hwang listened to my every word breathlessly. However calm of nerve he may be, he cannot escape the effect of the strange, heart-rending but still wonderful feeling that the role we have undertaken…My God, but we're up in the clouds!

Juan Hwang opened one of the wardrobes. To my great surprise, it was filled with golden-yellow and reddish-black Spanish wines.

"My case of samples!" he said, with a courtly gesture.

My first night in Geneva was beautiful. I fell asleep in the arms of a golden-yellow and reddish-black ecstasy. I dreamt I was lying in a great pool of blood, with my arms outstretched and a white flag pinned to my heart. The flag of peace.

20 January

A cold day, but the sunshine is lovely. The north wind has blown the wet snowfall away completely, and my headache as well. I wrote a long letter to Septemvir Utca. At home they have no idea of the commission that brought me to Switzerland. Mamma would fall in a faint if she knew; Papa would be proud of me, but he'd tell everybody in the Casino about it.

Monsieur Varaillet expected me at four this afternoon. We left our apartment early in order to take a long walk around the lake. Juan Hwang showed me the spot where Luccheni, the Italian anarchist, drove a file through the heart of Queen Elizabeth as she was leaving an excursion boat around the end of the last century. I heard a lot about that event from Aunt Louise, who was a lady-in-waiting to the queen and was at her side at that tragic moment. Aunt Louise's version of the affair kept changing with the years, until finally it was a certain Lombroso (?) who first pushed the queen overboard and then fired a revolver at the drowning woman. Since then Aunt Louise has turned quite deaf and can't even hear herself talk. The scene of the crime showed no sign of what had happened there. The thick bluish-green waves of the lake merely glittered, without evincing either memory or emotion. What a terrifying fate, to be a queen!

While we hurried toward the Rue Pradier, Juan Hwang advised me to say as little as possible to Monsieur Varaillet. I was not to pump him for information, because he couldn't tell more than he'd been instructed to do anyway. I was especially to refrain, he said, from smiling the way I usually smile, because it sets off my so-called charm. He told me to be dignified, to remember that I was a Dukay, and not to forget, above all, the importance of the matter at hand.

While crossing the Mont Blanc Bridge I had the feeling that two men were following us, with their hands in the pockets of their overcoats. At such times I have a dread of German agents. Juan Hwang assured me that it was of no importance, for everyone in Geneva watches everyone else, and it was even likely that the two men were afraid we were watching them.

Juan Hwang waited on the street while I called on Monsieur Varaillet. I must confess my heart was beating fast when I pressed the bell on the third floor. An elderly, stooped butler opened the door.

"Tout-de-suite!" he said, waving me into a room with an if-you-please gesture and then disappearing with my Spanish visiting card in hand.

The room was furnished in the atrocious taste of the Seventies. The chairs wore side whiskers, the vases wore whalebone corsets and the curtains wore thick, stuffed buns. I tried to imagine what Monsieur Varaillet would look like, for I had no idea whether he was young or old, fat or thin. Judging from the furnishings, I pictured him with a Makart bouquet in his buttonhole, with silk tassels at his ears and with a smile full of the white, walnut-sized, porcelain-headed upholstery tacks which gave his period sofas such a chilling leer. The scent of tuberoses in the room mingled with a smell of fried onions from the kitchen. The two smells I hate most. The minutes passed, and I held a handkerchief over my nose. Finally the door opened and the elderly butler reappeared. To my greatest astonishment he threw himself into an armchair, clasped his hands over a knee and said, with an air of preoccupation:

"Alors, Mademoiselle la comtesse…"

My conjectures had been wrong, for this was Robert de Varaillet. His manner of address told me that my false visiting card did not interest him, for he knew exactly who I was.

"Last night," he said finally, "I spoke with the secretary of the House of Parma by telephone, and Zurich informed me that the two quintals of pitch would reach Geneva this month."

I looked at him in confusion. He said with a dry smile:

"My dear Countess, you really must begin to learn our way of speaking. We can't be too careful. The two quintals of pitch refer to the two Bourbon princes. I understand you have an important letter for them from the king."

"Yes, but it's in double cipher. I have the strictest instructions not to open the letter and decode it until my meeting with the princes is certain."

"I shall let you know as soon as the two quintals of pitch arrive," Monsieur Varaillet said, with an emphasis which warned me against referring either to Bourbons or to princes in his presence.

Juan Hwang was not at the door when I left the house. But he emerged from among the passers-by, and greeted me as if we had not seen each other for a long time. I am hemmed in by hitherto unknown laws of caution. There is something frightful about it all.

2 February

Windy weather, but I went out for a little walk towards evening. I try not to appear on the street in Juan Hwang's company, for the two of us together are not exactly a commonplace sight and the cigarette vendor on the corner had a curious look in his eyes when he saw us together for the second time.

Every shopwindow in Switzerland is full of watches. As I was looking at a shopwindow I sensed that a man stood beside me, but did not turn my head. A few moments later he said, in Hungarian:

"Good evening, Countess."

His voice was rather kind and gentle than intrusive. I looked at his wan, pinched, ashen face, which was as fallen as if he had recently undergone a serious illness.

"How is it that you know me?"

"You nursed me in the Garrison hospital."

Wounded soldiers are completely unrecognizable in civilian clothes. It seemed to me that he was the soldier with the stomach wound whom I bathed on the day after the coronation.

"What are you doing in Switzerland?"

"I'm looking for an answer," he said absent-mindedly, fixing his eyes on the shopwindow. His clothes were neat enough, and his dark green hat seemed new.

"What is your name? I've forgotten."

"Krblfr."

The wind from the lake has a keen edge in these narrow streets, and now it blew the vowels of his reply away, like the chaff in a flour mill. I didn't want to ask his name again, but decided to call him Florian. In his face, in his entire personality there was a certain touching melancholy, a sense of fidelity and mysterious intelligence for which, at the moment, the name Florian was the best expression I could find.

"Au revoir, Countess," he said when I left him, and there was a peculiar stress in his *Au revoir.*

I told Juan Hwang of this curious encounter. In his opinion, Florian is a harmless deserter who thinks one bullet in the stomach has acquitted him of all duty toward his country.

4 February

The wind last night gave me a slight cold. It was stupid of me to go out with nothing under my dress but silk panties. I feel tiny, pinching pains in my bladder, but there's no need to go to a doctor, for I've had these pains before and I brought my pills along. I am impatiently waiting for Monsieur Varaillet's phone call, so I'll know when the two quintals of pitch will arrive. Poppy seeds or pitch? I swear I can't remember which. Something black, at any rate.

5 February

My cold has entirely disappeared, and towards evening I went out for a walk again. I can't stand being pent up in a room. Florian passed by unexpectedly as I walked along the lake. He merely tipped his hat and showed no intention of stopping to talk. It would not have pleased me at all if he had stopped. I don't know why I have the feeling that he is always close at hand.

6 February

A turbulent evening. During my usual evening walk along the Street of the Chanting Chicken I turned off at the little Place Grenus. The square was dark and deserted except for a closed auto parked along the sidewalk. Suddenly two men seized me, one held his palm over my mouth and gripped my left arm with his free hand while the other took me by the waist and lifted me as if to stuff me into the car. I couldn't scream; no more than a faint rasp came from my throat,

144

for I was half unconscious with surprise and terror. The sweaty palm over my mouth had a dreadful smell of machine oil. A moment later they dropped me, for a third figure had joined them. A savage fistfight began, which ended in a few brief seconds when the auto roared away at full speed and careened out of the Place Grenus, leaving only the third man behind, who was panting heavily as he picked up his green hat. It was Florian. He put his hands under my arms, for I was ready to collapse.

"Countess, why are you out alone at this hour?" he asked reproachfully.

While he helped me back to the apartment my wild heartbeat, which had seemed unbearable, slowly subsided, and I finally spoke as we reached the house. But my voice was too weak to say more than, "Thank you, Florian."

Juan Hwang was waiting for me impatiently, I fell into a chair and told him exactly, if fitfully, what had happened. Juan Hwang was pale as he listened. However long my pauses were, he offered no comment. Then, walking up and down, he calmly began to analyze the incident. He said my fear of being kidnapped by German agents was entirely groundless. The Germans, when they undertake such an assignment, aren't so careless. They have a great variety of techniques at their disposal; they would have used chloroform, to begin with. My attackers, in his opinion, were foreign deserters, of whom Switzerland is full right now. They might have been Italian, French, British, or even German. They had probably stolen the car and were on the prowl for women. They rob their victims, rape them and then abandon them. He was definitely opposed to notifying the police. As far as Florian was concerned, he said I shouldn't be surprised if he tips his hat next time and says: "Excuse me, Countess, would you be good enough to lend me twenty francs for a few days?"

8 February

For once Juan Hwang was wrong. We went for a stroll together at nightfall, but stayed on the Street of the Chanting Chicken, which is fairly well lighted and generally full of pedestrians. It seemed almost natural to meet Florian. I asked him up for tea, and when I made some discreet inquiries concerning his financial situation he said he had funds enough, and some friends besides; and he said he would be glad to oblige us if we were short of money. Florian's wrists are strong, and his hands are the hands of a tradesman. But his face is still ashen and pinched, as if he had come back from the tomb to visit the living. There is a quiet but powerful spirituality about this curious man. I've often seen the badly

145

wounded look like this when they recover as if by some miracle. When he left, Juan Hwang said his feeling was that Florian belonged to some sort of secret pacifist society which worships as fervidly at the altar of peace as certain sects do at the altars of their gods.

10 February

Madame Astade is ill with a bilious complaint, so we have no help for the time being. Juan Hwang scrubbed the floor, with gestures which would have done credit to an adagio dancer. I tried to prepare breakfast, but it was always the corkscrew rather than a spoon which came to hand when I reached into the kitchen drawer. I've hated corkscrews since childhood: sneaking, pushing creatures, they're among the worst looking, most characterless objects. Finally we sat down to breakfast. I'd put sugar into the salt cellars by mistake, sadly enough, so our eggs were sweet when we ate them. But they weren't bad at all,—it's a question of habit. We decided that domestic work can have a refreshing and calming effect on people—for half a day!

11 February

Finally the telephone rang. It was Monsieur Varaillet.

"The two quintals of pitch have arrived, Madame Vango, and if you're still interested you can inspect the samples at my apartment at five this afternoon."

And he hung up. I produced the two letters that the king had given me. One was the text itself, and the other was the key to the cipher. The king sealed the envelopes in my presence: the message was on white paper, and the key on blue. All I knew of the contents was that it set forth the four conditions of peace. One of the envelopes was sewn into the padding of my dark blue topcoat, and the other was in my box of medical prescriptions. I had written "For Hyperacidity" on the outside. Had they not been so carefully concealed, Juan Hwang would hardly have been able to restrain his restless curiosity. He has asked me more than once to take out the letters and decipher them, but I followed the king's orders implicitly. Now the time had come. Both of us were on tenterhooks, for the two little envelopes contained fateful things. I can hardly find the words to describe our feelings. Hospitals, hospital trains, battlefronts, barbed wire, burning towns, ragged prisoners of war by the thousands…heaven only knows what else was in our minds, although we felt rather than thought these things, and they made our hearts ache. The first paragraph on the white sheet of paper read as follows:

Black cosine anemone which hedgehog yellow Aunt Ilona hence drawstring.

I suddenly covered my face in terror and broke into a fit of nervous weeping. It is absolutely certain that if Juan Hwang had not been at my side, if I had undertaken the mission alone, if I had been alone in the same room with that message, I would have lost my mind. At that moment I was filled with a dreadful consciousness of probing into the most secret ganglia of the world's brain and finding nothing but a set of stupid, ridiculous, incoherent words. The other three paragraphs were couched in similar terms. The first, decoded, read:

Secret armistice with Russia. Reciprocal neutrality concerning Straits and Constantinople.

We continued decoding and came to the phrase, "The restoration of the Belgian Congo," which meant no more to me than the "black cosine anemone." What were they restoring, and where? The jungles, full of gorillas, or the extinct volcanos? Was this why Florian was shot in the stomach? My God, how dreadful it all is. What underground caverns of words, what black and bottomless pits of meaning are reserved for that simple, prayerful little word: peace. Juan Hwang placed a reassuring hand on my shoulder as I sobbed hysterically.

Finally we solved the last two paragraphs. "The Monarchy has no objection to the renunciation, in favor of France, of Germany's claim to Alsace-Lorraine." "Serbia, Bosnia, Hercegovina, Albania and Montenegro to be unified as a South Slavonian kingdom within the Monarchy. To be ruled by a Habsburg archduke."

When Juan Hwang had written down the final word he quietly placed his pencil on the paper, stood up and began to pace the floor with hands clasped behind his back, as is his custom when deep in thought. Several minutes later he sank into a chair as wearily as if he had walked thirty miles. He was unusually gloomy. I didn't ask why, for I knew his thoughts were lost in the labyrinths of international politics—he was thinking in terms of maps, straits, peoples and economic statistics. As for me, I continued to feel as I felt when we first began the decoding, that we were excavating the brain of the world with our delicate chisels and our silver hammers. The brain was in a state of complete decay. "Which hedgehog yellow...Aunt Ilona hence drawstring..." The secret language of diplomacy. International affairs in the highest sense.

Eight o'clock in the evening: I have just returned from the Great Meeting. This is how it happened:

At five o'clock precisely I rang the bell at Monsieur Robert de Varaillet's apartment. He opened the door again, and waved me into the room with the same if-you-please gesture. I showed no sign of agitation as I sat down to wait in the room that was redolent, as before, with tuberoses and fried onions. My heart was beating wildly. The sofa, with its white porcelain tacks, leered at me like a strange gigantic skull.

The door opened and the two quintals of pitch entered the room quietly, as if in a dream. No! Two splendid black panthers, rather. The Bourbon princes were dusky in the Italian fashion. One wore the uniform of a French officer, the other of a Belgian officer, and still they were as much alike as if they had been twins. Great golden epaulettes glittered on their shoulders, something to which my eyes have grown unaccustomed, for the uniforms of officers in the Austro-Hungarian Army are bleak, poorly cut and tasteless. The great golden epaulettes seemed like the foreshortened but shining wings of angels. And that's what they were, the two of them: angels of peace. When they entered the room it was as if a tremendous green, crackling spark had struck the air,—as when two high-tension wires meet. Yes, it was a moment of inexpressible magnitude. The dreadful war has been raging for two and a half bloodstained years, and now, for the first time, officers of the enemy's forces had entered the room where I sat with the king's secret letter in my black silk purse.

I stood up, for they were royalties. They introduced themselves politely, and there was friendship in the gleam of their fine dark eyes. In the first moments of meeting they treated me as two well-mannered young men would treat a young and, shall we say, attractive woman. Meanwhile a footman brought tea; I was so occupied with my thoughts that I didn't even look at his face, but saw merely the white-gloved hand as it moved before me. When we were left to ourselves one of the Bourbon voices took on a new tone of quiet seriousness.

"You have an important letter for us from our brother-in-law, Countess."

"Yes," I answered, and held out the envelope which contained the secret message in a French translation.

There was bewilderment on the prince's face as he turned the envelope and its contents this way and that. Finally he said:

"But this is a shoemaker's bill."

"Oh—excuse me!" I cried, and blushed to the tips of my ears. I hurriedly gave him the right envelope. The two pairs of dark eyes glowed at me smilingly. Men like to see women in sincere confusion, with a blush on their white faces.

The two princes stood by the window and studied the four brief paragraphs of the peace conditions for a long time, their faces immobile. They passed the letter from one hand to the other, and read it anew with deep concentration, mutely.

The two princes looked at each other and smiled, a long, querying, bitter, almost sarcastic smile. Then one of them, letter in hand, turned to me and said ill-humoredly:

"Countess, this scribble they concocted in Vienna is such a ridiculous, childish thing that we cannot submit it to Poincaré. A kingdom of South Slavonia! Under an Austrian archduke! Have they lost their minds? And the Monarchy has 'no objection' to the renunciation of Germany's claim to Alsace-Lorraine! It has an annoying ring, even to our ears. I can't believe my brother-in-law is responsible for such nonsense. Who composed this shocking document?"

"Uncle Cini, as far as I know."

"Who is Uncle Cini?"

"Foreign Minister of the Dual Monarchy. My mother's cousin. But I don't mind a bit hearing you abuse him."

They looked at each other and nodded with decision. Then they sat down and stared into space for a long time without saying anything.

"Would you be willing to return to Budapest tomorrow night, Countess?" one of them finally said. "We'd like to send our brother-in-law a long letter about this business."

"I'm willing to do anything."

"We'll send the letter to your apartment tomorrow afternoon."

When they accompanied me to the door, as we were saying good-bye, one of them gazed down at my feet and said:

"What pretty shoes. Did you buy them here in Geneva?"

Their eyes met in a smile. Once more they were simply young men whose every word was filled with hidden meaning, especially when their dark eyes were aglow. Two splendid black panthers.

12 February

I spent the morning packing and preparing for the trip. In the afternoon Florian came up, unexpectedly. I let him in, but told him I was terribly busy.

149

His visit didn't suit me at all, for I expected the princes' messenger with the letter for the king at any moment.

While we were talking, Florian suddenly surprised me with the following question:

"What sort of an impression did the young Bourbons make on you, Countess?"

"What young Bourbons?" I asked in confusion. "I don't know any Bourbons in Switzerland."

"The ones you met at tea yesterday, in Monsieur Varaillet's apartment."

I looked at him without drawing a breath for several moments.

"How do you know?"

Florian's pinched, ashen face smiled quietly.

"I served the tea. But you didn't even look at me."

Then he reached into his pocket and calmly produced an envelope.

"Here is the princes' letter to the king."

He stood up, said good-bye and left as quietly as he had come.

When the door had closed behind him Juan Hwang and I looked at each other speechlessly. After considerable pacing, Juan Hwang solved the riddle of Florian. Florian is a confidential agent of the court at Vienna, sent to protect me but perhaps to keep me under surveillance as well.

We left for Vienna on the evening train.

Chapter Five

14 February—Vienna

W E ARRIVED in Vienna at five o'clock in the morning, and by nine I was waiting in the king's anteroom at the Imperial Palace in Laxenburg, outside of Vienna. The Bourbon princes' secret letter was in my purse. I wore my Red Cross uniform, of which I've grown quite fond since the king said that its blue veil was very becoming.

The anteroom was filled with people restlessly waiting for an audience when I arrived. There were generals with briefcases under their arms, and civilians with swords at their sides. This last isn't quite true, of course, but that's how the scene affected me. None of those present ranked below chief of protocol or admiral. Their eyes popped with astonishment when I was the first to be admitted to the king's study by the adjutant.

"Guten Morgen, Gräfin"—the king came to meet me at the door. He wore an olive-gray field uniform, bare of every decoration but the Order of the Golden Fleece. His face and his glance were weary, but his eyes glistened with their "morning" blue. Around noon his eyes turn a lusterless gray-green. He kept my hand in his for a long time, and pressed it repeatedly. The room was filled with a peculiar grayish white mist through which, as if through fog, the outlines of the Louis XIV furniture, the gilt frames of the paintings and the deep crimson tones of the carpet emerged with a dull sheen. Suddenly a tall, long-stemmed black and yellow flag fluttered out of the fog and turned into a man before my very eyes. It was Uncle Cini, the Foreign Minister, whose black cravat and sallow countenance really made him look like the Austrian flag.

"Grüss Gott, Kristina," he said in a hoarse voice, and his fish-eyes stared at me. The snow outside cast a ghostly light into the room.

I delivered my letter, and the king moved to the window to read it. As he read, it was so still in the room—and, it seemed to me, in the whole snow-clad world—that the faint rustle of the paper, when the king turned the page, was an unbearably loud noise. Clearly depressed after finishing the letter, the king offered it to Uncle Cini, and his mute gesture was almost exactly like the gesture with which one of the Bourbon princes had handed His Majesty's letter to the other.

While Uncle Cini was reading the letter, the king raised the faint blue gleam of his eyes toward me and asked, in a low whisper lest he disturb the Foreign Minister:

"What do you think of the Russian developments?"

It was evident that the question had attached itself to his tongue like an ulcerous sore, and that he was constantly putting the same question to everyone nowadays, even to himself. I raised my eyebrows and nodded knowingly, for I could offer no opinion of the Russian developments. I hadn't the slightest idea what had happened or what was happening in Russia.

Uncle Cini's face froze as he finished the letter. He slowly placed the flimsy sheet of paper on a corner of the great French table. There was a certain finality in his gesture.

At that moment a terrible explosion shook the air and rattled the windows. I screamed, and threw my arms around His Majesty's neck. The door flew open at the sound of my scream and the adjutant rushed in. Uncle Cini was in the room with us, fortunately, otherwise the adjutant might have come to some very weird conclusions at finding me in His Majesty's arms. But he understood the situation at once, and was quickly gone. The explosion had been the result of a punctured tire on a heavy truck outside. The king, too, was deathly pale with terror. I could feel his heart beating furiously as I clung to him. Of the three of us, Uncle Cini was best able to conceal his fright; seeing the king's white face, he sought to make light of His Majesty's embarrassment and turned to me with a smile:

"Next time you're frightened, put your arms around me instead of His Majesty."

The king laughed, and a blush suffused my face. From the adjoining room, like an echo to the explosion, came the sound of a baby crying. One of the two doors of the king's study opens on his domestic life, the other on history. The king's eyes beamed merrily at my embarrassment as he offered his hand:

"Many thanks, my dear Countess. We'll let you know when we have need of you again."

A taxi was waiting outside the palace to take me back to Vienna, to Bösendorferstrasse. On the way a sentence came to mind, but I couldn't recall who wrote it or where I'd read it: "Kings are not born: they are made by universal hallucination." For the first time I seemed to understand the full significance of those words. The king was a human being. The "morning" blue of his eyes, the crying baby in the next room, the innocent *Apfelstrudel* kiss of long ago, and the furious beat of his heart...the heart, which "someday I shall hold in my hand," had given a sign of life just now, and was the heart of a living man. The king in him was all hallucination: the mob of briefcased generals and sword-girt civilians in the anteroom, with foreheads aflame—the mass of military, economic and political cares of the Monarchy. The way he stood beside the great French table in his study, with Uncle Cini all yellow and black behind him...it was as if his Foreign Minister were the two-headed eagle on the Austrian flag, holding the king's bleeding brain in its claws. No, not an eagle,—a vulture! This was the picture that stayed with me after our brief encounter.

I put the question to Juan Hwang at once: what did he think of the Russian developments? He had little to offer besides generalities. The Russian people, in his opinion, are no longer willing to tolerate the incredible depravity of the tsarist court and courtiers, nor the tsar's bloody ravings, which are counterbalanced by nothing but superstitious religiosity.

Juan Hwang particularly wondered what could have been behind the king's question when he mentioned Russia. The king must have had some disquieting news. Two possible sources of concern lurk in his question. One of these has to do with the Germans, whose stupid arrogance has been emboldened by the signs of disorder in Russia. This may be the explanation of Emperor Wilhelm's famous proclamation of last month, in which he thundered at the Entente in terms like these: "Our enemies have discarded their masks.... They repudiated our desire for peace, our humanity, and the honorable terms we proposed last December, with words of cruelty and hypocrisy" (he failed to add that the German peace overtures were made when Russia was still on a solid footing) "...Our enemies have confessed their thirst for conquest...they seek the annihilation of Germany... they seek to enslave the peoples of Europe...they are courting Greece for their own base purposes...but we have an answer for them...not our troops alone, but the very women and children of Germany are united in a common purpose and a common destiny, dedicated to ultimate victory or ultimate destruction!" The emperor was emboldened to make such a foolhardy speech not by the indications of Russian collapse alone but as well by the reassuring reports sent him by the German Ambassador in Washington. According to these reports, the American people are interested in nothing on earth but to make two dollars out of one. That peaceful, money-making nation cannot be dragged into war; but if it should become involved, the United States could not provide more than five or six divisions in the course of a year, and long before that time Hindenburg and Ludendorff will have done with their work. This stiffening of German self-confidence, in Juan Hwang's opinion, did not favor the king's secret hopes of peace. Now that the situation has changed, his advisors have hitched their own little wagons to the German star and may be expected to offer violent opposition to any peace proposals. Again, when Juan Hwang said this, I saw the picture of Uncle Cini holding the poor king's bleeding brain in his vulture-claws.

The other possible source of the king's concern: the Romanov throne. Kings don't like to see a great throne tottering in their neighborhood, even an enemy's throne.

16 February

I had a letter from Papa, in which he sent a copy of the latest letter from Uncle D. Uncle D. is Count Dmitri Ormovsky, who has a half-million-acre estate in Kazan and first came to Hungary in the year I was born. He belonged to the retinue of a grand duke, the tsar's cousin, who went hunting at Ararat. This was when the young Russian officer met Aunt Mira, father's youngest sister, who was said to be the most beautiful of the Dukay daughters. They were married, and have lived in St. Petersburg ever since. They usually spent a few months in Paris every other year, traveling westward through Hungary and always stopping over at Ararat or Septemvir Utca for a few weeks. Papa, too, paid them a visit well before the war, taking his most powerful hunting rifles, and they went after buffalo somewhere in the middle of Asia. With the outbreak of war their correspondence, instead of breaking off, has increased, which only goes to show that our circles, through the marriages they have contracted, exist at international altitudes and have means of finding their way to each other even above the welter of battlefields. Papa's correspondence with Uncle Dmitri, conducted through Stockholm with the help of Uncle Adam's mother (who is the daughter of a razor-blade manufacturer in Sweden), doesn't constitute espionage in any sense at all, for Uncle Dmitri is just as incapable as Papa of understanding the state of affairs. Uncle Dmitri's letter was written from St. Petersburg on January 10th, and he gives a detailed account of the assassination of Rasputin at a dinner between the night of December 29th and the morning of December 30th. Uncle Dmitri knew him personally, and tells how incongruous the bearded, booted figure seemed among the frock coats and glittering uniforms at one of the imperial receptions in the Winter Palace.

He never talked with Rasputin, but stood close to him once, and he says the old man's stink was something unbearable. Apparently he had never taken a bath in his life. But of course everyone courted his favor, for he dominated the imperial family completely with his filthy mysticism. It was a good thing they killed him, for he was doing great harm to the tsar's prestige. It was very cold that night, so they carried his body down to the banks of the Neva and threw it under the ice. Uncle Dmitri's letter was full of anxiety for the tsar's future. So Juan Hwang was on the right track when he discerned, in the king's anxious question concerning the Russian developments, his terror at the prospect of the collapse of a throne.

The date of the assassination of Rasputin gave me something to think about. On that dark dawn, on December 30th, when the ice floes of the Neva swept Rasputin's bearded body away, we were preparing for the coronation. I recalled all that happened from dawn to dusk that day. What an amazing dawn it was! Here a new throne rose from the fog, there the throne of the Romanovs began to totter. Yes, the history of the world is in wild career. I wonder where it will set me down? My left nipple is still a little swollen. At the moment of the explosion I held the king so closely that the Golden Fleece in his button-hole hurt my nipple.

19 February

I went to the Café Salzburg this afternoon, where the newspapermen cong-regate. Hugo Storm first took me there—he translated my "Goose-Girl" poem six years ago. They're nice boys, and proud of me, and they treat me as one of their colleagues. I'm particularly popular because I always bring a freshly baked coffeecake, which they divide carefully and eat with their coffee. Many people have begun to starve in Vienna. While they devour the coffeecake amid triumphant cries, the passers-by—and especially the children—stop outside and press their noses to the plate-glass window, looking at the cake as if it were some sort of miracle. White coffeecake! I hadn't been to the café for a long time, but they were all still there, with their galley proofs and their manuscripts. I wanted to talk to them because I'm beginning to wonder about events in Russia myself. The boys showed me the latest cabled reports, which came by way of Switzerland and made frequent references to two foreign words: *menshevik* and *bolshevik*. They'd looked up the two words in every dictionary and encyclopedia, but without success. At that point Edelsberg joined us at our table—the monocled veteran Viennese journalist who wears champagne-colored spats even in winter, speaks nine languages and is a noted polymath. Everyone listened while Edelsberg explained the meaning of the two words. Menshevik and bolshevik, he said, are variations of shashlik. Shashlik is mutton cut into tiny slices, grilled, and served on a spit. Menshevik is the same thing, but made of beef. Bolshevik, on the other hand, is made of pork, with the additional difference that a clove of garlic is stuck between every two slices of meat. But even the omniscient Edelsberg couldn't tell us more than this about the course of events in Russia.

Someone quoted Dostoyevsky to the effect that "Man is a pliable animal, a being who gets accustomed to everything." Hugo Storm declared that he, for one, was an animal who would have no trouble at all getting used to such white coffeecake with his coffee every afternoon.

5 March

A thin, distinguished lady entered one of the first-class compartments of the Budapest-Vienna Express. She made an unusual appearance, for her bosoms were as large as those of a peasant wet nurse, who can nurse four babies at once. Her thighs were as thick as if she were afflicted with elephantiasis. Her waist seemed uncommonly broad too. All this was out of keeping with her slender ankles and her narrow wrists. The Austrian customs guards took her off the train, hustled her into the customs office and took her clothes off in spite of every protest and threat. A few minutes later she left the office, but without the enormous bosoms, the swollen thighs and the broad waist. With great glee, the customs guards had drained her of fifty pounds of flour. This was her way of trying to smuggle flour to Vienna, to her starving daughter.

Could the woman be anyone but Mamma? This escapade illustrates her unbounded naïveté and her maternal heart of gold.

23 March

A very great day, and a historic date! We're still awake at three in the morning—Juan Hwang is pacing the floor as we discuss the events of the past few hours. My brain and heart are completely exhausted from thought and emotion. My nerves are still twitching because of the excitement I went through. Sometimes I fall asleep with weariness, but only for a few seconds at a time. The whirl of my thoughts keeps me awake, like the blaring of trumpets. I'll try to give an account of events in their order.

At about ten yesterday morning, when I was still in bed, my chambermaid

Margaret came in to say that a letter had arrived but its bearer would only deliver it to me personally. There've been such letters before—beggars or sly salesmen. But this time he wouldn't go away; he sent word that he came from Schönbrunn. At that I hurried into my slippers and put something on. I put my disheveled head out the door to find an older man in civilian clothes, hat in one hand and the letter in the other. His face seemed somehow familiar: it was that pastel blue-shaven face by which one can recognize the lackeys of court even in mufti. He narrowed his eyes at my uncombed hair; when I had identified myself he gave me the letter, bowed low and was on his way. My heart was beating fast as I slipped back into bed. The envelope was plain and cheap, and in it was a penciled note which read:

Please be at Apartment Eight on the first floor of No. 15 Blaue Lampe Strasse at six this evening.

There was no signature, but I knew the king's slanting, indistinct, unsteady handwriting.

Lying on my back, I stared up at the ceiling with unblinking eyes. My left hand rested on my throat—the gesture with which one tries to calm a furious heartbeat. My right hand, outstretched, still held the letter, almost as if the sheet of paper had been grafted onto my fingers. The king had invited me to visit him at a lovers' rendezvous.

Shortly afterward Juan Hwang entered the room. I handed him the letter without a word. He read it at great length, as if it were not a single sentence but a lengthy and involved text. After a long while he put the sheet of paper on the bed without comment, and fixed his eyes in space. I felt that he shared my thoughts. What was I to do that afternoon? Should I become the king's mistress? There was the danger, then, that I would remain a cheap little mistress and nothing more. Should I play the unattainable woman, whose virtue drives men to excesses of passion? The danger in this was that the king, who has little time for his personal life, would give up the chase early, and for good. Women are never wise enough to cope with a problem of this sort. In many cases it is the forbidden fruit which spurs a man's passion to the highest pitch; but nothing binds a man more closely to a woman than the intimacy of a love affair. A woman's body, above all things, has flavor, and fragrance, and fire. Virtue has neither flavor nor fragrance nor fire.

This afternoon may be decisive. The question is not merely whether or not to give myself to a twenty-nine-year-old man,—for this time the wonderful hallucination which the king represents has truly entered my life. Someday I shall hold the king's heart in my hand: I believe in the prophecy, which has echoed in my life with the mystery of all surpassingly wonderful hallucinations, and I believe that the ultimately great things of the world—God, love, even war itself—are painfully beautiful hallucinations. If the king were still unmarried, the path leading toward the prophecy would be almost too simple and straight. But the *Mountain* may still have amazing and momentous things in store.

Juan Hwang finally spoke:

"This letter sounds like a military order to me. Be at such and such a place at such and such a time. It has something of the flavor of a command about it."

Juan Hwang's gloomy words brought me back to earth. What he said was logical enough, for when I last parted with the king he agreed to send for me if there was need of me. But why to a private apartment on Blaue Lampe Strasse, in the fashionable northern suburbs of Vienna?

I spent all afternoon trying to decide what to wear. At first I thought I would put on my Red Cross uniform; in view of the fact that the king is profoundly devout, however, I was afraid the cross and, in general, the costume of virtue would have an unfavorable influence on the atmosphere of a clandestine apartment. I spent a long time going over the underthings I bought in Geneva last month, the latest Parisian creations, of the sort that only the French textile mills can instill with delicate, almost poetic piquancy. I selected a sheer, cobweb-thin rose-colored slip, trimmed with Alençon lace. After long indecision I decided on the perfume called *Chanson du Narcisse.* I put on my blue dress, which calls to mind the deep, warm blue of the summer sky. Blue, because six years ago, when we first met and when the king "pulled me from the well," I was wearing blue, but it was much lighter, of course. I felt there was a certain secret emphasis in this deeper, darker blue. I wore the little ruby earrings which Papa brought from India. I stood before the mirror for a long time, and was well satisfied. I brushed my hair back, straight, so that my face might be as open as my heart.

Juan Hwang accompanied me on the great journey. The windows of the taxicab were completely coated with mist, and we sat without speaking. It was as if we were sitting in an ark, which was rocking on ghostly waters. A strong snowstorm was swirling—the winter was expending its last ounce of strength on this late March evening.

"Be smart. I think we're at an important political turning point." Juan Hwang squeezed my hand when I left the cab in front of the house on Blaue Lampe Strasse.

My ring was answered by the same pastel-blue countenance who brought me the letter this morning. Once again he bowed deeply, and led me inside without a word. It looked like the bachelor flat of a cavalry officer. A glass cabinet was filled with silver cups and other things that are given as prizes at horse races. A large robe-covered couch, with an abundance of silk cushions, stood in a corner. I felt that each cushion was the gift of a different woman. They were probably the handiwork of middle-class "beauties," who seek by this means to make the memory of their brief, sinful adventure immortal in a man's mind. The fire had only recently been started in the tile stove and it was so chilly in those moments of waiting that my hands turned quite purple. Cold hands would never do. I drank two large glasses of the cognac that stood ready on a table, and warmed my hands at the stove. A pleasant giddiness seized me, and I could feel how everything around me was taking on the nature of a hallucination. The mute pastel-blue face that admitted me, too, had seemed pure hallucination.

All at once the door opened and a bearded man in yellow spectacles stepped in. The collar of his coat was turned all the way up to his eyes, and his soft hat was pulled deep over his forehead. Melting snowdrops decked his shoulders and the rim of his hat. He threw his coat and hat on the couch, then took off his yellow glasses and—the beard. It was the king. He wore a greenish-gray civilian suit. His face seemed uncommonly wretched. He gave me a casual, nervous handshake, and then said:

"My brothers-in-law have been on Austrian territory since dawn. This apartment belongs to one of my reliable men, who was once a fellow officer of mine in the Brandeis Dragoons. I arranged to hold the meeting here because I trust neither Schönbrunn nor Laxenburg. I no longer know which of the members of my entourage are German spies."

He touched my shoulder and looked at me apologetically.

"You realize that your life, too, is in danger?"

"Yes, Your Majesty."

"I ask you here," the king spoke anew, "because you're among the few who have played a part in this extremely hazardous thing from the beginning. It's possible that you may have to go on another trip, perhaps this very night. My brothers-in-law are bringing an important message."

He stood beside the stove and held a hand to his forehead for several moments. I didn't say a word, not wishing to disturb his thoughts.

I felt like less than nothing. And only a person who is ashamed not before others but before herself feels like less than nothing. At that moment I was ashamed of my rose-colored underthings with the Alençon lace, and of every one of the thoughts I had had about this meeting. What a wicked little female I am! But in the very moment of this shamed abasement I was reborn, for I felt I had truly become a participant in that mysterious and great hallucination which the king represented, standing beside the stove with the palm of his left hand over his forehead.

How often I have heard doctors say of a bayonet wound: "If the point of the bayonet had stopped a fraction of an inch short, the patient would have pulled through." How deep has the bayonet of war cut into Europe's body? To a depth of more than two and a half years by now. And now every day is another fraction of an inch. Juan Hwang once said—and this is what the boys at the Café Salzburg were saying, too—that the effect of war is manifest not in the mass graves of the battlefields or in the statistics of the army hospitals alone, but somewhere beyond, deeper, in the viscera of Europe, her blood vessels, the thin, invisible membranes of her body, the nervous network of dreamlike delicacy; and the extent of this debilitude will only be truly known, as evidenced in dull wits and twisted thinking, when the starving children of Vienna grow up. This last was Edelsberg's contribution, while he took great bites of the white coffeecake.

The state of the battle fronts today is an equilibrium of opposing forces. This means that the war may last for years. And every day the tip of the bayonet moves closer to the heart, or the liver, or the kidneys. But if the king succeeds in negotiating a swift, secret peace, the balance will be overthrown and Germany, enraged and rabid, will stumble, her fronts will rapidly dissolve, for every single German soldier will cast an envious eye toward the enticements of the Austro-Hungarian peace—the bayonet will come to a halt in Europe's chest, perhaps at a crucial point. Yes, in this hour, and here in this room, the fate of future generations might be decided, the question of Europe's survival.

The timid ring of a bell was heard in the hall, and the king started nervously beside the stove. Several moments passed, long enough for the newcomers to take their overcoats off. Then the door opened and three men in mufti entered: the two Bourbon princes and Florian, who had brought them here.

It was a touching encounter. As the king hurried toward them the foremost prince stopped with his chest outflung and clicked his heels in stiff military style, but the king put his arms around him. The king was deadly pale, and his lips quivered. He embraced his other brother-in-law the same way. I saw the scene only mistily, through my tears, but I'll never forget it. All of us in the room felt that this was not a simple meeting of kinsmen. Two officers of the hostile French and Belgian armies were embracing the emperor and king of the Austro-Hungarian Monarchy.

The king pulled himself together and said, with a slightly embarrassed and very human smile:

"Have a seat…"

At that moment the pocket of the king's jacket caught the eyes of one of the princes, and he even cocked his head to one side in amazement. The king's false beard was poking out of his left pocket, where he had stuffed it. The prince did not know what to make of the bunch of fur, but the king took no note of his brother-in-law's astonished look. They sat around the table, on the center of which stood a bowl of fruit. Florian poured glasses of cognac. They saluted each other with the glasses and with terse, unspoken thoughts.

"Have you brought a message for me?" asked the king, with a certain tension in his voice.

Some moments passed before one of the Bourbons replied.

"We had an opportunity to acquaint Monsieur Poincaré with the terms of your most recent peace proposal. Unfortunately the President of the Republic is of the opinion that the plan is less than nothing. The emphasis is on Alsace-Lorraine."

The king nodded thoughtfully.

"Next week I'm going to Germany, to the headquarters of the German Army at Homburg, where I shall hold a meeting with Emperor Wilhelm. I intend to do everything in my power to win German compliance."

Both the Bourbons began to shake their heads at once, slowly and negatively. Now the second one spoke:

"Your German trip will be in vain. It's completely hopeless to count on overcoming the insane arrogance of the German generals. But even if you should persuade Emperor Wilhelm you'd have gained nothing, for the Entente is no longer willing to negotiate with Germany."

"You must understand the situation, finally," his brother continued. "The Entente is willing to negotiate and make peace with *you*. But with Germany— *no!* They demand the unconditional surrender of Emperor Wilhelm."

The king, alarmed, peered first at one and then at the other of his brothers-in-law.

"A separate peace?" he asked in a faint, broken voice, and immediately glanced toward the glass cabinet at his back, as if to see whether a German general were hidden there. Then he reached for an apple, bit into it and began to eat greedily. Right now this was a sign of nervousness rather than hunger.

"I've asked the Foreign Minister to come," he said with his mouth full. "We must discuss this whole thing with him."

The princes offered no comment on this statement of the king. They began to talk of other things. When the conversation turned to Italy, the king's face turned red and his glance grew hard. No, no, he would make no concession whatever to Italy!

Once more the bell sounded in the hall, this time with vigor and determination. Soon Uncle Cini walked in, tall and lean, and again his sallow countenance and the fluttering tips of his black cravat made him look like a black and yellow Austrian flag.

After introductions and greetings had been exchanged he seated himself at the table. Florian and I, out of a sense of propriety and modesty, were sitting at a slight distance. The king gave a brief review of the situation and the discussion so far. While the king spoke Uncle Cini, with arms folded over his chest, cast surreptitious looks of appraisal at the two Bourbon princes, whom he held in contempt for some reason. When the king finished, Uncle Cini spoke up in a tone which suggested that he was the ruler and had listened as if to the report of a subordinate. I watched the faces of the two princes, and could see that this tone irritated them both. Florian's pinched, wan face, too, was full of suppressed passion. Uncle Cini said in a dry voice, while his eyes traveled above the others' heads slowly and disdainfully:

"The present military situation does not make it imperative, surely, for the Monarchy to sue for peace on bended knees. In any case, I cannot give my approval to the plan for a separate peace under any circumstances. Italy has earned the scorn of the entire world by betraying her allies. His Majesty cannot be called upon to betray the German treaty of alliance."

"The Germans betrayed the Monarchy long ago," one of the Bourbons said quietly and mildly, looking directly into Uncle Cini's eyes. "They've already promised the southern territories of the Monarchy to Italy. You're probably familiar, Count, with Bismarck's famous saying: 'I am morally prepared to commit the greatest rascality in the service of my country.' The Germans are good patriots. Right now this is as much as to say that my brother-in-law is faced with the greatest rascals in the world."

Uncle Cini replied lightly. In general, his manner of conversing with the princes was that blend of sweetness and over-fastidious courtesy which is always a sure sign, in high aristocrats, of passionate hatred.

"Let's not probe into the underlying reasons for our actions," Uncle Cini said, his eyes still swimming somewhere in space, "for we might easily come to the conclusion that Your Highnesses did not come here, under such perilous circumstances, in the interests of the Monarchy, but rather in those of France. And in Your Highnesses' view the ultimate interest of France can be nothing but the return of the Bourbons to the French throne."

The two princes' eyes met momentarily. Concealed in Uncle Cini's words they felt the delicate pinpricks of suspicion, underestimation and exposure. But an aloof silence of some moments' duration was their only reply. As was his custom, the king sat with his two outturned palms under his thighs, looking at each of the speakers in turn.

"What do you think, Count," said the second prince, reaching for an apple, "what do you think would happen to the Monarchy if—let's suppose!—if Germany were to win the war? Wilhelm would turn our brother-in-law out at the moment of victory, and Germany would engulf the Monarchy."

"These suppositions," Uncle Cini said calmly and disdainfully, fingering the cravat at his remarkably high winged collar with an easy gesture, "would take us very far indeed from the subject at hand. Neither Your Highness nor I can see into the future. We might also say that Russia or China will someday engulf the Monarchy. Let's keep to the present."

I don't know why Florian, in his excitement, suddenly came to his feet. But he stood behind his chair without moving.

Uncle Cini calmly continued:

"French illusions concerning Alsace-Lorraine cannot possibly interest us. Again I wish to emphasize that His Majesty cannot break the German treaty of alliance."

And now, unexpectedly, Florian spoke. His voice was hard and sharp, as if— after the feeble and flimsy silken threads of the conversation so far—he were snapping a heavy leather strap in the air:

"His Majesty has a much more important ally than Germany!"

All heads turned toward Florian at the unexpected exclamation. But Uncle Cini merely raised the glance under his lowered eyelids as high as Florian's knees. There was an element of good-natured patience in his gaze, but also the intimation that the speaker was no higher than a fair-sized dog.

Florian's voice snapped at the king with the vehemence of accusation and reproof:

"The king promised his people peace in his coronation address! It's not the people who write treaties of alliance, but elegant rascals of Bismarck's sort. The king can't break the treaty, no—but what about his promise to the people? Can he break that?"

Florian's pinched, ashen face was fearful and ghostly now, as he fixed Uncle Cini with an inflexible stare. His eyes glistened, for the somewhat bloodshot whites showed even below his pupils.

Now Uncle Cini's glance slowly rose from Florian's knees, stopping not at his face but somewhere above his head. His head thrown slightly back, he looked at the world over the tip of his large but delicately chiseled nose.

"My good friend, His Majesty is still not reduced to the necessity of being reminded of his given word. As you can see, His Majesty is doing whatever he can in the interest of peace at this very moment. But observance of the treaty of alliance is a matter of historical honor. And this is a matter which I am unwilling to argue with you."

Flashes of lunatic rage crossed Florian's face. Suddenly he pulled up his waistcoat, pulled out his shirt and exposed the ugly scar of a deep wound:

"And what's this? Take a look, Your Excellency! Don't be ashamed to look, even if you're unwilling to argue with me! What's this?"

The king rose to his feet and with a reassuring gesture he led Florian, who was clearly beside himself, toward the corner of the room.

Meanwhile Uncle Cini stood up too. He made a deep bow, and took leave of the princes with stiff ceremony. The king accompanied him into the hall for a moment. Florian still stood facing the wall, while his trembling hands tried to put his clothing in order.

The king returned, cleared his throat thoughtfully and carefully rearranged the chairs around the table. He was straightening the room. One of the Bourbon princes broke the silence when he sat down:

"Who decides the fate of the Monarchy? You, or your Foreign Minister?"

The king reached into his waistcoat pocket, produced a penknife, opened the blade and then placed an apple in front of himself.

Now the other Bourbon spoke:

"Monsieur Poincaré is expecting us. If you don't give us a letter in which you unequivocally acknowledge France's right to Alsace-Lorraine, then we might as well consider our mission finished."

After a few moments, since there was no reply, the two of them rose. And then Florian threw himself on his knees before the king. Wringing his clenched hands, he pleaded in a voice that was almost a moan:

"Your Majesty! I implore you! Write the letter!..."

Suddenly his head fell into the king's lap, and his shoulders began to shake with frenzied sobs. The king, without even looking at him, touched Florian's head with a fleeting, angular sweep of his left hand. The gesture bade Florian rise from his knees, but it also seemed as if he were seeking to give Florian his blessing. Then he calmly cut the apple in half. The two Bourbons stood motionless. An appleseed skipped from under the blade of the penknife to the other side of the table. The king reached for it, picked it up with two fingernails and placed it between his teeth. Pressing it to his front teeth with the tip of his middle finger, he began to gnaw the tiny, black, slippery appleseed. Meanwhile his gaze dangled, almost arched, in the vacant air, until it was all but frightening. I have never seen a human countenance peer so deeply into the infinite and, at the same time, into itself. With a quiet motion the king pushed the divided apple to one side and said, in a simple voice:

"Bring some paper and a pen."

Florian jumped up and ran to the next room for writing materials. The Bourbon princes resumed their seats.

It was already ten o'clock in the evening. And then began the composition of the letter, which was to last until one in the morning, for it takes exactly three times as long for three people to compose a document as for one. They weighed each sentence endlessly, pruned it, patched it, pronouncing it aloud the meanwhile for the others to hear. In the meantime we ate all the apples, for there was nothing else to eat in the apartment. The prodigious hallucination of history left us to ourselves. The atmosphere at the table was that of three impoverished petty officials arguing over a matter of family inheritance. When the king said, "I won't relinquish the South Tyrol!" it sounded like "I won't give up the brown bureau, Grandmother gave it to me while she was still alive!" Alsace-Lorraine figured in the conversations as if it were a tiny grape arbor on the outskirts of a village, with a few old pear trees and a reed-covered potato pit, which had to be surrendered—if with aching hearts—for the sake of unity.

Thus, composed on the night of the 23rd of March, 1917, in a small apartment on Blaue Lampe Strasse in Vienna, and addressed to Prince Sixtus, was written the letter in which Charles Habsburg, as head of the House of Lorraine, recognized the indisputable right of France to Alsace-Lorraine, thereby betraying his alliance with Germany. All this without the knowledge of his Foreign Minister.

24 March

This morning I went to the Stefanskirche and knelt in prayer before the altar for a long time. The Bourbon princes left in great secrecy at dawn, to show the king's letter to Poincaré. I prayed for the success of their journey. Betrayal, treaties of alliance…My God, what empty, false, hypocritical concepts they are! Tolstoy's words came to mind: "War is such a terrible, such an atrocious thing, that no man, especially no Christian, has the right, to assume the responsibility of beginning it." I've started to read *Anna Karenina* for the second time now.

26 March

As long as we have our wonderful forged papers, says Juan Hwang, why don't we go back to Switzerland? We left our apartment on the Street of the Chanting Chicken with the proviso that we might return in a few days' time. It's an attractive idea: I'm completely out of Egyptian cigarettes. I've begun to long for chocolates, oranges and dates. I can't stand the sight of all these starving people in Vienna any longer. Juan Hwang's principal reason for wanting to go to Switzerland is to learn all the sooner what the Entente's reply will be to the king's letter. His anxiety is so great that he spends hours pacing back and forth in the room, and when I speak to him he doesn't answer.

3 April—Geneva

Our first week in Geneva has passed uneventfully. Both of us are tense with anticipation, which means that food has turned tasteless, sleep gives no rest, everything has lost its flavor. The Swiss papers this morning say that the king's special train left for Homburg yesterday, after all, on its way to German Army Headquarters. The king and the German emperor will kiss each other on meeting, as monarchs do. No matter; the Sixtus letter must be in Poincaré's hands by now. According to the newspapers, Uncle Cini was dressed in the uniform of an Uhlan colonel for the meeting. I can almost see him now, left hand on his hip, standing beside Hindenburg with an easy grace, and I can hear his fastidious Viennese accent paying court to Hindenburg's North Prussian words as they grope their way forth from under the great pomaded handlebar mustache. Uncle Cini would faint on the spot if he knew what was in the king's secret letter.

14 April

This morning Juan Hwang unexpectedly announced that he is going away for a few days. His mysterious and marvelous sources of information have brought the news that the Entente is taking action on the king's letter. Besides Poincaré and Premier Ribot, only the King of England and Lloyd George know of the letter. It is said that they are presently planning to discuss the matter with Italy in secret conference. Russia no longer counts for anything. I'm not glad that Juan Hwang is going away. I am afraid of solitude. I don't like to be left alone with great hallucinations. Eczema has broken out on my left kneecap again.

20 April

A tragic day! I should draw a mourning border around this page of my diary. The Entente has answered the king's letter, and I feel that the fate of the world has been sealed. Juan Hwang returned at two o'clock this morning, and he was half mad with grief and concern. Here is his account of the events:

Yesterday morning in Savoie an elderly baker with a half-filled sack of flour on his back got out of a third-class compartment of the train from Turin as it pulled into the little diocesan village of St. Jean de Maurienne, in the valley of the Arc River. No one would have recognized him for Lloyd George, Prime Minister of England. A quarter hour later a very old nun with a masculine face climbed down the steps of another train: it was Ribot, Premier of France. Baron Sonnino, who had come to the little town in the disguise of a chimneysweep, was waiting for them. Their retinue of military, political and economic experts wore no disguise at all, for nothing about them betrayed the expert, not even their brains. One of the French experts was a childhood friend of Juan Hwang; this was how he learned the details of the secret conference. The baker, the nun and the chimneysweep began their discussions in a sacristy. Their great secrecy and their ludicrous disguises will seem incomprehensible to the eyes of future generations. It is all like the "black cosine anemone."

It would take too long to recount the interminable arguments of the baker, the nun and the chimneysweep behind the closed door of the sacristy. Lloyd George entered the conference with the intention of negotiating a separate peace with the Monarchy, for the British Army has just begun to take part in the land fighting around Arras, and it is in the British interest to weaken Germany by arranging the defection of the Monarchy. He was determined to slap Sonnino's mouth if Italy attempted to bite great chunks out of the southern, Italian-inhabited territories of the Monarchy. But Sonnino would not give in. He beat the table with his briefcase and nervously shook out documents which were meant to prove, by the terms of a secret Anglo-Italian pact, that England had promised the southern portions of the Monarchy to Italy in return for her entry into the war. During his harangue one of the papers fell on the floor and Ribot, with true French politeness, leaned down for it. But by the time his bald head reappeared above the table his face had turned completely purple, for a surreptitious glance at the document had revealed that England had also promised Italy certain regions which were reserved for France in the provisions of a secret Anglo-French agreement.

The conference ended in an ugly squabble. Lloyd George, the unctuous Welsh lawyer, managed to save the situation only by proposing that they compose a memorandum in which they would mutually undertake to ignore all future peace overtures, for such efforts only disturbed the unity of the Allied Powers.

A more despicable document had never been formulated in the history of the world. The meaning of the note issued after the St. Jean de Maurienne Conference was this: If King Charles, touched by some divine light, were to throw himself on his knees before the Entente and say, "Send me into exile, take away my every land, but put an end to this bloodshed," the Entente could not but answer, according to the note: "Go to the devil, young man, you're disturbing our unity!"

Lord, what have you done to the world?

I began to pack at once, to go to Ararat. After this I couldn't stand another moment in Switzerland.

Chapter Six

THE chestnuts are already blossoming in the park. Their fragrance, and the morning chimes of the chapel, the family surroundings and the faces of the old servants—all these recall the memories of my childhood. They curtain me off from the war, the king, the appalling hallucinations of history. I've taken refuge in a lovely hallucination of another sort: I have seriously set myself to write my novel about Chief Ordony, an ancestor of our family. I spend entire days in the castle library, and begin to feel quite at home on the Asiatic steppes of the great migratory period, from which seven tribes—our Hungarian forefathers—departed westward in the ninth century after the birth of Christ. One of the tribes was led by Ordony. Juan Hwang is a great help in my search for source material; his presence, fortunately enough, has not aroused the attention of the family, for he goes unnoticed in the tremendous castle and among the hordes of guests. Mamma is constantly reproaching me for deliberately avoiding the company. But they bore me beyond measure—right now only the novel interests me.

What could my ancestors have been like a thousand years ago on the steppes of Asia? I have merely to look out the window, where Russian prisoners of war are mowing the grass in the park. There are some wonderful types among them, Uzbeks, primitive Turkish profiles from the Caucasus, or slant-eyed Mongols. Asia has invaded our park at Ararat—quite tamely, to be sure. When we walk in the park the Russian prisoners take their caps off, spring to attention, and hold their scythes as if at rifle salute. They are mild, good men. They're grateful to be here, well treated and well fed. It's better to be here, mowing the grass under the blossoming chestnuts, than out on the battlefield, being mown down by death. None of the Russians are here by accident. Papa and Uncle Dmitri always enclose a list of names in their letters to one another. They requisition each other's protégés from the miserable prisoner-of-war camps, and put them to farm work on their own estates. Sometimes we all go down to attend one of their threshings, and watch them at their interminable, unwearying dances, which they do with arms akimbo and squatting on their heels. They have an incredible flair for dancing. They're always glad to sing for us, and their four-part folk songs are really beautiful. Juan Hwang is with them constantly, and by now he's collected more than two hundred words which the Russian and Hungarian languages have in common. These Russians have quickly learned to speak Hungarian. Their fluency is aided by the fact that the war widows in the village are more than willing to share the warmth of their striped blankets with the Ivans and the Nikolais. I imagine the Katushkas on Uncle Dmitri's estate do the same with our Hungarians. The people, if it were left to them, would gladly spend the whole war under their blankets like this.

Yesterday afternoon my brother Rere staged a great circus in the park again. He found the little cinnabar-red wagon to which I used to hitch my white donkey, Mici, when I was small. Mici had light blue eyes as large as plums. Since he has no donkey, Rere hitched himself into the harness and seated one of the Russians in the wagon, who spurred him on with a whip—playfully, of course. The game was Rere's idea, for idiots are children at heart. It was a hilarious sight to see a derby-hatted, jacketed count harnessed to the wagon like a draught horse, while a grinning Russian beat Rere's back with a whip. Everybody's sides shook with laughter.

Juan Hwang, standing beside me, did not laugh. Now, too, his countenance was transfused with the amazing hallucination which I've so often seen on his face when he is lost in thought. It is an unshakable theory of his that the springs of the rejuvenation of the world lie concealed in the great, primitive caverns of Eastern man; he says the peoples of the West are weak and decadent. I can't follow these thoughts of his, but his words always stay with me. Tonight, as I was walking in the park and thinking of one of the chapters of my novel, I stopped and began to listen. The four-part harmony of a Russian song came from the barns. It was beautiful and terrifying, as if all Asia were singing and the wind had swept the voices all the way from the Kirghiz steppes. The combined might of the harmonies, when they mounted to the climax of the melancholy song, almost seemed to be menacing the castle.

15 May

It's no use, I can't isolate myself from the outer world after all. The immediacy of war is brought home to us not only by the presence of the Russian prisoners, but by the great military map, too, which hangs in one of the downstairs salons.

It's Mr. Gruber's duty to move the tiny little colored flags forward or backward, according to the communiqués in the morning papers. Any one of his movements may possibly mean seventy thousand casualties. It's Zia's job to make the little flags, and she's very proud of it. She's only seven, but instead of sewing dresses for her dolls she manufactures paper flags to represent the battle fronts. After breakfast Papa stands before the map, smoking his cigar, his legs spread apart, and notes the shifting military situation with satisfaction or concern. In general, everybody discusses the military situation all day, and everyone's tone makes it seem as if he alone were in possession of great military secrets and is willing to reveal only fragmentary details. I feel but one thing, like a constant and incurable heartache: the war rolls on, and the point of the bayonet sinks deeper toward a fatal point in the world's body. The king is in my mind a great deal.

17 May

A lovely day, and a happy one. Writers like me are always pleased to see their work in print. I am especially proud because I submitted my manuscript under a nom-de-plume, Black Bird, and a literary magazine called *Full Moon* has agreed to print it. It's a little short story, and goes like this:

THE MYSTERIOUS LITTLE ANIMAL

Before falling asleep, King Mondolfred XVII reached for his glass and took another sip of milk, which came from goats fattened on white rose-petals. His chamberlain closed the heavy silk curtains of the canopied bed and tiptoed from the royal bedroom, which was now lit only by the little night-lamp under the image of the Holy Virgin.

A rank of motionless halberdiers stood guard along the corridors of the palace. The moon cast a ghostly light through the leaded, arched windows. It must have been about midnight when a curious little animal flitted over the marble floor of the corridor and, with a leap like a bouncing ball, succeeded in disappearing under the crack of the door at the main exit. It was as big as a rat, but somewhat rounder, and seemed purplish-black in the moonlight.

"What was that?" asked Andrew of Berulia, who stood nearest the door.

"A weasel, I think..." said the halberdier at his side.

"It wasn't a weasel," whispered another, more removed voice, whose owner spoke without budging his head from its rigid position.

"What is it? What are you talking about?" inquired a fourth voice.

"A curious little animal just passed by."

"You're imagining things," said the deep tones of Michael of Gorma, who could fall asleep even on his feet, open-eyed.

The halberdiers did not continue their discussion of the mysterious little animal. Silence and moonlight once more held sway along the marble corridors of the royal palace.

But the mysterious little animal appeared again on the following midnight. This time they all saw it; two of the halberdiers, in fact, watched it slither from beneath the crack of the door of the royal bedroom. Andrew of Berulia threw his halberd at the fleeing little animal. The halberd swept along the marble floor with a peculiar shriek in pursuit of its victim, and even caught up with it, but the little animal zigzagged from its path with an extremely clever leap and succeeded in escaping under the crack of the main exit once again, although this crack was so narrow that it hardly accommodated the edge of a halberd. Evidently the mysterious little animal was wonderfully skilled at changing the shape of its resilient body at will.

This time the halberdiers reported the incident to the lord chamberlain. The next night they stationed a guard in the bedroom, with orders to keep his eyes fixed on their sovereign. Under the influence of the goat's milk, Mondolfred XVII, his hands clasped on his chest, slept peacefully beneath the great canopy. The faint blue light of the night-lamp barely touched his reddish-blond beard. At about midnight the guard saw the strange little animal crawl from beneath the king's blanket. In a matter of seconds the corridor outside was in a raucous tumult. Every halberd flew after the fleeing little animal, but in vain. The rigid rank of halberdiers buzzed with excitement, and a number of them asserted that the little animal had no body but was a shadow. Next day the king's councilors spent all day debating how best to trap and destroy the mysterious little beast. They said nothing to the king about the matter, lest they disturb his rest. That night the master hunter stationed every bloodhound in the royal kennels outside the main exit of the palace. The caretakers leaned forward with the leashes in hand, waiting for the moment to release the dogs, whose bodies were already aquiver with the excitement of the chase.

Suddenly the shouts of the halberdiers and the metallic crash of their weapons were heard from the corridor. In the moonlight, the mysterious little animal could clearly be seen as it issued from under the door and zigzagged down the steps and toward the park. At that moment the caretakers gave a shrill cry and the motley pack of hounds set out on the chase like a whirlwind, amid a ferocious chorus of baying. Leaping over tall bushes in their fleet pursuit, the spotted bloodhounds seemed to be flying in the moonlight. The little animal, fleeing at lightning speed, took refuge in a corner of the high stone wall which surrounded the outermost stables. The baying of the dogs was suddenly insane and earsplitting. They tumbled over each other's backs, and for a moment the purplish shape of the little animal appeared on the whitely glistening fangs of one of the dogs. But it slid to earth again, and with a final exertion of strength it threw itself over the high stone wall in a tremendous arc. The howling dogs rushed to the wall, and their impetus almost allowed them to leap it as they flung forward in a wedge, but they merely grasped at the rim of the wall with their forepaws and fell back in a heap. The hunt had been of no avail.

The commander of the army himself took part in the next day's conference. The best archers, spear throwers and lancers in the royal army were stationed around the palace in close ranks. Battle fever seized every last soldier, while the king's councilors felt that their honor and dignity depended on the destruction of the little animal.

At midnight, when the tumult was again heard along the corridor, a shower of arrows and spears blanketed the steps outside. The fleeing little animal frantically sought a path through the dense forest of the soldiers' legs. One of the soldiers stamped on it with his hobnailed boot. The slippery little shape slid from under the boot and fled on, but its strength was clearly running out. The next moment the razor-keen spear of the champion spear thrower, John of Zorhin, found its mark. A triumphant shout rang out on every side. They crowded about the hero, who hastened toward the corridor with his spear held high, for the king's councilors were impatiently waiting. They brought a torch, the better to examine the captured prey.

A bleeding human heart dangled from the tip of the spear.

18 May

I told Juan Hwang that I've been writing under the pseudonym of Black Bird, and I gave him the short story to read. He said it was nice, but he wasn't as enthusiastic as I had expected. Of course he doesn't like the Habsburgs, and to his mind the king is merely a useful tool. I haven't shown my story to Mamma and Papa, for they're incapable of understanding symbolism of any sort. But I couldn't resist giving it to Uncle Fini. His opinion was discouraging. He maintains that writing of this sort is dangerously defeatist. Right now everyone must pray for a German victory. He explained the military situation, and the fiasco of the French offensive. His face was flushed as he spoke of German victory, and I could sense that he was a Schäyenheim through and through.

4 June

The days pass monotonously. The summer is unusually warm and stuffy this year. Sometimes I spend hours on a lonely bench in the park, sitting motionlessly in the perfect silence toward nightfall, when not even a breeze stirs the leaves. I still cannot help but respond to the frightful storm which is raging throughout the world. I envy Zia, and every child or grownup who is impervious to this feeling and can surrender himself to the pleasures of summer.

Another letter has arrived from Uncle Dmitri through Sweden, after a delay of about six weeks. The letter brought two items of sad news: the abdication of the tsar, for one, and the report that Miroshka (Aunt Mira) had one of her toes amputated because it froze during the January hunt. The tsar abdicated on March 15th, and the whole world knew about it a few days later, but Uncle Dmitri discusses the event as if it were a confidential family matter, cautioning us not to spread the news just yet. How amazingly naive people can be! The letter goes on to say:

> *After the assassination of Rasputin the court made a frenzied effort to salvage what could be saved and I myself had two audiences with the tsar. By the end of February the hunger demonstrations in Moscow and St. Petersburg had assumed the proportions of veritable revolution, and the government vainly tried to placate the Duma. It didn't do much good to issue warrants for the arrest of the leaders of the liberal parties. The government was forced to resign, and Iki became the new prime minister—a first cousin of mine, you may recall meeting him in my house. But when it seemed that the Lvov*

government was going to be able to keep things under control, a loud-mouthed lawyer appeared on the political scene, a man well known to me because he instituted a slanderous lawsuit against me sometime before the war; it had to do with the maintenance of a child, and he bribed witnesses to prove that I spent two nights with a woman called Olga Ilnova in the Georgia Hotel in Moscow, masquerading as a fur dealer by the name of Simirov; not a word of this was true, for I only spent a half hour talking with the woman in her room. So this filthy lawyer, Kerenski, seized power and turned my unhappy country into a republic. You know what the word 'republic' means, and if you don't know then I don't advise you to find out, for this Socialist blatherskite of a lawyer is beguiling the peasants with all sorts of promises of land distribution. But the Entente will soon make him swallow his words. Just yesterday I talked with Sir Evelyn Johnson, who told me in confidence that a part of the British battle fleet was already on the way, in the Baltic, and that England would set Russian internal affairs in order.

Papa was visibly downcast after reading the letter. He distributed an entire box of cigars among the Russian prisoners who are working in the park. This is something he's never done before.

10 June

According to the communiqués, the German star is in the ascendant. The king is much in my mind; I should like to be at his side, and to smooth his care-burdened brow. I am afraid he must have begun to regret the Sixtus Letter long ago, for events are proving that Uncle Cini was right.

Juan Hwang wanders about the park all by himself for hours at a time, aimlessly and wordlessly. There is always a great commotion about the map in the salon downstairs, the little flags are moved around triumphantly, and everyone has a comment to offer or a question to ask.

If I ever write a modern novel I shall use Mr. Gruber, Papa's secretary, as one of my models. One of the two eyes in his red, pudgy, cleanshaven countenance is green, the other brown. Despite his heavy body, he is exceptionally light on his feet. When he explains something, he stops the flow of air in one of his nostrils by placing a forefinger firmly against his nose. Then, at the end of a sentence, he uses this forefinger to prod the unsuspecting listener, who generally loses his balance. But he ends most of his sentences with a wheeze and flings his clenched hands so vigorously into the air that his arms almost fly from their sockets, and he snaps the fingers of the outflung hands without allowing one to see the lightning-swift gesture. He suddenly runs a few feet away, stops just as suddenly, looks at the victim of his eloquence over his shoulder with his two unmatched eyes, runs back and sometimes puffs up his face as he goes on talking, or rasps out an "*Oh-là-là*" in a curious throaty tone, throwing the accents high in the air at the close of a sentence, like a juggler with his little white balls; and he puts his questions as if he were deeply interested in an answer, but answers them all himself, bringing his face close to mine, and at these times his eyes flow together so thoroughly that one cannot know which is green and which brown. Mr. Gruber is German on his paternal side, while his mother was French. What can please such a man: Does he rejoice at the German advances, or mourn the French defeats? I can't make him out. I watch him because I can see myself in him, for I too am such a mixture, of German and Hungarian blood. Sometimes I feel a deep longing for Juan Hwang's oriental spirit, while at other times I can't bear his presence and am drawn to Uncle Fini.

27 July

After the French defeat at Champagne, with its great loss of blood, the latest Russian offensive has collapsed, too, and the German star mounts ever higher. Uncle Fini is as gay as a bird, for he's tight from early morning on. The air has been charged with excitement for weeks, and I've been unable to get on with my novel, nor am I inclined to keep this diary. The heat is unbearable, as if the whole world were aflame somewhere, not far away. This morning Juan Hwang offered the following analysis of the situation:

Kerenski, before launching his last frantic offensive against the Germans, implored his Western allies to approve the Stockholm conference on international socialism, for only a conference of this sort could bring about a truly democratic peace, not to mention the fact that such a conference might easily inspire the starving peoples of Germany and the Monarchy to rebellion. The member nations of the Entente, however, would not sanction the Stockholm conference, for they were afraid it would lend new strength to the revolutionary spirit of an already shaken Europe. However strange it may sound, the moderate Kerenski was as far from their hearts as the German emperor. They felt that Kerenski had no business interfering in international affairs—let him fulfill his contractual agreements and attack the Germans. Kerenski, like an obedient lad, attacked

176

them. Not only Russian corpses were left hanging on the barbed-wire barricades of the eastern front, but the Russian people's last vestige of patience as well.

26 October—Budapest

When hostilities began Emperor Wilhelm said the war would be over by the time the leaves began to fall. Since then the leaves have fallen three times, in the park at Ararat too. We've been back in Septemvir Utca for the past two weeks. It's now six months since I last saw the king, and I've had no news of him since then. I imagine he is happy, for the papers nowadays are full of the decisive victory gained by the combined Austro-German offensive against the Italians at Caporetto.

23 March 1918—Vienna

Five months have passed since I last wrote a word in my diary. I've made no progress on my novel either; lately my state of mind has seemed to demand a complete break with all worldly concerns. Like a balloon, aimlessly carried among the clouds by the wind. In the past few weeks I've been here in our house on Bösendorferstrasse with Juan Hwang. I came back to Vienna to be near the king. Sometimes I think he's forgotten me completely. The higher the German star mounts, the further away he seems to be. Large headlines in the papers report that the Germans on the western front have totally dispersed even the cavalry units of the English General Gough. Yes, the German star, and with it the star of the Monarchy, goes up and up, but at the same time the starvation here in Vienna has become really serious. I don't know what I would do without supplies from home. Mr. Gruber's fertile brain has organized an entire little smuggling ring for the benefit of my modest household here.

I've been wondering whether to request an audience with the king on some pretext or other. It's dreadful to think how far, how high, he's soared from me. Yesterday was Sunday, and I was all alone in the house, for the servants had gone out to amuse themselves in the Prater. From memory, I arranged the chairs in the downstairs salon exactly as they stood on that afternoon in May seven years ago. My God, how much has happened in seven years! I had a clear recollection of the king, still hopelessly far from the throne at the time, as he sat in a dark red-backed chair. I found my sky-blue dress in the storeroom, the one I wore then, and put it on. I acted out the scene of our first meeting. Everything around me came alive, the gypsy music and the fragrance of blossoming trees from the garden entered the room, which was full of voices and faces—still, it all seemed like a grievous hallucination. I threw the ball at the dark red-backed velvet armchair: *Apfelstrudel!* And I took off my earring to pay the forfeit and left the room, stopping behind the wing of the door to wait for my knight to come and pull me from the well. But he didn't come. Not for a half hour, not for an hour, and slowly it began to turn dark. Fear and a sense of hopelessness gripped me, I began to cry softly in the dark and stretched out my hand for the king's heart, which Frau Katz's prophecy had promised me.

Why has he abandoned me like this, for a whole year now? I served him faithfully, even at the risk of my life in Geneva.

I prayed for a long time tonight. I found this sentence in St. Ignatius Loyola's book: "Teach us, good Lord, to labor and not ask for any reward!"

17 April

The German star mounts ever higher and higher, crackling and glittering. Rumania has been at the Germans' feet since Christmas; the Treaty of Brest-Litovsk sealed the fate of a shattered Russia some weeks ago; and the papers this morning were triumphantly heralding the advance of the Germans from Yperen toward Paris in tremendous strength. Baron K., from the Foreign Office, called on me this morning. He says final victory is now assured, and that plans are already being drafted at Schönbrunn. Archduke Maximilian has been chosen to rule the new South Slavonic state when it becomes part of the Monarchy. All Rumania and the southern regions of Poland will come under Hungarian control. The Monarchy will be greater and more powerful than ever.

The king has vanished from my sight exactly as he did at the moment of his coronation. But this time he's gone further away, and to greater heights.

A momentous day—a fatal day. It came like an explosion after the flat and dreary monotony of the recent past.

20 April

Everything happened exactly as it did a year ago. I was in the bathtub at about eleven this morning when Margaret, my chambermaid, came in to say that a stranger wanted to speak with me personally. Margaret has no memory for faces. I told her to send him away—he was probably a beggar or a salesman. He wouldn't go; he brought a letter which had to be delivered in person; and the letter was from Schönbrunn. When I went to the door with my hair disheveled, the same narrowed eyes scrutinized my face. It was he—the mute, slate-blue countenance. He handed me the letter and disappeared. The letter was written on the same sort of paper, and again in pencil:

Please be at the apartment in No. 15 Blaue Lampe Strasse, where we met last year, at six this afternoon. Very important.

This time the last two words made it quite clear that the king was not summoning me to a lovers' rendezvous. Juan Hwang left home early this morning and hadn't returned by late afternoon. I left a short note to tell him where I was going; I could imagine how impatiently he would wait for me to return.

In the taxi I felt that the *Mountain* had trembled again and was on the point of baring its dark depths more deeply than ever before.

Again the slate-blue countenance opened the door, and the king was already in the room. Sadness overwhelmed the pounding of my heart: how he had changed in the course of a year! He seemed ten years older. His voice was mild and friendly as he hurried toward me and gave me his hand. Then his face suddenly turned gloomy:

"A fine mess of trouble your Uncle Cini has cooked up for me!"

This came as a surprise, for before this he had always talked of Uncle Cini as "my Foreign Minister." Now, all at once, it was "your Uncle Cini."

"What happened?"

"He made a very foolish speech. In answer to secret French peace feelers he declared that Alsace-Lorraine rightfully belonged to Germany, and that the Monarchy had never entertained any doubts about this German right. Thereupon Clemenceau flew into a rage and answered, via the Havas Agency, that the Foreign Minister was lying in his teeth, because the Monarchy had acknowledged the French claim last year."

My breath stood still.

"The Sixtus Letter?"

The king nodded silently.

"This morning I was called to the teletype. Uncle Cini was at the other end, in Bucharest, where he had just dictated the Rumanian peace terms. He was up in arms, and asked whether I had given my brothers-in-law a letter of some sort in this connection without his knowledge last year. I told him to calm down, I had given no written assurance of any sort. But he wasn't satisfied; he took a train at once and will be here tomorrow morning."

The king reached for my hand.

"Kristina, you were present at that meeting from beginning to end. Now listen closely to every word I say. You know what the military situation is: the Germans are pressing forward without pause. When a man is in great trouble he'll stoop to anything. That's what Clemenceau is doing with me right now. He wants to make the Sixtus Letter public. If the Germans learn about it, the allegiance of the Monarchy to the victors will have been in vain, all our sacrifices will have been in vain, the Germans will break us as a traitorous ally. If I know Ludendorff, he'll have me shot too."

He stared into the air, somewhat to one side, and at that moment his expression was as pitiful as a little boy's. His badly cut, loose civilian suit heightened his childish look.

"Please take a sheet of paper," he said, starting up from his thoughts, "and write down exactly what I say, for every word is very important. Here is what happened in this room last March. The five of us remained after Uncle Cini's departure. The two Bourbons, you, I and Oscar."

"Florian."

"No, not Florian," the king said with emphasis. "Oscar!"

"Oscar? What Oscar?"

The king pointed toward the door.

"The one who opened the door. Who delivered the letter. My most trustworthy man. His name is Oscar."

I made especial note of this, for I forget names very easily. The mute, slate-blue countenance was called Oscar, then.

"When I finished the letter to my brother-in-law Sixtus—" the king continued "—I looked around with the letter in hand, then gave it to Oscar to be put in an envelope. He took the letter and went into the next room for an envelope. Please underline that. *He went into the next room.* He stayed so long that I called after him: 'What's the matter? Can't you find an envelope?' and Oscar called back: 'I'm looking for one in the drawers of the desk.' Later, when he appeared in the doorway, the envelope was at his lips and he was licking it with his tongue in order to seal it. Did you write all this down?"

"Yes, Your Majesty."

The king stood up, crossed the room a number of times with hands clasped at his back, and then went out suddenly. When he returned a few seconds later

I could hardly recognize him. He wore the false beard, the collar of his coat was turned up to his eyes and his hat was pulled over his forehead.

"I must go now, Kristina, because there's a lot to do. Please be at Schönbrunn tomorrow morning at nine. At nine precisely. And read over what you wrote a number of times, so there'll be no mistake."

He took my hand in both his hands and said sadly, somewhat apologetically:

"I'm very grateful. Good-bye."

He turned quickly and left.

At home, to my great surprise, not only Juan Hwang was waiting for me but Florian as well, whom I'd not seen since the meeting with the Bourbons. After so long a time he made a worse impression on me than the king had done. His face was grayer and sharper than ever, and now he really looked as if he were not of flesh and blood. I had to tell them everything in the greatest detail. They listened wide-eyed, motionlessly. When I had finished Juan Hwang slowly pushed a chair to one side and walked to the window. Florian continued to stare into space with a rigid expression. Juan Hwang was the first to speak:

"The king is inexcusably stupid. He's under the spell of German victory. The king is deaf, and can't hear what's going on below him. The Monarchy is at the point where Russia stood last year."

Florian nodded wordlessly. Juan Hwang continued:

"Berlin and Vienna can hardly stand on their feet from starvation. You can hear open talk of a break with Austria in the corridors of the Hungarian Lower House. Vienna is full of socialists, while the Czechs...the king must be completely blind if he can't see what the Czechs are up to."

He waved his hand in angry disapproval. Now Florian spoke:

"There is only one thing for the king to do. When Uncle Cini calls him to account tomorrow, instead of repudiating the letter in such a stupid and cowardly way he must say: 'Yes, I wrote it, and I take full responsibility.' And if Uncle Cini's inclined to argue, he should have the idiotic rascal locked up at once."

"Shot!" cried Juan Hwang.

"The king must declare an armistice immediately, and take the head of his troops against the Germans. That's the only way he can save anything of the situation."

Juan Hwang approached me heatedly.

"Listen, Kristina, Florian is right: that's the only way. But the king is too cowardly for that. Fate has put this important role in your hands. You're a

181

bigger person than the king and Uncle Cini put together. Bigger, because you're beautiful and passionate. At moments like this it is always a woman's beauty and passion that determine the course of history."

Florian's ashen face quietly nodded.

"Tomorrow—" continued Juan Hwang "—you must unmask this childish falsehood of the king. You must seize the king and pull him down with you. Down? Up! If you do the opposite of what he asks, you won't be betraying him—you'll be saving his life."

"The king is a good, honest man," said Florian, "but he's terribly helpless and indecisive. I agree with Juan Hwang on every point. The future of the king, of the Monarchy, and of us all, will be decided tomorrow."

I can't recall how long the discussion lasted. I went to bed without a bite to eat, and my heart and brain seemed completely numb. The depths of the *Mountain* were open and menacing. The Great, Important Role, the role Frau Katz once talked about, had finally entered my life. Juan Hwang and Florian circled my bed with soundless steps, deep in thought, and occasionally, before I fell into a deep sleep, I heard words like these:

"Remember, Countess, the lives of millions of soldiers depend on what will happen tomorrow..."

"Pull yourself together and soften the king's heart. The king will listen to you. The king loves you..."

21 April

A few minutes before nine this morning I was already in the king's anteroom at Schönbrunn. The adjutant said no more than that the Foreign Minister was inside with His Majesty. The anteroom was full of high-ranking officers and statesmen. They were discussing the military situation in quiet, confident tones. Their words made the German victory appear an imminent reality, Juan Hwang and Florian were still circling about me like two shadows, and everything they'd said seemed like some excruciating hallucination. Here in the white and gold chamber every word—the Somme, Gough, Ludendorff, the Marne—and every military advantage of the Germans took on dazzling substance.

The adjutant opened the door and beckoned to me. My heart was pounding in my throat. Uncle Cini, with his fluttering black cravat, stood in front of the king's desk. The king wore his field marshal's uniform, with an array of stars, and—perhaps it was the glittering uniform in the ancient frame of the great room—Charles was now the king and emperor, mighty and majestic. He took a few steps toward me and greeted me in a noticeably cool tone:

"Good morning, Countess."

But while he shook my hand a warm, conspiratorial twinkle appeared in his left eye. Then he opened the conversation, with Uncle Cini standing beside the desk, tall and black and yellow.

"I asked you here, Countess," began the king, with an air of ill humor and severity, "because I want you to tell us precisely what happened when the letter which Prince Sixtus took from Laxenburg was given to him last year. Try to remember everything, and say nothing but the truth."

Then a sudden supplication filled his eyes, only fleetingly, but his glance penetrated my heart.

While I repeated the lesson I had learned by rote, slowly and quietly, Uncle Cini kept his cold, rigid fish-eyes fixed on me. When I finished he flashed a question at me:

"And so Oscar put the letter in an envelope?"

"Yes."

"In the next room?"

"Yes, I remember that distinctly."

Uncle Cini leaned against the table, folded his two long arms over his chest and turned toward the king with a sardonic smile.

"Your majesty, this incident of the envelope sounds altogether too simple. I'm afraid Clemenceau is right."

The king sprang from his seat and shouted in an impassioned voice:

"Whom do you believe? Clemenceau or your emperor?"

Uncle Cini was unmoved by the reprimand. He answered with the same smile:

"Your majesty, allow me to reply with a well-known anecdote. A tired traveler approached a farmhouse and asked the farmer to lend him his mule. The farmer said he was sorry, but he'd lent the mule to a neighbor just the day before. At that moment the earsplitting snort of a mule was heard from the stable. 'But your mule is right here!' said the traveler. The farmer turned red with rage and shouted: 'Whom do you believe? My mule or me?' "

Uncle Cini made a slight bow toward the king.

"The mule, of course, is Clemenceau."

All at once the smile left Uncle Cini's face, and his expression turned as hard as stone as he left the desk to fetch his attaché case, which was lying on one of the upholstered chairs. He took out an issue of *Le Temps*.

"Perhaps Your Majesty doesn't know the kind of proof Clemenceau has in his possession."

He spread the newspaper out on the desk.

"There! This paper reproduces a facsimile of the letter, written in Your Majesty's own hand, in which you admit the justice of French pretensions to Alsace-Lorraine."

The king took the paper in hand, studied the reproduction with care and then said calmly:

"That's not my handwriting."

Uncle Cini leaned against the table, folded his incredibly long, tentacle-like arms over his chest again and replied with a smile which combined a subordinate's deference with the most insolent sarcasm.

"Surely Your Majesty knows the story that's told about Count Bombelles, the physician of Emperor Joseph II. Bombelles was a great dandy, and once he told a group of listeners that a true gentleman would never wear yellow shoes. Someone glanced down and remarked: 'But Your Excellency is wearing yellow shoes even now!' Bombelles looked down at his feet and replied: 'But those aren't my feet!'"

Leaning back slightly, Uncle Cini looked at the king through half-lowered eyelids. The king didn't smile. He pressed the buzzer, which was set in the eye of an onyx fish resting on the desk, and when the adjutant entered he said:

"Bring that man in!"

We had to wait for a few moments, but no one said a word. Uncle Cini twirled his monocle rapidly, and the bright circle which the monocle described in the air was like a halo of disdain. The king stood by the window, facing partly away, and he gazed out into the park. I closed my eyes, for I was on the point of fainting.

When the door opened again I saw two armed guards show in Oscar of the slate-blue countenance, while they remained outside. Only the adjutant accompanied Oscar into the room, and then he left too. Oscar stood beside the white and gold door with head slightly lowered, like a man condemned to death. He held his hat awkwardly in his two hands. The king turned to him:

"Be good enough to tell us…"

Uncle Cini suddenly interrupted.

"There's no need, Your Majesty, It's the third time I've heard this story."

He began to shake his large, bony, clasped hands before the king's face:

"Your Majesty, I beg you to understand that it's no use. Do you think the French have lost their minds?"

The king looked Uncle Cini up and down coldly, and answered with a calm dignity which did not suit him, somehow, at that moment.

"Once again, Count, I tell you I didn't write that letter."

He struck the newspaper with his palm and exclaimed in a heated voice:

"This isn't my handwriting! Won't you take my word for it?"

Uncle Cini was still waving his clasped hands:

"What good does it do if I take your word? Clemenceau must have proof!"

"Monsieur Clemenceau will have his proof!" the king shouted. "Take a sample of this man's handwriting!"

He stepped to the table, took paper and pen and turned to Oscar:

"Sit down and write what I dictate."

Oscar dropped his hat to the floor and extended his wrists. They were handcuffed together. The king pressed the buzzer and, at a wave of his hand, the adjutant swiftly unlocked Oscar's handcuffs. Oscar sat down to the desk and rubbed his wrists before starting to write. The king began to dictate:

"The Monarchy recognizes the inalienable right of France to Alsace-Lorraine…"

Oscar wrote quickly. Uncle Cini put his monocle in place and took the sheet of paper in hand with a scornful smile. Then he nervously fumbled for the French newspaper and looked now at the reproduction, now at Oscar's handwriting. The scornful smile vanished from his lips.

I stepped closer and also looked at the two handwritings. My heart stopped. They were amazingly alike.

Uncle Cini was astonished and crestfallen as the king snapped:

"Look at those *t*'s, if you please! I never curve my *t*'s like that!"

Now Uncle Cini leveled his staring fish-eyes at Oscar's slate-blue face:

"How did you dare to commit this forgery?"

The lowered head did not answer. The king pressed the buzzer again and the adjutant appeared, replaced the handcuffs on Oscar's wrists and led him away. The king turned to Uncle Cini:

"Let Clemenceau know at once that we've found the forger and shall make him available so that Monsieur Clemenceau himself can examine the man's handwriting. Make arrangements to transfer the prisoner to the custody of the Entente somewhere. And now I'll send the German emperor a wire which I want

185

to compose with you. Sit down, please, and I'll dictate."

The king stood at the other end of the desk, with one fist on his hip and the other resting on the top of the desk. His voice had a metallic ring:

My dear Wilhelm—I have silenced Clemenceau's base and lying accusations. The voice of my cannon on the western front will give the French an answer for what they've tried to do. Faithfully, Charles.

He waited until Uncle Cini had finished the last word, and then he suddenly tossed his head:

"Does this message meet with your approval?"

Uncle Cini nodded without a word. The king stepped from the desk and softly clicked his golden spurs. The audience was over.

I didn't recover my composure until the taxi was at the door on Bösendorferstrasse. I hastened up the steps with an anxious heart. Juan Hwang and Florian met me with a crossfire of their mute, dry glances. It was hard to begin what I had to say. I started by stuttering something to the effect that the reality, the given situation, was other than the future, which we could not foresee. Then I gave a detailed account of what had happened, while the two pairs of eyes stared at me with growing coldness. When I finished, Juan Hwang was the first to speak. He was deadly pale.

"Is this true? Is this what you did?"

"I didn't do it," I said in fright.

He dashed to the door and seized the knob as if, in his anxiety, he thought to run somewhere, as if there were still something, somewhere, to be salvaged.

And then a dreadful thing happened. Juan Hwang suddenly sprang at me from the door and began to choke me, while he croaked in a stifled voice:

"Damned bitch! Damned bitch!"

We sprawled on the floor, with Juan Hwang's fingers at my throat, and I raised my eyes beseechingly to Florian. But Florian did not move, did not come to my aid. As his ash-gray face, cruel and mute, looked at me from above, it was the face of some unknown and terrifying Judgment. I saw no more than that he took his hat and left the room.

And Juan Hwang left me there on the floor. He rushed away with such violence that the heavy oaken door exploded with the sound of a deep-voiced cannon. As I lay on the rug, half unconscious, the explosion echoed somewhere along the empty corridor, and the echoes multiplied and grew louder until it seemed as if all the cannon of the battlefields were exploding near by, in frightful concert. I fainted.

26 April

This is the fifth day since Juan Hwang's disappearance. The scandal caused by the Sixtus Letter has subsided in the international press. What can have happened to Oscar? The French have probably executed him by now. The German troops are rolling onward like thunder on every front.

28 April

Baron K. visited me again for a short while this morning. He confided, under a promise of the greatest secrecy, that Schönbrunn is in a fever of excitement. Yesterday afternoon the queen rode into Vienna in her closed royal carriage to attend the opening of a new military hospital. When she returned at about eight in the evening, and after her carriage had entered the main gate of the park, two revolver shots were fired from beside one of the bushes, both of them shattering the windows of the carriage. The two horses shied, and broke toward the palace at a wild pace. No harm was done to the queen, and the lady-in-waiting at her side suffered no more damage than a bullet-hole through the rim of her hat. Since then detectives have been stationed behind every bush, and the military guard has been quadrupled. There is no trace of the would-be assassin. The incident is being kept in the greatest secrecy.

After Baron K. left I buried my face in my hands. I had the feeling, I don't know why, that Florian was responsible for the attempted assassination, although I had no proof of any sort for this. The question was suspended inside of me like a sinister garment—its very presence disturbing, dreadful, although its owner was unknown. Now it occurred to me that the other attempt at assassination, at the funeral of Franz Joseph, might also have been the work of...

Or Juan Hwang, perhaps?

Chapter Seven

GALA performance at the Opera tonight. Almost everyone in the thronged and brilliant house was an uncle or a cousin of mine. The entire Austrian and Hungarian aristocracy was there, as if they had come from the coronation in Buda with a prodigious leap over the intervening year and a half. They wore the same clothes and jewelry, and the splendor of the audience, the oriental regalia, the curved swords in their velvet scabbards threatened to surpass the performance on the stage in sheer spectacle.

I sensed something fearful, something sinister in the whole display, but Juan Hwang was not beside me to unfold the hidden meaning of these vague presentiments. And perhaps it's better that he's not at my side nowadays, with his eternal Cassandra-like prophecies.

When the king and queen appeared in the royal box, everyone rose and the orchestra broke into the Hungarian national anthem. Everyone sang, and the anthem was as moving and heart-rending now as at the coronation. But this time there was a certain air of triumphant intoxication about it, possibly because the full orchestra was so close to me, and the sonorous rumble of the majestic strains was truly beautiful.

When the chandelier overhead was dimmed I turned my head toward the royal box, but in the mist of darkness I could see nothing of the king except the two blurred patches of his snow-white gloves as he sat with arms folded in the box. Again so dreadfully far from me, and at such great heights! I've no hope of seeing him during his two-day stay in Budapest. Baron K., seated beside me, said that the king is very happy these days. According to the communiqué today, the Germans are approaching the Marne, and the fall of Paris may be expected in the space of a few short weeks.

29 May—Ararat

Spiteful people in Pest are whispering that the royal couple did not come to Hungary entirely without reason. The Viennese and Austrians are really starving now, and they came to court flour from the Hungarians; for all that the corn bread served in restaurants here is green with mold and half liquid, the knapsacks of our peasants are always stuffed with white loaves when they ruminate beside the ditch in the shade of an acacia. As far as Ararat is concerned, the war has hardly affected our kitchens. The estate steam mill puffs away uninterruptedly, and although the requisitioning is severe there is always enough flour that "spills" from the sacks to give us something to nibble on. The chef still sends written chits to the estate hunters, exactly as before the war, telling them how many deer, rabbits and pheasants to supply; oranges, lemons, dates and figs vanished long ago, to be sure, but no one can feel bereft after savoring the large, fruity, crisp cherries of Ararat, the golden-red butter pears, the velvety peaches that exude the fragrance of a freshly opened vial of perfume when one cuts them in half. The new chef, known simply as Mr. Barta, vainly competes with the memories which Monsieur Cavaignac left behind. Poor Cavaignac! Papa and his friends sit around the table drinking toasts to a German victory, while Monsieur Cavaignac, like a loyal Frenchman, is busy in one of the muddy, bloody trenches near the Marne, repelling the Germans as they push toward Paris. My brother György recently returned from the western front with a slight wound on his leg. It may have been the very rifle of Monsieur Cavaignac which inflicted the wound.

Leaning on his stick, György hobbles about the park all day and amuses himself by flinging pine cones for his dog to fetch. The pointer puppy tears after the pine cone with such vehemence that she can hardly stop when she's reached it, and often she tumbles head over heels. Her eyes are indescribably bright with happiness when she pants back with the pine cone in her jaws. And when she places it at György's feet her glance fills with the most beautiful pleading as she begs him to toss it away again. I can understand how this may entertain György more than anything else. A curious man, György. He is so different, with his short neck and round head, from the rest of us. Sometimes I have a feeling that it was not his calf but his soul that was wounded. He doesn't take part in the conversations during dinner, and offers no opinion either of the Germans or the French. Last week, when he received his medal for being wounded in combat, he threw it to the floor in a rage. This strengthened my suspicions, for I've examined his wound. We hospital nurses have considerable experience in such things. The path of the bullet runs diagonally through his calf And the bullet carefully missed the bone. Typical of a self-inflicted wound. If this is what happened, then György was right to do it. He's twenty years old and, as far as I know, he hasn't even been in love yet.

There are always a lot of children visiting at Ararat nowadays, and this makes for a noisy summer. Sometimes, when I pass the Chinese bathhouse, I can see slender, youthful bronze bodies diving from the high board.

I've not been in the Chinese pagoda since the accident, when I was fourteen, with the swimming instructor. Mamma's blue silk parasol bobs decorously from the direction of the castle when she makes her hourly tour of inspection in the bathhouse for fear that some harm will come to one of our little relatives, who are as oblivious to the war in their unbridled exuberance as the birds in the trees.

1 June

This morning Papa ran out on the terrace in great excitement and shouted for György. He called him to the large map, in front of which we were all crowding, even the servants. The Germans reached the Marne yesterday! The fall of Paris is a question of days. György didn't join in the shouts of joy, but kept on tossing pine cones to his dog.

2 July

Dull, dull days. There was a great storm today, and lightning split one of the old oak trees in two.

21 July

It was time for something momentous to happen, but as yet nobody knows what it means. A few minutes before nine this morning Mr. Gruber dashed into the,"flag factory," which is Zia's schoolroom:

"What's this? Aren't the new flags ready yet?"

He seized the ones that were finished and streaked away to correct the positions on the western front in accordance with the communiqués in the morning papers. Papa was already coming to take up a stand in front of the large map, with his feet spread apart and his cigar smoking deliciously. The progress of the flags has been noticeably wavering in the past few weeks, as if the mounting German star had come to a halt somewhere. General Foch's nondescript forces stopped the Germans on the outskirts of Paris, and even drove them back to some extent; but the positions this morning were even more surprising. The pinpricks of new and hitherto unknown little flags were striking roots in the map.

"What's all this?" Papa asked crossly, turning toward Mr. Gruber.

"American flags, Your Excellency," answered Mr. Gruber, bowing as he always does when someone addresses him.

"American?" Papa queried, wrinkling up his nose. As a matter of fact, there have been rumors of the disembarkation of American troops in French ports ever since the United States declared war in April of last year, but Uncle Fini, who is the American expert in the family, has been reassuring everyone that only a few hundred clerks and salesmen have been sent, and that French non-commissioned officers were drilling them with wooden guns far to the rear of the front. Uncle Andrew, who has excellent sources of information through Switzerland, seconded all this when he was here last week, and added that the lilac-cravatted clerks and razor-blade salesmen from New York were clapping their heels to the ground and practicing the manual of arms to the tune of, "Left, right, left! I had a good job and I left!"—and this was the full extent of American martial spirit. And now these little American flags appeared on the map all at once, foreign and intrusive, ludicrous and at the same time somehow disquieting. Were President Wilson to take one of these little flags in hand and examine it minutely he would collapse with alarm for the flags indicate that thirty-six of the forty-eight United States have been swallowed up in the ground. There are but twelve stars on each of the little flags. The remaining states vanished on the awkward hands of the flag manufacturer herself, by reason of that peculiar characteristic of gum arabic, which will stick anywhere but in the right place. Thus, for instance, South Carolina may be found on the tip of Zia's nose, all New England and Illinois on the lobes of her ears, eleven other states in the strands of her blond hair, and the rest on her thigh, where she scratched a mosquito bite. And other stars glitter on the arms of her chair and at the tip of her scissors. The "flag factory" filled the urgent order only by supplying twelve instead of forty-eight stars with each flag, but fortunately no one noticed this, for not even Papa knew what the stars were supposed to represent. The outrage was detected only when Uncle Fini appeared. All this has given me food for thought. Unquestionably our circles are the most cultured of all the classes of society, but we are completely ignorant of the world. Uncle Fini, too, knew how many stars there were on the flag and what they stood for only because he spent more than a year in America. He stood before the map for a long time with close-knit brows. In the afternoon everyone met in the library, as if by prearrangement. And we all began to read the history of the United States. The little flags suddenly heightened our interest in those few lilac-cravatted salesmen from New York.

2 August

The visitors have left the castle. The clamor of children's voices has subsided in the Chinese bathhouse. But every afternoon mysterious automobiles enter the castle gates. Strangers go into conference with Papa, and then disappear. Sometimes there are acquaintances among them, from the court at Vienna; Baron K., for example, or Uncle Lajos, who was a cabinet minister under Franz Joseph. During meals they all seem to lose their tongues. Even the most indispensable remarks seem a burden; everyone eats less, generally, and our eyes are fixed on our plates. The large map in the downstairs salon, too, no longer entertains the usual noisy, arguing crowds. Everyone visits the map in secret, and only to cast a few glances at it. The map is beginning to take on the role of some repulsive tumor which grows uglier by the day until the sick man will look at it only in the privacy of his own room and doesn't dare show it to a doctor for fear of hearing his own death sentence pronounced.

The air is imbued with a sense of great tension and terror. I sleep badly, and often get up at night to go walking in the park. Yesterday, at about two o'clock in the morning, I happened upon a figure idling along the row of plane trees that leads to the fishpool, and I was frightened at first, but I soon recognized Uncle Fini. It wasn't difficult to guess the cause of his sleepless vigil. But our self-discipline and discretion worked like a charm, and we began to talk of music, as if it were the most natural thing in the world to wander like timorous ghosts in the park at two in the morning. Uncle Fini left me after a half hour or so, but I sat alone by the fishpool for a long time. The gently moonlit sky was reflected in the very depths of the sleeping water. The silence was complete, and only the occasional bark of a dog sounded from the village, but at such a great distance that it seemed to come from another planet. The heavens have some appalling and portentous secrets in store for us. This much is certain, that the German comet is hurtling downward; and as I leaned against a tree with my eyes closed I could feel its approach, imponderable, of unknown size and heat, and I was sure it would strike somewhere in the park.

15 August

Uncle Peter, a first cousin of Papa and closely related, through his wife, to Ludendorff, who comes from a very old and noble Prussian family, has been attached to Ludendorff as a liaison officer of the Monarchy. It was really his thirst for knowledge that took him to German Headquarters, for Uncle Peter, although but forty years old, is a professional historian and a member of the Academy. This afternoon he arrived unexpectedly. He was surrounded at once, and we all hung on his every word. I shall try to give an accurate account of what Uncle Peter said.

We stood around him, Papa, Mamma, Uncle Fini, György and I. Mr. Gruber stood a little further away. The fact that he stayed in the room at all was a breach of discipline, but curiosity rooted his feet to the rug. Uncle Peter's every single sentence was followed by a flood of questions. He began by saying that the temper of the troops suddenly altered after the great German defeat of August 8th. Uncle Fini remarked that he still could not understand, on the basis of the communiqués, the reason for that defeat.

"Tanks! My God, so many tanks!" said Uncle Peter, cradling his somewhat smoke-colored countenance between two palms.

"Was ist ein Tank eigentlich?" asked Mamma, and there was a decided sense of insult in the accent of her "eigentlich." Uncle Peter pretended not to hear her question and went on to say that the reserves which went up to relieve the front-line troops were greeted with threats and ridicule from the trenches, with shouts that they were traitors and strikebreakers coming to prolong the war. Never before in the course of the war had this happened. On the 9th of August the imperial car drove up to Supreme Headquarters in a great cloud of dust. Inspection began after a hasty lunch, and every German soldier within a radius of seventy-five miles, even the casualties, was put on the alert. The imperial auto careened from one village to the next, and the emperor reviewed the ranks of soldiery with his marshal's baton in his paralyzed hand and holding the folds of his snow-white cape together, in a familiar gesture, with his other hand. His silver cuirass veritably blinded the sun with its farstrewn reflection of the afternoon rays. Uncle Peter, with the officers of the general staff, followed close behind. At seven o'clock the inspection came to an end, and a great council was arranged at half past eight in the Villa Ray, where Hindenburg had his personal headquarters. The flowing white cape mounted the steps with such a flutter that old General Plessen could hardly keep pace with it. Hindenburg, Ludendorff and the two aides, Captain Stocknagel and Uncle Peter, were waiting in the map room on the first floor. When he entered the room the emperor was noticeably pale. After curt introductions the aides retired to the adjoining room, which was separated by nothing more than a curtain. Neither of them, naturally, could withstand the urge to peep and eavesdrop. Ludendorff began by leaning over the map on the table and expounding the situation. This took a very long time. Hands clasped behind his back, Hindenburg stood beside the table like an angular statue carved of stone. Old Plessen stood with arms folded, while the emperor rested his elbow on the map. When Ludendorff came to the end of his recital, finally, the emperor sank into one of the armchairs without a word and, twirling his forked mustache, spoke only after a long pause:

"Well...yes. Fortunes of war. But we've been in more difficult straits. On the Marne, in,14, and in the days of the Brussilov offensive."

Ludendorff took a pencil in hand and addressed the tip of the pencil:

"Your Majesty, it's not the military situation alone that's catastrophic. What I requested Your Majesty's presence for is of much greater import."

The emperor turned his head provocatively toward Ludendorff, who was still studying the tip of the pencil. The emperor snapped:

"If we hold a public execution of several cowardly, loudmouthed rascals..."

Hindenburg's square, stony head shook in disapproval. The old soldier's voice broke from beneath his curly mustachios with an effort:

"The Fatherland is tired, Your Majesty. You cannot stem a tidal wave with toothpicks. I'm afraid we've already lost our allies. Reports from the Monarchy are very discouraging indeed. Turkey, Bulgaria—they no longer mean anything."

Plessen directed his gaze first at the emperor, then at Hindenburg, as if it were a table decoration which he wanted to place in safekeeping. Ludendorff spoke again:

"We've nothing left to do but to sell every inch of ground dearly when we retreat."

This pronouncement seemed in direct contradiction to the cautious movement with which he placed his pencil at a particular angle on the exact center of the map.

Once more the emperor proceeded to twirl his mustache assiduously, as if he sought to squeeze a solution from its strongly scented clumps of hair.

"And what about gas?"

Ludendorff paced the length of the room, and when he reached the wall he touched it with the tip of his middle finger, as if he simply wanted to take its temperature—with him, this was a sign of deepest thought.

"Gas?" he echoed. "It's true they won't be able to find an antidote to our mustard gas in less than a year, but this won't win the war—at most it will prolong it. Furthermore, one wonders what sort of gases *they* have. Our spies in Washington report that the Americans may have a great surprise in store for us."

The emperor twirled his mustache with flagging rapidity, and suddenly came to his feet:

"I shall expect you at Spaa tomorrow, gentlemen," he said, with an abrupt handshake.

"When did this happen?" asked Papa, after vigorously clearing his throat. Uncle Fini said nothing, but simply pinched his lower lip between two fingers.

Everyone stared into space thoughtfully, and nobody ventured to sit down. The lengthy silence, coupled with the fact that we all remained standing, was totally strange. Again Mamma asked, this time rather timidly: "Was ist ein Tank eigendich?"—but still she received no answer, which was the height of discourtesy on the part of the men. And then my brother Rere, who has lately been seized with a passion for uniforms, entered from the terrace. He slips into some sort of military apparel whenever he can. Last week he exchanged his jacket for the dirty, greasy, khaki-colored tunic of one of the Russian prisoners, and it took the most painstaking cunning to divest him of it, for he kicked and bit in protest. This time he had managed to gain possession of one of Papa's moth-eaten red Uhlan trousers from a storeroom upstairs. He wore these red breeches beneath his jacket, but without boots, of course, for in summer Rere is much addicted to barefoot pleasures. And this was how he entered the room, with a derby on his head, deadly serious and tiptoeing over the carpet lest he disturb someone. He came to a mannerly standstill beside Mr. Gruber, at some distance from the group which surrounded Uncle Peter. No one laughed at him, however outlandish his costume may have seemed, for there was something ghastly about his appearance, something dreadful and cruelly mocking. I began to reflect anew on Rere at that moment. Who was this human being? Was he simply a hollow and horrible caricature, or did his presence here on earth have some mysteriously meaningful message for us? I had already given this much thought. Now, as he appeared so unexpectedly in this shocking and at the same time ludicrous costume, I had a feeling that there was always an element of amazing, astonishing significance, portentous for the entire world, in Rere's every action, however senseless it might seem at first glance. Rere is unquestionably an idiot, but may there not be, in the mechanism of his understanding and of all idiots generally, a certain instinctive insight, stronger than ours and capable of grasping the covert, furtive secrets of the universe? For many of Rere's actions evince intelligence, tenderness and, often, manly chivalry. The trouble is that his love or rage is sometimes manifested in extravagant ways. Nevertheless I might even say that his deeds are frequently poetic, symbolic, admonitory and prescient. I recalled the scene of his performance in the park last year, when he amused himself by seating Ivan, a Russian prisoner, in the little red wagon to which he had harnessed himself, and I recalled the leer with which he endured the gentle, playful lashes of Ivan's whip. Everyone chuckled at the sight of him then—and since that time we've all learned a great deal more about the Russian revolution. There's been no news of Uncle Dmitri for an entire year. What has become of the Russian aristocracy?

Mr. Gruber inched Rere from the room with violent twitches of both his eyebrows. Rere complied with a mild grin, but I still had the feeling that there was some unintentional intention in his appearance—a secret of idiots. His devilish military masquerade and his naked feet seemed to tell the world: "Look at me—I'm the dissipate armed might of Germany and the Monarchy!"

I left them shortly afterwards, and didn't appear at supper either. My thoughts worked as sharply as if knives were whirling in my brain—it was the sort of headache that even the strongest pills would not relieve. I stretched out on my back at the head of the bed, with my eyes open in a rigid stare which added to my pain as they grew parched. Juan Hwang and Florian stood before me in our house on Bösendorferstrasse. My God, it was just a few weeks ago that the German comet was at its zenith, and only last April Juan Hwang and Florian were instructing me, amid entreaties and enjoinders, how to behave at Schönbrunn when the king confronted me with Uncle Cini in the matter of the Sixtus Letter. And when I returned, and when Juan Hwang sprang at me and tried to choke me! And that dreadful moment when, sprawling on the floor in fear of my life, I saw Florian's merciless, cruel, ashen face look down at me! What could I have achieved by acting on their advice? And what if I had persuaded the king to change his mind? Now that it's over I can't believe the possibility ever existed. The king would surely not have escaped with his life. Fate: the word exists, and is alive. The king now seems to me like Dhritarashtra, in the Indian epic, who ascended his throne blindly. He was constantly at the mercy of the winds, balancing on a single toe with his arms stretched to the heavens. No human agency directs our affairs. Our destiny is written in the stars. I trust but one serious science: the divination of the stars.

The dominant mood of the castle is as if one of the countless guest rooms upstairs were occupied by an unknown corpse, lying in state, a victim of murder or suicide or ptomaine poisoning who somehow belongs to the family but cannot be buried for some reason or other; and consequently the sweetish scent of death and decay, in the great heat, seeps with increasing strength through the drawn blinds. We have no way of knowing the identity of the corpse: sometimes he is called *Monarchy*, sometimes *Fatherland*, and sometimes simply *Ararat*. He lies barefoot in his coffin, in the glow of burning candles, dressed in red Uhlan breeches and a striped jacket, with side whiskers growing on a face reminiscent of Franz Joseph. I find myself completely confused by the physical structure of things and their inner meaning. Now, for the first time, I begin to understand the surrealist painting of Paul Klee, *La fuite du fantôme*, which hung over our bed on the Street of the Chanting Chicken in Geneva.

At meals the atmosphere at our usually gay and garrulous table seems to suggest that the castle and all our estates are marked for public auction a week from now, without a cent of collateral in Papa's accounts.

I alternately treat this abominable spiritual malaise of mine with doses of pills and the library. But neither one helps. Yesterday afternoon I made up a new game: I felt along the bookshelves with eyes closed, chose a book at random, opened it and placed my finger on a line of text. Then I opened my eyes and wrote the sentence down. This was my way of cross-examining the great spirits of the world. And here is the result: "The tender grace of a day that is dead will never come back to me" (Tennyson)…"To repair the irreparable ravages of time" (Racine)…"Monarchs ought to put to death the authors and investigators of war, as their sworn enemies and as dangers to their states" (Elizabeth Queen of England)…"String up the kings!" (Petöfi)…"Our revels now are ended" (Shakespeare).

I fled from the library, and from those strange ghostly voices. Passing the garages in the east wing of the castle, the gates of which still bear the ancient Renaissance ornamentation, I noticed a great black crack in the wall, like a dark blue vein in an old man's arm. The castellan happened to be going by, and he said that an architect who recently inspected the wall had discovered a dangerous shift in the ground.

Walking down by the fishpool, I found one of the swans lying under a jasmine tree. Its rigid yellow legs were fixed in a position which indicated a frantic grasp at the air and at life. Flies buzzed about the bird, and the feathers on its breast were overrun with maggots.

Apparently the world is full of pain, of cracks and maggots. We live by the grace of a happy blindness, but pupils grow out of our souls in hours of pain and panic, and with these, like cats and owls, we can see the world in darkness as it really is.

According to a report that arrived today, England has recognized Czechoslovakia as a belligerent power. This is the first official sign of the collapse of the Monarchy.

15 September

For weeks every newspaper has carried lengthy and colorful accounts of the public executions of deserters. One can sense from the style of the articles that they were written on instructions from above and are intended to serve as admonitory examples. These are those certain toothpicks with which they mean to stem the tide.

This morning a peasant woman, Mistress Lajos Ibrik by name, asked to see me. I had no idea why she wanted to see me in particular. I summoned her into my room, although I was still in bed. It is touching to see how these very poor peasant women dress when they want to put up a good front. Their heads are bound in a black silk kerchief, the single ornament of their lives. The silk kerchiefs are completely out of keeping with their plodding, earth-colored bare feet, which are coated with the dust of the highway. The village she came from was so far away that she had to set out, on foot, at midnight. I could hardly understand what she was muttering about, for she held a carefully folded clove-scented handkerchief in front of her toothless mouth and whimpered into it. Well, then, her son Laci had returned home for a little visit after a year and a half in the army, but the police nabbed him as a deserter, and now he was in great trouble indeed. She'd already been called to take leave of him. His execution was set for the day after tomorrow.

"I took the liberty of coming here," she added, "because my son Laci worked here in the bathhouse eight years ago…"

Not till then did I know whom she was talking about. Swimming Laci! Of a sudden I could see the lithe, savage animal as he dived from the high board in a graceful arc and swam under water like a seal. They say a fiery and mysterious bond links a woman to the man who takes her virginity. I've never felt anything of the sort toward that Swimming Laci. Perhaps I was too much a child. I had no idea what was happening to me there in the Chinese bathhouse.

And now, from a death cell, the unhappy boy had sent his mother to me—for he must have sent her, of course. I dressed swiftly, and an hour later I was driving toward Budapest with Papa's letter. General von Plitz-Sieburg, the present commandant of the municipal garrison who countersigns all sentences by courts-martial, was one of Papa's fellow officers in the Lebovice Uhlans. He received me very graciously, and we had a long conversation about Mozart, for he is a great music lover. I succeeded in obtaining a reprieve for poor Swimming Laci, whom the general was at first unable to locate in any of the guardhouses; he kept telephoning back and forth until I finally remembered that the prisoner's real name was László Ibrik.

22 October 1918—Budapest

Five weeks have passed since I last opened my diary. They have been dark days of lethargy, crowded with historic events and—for me—an incessantly upset-stomach. But now there is news: tomorrow the king will arrive in Hungary. He'll only be passing through Budapest on the way to Debrecen, that Rome of the Calvinists, where anti-Habsburg sentiment is strongest. This trip of his bears a dangerous resemblance to Emperor Wilhelm's hurried journey to Avenues, where he reviewed the German troops in his white cape and silver cuirass. But the magic charm has lost its force. The railwaymen in Galicia have adopted the Polish language for use on duty, and crack the skull of anyone who says a word in German. In Vienna they explain the king's journey by saying that he has fled to Hungary.

24 October

It was half a year since I had seen Juan Hwang. Today I was in the peers' gallery of the Lower House of Parliament even before the session opened, hoping he would appear at a meeting that promised to be stormy. Tension was high in the great gold and red chamber when the meeting was called to order. One could hardly hear the speakers for all the shouting. Juan Hwang was nowhere to be seen on the packed floor, but later the president called his name. He sat on the left of the House, surprisingly enough. His smart, lean figure inclined slightly forward as he leaned on his two fists. His glossy black hair tumbled over his forehead like a black flame. His voice was clear and metallic, although it contained no suggestion of rhetorical irony or persuasive eloquence—for this

199

very reason it had a declarative air. Tragic, commanding and almost surpassingly sad, his tone compelled a deep silence in a matter of seconds. He said things like this:

"Let us remain calm at this most catastrophic moment in our nation's history. The government which sold Hungary to the Germans must resign at once. We must come to a decision in the suit which has prevailed between Austria and Hungary for the past four hundred years. It is our duty to break with Austria at once and dethrone the Habsburgs. Hungarian troops must lay down their arms without a moment's delay!"

He said that much and sat down, visibly as exhausted as if he had poured out his whole soul with those words. After his speech the silence lasted only as long as it takes a spark to creep from the end of a fuse to the dynamite. Then the assembly hall suddenly turned into a madhouse. The president's bell vainly sought to quell the uproar. The president descended from the high rostrum as a sign that the session was closed. The deputies swarmed toward the exits.

I was swept out into the corridor, too, but I couldn't find Juan Hwang. It was almost as if he had been a disembodied voice during the meeting itself, a moving, human expression of the East, which was demanding the restitution of its hapless children, the Magyars, who had mistakenly found themselves on the German side.

I ran downstairs to the main cloakroom and asked if Deputy Juan Hwang had left. They said he had not. I waited for an hour and a half, until I could hardly stand on my feet any longer. The deputies began to leave for home in large and small groups. But there was no sign of Juan Hwang.

31 October

Terror entered the town about midnight, in a sloppy, black autumnal rain. None of us at Septemvir Utca went to bed. All night long we listened to the distant rifle-fire, which sometimes subsided and then broke out again elsewhere, foreboding in its very faintness. So this is what revolution is like. Papa smoked one cigarette after the other, although I'd never before seen him smoke anything but a cigar. György still held a pine cone he brought from Ararat, which for months has seemed to be grown to his hand. He kept turning it, busy with his thoughts. Mamma sat in an armchair beside the great white fireplace, lost in the folds of her mallow-colored dress, resting her cheek on a forefinger. Now, as always, she was as beautiful as a painting. All at once, in the midst of a long silence, she unexpectedly asked: "Was ist ein Tank eigentlich?"—as if the answer to that question would solve every mystery of life and the world for her. But no answer was forthcoming. At midnight, after a prolonged and violent burst of rifle-fire, she stood up and summoned all the members of the staff, marvelously preserving her pictorial composure. Her soft voice directed the packing of trunks, with attention for every item. A few moments later the many rooms were full of suitcases and trunks whose open mouths engulfed the jewelry boxes, the gold tableware, the furs and all the things that were most inclined to flee. Mamma wants to leave tomorrow for Willensdorf, in Austria, to one of the smaller Schäyenheim hunting lodges. Papa still has not decided. I looked into Zia's room, and saw her sleeping the deep, clear sleep of a child. A boarlike snoring resounded from Rere's room. My twelve-year-old brother János sprang from bed at the sound of gunfire and stood by the open window. When I entered, his first question was, "Where's the hunt?" and "What are they hunting?"

What is ahead of us in the dawn and the coming day? I know that Papa, Mamma and György, like myself, are constantly thinking of Uncle Dmitri's last letter, in which he gave details of the execution of the tsar's family in the cellar of the house in Ekaterinburg. He even wrote that the little tsarevitch, when his father carried him down to the cellar, asked: "Where are we going, Papa?" And at the last moment his father held up a blanket to ward off the bullets.

We're unacquainted with revolution, and for the moment we've nothing to defend ourselves with but our fear.

Later: As dawn approached the firing increased. At eight o'clock it was as thick and heavy as sleet. But news came that the soldiers were firing into the air without harming anyone. At this György and I took our courage in hand and went into town. We went on foot, György in his battle cape and I in my grayest Red Cross uniform. At the Suspension Bridge we met Uncle Lajos, whom I had never before seen walking in the street. The collar of his overcoat was turned up to his eyes, and as he hurried by he answered our greeting by closing his eyes and whispering nothing more than: "Dreadful…"

The street was jammed with every man, woman and child in town, and they were all drunk to a pitch of drunkenness which I had never seen before. Women, their hair in disarray, emitted curious moans as they threw their arms around the necks of the policemen's horses, which bobbed in the thick human flood and only occasionally raised their frothing manes above the brown torrent. The crowd seemed to have broken from the pavement like a water main. But it was not an alcoholic intoxication, rather the ecstasy of liberation. The people were dancing like howling dervishes about the corpse of war. Singing soldiers rolled by in overloaded trucks, aimlessly firing their rifles at the gray clouds as if in observance of a mechanized pagan ceremonial with the rites of which no one was familiar. There were masses of flowers, the final, simple white flowers of fall, which had come to the market for All Soul's Day tomorrow but were now strewn in a floral shower at the hands of the people. Rain was falling, mud and mire were everywhere, and as they pelted each other with flowers, and pelted the policemen's horses and the trucks, it seemed as if the black mud were turning into a white flower bed. Strangers rushed at each other, shouting, shook one another's shoulders and exchanged tearful kisses. György's face was pale as he gripped my arm firmly in the crush and whispered, "Wonderful!" Evidently the appraisal of revolution does not vary with one's social class but is a question of age. When we reached the square an unshaven soldier in a muddy cape and with his cap askew suddenly confronted György, holding an open pocketknife, and its whitely flashing blade lunged for György's jugular vein. But instead of piercing his neck it slid under the stitches of his insignia of rank. During the course of the operation the soldier leered broadly into György's face, and the whole thing seemed as if, with the officer's stars, he were cutting a cancer from György's flesh.

The rain stopped on our way back, but ink-colored clouds covered the sky, and although the Garrison church was ringing noon it was as dark as dusk outside. A number of open trucks rumbled by as we walked along the quay. They were full of troops too, but these neither sang nor fired their rifles. They stood erect in the open vehicles, with their fists thrust into the pockets of their capes. They were mute, devoid of all delight, and their faces seemed pitiless, as if some strange and menacing intent were driving them. Florian's face was in the first truck that whirled by. The pinched, ashen face was petrified to the point of immobility. It almost seemed as if he were leading the entire progress. But the trucks flew by so rapidly, thundering as they went, that I hadn't time to wave. And perhaps it wasn't he after all.

1 November

Papa and Uncle Fini have just returned from the royal palace in Gödöllő. They say little, but even from their few words I can sense that the anxiety and turmoil must be very great down there. The king is conferring with former cabinet ministers and unknown, muddy characters who happen in from the street. He's completely lost his head, and is frantically distributing commands, entreaties and decorations. Papa was awarded the Order of the Golden Fleece. The king granted the title of Prince to Uncle Fini, forgetting that Uncle Fini's ancestors were born princes for the last seven generations. Uncle Fini is visibly downcast by it all. Revolution has already broken out in Vienna as well.

This afternoon it was reported that the king would leave for Vienna on the afternoon train. The queen and the children will stay in Gödöllö for the moment, lest the king's departure be taken for flight. Austria, after all, promises the greater stability.

20 November 1918–Upper Austria

It's seven in the evening, and every window of our sleeping compartment is curtained. The king and queen occupy the first compartment. The queen is expecting her sixth child. The king is wearing the same civilian suit he wore in the apartment on Blaue Lampe Strasse. His emaciated face seems even smaller above that badly cut, loose suit. He rests his two palms on his knees and stares into space. The next three compartments are assigned to the five youngsters and the nurse who has charge of them. The rest of the compartments are for the retinue and the servants. I'm in the same compartment with Countess M., one of the ladies-in-waiting. We're on the way to a private castle in Eckartsau, on the remote approaches of the North Danubian slopes.

The train has been at a standstill on the open tracks for more than half an hour. The reason for the delay is that the Socialist workingmen in a near-by industrial town learned of the flight of the royal family, seized the railroad station and are unwilling to let the train pass. Louis XVI of France was similarly detained by the postmaster at Varennes. Our train left Vienna without commotion, though not in secret. The mood of the Viennese resembled the mood that prevailed in Paris during the great French Revolution: they were ready to flog anyone who harmed the king, and to kill anyone who cheered him.

Finally Baron K. returned after consultation with the local mayor. He brought bad news, which he hardly wanted to communicate to the king. The mayor had no armed force whatever at his disposal to restrain the workers. Baron K. turned to me with the thought that it might be better to try to reason with them. The words of a disinterested woman can be greatly helpful at such a time.

We set out in the mayor's car, which was waiting alongside the tracks. It was no more than six miles to the station, where a mob of thousands of workingmen was milling. But more and more kept coming, and the newcomers carried posters with the inscription: "Death to Charles! Tod dem Kaiser!" We struggled through the rain-drenched mob and directed our steps toward the baggage room, where the leaders of the workers had set up headquarters. We found three men in the poorly illuminated little room; I was dumbfounded to see that one of them was Florian. He wore a belt over an oil-spotted raincoat, with a large revolver in a leather holster. My heart began to beat faster, and I furtively indicated to Baron K. that I'd found a good friend. I touched Florian's shoulder as he was talking to the other two men, whereupon he turned his head toward me. But his face reflected nothing of my smile. It was the same pinched, wan face, but as he coldly fixed his yellowish-blue eyes on me he seemed a total stranger.

"May I speak to you for a moment?"

"What would you like?" he said impatiently, without moving. It was the same man I had known in Geneva, but an entirely new spirit possessed him. I explained my mission in a few mumbled words. I didn't want to speak out loud, lest the others hear, and my faint words were barely audible, for the wild tumult of the mob outside was growing stronger. Florian cut my words short:

"You know better than anyone else that the king betrayed the peace!"

"The king–"

"Please, there's nothing more to say!"

He turned his back on me and continued the discussion with his companions. They retired to a distance of several feet and brought their heads together. I wanted to approach him again, but someone grasped my arm and pulled me away. It was the mayor. He summoned me with his eyes and headed for the door. While we broke a path toward the car through the crowd, he whispered into my ear, still holding my arm:

"There's no time to lose. Their mood is growing uglier by the minute. The train had best return to the next station, where it can switch to another line and reach Eckartsau that way, even if it means a detour."

He was a white-complexioned, blue-eyed Austrian with side whiskers, of the old school that remained loyal to the emperor.

Later: I don't know what was discussed at the next station, but at about nine o'clock the train started through the dismal rain on a circuitous route to Eckartsau.

I sat in the corridor, on the conductor's seat. I wanted to be alone with my thoughts, for I could no longer stand Countess M.'s lamentations. Soon a bodyguard issued from one of the compartments, threw open a window and thirstily sniffed the cold, rain-scented air. In knee-high patent leather boots, with a striking uniform beneath his leopard cape, he looked like a heavy gold candlestick which the panic-stricken king might clutch as he foundered in the black surf, though it would serve only to pull him under all the more quickly.

Where were we headed, and to what end, in the black night? I began to feel a sense of infinite pity for the king. I was choked with tears as I tried to fathom the feeling that was in my heart for him.

I could clearly hear, now, the feverish, hollow beat of the Damask Drum. It was still before the war when a company of Japanese actors appeared in Vienna, and I went to all three performances for the sake of Seami's playlet. It was called *Aya No Tsuzumi*—The Damask Drum. The archaic little story told of a gardener who fell madly in love with Princess Kinomaru, and when one of the palace guards informed his lady of this the princess sent a message to the poor, lovelorn gardener, saying that a damask drum was hanging on a bough of a moon tree beside the Laurel Pool, and that she would leave the palace in secret and join him whenever he struck the drum. And at dusk the next day the gardener struck the drum. But the damask drum gave no sound, and the princess did not come. Each night the gardener struck the drum more strongly, but the damask drum remained mute. On the last day he beat the drum in a wild frenzy till dawn, when his strength gave out, and then, in a fit of desperate sorrow, he threw himself into the pool and died.

The rain was beating against the windows with increasing fury. I could recall the little play so clearly—the birdlike chirping of the actors, the noiseless tread of their felt-soled shoes, the princess's white face and almond eyes beneath the parasol of colored paper, the curious sets and the accompaniment of a hidden harp! While the train was hurtling toward Eckartsau, I closed my eyes and let my fancy feast on the remembered loveliness.

The door of another compartment opened and the nurse stepped out. As she sidestepped the bodyguard who was thirstily gulping the air, the two little white chamber pots which served the physical needs of the royal children flashed beneath her robe. She disappeared in the direction of the washroom.

The rain and the wheels of the train were humming softly now, almost silently, and the sounds wrought a change in me. I seemed to be the one who was beating the damask drum, with desperate, suicidal fervor.

But the king did not hear. He still sat motionlessly in his compartment, resting his two hands on his knees and staring impassively into space.

Chapter Eight

AFTER a silence of nearly five months, I'm impelled to make a note about my diary itself. On my tenth birthday I resolved to keep a daily record of important events. This was the first entry: "Mam'selle Barbier wore a mauve blouse today. Papa lit a cigar at five after four this afternoon. György went after a crow in the park with his new shotgun, but missed." And so on. Years later I paged through the half-finished diary because Dr. Freyberger wanted to know when I had my first attack of peritonitis and when I was operated. But the diary was discreetly silent on that point.

Right now I have the same feeling about the months which have remained blank in my diary since the flight to Eckartsau. The collapse of the Monarchy, followed by our own "Kerensky Revolution," then the rise to power of the Hungarian Commune—all, for some reason, have escaped the notice of my journal. It may be that in certain respects diaries are like living things, with the habits of trees, which sometimes fail to blossom. Perhaps they're at rest, or waiting for mysterious signs from storm and soil.

We've been here at Willensdorf since February, with two dogs and only the most essential staff. My parents didn't cross the frontier till March, after the outbreak of the Commune; Mamma was dressed as a peasant woman, Papa as a chimneysweep. Practically everyone in our set fled to the West. By now we've all learned that Bolshevik is nothing like shashlik, and bears no resemblance whatever to slices of mutton grilled on a spit. But as for what the Bolsheviks are doing in Russia and what their aims are, no one hereabouts has any idea. From time to time Mamma unexpectedly asks, "Was ist ein Bolshevik eigentlich?"— but no one ventures to reply.

The hunting lodge at Willensdorf has a slight smell of rats, but at least we're safe here. I've been reading a considerable number of historical works in connection with my Ordony novel, and so I know that for the past fifteen hundred years these high Austrian Alps have borne the brunt of the vast waves which have invaded Europe like a torrential flood from the endless Asiatic plains between the Caspian Sea and the forest belts of Siberia. Now they have inundated the Hungarian lowlands once more, as in the time of the Völkerwanderungen, and later the Tatar, Kuman and Turkish invasions. One of the waves of the present flood has splashed as far as Bavaria, where the Communists have also seized power.

The royal family is in Switzerland, in a safe place in Prangins. At the moment that's all I know of them.

Willensdorf is two hours by auto from Vienna, and so we often go to town. Only the main floor of our house on Bösendorferstrasse is open. It would be dangerous to hire new servants. The very concept of a trustworthy new footman has vanished since the revolutions began. A former colonel who found it impossible to collect his pension asked Papa to take him on as a valet. Papa brushed off his request by saying that he trained his valets to be colonels but did not care to train colonels to be valets.

Events have wrought an incredible change in every phase of one's way of life. Every word, every idea, every truth has changed in meaning. Yesterday Baron K. told me he'd been a most conservative man all his life—he even used shaving cream sparingly—while his brother Alfred ran through his share of their patrimony in a few short years. Alfred gave big dinners, and drank three bottles of French champagne a day even when alone. The situation at present is that Baron K. hasn't a cent to his name, having lost his fortune in war bonds, whereas Alfred is living in high style because his valet made a practice of storing empty champagne bottles in the attic and consequently accumulated a twenty-year supply. One gets an unbelievably high price for old champagne bottles with well-known labels in Vienna today. They are filled with spurious liquors and sold at fantastic rates in night clubs to the new *Schiebers,* the profiteers who are riding the crest of inflation. According to Baron K., his brother Alfred's case is the best possible comment on the economic structure of postwar Europe.

One has to step cautiously on the sidewalks of Vienna to avoid treading on the outstretched wooden legs of the disabled veterans who sit by the walls. They hawk their goods in faint voices: shoelaces and flints. They remind me, somehow, of the refuse bins in military hospitals, filled with amputated limbs and bandages brown with blood and pus.

21 April—Vienna

This morning I had a premonition that something very important would happen. Dark vernal rain clouds covered the sky, but the rays of the sun broke through the cloud openings in broad, golden-lilac sheaves. Boucher painted a landscape like this, with a lightning-blasted tree stump in the foreground, of which I'm very fond. Such strange displays of the weather always augur something of significance for me.

I left the Stefanskirche at about noon after praying for a long while, for today was the first anniversary of that great, fateful scene in Schönbrunn when the king repudiated the Sixtus Letter in Uncle Cini's presence. Good Lord, was it only a year ago? How much has happened in the course of a single year! A wagon heavily laden with bricks was creaking through the square in front of the church. Two white Lipican horses of the most noble stock were pulling the wagon, two beauties with arched necks, long tails and rosy nostrils which made it impossible not to recognize them as horses from the royal stables. A year ago they were hitched to the carriage of the emperor, perhaps, or of one of the archdukes.

I was on the way to the Graben when I suddenly saw Juan Hwang approaching in conversation with two other men. He recognized me, looked at me and said nothing. But his glance said more than any greeting. I walked on without looking back, and stopped by the great baroque pillar which commemorates the plague. I knew he would come. And come he did, a few minutes later. He stepped close to me, took my hand, looked deep into my eyes and said quietly:

"Will you have dinner with me? That's a beautiful hat you're wearing."

This was the extent of our reconciliation. As simple and as shattering as that.

Men—listen! Beat a woman, stamp on her with your heels, but when you're once seized with a fiery desire for forgiveness don't kneel before her, don't weep and wail—simply tell her, casually, without a hint of flattery: "That's a beautiful hat you're wearing."

You cannot frame an apology in more meaningful words. Not because women are vain and foolish, no. But there is nothing lovelier, more dramatic, than a dramatic scene unperformed. Lessing put it this way: "True dramatic dialogue is the art of omission."

5 June 1919

The tempo of life has quickened in our Bösendorferstrasse house. Papa confers with financial and political bigwigs behind closed doors, in daily anticipation of the fall of the Hungarian Commune. Mamma stages elaborate tea parties, which are occasionally distinguished by deadly dull recitations. News of the outside world flows into our house by way of Switzerland, and we've already re-established contact with the royal family as well, if only by mail. Our legitimist circles are hard at work. We have news of Ararat fairly often too. Most interesting of all, to me, is that the People's Commissar at Ararat is Lászlo Ibrik, alias Swimming Laci. I'm twenty-three now, so he must be at least twenty-seven. They say he's behaving in a most insolent fashion. His first move, when he occupied the castle "in the name of the people," was to demand striped trousers and a monocle, for he wanted to dress like a count. I take a different view of the motives of his behavior, to be sure. I wonder what picture he has of me in his imagination, and what I mean to him? According to the reports he walks back and forth in the rooms all day, plays billiards by himself, strums on the piano with one finger for hours, has the table set for himself alone in the great dining hall and is served by three footmen, eats roast duck with red cabbage at every meal and throws the bones on the carpet behind him. To my way of thinking, these are all variations on the theme of unrequited love in a hopeless heart.

1 August 1919

The Hungarian Commune has fallen. Like a pacified flood, the spiritual influx that broke from the East has retired to its Asiatic riverbed. Pacified? For those who take it so. Fortunately we've managed to come through swimmingly.

We're rushing back to Willensdorf to pack our trunks.

Our exile is over.

3 August—Ararat

We arrived yesterday afternoon, and today the past already seems like a bad dream from which we have just awakened. The familiar faces of the old servants in the rooms and along the corridors, the liveries of old, the black frock coats of the footmen, the chambermaids in light blue. And the Russian prisoners who used to mow the lawns are gone from the park. Mamma assembled the servants for roll call: only one of them, a footman called Józsi, became a Communist, and he landed an important position in Budapest. I remember his longish face well. Monsieur Cavaignac is missing, and Mr. Johnson the English stablemaster, and Mam'selle Barbier and Miss Wenlock. But we brought a piece of the West back with us in the person of Zia's new French governess, Madame Couteaux. She's an amusing old harridan.

I hear that Swimming Laci escaped to Russia.

8 September

In 1871, after the failure of the short-lived French Revolution, fashionable Frenchwomen used the tips of their umbrellas to poke out the eyes of captured Communards. Public opinion here in Hungary has been possessed by a similar hysteria. Eagle-plumed counterrevolutionary officers patrol the highways. Yesterday they captured József, the footman, and shot him in his tracks. Juan Hwang, who's been visiting here at Ararat for the past few days, says these patrolling officers express the mood of all Europe. French and British troops have landed at Archangel, while from Poland Russian counterrevolutionary generals with British arms are advancing toward the Ukraine to suppress Bolshevism.

In the evenings Papa sits on the bank of the fishpool, and it is clear to see that he is perpetually reflecting on the future of the world, something he never used to do before. He's already fifty-one years old, and his hair has begun to turn silvery gray at his temples. Yesterday I settled down beside him and tried to divine his thoughts. He pensively scratched the bristles of his mustache, which has turned into a thick English mustache in the course of time, with the crippled stump of his left forefinger, and his impassive eyes watched the opalescent reflection of the summer twilight in the lilied mirror of the pool. He was always fond of these twilight hours. Now he was back, and everything was the same as before. The fishpool was the same, though covered with water lilies, for it is one of the less attractive characteristics of revolution that its adherents neglect to clean such fishpools properly and efficiently. Once the water lily has taken root, its extermination is almost impossible. The mucous, lacy, gray-green leaves covered the mirror of the pool like a torn, jagged tablecloth on a wide, brightly varnished table. The pool, clear as crystal, was arrayed in revolting rags. Papa felt that the whole world was somehow like that. He was in the grip of a feeling that had no substance, had nothing but an unusually low temperature. The cold sensation around his heart was a very delicate fear, one of the violet-hued nuances of the fear of death. It was the sort of fear that manifests itself in short, unexpected twinges while a man shaves in the bathroom, or between two spoonfuls of soup, or during a game of cards, makes its presence known by unprovoked and eccentric apparitions, gentle and momentary little contacts, mysterious winks of the eye as if in encouragement of an awareness of its constant and close proximity. Papa did not fear his own death; he is too brave, too cynical, too much a Catholic for that. He feared the death of a way of life, which cannot precisely be called the death of the aristocracy. And in the destruction of this way of life he saw the loss of his own children, whom

211

he considers neither wise nor strong enough to hold their own in the new shape of things. This was what Papa felt, faintly and yet clearly, as he scratched the bristles of his mustache. The pool was empty. The park was empty. The whole country was empty. And the firmament above was empty. It lacked a king.

18 November 1919—Budapest

Social life at our house on Septemvir Utca has never been so active, perhaps, as it is nowadays. Mamma gives tea parties for a hundred or a hundred and fifty guests almost every day, partly in the interest of all sorts of institutions for war orphans and disabled veterans, and partly for Catholic and legitimist purposes. It is not the personages themselves but their purses that she invites to these charity teas. But purses usually don't care to venture out alone, unfortunately, and so their proprietors come too. Consequently the company at these teas is very mixed. The so-called *nouveaux riches* are there, whose hands are thicker and redder than those of employees in the downtown section before the war, in London's City or in the old Hanseatic towns, while their refinement is correspondingly thinner. They eye the art treasures in the Septemvir Utca house with glances which suggest a sense of personal insult. One woman went so far as to comment:

"I'm dickering right now for a painting by Raphael, the famous German artist. Kornstein, on Váci Utca, wants one hundred twenty thousand Swiss francs for it."

Her daughter, seated at her side, retorted with a frown of disdainful annoyance: "How can you be so silly, Mamma? Kornstein's shop isn't on Váci Utca!"

Newly formed political groups and secret military societies of every sort are introducing anti-Semitism into Hungary as diligently as the cultivation of potatoes was encouraged in the eighteenth century. Wealthy Jews are thronging to the protection of the Catholic Church, and at the same time they mount inordinately extravagant dinners, with mock turtle soup, caviar and Chinese sparrows' nests, always trying to have a bishop or so among the guests. In this capacity Uncle Zsigmond, too, was present at such a dinner in the interest of the legitimist cause. The mistress of the house, a recent convert to the Church, smiled her most beautiful smile as she raised her glass to him with the toast: "Long live Jesus Christ!"

10 December—Vienna

I've been in Vienna for several days, in need of a real rest after the rigors of

Septemvir Utca. I rather like the quiet elegance of the house on Bösendorferstrasse, with the mute memories that walk its rooms. It was time to leave Budapest, if only because Mamma wants at any cost to marry me off to one of my cousins. Apart from the fact that he strikes me as homosexual, my instincts are firmly opposed to the *Insucht* of aristocracy.

I was at the Opera with Juan Hwang on Saturday. They were playing *Die Tote Stadt*. Could the title have been chosen by pure chance? Vienna is truly a dead city—the great decapitated head of the Monarchy, no longer linked to its trunk and to the limbs which live and move by themselves. Its blood circulation is truly amazing. During the Commune it was packed with fleeing aristocrats, and now with fleeing Communists.

But this decapitated head can still laugh heartily. Yesterday we went to a little cabaret where the entire audience—myself among them—laughed itself silly over a skit called "Napoleon's Umbrella." It dealt with the fact that the *nouveaux riches* of today will buy any old moth-eaten thing if they can be persuaded that it is an antique. A salesman offered Napoleon's umbrella for sale, not knowing it was the customer's own which had been placed on the counter and was accidentally mixed in with the saleable stock. After the performance, when we were having supper at a restaurant, Juan Hwang, who always thinks along broad, encompassing lines, launched into the following analysis:

"Two things characterize the mentality of Europe today. The gray suede gloves, for one, which Clemenceau is absolutely unwilling to remove at whatever conference; and Lloyd George's latest speech. Lloyd George asserted that Europe has arrived at a major crossroad, and must decide between free enterprise and Communism. He cast his lot with free enterprise, but went on to say that if private capital continued in its unprincipled attitude toward the misery of the laborer and the passionate, hopeless desire of so many millions of unemployed for work, then the system, in his view, was bound to collapse for its own lack of conscience. Everyone understood and agreed with this position, but promptly forgot his qualification. The world is full of unemployed and dissatisfied workingmen. Opposing them are those who buy or sell Napoleon's umbrella. Private capital has started a shameless round of speculation. There is an incredible shortage of housing in England, but it's impossible to undertake any construction because speculators have inflated the price of building materials. And as far as the price of basic commodities is concerned the same situation prevails everywhere. The war produced various sorts of rationing and price control agencies—in Hungary we had the War Production Agency, and the Coal Distribution Board, and the Clothing Central—but speculators quickly undermined the fundamental structure of such an incipient collectivist economy, viewing it as a dangerous form of competition. They forced the government to withdraw to its police stations, schoolrooms, revenue bureaus and hymnals. Shoe leather met the first stirrings of collectivism in open conflict, and shoe leather proved the stronger. The future of Europe, and of international affairs as well, is in the hands of a stupid, grasping bourgeoisie. Clemenceau's gray suede gloves are indicative of Europe's reluctance to shed certain of her moldy ideological trappings."

A policeman, dressed in a spinach-green uniform and a flat vizored cap, passed our table. Juan Hwang pointed at the officer with a wave of his thumb:

"The new uniforms of the Viennese police were the gift of a *Schieber* who belongs in prison."

When we asked for the check the headwaiter, who has known me for a long time, inquired after Papa and Mamma. But he no longer addressed me as Countess. The Socialist Government of Vienna has forbidden the use of aristocratic titles. But it's all in vain, for people are fond of titles. In 1789, when the United States elected its first president, the senate wanted to give George Washington the title of "His Highness." Washington expressed a preference for "His Mightiness."

3 January 1920

We spent the holidays very quietly. I always shiver on New Year's Day, and my teeth chatter as if I had dipped my feet into an invisible and ice-cold sea.

We've had news of a death at home. Everyone is alike at birth, and dissimilar in death. The circumstances of a man's death reveal his occupation, his character, his entire personality. He falls on the battlefield: a soldier. She drinks lye: a lovelorn little servant girl. Shot while trying to escape: a burglar. Heart failure: a bank director. Thrown from a horse while taking a jump: my grandmother.

Grandmamma Jefi died yesterday, of a broken back. She was sixty-five. By way of punishment Papa shot the horse called "Lightning," which seems hardly fair, for Papa always hated his mother-in-law while she was alive.

26 June 1920—Ararat

Diary, wake from your rosy dreams: black banners flutter at the towers of the castle, and the balconies are draped in black. They have signed a peace treaty in Trianon which has bereft our thousand-year-old land of two-thirds of its territory. Papa wept when the news came. I saw similar emotions on the faces of the peasants. Only in the extremity of pain is a people truly united.

The proportions of our estates, in a reduced country, seem even larger. This is a rather frightening feeling. György probably had this in mind when the two of us were sitting in the park on the marble bench, ornamented with Empire wreaths, where Grandmamma Jefi used to sit in silent dignity after she had quarreled with Papa. György is already twenty-two, and is attending technical school. He's the first Dukay who's ever sought a degree in agricultural science. And he also wants to study law and political economy, preferably abroad. There have been members of our family who collected Brazilian butterflies, riding crops or tufts of women's hair. György is the first with a passion for collecting degrees. From some words he's let drop I can see he has great plans for the time when the entail will become his, but he never talks to Papa about them. Father and son: two entirely different worlds. György is now at the transitional age "when regrets come to resemble hopes and hopes are beginning to resemble regrets," as Turgeniev says in his *Fathers and Sons*.

A sultry summer calm prevailed as we wordlessly watched the mourning-draped castle. The banners dangled languidly, motionlessly. But all at once a breeze stirred, the desperate, dust-filled herald of a summer shower, the boughs began to buzz, the banners came to life in the twinkling of an eye, their black stuff fluttered with wild furor in the wind, the drapes on the balconies began to flutter and snap like great witches' wings, fugitive and fearful. The violent burst of wind swept not only leaves and broken flowers on high—it also stirred the sorrows inside of me. Words, images, voices whirled in inner turmoil, and when a flash of memory recalled the picture of the two white horses from the royal stables as they pulled the brick-laden wagon with strained sinews, I began to weep aloud. Sobs shook me so convulsively that György was impelled to take me in his arms. When he asked why I was crying, I couldn't tell him it was because of the two white horses, for this would surely have sounded completely stupid at that moment.

7 September 1920

Feri Kontyos, the son of the estate blacksmith, stood at the very spot in the salon downstairs where the large military map used to hang: after five years in a prisoner-of-war camp, he had just returned from Tashkent with a Russian wife and two children. Their train managed to cross the hunger-stricken areas only because they filled the coal tender with bread and tossed loaves to the starving hordes which tried to stop the train by force of arms. During his imprisonment he worked as a stonemason in Tashkent, and he says the Russians are very kind people. This was meant in part for his wife too, who stood speechlessly because she doesn't know a word of Hungarian, She's a simple little blond woman with a heart-shaped face and two frightened blue eyes which she kept closing from time to time, as if dazzled by the furnishings of the castle, by Papa's giant cigar and Uncle Fini's snow-white spats.

A great discussion of Russia began after they left. Uncle Peter was present too, as well as Dr. Kliegl, whom Mamma brought from Vienna as a tutor for János. The discussion led nowhere, but I was particularly struck by what Uncle Peter said, for he likes to take a scholarly, dispassionate view of things. He delivered a veritable little lecture on the theme that the World War should have been considered a divine admonition, a warning that Europe must inspect and overhaul the laws by which men live in community. Instead, Europe has been satisfied with a few inane peace treaties and the dominion of profiteers who are compromising the principle of free enterprise once and for all. Europe has ceded the opportunity for great and altruistic experiment to the Russians. But instead of saying, "Look, children, you have an immense and backward country, it's very right for you to test something entirely new on your own skins, we'll watch you and help you and we'll see what's to be done if something worthwhile comes of this dangerous experiment"—instead of saying this, Europe sent French and British troops to beat out the brains of the experimenters. And when they saw the streetlamps sprawled across the sidewalks in St. Petersburg, when they saw that the shops were closed and that the people were wearing bark sandals instead of shoes, they said: "It's a shame to waste gunpowder, this Communist system will collapse of its own accord in a few weeks"—and they withdrew their troops.

"Es war die grösste Blödheit! The very height of stupidity!" Uncle Fini interrupted with an impassioned outcry. "As long as they were there, half a company of British soldiers could have taken care of that handful of Jewish Communists, and Europe would not be in such a state of tension now."

Uncle Fini sprang from his seat, raised his clenched thumb and forefinger on high and exclaimed with oratorical fervor, carving out every word:

216

"Nothing exacts a greater revenge than a job of work half finished!"

Then, like someone who has hit the nail on the head, he threw himself back on the couch and wrapped himself in his extremities, crossing his knees with decision and folding his arms over his chest as well.

"I'm not debating that point right now," Uncle Peter continued in a gray tone, "but the landings at Archangel and the support of the counterrevolutionary Russian generals achieved one end alone. They convinced the Russian people and their leaders that Europe is their deadly enemy. And consider the present starvation. You heard what the Kontyos boy said. And I've heard from other sources, too, that the starving people have been eating grass and dirt in their agony, and have even torn corpses from their graves. Never before in all history has there been such a drought. It's said that thirty million people have perished from hunger. At the same time Europe's granaries are stuffed with wheat. The world has never been so devoid of brotherly love and humanity as it is now. Only the Quakers have sought to help. Europe has let the Russians know that there is no mercy for them from the West."

At this point, when Kliegl began an elaborate and windy oration on the differences between Eastern and Western culture, I left the discussion. Later Mamma also crossed over into the little salon and didn't notice I was there. She began arranging her porcelains and talking to herself, as she always does. Suddenly she set down the Copenhagen goose in her hand and asked the little porcelain figure, raising her two palms: "Was ist ein Bolshevik eigentlich?"

9 October

Papa was completely beside himself when he returned from hunting today. He'd been hunting on the farm from which the new Czechoslovakian border has cut eight thousand acres. He fired at a rabbit, and it's common knowledge that a rabbit usually makes one long, final hop when it is shot in the neck while on the run. This rabbit tumbled over the new boundary line. A nearby Czech frontier guard ran up and collared it at once. A great argument broke out over the right of possession. The frontier guard claimed the rabbit as Czechoslovakian property. Papa maintained, however, that the rabbit had started its leap on Hungarian soil, had received the fatal shot on Hungarian soil and was carried across the border only by the force of gravity. They almost fired on each other in the heat of argument. Papa is in a rage and says he will take the case to the International Court at The Hague.

One of the new national frontiers runs right through the middle of a billiard table in a little provincial café.

1 January 1921—Budapest
Again a new year. Brr!

6 February
Empty days. Such empty days are like the corpses of people who commit suicide for reasons unknown.

Thank God Monsieur Cavaignac is back and looks none the worse for wear. He gets together with the rest of the servants each evening and fights the war over again in his atrocious Hungarian. Mr. Johnson, too, has been back for the past six months. He was awarded a medal for valor under fire, but he doesn't say a word about his war experiences.

19 March—Vienna
I'm going to be twenty-five this year. Historians refer to this span of time as a quarter of a century. Appalling thought.

24 March
Today makes two weeks since we came to Vienna. We returned from the Opera at about eleven tonight. We made a supper of cold chicken and Juan Hwang went right to bed because he was very tired. I wrote two letters, to Mamma and Zia. It's a bad habit of mine to prefer to write letters in bed, first because it gives me a backache, second because I've ruined several blankets by spilling whole bottles of ink. It was not quite midnight when my chambermaid Margaret entered in a fright and said a man wanted to see me about a very urgent matter. She said he looked something like a detective. I sent word that I'd gone to bed and he was to return tomorrow. Margaret came back with the news that the individual wouldn't go away and said he was from Schönbrunn. At that I sprang from bed. Good Lord, the ink! The word "Schönbrunn" moved me like a magic charm. Could it be Oscar? Was Oscar alive? If not Oscar, it was still a messenger from the king, certainly.

In slippers and dressing gown I dashed into the corridor, which was only faintly lighted by now. A bearded man was waiting for me, his face half covered by large leather-rimmed motoring goggles. He held a smallish suitcase in his hand. He didn't move, whereupon I stepped closer to him. I recognized the greenish-gray cloth of his suit. The king!

He slipped the goggles over his head, but still did not remove the beard. He pressed a forefinger to his lips and looked around timidly.

"I've just arrived in secret from Switzerland. Who are your guests? Am I safe here?"

"There's only one guest in the house, Your Majesty, and you can trust him."

"Who is the guest?"

"Juan Hwang."

He began to search his memory.

"Yes, I remember…the deputy who proposed my dethronement in Parliament. Won't he betray me?"

"No, Your Majesty. I'll stake my life on it."

"The servants?"

"Only my chambermaid is in the house. And the doorman downstairs. We can trust them both."

Thereupon the king took off his beard and pocketed it.

"Later on I'd like to talk with your guest too. I like to see my noteworthy enemies face to face."

I led him into the drawing room, where he threw himself into an armchair wearily.

He placed the cheap little fiberboard suitcase on the floor beside him. His shoes were dusty, his suit wrinkled, his face unshaven.

"Dear Kristina," he said with a friendly and somewhat embarrassed smile, "above everything else, I'm hungry."

"Would Your Majesty like to wash in the meantime?" The king examined his soiled hands with care. "Well, it wouldn't do me any harm. I traveled third class. My name, moreover, is Charles Ringl, and I'm a tailor's assistant by trade. I'll tell you why later. Can you put me up for the night? Or rather: are you brave enough to put me up? If the Socialists of Vienna learn I'm here, you might get into trouble."

I took his little suitcase in hand and led the king toward one of the guest rooms. We had quite a tussle over the question of carrying the suitcase. He won in the end. While the king changed I saw to the preparation of his supper. I roused Juan Hwang from a deep sleep.

"The king is here!"

"I know," he said. He closed his eyes and went back to sleep. I shook him again.

"Wake up! The king is here!"

"Which king? Franz Joseph?"

I threw a glass of water in his face.

"Get dressed at once. He wants to speak with you."

I pulled his covers off and helped him dress, meanwhile telling him the details of the king's arrival. His befogged face gradually came to life, but he still kept trying to slip his jacket over a pajama coat.

I hurried back to the drawing room where, to my greatest surprise, the king was waiting in the full uniform of a field marshal, with all his decorations. He was freshly shaved, and gold spurs jingled on his patent leather boots. The little suitcase had worked wonders. I could only explain his quick change with the thought that he didn't want to meet a Hungarian politician of the Opposition while dressed as a shop boy. The marshal's uniform wrought a change in his tone, his gestures, his expression.

"Now I can tell you," he said with a smile, "why I chose the trade of tailor's assistant. When the customs guards opened my suitcase at the Swiss frontier I had to be able to offer some sort of explanation for the uniform."

The supper which Margaret wheeled in on a little table would have been entirely suitable for a tailor's assistant, but it seemed altogether scanty in view of the marshal's uniform. Cold chicken, salad, cake, compote, and a bottle of wine.

"Splendid!" the king exclaimed, and addressed himself to the food wolfishly. I had ordered Margaret not to look at the guest while serving supper. She made every effort to comply, and this lent her eyeballs the rigidity of a painted doll's. Occasionally, however, her rigid eyes darted like lightning toward the king, as if Margaret's glance had been made of rubber and could be snapped back and forth. And her fixed eyes filled with terror almost to the point of weeping, as if they had glimpsed a ghost come home.

In her presence the king conversed in English, which he speaks with a strong Viennese accent. His *i*'s sounded like Austrian eggs: *Ei.* His *v*'s tended to become *f*'s.

"I'm faced with a crucial decision," said the king, struggling with a drumstick. "I want to leave for Hungary tomorrow morning. I thought of your auto; I hope it's supplied with the necessary papers to cross the border."

"Is Your Majesty expected in Hungary?"

"No one knows of my coming. It's best that my arrival in the royal palace in Buda be a surprise. It took me from early morning till now to make the trip from the Swiss border to Vienna. In the course of the long trip, and wearing my false beard, I entered into conversation with my fellow travelers, who were tradespeople or Tyrolese peasants. While I was their emperor it was good to know that they called me simply 'Karl.' They never called Franz Joseph by his name. He was simply 'Der Kaiser.' I, 'Karl,' stood closer to their hearts. Their use of the name was a pat on my shoulder, an embrace. And now...a dreadful people, the Austrians. A broad-beamed fishwife sat across the way from me somewhere near Innsbruck. I brought the conversation around to myself, and began to praise myself a bit, saying what a stout fellow that Karl was, for he didn't start the war and when he ascended the throne he wanted nothing but peace. You know what that fishwife said? *Karl? Der bödl Kerl!* Churlish Charles! And then she gave me a detailed account of the way I had repudiated the Sixtus Letter."

Preoccupied, the king scraped the last drop of juice from the compote dish with his spoon.

"Well, yes...that was my mistake. I must confess I dream of it every night, like a gambler who had to choose between red and black, and chose black, and lost everything on a single turn of the wheel. Your Uncle Cini—pardon, my Foreign Minister—that alabaster-fronted ox held me in the hollow of his hand, too much so. If only there had been someone to stand beside me then, and shake me a bit!"

At these words he closed his eyes of a sudden, so deep was the pain in his heart.

Juan Hwang entered the room like a phantom, as if on cue. He made a low bow to the king, who rose and offered his hand with a friendly smile.

Margaret brought coffee, and we settled into armchairs. The king continued talking in the same lively tone he had used with me, but his liveliness did not seem entirely natural, as if he had taken some sort of stimulant. I could understand his mood: it was a blend of happiness, uncertainty, hope and fear, at their height. And I imagine he meant, by his show of good humor, to seem casual to Juan Hwang. He turned toward me, but his frequent glances at Juan Hwang indicated a wish to share his story equally.

"Do you know the origin of the name Habsburg, Kristina? In my childhood my father told me of one of our ancestors, Ruelf, who lived in the tenth century and was a respectable and industrious robber baron in the best traditions of the Middle Ages. When he had collected enough gold from the treasure-laden caravans of merchants on the Moravian highway, he built a capacious feudal fortress on a mountain peak. He was overwhelmed with happiness at the thought of having his own fortress, and even when he had declined into senility he

221

continued to repeat, whether to his retinue or in solitude: Ich habe eines Burg!'
But since he spoke Middle German with a thick tongue and mouthed the words,
I've a fortress of my own!' this sounded like 'Hab' 's Burg!' I don't know how
much of the story is true, but it's certain that I'm the first Habsburg who can say
of himself: 'Ich habe keines Burg!'"

We laughed politely. Meanwhile Juan Hwang let me know, with a furtive little
lift of his eyebrows, that he wanted to be left alone with the king. I collected the
coffee cups as a pretext for leaving the room. But I didn't close the heavy oaken
door all the way, I stopped to listen.

"I'm very pleased to have a chance for a talk with you," the king began. "I'd like
your opinion of my plans to return."

"Your Majesty is going to Budapest in order to reoccupy the Hungarian throne?"

"Naturally."

"I consider it a particularly unfortunate idea."

"Why?" came the astonished, somewhat offended, drawn-out query. "During
my stay in Switzerland the Hungarian people have given touching evidence of
allegiance to their crowned king. No, I don't mean the aristocracy alone. I've
received carved shepherd's staffs and rustic embroideries as gifts, accompanied
by letters painstakingly written in a peasant hand. Last week a great goat's-cheese
arrived. I hate goat's-cheese, personally, but a round cheese like that can contain
the heart of an entire nation."

"Your Majesty, the Hungarians are undoubtedly loyal to their king. But they
are no friends of the Habsburgs."

"How do you mean?"

"For three and a half centuries they've fought a ceaseless battle for liberation
from the Habsburgs."

"Don't forget that the East would have engulfed Hungary long ago if it hadn't
been for the Habsburgs. Even you cannot deny that Hungary flourished both
economically and culturally during the Habsburg centuries!"

"Aside from that, Your Majesty—it is only an apparent independence that the
Hungarian people enjoy today. Political pressures from the outside—"

The king interrupted him.

"I'm assured of the support of the Entente. Otherwise I wouldn't even have set out."

"I don't know and I shan't ask which Entente circles persuaded Your Majesty
to make this trip. This much is certain, however: Czechoslovakia, Jugoslavia
and Rumania will mobilize at once. The Little Entente has every reason to refuse

to tolerate a Habsburg on the Hungarian throne."

While speaking, the king occasionally stood up and stalked the length of the room. At such times Juan Hwang also rose—one could be sure of this from the little noises which accompanied their movements.

"I'm glad to have your opinion, and I've heard it with interest," said the king, "but my decision remains unchanged. So you consider my return to be completely hopeless?"

"Nothing is hopeless, Your Majesty. It's completely hopeless only as Your Majesty pictures it. I strongly urge you not to submit yourself to an ugly humiliation."

"Nothing is hopeless, you said. What would your solution be?"

"I don't feel I have the right to advise Your Majesty."

"Your opinion both interests and gratifies me. I wish you would accept the title of count as a mark of my gratitude."

"Thank you, Your Majesty; but for various reasons I cannot accept."

"Let's hear your solution," the king pressed him.

"Do I have Your Majesty's permission to speak quite candidly?"

"I very much wish you would."

I brought my ear close to the crack of the door, the better to hear every word. I recalled that I had stood the very same way behind this very door ten years ago, waiting for the little captain of Dragoons to come and rescue me from the well. The memory of that tentative kiss rang in my recollection like the sound of a musical clock. Ten years—ten years ago next May. How amazing it was that this strange romance of mine and the workings of the world had brought me back here, behind the heavy oaken door!

"The Hungarian people are faced with a curious dilemma today," came Juan Hwang's voice. "They would like to have on their throne the man whose forehead the crown of St. Stephen has already graced, for they have a religious faith in the magic of the crown. At the same time they don't want a Habsburg. Why does Your Majesty want to return in your capacity *as a Habsburg*, when this name implies not only the restoration of the Hungarian throne but of the entire Monarchy—however much you may deny it—and would surely lead to war?"

"Therefore—"

"Your Majesty can regain the Hungarian throne only by dropping the name of Habsburg and—"

"And?"

"—and marrying a Hungarian."

The king sprang from his chair as if he had not heard aright. My hand leaped to my heart. Had Juan Hwang gone mad?

"What did you say?" the king asked with irritation.

"I'll repeat it," Juan Hwang replied calmly. "Your Majesty must drop the name of Habsburg and marry a Hungarian girl. Before you begin to reflect on this, Your Majesty, remember that a smile is never enough to recover a lost throne. Sometimes weapons will serve, and sometimes a masterly trick. Sargon I, king of the Akkadians, in the third millennium B.C., regained his throne only on condition that he burn his wife at the stake. But they tied a slave, clad in veils, to the stake instead, and the king lived happily with his wife till the end of his days, for a secret door led to her room from his bedchamber. I could cite almost identical instances in the Chou Dynasty of China, the Merovingian Dynasty and even the history of the Bourbons. Consider this, Your Majesty: one fine day the Havas Agency announces the sad news of the queen's death in a skiing accident in Switzerland."

"My wife can't ski," the king interjected nervously.

"So much the better! It will seem that much likelier for her to have fallen into the very deepest crevasse. I can recommend Hurdl Pass in the Canton of Valais. They've never found a single one of the tourists who disappeared in those icy wastes. At the moment of the accident Her Majesty, with a new hair-do and spectacles on her nose, will be sitting by the fireplace of a little Swiss hotel under the name of the widowed Frau Schmidt, knitting a warm waistcoat for little Crown Prince Otto or perhaps reading a good book. The world will mourn her with due respect for a while and will forget her completely after three days. They'll even forgive her for having been a Bourbon. Don't forget, Your Majesty, that the Bourbons have always brought misfortune to the Habsburgs. Think of the daughter of Maria Theresa, who married Louis XVI and found herself on the guillotine."

"My wife is ready to make any sacrifice," the king said softly and thoughtfully. "But your plan is so fantastic that I'd be laughing out loud at this very moment if you hadn't reminded me of Marie Antoinette."

"It's no more fantastic than the fate Your Majesty decreed for Oscar in connection with the Sixtus Letter. Keep in mind, Your Majesty, that the history of the world is a series of wild adventures and horror stories. The less likely a thing seems, the closer it is to historical truth. The nineteenth century accustomed all mankind, and kings most of all, to the comfortable mentality of, say, a notary public. We're in the twentieth century now, however, and have just lived through an appalling World War. I'm willing to wager that Chevalier Ruelf would agree with me."

The king laughed, and then rose.

"Thank you for this very interesting talk."

At that I entered the room, exactly as Juan Hwang was leaving. The king glanced at his watch.

"Three in the morning! I shan't have much sleep. Someone is coming for me at eight to accompany me to Hungary."

He was visibly exhausted. I led him to his room.

25 March

After breakfast Charles Ringl, tailor's assistant, took his suitcase in hand, for the auto, with a stranger at the wheel, was already at the gate. At parting he looked deep into my eyes, and I made the sign of the cross on his forehead. He hurried away without a word, clearly moved. He was near the door when I hissed after him in alarm. I signaled to him mutely that he'd forgotten to put his beard on. He smiled, pulled the mass of hair from his pocket and donned it carefully before the hall mirror. I was panic-stricken to see that the porter, Hans, was already standing motionlessly at the door of his booth, hands clasped behind his back, and had observed the whole scene. As the king stepped through the door I turned to Hans with a confused smile:

"A film actor. On his way to the set."

Hans nodded speechlessly and gloomily. It seemed impossible that he had failed to recognize the king. Fortunately Hans is very stupid, and dull heads are the most trustworthy.

I had half an hour to make the Budapest Express.

25 March—Budapest

Half past seven in the evening. The windows were bright in the Buda Fortress. The King had been in conference with the Regent for hours. My automobile, with the same stranger at the wheel, was waiting for the king before the iron gate of the main entrance, where enormous two-headed bronze eagles were ruffling their wings on top of the pillars. In the back seat I recognized the little fiberboard suitcase which must have contained the threadbare civilian suit, with the false beard in the pocket of the jacket.

I was walking back and forth before the gate in the dripping rain. A few minutes before eight the bugles resounded from the direction of the inner court, blowing the call to arms. This meant that the king was on his way. I could hear the shouted commands and the slap of rifle slings as the guards presented arms.

And there came the king, the golden trimmings of his marshal's uniform glittering through the rain in the light of the lamps. His steps betrayed a boundless melancholy as he approached in the company of Baron K. The bugles were still blowing, and their call was like a fanfare in final farewell. I was not far from the auto when the king mounted, but he did not look at me although I felt he knew I was standing beside the pillar. The embarrassed little smile on his pallid countenance must have cost him a tremendous effort. Baron K. took leave of the departing automobile with a low bow. I stepped to his side and asked in a whisper:

"What happened?"

He replied with a gesture merely, turning his two palms to the rain for an instant. He too was deadly pale with emotion.

Juan Hwang had been proved right again.

Chapter Nine

THE DAYS have been fearfully bleak since the king left. But yesterday something did happen. At about six in the afternoon a bearded, unkempt man in bedraggled clothes appeared at our door on Septemvir Utca. He insisted on speaking with Papa, but the porter refused to admit him, naturally. He spoke not a word of Hungarian, and very little German. The porter was about to throw him out, despite the stranger's vehement protests, when Papa, who usually leaves for the Casino at that hour, came walking downstairs. Having thoroughly searched the visitor's unruly beard with his piercing glance, he gave a sudden shout and embraced the vagabond wanderer. It was Uncle Dmitri, with whom all correspondence had ceased soon after the Russian revolution. We were all convinced that Uncle Dmitri, too, had been executed by the Bolsheviks. After three years in hiding he finally managed to make his way through Poland, reaching our palace and Papa's warm embrace in a tattered, starved state. Of his half million acres in Kazan, only the rags he wore on his back remained. In a matter of hours Uncle Dmitri underwent a remarkable transformation. They hurried him into a tub and burned all his clothes in the courtyard while he bathed. When he stepped from the tub he found Papa's barber ready for him, equipment and all—Mr. Husnik, who had been summoned as urgently as a skilled specialist to the bedside of a seriously ailing man. By dinnertime Uncle Dmitri was outfitted in one of Papa's smoking jackets, and he resumed the conversation almost where he had left off ten years ago, when he had last stayed with us on his way to Paris. His wife, poor Aunt Mira, died the year before last while they were hiding in a Polish village called Hirlice, where Uncle Dmitri wrapped her in a tablecloth, dug her grave himself and set up a simple wooden cross on which, as he said, he carved only the words: *Tempora mutantur.*

But this afternoon he too repaired to the Casino, to try his luck, after so long a time, at the baccarat tables. With Papa's money, of course. Evidently the phrase *Tempora mutantur* applies only to the dead. The living change, from the moment of conception, not one whit.

Nightgowned, my hair uncombed, I stood in the middle of the room in an agony of apocalyptic disorder. The contents of my wardrobes, my drawers, my suitcases lay strewn in confusion over the bed, the carpet, the chairs and tables. Once again my chambermaid Margaret pulled open the empty drawers—no, no sign of it—my diary was lost. Since morning I had sought it in vain, and it was almost as if my whole life were lost. And now there was nothing but chaos: stockings dangling about the room, bundles of love letters, medicine bottles, jewelry, rolls of cotton, dancing shoes, everything that makes up the botched, useless life of a woman like me. I always kept my diary—a green leather-bound book with a lock—in my little jewel box. I clearly remembered returning it to its usual place on the evening of March 25th, after I made my entry about the king's unhappy departure; I had the keys to the box and the book, but the diary was gone, although none of my jewelry was missing. It was incomprehensible and unnerving. I had already telephoned to Vienna and to Ararat, and they'd been searching everywhere ever since. I was convinced that inanimate objects have souls, characters, desires and a capacity for revenge.

Then they found it. András, the castellan at Ararat, telephoned at about noon to say the book had been in the drawer of my writing desk and was already on the way by messenger. The diary was found, but I was lost. If my memory could betray me so, then I was at the point of distraction.

Yes, I am lost and preparing for death as for a beautiful, distant, limitless journey, rocked in the sweet and gentle mercies of my most potent sleeping pills. I have lived almost twenty-five years. Life holds nothing for me. This last week, from Friday to Friday, during which the king's second return took place, sealed the fate not only of the Habsburg Dynasty and of Hungary but of my own life as well. Before I die I want to record the events of this final week; if I leave my Ordony novel unfinished, I can at least bring the diary to a close.

Dr. Freyberger came at four in the afternoon. He's been my personal physician since childhood; for twenty years he's been peering into me like an X-ray, and he knows my vertebrae, my liver, my pulse better than the ticking of his own watch. He knows my eczemas, the buzzing in my ears, my hay fever, my menstrual disorders, the little black mole under my left armpit, my neuralgia, my bleeding gums and my bad dreams better than he knows himself. Besides Mamma, he is the only one who knows of my childhood accident in the Chinese bathhouse.

I told him I intend to kill myself tonight. He was neither to try to talk me out of it nor to raise an alarm; I would not be thwarted. To my great surprise, he did not try to dissuade me. In his usual quiet, somewhat sorrowful but always reassuring tone he said only: "Everyone has the right to do what he wants with his life." When I asked him what the effect of these pills would be, how they worked and how long consciousness would persist after I had taken the fatal dose, he said there were no corpses among the professors of medical science—what I asked was, consequently, a secret known only to death itself. He took leave of me with a simple "Au revoir"—it sounded as if he were arranging a rendezvous in the next world. When he left I sensed how much that stoop-shouldered, ugly man had meant to me throughout my life—how much peace, how much wisdom, how much reassurance and warmth. My recollection of him at that moment came to me as to a woman who had been dead for the past twenty years and walked the earth only in thought, as someone else might walk the golf course on Sundays.

Before I begin the record of this fateful Friday I had best give a brief account of the past seven months.

Since the king was shown the door in the Buda Fortress so delicately, gently and despicably at the end of March I'd not once seen Juan Hwang. Nor did I long for him, for the knowledge that he had been right again would have made me feel small in his presence—a feeling akin to ptomaine poisoning. Affairs of state both internal and external quieted down after the king's departure. In secret, however, the legitimists were more active than ever. This summer, too, foreign automobiles kept coming to Ararat and daily conferences were held behind the closed doors of Papa's study; Mamma and I were not invited to attend, of course, but we knew that the king's emissaries kept him in constant touch with Hungary. They were preparing for something, and it could be nothing but the king's second return, this time more carefully planned. I had not a moment's confidence in any of it.

From April on, Mamma made frantic efforts to marry me off. Ever since the *Apfelstrudel* scene of ten years ago she had suspected that my heart was filled with reckless dreams which centered on the king; but now she assumed I had been cured of that malady, and she exerted all her strength to bring about a wedding. It was an old fear of hers, the fear that I would be involved in a dreadful scandal sooner or later or end my days, like Baroness S., in some Balkan brothel; this fear returned with all its former pangs, like the rheumatism of poor Grandmamma Jefi. It may be that she heard of my friendship with Selley. Selley was second-rate, as actors go, but he reminded me of C., the French prize fighter—a more tender, more fashionable edition, to be sure. His name was but an *h* short of the name of the poet who wrote the "Hymn to Intellectual Beauty," with those lines I love so much: "The awful shadow of some unseen Power floats tho' unseen amongst us." And his spirit, too, had something of the English Shelley's delicate fire. I was certain no one noticed us when we used to have supper in little Buda taverns during the summer. I've never in my life seen a dirtier, more disorderly bachelor flat than his. But he was very amusing. Two ornately framed, autographed photographs hung on the wall: one of them represented the dark-eyed Latin goddess with whom he once appeared in a guest performance—*a mio carissimo amico, Eleonora Duse.* The other was a picture of a bald, middle-aged man, with this touching dedication: *Maestro! I beg you, please pay something on account! Sam Bloch, English tailor.* My affair with this Shelley-without-an-*h* was like a summer storm: warm gusts of wind, lightning, thunder, and then airy laughter. When he lay sobbing at my feet amid protestations of love I listened to him as to the sound of the great organ in the Stefanskirche, for marvelously deep tones have always moved me. He called me his queen, his white swan, his black orchid, he had special words for my skin and my breasts—words in which I sometimes detected the accents of Verlaine and Rilke. Once, after one such burst of love, he suddenly stood up and slapped my face with full force. Later, when we came to our senses and I asked him why he had done that, he replied, "I happened to think of something."

Meanwhile offers of marriage swarmed around me, as thick as mosquitoes. Archduke L. appeared at Ararat again; at present he is the assistant manager of a brewery in Vienna, and has been wearing the same raincoat for years, both summer and winter. The beer he brews is atrocious, but it has a lovely name: Habsburg Hops. His hands are as thin as a cripple's. Mamma and I repeated our "Erich" scene of ten years ago—my first proposal—when His Beeriness asked for my hand in marriage. All our relations joined with Mamma in trying to marry me off. They lay in wait for the right moment to strap me into the straitjacket of marriage. Aunt Julia lent her support to the Greek Ambassador's suit, and when we were alone she rolled her eyes skyward and declared she had never seen a more attractive masculine profile. Apart from the fact of the Greek's long name, in which the words *Acropolis* and *Protagoras* occurred several times over, His Excellency was, in my view, more like an Austrian station master than Praxiteles' *Hermes*.

In past centuries the heir to the Hungarian throne was given a section of the country at a time on which to practice the art of ruling. On a similar basis, Papa gave György full administrative control over our game preserves and forests. György immediately went into business, charging hunters from abroad two hundred dollars for each stag they shot and fifty dollars for each mouflon ram. Thus a fascinating international set appeared at Ararat in September, among them Monsieur Fragonard, a Belgian arms manufacturer with a rounded belly and a little cinnabar-red mustache, whose ancestors included Honoré Fragonard, the great rococo painter. It was Uncle Fini who whispered his honorable intentions in my ear.

After all the many refusals Mamma gave me up with a fine sense of melancholy and a vain hope of keeping my lunacy a secret as long as possible. It was no surprise to find her thinking of me that way, for even I was no longer able to understand myself. "The awful shadow of some unseen Power…" Yes, Frau Katz's prophecy was still alive within me this summer, like a disquieting stab of pain, strange and sinister.

Now I know it was the approach of death. It was the ultimate secret in the depths of the *Mountain.*

Last week, on the 20th of October, the king appeared on the Hungarian horizon at dawn like some fateful comet running its final course in a ghostly parabola. He came by plane, and was accompanied by the queen. They landed on a meadow in western Hungary, and were lodged at a near-by castle. Half an hour later we were informed of their arrival by a telephone call to Septemvir Utca. Papa flung himself into an auto at once and hurtled away. Thereafter our private telephone kept ringing constantly, and messengers came every half hour only to hurry off five minutes later. We were besieged by newspapermen who were present at the events as they occurred; reports arrived from various sources.

This was the situation by evening: the king planned to enter Budapest the next day at the head of divisions which had rallied to him from the western garrisons, while loyal troops in the capital were to arrest the Opposition forces during the night, so that the capital would be festooned with banners and the people cheering with joy as they welcomed back their king.

At one o'clock in the morning we were informed that the royal couple had been awakened and removed to the barracks at Sopron, for the castle was not considered sufficiently safe. The guards at the barracks were trustworthy; but the king and queen had nothing better than a military cot apiece to sleep upon.

The next morning—Friday morning—the troops passed in review in the courtyard of the barracks and took an oath of fealty to the king, who wore a field

231

uniform with a bayonet at his side, devoid of all decorations. The commandant of the barracks was promoted from major to colonel. Papa reached Sopron at six in the morning and telephoned every half hour from then on. Uncle Fini was on duty by the telephone here, and beside him stood Baron K., who hurried off on secret errands from time to time.

In the morning the royal couple appeared in the streets of Sopron, where the inhabitants of the town—German-speaking, in the main—accorded them a great ovation.

At noon the king named Papa his Master of the Equerry. In Uncle Fini's opinion, it was but a question of days until Papa's branch of the family would be elevated to the dukedom which King Leopold II had granted to György Dukay in 1791 and which became extinct with the latter's death in 1829. Mamma's face was flushed with excitement as she paced from room to room, arranging her porcelains. Meanwhile she kept humming that old Viennese catch, "Ach du lieber Augustin, Au-gustin!" ...I hadn't heard her hum since my childhood.

At eleven that evening the royal couple boarded a train at the Sopron station, and the loyal troops were also entrained. We didn't close our eyes all that night. From time to time I opened a window and listened. The night was quiet. At three in the morning Papa telephoned to say that the train was still waiting in the station at Sopron. Uncle Fini found the delay inexplicable, and was beside himself with rage.

At nine on the morning of the next day, Saturday, we learned that the royal train was advancing very slowly because the bridges in its path had to be seized one by one lest they be blown up. Uncertainty, perplexity and fear reigned in Budapest during those hours. I ran over to the Garrison church but was unable to get inside; it was so crowded that people were even kneeling in the street, all of them praying for the king. At noon there was a great ringing of telephones: the garrison at Győr, only seventy-five miles from Budapest, had taken an oath to the king, whose train was met with martial music and the national anthem at the station. Papa, too, delivered a speech to the people through a window of the train. I wish I'd been there—I've never heard him make a speech. I'm afraid he probably began as Uncle Géza once did: "My dear peasants!"

At three in the afternoon the train was at a standstill on the open tracks; the rails before Komárom had been dynamited. Meanwhile representatives of the government, in automobiles and by special train, had gone to meet the king, to inform him of the Entente's protests against a restoration and to persuade him to turn back. At the advice of his staff officers, the king refused to receive them. The train set out anew, but it was eight in the evening before the wrecked rails were repaired. National anthem, martial music, flags and speeches at the Komárom station too. They were only fifty miles from Budapest.

At about nine o'clock Mr. Gruber came home from the city. He called me aside.

"I'm worried about His Excellency. It's disquieting to know that he's on the king's train. The Budapest Garrison is on the alert, and the government forces are going to defend the city. They're distributing arms even to the university students. I'm very much afraid that civil war is going to break out. They've given the troops to believe that the king is leading Austrian and Czech divisions against the city."

At eleven Papa telephoned to say that the royal train had halted for the night. At that we also went to bed.

The next morning, Sunday, the telephone rang again; the train had started and was but twelve miles from Budapest.

Soon, however, at about eight o'clock, came shocking news: infantry on near-by hills was firing at the king's train. The king was reluctant to order an attack, for he hoped to avoid bloodshed. A priest was summoned to hear the king's confession in the office of the railway station; this took some time. Then he wanted to enter the village and attend Mass, but it was impossible because the road leading to the church was already under fire by then. Thereupon he commanded that a military Mass be celebrated alongside the train. But it all took hours, for it was difficult to locate a bell, sacramental wine, a pyx and a cross. During Mass he, too, knelt in the mud beside the tracks. His staff officers gnashed their teeth in fury, for each moment brought more reports that unopposed government forces were occupying the most important points before them.

At noon the train was waiting, and the generals implored the king to give the order for an attack. But the king decided to face the hostile and misguided Hungarian troops alone. He still had faith in the magic of his crowned head. He went so far as to mount one of the locomotives. Papa and Uncle Zsigmond and others went with him. But the separate locomotive had hardly started when the cannon rang out too, and the locomotive had to stop under the threat of a heavy barrage. The engineer would go no further.

At two o'clock in the afternoon the king's own division of guards began the assault. Casualties streamed in, one after another. Meanwhile negotiations continued by telephone between Budapest and the king's men. Each side called on the other to surrender, or—the gallows.

From this point on I don't know exactly what happened that afternoon. At seven in the evening my chambermaid Margaret shook me awake on the rug in front of the fireplace, where I had slid from the armchair in a sleep of exhaustion. She told me in a whisper that Juan Hwang wanted to talk to me urgently. She led me to the basement, and on a bed in one of the servants' rooms I found György, his clothes dripping with blood.

"I didn't want to have him taken to a hospital," Juan Hwang whispered, "because his name would appear on the published casualty lists."

The situation was clear to me at once. György was one of the university students who had taken arms against the king. And taken arms against his father as well! My God, if Papa ever found out! No, he must never know. György's trousers were covered with mud and torn at the knee; he had crawled up to the firing line on his stomach along the rocky hillside. The wound in his shoulder did not seem serious, fortunately. I ran for my bandages and sent Margaret for Freyberger. Juan Hwang was covered with mud too. He wore a cartridge belt over his fashionable fall overcoat. Not till that moment did I notice a Mannlicher, with bayonet fixed, leaning against the wall in a corner. He took the weapon in hand and rushed back to the firing line.

News of an armistice came at about midnight, and negotiations were begun at dawn.

At nine o'clock on Monday morning Uncle Zsigmond telephoned to say that the end had come. He said a short prayer into the phone—God save our country from the ravages of a bloody civil war. The terms offered by the government were unacceptable; they demanded the king's immediate abdication and his departure from Hungarian soil. His staff advised a swift, determined attack at once, but by then that was out of the question. The loyal troops were faltering, were beginning to murmur that the king had betrayed them, for he had no support from the Entente. They suddenly started to wonder which of their two sworn oaths—the one to the king, or the one to the Regent—was valid. The officers too began to feel as if cut in half by the swords of East and West. Fate whispered of a general's rank, of a baronetcy, at one ear; and at the other, of the gallows.

The battle was still raging in the afternoon. When I opened my window I could hear the distant cannonades. Mamma continued to stalk from room to room, arranging her porcelains, but the flush had vanished from her face. Uncle Fini sat beside the silent telephone and gnawed his nails.

And the telephone did not ring until seven that evening. The king's forces were completely surrounded. His train had been forced to retreat toward Komárom. On the way the king himself had advised his officers to change into civilian clothes, jump from the train and flee to safety.

At eight in the evening the king was taken prisoner.

At about noon the next day, Tuesday, András the castellan phoned to say that the royal train had passed through the Ararat station ten minutes earlier. The king and queen were being taken to the cloisters at Tihany under military guard. All shades were drawn at the windows of the train.

Wednesday, Thursday...I can no long remember those hours. Papa and Uncle Zsigmond were also taken prisoner. The newspapers of the entire world were buzzing; the Council of Ambassadors voted to send the king into exile. Mamma was completely speechless for two days. Uncle Fini had vanished somewhere. Mr. Gruber comforted Mamma by saying that the prisoners would be granted an amnesty. György was still in bed; we told Mamma he had a bad case of influenza.

On Friday the royal couple was escorted to the Danube and placed aboard a British gunboat, the *Glowworm,* under the supervision of officers of the Entente. Aunt Julia was present at the moment of their final farewell. Once again, before their departure, the king appeared on deck and gave a mute salute to the spectators on shore. The bayonet was no longer at his waist, for he had taken it off and thrown it on the table in front of the Entente officers at Tihany.

At five o'clock in the afternoon the *Glowworm* set sail, taking him into perpetual exile on the island of Madeira.

That's the end. *Consummatum est!*

Why didn't I make an effort to reach the king in these past few days, to be at his side in those fateful hours? My conscience had beaten me to my knees. For it is all my fault. I didn't take the advice of Juan Hwang and Florian: I didn't sway the king when he repudiated the Sixtus Letter.

And now—come, death!

6 November 1921—Orient Express

I've decided otherwise. I'm on the way to Lisbon and from there to Funchal, the capital of Madeira. I shall share the king's exile as long as I live. This is, after all, a more beautiful death.

Chapter Ten

THE EXCERPTS cited from Kristina's diary so far have cast no new light, essentially, on the Habsburg tragedy; at most they have brought us closer to the march of events by enabling us to see them through the personal experience of an eyewitness who was, in her dreams and desires, herself a participant in that tragedy.

This final section, however, contains details which have not hitherto been made available to Habsburg literature. Up to this point it has been necessary to condense certain parts of the diary, for Kristina, like all diarists, sometimes tends to chatter about irrelevancies for pages on end. But the following pages are reproduced in their entirety.

26 November 1921—Somewhere on the Atlantic

Yesterday I boarded ship at Lisbon for the three-day voyage to Madeira. The sea is brilliant with sunshine but very rough, unfortunately. I have spent the whole day lying in bed, and this tiny cabin makes me feel as if I were locked in my own coffin. And I have every reason to feel like a corpse.

28 November

I felt wretched this morning, but crept out on deck nevertheless. The purser says we shall be in Madeira at three this afternoon. The island has no harbor; larger ships stand about a mile offshore and discharge passengers to Funchal, the capital, by motor launch.

Later: At two o'clock this afternoon the island came into view on the western horizon. The binoculars trembled in my hands when I glimpsed the palm trees on the waterfront of Funchal, and behind them the Hotel Azuria, glittering whitely in the sunshine. It still looked no larger than a lump of sugar. The motors of the ship seemed to gather all their strength, and the sunlit waves of the ocean joined in a wild dance. Gulls appeared to shriek with pleasure about the smokestacks, as if they too sought to help the ship on her way. A sudden breeze sprang up—it was as if the winds lent all their force to speed the ship shorewards. Through my binoculars I could see the HOTEL AZURIA grow larger. By now it was as large as a hatbox. The white rays it cast were almost blinding.

The king is staying at the Hotel Azuria.

29 November—Hotel Azuria

Senhor Camilo Camillian, the hotel manager, greeted me with exceptional graciousness when he learned my name. He told me, in answer to my questions, that the king and queen had reached Funchal eight days ago. Acting on the instructions of the Council of Ambassadors, he placed the twenty rooms of the Villa Amalia, a completely separate wing of the hotel, at the disposal of Their Majesties, who are now living in total solitude. They see no one. The king occasionally appears in the tiny garden of the villa for a breath of air.

Senhor Camilo Camillian is a short man with a goatee, and wears a frock coat of perfect cut. The strength of his perfume very nearly made me faint. His features and the shape of his head reminded me of the stuffed ibex head in the billiard room at Ararat, of which I was so frightened as a child. Nothing is more terrifying to me, still, than the yellow and apparently square eyes of a goat.

I need rest, and intend to stay in bed all day today. But tomorrow I shall request an audience with the king.

30 November

This morning I took a long walk in town and learned a great deal about the island which has become England's new St. Helena. Funchal, the capital, extends along the level water-front, and only at the back of the town does it cling to the steep mountainside, like the train of a woman hurrying from the mountains for the summer. She did not forget to bring her bathing suit: the palm trees on the promenades, the tropical plants in the tiny parks make a modest covering for the nakedness of the shore. The town itself is no different from the little Latin towns on the Mediterranean coast, which boast a few trolley cars and automobiles, a few palatial hotels and bank buildings at the front, while at the rear the little gardens pressed between walls of stone and the narrow little streets bounded by vineyards frantically seek to escape the choking heat by fleeing up the mountainside. The whole town is full of indecision: the seashore longs for the mountain and the mountain yearns for the seashore.

The huge mountain towering over the town has evidently resisted all attempts, ever since the first Paleolithic man landed here in his dugout canoe, to give it a name with human reference, considering such nomenclature to be beneath its dignity; thus, even unto the present day, the mountain has simply been called *Monte*. At the midriff of the mountain, surrounding a great two-steepled church, lies a tiny village whose inhabitants, all workingmen, travel back and forth by a cable car which runs only in the morning and the evening. The island has a population of about one hundred fifty thousand people, all of whom speak Portuguese, although they are a motley of the major European races, the Latin, the German and the Slav. Practically every state in Europe is represented by consuls who usually receive no salary but are permitted to post the national crest at the door of their apartments, to print resounding titles on their visiting cards, to wear minor decorations and, generally, to give the peaceable population the impression that they are human battleships.

1 December

The waiter who serves the royal couple in the Villa Amalia is called Artur. I asked Artur to give His Majesty a brief note in which I requested an audience. At about eleven in the morning I was sitting in the hotel lobby, which was completely deserted, when—to my great surprise—someone put a hand on my shoulder. It was the king. He wore a gray civilian suit, and seemed somewhat thinner than when I last saw him. Apparently he is growing a long mustache, and this has altered his features. He did not allow me to rise, restrained me with his hand on my shoulder, and sat down himself in the next armchair. How strange it was that he greeted me without a word, only with this gesture and a smile! It was as if he were already a ghost. Nor did a single sound come from my throat. There was something embarrassed and boyish about the king's smile. Boys who fail a make-up examination generally smile like that. The king seemed ashamed, even in my company, of the failure of his second effort in Hungary.

"So you're here!" These were his first words, and there was a trace of emotion and gratitude in his eyes as he looked at me. We started to talk, and when I inquired about his trip he briefly recounted that they had been obliged to leave the *Glowworm* at the Lower Danube because the waters were too shallow. They took a train to the Black Sea, where a British cruiser picked them up and brought them to Madeira. He kept gazing about nervously while he spoke.

"Can I do something for you, Your Majesty?"

"I'd like to speak with the hotel manager. I find our bill too high, I have no secrets from you—I arrived in Funchal with very little money. You know, perhaps, that my children and the staff are still in Switzerland. The queen and I occupy only two rooms, but the hotel charges for all twenty rooms of the Villa Amalia, together with board for twenty people. That's overdoing it, I think."

Indignant, I hurried to the manager's office and informed Senhor Camilo Camillian that His Majesty wanted to talk to him. He dashed into the lobby, bowed to the ground before the king and kept on bowing as he ushered His Majesty into the office. The king beckoned to me surreptitiously. I had the feeling that he was afraid to be alone with the perfumed goatee, and when Camilo Camillian asked how he could serve His Majesty, the king turned to me in confusion:

"Perhaps the Countess would be good enough..."

I told the manager what was in the king's mind. Camilo Camillian's right hand suddenly gripped his goatee and dangled there for a few moments.

"It is a hard problem—but we shall find a solution, of course. It has probably escaped His Majesty's notice that he and Her Majesty the Queen have every right to consume twenty breakfasts each morning, twenty dinners at noon and twenty suppers at night and, what is more, our directors have no objection if Their Majesties wish to avail themselves of all twenty rooms; consequently it is their right to get up at every half-hour of the night and move to another freshly made bed in another room..."

I sprang from my chair, but Camilo Camillian stopped me with a fresh torrent of courteous and kindly words.

"—please, I have not finished. I simply want to clear up the matter of their rights. If Their Majesties should object to this arrangement for any reason whatsoever, we would have no alternative—let us assume they wish to occupy four rooms in all—we would have no alternative but to open the other sixteen rooms to strangers, for the applicants are legion—legion!...Be good enough to look at these telegrams from Sir Henry Robertson, and Prince Obbialero, and Mr. Haywood, all begging for rooms. These arrived this very morning, and that pile on my desk consists of similar telegrams. Your Majesty must realize that as manager of the hotel I must protect the interests of the stockholders..."

The king stared sadly into space, and his expression made it plain that he regretted this excursion to Senhor Camilo Camillian's office even more than his last trip to Hungary, where gunfire had greeted his train. The final phrase, "I must protect the interests of the stockholders," rang ominously in his ear, perhaps even more ominously because Senhor Camilo Camillian, who spoke perfect German, interspersed his speech with occasional Portuguese words when excited. This was the voice of an entire social order, and it was as close as this voice had ever come to the ear and purse of a monarch whose throne had been the mainstay of that order. "The interests of the stockholders"—yes, he had heard this expression, with a dying fall, in the laments that called him back to the throne during the days of the revolution. The interests of the stockholders must be protected! In bygone days it had been, "Dalmatia must be protected"…"Transylvania must be protected"…"France insists on her claim to Alsace-Lorraine"…or "Turkey will not surrender the Bosporus." The king knew what such ominous phrases meant, and he also knew that as a sovereign prince he could not deny their sanctity, for they supported the throne itself. Yes, the interests of stockholders in the Hotel Azuria must be protected. Without a word the king reached for his wallet and produced one thousand four hundred eighty-five Swiss francs in payment of the hotel bill for the first week. Senhor Camilo Camillian made a deep bow as he accepted the money, and it was impossible to know whether the bow was intended for His Majesty or for the banknotes.

6 December

I was invited to take tea with Their Majesties this afternoon. The queen's condition is very much in evidence by now. Good Lord, her eighth child is on the way, and it was only a short time ago that they celebrated their tenth wedding anniversary. Both of them complained of the fact that the garden of Villa Amalia is about ten paces wide in all, and its iron railings are surrounded by gapers from morning till night.

"We dare not venture into the garden until nightfall," the king said, "otherwise we would feel like a pair of gorillas newly arrived in the zoo. When an excursion boat visits Funchal, the situation is completely intolerable. People trample each other to death at the railing."

"Tell about the Englishwoman," said the queen, who was busily knitting. She was making a warm little jacket for the coming baby.

"Oh, yes!" laughed the king. "On one of the quieter afternoons an elderly Englishwoman with thick eyeglasses haunted the railing of Villa Amalia until she succeeded in attracting the attention of a valetlike sort of chap as he stepped out of the villa. She called him to the railing and offered him a bribe of five pounds if he would let her inside and show us to her. She wanted to know whether it was true that we were kept in chains. The man showed his sterling character by turning

240

his back on the intrusive Englishwoman and disappearing into the villa."

"Who was he? Artur?" I asked.

"It was I!" cried the king, and he threw his head back in laughter. The queen, too, laughed heartily. Then the king struck his forehead with his hand:

"But what an ass I was! I should have taken the five pounds!"

A wonderful sense of happiness ran through me, although I did not join in their hilarity. Surely God must love people who can laugh like that.

14 December

Apparently wonders will never cease. I was sitting in my room this afternoon when Juan Hwang unexpectedly stepped in. He stood in the door, and for a long time we looked into each other's eyes speechlessly. I was paralyzed with surprise. Juan Hwang looked haggard. He came to me, kissed my forehead and then asked, in the tender voice one might use to ask an invalid how she feels:

"Can you live without me?"

It was in words like these that he always gave me to understand that he could not live without me. I shook my head, quietly and feelingly. He laughed, a kind, endearing laugh, then sat down at my side with that lithe pantherlike movement which I so admire in him. He put his arm around me, and we gazed into each other's eyes, not with the moist, melting gaze of lovers but with the fidelity of our unhappy, tragic friendship. Then we started to talk, and told each other all that had happened since we were last together.

Juan Hwang took the room next to mine, and by moving the wardrobe a little to one side we cleared the adjoining door. There are hardly any guests in the hotel; naturally, not a word was true of the telegrams to which Senhor Camilo Camillian had referred in the king's presence.

After supper I went to bed, while Juan Hwang walked up and down in my room. We talked for a long time. Occasionally he stopped and leaned against the wall, and at these times darkness swallowed him completely, for my little reading lamp was the only light in the room. Then his voice sounded as if it came from very far away, like a voice heard when one is half asleep.

The conversation so terrified me that I cannot recall exactly what was said. He began by repeating the substance of what he told the king on Bösendorferstrasse last spring. He did not know that I had been listening at the open door. Roughly, the gist of his remarks was this:

"Even the king can no longer doubt that he cannot regain the Hungarian throne by the means he has employed so far. It seems as if all hope were lost. Seems, mind you. In their deepest instincts the Hungarian people are still loyal to the crown. It is only as a *national* ruler, however, that Charles can return to the Hungarian throne. This means that he must become a Hungarian himself, renounce the name of Habsburg and marry a Hungarian woman."

"Are you mad? How can you even imagine such a thing? Wholly apart from the fact that the king loves his wife, there can be no question of divorce in any form whatever."

And Juan Hwang's reply came from beside the wall, out of the darkness:

"A Roman writer, Artius, once said that the hog feeds on acorns, the stork on snakes, and history on human lives. Sometimes it swallows a hundred thousand soldiers. Sometimes a single man. It is still a more beautiful thing to depart this vain, brief, earthly life under the sinister but splendid stars of history than to die of appendicitis. Death at the hands of history is the only death which contains the seed of life, like a cion grafted on a tree. The king did not accept my suggestion, which was to dispose of the queen by means of a trumped-up accident—namely, her death while skiing in Switzerland. Now it is up to us."

A second later he added in a quiet voice:

"The queen must die."

I covered my face in terror and shrieked plaintively:

"No, no!...Don't say any more!"

At that moment, although I had no proof, I was entirely convinced that Juan Hwang had been involved in the attempts on the queen's life, first at the funeral of Franz Joseph and later at Schönbrunn.

"Get out of my room!...Get out!" I cried, still covering my face with my hands.

Later, when I regained my composure, Juan Hwang was no longer in the room.

20 December

In the mornings I take my portable typewriter over to the Villa Amalia for an hour and help the king with his correspondence. He dictates touching letters to his children and to his grandmother, Archduchess Maria Theresa, who is with the children in Switzerland. The king still has a large correspondence. He receives letters from all over the world. An elderly Hungarian teacher writes from Rumanian-occupied territory, asking for help in the reinstatement of his pension. A Tyrolese game warden writes to ask whether His Majesty would like to buy a hunting rifle at a low price. A woman in Zagreb asks the king not to throw away the outworn clothing of his children but to send the clothes to her, for she has eleven youngsters and her husband was killed on the Italian front. All this is as if the decaying corpses of the war were still muttering, still bleeding. This is what has remained of the Monarchy. I answer all such letters, beginning them all with "On behalf of His Imperial Majesty I regret to inform you…"

Everyone makes demands on the king, who sometimes stands staring into space, lost in thought, for he has no idea how he will manage to support his family. Yesterday he complained again that the exorbitant hotel bills were becoming an ever greater source of concern.

I wrote a long letter to Papa tonight, and gave him a frank picture of the situation. Evidently the home front has still not recovered from the recent events.

1 January 1922

The days pass with unvaried monotony, and there was nothing of note to mark the holidays. I wonder what the new year will bring? Since our last conversation Juan Hwang has avoided all talk of politics, and thus we manage to get on without quarreling.

Still no news from home. There has been no answer to my second letter to Papa, although I myself begin to be short of funds. I feel very weak nowadays. Eczema has broken out on my left kneecap again. This is a result, I think, of the local climate and the diet here.

6 January

The queen has finally received permission to visit her children in Switzerland. She leaves tomorrow.

7 January

A dreadful day. The queen went aboard ship before noon. I went along in the motor launch, too, to see her off, and when I returned there was a letter with Juan Hwang's handwriting in my room. The letter consisted of one short sentence without signature:

I've gone away.

I collapsed into a chair, and may even have been unconscious for a while. Why has he gone away? Where has he gone? Once more I could hear his voice: "…the hog feeds on acorns, the stork on snakes, and history on human lives."

What must I do? Should I warn the king? Should I wire the queen and notify the police in every country of the world?

"...the sinister but splendid stars of history..." I am afraid I shall go mad. I am completely helpless. I went down to the little Carmelite chapel and knelt in prayer for a long time.

13 January

This morning the king showed me a telegram from the queen, announcing her safe arrival in Switzerland and reporting that she had found the children in good health, except for little Archduke Robert, who was in bed with appendicitis. The queen will stay in Switzerland until Robert is entirely well.

O God, please protect the queen and keep her from harm.

17 January

Nowadays the king and I are completely alone. I not only attend to his correspondence in the forenoon but spend the afternoon hours with him too. Sometimes we play cards. This afternoon, when we wearied of cards, we began to play *Apfelstrudel,* to renew the wonderful days of our youth in Vienna. The king is in a good mood, and keeps count of the days until he can see his children once more.

Tonight, when I was alone in my room, a terrible anxiety seized me again. I recalled the day when Juan Hwang showed me the spot on the bank of Lake Geneva where Luccheni, the Italian anarchist, drove a file through the heart of Queen Elizabeth.

20 January

Another telegram: Switzerland has ordered the queen and the children to leave the country at once. Nothing is more indicative of the kindness of the Swiss Government than the fact that little Archduke Robert has been granted permission to stay during the period of his convalescence—only until he recovers, of course, after which he too will be driven out. This is Switzerland, that land of milk and honey which managed to stay out of the war. Apparently the entire world has forgotten the meaning of the word mercy.

My heart was beating wildly when I woke from a short nap this afternoon. I had dreamt that the king was once more being crowned in Buda, amid great pomp and splendor. But instead of a frosty December snowfall it was a beautiful day in May, and I was the queen.

I am sick at heart. I wish I were a schoolmistress in some remote little Hungarian village. I would have a garden, with an old walnut tree at its center. O God, keep the queen from harm, protect her from the sinister stars of history.

2 February

This was the most wonderful day of my life. The queen arrived with the six children. I stayed on shore while the king took the motor launch to meet the ship—it was the *Avon*. When they returned the king headed straight for the Villa Amalia with his smallest son on his arm. The other five youngsters flocked after their father like noisy sparrows. The whole scene was so touching that onlookers stood with tears in their eyes.

7 February

When I went down to dinner at noon today, I found Juan Hwang in his usual place. He greeted me as if he had not been away for even half a day. He did not say where he had been, nor did I ask him. He seemed in low spirits.

14 February

The staff of the royal family arrived from Switzerland this morning. The poor queen has really been in an awful state, with all those children to care for.

The king showed me a letter, signed by Camilo Camillian, which he had received from the management. Dripping with servility, the letter stated, with deepest regrets, that the management could wait no longer for payment of the bills due. The king has been unable to pay his hotel bills for the last two weeks.

I cannot understand why my letters home have not been answered.

21 February

The king is happy because his situation has improved for the moment. A noble-hearted Portuguese gentleman, hearing of the difficulties of the royal family, has offered them the free use of his villa, which stands empty on the Monte.

28 February

The royal family and their retinue moved up to the villa on the mountainside yesterday. They made a party of seventeen, including two ladies-in-waiting, an Austrian and a Hungarian tutor, two chauffeurs, the queen's chambermaid, the Swiss nun who has charge of the smallest children, and the wife of one of the chauffeurs. They were accompanied by Count Dalmea of Spain and his wife. Nineteen people in all.

4 March

Everyone is in high spirits: little Archduke Robert, completely recovered, has arrived with his great-grandmother, the elderly Archduchess Maria Theresa. The whole family is finally united. But the occupants of the villa now number twenty-one, and the accommodations are very meager. This evening I sent the following letter to Septemvir Utca:

Dear Papa—I cannot understand why there has been no answer to my letters. Hurry, please, and help the royal family before it is too late. Let me give you an idea of their situation.

The Villa Madaro is built on the side of the Monte, at an altitude of about fourteen hundred feet. The garden is large and attractive, but the vegetation at that altitude is not tropical at all. The villa is a one-story affair, painted reddish yellow, and from one of its windows there is a lovely view of the mountainside, of Funchal and the ocean. The villa is small at best, for it was built with the three members of the Madaro family in mind.

Inside, a tiny foyer opens on an octagonal hall. The living arrangements are as follows: the seven children and the Swiss nun live in the three rooms on the left. The larger room on the right is occupied by Archduchess Maria Theresa, and beyond is the dining room, so small that meals are often served in three sittings. The next two rooms—cubbyholes, really—house the two ladies-in-waiting. The king and queen selected the two little mansard rooms in the attic for themselves; there they can enjoy a certain degree of quiet, for traffic downstairs is brisker than on the main street in Funchal.

In the smaller building, not far from the house, are the kitchens, the pantries, several gloomy storerooms and two tiny attic rooms which have been assigned to Count Dalmea and his wife. The two tutors—one is a Hungarian priest, the other a schoolmaster from the Tyrol—live in the greenhouse, which is lit only by oil lamps! The rest of the staff is billeted in an overcrowded porter's lodge.

I write of the accommodations in such detail only to show you that the situation could not possibly be more miserable. Papa, Mamma—if you could only see how wretched it is! Please, Papa, think of the eighty rooms that stand empty at Ararat, not to mention our other houses, on Septemvir Utca and elsewhere. Fate has been kind to you—the staff at home still numbers about fifty, even in days like these. I shan't speak of "national chivalry"—but how can you and Uncle Andrew and the others betray your consciences by allowing your king to suffer so, when you all owe your fortunes to the Habsburgs? If you dont believe me, send a commission of inquiry—but do something to help, do something as soon as you possibly can.

6 March

This morning, when I went up to the Madaro Villa, I found great confusion in the hall. The king was in his shirt sleeves, sawing a plank in half. The Hungarian priest's cassock was covered with sawdust too. They were building a little chapel beneath the stairway in the hall. I watched them for a long time, and recalled the crimson velours and the Gothic heights of the Matthias church, and the magnificent splendor of the coronation. But I think this little chapel must be dearer to the heart of God.

By noon the chapel was ready, and the priest conducted Mass. The king and little Otto were the ministrants.

7 March

This morning the king, the older children and the two chauffeurs went into town, to the outdoor market place, where they bought thirty hens and six roosters. The king himself carried two of the heavy baskets. His plan is to raise chickens in the garden, where a chicken coop stands empty. I met them in front of the Hotel Azuria, and attempted to relieve the king of one of the baskets, but he protested with a laugh. He said placidly:

"Now I have fewer Swiss francs than children left. But I think the chicken yard will give the children a great deal of pleasure, for each of them will have his own duties and responsibilities. I've discovered, furthermore, a marvelous secret of economics. These hens will lay fresh eggs every morning, and the little chicks will grow up to be fat chickens, and then we shall be able to eat them…"

8 March—Villa Madaro

At two o'clock this morning I was roused from sleep by Juan Hwang, who had just returned from town.

"Wake up," he said, paler and more nervous than I have ever known him to be. He switched on the light and began to pace the room like a madman. I jumped from bed and put something on.

"I've just learned," said Juan Hwang, throwing himself into a chair, "that there is a conspiracy afoot against the king. They want to murder him!"

"The king?"

Juan Hwang nodded gloomily.

"It's a very serious affair. I've not been able to find out who is behind the conspiracy, but I have a feeling that it has very powerful support. The king is a burden to the major powers of Europe; as long as he is alive, they must constantly expect him to make trouble. One thing, however, I did learn for certain. The execution itself has been entrusted to that little devil with the goatee."

"Camilo Camillian?"

Again Juan Hwang nodded gloomily. Standing in the middle of the room with a blanket about my shoulders, my knees began to tremble. I had no reason to doubt Juan Hwang's words, for his intelligence of this sort always proves to be correct. He has secret sources of information in the political underworld. I began to dress hurriedly, but Juan Hwang stopped me.

"What are you going to do? Run to the police? Tell the king? At the moment this would not only be purposeless but dangerous to boot. As long as we don't know what forces we're up against, we can do no more than watch and wait."

We talked until dawn; I did not go back to bed. By early morning I was up on the mountain, and I spoke with Count Dalmea first of all. Acting on Juan Hwang's instructions, I did not tell him exactly what was going on, but I cautioned him to keep the iron gates of the villa closed at all times. Dalmea reassured me by saying that the gates were always locked, and called my attention to his wolfhound, Ripp, who allows no strangers to enter the grounds. Ripp is really a terrifying beast. A dry, green light burns in her eyes, her jaws are constantly dripping with saliva, and her coat is bristly. She is so lean that one can count her ribs, although she devours great quantities of food.

I talked with Anna, too, the wife of one of the chauffeurs. I warned her to taste all food that was served to the king.

I carried out all of Juan Hwang's instructions conscientiously, but as I stood in the garden I somehow felt that the entire conspiracy was a fantasy of his. On the little slope in front of the villa stands a lovely silver poplar, and at that moment its loveliness was further enhanced by the fog. The tree was planted in celebration of Napoleon's death. I am afraid the celebration was somewhat premature.

Spring has come, but the garden is still clad in fog. Now, in the early days of March, the two-thousand-foot Monte begins to doff its snowcap, as if in greeting to the incoming season. The consummation of this gesture will take four weeks—as Count Dalmea explains it, mountains move less quickly than men. When the mountain sights the approach of spring, clad in the blue-and-gold veils of the sea, it begins to cry with joy, and its tears flow in streams toward the ocean. A swollen little brook runs through this very garden. Down in Funchal the heat of summer has set in, but up here the Monte is still bathed in the apocalyptic mists of its miraculous metamorphosis. Warm fog covers the Monte from the middle downwards, and it will take the oak trees only eight days to blossom in this fog.

9 March—Hotel Azuria

The king went shopping in town this morning, for tomorrow is the fourth birthday of little Archduke Charles. By the time he reached home, in the afternoon, the birthday boy was in bed with high fever, and neither the cake nor the doll house gave him any pleasure. The queen and one of the chauffeurs are also ailing, and so I have had ample use for my knowledge of nursing. This has been the first time in a long, long while that I have worn my Red Cross nurse's uniform. The Swiss nun and I ran from one bed to the other, thermometer in hand.

12 March

I was up in the Villa Madaro this morning. I found the king feeding his chickens in the chicken yard; three days ago little Archduchess Ethel was stricken with pneumonia, and yesterday little Archduke Felix took to his bed with the same complaint. The labor force is bedridden, thereby increasing the servants' work, and so the king himself volunteered to feed the chickens. He was wearing a shabby green apron, and had just filled the troughs with water.

"Believe me," he said, "the management of such a chicken farm is no less demanding than the responsibilities of rulership."

He strewed corn from the pockets of his apron with a somewhat awkward motion:

"Pi-pi-pi-pi-pi!...Keep your eyes on that fluffy little chick with the bare neck. She behaves just like Slovakia. And those two little roosters over there, the white and the reddish brown, are constantly squabbling, like the Serbs and the Croats. That great fallow rooster, on the other hand, terrorizes the whole company, and even tried to take a nip at me before. Pi-pi-pi-pi-pi!"

"Hungary?"

"Yes!" laughed the king. "And I shall cut off that gorgeous blue-black tail of his by way of punishment, and pin it on my hunting cap."

14 March

This morning the roosters, the hens and chickens waited in vain for their caretaker to pour fresh water in the troughs. For days the king has concealed his rising fever, even from himself, but now he too is bedridden.

17 March

It is ten o'clock at night. I have just left the Villa Madaro after nursing the king all day. I want to enter these few lines quickly, before they fade from my mind. Yesterday the children kept running into their father's sickroom, but from this morning on they were strictly forbidden to enter. Now they are only allowed to stand by the door towards evening, to say good night. I happened to be there when the four children—the other three are still sick—climbed the narrow stairs which lead to their father's attic room and stepped into the doorway, one after another. And one after another the four childish voices called, with exactly the same intonation, "Gute Nacht, Papi!" There was something heartbreaking about it. Drowsily, but with marked tenderness, the sick man's voice echoed them: "Gute Nacht, Otto...Gute Nacht, Robert...Gute Nacht, Rudolf...Gute Nacht, Franz Joseph..." It sounded like six centuries of Habsburgs taking their final leave of the world. The king called them each by name, in turn, although the four shrill greetings of "Gute Nacht, Papi" must have been very much alike through the closed door.

Juan Hwang says the king's illness is not serious. He is still disturbed by the conspiracy, which I have almost forgotten. He says he is on the right track and will soon know more about the matter. The danger, in his opinion, is not past. Quite the contrary!

20 March

This morning I met Count Dalmea in the garden of the villa. He wore a broad-rimmed straw hat and a light summer suit with a rose in his buttonhole, a costume which seemed strange in the fog—for the garden is still covered with fog. He had just left the king's sickroom, and he said the king was planning to hunt mouflon on the Isola Deserta next week. The king had practically no fever this morning. Count Dalmea was on his way to town, to make arrangements

250

for the hunt. While he led me through the garden his dog, Ripp, kept hovering about our heels. She would vanish into the fog for a moment, and then reappear. However fond I may be of dogs, I can't bear the sight of that repulsive beast.

21 March

Last night the king's temperature was 102.2°, and this morning it was 101.6°! When I went up to the villa before noon, Archduchess Maria Theresa called me aside and said it was really time to call a doctor, for so far neither he nor the sick children have had medical attention! They are so short of money that they have been reluctant to consult a doctor. I returned to town immediately and at about noon, after much telephoning, Dr. Nuno Roteimon and Dr. Leito Aldao came to the hotel. Aldao, the younger of the two, speaks English fairly well, while old Roteimon speaks only Portuguese and a few words of German. I told them what I wanted, and they left for the Villa Madaro at once. Their diagnosis was bronchial catarrh, not disassociated with the dull spots they seemed to hear on the right upper lung. Both of them declared that it was not serious. They have promised to return tomorrow. Count Dalmea accompanied them into town to buy ammunition for the mouflon hunt.

22 March

Early this morning I was already at the Villa Madaro. After Mass I sat in the hall and waited. Young Dr. Aldao was the first to descend the narrow steps from the sickroom. He hurried to my side and whispered, almost poking his nose in my ear: *"Inflammation of the lungs!"* Pneumonia—everyone was speechless when they heard the news. The physicians were wondering where to place the king, for they found the little attic room unhealthy. After studying the premises they decided to move the sick king into the large downstairs room where Archduchess Maria Theresa has been living. The queen went up to the sickroom to discuss this with the king, but she soon returned to say that the king would not agree to the arrangement because he did not want to inconvenience his grandmother. Old Dr. Roteimon's face stiffened, and he sent the queen back with the message that there must have been some mistake, he had not suggested the move to His Majesty as a request but as the command of a physician. While the queen was upstairs young Dr. Aldao stood by the window and gazed out into the garden, where the heavy, white fog was slowly curling. He beckoned me to his side and whispered:

"Who advised the king to move into this villa?"

"I'm afraid it was an economic necessity."

"Do you know that no one has moved into any of the neighboring villas yet? The Monte is very hard on the lungs in March. The native population knows this very well, but of course it's not noised about because of the tourist trade. During these weeks the Monte is like a wild beast in its mating season—it does not like to be provoked by our presence."

Dr. Aldao turned back to the window and kept on studying the fog, which crept about the trees of the garden as if preparing to launch an attack in full force on the Villa Madaro.

Meanwhile the chambermaid and the Swiss nun had spread clean sheets on the bed in the downstairs room, and the king was already descending the stairs, in pajamas and slippers, with a winter overcoat about his shoulders. But the queen had to support him, for he could hardly stand on his feet. I preceded Dr. Aldao in hurrying to the stairs to help support the king, although there was barely room for the three of us on the narrow stairway. This was the first time I had seen him since he fell ill, and he was a pitiful sight. The hair has turned gray at his temples and at the roots of his mustache. And to think he is only thirty-three years old! The doctors prescribed linseed applications, and quinine for his fever. So much for their medical knowledge.

Later, at home, when I told Juan Hwang what young Dr. Aldao had said about the fog, it was clear to see that he was very deeply impressed.

27 March

"The Kingdom of God is a vast music…" The Rilke poem comes to my mind. The king has received the final sacrament. I was there in the room, but it is impossible to describe what I saw and felt.

At four o'clock this morning all of us were still keeping a sleepless vigil in the hall. The two doctors spent the whole night at the sickbed. Old Roteimon was the first to leave the sickroom, and he stretched out his hands as he spoke: "*The heart! The heart is failing!*" He spoke in Portuguese, but everyone knew what he meant.

The king has been unconscious since one o'clock. Someone telephoned, while others began composing telegrams.

30 March

The king has regained consciousness! His fever has abated, and his heart has recovered its strength. According to Roteimon, he is out of danger. They took the children in to see him for a few moments. Then Dr. Aldao drew some blood from the spinal region. Count Dalmea came into town with me to make new arrangements for the mouflon hunt.

31 March

Disturbing news: inflammation has attacked the other lung, and the king has been in a coma again since this morning. They gave him an injection of turpentine, and some adrenalin towards nightfall. I can no longer keep my eyes open. I returned to the hotel around midnight, after falling asleep in the car. Juan Hwang was waiting impatiently. When I gave him an account of the gravity of the king's condition, he was seized with sudden rage. He gnashed his teeth and beat the wall with his fist:

"The swine! He's outwitted me, that swine!"

"Whom do you mean?"

"The goatee! He tricked us all! I myself thought he meant to kill the king with a revolver or a dagger, with poison or a bomb! But no! He was much more ingenious than that! He killed him with hotel bills! He killed him with fog! He hounded him up to the Villa Madaro! Now—now I can see what the fog was for!"

I felt that Juan Hwang was right. And I began to understand why there had been no answer to my first two letters to Papa. Camilo Camillian has probably been withholding my mail.

1 April—Villa Madaro

At seven o'clock this morning Artur, the waiter, woke me from a deep sleep to say that I was to go to the Villa Madaro immediately. I threw on my clothes, Juan Hwang was fully dressed and waiting for me, and we left together. A heavy fog hid the garden. They were just preparing a fresh bed for the king when we arrived. He was conscious, but succumbed to fits of fainting from time to time. We opened the window. The fog glided into the room, as white as a ghost come to take the king away. Dr. Aldao administered oxygen, and the Swiss nun kept sliding hot-water bags under the blankets. At half past nine he took a sudden turn for the worse. The fever rose alarmingly, and the pulse weakened. But the

253

king unexpectedly recovered consciousness and raised himself somewhat in bed. He said, in a clear, calm voice: "Ich möchte..." And he said no more, but everyone knew what he wanted, and the Hungarian priest brought the Eucharist. When the king had received it he asked for another pillow at his back, and his voice, again, was completely clear. At half past eleven Dr. Aldao wheeled away the oxygen tanks, for they were no longer in use. A cold sweat covered the king's face.

At twelve o'clock the door opened quietly, old Archduchess Maria Theresa took the ten-year-old Crown Prince Otto by the hand and led him inside. There is nothing more touching than the face of a frightened child.

One final injection. Dr. Roteimon released the king's wrist, took his watch from his waistcoat pocket, and the room—which had heard nothing but whispers for some time—suddenly filled with his strong, slightly quavering voice as he said, almost too loudly, almost at a shout: "*Twenty-three minutes after twelve!*" It was in Portuguese, but everyone understood, for we all looked at our watches. And we understood, too, that the king was dead.

Juan Hwang seized me by the arm, pulled me to the window and whispered, in a completely distracted voice, pointing at the garden through the open window: "Look!"

Terror-stricken, I covered my face to hide the sight I saw out there. Now, for the first time, the fog had lifted from the Villa Madaro, and brilliant sunshine flooded the entire garden. The fog had fled, like an assassin, from the scene of the crime.

Five o'clock in the afternoon: There are days that are longer than life itself. I am all alone on a bench in the garden of the Villa Madaro. The poor king would have done better to fall at the head of his troops on the battlefield, or to succumb to the gunfire of the revolutionists; it would have been better for him to die on the altar of peace at the hands of the secret German executioners. History will never forgive pneumonia, the oxygen tanks and the cupping-glasses.

Once, before the war, we went to the circus in Vienna, Papa, Mamma, Uncle Fini and I. The circus attendants brought in a life-size, costumed wooden doll, carried it around the front rows by the armpits, manipulating it to show the spectators that its face was really painted wood and how rigid its eyes were, how stiff its hands and feet. Finally they accidentally dropped the wooden doll, and it landed with a crash on the ground. Then came the surprise. The wooden doll, motionless up to that moment, slowly raised one arm and regained its feet with awkward motions, as if driven by an ingenious mechanism. The climax of the act was when the doll began to sing and dance with great cleverness, very entertainingly, and it ran from the ring amid rounds of applause, for the doll was really a human being. This was what happened to the king. Here, in Funchal, I watched him turn into a human being. This was the man they propped on the throne in the middle of a war which he did not start. During his reign the Germans and his councilors were constantly scolding and abusing him, for if they had not watched him closely he would have made peace at once, like a naughty child with an obsessive idea. This was the man they killed—Juan Hwang is right—with hotel bills and fog, but more with hypocrisy than anything else, in my opinion. Count Dalmea tells me he has just been informed that the wealthy bankers of Funchal, when they learned of the king's straitened financial condition in January, voted to give the royal family unlimited credit. The only trouble was that they neglected to let the king know about this generous offer. As for the Austrian and Hungarian aristocracy—! And the wealthy prelacy—! Papa is an exception. Papa finally took action, after I went to the telegraph office last week and sent him a long, beseeching, peremptory wire; fifty thousand Swiss francs arrived with a promise of further remittances. And there were other exceptions who did help. Exceptions? No, not exceptions! Their help was neither sufficient nor did it come on time. The king is dead—this speaks more eloquently for their help than anything else. They were disgracefully craven and heartless toward the king, all of them, every one, the Council of Ambassadors, the Swiss Government, all the potentates and maharajahs in the entire world!

One of the chauffeurs told me that Ripp, Count Dalmea's dog, gave birth to a litter of nine puppies this morning. Brr! Cold chills run down my spine when I think of that frightful beast.

Later: They have decided to perform an autopsy. The funeral will take place only five days from now, and a tropical heatwave is raging.

Midnight: At nine o'clock at night Dr. Roteimon and Dr. Aldao entered the dead man's room, together with a third doctor whose name I don't know. The dead king lay in bed with his chin bound, and his face was already bristled. The doctors unwrapped their instruments and set to work. As assistant, I was in my white gown too. Scalpels, scissors and odd-shaped saws glittered in the light. They sat the corpse up in bed, took off his shirt and stretched him out again.

They opened up his chest and extracted the king's heart. Then they squirted a solution of formaldehyde into the arteries to keep decomposition from setting in.

I was holding the metal tray when Dr. Aldao placed the extracted heart in the tray—an ugly, purplish, bleeding mass of flesh. The edges of the main arteries were white where the surgical scissors had pierced them, and the blood was still oozing out.

Suddenly the tray began to tremble in my hands. Like a sinister bolt of lightning, Frau Katz's prophecy struck through me: "And someday you will hold the king's heart in your hand..."

Dawn: The autopsy took more than two hours. Later, sitting on a chair in the hall, I fell asleep from sheer exhaustion. It was already light outside when I opened my eyes. I started for home, but took a long way toward the main gate, for I wanted to give the chickens some fresh water. I felt I owed this to the king's memory. And I wanted to see, for the last time, the bare-necked little chick, Slovakia; and the two little squabbling roosters, one reddish brown and the other white, the Serbs and the Croats; and the great, domineering fallow rooster, Hungary—all that remained of the Monarchy.

The refuse pit is behind the chicken coops. I don't know how it could have happened—the doctors probably threw the king's heart into the pail and the servants, not knowing what it was, threw it in the refuse pit.

When I passed by, Ripp was standing at the brink of the refuse pit and gnawing on something. I recognized the king's heart between her teeth just as she gulped it down.

Chapter Eleven

SERIOUS and trustworthy memoirs have described the king's exile in Madeira, his last days and the circumstances of his death, exactly as Kristina's diary depicts them, with the difference that these memoirs make no mention of Kristina Dukay's presence in the king's following. This does not exclude the possibility that Kristina was actually present in Funchal; one must assume, at best, that the chroniclers did not mention her name because they did not consider either her person or her presence to be noteworthy.

This diary is full of statements which do not always correspond with historical fact. It is a matter of common knowledge that the Bourbon princes met the king's secret emissary not in Geneva but in Neuchâtel. There was never any attempt whatever on the life of Queen Zita. It also seems wholly improbable that King Charles would have given a young woman like Kristina Dukay so important a part to play at secret conferences on the outcome of which not only the fate of the Monarchy but of the entire world, so to speak, depended. There is no doubt that Kristina did know the king, and was often in his company; but in general there is no historical proof of any sort for all that is said by the diary to have taken place between Kristina and the king.

One of the historians who read Kristina's diary while it was still in manuscript characterized it with these words: *A pack of audacious lies.* We must note, however, that this very same historian recorded falsehoods of the most brazen sort without blinking an eye.

He called attention, for example, to the names which appear in the diary. There is no hotel known as the Hotel Azuria in Funchal, nor has anyone there ever heard of a hotel manager with a goatee who called himself Camilo Camillian. The names of the physicians in attendance were actually Leito Monteiro and Nuno Porto. The royal family, after moving to the mountain, did not live in the Villa Madaro but in the Villa Rochemachado; otherwise the description of the villa is entirely accurate. Among the faithful followers who volunteered to stand by the king in his travail were Count Almeida of Portugal and his wife Donna Constanzia da Gama, but the records fail to mention a Spanish count called Dalmea. It is true that on the night of the king's death the two physicians,

Monteiro and Porto, did remove his heart, if only because it was a tradition to remove the heart of every Habsburg after death. But Queen Zita preserved the heart as a holy relic, and thus it can hardly be true that a nonexistent Spanish count's wolfhound, Ripp, consumed the king's heart in a refuse pit on the following morning.

For all this, Kristina's diary cannot be dismissed with the statement that it is a lie. According to the general conception of a lie, the liar must wish to make an untruth seem true, intending thereby to mislead his fellow men. A person who makes assertions like the assertions of Kristina is not a liar, however, but—a poet. It is of no importance, really, whether Kristina or a policeman in civilian clothes acted as the king's secret emissary, nor is it important whether Uncle Cini or Florian or entirely different people were present at the fateful meeting at Laxenburg. What is important is the spirit which permeates this monumental drama.

Viewing Kristina's diary in this light, we come to the surprising conclusion that her every single statement conforms to historical fact.

But before undertaking the task of demonstrating the historical authenticity of this strange diary, we must familiarize ourselves with Kristina's final fate.

From Funchal she went to Spain, where she spent a number of restless years, sending her family the briefest of letters which contained only a fragmentary account of her life abroad. Letters to her father were particularly colorful, heated and turbulent, especially those in which she asked for money. Sometimes she unexpectedly turned up at Ararat or on Septemvir Utca for a few weeks, only to vanish again. Acquaintances often saw her at the gaming tables of Deauville or Monte Carlo, and her photograph occasionally appeared in the society sections of cosmopolitan magazines, dressed for polo, or with a hunting rifle in hand, or with a fishing reel and a giant swordfish or a record-breaking tuna hanging head downward in the background. Once she was voted the "best-dressed woman in the world"—another time she barely managed to extricate herself from a notorious scandal that had to do with forged checks, a widely publicized affair in which, however, she figured merely as an intimate acquaintance of one of the Canadians who were involved.

Toward the end of the Thirties she evidently wearied of endless wandering, of life in hotel rooms and sleeping compartments, for at that time she took up permanent residence in the home of her parents. By then she was forty, and the dark hair which had coruscated with the hues of burnt bread-crust was beginning to turn gray at her temples, but she did not dye her hair. She was generally seen on horseback, whether at Ararat or on the streets of Buda.

In the fall of 1939 she married Ivan Borsitzky, a Hungarian diplomat, and this move afforded Countess Menti great consolation. But Kristina divorced Borsitzky, for reasons known only to herself, after two weeks of marriage, and was sickly for a period of months. In the following year she married again, surprisingly enough; this time she became the wife of her physician, Dr. István Freyberger. Kristina was forty-four years old, while the physician was sixty.

Kristina survived the Madeira tragedy by twenty-three years. In January of 1945, after Soviet forces had occupied Budapest and while the ruins of the capital were still smoking from the fires of the siege, a commission of twenty members set out through snow-covered streets toward one of the Ghetto houses, to view the slaughter and to prepare a notarized deposition similar to the one which was made at the graves in Katyn Wood. In the courtyard, among the hundreds and hundreds of bodies piled in a frozen mass, there was the emaciated corpse of a woman, stripped of all clothing and covered with nothing but a tattered horseblanket. One of the university professors on the commission was surprised to recognize the features of Kristina Dukay. Her legs, naked to the thighs, extended from beneath the blanket, and the carefully groomed toenails were tinted a dark shade of mauve.

István Freyberger was of Jewish descent, somewhat stoop-shouldered, a physician who was not accounted a notability among medical men. We do not know the advantages of this marriage, but we may suppose that Kristina discovered the ultimate tranquility of life, its valedictory loveliness, in that gentle, wise man when she married him at the age of forty-four. We know that Kristina was tormented with various minor ills from childhood on, buzzings in her ears, cramps in her heart, twitches in her stomach, eczemas. It is likely that her sensitive flesh took comfort in the constant proximity of a physician. But we do not mean to detract from the somber splendor of Kristina's death, which was worthy of the embattled and embittered life she led, a life of majestic dreams. The marriage lasted for five years, and those who knew them said their union was touching in its tenderness. They were happy. When the Jews were faced with their extreme ordeal under Nazi domination, Kristina shared her husband's fate. Her death occurred without either pathos or heroism. What happened was this: when the executioners of the Arrow Party arrived to take her husband away, she protested, verbally at first, and then she

259

began to struggle with the two young murderers, who simply shot her down.

This diary of hers, which was found in a locked drawer, was originally written in German; apparently that language came most easily to Kristina. In the description of the Geneva apartment which she occupied in 1917, Kristina mentions that Paul Klee's *La fuite du fantôme* hung in her bedroom. Paul Klee painted that picture in 1929. Thus Kristina betrays that she wrote her diary well after the fact, perhaps in the years that preceded her death. This is indicated by the evidence that she no longer remembered certain names. She viewed things from a perspective of nearly twenty years, as the simple wife of a stoop-shouldered physician; on first reading her diary we felt like an astronomer when his spectroscope first detects the faint but fabulous light-signals of a star which exploded eons ago.

To interpret those signals was no easy task. We were thoroughly puzzled by the mysterious person of Juan Hwang, for the diary asserts that he was a member of the Hungarian Lower House in 1918 and even made an important speech at a decisive moment. There has never been a member of the Hungarian Parliament by the name of Juan Hwang. Kristina clearly used this name to conceal someone's identity.

We chanced upon the source of this strange name in the annals of Chinese literature. During the seventh century after Christ a learned Buddhist of great piety set out from Sian Fu, the capital of Shen-si Province, and spent sixteen years in India. He wrote a book about his long journey, *The Record of the Western Countries,* which is considered one of the classics of Chinese literature, for he was among the first Chinese to penetrate to the occident. It is probable that Kristina, while engrossed in research for her novel about the Ordony chieftain, read some works which dealt with this Chinese Marco Polo, and that the name of Juan Hwang—also known as Yüan Chwang and Hsüan Tsang—took root in her imagination and blossomed there.

According to our supposition, the Juan Hwang of the diary is nothing but the oriental spirit—transplanted to the west from deepest Asia, at odds with itself—which was present in Kristina's spiritual complexion. When Kristina writes that she slept in one bed with Juan Hwang, in their ground-floor apartment on the Rue Chantpoulet in Geneva, we must think of something more than mere physical love.

Perhaps it was not Juan Hwang who wanted to kill the queen, but Kristina herself, who was not completely unjustified—after the *Apfelstrudel* kiss in the spring of 1911—in abandoning herself to a wild dream of becoming queen of Hungary. Perhaps she clothed her desires in the guise of Juan Hwang, whose political function is a historical actuality.

It was the spirit of Juan Hwang who repulsed the king at the outskirts of the city when he was pleading for the Hungarian throne, and it is the spirit of Juan Hwang who has been ousting German-blooded rulers from the thrones of Eastern Europe for centuries. The figure of Juan Hwang is that living bond of blood and instinct which still binds the Hungarians, Bulgarians, Rumanians and—to some extent—the Slavs of the Danube Valley to Asia.

Pursuing this strand of symbolism, we can also unmask Florian. We first encounter him as a wounded soldier in a military hospital. Then he unexpectedly turns up in Geneva, and later in the most confidential councils of the king. He appears wherever the interests of peace can be served, and when the king, losing his courage and his equilibrium at the climax of the tragedy, abides with the Germans, Florian leads the raging, revolutionary mob against the monarch.

In our view, Florian bears a strong resemblance to the Unknown Soldier. Florian is the stomach wound in the delicately chiseled and diplomatic phrases of Uncle Cini. Florian is the historical reality who was, verily, present at the fateful conferences in the imperial chateaux at Laxenburg and Baden. He was more truly present than if he had merely stood beside the table—he was present in the king's heart, for the young king's heart truly went out to his suffering soldiers.

Camilo Camillian: in all probability, Kristina intended this perfumed goatee to symbolize the ruling classes of Europe, whose heartlessness truly despatched the unhappy king to his death, after which they wiped their hands on lengthy telegrams of condolence. The historical fact is that the Council of Ambassadors exiled an unhappy family to a desert island, for there is no more deserted island in modern civilization than an unpaid hotel bill.

In conclusion: Ripp, the ferocious wolfhound. Again historical truth comes to the defense of Kristina's journal. For Ripp did devour the king's heart on the brink of the refuse pit. It was not a flesh-and-blood heart but another, the parcel-carrying, chicken-raising, chapel-building, paternal heart of someone who was a simple little man, who did not disdain to take needle and thread in hand, who loved his wife, loved good cheer, loved an occasional glass of wine, loved peace and loved God, would have liked to do some great good and was surprisingly similar to the many, many millions of his respectable fellow men if only in that he proved too weak, too inept and—in moments of decision—too simple to achieve his "great good."

It was this gentle heart, the heart of millions upon millions of peaceable men, that was devoured by Ripp, the ferocious wolfhound, who was nothing else than the bestiality of the European spirit which truly spawned a litter of nine on the brink of the second World War. In the final analysis, then, Kristina's diary turns out to be a combination of truth and poetry.

In the further course of our story we shall meet Kristina again, but only in a supporting role. The chapters that follow will deal with the years which were crowded between two World Wars. And, as these years dance their way to destruction, the principal figure will be the younger Dukay daughter, Zia—who, at the time of the king's death in 1922, was only twelve years old.

3. The Copperplated Twilight

Chapter One

MANDRIA, solitary village on the minuscule island of the same name, is in the northeastern reaches of the Adriatic, close to the Dalmatian coast and to those steep, violet-hued cliffs which, ten miles in the distance, overshadow and conceal ruined gates of ancient towns, patron saints resting in silver tombs, bands of determined and desperate smugglers, reeking fishmarkets—and concealed, seven hundred years ago, the melancholy of a Hungarian monarch who fled from the Tartars and took refuge along these misty stretches.

The island of Mandria belonged to the Austro-Hungarian Monarchy for several centuries, but after the World War it became part of Italy and thereupon fell victim to the erroneous notion that it would remain so forever. As a consequence of this mistaken idea the principal square of the village was named Piazza Vittorio Emanuele, a formality which was both unnecessary and superfluous for a variety of reasons. First, the village had no other square but this, and so it was needless to suppose that someone might confuse this square with another. Furthermore, had the triumphant King of Italy seen the square, with its ornamentation of fish-guts and rotting tomatoes, where children, in full daylight (and adults, but only after nightfall) performed functions the performance of which is generally restricted by modern man to the confines of modest and narrow enclosures—had he seen this square, he would surely have protested against such an application of his name. Properly speaking, it was not even a square, for most of its expanse was occupied by a shallow, concrete-lined lagoon, an extension of the harbor, that gave shelter to the smaller craft and was littered at the bottom, like a somewhat singular aquarium, with black and crimson rags, the discarded hulks of bedraggled skirts and trousers, with yellow halves of lemon, the silvery hollows of empty tin cans, with lacquered but leaky and rusting chamber pots, all of which glittered with the colorful splendor of tropical fish. The name of the dwarf-dimensioned king was accustomed to tremendous, beautiful Latin squares. But we cannot take it amiss that Mandria named its only square, which had borne the name of Franz Joseph for thirty years, after Vittorio Emanuele, for it was an age when streets, squares and bridges the world over took on new names with the persistent regularity of swindlers and confidence men.

The island was most easily approachable by motor launch from the ports of Zara or Lussin, and this is worth knowing because Mandria was a watering place and resort, or at least it was so advertised in the informative brochure that enumerated, to the credit of the island, such attractions as the newly built *bagno* and the Francesco Ferdinando Promenade, a thoroughfare which guilelessly meandered along the seashore without the slightest suspicion that a few years later it would be slapped in the face with street signs that read Corso Mussolini.

Among Mandria's other attractions were the golden chalice on the altar of the Church of San Simeone, the work of Mediolani and the gift of Elizabeth of Anjou; the eighteen liras per diem charged at the Pension Zanzottera; the running water at the Albergo Varcaponti; the uniform perfection of service; the remarkable ocean air; and other irresistible advantages. The informative brochure, however, failed to inform anyone of the fact that Mandria had no supply of drinking water, and that the island was inaccessible for weeks at a time when the seas were rough. It also failed to note that the plumbing at the Albergo Varcaponti had been out of order since before the war and was still unrepaired. According to Occhipinti the druggist, who was known for his pithy sayings, the brass plumbing of the hotel would improve only if the glottal plumbing of Signor Varcaponti himself broke down. The signor and his nautical beard could be seen all day long on the terrace of the Trattoria Marica, a bottle of *vino rosso* half empty at his side.

The postman brought a daily burden of printed folders and announcements from every part of the world to the Dukay Palace on Septemvir Utca. The Dukay name attracted as well the advertisements of department stores in London and the catalogues of small-arms firms in Belgium as the brochures of French, Swedish, Dutch or American business houses. The world gave notice of steam yachts, stylish brassières, secret gambling dens, breeding animals, astrologers, automatic corkscrews, trained white mice, Greenland cruises, rejuvenating drugs and the jubilee celebrations of German singing societies to the Dukay Palace. This terrestrial globe was never so rich, and never offered its merchandise so resourcefully, as after the first World War, although at that time all international commerce had something of the air of a clearance sale about it. History teaches us that it is not the dictators who can foretell the future, but rather the dealers in second-hand clothes. Deauville, Biarritz, Carlsbad, Venice and the rest, world-famous hotels and sanatoriums, like poor relatives, sent news of themselves from time to time lest the Dukays forget them utterly. No wonder, therefore, that in the flotsam and jetsam of price lists and catalogues the Mandrian prospectus too was swept, like a stark message carried along the ocean tides in a bottle, up to the shores of Septemvir Utca.

Quite by chance the prospectus was fished out of a wastebasket by Zia, youngest of the Dukay children, who was nurtured, as we already know, under the wing of old Madame Couteaux—Berili, as the little girl called her after a favorite Teddy bear of childhood.

The trilingual prospectus captured the youngster's fancy. Perhaps it was the word *Mandria* itself, which has a truly strange music. The name hums with mild and laurel-scented zephyrs, especially after a perusal of the prospectus. It is impossible to know precisely what it was that enchanted the child's spirit. Perhaps it was the golden chalice of San Simeone, or perhaps the sea, which the cheaply colored prospectus painted such a blue as in reality it never is—or perhaps the running water of the Albergo Varcaponti, which became, in her imagination, a fairy brooklet bubbling in every room. It is more likely that the wells of fantasy in the childish soul simply seized on Mandria as a polyp's tentacles will seize the colored rag dangling for bait. Girl-children make very early and very ceremonious preparation, both in body and soul, for what is to follow. Young birds are known to carry blades of grass and twigs in their beaks long before nesting time, and girl-children collect the prospectuses of distant, unfamiliar resorts and the autographs, carelessly scribbled and dispensed with regal disdain, of third-rate movie stars. Zia was content with Mandria. At the age of seven she had already decided to spend her honeymoon on Mandria, although she did not know at the time that honeymoons consisted of more than meals and social conversation. She was like the rabbit-eared Princess Oasika in the Brahmanic tale who borrowed the wings of a falcon and with the help of elephants and tigers built, on the Hill of Oranges, a crimson citadel of yellow towers, with no other materials than her own vague desire. This German fairy story was printed in Leipzig and made available exclusively to the children of the wealthy at an outrageous price by a metropolitan bookseller. The book, beautifully illustrated and printed in Gothic letters each the size of a young swallow, was given to Zia as a Christmas present one year, and on the very next birthday of Countess Menti she recited the entire poem without a single error; at most she said Oakisa instead of Oasika, but fortunately this slip was noted only by Fräulein Elsa, her governess at the time, who punished her for it by making her kneel in a corner after the party. This was one of those occasions when her loving brother, the halfwitted Count Rere, smuggled to his kneeling sister's side an empty cartridge shell and another of the usual little offerings, bleached to whiteness, that he had found in the park.

With the passing of years we shall see how Mandria decided Zia's fate. A single word, a mood, may have hardly any luster or pulse or meaning when it penetrates the soul of childhood, yet it will still strike root there, throw out its leaves and become the signpost of a capricious destiny. Primeval forests sprang up so, when a solitary bird of passage circled the desert plain, a tiny seed undigested in its droppings.

Not every human soul is fertile ground for dreams and visions. In most cases the heavy physical exertion of swimming meets, piano lessons or self-abuse serves to dispel the redeeming or murderous visionary angels of adolescence. But the soul of young Terézia Dukay was a hotbed for visions. Behind the golden orange groves of Mandria a further dark vision took root and this she called the Copperplated Twilight, for it was in such strange and meaningless phrases that she expressed inexpressible things to herself, without even speaking the words aloud. The Copperplated Twilight had its origin in the palace library, where she came upon an old French etching, a representation of Marie Antoinette. Out of this picture developed her story of an autumnal dusk.

Madame Couteaux had now been at Zia's side for three years, and the eleven-year-old little girl already spoke an excellent French. From the very beginning her language knowledge grew swiftly, as a newborn infant grows in weight and frame when the mother's milk flows amply. And, like a big-bosomed peasant wet nurse whose gushing milk stains her shift even after she has suckled the fusty scion of wealth at her breast, Berili was a source of rich and flavorsome milk for this child who had taken the place of the departed Louise in her heart. From morning to night the Gallic language poured from Berili, her agile mouth overflowing with improper little stories or lengthy tales, village vulgarities or tuneful nonsense-rhymes, and at these times the pea-sized birthmark with its bouquet of crescent-shaped hairs above her left lip bobbed in constant and rhythmical accompaniment.

The first poem she taught Zia was called "Le roi Dagobert." The verse told how the good King Dagobert put his breeches on backwards one morning when he went out hunting, and how he fled helter-skelter at the first sight of a rabbit—this good king who that very day had ordered every last man in his army to die a hero's death on the battlefield. And when the devil came to call for him in his old age, the king begged St. Elias to do him the kindness of dying in his stead. On the occasion of Countess Menti's next birthday Zia guilelessly recited this poem, with the result that after the festivities the countess summoned Madame Couteaux for an urgent interview and concluded an agitated and reproachful harangue by prohibiting any and all further mention of the poem about good King Dagobert. This was the first open conflict between the meridional spirit and the Dukay Palace.

Berili's educational methods were other than those of Fräulein Elsa. She gave no long, tearful, moral lectures when the child missed a piano lesson or an hour of penmanship. She never sent her to kneel in a corner. Animal-like in her passions, she simply slapped Zia's face roundly, for all that corporal punishment was strictly forbidden in the Dukay Palace. On the other hand, she found it the most natural thing in the world that Zia should instantly return her slap. Often they spat out at each other. Thus their mutual friendship and love and fundamental respect for each other deepened from day to day. Berili was essentially full of cheer; nevertheless, it was she who imbued the girl's spirit with the mute and fearful anxiety that was to be the wellspring of decisions made at crucial moments in her later life. It is a common burden, this heavy and mysterious fearfulness, of all human souls. The terrifying ritual ceremonies and loathsome blood sacrifices of primitive religions, whether those of prehistory or of "stagnant" civilizations, of Eskimos, nomads or Polynesians, have their origins in this great fear. Man fears something, and most often it is death. Frequently, however, he fears life, and this is the more dangerous species of fear. The fear of death leads toward life, but the fear of life conduces to death. Relatives and the police cluster in bewilderment around the bodies of youthful suicides: it was the great fear that killed them. In most people this open scar finally heals of itself, but there are sensitive and delicate nervous systems in which the wound merely continues to throb ceaselessly under its thin film of tissue. The fear is variously manifested in adults. There are men, valiant warriors or wresting champions, who for some unknown reason are obsessed by a terror of turkeys, and others who cannot bring themselves to eat rice pudding. Professors of the new psychology refer such aberrations of fear to the injuries of childhood. Without knowing or willing it, Madame Couteaux inflicted a grave injury upon the soul of the little girl entrusted to her care.

✛

The incident took place in the fall of 1922, on an October afternoon in the palace on Septemvir Utca. Twilight had descended over the rooftops in Buda, and the atmosphere had an odd, dull, coppery glint that seemed, under the vaulting arches of the room, to have seeped down from a distance of many bygone centuries. Such a curious and rarefied modulation of light and air is necessary, evidently, to the presentation and birth of stories, legends, wonders or fears. So the Gospel, too, came about, in "a rushing mighty wind," as we know from the letter written by Luke the Evangelist to the physician Theophilus. Tongues of fire came down upon the human spirit and Peter, who was—according to his contemporaries—a mild and cautious man, began to speak the ardent words of Joel, the ancient Hebrew prophet.

Madame Couteaux was sitting by the window and stabbing a half-finished stocking with her knitting needles, for she refused to acknowledge the invention of the power loom, as far back as the eighteenth century, in England. Not only her stockings but the lace fringes of her flannel drawers were manufactured by her own hand. Zia sat in a corner of the large tapestried sofa, as small as she could draw herself up to be, her fist pressed to her chattering teeth. She was listening to a story. The role of Joel, the ancient Hebrew prophet, was at this moment being played by Lucien Veyrac; Berili's grandfather, who died in 1866 and had served in the armies of General Lafayette as a youth. In the Sixties he had passed his ninetieth year, and, as the Parisian papers of that period said, he was one of the nineteen men left alive who had borne arms in the glorious French Revolution. The children of the Carcassonne cheesemaker had grown up and scattered around the world; only eight-year-old Marianne, known at present as Berili, remained at home and so she not only knew Lucien Veyrac but was at her grandfather's side from morning to night in the declining years of the aged veteran. In the diligent cheesemaker's home, where all had a hundred hands, no one had time to waste on them. It would have been impossible to say whether the child was put in the care of the old man or the old man in the care of the wise youngster. Grandfather Lucien wore white stockings and knee breeches,

272

and still combed his hair into a pigtail at the back. He even played the violin with tremulous fingers now and then, but he had to be watched closely, for once he almost set fire to the house, and occasionally, mistaking the bottle for wine, he took a swig of petroleum, and another time he accidentally missed his chair, sat on the floor and was unable to stand up for fully half a day. Those years of Berili's childhood were spent on the knee of one of General Lafayette's former troopers, under the branches of Grandfather Lucien's tales, and the yellowing leaves of a great historical epoch fluttered into the little girl's heart. We must suppose that Lucien Veyrac did not lie to his granddaughter, or at least no more than the proprieties of storytelling demand. However this may be, the faded dove-blue cape with its metal buttons and the withered body in the cape, against which the child used to nestle her cheek, were still part and parcel of the glorious French Revolution. And now the stories had such an immediacy, as Berili passed them on to Zia by word of mouth, that the intervening hundred and fifty years seemed to vanish and the clock in the Copperplated Twilight could almost be heard to resound with the fiddles playing "Richard, oh my king! Abandoned of the world!"—playing the ancient song in the Salon d'Hercule; for Lucien Veyrac, able fiddler that he was, belonged to the military orchestra and in this capacity he was present at that memorable banquet given in honor of the king and queen by one hundred Swiss officers, Flemish officers and the officers of the National Guard at Versailles, the last soldiers to maintain their allegiance to the sovereign in a France already torn by revolution. Champagne flowed freely and the glasses rang, voices were raised in song and impassioned speeches. The latter, to the best recollection of Grandfather Veyrac, were remarkable for their stupidity, as speeches have generally been throughout history whenever military men chose to congregate en masse and declare themselves. Visibly exhausted by the day's hunting, the king sat in his place. Finally the doors of the royal reception hall swung open and the queen appeared, the dauphin in her arms. The walls reverberated with huzzas as the officers sprang to their feet and hundreds upon hundreds of swords were whipped from the scabbard, though not in order to subdue a revolution at that very moment but merely for the sake of the spectacle, to greet, with drawn swords in the right hand and brimming glasses in the left, their queen—who presented a truly majestic and melancholy aspect with the little dauphin on her arm. Hungarians, who are familiar with the details of their own history, know that the ill-fated Marie Antoinette found the stage directions for this scene in the archives of the Habsburg family, and took as her model that

273

affecting and effective tableau of her mother the Empress Maria Theresa at the Diet of 1741 in Pressburg as she made an appearance before the sword-rattling and mustachioed Magyars, holding the heir apparent in the selfsame way and evoking the same response: a flash of swords from their sheaths to the famous cry of "Moriamur pro rege nostro Maria Theresa!" This picture, Mother and Child, never leaves the gruff masculine heart unmoved, particularly when the Mother is a bona fide queen and the Child a veritable heir apparent. Perhaps unwittingly, the major-domo at the Viennese court had taken his inspiration for this tableau from Raphael or from Botticelli: the Madonna with the child Jesus on her arm. There was something calculated and theatrical in the queen's entrance, reminiscent of benefit performances given by debt-ridden old actors, who choose to play their most heart-rending scenes on these occasions because the bailiff is hot on their heels at home. It is a scene for troubled queens: the child cradled in arms. Besides Maria Theresa's and Marie Antoinette's, there is another such scene, the third and last, in Habsburg history: widowed Queen Zita with little Otto, the crown prince, on her arm. But by that time the roomful of sword-waving gentlemen was wanting, and the picture itself, the Mother and Child, reached Hungary only as a photograph sent from Lequeito, and its result, instead of summoning swords from scabbards, was to extract purses from pockets—and these from the pockets of only a few Hungarian aristocrats, Catholic bishops and Jewish industrialists who lent their support to keep the legitimist ideal alive in the person of the throne-bereft and persecuted royal family, very properly finding the heritage of feudalism and the expansion of nineteenth-century capitalism on firmer ground in the proximity of the throne than on the back of all sorts of catch-as-catch-can movements and revolutions that made prime ministers of throaty suburban solicitors and grime-coated locksmiths' apprentices.

It was a further observation of Lucien Veyrac at the banquet in the Salon d'Hercule that Marie Antoinette's legs were dumpy and thick, the lines of her face were hard and her hands were no prettier. The nails of her fat fingers were ridiculously short—as Berili recounted the story in its smallest and most vivid detail, breathing a ghostly life into the queen of the Copperplated Twilight, she did not fail to mention that during intermissions the musicians nudged each other and pointed their horsehair bows at the handsomely mustachioed Swiss and Flemish officers who had had affairs with the queen. Berili did not realize that in the recital of these details she was trespassing on the most sacred precincts of the Dukay house, for the little girl curled up in a corner of the tapestried sofa and listening to her tale was born of a Schäyenheim princess and therefore accounted Marie Antoinette as a kinswoman. The beheaded French queen, if only remotely and mistily, was linked by familial connection to the palace on Septemvir Utca, at least in the eyes of Countess Menti, whose calculations were not unreasonable in that Prince Rudolf Schäyenheim had married Marie Antoinette's cousin, the Archduchess Elizabeth of the House of Habsburg. The Dukay children, however ignorant they remained on the score of other matters relative to sex, were duly informed of this aspect of their origin from the cradle on. Berili knew nothing of all this. Energetically poking her long knitting needles into the stocking, she continued her disrespectful remarks about "that Austrian slut." She had no idea that at this very moment the Copperplated Twilight was pitching a tent of sinister witchcraft in the heart of the eleven-year-old little girl.

Grandfather Lucien saw more of the glorious French Revolution than merely the boisterous banquet in the Salon d'Hercule. "Sais-tu, ma petite—" knitting needles stabbed at the stocking "—this whole lousy business started because France had an addle-brained king—un roi completement gaga—who could not even manage to finish school properly. He was unlucky enough to marry a slut, that Marie Antoinette. It helped her not a bit that she was the sister of the Emperor of Austria—she was a slut. And what a slut! Ah, quelle garce!"

Cautiously poking one of her knitting needles into an ear to fish out some of the earwax therein, Berili pronounced these words as if she had known Marie Antoinette as intimately as she once knew an oystermonger she had lived with for ten years in Toulon, a Madame Rabaut, who was of socialist persuasion in her amours and scorned not even the bedraggled streetsweeper Gerard. This, by the way, is how the links in the chain of an oral tradition are forged by those who resurrect the cloudy figures of history—by association with their own familiars, whose gestures and glances and habits the storytellers borrow. Their characters are pieced together out of living men, relatives, friends, acquaintances—their thievery even extends, in fact, to the lineaments of unsuspecting strangers, and in this respect they hardly differ from the pickpockets who frequent trolley cars. They are precisely like novelists, these raconteurs. Thus Berili cannot be blamed for her slight confusion of Marie Antoinette with the oystermonger. Many others, from Carlyle to Stefan Zweig, have caught at the storied skirts of the unhappy queen in an effort to snatch her fleeing figure back into reality.

"Antoinette," Berili continued, using the queen's Christian name as she was perfectly entitled to do, for it is a right of address in regard to kings and queens that storytellers have reserved for themselves from ancient times, "Antoinette was a terrible spendthrift. She had a lover called Colombe" (Berili to the contrary, history knows him officially as Calonne) "whom she wound around her little finger. Let him root in the earth for more money if need be! Because what else could such a fair-haired boy become but Finance Minister? Finance Minister—naturally...naturellement ministre des finances!" She gave the stocking another vigorous jab with the knitting needle, from which she had already cleaned the earwax with a swift brush against her skirt, for such nose-and-ear-pickers commit their nuisances in the happy belief that these surreptitious motions of theirs go unnoticed.

"Where was that rascal Colombe to get this tremendous lot of money? From the people. From the poor! They squeezed the money out of the poor oppressed people to give that Austrian slut her dinners, and wax candles, and champagne, and silks and powders—because in those days the fine, rich gentlemen did not even have to pay taxes...who bore the burden? Naturellement le peuple!"

Berili's meandering tale occasionally happened upon a historical truth. They passed each other, these two, and sometimes strolled along together for a few paces, but without any desire on either side for closer acquaintance.

"My grandfather used to say that they were nine brothers and sisters, and so poor that their mamma often gave them no more than a paper-thin slice of bread and butter each for supper. And where do you think their mamma got the butter? Butter! Well, what do you think? Que penses-tu? At that time their mother was nursing her youngest child. She always had a youngest child at the breast. Their mother squeezed out her own milk, churned it and smeared a thin spread of butter on those thin little slices of bread. Human milk! Beurre humain! Fortunately she had a good flow of milk. The poor thing did this in secret, but Grandfather Lucien was ten years old by then, and he saw her, and he knew all about it."

"What was Grandfather Lucien's father?" Zia asked from the corner of the sofa, speaking in the childish voice that has been muted and warmed through by a story.

"He was a wheelwright. But there was hardly any work, and when he made some money they took it away in taxes at once. Grandfather saved the entire family by becoming a footman in Marquis Raverney's castle."

"Did he get such a big salary?" demanded Zia, wanting to tilt the scales in favor of the aristocracy.

Berili twisted her head in the direction of the sofa and cast a scornful glance at the youngster.

"Sometimes you ask stupid questions, dear. Big salary! For a little bus boy! In those days! But Grandfather was a clever and quick little boy, and he loved his brothers and sisters, and he was God-fearing, and so he stole as much as he could carry from the castle. Fruit, cheese, roasts...one dark night he carted a whole sack of wheat home from the granary. Mais naturellement!" Berili lifted the two knitting needles into the air, without any further explanation. Then she continued:

"Luckily he wasn't ever caught. He spent four years in the service of the castle. Then came the trouble. The big trouble! It was in 1799, on the twenty-eighth of July, at nine o'clock in the evening." (Here Berili erred by ten years, but this sometimes happened to Tacitus too.) "The village lay in a tolerably secluded spot, and the post passed through no more than once a month, so they had no idea, in the castle, that revolution had broken out in Paris two weeks before, that the people had stormed and taken the Bastille and liberated the innocents the rascally Colombe had imprisoned there at the behest (of course) of the king and queen. Well, no one in the castle had any idea what was simmering in Paris. There was partridge and truffles for supper, with a red wine sauce. *Perdreaux truffés!* In addition to Grandfather, three other footmen, Jean, Michel, and Paul, were serving the meal, all of them in fine livery with silver buttons. Pink tapers glowed in large candelabrums on the table. A musical clock was softly playing the song that begins 'Au clair de la lune.' There were ten people seated at the table, Marquis Raverney, his wife, the eldest daughter Jacqueline, Pierre and George—both of them were fully grown—and besides them the two smaller girls, six and seven years old, the two governesses and a visitor, old Count—now, what was his name?"

(Zia leaned forward to listen. The picture was perilously close to the dining rooms of the castle at Ararat or the palace on Septemvir Utca.)

"The marquise was a thin blonde, with a very long nose and a tiny mouth under her nose. Grandfather used to say that they knew her for a quiet, good soul. Marquis Raverney had three corporations—a big one on his belly, a smaller one under his chin and an even smaller one on the crown of his bald dome, where a swelling had grown to the size of a walnut. This was Michel's description, whose head was always full of such nonsense. The marquis was very fond of a waistcoat that was colored a poisonous green, and he always wore a gold watch as big as a potato in each of its two pockets. Grandfather had nothing bad to say about him. Generally they dined on the terrace in the summer, under the chestnut trees by the light of lanterns, but that day there had been a heavy shower in the afternoon, and rain was still threatening in the evening. So they ordered the table set in the dining hall, which had double doors that opened on the terrace and let the good cool-smelling rain-drenched air pour in. It was around half past nine, and Grandfather was just passing the partridge to the marquis, when a growing hubbub of voices was heard in the park, the voices of men and women, more and more voices coming ever closer. Within a few seconds a whole regiment of people, all wet to the skin, trooped into the dining hall from the terrace. They were shouting and shoving each other, some were drunk, many carried table legs, rusty pitchforks, or ancient shotguns, and even the women had all kinds of clubs out of the attic, and then there were laths and vine-stakes tipped with knives or sword points...bâtons ferrés...They were all villagers, but there were some strangers from other villages too, and you couldn't hear what they were shouting in the great clamor. Tollier the carpenter, who was the drunkest of all, skipped to the side of the marquise with a polite pirouette and holding the scruff of her thin neck in his shovel-sized hand he said: "Ah, Madame, notre bonne marquise!"— and then pushed the marquise's forehead down into the fine gilt-edged plate that was full of wine sauce. Someone grabbed one of the tips of the tablecloth and pulled it off the table—chinaware and glasses were shattered...the candelabrums tottered and fell...the candles rolled away on the floor...one of them was still burning and it set fire to the heavy lace curtains at the window. The burst of flame started a scuffling and a shouting that would freeze the marrow in your bones. It must have been horrible...."

"Did they hurt them?" Zia's voice chirped fearfully. Berili raised her eyes to the ceiling and said only: "Mon Dieu!"

"And the footmen...your grandfather...didn't he protect them?"

Berili twisted her head toward the sofa once more. For a few seconds she plied her knitting needles wordlessly. Finally she said:

"His own father was among them."

Then, as if in protest against the unspoken thought, she threw her hands in the air to dispel all suspicion from four generations of the Veyrac family:

"But he didn't touch anybody! Ah, non, non! Lui, il n'etait pas un de ces types-là! He wasn't that sort. It's true he had his axe along, but he only worked on the walls. He stood on a chair and cut to pieces all the old family portraits and the framed sheepskin records of the noble Raverney line. He worked his way from room to room till dawn, having been a diligent man all of his life. And Grandfather Lucien didn't take part in the obscenities either. He didn't lay a finger on anyone. But two of the footmen, Michel and Paul, who had stood there poker-faced and were passing the silver trays just a few minutes before—they certainly put their shoulders to the wheel…Oh, mon Dieu!"

"Did they kill the little children too?" Zia's tearful voice came from the corner of the sofa. Berili replied evasively:

"Grandfather used to say that when dawn broke, the corridor of the castle—inlaid with large smooth marble blocks, it was—when dawn broke the corridor had a long uneven red stripe running along its length, like the trail of a whitewash brush dipped in red paint…Ah, le pauvre!…They had dragged the marquise along the corridor by her hair."

Zia buried her face in a silk cushion. She had before her a picture of the corridor in the castle at Ararat, as a massacred Countess Menti was dragged by the hair along its marble floor.

Berili noticed her movement and continued reassuringly:

"Such nastinesses weren't committed everywhere. In some of the castles they only drove the owners away. And sometimes the lords and ladies had already disguised themselves in peasant clothes and fled."

Berili thoughtfully rolled up the half-finished stocking and stuck her long knitting needles neatly into the ball of wool.

"It was a long time ago…let's forget it!" she concluded.

She limped away to her own room. She limped because she suffered from arteriosclerosis. Hardening of the arteries periodically gave her stomach cramps and made her lame.

Zia was left alone in the room. The Copperplated Twilight grew darker and darker. She was almost ready to start screaming. Shivering, she huddled in a corner of the sofa, and pressed her tiny fist even more convulsively to her mouth. It was hardly more than three years after the return from Willensdorf, where they had fled because the "Connumist" revolution had broken out in Hungary.

This mispronunciation of the word stayed with her, just as she had long referred to oranges as "noranges," but she still had no idea what the Connumist revolution was. They had already been in Willensdorf for a number of weeks when Count Dupi and Countess Menti arrived. Count Dupi was dressed as a chimneysweep, and Countess Menti as a peasant woman, a kerchief over her head and a basket on her arm. With good will on all sides, Count Dupi might indeed have passed for a chimneysweep, but Countess Menti's appearance, despite the petticoats, starched shirts, motley stockings and red Szeged slippers, simply screamed out her Schäyenheim origin, for she spoke Hungarian badly and even rolled her *r*'s, not to mention the whiteness of her thin hands and her face which, framed in a peasant kerchief, made her look like a Meissen porcelain pitcher. This affair of the disguises was as purposeless as if someone had tried, by means of a few pieces of clothing, to turn a giraffe into a poodle. It all seemed very amusing at the time, and the laughing children hopped and danced around the masquerading parents who, because they had successfully crossed the border, attributed their accomplishment to the cleverness of their costumes, not knowing that Mr. Gruber the secretary, who arranged the escape, had so thoroughly bribed the two Austrian guards on duty at the border that Count Dupi and Countess Menti could have crossed the Bruck bridge had they been dressed like the German emperor and empress, with crowns on their heads and purple robes about their shoulders, for the guards would have turned away their eyes with the same modesty.

Of all this only so much remained in Zia's childish mind, that Papa and Mamma too had put on peasant disguises. Why had they dressed in peasant clothes, like the French aristocrats in the days of Grandfather Lucien? Were they afraid too? Her head swam with so many mysteries.

It was particularly the memory connected with a certain roast goose that now began to disturb the child. It had happened the year before last, in August, at Uncle Paul's. Uncle Paul had also married a Schäyenheim girl, and he lived in a castle quite as large as the one at Ararat. Such castle-dwelling kinsmen visited each other frequently, and on such occasions their guest rooms were full for weeks without respite. Countess Menti took Berili and Zia and went to pay a ten-day visit at Uncle Paul's, who happened to have an unusually rare and distinguished visitor at the time: a real, live little elephant that was hardly larger than a heifer. Uncle Paul had bought the elephant for the amusement of his children from a wandering circus that had gone bankrupt, and he planned to deed the beast to the zoo when it grew up. The little elephant was completely at his ease as he paced the park, as if his own ancestors too had been born to such places for hundreds of years back, and he congenially tolerated the shrill, joyous outbursts of the children prancing about him. Adalbert's expression —Adalbert was the elephant's name—was full of shrewd wisdom. His shiny black eyelashes of finger length resembled the long eyelashes of the clay-tinted lady who had made a motion picture in their castle that spring, with the difference that the actress, at the end of a sequence, using her fingers for tweezers, carefully removed the eyelashes and gave them into the care of her wardrobe mistress, something that Adalbert could not do because, on the one hand, he did not retain a wardrobe mistress, and, on the other hand, because his eyelashes were real elephant eyelashes, as Countess Menti explained the phenomenon to the incredulous children. Adalbert had a dazzling talent as a juggler, however much his form and extremities belied the possibility of such accomplishment. His apparatus was an enormous meter-wide balloon filled with air which never touched earth once it had been thrown to him, for Adalbert, without seeming to move, used now his head, now his trunk, now the tip of his tail to keep it constantly in the air. He merely flicked the tip of his tail imperceptibly, or lifted one of his stubby hind legs, and the ball bounded into the air again without Adalbert having even looked at it, almost as if he had long-lashed eyes on the bottom of his padded feet or on his rump. And when he finally tired of the game he would suddenly twist his trunk to one side like a baseball bat and give the balloon so mighty a blow that it flew into the topmost branches of one of the near-by trees. He seemed to address the rubber sphere as if it were a giant fly: "Now that's enough, let's have no more nonsense around here." One could laugh himself to death over this, and to be sure there was no dearth of childish laughter.

The ten-day visit with their cousins and Adalbert started beautifully, but on the second day that certain roast goose made its appearance at dinner, which was not in itself unusual. Footmen circulated the silver platters exactly as it was done at home, and they were all engrossed in the enjoyment of that fine, crackling roast goose when Aunt Stefi, with the customary nod of her already graying, crane-blonde hair, spoke up in a sweet voice from the head of the table:

"Wisst Ihr, Kinder...do you know what kind of a roast goose this is, children?"

And she related that the head gardener had confiscated an old peasant woman's two geese; in defiance of a strict prohibition they had been foraging on the park preserve, but Mr. Hörcher the head gardener had espied them, for Mr. Hörcher had the eyes of a hawk—er ist ein Mann mit Adleraugen—and like a hawk he swooped down upon the geese.

Aunt Stefi made a great hit with the picture she conjured up of Mr. Hörcher's eyes swooping down on the geese, and the children broke into screams of laughter. But then an unexpected and peculiar thing happened. Countess Menti put down her knife and fork, dropped her napkin on the table, stood up and left the room. She was visibly pale. Aunt Stefi and Uncle Paul looked at her with amazement, and the footmen too followed the departing countess with their eyes, but the latter did this without moving their heads. A sudden coolness descended over the table, a palpable coolness of which even the children were aware, for they felt it on their skin although they did not know what it meant. Some part of the secret was revealed to Zia a little later, but she told no one about it, not even Berili, who vainly stabbed at the child with the pinpricks of her impatient and curious queries: Qu'est-ce que c'est que ça? Qu'est-il arrivé?

Countess Menti's room was beside their own, and only a thin door separated the two. After dinner Uncle Paul and Aunt Stefi sought out the countess in her room and there, behind the closed door, a quarrel broke out. Zia stole to the door and eavesdropped. It was the first time she was privy to the secrets of her elders. So agitated was the exchange of words, which took place in German, that she understood little of it, but the very fact that her mother, whom she had never known to raise her voice, was now quarreling heatedly—this fact itself was as unusual, even terrifying, as if a new and strange Mamma had entered the world. But one sentence was quite clear to Zia as Countess Menti's voice lashed out in a sharp and imperious tone:

"Wenn jemand ein Rittergut von sechzigtausend Joch hat, isst er keinen solchen Gänsebraten! Nobody with sixty thousand acres of land has to eat such roast goose!"

Berili, her face flushed, stood behind Zia and her sparse gray hair almost crackled with excitement as she nudged Zia with her questions: "Que disent-ils? Qu'est-il arrivé?"

But Zia just wriggled her shoulders and eyebrows, and did not communicate even the one clearly heard sentence to Berili, for she felt that it concealed some family disgrace. Berili was thrown upon the resources of her own brand of logic. She spread her arms plaintively:

"Mais je ne comprend pas...I can't understand it. The goose was entirely fresh—I didn't smell anything wrong. I've got a nose, haven't I?"

But the nine-year-old child knew by then that the roast goose stank. It was not the stink of spoiled meat, but something else, a more profound stink from which Countess Menti—who was a sensitive soul—recoiled. Within an hour the car was ordered to the door and they departed. The countess left without any farewell. Probably other things contributed in the course of the years, but this was the beginning of a lifelong estrangement between Countess Menti and Uncle Paul's family.

At the time Zia had only a dim comprehension of all this. Now, as she sat in the midst of her Copperplated Twilight, abandoned by Berili and alone with Grandfather Lucien's story, she began to feel that there was a sinister link between the roast goose and the bloody corpse of the Marquise Raverney. And now, too, she began to sense the connection between this affair and the story that Uncle Dmitri began to tell at dinner in the presence of them all one night last spring, whereupon Countess Menti had silenced him with a curt English phrase and Uncle Dmitri suddenly shifted to the subject of horses. Uncle Dmitri's arrival brought Zia the same mysterious message from Russia that had resounded in Grandfather Lucien's story, a message which seemed to indicate that payment would some day be demanded for the roast goose, the little elephant, the tall, pearly-branched fountains in the park, for everything that surrounded her. These obscure associations met, mixed and mingled in Zia's soul for the first time that late October afternoon. A dim sense of responsibility took root in the child's soul during the dusk of her Copperplated Twilight.

Berili was still exploring the closet of the adjoining room, for Berili was always searching for something although she never really knew what it was. One might suppose that Madame Couteaux had wreaked a cowardly revenge of the common people upon the little countess entrusted to her care, purposefully poisoning her with an instillation of fear. Berili was innocent. The faucet is not to blame if it sometimes spurts brown water rather than clear. The fault is not in the faucet, but in the rust of the pipes built into the wall and under the ground.

Chapter Two

LIFE WAS divided between the palace on Septemvir Utca and the castle at Ararat, so that the summer months were spent at Ararat and the winter on Septemvir Utca, while the spring and fall were spent in the villa at Reichenau, outside of Vienna, or perhaps in Nice. As in the castle at Ararat, so in the palace on the hills of Buda each child was allotted a suite of three rooms, one for himself, one for the tutor or governess and an intermediate parlor for socializing. Zia's rooms at Ararat were on the mezzanine of the south wing. Kristina's adjoining suite had been empty now for three years. Following the death of the king, Kristina had gone to Spain, and every half year she sent each of her brothers and her sister a terse postcard which, with its pictures of palm trees and indigo seashores or of mauve bougainvillea clustered along the gleaming white walls of a Spanish side street, was like a tiny feather dropped into the heather or the underbrush by some exotic bird of passage—but Kristina herself never put in an appearance. She had vanished somewhere in the clouds of the royal tragedy. The rooms of young Count János were in the north wing, and there György's suite lay empty, for he was now in his first year at Cambridge as a student of international law and political economy. He was the only Dukay ever to take a degree in the agricultural sciences, and he had done this while still in Hungary, for of all the Dukays he was the first to prepare with so deeply felt a sense of obligation for the assumption, upon the death of his father, of the estates. János was a private student in the sixth form of a parochial *gymnasium* in Budapest, and the tutor Dr. Kliegl was in charge of his education. Count Rere and Mr. Badar had rooms along the corridor of the ground floor, near the servants' quarters, which arrangement itself indicated that the half-witted Rere was not thought to be entirely human.

Before the war the castle used to resound with the din of children and the babel of the German, French and English tutors and governesses, but it had since grown considerably quieter. These children's suites in no way resembled the cheerful rooms of well-to-do middle-class youngsters, syrup-sweet with fragile white curtains and painted furniture. Here the bedchambers were vaulted, with heavy draperies, dark furnishings as old as Methuselah and cloudy old paintings, reminiscent—like the rest of the rooms—of the fact that the Dukays, as members of the Ordony clan, were already a thousand years old at birth. Even in the pink flesh and tender bone-structure of Dukay infants there was an element of the human fossil.

The honey of motherly love was as far from Countess Menti's heart as the voice of the nightingale from the throat of an ostrich. She had expended all the fine animal passion of her maternal instinct on her first-born half-wit child. She felt no mother-love, in the conventional middle-class sense of the term, for her other children. And it would not have been fitting for a princess *née* Schäyenheim to inquire after the didies of her little ones, to rock them on her knees or to murmur sweet nothings to them in a ridiculous voice, not to mention other things that even middle-class women do, such as to chew the white chicken meat thoroughly, bind it well with their own saliva and then push this pabulum between the toothless jaws of the flourishing offspring with their fingers. Even in her relations with the children Countess Menti maintained the cool distance that her rank demanded. The apartments on the main floor of the castle were not only geographically but spiritually at a distance from the children's rooms, into which she ventured only infrequently and by accident. But the fact is that her presence was not required, for the parental responsibility was fulfilled by the provision of a separate and distinct governess or tutor for each child. And this person, whether governess or governor, was expected, according to Countess Menti's most precise estimation and understanding, to *govern,* in the literal sense of the term. The function of the governor (or governess) within the organization of human society is like that of the umbrella or the bicycle, the handles or spokes of which may conceivably be of various manufacture—the governor (or governess) may be French, or English, or German, man or woman, young or old, but in the final analysis he is a *governor* and nothing else. The fact that these governors (or governesses) might be inhabited by human beings, whose individualities and spiritual capacities are reflected in children, was completely beyond Countess Menti's comprehension, just as she saw no more of the footmen in the castle than the livery that contained mechanisms equipped with extremities to open doors, pass platters, make low bows, equipped with rapidly pumping legs to hurry away in the execution of an order, with lips that moved in answer but asked no questions, eyes that did not see, ears that heard nothing more than the requirements of a command. It would be wrong to suppose that this attitude toward the servants sprang from dull insensitivity or overweening pride on the part of Countess Menti. It was the art of ruling that required her to consider inferiors in this way. Count Dupi, whose tumultuous youthful career and light-hearted genial spirit had brought him much closer than his countess to life and to people, was obliged to take the very same view of tutors, governesses and servants.

Thus the Dukay parents had no idea in what different directions their two youngest children, Zia and János, were proceeding toward the fulfillment of their several destinies, there in the north and south wings of the castle under the tutelage of Madame Couteaux and Dr. Kliegl—Zia toward a life of health and light, János toward the outermost and most despicable limit of destruction. They did not know and could not measure the extent to which the two disparate destinies would be the result of early training, but we, considering the children's fate and our story in retrospect, are compelled to take a stand with Taine, who maintained—in the great controversy that raged at the end of the century—that besides race and time, environment is of signal importance in the determination of motives. Going even further, the fate of the Dukay children challenges us to contemplate a more audacious hypothesis, to believe, in contradistinction to the now outmoded doctrine of predestination held by the Bishop of Hippo, that education is capable of producing *entirely new* men, men who are independent of the industrious genes and chromosomes and their accomplishment in the workshop of maternal flesh, independent of inherited traits generally.

We consider it an unusually happy achievement to have established the concept of the Dukay children, descendants of the Ordony clan, as *human fossils*. But if this attractive poetic metaphor is to survive the test of truth, we must continue by saying that in the case of Zia the fossils were corroded and dissolved by the acid of the Carcassonne cheesemaker's daughter. In their conviction that Madame Couteaux's influence on Zia did not extend beyond the bounds of French language instruction, the Dukay parents fell victim to the kind of error committed by someone who takes concentrated sulphur salts instead of castor oil as a cure for constipation. In the chambers on the main floor of the castle Countess Menti and the aging and increasingly serious Count Dupi—but especially Countess Menti—made every strenuous effort even after the collapse of the Habsburg regime to preserve, within the constitution of their own souls, in the climate of their castle and the comportment of their servants, the observance of the most noble baroque forms of the ancient Hungarian upper class, while on the mezzanine of the south wing of the castle their youngest daughter was subject to influences beyond their control, the like of which had never before penetrated those ancestral walls. During the drive back to the castle from their Austrian exile, after the short-lived Communist revolutionary episode, when Count Dupi learned in the course of conversation with Madame Couteaux that her first name was Marianne, it was more to parade his own wide reading knowledge than for anything else that he asked, with a comic wink: "Connaissez-vous Marianne?"— and how could he have suspected that this ugly old Frenchwoman not only knew Marianne but in the very fundament of her soul *was* the red-capped Marianne herself, the deathless and demoniac spirit of revolution, eternally young? One might suppose from all this that Madame Couteaux, disguised as an instructor of French in gentle dotage, had wormed her way into the interior of the vaulted castle at Ararat with objectives comparable to those of secret agents during an actual revolution, who pile suitcases full of dynamite around the piers of bridges in the dark of night and blow the streamlined luxury express, with its ill-fated and unsuspecting passengers asleep in their silk pajamas, sky high.

Nothing was further from Berili's mind than such an objective. She was one of those people who have no objectives at all, who simply exist, but existence itself is a greater matter than an objective. Berili's existence at Zia's side was the constant presence there of the reaches of southern France, and nowhere in the whole wide world is there a single point where human gaiety glows with so bright and consuming a flame. They respect nothing, these people, that men in general esteem worthy of respect. They are a God-fearing folk, but this does not prevent even the grown-ups from pinning a note that reads, "Lover, come back to me" to the back of the rector's coat as he ambles down the street, or from playing other similar pranks. During the Elevation of the Host, in the most reverent moments of the Mass, their humility is deep and sincere as they kneel on the cathedral stone at the sound of the tinkling bell, but while they are getting to their feet they cannot refrain from pinching the bottom of the woman in front, however much of a stranger she may be, but they do this as if it were an accident or somehow part of the process of standing up, and therefore their faces retain the look of high seriousness suitable to divine worship. They lack the capacity for respect of the forms of society, of the bleak beauties of tradition or the stirring pomp of national patriotic observances, although there is hardly a race more closely attached to its heritage and more thoroughly imbued with love of country. They have given birth to the village mayor who makes the dedicatory exercises an occasion for civic celebration when the first public urinal has been successfully erected on the village square, and who is the first, after the echoes of official speeches have subsided, to step up—hat on his head, bulky overcoat on his shoulders, his cat-whiskers reminiscent of de Maupassant, his dignity majestic—to step up and consecrate this truly useful, nay, indispensable vessel of public health and welfare, while the village fife-and-drum corps renders the French national anthem. And from among them, too, sprang that principal of the girls' reform school who incorporated the most devastatingly beautiful moral concepts in a volume called *The Salvation of Womanly Virtue* but had nevertheless to be thrown out of his post because a noticeably large number of his adolescent charges broke out in pregnancy. The fact is that the principal, a confirmed and methodical practitioner of education by illustration, or "learning by doing," used to summon the wayward girls of his institution to his room one by one, and later dismissed them with these words: "Now you know, my child, what it is you *must not do!*" These were people who prepared for the occasion of a benevolent visit from their betters by hastily and furtively dipping their hands in the washtub, in order to greet the dignitaries with a wet handshake as well as a low bow; they were willing to risk their jobs or their commercial licenses for the sake of the most insignificant joke. Berili served these and similar incidents up to Zia as a daily diet. The inhabitants of her stories respected neither suffering nor death. Madame Couteaux was tortured by the hypertonic cramps that accompanied arteriosclerosis, and from time to time she was seriously crippled. She might turn pale with pain, or be coated with perspiration, but when she recovered her breath for an instant she immediately made a smutty joke. This type of person did not indulge in self-respect either. In those days Berili was already approaching seventy. She wore flannel drawers that fell below her knees and were edged with a zigzag fringe of lace, and when Zia, while they dressed in the morning, asked to look at her breasts out of childish curiosity because she had never seen a female bosom, Berili modestly turned her request aside:

"What do you want to see those two dried figs for? Une paire de figues desséchées!"

Beril's breasts dangled so noticeably under her dress that only a few days after her arrival she was constrained by Countess Menti's tactful direction to don a corset, and the high corset squeezed her sagging old breasts into the shape of long loaves peeping out of a bakery basket. Her feet were knobby and the veins at the back of her knees were blue-black with varicosis. Her shoulders were stooped, her hair disheveled and uncombed. Standing barefoot and in drawers before the mirror while dressing, her mouth was not still for an instant:

"Look at that ugly old witch! Pfui! Look at those feet! Regardez ces pieds!" She scolded and scorned herself with such sincere wrath that Zia doubled over with laughter.

Her omnipresent disrespect was, in the final analysis, the expression of a boundless worship of life, youth and beauty. This human type has most recently been metamorphosed into art for us by Pagnol and Giono, and probably with greatest success in the characterizations of Raimu. Madame Couteaux was the female counterpart of Cézar in *Marius* and of Giono's baker. The Carcassonne cheesemaker's daughter herself bore a resemblance to a cheese from the south of France, in which the blandness of milk combines with the spicy fragrances of the Espinous hillsides, the salty whitecaps of the Gulf of Lions and the weathers of the Pyrenees. This mass of flavors is a little sharp, a little malodorous and a little rotten, but kneaded with tremendous quantities of sunshine. The great Cheesemaker who created the world added a pinch of the wrath of rodents, a dash of the whey of gossip and a sprinkling of all the many spices of prevarication, too, when he concocted the spiritual frame of Madame Couteaux. Berili's character was clean and clear but blemished by tiny blots, as the white apron of a cook is spotted with splashes of sauce. For example, she talked far too much even when alone; held inanimate objects in conversation, scolded them, called them to order, praised them, greeted them or bade them farewell according to her mood. Thus everything about her came alive, took on a distinct face and had a distinct character, whether kind or cruel—her clothes, her diminutive scissors, her false teeth, her knitting needles, the corset Countess Menti had made her put on, the furniture and the dresser drawers. She loved and brought to a high degree of perfection the art of conversation, which consists principally in passing not altogether unbiased judgment on our fellows. She took two days off each month, and spent these Sundays at Budafok, where she had discovered several French families in the champagne distillery and the enamel factory. How she discovered them is clear only to those who are familiar with the secrets of insects or fish, which congregate by instinct in the vastness of forests and oceans. Budapest never had a considerable French colony. The war years swallowed up even the few castaway Frenchmen who had happened into the city, so that the members of the little French group at Budafok seemed to be museum pieces. And, to be sure, that was what they were: Monsieur Gaston Deleriaux and his wife Germaine at the distillery, and Monsieur Bottin, with his mother and his older sister, at the enamel plant. Madame Couteaux became the sixth member of this miniature colony. She spent her Sundays with them, quarreled and made up, brought them presents and accepted gifts in return, and although Zia had never seen the members of the colony, Berili carried so many precisions home with her that their figures gradually came to life, until Zia was able to picture Monsieur Deleriaux as he applied the wax to his mustache, a sharply pointed embellishment which was said by Berili to resemble a carnation and to contain more dirt than wax. Zia knew that Germaine's hips were a little crooked, that the mouth of fat Monsieur Bottin had a sour odor, that old Madame Bottin was as deaf as a stone and that Mademoiselle Bottin, who was in the throes of an affair with Monsieur Deleriaux, was past fifty, for all that Monsieur Deleriaux took her for thirty-seven.

Besides these living creatures, Berili enjoyed an even more populous and gaudier society: the memories of her childhood, her girlhood and the subsequent years in London, out of which the human figures stepped forward with as much vividness as those of the Sundays at Budafok. Thus the three rooms which concealed an adolescent countess and an old French governess in the south wing of the castle or in the Septemvir Utca palace were noisier and more colorful than anyone could have imagined. When the two of them stepped out of their rooms they made a proper and prescribed impression, the Countess Zia and the old Frenchwoman; but when they were alone the picture changed, and they were like the mother bear and her adopted fawn in some refreshing forest tale. We already know that in the very first moment of their meeting at Willensdorf Madame Couteaux had locked the thin-limbed ash-blond little girl into her heart, hardly knowing who she was but veritably sweeping her into the vacancy left by poor Louise, whom the influenza epidemic had taken away.

From all this it can be seen that nothing was further from Madame Couteaux than the concept that endows a governess with the attributes of a certain method, culture and purposefulness. With the best will in the world, Madame Couteaux could not be called cultured. She knew of Napoleon and had her opinion of him—le pauvre petit caporal—simply because this had been her grandfathers opinion of the emperor on the basis of personal impressions. Moreover, Madame Couteaux knew of Archduke Rudolf and the catastrophe at Mayerling, because the romantic background of that misfortune created an even greater stir in the salons and kitchens of Europe at the turn of the century than, later, the news of the outbreak of war. Careless and thrill-hungry men and women feasted their salacious imaginations on that erotic history. Berili, too, retailed the incident to Zia during a "history hour" exactly as she had heard it in the kitchen of the London hotel: the crown prince had committed suicide because, in the course of a drunken Black Mass on that memorable night, Baroness Vetsera had cut off the archduke's genitals with her scissors. This was the full extent of Madame Couteaux's knowledge of history. Her other cultural capacities included a formidable skill at knitting stockings, and with ladle in hand she could mix salt, pepper, white wine, thyme, laurel leaves and other spices as artfully as a master violinist melds harmonics, for it is well known that the art of cookery achieves its highest perfection in the regions stretching south from Lyon.

Berili's lack of culture hardly meant that she had no feeling for the mysterious flashes of artistic beauty with which life is abundantly full, however few are those who notice and understand. This sensitivity is only adequately described as the peculiar strength of folk poetry, which has not only expressive but receptive capacities as well. There are people on the lowest levels of society, stevedores, portside prostitutes ravaged by disease, impoverished seamstresses, who see the lurking wonders of life more clearly than all the marble-fronted presidents of academies. Madame Couteaux was of this perceptive, enthusiastic breed. Not one bashful wonder of the whole wide world, however small and retiring, could escape her agitated exclamations of "Ah, ça, c'est magnifique!" When she went walking in Buda with Zia and came to the Renaissance gate of an old house, her deep hoarse voice began to gurgle with "Ah, ça, c'est magnifique!"—although she had no idea that the stone wreaths of the old gate had been identified as Renaissance by the presumption, unknown to her, of human intelligence. The old stone steps on Gülbaba Utca received her highest decoration, "Ah, ça, c'est magnifique," when they happened to be passing that way in the twilight hours. They went on boat rides along the Danube, and when an island of willow trees loomed up out of the pearly mist in the lap of the enormous stream, Berili cried, "Ah, ça, c'est magnifique! Comme un bateau vert, qui avance! It's like a green boat gliding!" In the fine frenzy of her admiration she seemed to sing the words. When the meadows around the castle or along one of their village walks were being mowed, and the rhythmical swing of the mowers, the color of the meadows and of the sky which framed the picture, and the picture itself abounded with the gentle music of motion…"Ah, ça, c'est magnifique!" This "Ah, ça, c'est magnifique" was as much a part of Madame Couteaux's being as the large, ugly birthmark next to her nose, with its crescent-shaped white hairs. The wash of the brook swept over mossy stones, and the branches of fern broke the sunlight into golden-green stripes over the play of the water. Berili narrowed her eyes and cupped her gnarled old hands to isolate this detail in the basin of the brook: "Ah, ça, c'est magnifique!" When she saw a barefoot peasant girl in the village, she stopped her and pointed out to Zia the magnificent perfection of the blond nape below the girl's upswept braids. And so, without any pedagogical intention, merely by the outpourings of her own love of life, she widened the horizons of the world in Zia's soul, and taught her that the flashing brilliancies of life could be found not only in the castle and in the palace on Septemvir Utca, within the closed circle of their own existence, but everywhere, strewn throughout the world. This method of education was in itself a revolutionary act.

On her twelfth birthday Zia was presented with a camera by Count Dupi, the only member of the family who occasionally trudged upstairs, always with something for his little "cricket"—parasols, jewelry, gloves, opera glasses and, finally, a camera. Thereupon Zia, whenever she went out strolling with Berili, took pictures continually. At first it was Berili who called her attention to the beauty in objects around them, but soon she developed an independent eye for those evanescent hummingbird gleams: the dachshund puppy, flat against the ground, cautiously stalking one of the unsuspecting stone lions of the Suspension Bridge; the general, attaché case in hand, as he angrily scratched his bottom while hurrying to the office; and the old hack horse, patiently pondering the creation of the world.

Madame Couteaux was without literary learning as well, though she read a good deal in her boredom. She ferreted out the French books in the castle library and stored them in her room. As a mouse in the storeroom can tell the difference between the raisin box and the keg of nails, she too knew what literature to choose for her ancient eyes to chew upon. She would shatter the long silence of reading with a shout, brushing the strands of gray hair over her ear: "Ah, ça, c'est magnifique! Ecoute ça, c'est bien trouvé! Just listen, how well it's put!"

She would read a few lines of Anatole France, for example, aloud to Zia, carving out each word: "*Chaque foil de son corps avait sa goutte de sueur...*" This recital tells of the red-faced, fat country parson struggling up the hillside in the heavy summer heat, as he takes his jacket off and opens his shirt, while on every single hair of his eyebrows, his arm and his chest a pearl of iridescent perspiration glistens. Berili had a talent for picking lines like this out of her books, and she fed them to Zia like sweet grapes.

Although her memory was fading and fragmentary, she had a cropful of cruel little verses from the anonymous pen of meridional folk humor. It is a variety of popular poetry which is happy only when transgressing the boundaries of propriety. Madame Couteaux not only recited these verses but sang them in a hoarse voice and even accompanied them with a dance, usually while dressing, and as she sang and danced Zia—who was, in any case, inclined to explosions of laughter—Zia rolled on the floor with roars of glee.

The popular poetry of every language is replete with furious pranks and wordplay, as when a single word in the most sarcastic line of verse is suddenly split in two, and a pause or a wordless melody is thrust between the syllables. This is most effectively done with words the first syllables of which accord with the first syllable of another and most improper word, and at this point the listeners all hold their breath, as if threatened with a blow, lest someone proceed to take his trousers off. But all goes well, because the narrator always concludes by turning the first syllable into a thoroughly respectable word. For instance, in the French language the word *cul* means backside, while *curé* means priest. Thus, if the little verse hums no more than *cu...cu...u...*, it is impossible to tell whether a bishop or a backside will emerge from the gap. Of course the word turns out to be priest, or *curé,* and the verse not only disclaims all responsibility for naughtiness but heaps its mute rebuke on those who dared to entertain naughty thoughts.

One such poem, performed daily with music and ballet by Berili and Zia while they dressed, went like this:

> *La haut sur la montagne*
> *Mironton-ton-ton mirontaine*
> *J'ai aperçu un cu...*
> *Un curé de campagne*
> *Miron-ton-ton-ton mirontaine*
> *Qui conduisait son trou...*
> *Son troupeau de fidèles*

Mironton-ton-ton mirontaine
Qui allait faire un pé...
Un pèlerinage
Mironton-ton-ton mirontaine
Pour aller voir la Vièrge.

The explicit and pious significance of the poem was that "High in the hills I saw His Reverence leading his flock of the faithful on a pilgrimage to see the Blessed Virgin."

In view, however, of the fact that the first syllable of the word *troupeau* (flock, herd) means *trou,* or hole, while the first syllable of the word *pèlerinage* refers to an intestinal eruption, the implicit meaning of the poem was clear to all: "High in the hills I espied a backside leading its own hole, preparing to release an intestinal eruption and on its way to see the virgin." Naturally, not the Holy Virgin.

The childish spirit is exceptionally receptive to these rough but innocent jests of folk humor. It is therefore understandable that Zia, in the course of her very first French lessons, when she was only nine years old, was already singing and dancing to the rhythms of this little verse with childish abandon.

Then there were other verses, similarly dipped from the well of popular poetry in the Midi, which did not think it necessary to conceal their message in truncated syllables. Such a one was the rhyme about Little Amélie, a favorite in the repertoire of the Berili-Zia Song and Dance Duo, also performed in nothing but drawers, though without audience:

La petite Amélie
M'avait bien promis
Trois poils de son con
Pour me faire un veston
Le poil est usé
L'habit est foutu
La petite Amélie
N'a plus de poil au con!

The burden of this "nursery rhyme" was that little Amélie had promised to make a suit for me out of three hairs plucked from a certain place on her body. The suit was exposed to such continuous and uninterrupted use that it wore out completely, and poor little Amélie did not have a single hair left on that certain place.

Specialists in French folklore, and Gallois in particular, have written countless appreciations on the compact excellence of this rhyme, the original version of which dealt with *Tante* Améliwe, in real life a cousin of Philip of Orleans. They have praised it for its marvelous felicity of expression, remarking especially the numerous ambiguities lurking in the word *trois,* for the circumstance that Princess Amélie had no more than three hairs left at the time she made her promise is far more eloquently indicative than whole volumes could be of the king's cousin's matchless enthusiasm for the opposite sex. The scholars drew these conclusions from the long history of the poem, because it is a motif that appears in all popular poetry, as well in the Hungarian legend of the *Körösi lány* as in the English "Sweet William's Farewell to Black-Eyed Susan."

The fastidious reader might accuse us of a pornographic purpose in probing the coarsenesses of folk poetry. He is wrong. It must not be forgotten that an account of young Terézia Dukay's spiritual progress would be incomplete without a precise and conscientious catalogue of these details. They freed her from the musty darkness of prescribed breeding, and this liberation made it possible for her, at later stations of her life, to recover and lift herself like a light-winged bird out of the dark ruins on the paths of history among which the Hungarian nobility was soon to disappear, just as in Mirabeau's time the French and in Lenin's time the Russian nobility disappeared. And there is something further. In their song, their music, their laughter, almost unnoticeably these little rhymes gave Zia the sexual enlightenment the lack of which sometimes strikes a dreadful wound in the soul of young girlhood. She greeted her first menstrual period unafraid, as a phenomenon of life. At the age of twelve she knew everything, while at the same time sixteen-year-old Count János still believed that children came out of their mother's navel without the slightest male intervention.

It need hardly be said that neither Countess Menti nor the chaplain of the castle, the Reverend Alajos Galovics, had any conception of Madame Couteaux's training methods and scarcely suspected what pagan ceremonials of southern French folklore were conducted behind the closed doors of the nursery. Had they known of it, they would have fainted into each other's arms with revulsion, and if all this had taken place in the Middle Ages Madame Couteaux would have

295

been condemned for a witch and burned at the stake in the castle courtyard, a fate well deserved according to the moral standards of the period. But no hint of it leaked out, because Zia sat at the large family table during mealtimes with an ethereal aspect of lilylike innocence suitable to her youth and rank, while Berili wore the venerable mask of her old age. But under the table they occasionally kicked each other and giggled into their napkins, despite the flood of dinnertime ritual about them and the atmosphere of solemnity that hovered over the tablecloth. They were accomplices, little seditionaries in secret mutiny against the environment, and when they pulled in their shoulders and giggled or thumbed a nose at the rigid pomp of their life, they were as the electric sparks of the approaching tempest.

Chapter Three

A T THAT time a philosophical school in Mödling was wrestling with the difficult problem of classifying Man into two main categories, according to his character traits and his modes of thought. There was a crying need for this; after the first World War the casual reader of newspapers often dropped his favorite journal in consternation and went to bed with a headache. It was no longer possible to steer a clear intellectual course, to understand why General Zeligovski of Poland had staged a military coup, why the Italians had sent a fleet to the island of Corfu, why the Druse were on the move, why the Spanish Minister Dato was assassinated in Madrid, what the significance was of the Vidovdon Constitution in Jugoslavia, why Sultan Mehmet was forced to flee, what was the ultimate goal of the Leaguists, Separatists, Zionists, Legitimists— the ramifications of the international scene were more difficult to follow than Einstein's Theory, which in those years was creating the greatest upheaval ever known in man's mathematical self-respect. In restaurants the guests waited in vain to order a meal, for the waiters retreated into corners to discuss relativity. Men well known for their stupidity declared with mysterious nods that they understood the new concept, although they did not offer to elucidate and their apologetic silence was accompanied by looks of pity: "*You* couldn't understand it anyway!" Toward the political formulations of the world about them their attitude was the same, and in the meanwhile the -isms and -ists of Europe multiplied like toadstools after rain.

This was the lamentable condition that the philosophical school of Schmidt and Kopper hoped to remedy. They determined that there were two types of human beings: the *tiller of the soil* and the *breeder of beasts.* They started the classification with Cain and Abel and pursued it through all human history. According to Schmidt and Kopper, Cain was of the tiller type, while Abel was of the breeder type. The difference between the two types was that the tiller represented the man of *established order,* who measures out the land with his own steps or a rod, draws borders and boundaries, and cuts a *straight* furrow with his plow, while the breeder simply depends upon the reproduction of his animals, which wander *freely* as they graze and stray along *irregular* paths. Breeders are not slaves to regulation or precedent, heritage or tradition, and are therefore capable of greater achievement in every branch of life, for the more *perfect* a system the more sensitive it is to deviation and disturbance. "Systematisch" Berlin is typically a tiller. All eyeglasses and slide rules. On the other hand Paris—in whose tiny theaters haloed Saint Peter turns cartwheels and sings saucy songs the meanwhile—Paris is a breeder. In her great automobile factories the emigrant Bulgarian iron-workers put their heads together with Cuban comrades in an effort to arrive at a common denominator of ideas. Futurist poets, cubist painters and musicians declare war on the time-honored meaning of meaning in the cafés of Montmartre. In Paris even the fluid brains of the oysters seem to be pondering some vague conspiratorial meeting of minds. This is why Berlin, even with fifty million inhabitants, would remain a village, while Paris, with her population reduced to one hundred thousand, would still be a capital.

Arnold Toynbee had already scribbled the outline of "A Study of History" on a scrap of paper, had already decided that there were two types of men: the *Ptolemaic* and the *Copernican.* The former still believes that the sun revolves around the earth, while the latter has realized that it is *we* who revolve around something, in concert with our national histories, our political parties, our bureaus of internal revenue, our prayer books, toothbrushes and ulcers. The tiller and the breeder are as readily discernible in this concept as in the speculations of du Nöel, who separated men into *Adaptors* and *Evolvers,* those who conform and those who reform.

Unfortunately these worthy abstractions are not applicable here, if only because they do not serve to illustrate the difference which obtained between the mezzanines in the north and south wings of the castle at Ararat. In our estimation, there were two main types of men in those years after the first World War: the *Deferent* and the *Irreverent.* This duality is not at great variance with the groupings of Schmidt-Kopper, Toynbee or du Nöel, and it has the advantage of being more readily applicable to the flannel drawers of Madame Couteaux and the arms tightly clenched behind Dr. Kliegl's back. At the same time its paradigm is mirrored throughout the world, and especially well reflected in the Europe of the Twenties.

In their hearts the Deferent stood ready to forge a veritable god of an Austrian housepainter who was still sipping lonely beer in a Munich *Bierhalle.* Men seemed to be seized with a thirst to indulge in every form of deference, and hungrily sought for the objects of their veneration. The power of the new dictators, Kemal Pasha,

Mussolini, Pilsudski, Primo de Rivera, Camera and Waldemaras, was born in the amniotic fluid of deference. Seemingly opposed political tides met at the springs of deference, met in secret but not by chance, like an instructor of mathematics (who has six children) meeting his older students in a brothel. They pretend not to know each other, but their intentions are the same. Deference sought its own level in every direction. Turkish poets wrote odes in praise of Kemal Pasha, who was often so drunk that he used to fall over the railing of his box in the cabarets of Ankara and land like a log in the midst of the dancing couples. The somewhat exaggerated Roman features of Mussolini were cut in cardboard like giant coupons and reproduced like cheap wallpaper. These black cardboard profiles covered the walls of even the tiniest hamlets and swept over the body of Italy like ants over dead horses. Deference knew no boundaries. Photographs of Archduke Otto appeared on the front page of Monarchist rotogravures in Hungary with the caption: "The Rightful King and His Favorite Bicycle." Tears came to the eyes of men and women as they paid homage to the bicycle. They began to hold veritable orgies of deference, as if suspecting that some enormous disrespect was threatening the entire world. They invented new titles in order to be more deferential toward each other. Death notices, listing ankle-length genealogies, simply swarmed with phony titles of nobility. Cheap one-family villas smeared baroque embellishments of plywood on their foreheads by way of description.

Naturally, the greatest orgies of deference took place in the realm of international politics. As a result of their thirst for respect, people began to dye their shirts in different colors, even those parts of the shirt which came into contact with not entirely respectable parts of the body. The glow of deferential Europe was augmented by rays from the land of the Rising Sun, where Japanese pilots committed hara-kiri if they accidentally flew over the Palace of the Tenno and thus violated the deference due their emperor. When Japanese Ambassador Shiratori let it be known through secret diplomatic channels that Japan was willing to sign a three-power pact with Italy and Germany, the pact became a historic meeting place of the Deferent. The members of an agricultural mission from Tokio arrived in Rome and noted with consternation that the Italian officials who had appeared to welcome them in the hotel lobby wore top hats and frock coats. The fact of the matter was that the Japanese were dressed in nothing but gray suits. Excusing themselves for a moment, the sons of Nippon trampled over each other in their haste to regain their rooms, and soon descended the marble staircase of the hotel in frock coats and top hats. But the Italians were nowhere to be seen. A half hour later they returned, having changed into light gray suits lest their Japanese colleagues be embarrassed. Thus the world chased its own tail out of deference, until the Deferent reached the point where the innermost sanctuary of deference was established: in the gas chamber. All this started in the early Twenties, at which time the thirst for deference bobbed up in legislation too. In Hungary they wrote a code of deference into a law. Franz Joseph had had no need of such a law, for he was authority itself. But something had to be piled under the shattered ruins of the Monarchy to support its collapsing beams. The Regent of Hungary stemmed from the lesser nobility, and the institution of the regency itself had to be kept alive by incubator methods. The principle of deference spread downward from above with the speed of a contagious itch. The Federations of Chimneysweeps discovered that they possessed qualities which were evocative of deference, and they in turn demanded that a comedy called *The Chocolate Love* be forbidden the stage because a chimneysweep was represented as deceiving his wife in the second act. The motion picture *"Go it, Gypsy!"* showed an easygoing newspaperman borrowing ten pengös from his friend. The Guild of Rural Newspapermen mobilized torchlight parades in protest, and the scenarist was obliged to make a public apology on his knees because the producer's investment was in danger. He declared that such newspapermen did not in reality exist; only one had he known to sink so low, and that was himself. Everything was done to preserve deference in its every form, and when this did not succeed in sufficient measure there were those who began to suspect that deference could not be artificially engendered.

So far we have seen the tillers, the Ptolemaic or adaptor type. In opposition to them stood the breeders, the Copernicans or evolvers: the *Irreverent*. We may say without hesitation that Madame Couteaux belonged to the category of the Irreverent, while Dr. Kliegl the tutor was the very prototype of the Deferent.

The tutor wrote his doctoral dissertation on Metternich, and it was entitled *Metternich and the Status Quo*. Dr. Kliegl understood the concept of a status quo to mean exactly what it had meant to Metternich: Let everything remain as of old! Therefore the European thrones which were overturned by Napoleon— that mad Corsican bull—must be reinstated. Metternich being the true spring of legitimacy, Dr. Kliegl had a broad and profound basis for his conviction that the exiled Charles IV should be re-established on the Habsburg throne. His firm conviction was in no way shaken by the incidental circumstance that the revolutions of 1848 in Paris, Vienna and Budapest had thoroughly mangled Metternich's doctrine, nor was he disturbed by another anomaly, the fact that in 1815 Metternich was the representative of a victorious Austria at the Congress of Vienna, while Dr. Kliegl was backed by an Austria which carried hardly more weight than a single drooping feather of the vanquished rooster after a cockfight.

It would be wrong to suppose that the Hungarian aristocrats who fled the Communist revolution and escaped to Vienna in 1919 spent their time snoozing, or that in the great confusion of the burgundy-brocaded rooms at the Hotel Sacher, so reminiscent of the age of Franz Joseph, nothing happened beyond an occasional interchange of wedded bedfellows among the young countesses—a phenomenon that can be attributed to the power of revolutionary whirlwinds, which not only loosen the shingles on the housetops but relax the bonds of marriage as well, to the cry of "What the hell! It doesn't matter anymore!" It was the time when Prince Fini observed that "When a man asks a woman to be seated nowadays, she pretends to misunderstand and stretches out on the bed."

More than this happened in Vienna. Serious conferences took place in the interest of restoration, similar to the royalist activities of French noblemen who escaped to northeastern Germany after the glorious revolution. One of the seats of these conferences was the Dukay palace on Bösendorferstrasse, where the white tiled fireplaces often echoed with weighty addresses. On one such occasion a young man of thirty stepped up to the tiny gold-legged table that served as a lectern. His high forehead and indeed his entire aspect bore a pleasant resemblance to Grillparzer, without the thick blood of the nineteenth-century Austrian dramatist but with his sublime vigor and his threatening impulsive nervosity. His voice had a slightly dreamlike tenderness which betrayed the *Schöngeist,* the beauty of soul dormant within. Not many of his listeners knew who he was, for attendance at such gatherings was drummed up on the basis that "Les amis de tes amis sont mes amis," any friend of yours is a friend of mine. The speaker's topic was "Metternich and the Status Quo." His lecture was a great success, for he made quite clear the historical necessity of returning Charles IV to the throne. Only lectures like this can be profoundly successful— lectures that elect to follow the strand of logic in the crazy-quilt fabric of history which leads to the listeners' desires. Danton would scarcely have achieved any degree of success with such an audience, although he, too, often mounted the charger of historical logic in his addresses to the National Convention.

Just as Marie Antoinette had once engaged in thick correspondence with the Comte d'Artois, the Prince of Bourbon and other titled supporters of the royalist cause who had taken refuge abroad, so Queen Zita's letters, postmarked from Switzerland and addressed to Hungarian legitimists, began to arrive in Vienna. Count Dupi himself treasured two such letters from Zita, sent to him by way of Kristina.

In August of 1919, when the Dukay family regained its ancient seat after the collapse of the Hungarian Commune, Countess Menti's first act was to send Otto Kliegl an invitation to become the tutor of her son János. Count Dupi left the education of his children entirely in his wife's hands, for at that time he was constantly occupied with the affairs of the recovered estates. In any case, his son János did not move him to enthusiasm. He referred to the boy as "the German puppy," because young Count János was typically Schäyenheim, with cold blue eyes and a narrow, firmly set jaw.

Dr. Kliegl arrived at the castle in the first days of September. His modest luggage contained two suits: one dark blue suit and a tuxedo. The latter was tight in the shoulders, and its sleeves were a little short, but Dr. Kliegl knew that to enter a nobleman's castle without a tuxedo was tantamount to going naked. But something else he brought along was far more important than his clothes: it was his deep and reverent devotion to the aristocracy, the cornerstone of his entire historical perspective; Metternich too had held that the two mainstays of the monarchical principle were the Catholic Church and the aristocracy. To Dr. Kliegl every born aristocrat was an exceptional, extraordinary being, as saints are to practicing Catholics. His gestures and even the modulations of his voice were tuned to this devotion. He took charge of Count János, who was then thirteen years old, as if the boy were a Holy Grail which it was his task to fill, drop by drop, with the clear wine of learning and morality. The tutor was a frail, light creature, and the leanness of his physique enabled him to move noiselessly. His walk was effortless and silent. Conversing in the midst of a social group, he could tie so tight a knot of his arms, high on his back near the shoulder blades, as to make it seem that those extremities were entirely boneless. An attitude like this is always expressive of a strong inner tension, is referred by the doctors of the soul to the realm of the inferiority complex, and often points to the repression of unconscious but powerful aggressive impulses directed against the immediate environment. For the time being, Dr. Kliegl betrayed no awareness of such desires, for he was all humility, zeal and gratification. All this contributed to the deep impression Countess Menti made on him when he caught his first glimpse of her in Vienna. That cool and pleasant air of refinement emanated from a truly beautiful woman. The lines of her handsome waist and slim legs, attractive without the coquetry that well-shaped feminine legs can rarely avoid, her long thighs, the perfect balance of her figure, the wide shoulders that seemed to move as easily as the neck of a bird although they moved only infrequently, the noble arch of her throat, which she could stretch to improbable length in the expression of doubt or disfavor, her ash-blond hair, exquisitely shot with the first shades of gray, and her eyes, her marvelously blue eyes, rendered even bluer by the white frame of her face and replete with a combination of haughty humility and supercilious boredom—all this, to Dr. Kliegl, represented the ideal of womanhood, and after no more than three meetings in Vienna the young professor found himself lifted by pure love to heights such as only truly religious spirits can scale. This rare capacity for transfiguration, this latent Gothic surge seems to be peculiarly characteristic of the German race in its Austrian reaches, and is expressed as well in the music of Mozart and Haydn as in the lyrical symbolism of Stephan George and Hugo von Hofmannstahl. Needless to say, Dr. Kliegl's transfiguration lost none of its potency when he learned that the countess was born a Schäyenheim princess, or when he discovered her Habsburg connection from a chance remark.

Following his arrival the conversation at dinner turned to the question of the king, and Dr. Kliegl took the lead albeit modestly, apologizing in all directions every time he opened his mouth. Later, when various solutions of the general political situation came up for discussion, he cautiously essayed an anti-Semitic statement or two, but these were only reconnaissance patrols in territory as yet unexplored. When his remarks found no echo, he steered the conversation to other topics.

After dinner Countess Menti retired to the little green salon with Dr. Kliegl to discuss the details of Count János's education. A footman placed a tray of decanters at their side, to wash the splendid meal down with thimblefuls of fiery French liqueur. Dr. Kliegl outlined his pedagogical principles. Ideas sprang lightly from his fine Grillparzer forehead, and the words issued from his mouth with the lightness of feathers. No one spoke the Austro-German tongue more elegantly than he did, without a taint of the drawling Viennese dialect. He pronounced the word *deutsch* as *theutsch,* even as Klopstock used to write it, betraying the word *teuton* lurking there.

Everything had begun so wonderfully. The unexpected pomp of the park and the castle on arrival. The elaborate scale of aristocratic life, at which the salon and its white fireplace in the Dukay Palace on Bösendorferstrasse had barely hinted. The dinner, the lofty level of conversation, and now the brilliant beauty of the little salon, and the countess—few and far between are the occasions when a man is so suddenly presented with an abundance of life's gifts. Dr. Kliegl's pedagogical lecture, accompanied by Countess Menti's gentle nods, dealt with the necessity to keep the young count as far as possible from the harmful influences of life, to temper his thought and character to the unique salvation of the Catholic Church and the requirements of his noble birth and high estate. Dr. Kliegl brought his performance to a well-rounded if abrupt period and stood up to make his departure. With a delicate and gracious gesture, however, the countess waved him back to the armchair, which was upholstered in light green velvet. It was an exquisite shade of green, matched only in the plumage of one or two species of tropical birds, and there only in fragmentary glimpses. One of the lighter green hues, it bordered on blue. Dr. Kliegl did not rejoice in the countess's gesture of delay, for he had a particular reason to seek solitude. The countess reverted to his lecture on "Metternich and the Status Quo," the main argument of which she had faithfully kept in memory, but there were some aspects, especially in connection with the machinations of Talleyrand, on which she desired enlightenment in greater detail. Dr. Kliegl crossed his legs, knotted his thighs together like the lattice on a pie, jammed the tip of his right elbow to the side of his skull, pressed a fist to his cheek, locked his left hand over his right wrist and sought meanwhile to give the impression that these movements were indicative of his concentration on the countess's query. Unfortunately this was not the case. Dr. Kliegl began to regret, immoderately, the little glassful of fiery liqueur. During dinner he had not been able to withstand the temptation of a foaming glass of blond beer, after which he had indulged generously in wine spritzers, and all this was not without effect. No, it was not the effect of alcohol. Dr. Kliegl had never been so sober as he was at this moment. But from birth his *musculus constrictor vesicae* had been weak. The Viennese physician whom he plaintively consulted on several occasions had explained that if the tiny muscular mechanism between the bladder and the urethra is weak, then the micturitive impulse is overpowering, while the bladder itself is incapable of retaining large quantities of liquid for any length of time.

Countess Menti especially wanted to know how Talleyrand had managed to succeed, after all that had happened—*all* that had happened!—in having France recognized as a major power at the Congress of Vienna in 1815. The question could not be answered in a word. In the meantime that single thimbleful of fiery liqueur had found its way through the stomach and liver to the bladder, and was creating a greater commotion there than Napoleon's return had created at the Congress of Vienna. Dr. Kliegl resorted to the most harrowing spiritual and physical exertions in order to fly from the prison of his own eloquence on the one hand, and on the other hand to escape from the room without mishap as soon as ever he could. The exquisite little green salon had lost all its charm for him, and resembled rather a torture chamber. At this point he no longer dared even to stand up, feeling that to relax the pressure of his thighs would have serious consequences. But in the event that he were to succeed in getting to his feet, by the time he found the particular door he sought in that enormous and— to him—still unknown castle, it would be too late, for in such circumstances these doors manage to hide with remarkable dexterity and well-nigh stubborn cruelty. Twice in the course of Dr. Kliegl's lifetime he had experienced similar difficulties, which is why he took his complaint to the physician. Introspective people burdened with feelings of inferiority lack the natural assurance that enables others, in similar straits, to rise above the momentary pause which ensues when they have to leave the room for a short time without further explanation. While Dr. Kliegl's sentences probed the mysteries of Talleyrand's character, his locked thighs were trembling with the effort of his exertion, his face almost imperceptibly took on a lachrymose look, and at that instant he was aware of an unexpected warmth suffusing his trousers. But he did not abandon hope entirely, thinking himself fortunate to have changed, before dinner, from the gray traveling suit into his dark blue, the color of which is known not to betray dampness. Countess Menti's sensitive spirit must have awakened to her guest's physical agonies, for when he rose this time she no longer delayed him, although they had not really exhausted the subject and Wellington still remained to be discussed. As he bowed over her hand Dr. Kliegl cast a stealthy look at the green armchair he had been sitting in, and what he saw left an eternal scar in his heart. A dark stain about as broad as his palm on the accursed light green cloth simply shouted the presence of a damp infiltration, as if ink had been spilled

305

there. Dr. Kliegl tottered up to his room and was so consumed with shame that he tumbled into bed and, pleading fatigue, did not make an appearance at supper. A world had fallen apart inside of him, together with Metternich and the Congress of Vienna. How wretched and disgusting life can be! How clumsy and repulsive the flesh, when the soul is fluttering on the most exalted heights! Would the monstrous dark patch of dampness dry without leaving a mark on the exquisite cloth? It was not likely. Urine has a corrosive effect, especially on such dyed fabrics. Not only the scientists of I. G. Farben but every puppydog has demonstrated this in countless experiments. It was impossible that the countess should not have noticed that shrieking black blotch, not have known what had happened. Perhaps, after such a debut, he would even lose his position. This dire anxiety of Dr. Kliegl revealed that he had no comprehension of Countess Menti's spiritual composure. Her spirit was full of a vast capacity for forgiveness in the face of this and similar kinds of physical weakness, for she was Rere's mother, she was the one who insisted that Rere remain in the castle. And when Dr. Kliegl's overwrought imagination went so far as to conjure up an image of the armchair with the whole distinguished family grouped about and laughing at him, he was only testifying to the pettiness of his own soul, because Countess Menti would finally have taken the blame on herself rather than submit a fellow creature to laughter and scorn. But the tutor was incapable of realizing the full dimension of the countess's personality, and the next morning, when he heard hammer blows on the terrace and looked out of the window, he felt as if the nails were being driven into his own coffin. Out on the terrace a carpenter was re-covering the chair with fresh cloth.

For weeks, when Dr. Kliegl went to sleep, the light green velvet with its dark spot about the size of a palm appeared behind his eyelids as soon as he closed his eyes, exactly as he had seen it in that stealthy instant while kissing the hand of the countess. This could arouse great mental anguish in a man who was the child of a minor Austrian civil servant and had grown up in the reverent, almost worshipful atmosphere of deference and good manners that prevailed in the parental house. His childhood had been as empty and unsmiling as a rainy afternoon in Salzburg. He lost his parents at an early age and found his way to the home of an aunt in Hungary. He spoke Hungarian well, but one could sense his contempt for the words even as he pronounced them.

Should we care to make the tutor's pedagogical operations a subject of our investigation, it were best to employ the comparative method. If the personality of Madame Couteaux can be compared to a round, heavy, taste-packed, fragrant, glowing cheese from the Midi, then Dr. Kliegl was comparable to a soggy, massive Austrian bean pie, which is distinguished for the fact that its flavor is neither that of the bean nor of a pie. Nevertheless, a pleasant, nourishing pastry. For those who like it, that is. On the other hand, if we speak of the Dukay children as human fossils and maintain that the Zia-fossil was corroded and dissolved by the acid of Madame Couteaux's meridional spirit, then we may say that Dr. Kliegl dried the János-fossil to a further degree of hardness and sought to deprive it of its natural moisture. In her own rough and sometimes ribald way, Madame Couteaux instilled in Zia a love of mankind and of all its members, opened the doors of life for her in many directions. Dr. Kliegl locked the boy in, closed all the windows around him, taught him self-immolation instead of humility, and stimulated him to spiritual self-abuse by the repeated application of his tutorial theories of history. We have mentioned that Count Dupi bowed to the temper of the times after warfare and revolutions had subsided, and among the orders he promulgated for the staff was one which prohibited the footmen from helping his sons put their shoes on. Let them put their shoes on themselves, with their own hands! Dr. Kliegl did not approve of this order, and he not only permitted but actually encouraged the footman Joseph to continue kneeling at the bed and helping young Count János with his shoes, for he considered even the most minor infraction of established rule, of the status quo, to be dangerous. And he was completely right. History cannot be made by compromise in either the one or the other direction, otherwise what would become of the conflicts which create history? At the same time Berili, for all that the general order concerning shoes did not apply to the female members of the family, chased Julia out of Zia's presence like an angry hen on the first morning the chambermaid approached the little countess's bedside with some such purpose in mind.

For years the dark stain, shaped like a raven squatting on the green armchair, kept returning to Dr. Kliegl's imagination.

We have been obliged to consider the tutor's illness and the painful consequences of his condition in the interest of character study. So dark a blotch on an armchair will make a man spiteful, vengeful and cruel not only toward individuals but, eventually, toward the entire world, should the occasion

307

present itself. We know of Robespierre that he was a highly cultured being aglow with the most sublime principles. As a result of the mischance that this illustrious mind was forced to inhabit an imperfect body with an imperfectly wired nervous system, one thousand three hundred seventy-six victims fell to the guillotine during the not quite fifty days of his regime, according to contemporary records, and history made of this a hullabaloo that has echoed for centuries. Dr. Kliegl's weak *musculus constrictor,* through the manifestation of its influence on young Count János twenty-five years later, in the fall of 1944, claimed many, many more lives than Robespierre's reign of terror.

Chapter Four

THE HEAT of July in the summer of the following year, in 1923, was stifling. During the summer months the family used to dine on the wide, breeze-swept terrace, but now they took refuge from the heat in the central dining hall, with its cool, thick walls. They even drew the curtains at the windows and lit the chandeliers. Out of deference to the guest, Rere and Mr. Badar were not asked to sit at the table. The guest was indeed a distinguished personage: His Excellency Count Zsigmond Dukay, a consecrate bishop of the Catholic Church and a first cousin of Count Dupi. His consecration had occurred twelve years ago, when he was barely thirty-eight years old, and during the brief reign of Charles IV he had played the role of a veritable privy councilor. It was part of a centuried heritage for the Dukay clan always to number a prelate among its members, and having assumed the sacrifice, or accepted the honor, in this generation, Count Zsigmond turned out to be a truly worthy Prince of the Church, known for his high cultivation and glowing humanity. The members of his diocese rejoiced in *The Still of Night,* a prayer book that he had written in a most elegant style. An estimate of the bishop must not take into account the malignant rumors, in all probability baseless, that His Eminence was homosexually inclined and not averse to the celebration of a Black Mass or two. These misunderstandings originated in the startling thinness of the voice which issued from the bishop when he opened his mouth, for he sported a gigantic, broad-shouldered frame and one expected deep, booming echoes from such a barrel-chest. The rumors also held that the bishop used cosmetics. This too was a base slander, although it is indubitable that an almost imperceptible blue-green shadow paraded across His Eminence's upper eyelids, while his eyebrows appeared to be somewhat unnaturally dark and there was a suspiciously blue and red coloring to his face. All this, however, offered no proof of the rumors. Eminent and illustrious figures of society can rarely avoid the bite of such sinister gossip, just as the stone images built into the sides of a cathedral are forced to suffer the white tracery of pigeons and sparrows splashed on their shoulders, and on their hands locked in prayer, and on their nosetips, and have no recourse because the Lord God created not only saints but ignorant birds too.

As the bishop sat at the right of Countess Menti, with the heavy gold pectoral cross on his neck and the tiny violet biretta on the crown of his head, an even more than usually gloomy and solemn atmosphere hovered over the table, its temperature most exactly reflected in the reverent expression on Dr. Kliegl's face. Footmen passed the jellied saddle of venison with vinaigrette sauce, one of Monsieur Cavaignac's most perfect compositions. Outside the heat raged, until it was impossible to touch the wrought-iron gratings on the terrace with a bare hand. Through the thick walls into the curtained, well-lighted interior of the dining hall seeped the heat, and everyone's sweat glands began to perspire in corresponding measure. A tiny drop of perspiration trembled at the tip of every hair in the bishop's thick, bushy eyebrows. Berili, seated at one end of the table with Zia at her side, turned to the little girl and her hoarse rumble of a voice, which was incapable of a whisper, began to intone, like a Biblical quotation:

"Chaque poil de son corps avait sa goutte de sueur..."

A morsel of jellied venison skipped from Zia's tongue to her plate and she was seized with a laughing fit which she vainly sought to hide behind a napkin. Her head bobbed under the table by way of escape.

Countess Menti and the bishop were conducting their conversation in English, because Count Zsigmond was fond of the language and spoke it with Cantabrigian colloquialism, and because its peevish gutturals and drawling accents suited his mobile lips, the soft muscles of his face and the effeminate nature lurking in the heavy Renaissance body. Their discussion was focused on the ways and means of reorganizing the Catholic Women's Union, of which Countess Menti was president, so that the women would play less bridge and cover more areas on their bodies than the remarkably minute swimming dresses they wore allowed them to do. In the latter connection Countess Menti had twice summoned the Minister of the Interior to her presence, and their conferences had been fruitful indeed, for since then gendarmes in plumed shakos patrolled the beaches of the Balaton and measured the women's bathing suits with a centimeter rule to insure that they were within the prescribed limit. The conversation, therefore, flowed along these highly serious, we might even say exalted, lines.

At first no one noticed that Zia had disappeared, like a magician's rabbit, into the depths. But quacking, gasping noises began to come from under the table. All heads turned in her direction, and there was a sudden silence. The silence itself was so menacing that Zia's head emerged from the deep at once. Her face, however, was the face of one of those unfortunates who look frantically around when an altogether uningestible mass of liquid is stuck in their throats. Countess Menti's neck stretched forward with a movement of which only birds are capable. Her eyes fastened on Zia like an ice-cold, steel-gray manacle. It seemed almost incredible that the gentle Countess Menti, "die gute Menti," should have such a look in her possession. The effect of the look was as if a Mother Superior had unexpectedly drawn an assassin's knife with lightning speed from the sleeve of her habit. A single and scarcely perceptible flash of that look brought Zia to her feet and ordered her out of the dining hall. The impertinent little countess took flight.

Countess Menti's face instantly modulated into the face of "die gute Menti" once more, and she turned to the bishop with a smile that was gentle and apologetic but majestic as well:

"I beg your pardon…dear me, these children!…"

Count Zsigmond nodded his forgiveness. He launched a new English sentence in which, with all due respect for the idiom of Cambridge, we cannot but admit that there was something of a whine.

Understanding the pronouncement of Countess Menti's look to mean that Countess Zia would not be permitted to continue her meal, the footman discreetly cleared Zia's plate from the table. For a moment it seemed that Countess Menti's rigid self-discipline had banished all signs of a badly bred child's outrageous behavior from the solemn formality of the hall.

Then, unexpectedly, the outrage broke out in good earnest. Clutching a wizened old hand to her mouth with such force that her dentures were pushed out of place, Madame Couteaux suddenly emitted a peculiar hoot, reminiscent of the singular calls often heard in the ominous profundity of a forest or on the wasted sands of a desert plain. At once all eyes were upon her. This time Countess Menti's neck stretched to an incredible length, and immediately the Schäyenheim look appeared in the working of her eyes, prophetic of catastrophe. Like a crane, the steely look lifted Madame Couteaux's ancient body from its chair and wafted her toward the door. Berili's face was red now, and full of anxiety. We have mentioned the way she suffered from hardening of the arteries, which not only inflicted internal agonies but burdened her with a recurrent limp. And so, limping, she struggled to the door, clutching at the air before her as if it were a banister.

Lines of anger and offense settled on the bishop's sensitive face, like the sudden apparition of wolves and eagles on a mild and pleasant meadow. With the crippled forefinger of his left hand Count Dupi brushed the bristles of his mustache in annoyance, and in that thick but flavorsome Hungarian tongue, which was not in the command of every nobleman, he growled in the direction of the departing Couteaux:

"Mit röhögnek ezek a marhák? What are these idiots tittering about?"

It was not a voice of incensed anger but rather of indignant protest, as when someone is banned from an exciting and amusing game. Count Dupi liked a good joke, in whatever vein of laughter, for he had spent most of his youth in the company of frivolous cavalry officers, prostitutes, waiters, gypsies, actresses, writers and other attractive good-for-nothings. There was jealousy in the rumble of his voice at the moment.

Seventeen-year-old Count János sat with his face motionless, and written all over it was, "Watch me vindicate the honor and dignity of the Dukay progeny." Dr. Kliegl was observably pale, with terror in his eyes, as if a divine thunderbolt were about to strike down upon the table.

Once more Countess Menti achieved a miracle of self-control. She addressed herself to the jellied venison with unfaltering delicacy of gesture, spearing ridiculously tiny morsels on her fork, manipulating her utensils and negotiating the business of nourishment with such an artistry that the heavy silver seemed to move over the noble chinaware like lacemakers' needles in ancient Venice.

Henri Bergson, McRoy and other great thinkers have made valuable contributions to the wealth of literature on the psychology of laughter, but they have not yet been successful in clarifying the mystery of its contagion. Contrary to rule, the silver-haired old castellan András Hidi, who was dressed like an under-sheriff of the past century, moved from his prescribed post six paces behind the table and went to the serving board where, with his back turned, he began to shake as if a mysterious current had been plugged into his flesh. Nothing like this had ever happened m the forty-two years of his service, and the performance was even more remarkable in view of the fact that he could not conceivably have known what the little countess and the old French governess were laughing at. Only the footmen noticed the castellan's shaking shoulders at first. Three footmen were on duty, with white cotton gloves, white ties at their throats, their coats studded with large, flat silver buttons which bore the woodpecker crest and eleven-pointed coronet, their checked waistcoats edged in blue and red stripes of the Dukay colors. Three cleanshaven men, who moved only by rote. Three men with the ancient commandment of discipline and humility in their blood, descendants of the Sklav and Khazar tribes, whose fathers were the faithful servants once slaughtered at the graves of their Hun and Turkish masters. Nevertheless, the rigid masks of the three men began to twitch, their lips grew narrow, the skin of their nostrils tightened and the silver trays began to dance in their hands.

The bishop sensed the mysterious electrical storm around him and imagined he had caused it by speaking English. He switched to Hungarian and brought up the subject of the king. He confidentially related the happy tiding that Otto, the "rightful" king, now eleven years old, had just received his first bicycle. So artfully did he avoid mentioning the person who gave Otto the bicycle that it was immediately apparent that the bishop himself had been the donor.

But it did not help. Old András the castellan had disappeared by now, and the silver trays were teetering even more perilously in the hands of the footmen. Imminent danger threatened the authority of the Church and the baroque pomp of the noble board. Seconds later the three footmen vanished, and the bishop felt as if his ministrants had abandoned him at the altar in the middle of Mass. Countess Menti started to grow pale. She slowly reached for the little silver bell that always stood ready at the side of her plate. She rang sharply. She rang once, then again—no one came.

In the meantime Berili pulled a somber face as she limped up the marble staircase, with the real banister of the gilded railing under the clutch of her hands now. Zia waited for her impatiently. As soon as they were alone behind the closed door, the two of them fell into each other's outstretched arms, hooting, wheezing, gasping for breath as the laughing fit raged on. They stumbled from one chair to another, holding their sides, dripping with tears, perhaps no longer even recalling what they were laughing about, like a rattling, glistening downpour that has no idea why it does what it does. Sighing and moaning, they tottered to their beds in a sweet agony of laughter.

Elizabeth, the chambermaid, listened with her ear glued to the door. Ignorant of the reason for their laughter, she was frightened at first, and then she began to smile, and then her hands crept to her stomach and a moment later she too was off, rollicking down the long corridor as if she carried the blessed flame in the white folds of her pleated apron: meaningless, wild laughter. Seconds later revolution broke out in the entire castle. No, no cause for alarm—it was only a mild explosion of spirit, but peculiar and foreboding still, almost incomprehensible. Out in the courtyard the brooms came to a halt in the hands of the porters, and when one of the kitchen boys staggered into the great kitchen, doubled over and clutching his belly, Monsieur Cavaignac made for a ladle to crown him with, but in the next instant he began to snort and grunt also, his tall duckcloth cap rocking with laughter. So the flame advanced, through the hearts of the scullery maids toward the laundresses and charwomen, and from there to the stables. The red-coated coachmen were already laughing, until Mr. Johnson, the shovel-faced English stablemaster, was obliged to bare his yellow teeth too.

What were they laughing about? They did not know. Perhaps it was an unconscious revolt against the monotonous and rigid life of the castle. Perhaps it was the kind of laughing urge which so often challenges the drawn-out sermon or the too dreary funeral oration. Or perhaps it was all the forerunner of what was actually to take place within these walls twenty-one years later, in 1944: in the gallery of ancestral portraits gun-shots dapple Ferenc Illyeshâzy's leopard-skin cape, bayonets shred the old canvas on Katalin Dukay's midriff, axe-blows grope for the pigtailed skull of Palatine István, boots crush the crystals of the Venetian chandeliers underfoot, the walls are plucked, like chickens, free of their embellishments, the cherry-red, golden-yellow, apple-green silken draperies are ripped from the ceiling, and crowbars shatter the French mantelpieces. Why, why, why? Perhaps it is the blind, unquenchable revenge of the Sklav and Khazar fathers, because they were once slaughtered merely for a show of pomp.

Peering from the window, Berili and Zia soon saw the bishop's enormous, dark blue automobile disappear beneath the chestnut trees, the gravel of the courtyard crackling under the fat balloon tires. A few seconds later came the sound of steps along the corridor, and Hilda, Countess Menti's first adjutant, known to Count Dupi as the One-Eyed Regent because of a paralyzed and swollen eyelid, appeared in the room, an occurrence in itself unusual. She informed Madame Couteaux in a dry voice that Her Excellency the Countess had asked for her.

"Tout de suite!... Tout de suite!" Berili waggled her decrepit fingers in the air by way of reassurance, but the One-Eyed Regent stood motionless, indicating that she would brook no delay in the execution of the order to conduct Madame Couteaux to a hearing. Berili had time only to adjust the alignment of some music albums on the piano with great care, a gesture that was completely fruitless at this moment. Before she stepped through the door she cast a swift glance at Zia's pale face.

As they approached the countess's apartment on the main floor, Berili grew increasingly pale. She was well aware of the danger that threatened her. She knew with what cool terseness the countess was accustomed to introduce changes in the castle staff of fifty-eight, and against her decisions there was no appeal. Often there were weeping, overwrought faces in the servants' quarters.

The countess received her in the little green salon. A forefinger supported her sad, preoccupied face. The One-Eyed Regent bowed and departed, leaving them alone. Berili could almost hear the beat of her own heart. She stood before the countess as before a general, like a militiaman whose old, bent body is not suited to the attitude of attention. Finally the countess spoke:

"Chère madame," she began, and for a brief interval she gazed down at the carpet, without moving her forefinger from her face. To Berili's understanding the tone of her voice implied only one possible conclusion to the sentence: "...you must give up your position!" And she also knew what that simple statement would mean to her. In a few years she would die in one of the poorhouses of Toulon, without money for medicine to ease the recurrent and increasing agonies of her hardening arteries. But she was even more terrified at the thought of losing Zia.

She cast herself into the breach of the momentary pause with all the strength of her race. Should the countess pronounce the word of dismissal, her fate was sealed. A word once given in that house was never recalled, neither upon reflection nor in apology.

"Excusez-moi," she blew the fire of her breath upon the flicker of the brief pause, melting and widening the narrow opening of time in order to wriggle through it with her whole body. Now the countess gave her a glance for the first time. The glance said: All your excuses are in vain.

But Berili's tongue began to buzz, like a pneumatic drill that can go through concrete blocks. Her hoarse voice caught the flame, and the vigorous gesticulation of her arms gave encouragement to the words. She was the daughter of Danton's daggers at that moment, and what she said was not defense but impassioned accusation. An accusation directed against an old fool called Madame Couteaux, who was a disgrace to mankind and whose abominable behavior—sa manière a-bo-mi-nable—could only be attributed to the aberrations of second childhood.

But no, no, even that was no excuse for what had happened. Ah, non, non, non! Her face was aflame, her eyes shone as she crushed herself like a worm. There was, there could be no forgiveness, none, none, none! Her knotty feet stamped the floor:

"Im-par-don-nable! Im-par-don-nable!"

She stretched out her arm and shook a finger at the door:

"Out with her! Out of the house with the old wretch at once!"

And she pronounced the fear that lay most deeply in her heart:

"Let her go back to Toulon and perish in the poorhouse!...and it's not enough, no, still not enough punishment for her!..."

Only cardsharps unmasked in the dark dens of Toulon can defend themselves with such fire and stormy eloquence, such psychology and daring, captivating and confusing the hastily summoned gendarme, repressing not only his words but even his breath. What could poor Countess Menti do but nod in approval as the French holocaust raged in agitation before her.

At the end of her long and thunderous denunciation Berili came to a brief pause, clenched her gnarled hands at her stomach and said, her voice softer but in a tone of final judgment:

"Non, non…there is no way out…she must be dismissed at once."

Berili knew that in pronouncing the final judgment herself she violated the unwritten law of the castle, for the right of final decision belonged to the countess. She threw one more statement at herself, still as if she were a third person about whom she was unconcerned:

"…she won't live much longer anyway, with her hardened arteries…"

Countess Menti knew of her illness. And because she was "die gute Menti," the Schäyenheim princess of a few moments ago was already beginning to thaw. After a short interval she asked, without moving her face from the forefinger:

"And what was the reason for this rudeness?"

Berili raised her two arms toward the ceiling in perplexity. Now she was audacious enough to step closer and pound the arm of the chair with a finger for emphasis as she explained that the cork of a wine bottle had turned up beside Countess Zia's plate and the little countess, "la pauvre petite," was so confused by the presence of His Eminence and her awe of him several ecstatic exclamations of "Ah, qu'il est magnifique!" delivered with face lifted to the heavens, flew out in the direction of Count Zsigmond—in her confusion the little countess took a mouthful of cork instead of bread, and the innocent childish creature began to laugh at this. "C'est tout!"

After brief reflection Countess Menti declared that it was nothing to laugh at. With a nod she indicated that the hearing was at an end.

Berili had survived her hour of trial. But while the interview was going on, Zia walked the floor of their rooms, her face white. She knew that her mother intended to dismiss Berili. She also knew that her pleas could be of no avail. Although she was only thirteen, her Dukay blood began to swell and glow, the spirit that recognized no obstacle and tolerated no contradiction. She sprang from a chair and with arms upraised she shouted to herself:

"No, no, I won't let them take Berili away!"

She felt secure in her decision. Her mind fled to her father, to the gruff voice of Count Dupi. Papá and his gruff voice were still the final authority in the castle and the entire Dukay dominion.

At the moment of departure the bishop's visit was marred by another painful incident, and it was fortunate that the inhabitants of the castle did not hear of it.

We are acquainted with Count Rere's habit of wearing striped jackets and a derby all the year around, for his primitive nature did not respond to climatic change. The only allowance he made on days when the heat was stifling was to take off his shoes and stockings; it goes without saying that he immediately forgot these articles under some tree or other in the enormous park, and the castle staff was mobilized for more than one searching expedition a day. Sumi, the spaniel pointer, often made a triumphant appearance with one of Count Rere's shoes, bearing it as if she were on a hunt and the shoe were a pheasant.

Count Rere was accustomed to discard a great many things. We know him for a passionate reader. He read Baudelaire for long hours as ecstatically as he read a seed catalogue if it happened to come into his hands. He did not read the words but only the letters, his lips in constant motion as if he were chewing on pumpkin seeds. His passion for reading wreaked considerable destruction in the castle library, for he took volume after volume on his solitary wanderings, and when his capricious brain was bored with reading he cast the book away like a gorilla discarding an orange after his thirsty black lips have sucked out the juice. Thus the gardeners and the men hired to mow the lawns often came upon beautiful leather-bound books, sun-faded under a bush or rain-drenched at the side of the brook.

After dinner Count Rere was walking along the edge of the brook, cooling the enormous soles of his feet in its rippling waters. His stylish striped trousers were rolled to the knee, and his naked hairy legs shone with damp mud. At bottom he was an ordinary mud-scuffing gypsy, while from the knees up, in his British trousers, jacket and derby he turned into a perfect picture of a count, and the picture was blemished only by his numerous optical devices, his rings and the cannibalistic collection of stolen keys he carried. Over his shoulders swung the enormous racing binoculars, which he had yet to remove from their leather case. Taking long steps, he strolled along the basin of the brook like some strange marsh bird, the good-humored, happy little grin of a halfwit on his face. When he espied the bishop's departing automobile he sprang from the brook, splashing in agitation, and with several powerful leaps he launched out after the car as it swayed delicately along the undulating roads of the park, like a ship on the waves of the ocean. Count Rere clambered onto the trunk at the rear, unable to withstand his childhood love of taking a ride. He looked like a black monkey as he perched there. It is a primordial desire: to be borne along by the strength of some strange external energy.

At the large grilled north gate the gatekeeper, decked out in the regalia of Maria Theresa's time, was well acquainted with this habit of Count Rere, and had frequently swept the count from the rumps of departing automobiles before swinging the gate open. This was the way it happened now. However, it was not only Rere's delight at hitching a lift that had attached him to the trunk of His Eminence's car, but familial affection as well. Rere was familiar with, and kept close account of, all family connections. He knew precisely in what degree of kinship he stood with every member of the Dukay clan. Rere took pleasure in being related to someone, and seized any opportunity of shaking a relative by the hand—in the opinion of many, he was far too aggressive. While the gatekeeper fussed with his heavy gate and the vehicle idled for a moment or two, Rere opened the automobile door with the most benign smile of fraternal fondness on his face and extending his dirty right hand, on the thumb of which he wore a seal ring, he leaned over to His Eminence the Bishop and croaked, his voice full of emotion:

"Hal-lo, Thigmond!"

The bishop's sensitive features were eloquent with fright and disgust at the sight of the grinning horseface under the derby. He drew back into the dark blue cushions of the automobile and defensively extended the exquisitely shaped hand, as white as a woman's, on which he wore the pontifical ring of his office, the emerald to which the archduchess herself used to press her lips. Commandingly he waved the hand at Rere in dismissal. Such gestures never insulted Rere. Once more he covered the bishop with a grin that dripped with love, and closed the car door obediently. Then, arms akimbo, one muddy leg proudly thrown forward, he stood at a distance of a few paces waiting for the automobile to depart, a flushed smile of embarrassment on his face, like someone who has just been awarded a medal of high distinction. Later, his calves dappled with drying mud, he straggled back to the brook, to surrender himself once more to the minor pleasures of life and the summer season.

Under the effect of the excitement they had experienced, Zia and Berili were unusually quiet for the next few days. They went about on tiptoe even behind the closed door of their apartment. But several days later out came the merry strains of *Miron-ton-ton-ton mirontaine,* out of hiding came the impudent little songs about the provincial priest and little Amélie, like cautious game fowl after the echo of the shotgun has subsided. Hardly a week had passed when Berili's clumsy feet began once more to move in a dancing shuffle beneath her knee-length lace-fringed flannel drawers.

Chapter Five

NOT FAR from the Arc de Triomphe, in the Seventeenth Arrondissement of Paris, there languished an exceptionally desolate little street, its pavement as aloof and forbidding as a floor that has just been thoroughly ploughed by a careful broom or a vacuum cleaner. The street sign, its white letters gleaming on a light blue background—these colors, too, contribute to the smile of Paris—wore this unusual inscription: "Rue Général Ferreyolles Voie privée Circulation interdite." Why the street was in retirement, why it was closed to traffic—even the most ancient denizens of the quarter did not know, and in all probability the prohibitions were no longer in effect. It was a short street, with four mansions on one side narrowing suspicious eyes at four other mansions across the way. With their tall, steep slate roofs, they were like gray-kerchiefed old maids who are not on speaking terms for some reason or other. These mansions were built in the days of Emperor Napoleon III, on the shaky ground of the period when, in 1848, the Republic displaced the Orleans Monarchy and was itself succeeded by the Empire, and it was understandable if the marks of anguish and anxiety lurked on the foreheads and faces of the spinster mansions, for at that time Bismarck had already been made a count and the newly united Germany, mustache sharpened to a military point, wearing a steel helmet that was like the lid of an urn, shod in enormous cavalry boots, was approaching Paris with long thumping steps.

It was in those days that Peter Dukay, Count Dupi's father, had bought the mansion at No. 4 from General Bonaparte's son, the Marquis de Ferreyolles, who married Suzanne Dukay. The house was comparatively small, but considering that the pigskin suitcases, embossed with the blue-red Dukay colors and the eleven-pointed coronet, had appeared in the mansion only at infrequent intervals during the past eighty years, as infrequently as some of the rare arctic species of wild geese are to be seen over the Seine, it proved sufficiently large to shelter the Dukays who happened into Paris from time to time. To the left of the enclosed little courtyard, which had breathed deep the sweet savors of Empire, stood a fitting relic of the past century, Chapu's statuette of Nike, the ancient bronze now green with age and on her face a look of reproach for the oblivion to which

320

her beauty was committed. Facing the entrance was a line of three large double doorways, and over the center door hung a horse's head in marble, betraying the secret that the closed doors concealed: these installations had been stables and carriage houses at a time when the Bois entertained nothing more than coaches. Prince Fini, who often exercised the right of kinship to take advantage of the free lodging in Paris, was known for his cutting observations, and he declared that the marble horse's head above the entrance to the stable belonged in the gallery of Dukay family portraits, an observation which was not entirely groundless, for when Prince Fini once placed a derby on that rather ill-conceived likeness of a noble steed, the resemblance of the horse to Count Rere became strikingly apparent. In these antics there was always something of the innate Schäyenheim contempt for the very thought of the Dukays with their Hun-Turkish blood, for they were, after all, the descendants of an Asiatic horde.

At the right of the courtyard was the entrance to the apartment of Mr. Emanuel, who, with his wife, served both as doorman and caretaker, an acquaintance of ours from before the war of whom we know that for long months and often for years he had surreptitiously rented the orphaned rooms and crested linens of the little palace to international adventurers in search of pastoral retreat, had in fact built up a substantial practice from which the income, in the course of two decades, enabled him to purchase a villa on the outskirts of Houlgat.

In the autumn of 1925 four taxicabs arrived from the direction of the Gare de l'Est, and the four taxicabs occasioned an extraordinary bustle that must have been offensive to the secluded little Rue Général Ferreyolles. Some days before, Mr. Emanuel had received his telegram of advance notice, in time to evict the first-floor tenant, an elderly silk manufacturer who came up from Lyon to deceive his wife once every month, and to clear the second floor of its tenant as well, a Turkish cigarette dealer of unpronounceable name who was recommended to Mr. Emanuel through subterranean channels and had set up a temporary harem in Count Dupi's bedroom. Since the receipt of the telegram Mr. Emanuel's face wore the marks of deep mourning, for the terms of the wire augured a long sojourn.

But it was with the enthusiasm of old that his gold-braided doorman's cap performed its tremendous arc and scraped the sidewalk when Count Dupi struggled out of the narrow taxi. The French language, as employed by Mr. Emanuel in greeting his long-lost master, rang with a melody which only the members of the Comédie Française can emulate, and these only in the tragedies of Racine.

"Bonjour, Monsieur le comte!"

Then, directing his song at Countess Menti, with another sweep of the gold-braided cap to the sidewalk:

"Bonjour, Madame la comtesse!"

"Bonzhur, Emanuel," growled Count Dupi, with an affable smile, and instead of shaking hands he patted the shoulder of the squat, long-nosed Frenchman, on whose head a few strands of camel's hair were graying and in whose deep sockets two lively crow's eyes shone. Count Dupi's amiable growl and somewhat sentimental smile were not intended for Emanuel, whom he knew to be the world's most depraved rascal, but for Paris, his own Paris, of which not only Emanuel but he too, "Le comte Dupi," had once been part and parcel, to such a degree of popularity that his picture—with gold-knobbed walking stick, monocle, the well-known top hat, the swallowtail cutaway currently fashionable, a perpetual white carnation in his buttonhole, his mustache still pert and twirled to a smart point—this picture often appeared in the humorous periodicals of Paris, and one of these caricatures represented Count Dupi as strolling in the afternoon crush on the Boulevard Madeleine with a posture which only Paris can attribute to oriental nabobs, a broad smile under his sharpened mustache and on each arm a beautiful woman wearing, in the style of the period, ostrich-feathered hats the size of millstones, elbow-length gloves, shoes with heels of exaggerated height, but otherwise completely naked. This was Count Dupi's first visit to Paris after an absence of eleven years. As he patted Emanuel's shoulder, the old, prewar Paris welled up within him.

Countess Menti acknowledged the modulations of Mr. Emanuel's floor-scraping singsong greeting with a cool nod. There was something wonderfully exclusive in her carriage as she waited for the others at the door. Faithful to her marriage vows, she had never deceived her husband, but in thirty years of married life she had learned a great deal about Count Dupi's shabby affairs. In her eyes Paris was nothing but a gigantic brothel. In any case, she despised the French. At that moment, standing in the door-way, supporting her neck with a forefinger, she was again the Schäyenheim princess who had just set foot on what was still enemy soil, who was unable to forgive these diminutive, excitable and, in general, physically dirty Frenchmen for having wrested the flag of triumph from Hindenburg's iron fist. She did not forget that of the three Allied officers who had treated Charles IV as a common prisoner on the Danubian gunboat, one had been a Frenchman, and therefore she hardly acknowledged the greeting of Juliette, Emanuel's wife, who appeared on the threshold to welcome the noble family. And she particularly did not forget what a Schäyenheim could never forget, that this rabble of a people had decapitated Marie Antoinette.

Mr. Emanuel observed to himself that Count Dupi, who was then fifty-seven years old, had aged considerably in the past eleven years. However, while he unloaded the suitcases and the other arrivals from the taxicabs, he expressed just the opposite of this observation in an inexhaustible flood of words.

"Vous avez bonne mine! Vous avez rajeuni!" he called over his shoulder, his eyes not leaving the count's face for a second.

Nineteen-year-old Count János and his tutor Dr. Kliegl alighted from the second taxi; from the third came Zia, now nearly fifteen years old, with Berili; while in the fourth cab were the One-Eyed Regent, the chambermaid called Elizabeth, the major-domo Herr Jordan, and the footman known as Joseph. The family and its escort of six filled the little palace. Only two rooms remained unoccupied, and in the ensuing days György arrived from Cambridge while Kristina ran up from Spain.

The parents retired for extended and individual talks with the children they had not seen for so long, and soon discovered that they had very little to say to each other. György, who was already twenty-seven years old, had developed a broad set of shoulders in the boat races at the university. But his neck is still a bit stocky, Count Dupi reflected. Privately he studied the heir to his estate and title, whose round head, slightly short frame and friendly moss-brown eyes bespoke the Ostyak blood of the extinct Zoskay branch, which cropped up no more than once or twice in every century among the lithe, eagle-beaked Dukays, like a humble relative who dares venture no further. The father addressed himself to these conferences with a cautious objectivity, and the son with a courteous and generous frankness, as if Count Dupi were discussing the bestowal of a responsible sphere of employment on a young man whom he now met for the first time in his life. The youth did not make a bad impression on him. György did not ask for money, and he had never accumulated debts of any sort.

Kristina's demands were that much greater. She announced her imminent departure for Tokio, since it was the year of Hirohito's accession to the imperial throne.

"Are you going alone?"

"Count Harakoshi will go with me. He's very close at court."

Kristina's nails were stained a dark red.

"Only improper women wear such things," observed Countess Menti, who had a gift for refined expression. However, Kristina proceeded to inform her mother that Queen Ena of Spain wore the same shade of nail polish.

"Tell me, Kristi," Count Dupi inquired the next day, "is it true that you paint your toenails red too?"

"Of course."

"Let me see."

Kristina kicked off her light crocodile-skin shoes and peeled the silk stockings from her legs.

"Mhm..." Count Dupi studied the crimson toenails. He had never seen anything like this. He could not have seen anything like this, ever, for Kristina's toes were among the pioneers. Later Zia came in. And then the brothers. Kristina exhibited her legs as if they were rare birds she had captured in Andalusia. Countess Menti turned her eyes away. She recalled that Kristina was already twenty-nine.

They had planned this Parisian visit to last three weeks, to introduce János and Zia to the noteworthy sights of the city on the one hand, and on the other to enable Countess Menti to enlarge and refurbish her wardrobe, to discuss the purchase of some precious stones with M. Cartier himself, and to take the family to performances at the Opéra and the Comédie Française without which their culture would have been as unsatisfactory as a ragged shoe.

Sometimes Count Dupi isolated himself from the family and went alone to the Folies Bergères or Le Rat Mort, but on these occasions he always felt as if he were in a cemetery. The past decade and the intervening war had seen a whole world into the grave. Waiters, hat-check girls and proprietors no longer trampled on each other in their haste to greet him when he stepped in, no longer did he hear the whispers of "Le comte Dupi!" around him—he counted for as much of a guest as the grocer from Amsterdam and the lawyer from Barcelona or anyone else who had the price of admission to the gay thresholds of Paris.

He sat alone at a small table and ordered champagne, but scarcely tasted it.

A top-hatted man courted a woman on the tiny stage of L'Enfer. His flow of passionate appeal was as clean and high-minded as if intended for a graduation speech in a school for girls, and his audience justly took this alone to be suspect. Everyone knew that such flirtations on the stage of L'Enfer could only lead to some obscene conclusion. The top-hatted actor declared himself in lily-white words of love, in the midst of which he had considerable difficulty with the topper: he could not find a hat-rack, he could not find a chair, he had no place to put it. In his excitement he passed the hat from one hand to the other, which embarrassed his efforts to embrace, however worshipfully, the object of his affections. Again and again, as the words poured from him, he looked around in vain, and this was amusing in itself. The audience fidgeted, its eyes shone, waiting for the solution to the problem of the hat-rack. The actor's declarations of love grew steadily more heated, and apparently his body as well as his soul caught fire because the missing hat-rack appeared, if not at the usual height, it appeared and the actor hung the hat on his own flesh through the cloth of his trousers; and when the hat was truly in place, as if suspended in air, and the audience that had been mutely listening broke out in an explosion of whinnying and screaming laughter, the actor timidly snatched the hat from its biologically temporary hook and continued the fine flute-song of his courtship with the most innocent face in the world. But it was impossible to hear the rest, because the audience was rolling with laughter. The entrance fee was five francs. Paris purveyed the essence of audacious gaiety at an unbelievably low price, and, rude and crude performance though it was, Molière seemed to lurk somewhere in the background.

Count Dupi contributed only a grudging half-smile to the general screaming and whinnying. He did not stay to see the rest of the program but departed, almost sadly, with the feeling of someone who has left an unpaid bill behind him. The demand was for his wild humor of old, and he was no longer capable of paying in this coin. He was out on the street when the waiters, who sported horns and were dressed like devils, ran after him with their long cloth tongues hanging out and accompanied him, bowing, all the way to the street corner, in gratitude for the thousand-franc tip he had left under the plate, a sum so unusual in Paris at that time that at first they could not believe their eyes. Like a carpet of roses they cast before his feet their reiterations of "Au revoir, Monsieur," not realizing that this elderly but still slender and tall gentleman was the ghostly apparition of Europe at the turn of the century. Count Dupi paid no heed to the troop of devils thronging about him with their dark brown cowls and unsteady horns. So might a lion tread his way among the baying hounds. He vanished from the mobs of Montmartre.

By the second week he had surrendered to his fate and remained at Countess Menti's side in the box at the Opéra, and dozed through Debussy's most fetching arias, since his own taste for music ended with the gypsy variety. Countess Menti placed her elbows on the balustrade and clutched her throat with a gesture common to music lovers. Her capacity for musical appreciation withstood the sternest test.

As for the youngsters, they followed completely different paths in making the acquaintance of Paris under the direction of Dr. Kliegl and Madame Couteaux. They went their separate ways from the very first day. Dr. Kliegl spoke French like an early edition of one of the Hungarian-French drill pamphlets so often found in the second-hand bookshops of Budapest, which contain exercises in sentences like these: *The painter loves (is in love with) his grandmother. The camel entered (walked into) the room. Give me (let me have) that flea.* Contrariwise, from the moment the Orient Express touched the French border at Basle, Berili threw herself into her native language like a trout released into a running brook from a stale fishmarket pool. In a matter of seconds the pectoral and dorsal fins of her God-given loquacity became one with the torrential spring of lively fresh water. The next morning, although she had no shopping to do, Berili went down to the market place, took her place in line with the other women, wormed her way into their conversations, took part in the eloquent play of their shrewd glances, their wry laughter or the cheerful protestation which sounds, to a stranger, like the noisy intake of soup flavored with the mysterious spice of the mother tongue. Despite the fact that she had no personal stake in the matter, she joined with them in scolding the high costs; during those years Paris swam in abundance and low prices, but in every period and in every part of the world the established price has invariably provoked the selfsame tempest in market baskets and shopping bags. As if contact with her native land had suddenly cured Berili's intermittent lameness, she seized every occasion to dash into the neighboring streets, prowl in the little shops and, without any intention of buying, to peer behind the counters and peep behind the curtains that separated the store from the living quarters where the shopkeeper, in shirt sleeves, took his dinner with his family. Berili sampled the various dishes, was overwhelmed by the flavor of the *moule marinière,* imprinted the seal of her praise on the various Yvonnes, Germaines and Madeleines from elbow to eyebrow, and the reticent French people, who never hated foreigners so heartily as in the mid-Twenties, not only accepted the pushing impudence of Madame Couteaux as natural but even reciprocated with the greatest affability. Without pause for ceremony Berili became a member of the family for those few minutes when she burst in upon them with her impulsive visits only to hurry off at once, like someone pressed for time enough to carry out all the urgent obligations of seeing the homeland once more. She called out to janitors as they swept their courtyards. She stopped postmen on the street, clutched the strap of their mail-pouches with her dry old hands and would not let them go until she had exhausted a garrulous stock of talk with the red-faced, black-mustached fellows, deploring their low wages, threatening the Postmaster General of France with her umbrella—and then suddenly left them in the lurch, just as suddenly as she had seized on them with her love. She cavorted and rejoiced in the tropical lushness of the French language like a parrot freed from its cage. She rapped on the window glass of dress shops in which pallid Susannes and Amélies were plying their needles, waved to them with extravagant motions, pulled long and expressive grimaces at them by way of conversation and searched the dimness for a glimpse of their faces. She seemed to surmise the presence of her lost Louise in the depths of these workshops, Louise of the incredibly delicate eyebrows and translucent ears whom the influenza epidemic of 1918 had claimed for its own. It took days to satiate her wizened heart with the juices of old, and her agile nostrils quivered as she sniffed the pervasive odors of the more remote and dirtier streets, the unmistakable conglomerate aroma of rotting bananas, garlic, oyster stalls and cheap soap that distinguished the Rue de la Revolte or the Rue Cambronne. The blessed reek of Paris was purest balm to her thirsty lungs.

Count Dupi raised the crippled stump of his left forefinger in the air and addressed himself to Dr. Kliegl when the latter was on his way to a sightseeing tour of the city with János one evening:

"Just be careful!"

With a mute bow the tutor acknowledged the admonition, which he could hardly take as other than a warning to be cautious at street crossings. It is true that traffic in Paris was probably never more formidable than in the victorious decade following the war. But Count Dupi had something else in mind. He

327

thought it natural for an experienced tutor to take the "German puppy," whose mustache was beginning to blossom and who was in Paris for the first time, and dip him vigorously in the erotic enticements of the cosmopolitan quagmire. And he knew from his own precedent that caution was required in this realm of activity. When the theaters had emptied onto the wide boulevards in the early hours of the morning, mysterious figures stepped from the shadow of the buildings at the sound of strolling foreigners, whose walk they could recognize even from a distance, and accompanied them for miles, clinging firmly and confiding in a whisper that they knew a place where men joined with men, or women with women, or men with goats, or women with dogs, or perhaps men with suckling infants, in the observance of the customary rites at the altar of love, all in confirmation of the writings of Suetonius, the Roman author who recorded similarly incredible things in the comportment of the emperors at the time of Nero. With Dr. Kliegl at his side, Count János was in no danger of stepping into that filthy quagmire. The tutor was intent on introducing his pupil to the purest beauty of life, and only the loftiest stairways of the cultured world led in that direction. For there was a Paris of that sort too—properly speaking, this was the real Paris, aloof and ethereal, hovering and almost hidden in the din of the avenues, the lanes, the malodorous brothels, the champagne bottles popping in the international casinos. This Paris was the treasure house of poetry, of music, of art, of the most noble relics of history, a jewel box for the spiritual wonders of mankind. It was toward these heights that Dr. Kliegl led Count János. They set out every morning at ten o'clock, after consuming an enormous breakfast.

"The old Opéra stood here—" the tutor stopped his pupil in the midst of traffic "—in February of 1820 Prince Berry was murdered here while watching the dances of Virginie Oreiller, with whom he was in love."

Then they passed on.

"In this house," the tutor stopped once more, "lived Lulli, director of the Royal Academy of Music, born in 1633 in Florence, died in 1687 in Paris."

They continued on their way. The tutor came to a sudden halt. A strikingly handsome pigtailed chambermaid leaned out of the ground floor window in one of the houses on the Rue de Rivoli. She happened to be shaking the dust from a small rug onto the heads of the passers-by precisely when Dr. Kliegl raised his arm to point. The pigtails noticed his gesture, the rug stopped shaking, and for a few moments the attractive girl gazed at the two unknown men with a smile; then, when the elder one continued to point in her direction, she laughed and shook her pigtails in unmistakable indication of her willingness to become better acquainted.

"That is the room where they assassinated Admiral Colligny on St. Bartholomew's Eve, in 1572," the tutor continued his explanation, arm upraised, completely oblivious of the chambermaid. The two men might have been equipped with those miraculous spectacles which exclude the rays of the sun but reveal the hidden structure of the skeleton in a phosphorescent light. To the great disappointment of the pigtails, they walked away.

The equestrian statue of Louis XIV, which was one of Bosio's works, or the comic and tragic Muses carved by Seurre on Molière's fountain—each one of them was accorded a few explanatory phrases. Lean in its Gothic beauty, the cathedral of St. Germain l'Auxerrois seemed almost to stand in splendid isolation. One had to stop and explain that twice daily the carillon rang out the "Marche de Turenne" and played the most exquisite French songs, among them the ancient song of Chapnis, in all their nobility, while the hands of the clock showed not only the hours but the days as well and even the phases of the moon. Dates, names and facts simply poured from Dr. Kliegl, and Count János had every reason to pay homage to the dazzling profundity of his tutor's knowledge, not suspecting that the tutor was wont to forget his store of names and dates by the very next day, having memorized them the evening before out of that very useful little volume known as the *Guide Bleu.* Before going to bed he dedicated one whole hour to research for the coming day's excursions. No matter the means; what matters is that *at the time* he made his explanations he knew what he was talking about, knew it, we may add, accurately and conscientiously. Naturally he was the one who determined the itinerary, and he carried the necessary information in his head like fast-spoiling foodstuffs. In this way they covered the Louvre, the École des Beaux Arts, the Pantheon, Fontainebleu, Versailles and whatever else they could crowd into the space of three weeks. All the road signs along the highway of historical relics and on the footpaths of art pointed in one direction: palpable proof that this abundance of beauty could only have originated in an age of kings and emperors.

As he hobbled in at midnight and learned from Emanuel that his son was not yet home, Count Dupi assumed with a murmur of satisfaction that the rascal was treating the female citizens of France to champagne somewhere on Montmartre. His assumption was entirely groundless. They sat over a single glass of *fine* on the deserted terrace of some quiet café, and the subject of the tutor's lecture was that

French culture could not have reached its present stage of development without German influence. When a daringly painted *grue,* as the French language has named these swamp birds of the evening, stopped at their table now and then with an inviting smile, an imperceptible gesture of Dr. Kliegl waved away her insistence without a moment's pause in his address, as a bishop will shoo away the fly that settles on his nose during the sermon.

Berili and Zia followed another road. From morning to night they thirstily feasted their admiring eyes on the shop windows. Hand in hand they tugged at each other, with continuous cries of "Regarde ça!" Look there, look at this, look at that, whether it be women's underwear, automobiles, shoes, perfume bottles or fountain syringes—Berili in particular afforded even the most minute object the benefit of her tremulous "Ah's" and shouts of "Ça, c'est magnifique!" with arms uplifted and waving, all of which contained a large proportion of pride, as if she herself had assembled the French automobiles, resplendent on gleaming black rubber tires, with her own long knitting needles, and all the products of French industry as well. A considerable sum of money was at their disposal for shopping purposes, but this interested Berili less than the artistry and excitement of a close-driven bargain. From her expression, when she stepped into a shop, she might have been taken for the secret agent of a price control commission. It was with the greatest indignation that she took cognizance of the fact that they had the temerity to ask one hundred and twenty francs for the bright green gloves which had caught Zia's fancy in the window. She summoned the proprietor and scolded him from top to toe because the same gloves cost seventy francs on the Rue Royale—an assertion, incidentally, that had no basis in fact—until the proprietor would have been glad to let his goods go for nothing if only to terminate the flow of abuse and accusation that so entranced his other customers. When they left the shop, laden with packages, Berili winked at Zia and nudged her with an elbow, and these gestures called for acknowledgment of her consummate skill. Certainly she knew Paris well! She recalled the address of Madame Goujon, widow of the sometime druggist in Never, who used to live on the Rue Payenne and concocted the world's most wonderful homemade jasmine-scented hand lotions for a quarter of the price one paid in shops. Let's go to Madame Goujon's! By sheer coincid-ence the old lady was still alive, and not only lived at the same place but had raised the price of her lotion no more than one franc in the course of the past twenty years, something that Berili did not fail to remark reproachfully although that French franc was no longer worth a tenth part of its former value.

On the occasion of one of their journeys they happened into the Musée Carnavalet. The entrance simply sucked them in although museums and galleries never figured in the plans for their daily excursions. Berili, too, was on her first visit to this storehouse of the city's historical past. At first they wandered idly in the costume gallery, then they suddenly found themselves in the Louis XIV wing on the first floor. In the glass cabinets of the Salle du Temple they discovered Marie Antoinette's worn white cotton stockings, the monarch's razor and, in a corner, the guillotine itself. All at once Zia felt the depression of her Copperplated Twilight mood. Grandfather Lucien's story came to life around her, and a cold shiver ran down her spine. So, after a hiatus of years, the Copperplated Twilight was making its presence felt, like a sudden agonizing earache or a pang that goes through the liver like a knife. She pulled Berili away from the guillotine, although the latter was no more moved by that contraption than by one of the antique looms. Zia communicated her inner commotion in a whisper: "Allons, chérie!"

Out in the sunshine she recovered herself, but for a long time before retiring that night she continued to see the vision of Marie Antoinette's white cotton stockings, their every single thread, where an occasional rip had been awkwardly darned. This was what the unfortunate woman had worn in the dungeon of the Temple before they beheaded her.

The days of the three-week sojourn in Paris vanished rapidly, like slices of a large frosted cake. Only a few slices were left on the platter, the departure was planned for Thursday, the sleeping compartments had been reserved at the railroad station. One afternoon Zia burst into her father's room. Count Dupi was reading the lead editorial in *Figaro,* which dealt with the Greek Army's violation of the Bulgarian border and its veritable battle with Bulgarian sentries at the Demir Gate. Zia curled up in his lap, as she used to do when a little girl. Count Dupi suspected that her kittenish blandishment was prefatory to some important request.

"Papa, let us stay on a while longer. Berili and me."

"What on earth do you want to do here in Paris?"

In lieu of an immediate answer, Zia thoughtfully twirled the end of one of Count Dupi's thick eyebrows, as though it were a miniature mustache.

"I want to study photography."

This idea had struck her the day before. During one of their explorations she had espied Hugo Mongés's albumlike book, *Le photo artistique,* in the window of a large bookshop. The book cost five hundred francs, and for once Berili's skill at haggling failed to produce any effect whatsoever. But Zia thought the book well worth while, whatever its price. In word and picture it proclaimed the novel theory that true photography was on a level with painting. In those days Mongés was the Picasso of photography in Paris. He was one of those who liberated photography from its prison of fleecy clouds, surging seascapes, homing kine, falling leaves, village festivities and other banalities. He was the one who gave notice to amateur photographers the world over, as their equipment improved from year to year, that it was possible to photograph subjects other than grandma with a favorite cat in her lap, or the "good-looking" cousin as she stretched her length against the sky in a leap on the tennis court—that there were secret flashes of meaning, whether sad or gay, in life and its objects. They had begun to take note of him before the war, when he won first prize at a photography exhibition for his picture of a refuse pail outside a suburban gate, with eggshells, empty bottles of hair tonic, a pair of ragged children's shoes and some butter-brown potato peelings all curled like snails over the edge of the pail. The judges observed that the picture, aside from the excellence of its lighting effects, was serious in content.

The album contained a choice selection of photographs by Mongés. Another picture, also a prizewinner, was called "The Wager," and represented one of the tremendous marble ponds in the park at Versailles, a sleeping pool of magic beauty. At the edge of the pool stood two mischievous, barefoot street urchins, five or six years old, their legs wide apart, their hips strained forward. They were competing to see which one could propel the loftiest and longest liquid stream into the middle of the pool. Before Mongés, only the puffy stone angels of an ornamental fountain were allowed to perform such acts in the realm of photography. A third picture showed a violin on a table, in the company of a half glassful of milk and a broken piece of bread. The A-string of the violin had snapped, and was curled around the neck of the instrument. There was something cruel, something merciless and frightful in the curl of the string. It seemed to be choking the violin with murderous abandon. The photograph was a somber ballad of unrequited love, and the musician, though not in the scene at all, stood revealed. Zia sat up late into the night, devouring the photographs and the accompanying annotations with her eyes. Paul Ducreux had written a foreword to the album, and he dipped the flag of modern French painting in recognition of the mastery of Mongés. Zia, a passionate photographer, scrutinized the pictures like a provincial painter who first glimpses a Rubens canvas after a lifetime of depicting boar's heads for the signboards over neighborhood butcher shops. What would happen if she presented herself for instruction in Monsieur Mongés's studio? The thought of it so excited her that she woke Berili, who was sleeping in the next room and emitting little snores, each snore as sudden and startling as if it were intended to frighten someone from her bedside. When she was finally aroused, and understood what was in Zia's mind, Berili sat up in bed and locked her dry old hands in prayer. "Quell' idée!" Only the good Lord could have prompted such a wonderful idea! For days Berili's heart had been slowly breaking at the thought of departure. Now this child had roused her from a bitter dream with the prospect of spending the entire winter in Paris! Ardently she cradled Zia at her breast and rocked back and forth: "Oh, mon enfant! Mon enfant seul!"

Count Dupi murmured audibly and at great length as he listened to Zia's exposition of her plan. He leafed through the album with her carefully, but made no remark. It was sheer cunning on his part; he wanted to prolong the decision, to provoke every shade of flattery from Zia. For this was indeed his only real delight, when the "cricket" nestled in his lap from time to time, put her arms around his neck, rubbed his mustache with her fist or twirled his eyebrows. There was no request Zia could make that Count Dupi would not have fulfilled. He was pleased, too, that her mind ran on such serious and practical matters. As a hobby it was worth more, at any rate, than if she were to breed Angora rabbits or collect the prescriptions of Indian dervishes.

Around noon of the next day Hugo Mongés put in an appearance on the street named after Général Ferreyolles. He knew whom he was honoring with a personal visit, for in those years the name of Dukay still had a popular ring. The master looked more like a wine merchant from Arras than the pioneering apostle of photographic artistry. He was a fat, substantial man, and his face was as whitish-gray as if he had already been condemned to death by some deep-seated kidney ailment. The tips of his compact mustache were sharpened to a point, and as he kept turning his head from side to side with a restless motion the fragrance of perfume exuded from his mustache like sparks from Greek matches.

He thrust his pudgy chin somewhat forward, a self-conscious attitude closely connected with the remarks of Ducreux in the foreword to the album. The narrow crimson ribbon of the Legion d'Honneur bloomed in the buttonhole of his jacket, which was of poppyseed-gray cloth. The nails of his ten fingers bore the ineradicable stains of developing acids. He had no idea, at first, why the Hungarian count, whose name he pronounced *Düké,* wanted to speak to him.

The conference took place like a meeting of monarchs. Monsieur Mongés soon understood what was under discussion, and when the talk turned to the economic aspects of six months of instruction his right palm clutched his chin as if that round parcel of flesh were in sudden danger of falling to the ground. For a few seconds he was lost in thought, his eyes searching the air, and then he pronounced a sum. Count Dupi could hardly believe his ears. It was so small. The eyes of the master, however, followed the announcement of his asking price with an expression which seemed to indicate his fear that the count would immediately telephone for the police. Monsieur Mongés asked to see his prospective pupil. When Zia stepped in he hastened to her, took her two hands in his and did not release them for some time but kept looking at her with eyes that were almost tearful, as though it were a matter of the girl having been purchased in infancy by the count as a stolen baby from some wandering gypsy, and it had just become known that Zia was the long-lost and newfound child of Monsieur Mongés. The speechless reunion of father and daughter could hardly have been more touchingly portrayed.

The departures began on the following day. Kristina left for Madrid in the morning, while in the afternoon György returned to Cambridge. On Thursday evening the Dukays mounted the *Wagons-Lits* of the Orient Express for the journey back to Hungary. Only at the last moment did Mr. Emanuel learn that the young countess and her elderly companion were to spend the entire winter in Paris. His face turned white. Offhand, he could not even estimate how devastating an economic blow this was to him. His smiles, as he bade farewell to his master and mistress, turned as sour as if he had spent the whole day eating unripe pears. He broke the awful news gently to his wife Juliette.

Had Berili been the very Angel of Forbearance, to whom loud words and the heat of argument are unknown, it would still have been difficult to avoid a clash. Thus, on the morning of the next day, a quarrel broke out. Juliette stood with arms akimbo in the middle of the courtyard and shouted at one of the upper-story windows, where Zia was vainly trying to pull Berili out of verbal range.

Mr. Emanuel intervened in the interest of conciliation, with the result that a few moments later he was shouting up at the window even more vociferously than his wife. A pipeline fractured or a water main burst was nothing to the stream of epithets with which they flooded each other. The vilest phrases exploded in mid-air like bombs. *Vieille garce, va! Et va donc, fils de pute!* It was with the catapults of the idiom current in the northeastern provinces that Emanuel and Juliette propelled their heavy charges toward the window, while Berili poured the fiery pitch of southern French recrimination on the neck of the attacker. They brandished mops, and threatened one another with the police. Finally, after vast expense of blood, they came to their senses. All this did not prevent Mr. Emanuel and Juliette from going to the motion pictures with Berili every Sunday, especially since she paid for the tickets. They patched up their quarrels every half hour, handling each other at these times with all the gentility, the respect, all the polite shadings of obsequious courtesy befitting the descendants of the French age of chivalry.

Punctually at ten o'clock every morning Zia appeared at Monsieur Mongés's studio, which was built into the fifth-floor attic of a building on one of the side streets of the Avenue Victor Hugo. The studio resembled neither his album nor the eloquence of Ducreux's foreword. It was an impoverished little photographic studio, like hundreds of others under the roofs of Paris, with sun-faded green curtains and several sticks of lame, gilded furniture. The sole assistant, on whom the more arduous part of the work devolved, was Madame Mongés, and she spent the entire day dipping photographs in emulsion trays of various size. But, in view of the rooms in which Baudelaire or Verlaine lived or died, it is certain that this environment did not diminish the merit of Monsieur Mongés's art. As an instructor, too, Monsieur Mongés was first-rate. Each day he set out into the wilds of Paris with Zia. They carried similar cameras on their hunt for subjects, and photographed the same scenes. The resultant photographs, developed and enlarged, furnished material for their study. Why was one picture good and the other poor? What was wrong with the use of lighting? Where did the statement falter, where were the objective resources inadequate? Critical derogation and praise were applied to the compositions of master and pupil alike. Zia proved not only an enthusiastic student, but an intelligent one. After the first few weeks she already knew the fundamentals, the relation of background to predominant forms, the principles of lighting, and especially the subtle accents of "musical" and "dramatic" statement. Monsieur Mongés employed those expressions. "The competent photographer can arrange light and shade like the folds of a backdrop…The art of dramatic statement is the art of omission…It is not altogether imperative for the Eiffel Tower to grow out of the hat of your central figure, like a pheasant's tail…Wait, let's drench that stone stoop with a few rays of light…."

The master was assembling a new album of twelve "cantos." What does the average Parisian do in the twelve months of the year? There were fleeting glimpses of his place of work, the kitchen in his home, the physician's waiting room, the motion picture box-office, the bedroom, all in accordance with the season. The human tragedy in twelve scenes. There were only twelve pictures, but each was full of gay complaint, of bitter laughter, rebellious boredom and constrained apathy. It promised to be a beautiful piece of work. Dante might have composed his *Inferno* as Mongés prepared his album. Right now he was working on "July." When Zia entered the studio one morning, the stage was already set. A sprawling sofa, a little table alongside, champagne glasses, a bottle of soda-water and a half lemon exhausted of its juice—the emblems of scorching heat, of the dog days. A few seconds later a man and a woman, completely naked, stepped from the darkroom, which also served as a dressing room. Monsieur Mongés labored as if he were on the tremendous stage of the Opéra. He called the woman *Madame*, but addressed the man as *Monsieur le général*.

"Let us imagine a hot Sunday afternoon. You haven't the money to go to Deauville, so you've taken off your irksome clothes and let down the blinds, though the sun penetrates the chinks nevertheless. Madame, please stretch out comfortably on the sofa, gaze at the cigarette smoke and think of your lover, who is far away. You are playing a married couple now. General, sit on the edge of the sofa, beside your wife. Think of your consumptive lungs, and of your low salary. Outside the sidewalks are melting. No, please, this is not a pornographic display! General, I want you to sit covering your wife. Lean forward, put your elbows on your knees so you cover yourself. We are not interested in your charms."

"Is he a general?" Zia asked in a whisper.

"No. He's a model who hasn't eaten in two days. I call him general because there's a red stripe on his leg: it's the mark left by his garter. A fine motif! The pale, tortured flesh of modern man. Are we ready?"

After the first exposure the general, stark naked, paced the studio floor as though it were a military induction center or the examination room of a urology clinic. It was the first time in her life that Zia had seen a man naked. She had imagined it would be totally different. A mild disgust and revulsion seized her.

Zia also became familiar with accessories, cameras, lights and chemicals. "'Acquaint yourself with the materials you use,' the aged Perugino said to the youthful Raphael. 'Bind your brushes yourself, and mix your own paints.'"

Monsieur Mongés cited this quotation when he first put Zia into a white laboratory smock and stood her by a water tap to rinse photographs. Perhaps the aged Perugino never said anything of the sort to the youthful Raphael, but the words are not important. It is the melody that counts. Monsieur Mongés was practical enough to use Zia for the darkroom work that his wife could hardly cope with any longer. There were three papier-mâché trays, a black one for fixer, a white one for water and a yellow one for developer. The screw-in infrared bulb, the drying racks, the diffuse light and the bromide baths, orthochromatic and panchromatic development, orange and red filters, the mirror-reflex apparatus, the spotlight, the spraying lamp, the contact printer, the enlarger, the glossy papers, the scissors, the knives, the chemical scales…Zia came to know something new: the feverish savor of industry, the ultimate secret of which the beavers, the ants and the bees have not yet revealed to man. Every day Monsieur Mongés escorted her downstairs as far as the door, and bade her farewell with a deep bow.

On her way to the studio Zia passed through the Bois each morning. Berili always cautioned her:

"Watch out for the men. The Bois is especially dangerous."

And she told how, while she was knitting in the Bois one day, her twelve-year-old Louise strayed from her side and then came running back, her face pale, because a fine old gentleman had stepped from the bushes and, instrument in hand, had asked Louise to help him "calm the little fellow down." "Ils sont les nervosés! They're off center, all of them, armed with candies, and coins, and little pieces of jewelry. The young ones all have the clap. Take care, mon enfant."

It did not take much prompting to warn Zia away from this side of life.

It is a shame that in Paris, too, time passes. The arrival of spring along the Avenue Foch was virtually heartbreaking, with its splendor of colors and gleams. But it was necessary to prepare for departure. As a farewell gift Zia sent Monsieur Mongés a heavy silver cigarette case engraved: *To the Master, from his Grateful Pupil.* Madame Mongés received a diamond ring.

Mr. Emanuel conducted the travelers to the train. Once they were gone, he stepped out of the Gare de l'est with the expression of someone leaving the gates of a sanatorium, cured after six months of serious illness.

The train was passing through Châlons-sur-Marne. Vast French military cemeteries came into view here and there, with thick clusters of crosses like the rank vegetation of death. They were approaching the border. France grew smaller, smaller. Smaller grew the wide green mirrors of the spring flood-waters in the midst of which stood young birches holding their scant white shifts up to their knees, as in the landscapes of Millet. French *cheminots* were seen less often standing by the tracks, with swollen shoulders stuffed into faded blue jackets.

Berili sat by the window and stared out. Outside, in the corridor of the sleeper, a middle-aged German couple faltered indecisively. The woman must have been in her ninth month, for her rounded belly looked as if an open umbrella were concealed under her dress. She blocked the narrow corridor completely. They were genteel, modest and misfortunate. It was impossible to find a seat on the crowded train. Finally the husband, with his mildest "bitt' schön," bowed his way into Zia's compartment. Could his wife sit down for a while? Naturally, Zia invited them both to come in. They did not speak a word of French.

France grew smaller, smaller. The red-capped French customs guards had abandoned the train to its hopeless fate. Berili continued to stare out of the window. Her face was ash-gray. So lame had she been at the moment of departure that she managed to mount the train only with Mr. Emanuel's help. And now, as they left the border behind, the furtive tortures of arteriosclerosis began to twist at her veins once more. As she looked out of the window the marks of farewell and death were written on her face, on her wide dark blue lips, on the very crescent-shaped hairs of the mole beside her nose. She knew that she would never see France again. The experiences of the past six months filled her with dim foreboding. Was she able to see into the future? Hardly. It was like the apprehension of a child who sees her mother after a long absence and searches her expression in secret fear that she has caught a cancer or will be struck down by a trolley car within the next few days. Berili felt that she should not have left her homeland to itself at this time, that her presence, for some hidden reason, was imperative and indispensable; it was as if the destiny of France depended on the continuance of her fierce quarrels with Mr. Emanuel and Juliette. In her absence the Eiffel Tower might easily wander off, perhaps, to take up its stand, with legs widespread like an enormous iron giraffe, somewhere above the forests of Vincennes; or the beautiful bridge of Louis Philippe might decide to settle down like a pig in the mud of the Seine; or the metal shutter in front of Monsieur Franquet's woolens shop might close, with a horrible message for the world on the handwritten note posted outside.

Zia kept an anxious eye on Berili, who must have sensed something in her glance; she cleared her throat curtly, surveyed the German woman for a moment, and then began to murmur:

"Ah ça, je me demande, pourquoi ces sales boches fabriquent-ils cette masse effrayante d'enfants? I'd like to know why these dirty Germans manufacture such a mess of children?"

They were in Switzerland. The telegraph poles darted past the windows with a sarcastic hoot, like witches mounted on broomsticks, and the green hillocks on the horizon were hobbling in the opposite direction too, as if they all wanted to emigrate to France. When the train goes east, the heart seems to feel that everything is hastening westward.

Came the Swiss conductor, who spoke both French and German. He gently tried to oust the Germans, who had no sleeper reservations, from the compartment. His "bitt' schön" became less mild, but without result. Suddenly, with a great rush of words, Berili threw herself into the fray. She began with excessive politeness, but in the third sentence she was already calling the conductor by his first name, and scolding him like a child. Didn't you ever have a mother? Did you drop from the sky? What are you? Are you a man? You're Swiss, you are, you managed to stay out of the war, and yet there isn't so much humanity in you as the dirt under my fingernail. The compartment is ours, the lady is our guest, it's none of your business. Regulations! Look in your heart, my fine friend, and see how many regulations you've kept in your lifetime!

Arms akimbo, the conductor enjoyed his scolding with a smile. Several branches of his family were French, and the old woman reminded him of one of his aunts. He adopted her familial tone, and addressed her with the familiar thou:

"Don't be so generous, *toi,* at the expense of the Wagons-Lits Company. You won't lose your job, but I will."

He took the Germans with him, but his heart had softened and he promised to find seats for them. As they progressed along the narrow corridor the German woman's enormous belly formed a veritable blockade against European trade and traffic. People fled to their compartments and to the washrooms at her approach, and those who were unable to fit in anywhere else retreated to the next car, like the members of a Bulgarian tourist excursion all of whom abandoned their entrenched positions. Faces reflected gentle courtesy but terror too, as if the huge German belly were threatening to give birth to another eighty million Germans right there on the train.

They had long entered Austria, and the train climbed so high in the Tyrolean mountains that they might have been riding on an airplane. The little villages below looked like playthings.

Berili was strangely speechless. In the twilight glow of spring that came from the snowy peaks the sallowness of her face was frightening.

"Do you feel sick?" Zia asked softly.

"Pas du tout! Not a bit!"

They had dinner and retired early. Zia clambered into the upper berth. They fell asleep quickly, omitting for once their whispers and mutters after going to bed.

All night the train crept along the Austrian mountain passes. In the morning the sun shone and they were approaching Vienna when Zia woke up. There were noises in the corridor, and soon the conductor knocked to indicate that they would reach Vienna within the hour. Zia called to Berili, but there was no answer. Fearing the worst, she climbed out of bed.

Madame Couteaux was dead. Her mouth was partway open, as though she were about to say something. The glazed look of death peered through her half-open eyelids.

Zia was still not certain what had happened. She began to dress hurriedly, as if Berili's life depended on whether she could find her barrette in time.

She rang. The conductor came. She simply pointed to the corpse. Then two strange women came to arrange the body somewhat, and in the meantime they threw questions at Zia. One asked her sympathetically, "Was she your mother?" And Zia answered in confusion, "Ja...Nicht..."

The corpse took possession of the entire compartment. The train clicked on monotonously. Zia sat on one of the little jump-seats in the corridor and wept, burying her nose in a handkerchief. Sometimes the hand of a foreign woman rested on her shoulder in compassion, and then she courteously stopped crying for a few moments.

The travelers were talking of the fatality. Soon the conductor arrived with the news that the German woman had given birth to a healthy boy on the wooden bench of a third-class coach during the night. In one of the compartments someone was heard shouting an explanation to a deaf old gentleman:

"An elderly Frenchwoman died on the train, and a German baby was born...."

The words sounded like a threatening pronouncement of history.

Zia went into the compartment from time to time and kissed Berili's forehead, which was rapidly growing cold. Then she returned to sniffle at her place. The conductor reminded her of the need to send a telegram to Budapest from Vienna. It would be best if the hearse were waiting at the station.

The death of Madame Couteaux caused no greater concern in the palace on Septemvir Utca than if the key to one of the suitcases had been lost en route.

They buried Berili the next afternoon in a little cemetery on Buda. Besides Zia, the noble family was represented by Mr. Gruber, the secretary, and the staff by the One-Eyed Regent. The three of them were the only mourners. No one else.

But wait! Here are some others. Zia recognized them although, to be sure, she had never seen any of them before. They were the members of the little French colony, Monsieur Deleriaux from the champagne distillery, whose pointed mustache contained more dirt than wax, with his wife Germaine, whose hips were a little crooked, old Monsieur Bottin and his halitosis from the enamel plant together with his mother, who was as deaf as a stone, and his sister Mademoiselle Bottin, who falsified her true age by eighteen years and was in the throes of a clandestine affair with Monsieur Deleriaux. Yes, it was they. Unlikely creatures, figments of the imagination who were even now only exceptionally on an excursion into reality and would return to the realm of fable again after the funeral.

Mr. Gruber and the One-Eyed Regent, in their official capacities, suffered through the funeral with the expression of witnesses called to testify at the trial of one Madame Couteaux, who had committed the misdemeanor of dying.

When the priest concluded, Monsieur Deleriaux stepped to the open grave. The tears dripped along his mustache and his jaws shook, as if he wanted to chew something thoroughly and quickly before beginning his valedictory. What does a Frenchman say on such an occasion? He brought the farewell greeting of the French people to its homeless daughter, and he reassured the deceased that this little plot of foreign soil was now a part of France.

All the members of the colony sobbed out loud. Mademoiselle Bottin was on the point of moaning. Zia felt that they were mourning not Berili but themselves, the pain of exile bursting from their hearts.

The next day, in the depth of a bureau, Zia found Berili's last will and testament, in the tone of which there was a grave munificence, as if the disposition of vast estates, corporate securities and industrial interests were involved. She left her knitting needles to old Mamma Bottin. The corset with which Countess Menti had burdened her went to Madame Deleriaux, in view of her crooked hips. Her umbrella was willed to Mademoiselle Bottin, and her clothes, shoes and linen were also divided among the three ladies. Monsieur Bottin received the worn, checkered English suitcase with which Madame Couteaux had alighted at the little Willensdorf station six years ago. Her gold wedding ring went to Monsieur Deleriaux, whom Berili always used to tease with the suggestion that he divorce his wife and marry her instead. When leaving she regularly honored him with a confidential, coquettish wink.

She bequeathed her prayer book to Zia. There was, in this, a certain willful contradiction to the life she had led, and perhaps an element of repentance for the unseemly songs.

On a sealed envelope she had written: *Pour mon cercueil et pour mon enterrement.* For my coffin and for my burial. There were three thousand-crown notes in the envelope, put aside from her salary in the early years. This marked the peasant in her. Old beggar-women, too, hide the money for their coffins, viewing everything that awaits them after their death on earth with suspicion.

Some years earlier, the three thousand crowns would have afforded quite a charming little funeral. Berili had forgotten only one thing. After the war a dire disease attacked the blood vessels of most nations, and the white corpuscles multiplied to an alarming extent. In the meantime the value of Hungarian currency tumbled so far that three thousand crowns would not even buy a box of matches.

Chapter Six

FOUR years passed after the winter in Paris, and the world hardly changed in those four years. From the fall of 1925 to the fall of 1929 old Europe stopped to rest a bit on the road of time, because the sun was beginning to shine with undue warmth. He took off the veteran's tunic that rattled with so many military decorations, sprawled under a tree and started to eat. In one sitting he consumed some four million automobiles, purchased mainly at the American grocery store but in part home-grown. Then he lit his pipe and stared into the smoke rings. There he saw Briand and Stresemann as they embraced each other in the Locarno Hall of the British Ministry of Foreign Affairs and solemnly vowed, before the eyes of the world, that France and Germany would never take arms against each other again. Germany joined the League of Nations, which pleased the men at Geneva so much that they all threw their hats to the ceiling and immediately terminated the military surveillance of Germany. Europe's Foreign Ministers no longer had time for the golf links, not even on Sunday, so busily were they signing treaties of friendship—the terms of the Italo-Abyssinian agreement were especially moving. The whole thing gave the impression of someone stopping a total stranger on the street to say: "Excuse me, sir, but would you be good enough to step into that tavern for a glass of wine with me? And let us sign a contract never in our lives to kick each other in the pants." This is what a French and a German writer did, publishing—for all the world to see—the correspondence in which they entered into a mutual obligation, although they had never met personally, to refuse to wage war against one another in the future. Both of them were practiced draft dodgers. French engineers began construction on the Maginot Line, while wise men gave doubting Thomases the assurance that the elaborate entrenchment, this new *Van-Li-Chang-Cheng*, was not intended to ward off the attacking Germans but merely to relieve unemployment in France. Later we shall see that this hypothesis was correct. The world brooked no disturbance while it snored away in dreams of peace. England and the Soviet Union may have severed diplomatic relations for a second or two, but this caused no greater commotion than the roaring of two lions over a haunch of horsemeat behind the iron bars of the zoo at feeding time. Oil was the cause of this little misunderstanding.

After the World War, Europe shook itself like a dog climbing out of a river and, as the anti-royalists said, shed seven parasitic insects: seven ruling thrones. To aggravate the royalists, the anti-royalists began to elect Queens of Beauty. Paris, of course, was in the forefront. The festive event took place in the Opéra, and the President of the Republic was the first to kiss the newly elected Queen. Smaller nations hastened to emulate Paris, with the difference that the chiefs of state did not kiss their Beauty Queens in public, for that would have compromised their dignity. It can be said without exaggeration that in the second half of the Twenties the majority of the people, especially in central and southeastern Europe, were occupied with beauty contests, which worked a substantial increase in the worshipful reverence of feminine beauty. Every race wanted to prove that it had the most beautiful daughters, but the malignant partisans of racial theory did not approve because the Bulgarian Queen of Beauty proved to be the platinum-blond daughter of a Swedish mining engineer who happened to live in Sofia, while the Polish Queen of Beauty was the daughter of a Greek horse trader. The dream of the future, the United States of Europe, was made manifest in the image of Miss Europe, photographed in a bathing suit just as she was about to test the warmth of the ocean with her pretty toes. Even the imminence of world government cast its shadow in the person of Miss Universe. In the space of seconds the beauty queens became film stars and the wives of South American millionaires. "Hope is reality!" Guillaume à Aquitaine once sang, and the bright angel of hope made herself equally at home in the noble residence of the Greek Orthodox Patriarch in Bucharest, behind the counters of department stores in Brussels and in the bordellos of Warsaw, wherever the Creator had enlisted young girls in various spheres of activity. Retired admirals, active mill managers and unemployed sculptors vied with each other in the general tumult to become members of a commission of judges. The members reputedly allowed themselves to be bribed by the candidates, but it is inconceivable to connect serious judges with material corruption.

Do you remember how wonderful Europe was toward the end of the Twenties? Historians, begone! Go elsewhere. As for us, we are on the trail of the bones and tusks of an extinct Dinotherium along the undulating plains and treeless wastes of memory: Europe's extinct high spirits.

The tremendous antediluvian creature must have been extremely attractive, for one phrase began to occur more and more frequently in the deadly boredom of America: *doing Europe.* The colloquialisms both of Dallas and of the East Side became commonplaces in the neighborhood of the little one-story houses along the streets of Buda, and the sheep herded by American Express often made discoveries as surprising and poetical as only people from afar can do. They established, for example, that the houses in America are larger than those in Buda, while the firmament is much wider over Buda than over New York. However we take it, this conclusion at least meant a greater gain of territory for the dismembered little country than did the revisionist articles of Lord Rothermere, which were causing such an acceleration of the national heart-beat in those years. Doormen in posh hotels along the edge of the Danube were assaulted by tourist parties with the problem of what to see. And the answer came as if from a phonograph record:

"See the church of St. Matthias. See the Fisher's Bastion. Go to the pool at the Hotel Gellért—it has artificial waves! And every day before noon a real archduchess goes swimming there—you can even touch her!"

Yes sir, you could have touched her, had you wanted to, without additional charge. In the shallow water of the *Hullámfürdö* there really floated a corpulent archduchess. This is how the king of beasts must take his ease in the African bush. The artificial waves agitated her large breasts and soft belly until it seemed that they were nodding in encouragement of tourism at the shoe wholesaler from Chicago who swam round and round the Royal Highness and wondered whether he dared touch her. Finally (as the American spirit is always ready for a large-scale venture) he took a deep breath, pretended blindness behind his thick spectacles and swam straight into that fleshy abundance, managing to struggle free only with the greatest travail, as if from a soft mud bath in history, amid stammers of "Oh, I'm so sorry!" But at home he told members of his club how he had spent fully seventeen seconds in the lap of a veritable Habsburg archduchess.

What else happened during those four years? Oh, yes: Having insufficient reverence for the Atlantic Ocean, Lindbergh flew across that body of water. In general, there was considerable action on the Irreverent front. The irreverent miners of England went out on strike. Three irreverent individuals made unsuccessful attempts on the life of Mussolini, although according to some sources the attempts were engineered by the Fascists to prove the invulnerability of the Duce. In Hungary a clandestine group of patriots invented a new secret weapon that was completely noiseless and had the important advantage of causing no harm to human life or property, but was still considered effective enough to force France to her knees for having trussed the mutilated body of Hungary in the straitjacket of the Little Entente. The secret weapon was a rather delicate printing press that began to turn out counterfeit banknotes of France in great quantity. Reckless and resolute Hungarian patriots were found to pack their pockets with the product of the secret weapon, steal across the several borders and begin the destruction of French economic life. They ordered caviar and crêpes suzettes in the restaurants and threw money around the casinos in a way that Count Dupi could not have approximated even in the good old days. Unfortunately the product of the secret weapon was easily detectable at a distance of ten paces, a fact which caused great damage to the good name of the Hungarian printing industry. But they were still the heroes of a new humanism, those who distributed thousand-franc notes instead of wounds. Official circles in Hungary indignantly condemned the sneak attack and ordered an energetic investigation of the counterfeiters which led to no result at all for a long time because the national chief of police himself was the head of the ring. A new theme enlivened the couplets of Parisian floor shows, but otherwise there was little damage. Europe continued to beam with good humor.

Rumania produced an organization with the splendid name of the Iron Guard, while in the autumn of 1928 the Albanians elected Zog to be their king, a development that aroused great excitement among the maiden ladies of Hungarian aristocracy. Formerly an humble infantry lieutenant of the Monarchy, he was at least single, and although the throne on which he sat loomed no larger than the pea in Rustician's tale, it was at least a throne. Kristina traveled to Albania because it was the opinion of her Spanish doctor that her tracheitis could improve only on the Albanian seashore.

And nothing more interesting happened in the environs of Septemvir Utca either. Zia ordered a handsome tombstone for Berili, and often went to visit her grave. Later she went less often. Last year she went only on All Souls' Day. In November of the past year Count Dupi celebrated his sixtieth birthday in the narrow confines of his family circle. Of all his children only Rere and Zia were present, because György was still in America and János was pursuing his agricultural studies in Leipzig, having taken along not only Dr. Kliegl to do his thinking for him but the footman named Joseph as well, so there would be someone to pull his shoes on in the morning, for German valets were so swollen with the national self-consciousness of Hitler's speeches that they no longer undertook this service. Countess Menti devoted all her time to the Catholic Women's Union; in her speeches as president, she continued to reform the morals of the world with high hopes of success. Zia installed a tiny photographic darkroom in the palace on Buda. Recently she began to take an interest in portrait photography. Not only the entire palace staff but half the inhabitants of the village at Ararat were exhausted as models.

Zia was now past eighteen, and in the opinion of those who understood such things she was not accounted one of the "dazzling" beauties of Hungarian aristocracy, one of those whose names were common currency. Her eyebrows were a little too thick, with stubby irregular hairs, and eyebrows like hers deprived a woman of the dreamy mystery which high, arched, narrow eyebrows can lend the feminine face. Women overcame this obstacle by having their eyebrows entirely uprooted and penciling thin lines over the agonized skin. The popular tea-shops, the theater lounges and the fashionable city streets began to fill with imperfect imitations of Tutankhamen, all because a quarrelsome Egyptian Pharaoh grew bored with the sublime quietude of the nether world and unexpectedly stepped out of his four-thousand-year-old golden tomb. The habit of depilation gradually found its way down into the armpits of women, and ranged even further. After retiring and turning off the light, unsuspecting men often found that the customary groping of their hands met with a great surprise.

(Fifteen years later the world, too, meets with a great surprise: *ripmaus* is rife. What is ripmaus? Impossible to say, exactly. It is some unexpected and intangible criminal act of cosmic dimension for which we have no suitable word, just as there was no word for oxygen before Lavoisier. A murky, liver-spotted criminal act, shapeless, astonishing in extent, and we now know that it was committed by an old man, an old man with a beautiful high forehead. Turning his ragged pockets inside out, we find red-tinted toenails, uprooted eyebrows, armpits and other cavities cleanshaven. Possibly all this has no connection with the crime, although the blood-red nails seem suspicious. We must examine it all, the bread crumb, the wisp of thread, the airplane, the forged treaty of alliance, the atom-seed awkwardly forced open. Where are they from, how did he come by them, how long has he had them? And what is this medal of the Virgin Mary about his neck, from the time of Augustus Caesar? Why does he carry that futurist poem, written in 1927 by a Parisian poet, beginning: "There is a sewing machine in the blackboard chalk…" Let us see his other pocket. A confidential world-wide catalogue of distinguished homosexuals? Worthless. We know all this from the report of the inquest that followed the fall of Rome. What about the rest of his pockets—where has he concealed that sharp little knife, one scoop of which suffices to sever the *vas deferens* and presto, you're sterilized. We must cross-examine him: where, when, how often and in what low dives did he consort with the Church, with Literature and with Learning. Ripmaus. The word was used by a two-year-old child whose mother they ravished before her very eyes after shooting her papa for his show of resistance. Ripmaus: riot, rape, panic, murder, suspicion…We still do not know what mists the ill-omened little star of that word was born in. The child said: "When the ripmaus came…")

A hairdresser in the city, the whispering Mr. Kudera, advanced tactful and delicate hints, but Zia spurned the suggestion that she have her eyebrows plucked. And she was right. People look beneath unruly eyebrows like these with the sensation of ringing at familiar doors, behind which the furniture and chinaware are old acquaintances and the dog too barks in a friendly fashion. This effect was heightened by the warm gaze of Zia's eyes, which were as green as the bud of an apple. She sat for Count Joachim, who was well known in artistic circles as a portrait painter.

"If I can match the color of your eyes," he said during one session, "I'll be satisfied."

An English pipe in his mouth, he talked incessantly.

"Your mouth isn't easy either. There is something at the corner of your lips that reminds me of fledgling birds. And where did you get that nose? Nowadays you see the straight Schäyenheim nose only on the statues of Polycletus, while the Dukay nose has that slight hook of Caucasian camel drivers. Dollin would call it a saber nose."

"What's wrong with my nose, Uncle Himi?" Zia held her head still and kept her eyes in the desired direction.

"You have a very charming little nose, but it has a wee touch—how shall I say it?—a wee touch of Slovak. *You* know. Don't move, I'm doing your nose right now. Odd: your nose is just the slightest bit off center. There is something inviting about such noses. Are you still a virgin?"

"Not yet," answered Zia, her thoughts elsewhere.

Count Joachim started to smile, something he rarely did.

"A splendid answer. Next week I'm going to Vienna to paint Professor

Freud's portrait. He'll be very pleased with your answer. He dotes on such slips of the tongue."

Zia paid no attention to the buzzing of Uncle Himi's Henry IV beard, which was the color of hard rolls, because she was wondering what cameras to take on the mouflon hunt tomorrow. In any case the subject did not particularly interest her. But not because she had a frigid nature. No, she was not frigid. Her lithe, attractive body was often visited by desires which were like mild zephyrs in a blossoming tree. But Zia longed for something of unearthly beauty, for the purity of celestial love that is often like ethereal music in the heart of a young girl. This kind of desire came into man's possession sometime in the distant past, beginning perhaps in the Aurignac period when the first visions appeared to the hollow beat of drums, and has since been the only means of differentiating between man and beast. Zia waited impatiently and solemnly for the first flowering of love, but it refused to come. When she graced the Park Club with her slender, supple waist from time to time, she was instantly surrounded by young men who, for all that they were known by names—Kuki, Sigi, Fufu, Ubi—more suitable for household pets, were of a type not to be scorned, their fine figures tempered by tennis and horsemanship, hunting and skiing; and if there was an example or two of the roisterer withered in night clubs or at the gaming tables, they were still handsome lads in general, not in the sense of *beau garçon* but in the heritage of the race, with a fine nose here, a well-cut mouth there, long flat eyes or sharp profile, and particularly distinguished by the gentle breeding of gesture and courteous modulation of voice that the sons of country gentry, Sabina landlords and Jewish manufacturers, in their efforts at emulation, translated into hunched shoulders, crooked arms, drawling accents and entrancing idiocy. To the latter the morning hours were known as the "ma-tin-al-is," by which they meant the early forenoon, and when they went to the *Gerbeaud* to eat hot little pastries stuffed with chopped meat they ordered "vol-au-vent," as they had heard Countess Carlota pronounce it, and the next day they were contemptuous of their parents because of the word "haché." They had their hair cut at Fröling's, because Prince Andrew once entered that barbershop by accident, and they were lulled by the happy delusion that all this compensated for centuries of insufficiency, in bone, blood, nerve and intellect. They were like garbage trucks. Like a vast mob of fans marching in emulation of their favorite star: they had only the husks and scraps of refuse to work on.

There was not one among the imitators, nor even among the imitated, to interest Zia. But she liked to be with them, because she was young; she was fond of tennis, and of dancing, and she especially liked to laugh. The corners of her lips, reminiscent of fledgling birds, impatiently awaited the nourishment of laughter. Youth is generally high-spirited. But something inexplicable happened after the World War: the youth of the middle class and the working class lost its good humor of old. Gaiety was prevalent only among the offspring of the peasantry and the aristocracy. Nature protected the popular humor of the people, even in adversity, because they lived close to nature, and the people protected the humor of the aristocrats, who lived as far as they could from the very people that cared for their carefree existence. In between, in the offices and factories, an ink-stained and artificially manufactured humor prevailed. The workers were badly paid, and from the expropriated parts of the country, which was now a third of its former size, came a vast flood of ousted Hungarian officials, like a stream of blood from a torn artery. These simply vegetated now, or pushed the stay-at-homes out of a job, and that was no laughing matter for the middle class. If you really wanted a good laugh you spent an evening with young Count Sigi, who delivered interminable political addresses when completely drunk and was devilishly clever at imitating the gestures and intonations of his father the cabinet minister. Exploiting deliberate errors of pronunciation and slips of the tongue to the full, he filled his historically portentous speeches with the most scandalous obscenities. It is said that a secret known to two people is no longer a secret. But this is utterly wrong. Pensioned editors of telephone books from Sables and bear-breeding landowners from Zola traveled long distances to hear Count Sigi orate, but not a single word of his orations reached the minister-daddy's ear, with such remarkable fidelity did the great public keep the secret. The sly public made a fatal mistake: they should have laughed at the minister-daddy's speeches instead. To those, however, they listened with awe.

Now that Zia was an eligible young woman, the good-natured youths of the aristocracy were often present at the balls in the Dukay palace or at the hunts from Ararat, and even in her sleep Zia sometimes broke into laughter over some of their *mots* or some of their pranks. There was the affair of young Baron Ubi, who was invited to a party at which everyone was to wear children's clothes. Ubi dressed as a three-year-old boy and carried a toy cane which bore a horse-head, bridle and all, at one end. He arrived late, after the company had already gone in to dinner. Ubi galloped madly into the dining room with a paper shako on his head, and immediately realized that he was in the wrong apartment, for all the guests were in evening clothes. The manager of a tobacco plant was celebrating his thirtieth anniversary, and the master of ceremonies was in the middle of his encomium. For the sake of the greater effect Ubi had let his shirttail hang out of his back-button jumper, had even stained part of it brown; undaunted, diminishing neither his yowls nor his wild career, he whipped his steed around the table like a racer approaching the finish line and then disappeared like a whirlwind. After his departure the solemn company broke into two factions. The majority held that nothing had actually taken place, so unlikely did the incident seem. Yes, these young men were gay blades, but the stuff they were made of was not suitable for the kind of love Zia was patiently awaiting.

However true it was that aristocratic society broke out of its bandbox after the war—Countess Sophia declared an end to discrimination and announced that she for one would address a sisterly thou to the women with whom she made the collection rounds on Children's Day—however true this was, the members of the nobility still preferred to mix most freely with foreign diplomats. Zia was somewhat beguiled by the Argentine military attaché, whose face was plum-blue from shaving. Zia confessed this inclination to her very good friend Elizabeth, and the "dazzling" flaxen-haired beauty in turn made no secret of the fact that he was the very man to whom she had presented her virginity. Within a week Elizabeth informed Zia that she had consulted Señor Calandra and found him willing to accept Zia's virginity too, especially since he would be unoccupied for the next few days. Zia was touched by so much unselfishness, but refused the offer with decision. Those who have shaken their heads, if only in fancy, over the training methods of Madame Couteaux, may now withdraw their head-shakings. At the appropriate time Zia had been given a full insight into the secrets of sex, with all its regular and irregular conjugations set to music, versified and rhymed, and in the depths of her soul there remained an element of loathing for the beast in man. It was as if Berili had purposely aroused this loathing in the child, wisely knowing that a healthy little dose of loathing, administered in the proper proportion, is the most dependable chastity belt. Elizabeth had spent six years as a student at the Sacré Coeur.

Early one September morning Count Dupi hobbled up the stairs and entered Zia's apartment.

"Look, cricket," he fell into an armchair with a jolt, "wouldn't you like to come with me?"

"Where?"

"Venice. Let's sneak away for a while."

"'Aw...that's a *wonderful* idea.'" Zia did a splendid imitation of Miss Roberts, the daughter of the British ambassador. "When do we start?"

Count Dupi reached into his waistcoat pocket and consulted the thin, worn gold watch that had not left him since he was a lieutenant of Dragoons.

"Let's leave in a half hour. We can have dinner at nine in St. Mark's Square."

Shortly afterward the large touring car drew up in front. Oscar the chauffeur, who for some unknown reason resembled a Persian fur dealer, scrutinized the map. If they started now they could be in Venice by eight o'clock, allowing for two blowouts. His Excellency the Count and Countess Zia came downstairs, with several footmen in their wake carrying the pigskin luggage with the red and blue stripes, suitcases that were so old they had taken on the color of well-smoked meerschaum.

They set out. One more ta-ta for Mamma and then another for Rere, whom they sighted in the park with a mop in hand. He stared after them from beneath the rim of his derby as if he were seeing an automobile for the first time in his life.

The two of them liked to steal away like this, together, from time to time. Count Dupi's rumbling voice took on a new warmth when he could introduce Zia to one or two of his friends in a dining car or a hotel lobby:

"This is my daughter."

He was pleased with this supple-waisted lady, with her eyes of apple-green. Beyond paternal affection, the company of a pretty woman was still as necessary to him as a rosary to a nun. She proved a good traveling companion. They jabbered a great deal of nonsense, but this helps to relieve drowsiness and is especially effective against the sirocco encountered on Italian soil. It developed that Zia, inexplicably, had never been in Venice before. In his morning paper, Count Dupi related, he had read that a famous German repertory company was to present an outdoor performance of *The Merchant of Venice* in the Piazza San Tomaso on the following day.

They were in the neighborhood of Klagenfurt. The powerful automobile did well over seventy miles an hour on the open road. Unlike the Hungarians, the Austrians had realized that to maintain their highways in superlative condition was an excellent investment, because the number of vehicles in Europe was increasing and these were drawn to good roads like bees to honeysuckle. Count Dupi was lulled to sleep, always and inevitably, by the monotonous hum of the motor. Zia studied the face of the sleeper. Poor Papa, he was growing old. Then she looked out of the window at the roadside juniper trees, so typical of Austrian highways, as they rapidly snatched at the past and staggered backwards. Their branches seemed to be patched together with scraps of red velvet.

Zia could not have imagined what awaited her in Venice. How could she have known—a girl's first great love arrives more stealthily than the first snipe in the slate-blue twilight of the budding March forests. She began to read *The Merchant of Venice,* of which only a French translation had been available in their library.

They arrived on schedule and found the Piazza San Marco crowded with their acquaintances, almost as if they had brought all of Budapest along. Like Zia and Count Dupi, the friends and acquaintances had come for the outdoor performance.

"Tickets?" Princess Karola laughed in disbelief. "They're not to be had. Perhaps for love, but not for money."

It was always impossible to divine Count Dupi's method of solving such problems. On the following night, however, he was in the front row with Zia, not far from King Alfonso of Spain and the American Secretary of the Treasury, Andrew Mellon. The stands, newly built for the occasion, were jammed with men in dinner jackets and women in evening clothes. It would have been difficult to ascertain whether Shakespeare or the couturières of Paris constituted the main attraction. Certainly the gown of one Mrs. Ryan was more widely discussed than the tragedy by an English genius. As for the performance itself: here again it was possible to distinguish the Deferent from the Irreverent.

"Aw...this is *wonderful!*" shrieked Miss Roberts; naturally, she was there too. The Schiaparellis and the Molyneux found the spectacle ravishing. Not so the Irreverent. Near the center of the stands, in the midst of the ceremonious pomp of dinner jackets, sat two men in street clothes. Amid such an array, the tieless, open-collared privilege could only pertain to the intellectual. And that is precisely what they were—two Hungarian writers. The one with the mustache was called Pognár, because a German official had misspelled the name of Bognár when making an entry back in the days of German domination. Hungary's fate was sealed when Magyar grandfathers surrendered their bony names to the attacks of German inkwells, to the onslaughts of pens wielded by Austrian penpushers with hair in their ears. The sons and grandsons wore the resultant misshapen names like broken noses or ugly scars. Indeed, in the preceding season one malicious critic of a play by Pognár had not failed to remark that "Pognár's whole auctorial personality is nothing but one great slip of the pen." The other writer was called Paul Fogoly. The Fogoly name had been more circumspect, had carefully eluded the grasp of recording secretaries in the age of Habsburg rule, for it was a Magyarization of *Fürst* effected after the Austro-Hungarian Compromise. Since then the Magyar blood poured into the Fürst cup had washed away all traces of German antecedence.

The two of them—we have met them before—belonged to the type that is part author, part journalist. They must have been about the same age, between thirty and forty. They worked in the same editorial room and were in love with the same girl, with Eva Kócsag, the popular and thoroughly scatterbrained actress who was known as *artiste* even to stagehands. They were constantly condemning one another's articles and plays, and each dreamt of the other's sudden death. But they were not hypocritical enough to hide their dreams. Pognár often stopped at Paul Fogoly's desk with a beaming face:

"Say…what do you suppose I dreamt of you last night?"

"I know. A trolley car cut me to ribbons."

"Much more horrible. Your new play was a success!"

All this was indicative of the openheartedness of their characters and the sincerity of their friendship. When one of them went away to work on a play, the other turned up within a few days to heckle him. That was how they happened to meet this time, too, in Venice.

The performance was under way. Bassanio, Lorenzo and Gratiano were just entering upon the street scene of the first act.

Pognár surveyed the resplendent little square of St. Thomas.

"Look at all the freebooters on the rooftops and in the windows. We might almost be watching a hanging in the prison courtyard at home."

The word "hanging" elicited a quiet protest from Paul Fogoly, who knew his friend's way of thinking. When Pognár had subsided, Fogoly asked:

"And who is to be hanged here?"

"Shakespeare."

Paul Fogoly had no comment to make on this remark. His silence signified agreement. Neither of them liked German acting. In their opinion only the French and the Russians knew how to act. And, well, the Hungarians. Famous

Hungarian actors? Pethes! Csortos! In this connection they never continued the catalogue, but the name of Eva Kócsag sprang to the minds of both of them, and completely without justification, for Kócsag the *artiste* was certainly...

The breeze snatched the words from the mouths of the actors and whirled them toward the rooftops like scraps of paper. Nevertheless, the Dresden accent was still evident on Bassanio's lips.

"How much better the original is," came from Paul Fogoly's cleanshaven face, and he began to quote:

> *"O my Antonio! Had I but the means*
> *To hold a rival place with one of them..."*

Beside them sat a theatrical scout from London whose female companion had already informed him that their noisy neighbors were rude because they were Hungarians. Now he pricked up his ears at the sound of the English quotation and turned to his lady:

"How very interesting...I never realized that the Hungarian language was so similar to English!"

Unquestionably Paul Fogoly's English accent was deplorable, and if he had quoted Shakespeare in Swahili the difference would hardly have been great. But Paul Fogoly knew several of Shakespeare's plays completely by heart, and in the original English. Let Western Europe match this if it can!

"Look at the moon," murmured Pognár.

Assuredly the moon's behavior was fantastic. It was almost full, and cavorted among the patches of cloud in a frenzy. It seemed to be running circles around the Piazza San Tomaso.

"Look at him laugh," Pognár continued. "He's laughing at the spotlights."

The spotlights were shining on Portia's robe at the moment.

"I ask you! According to the play, we are in Portia's house. If the moon knew the stage directions, he wouldn't be on stage right now. But he doesn't know them. And what's the entire Piazza San Tomaso doing in Portia's house? That's why I think outdoor performances are a lot of nonsense, you see. A play written for the stage, which is to say for interiors for the most part, cannot be performed outdoors. The wind sweeps the actors' voices away—although that's not much of a loss here. Look how beautiful the moon is! Like glistening soap bubbles washing over those fine old rooftops. Divine! And Reinhardt wants his ugly spotlights to compete with that! Here's Shylock, finally. How do you do, Mr. Shylock. Not bad make-up. But listen to the makeshift platform creak under his sandals. Now look at those marvelous four-hundred-year-old little Renaissance stone bridges. How firmly and yet with what daintiness they grasp the narrow banks of the canal! That bridge doesn't creak, my friend. Lord, Lord, how still the bridges can be on such moonlit nights! How beautiful it would be here in the Piazza, with only the moon and, if you'll excuse me, without Reinhardt."

Paul Fogoly recalled that a year ago Reinhardt had turned down Pognár's play, *Children Grow Up*.

"You're completely wrong. The performance is excellent. Keep your mouth shut, I can't hear a word."

"I wouldn't say that the performance is poor. But do you know how it impresses me? As if they were to take a framed landscape of a forest scene and hang it on a mossy stump, amid the magnificent Gothic obscurity and the dizzy heights of the branches, where the breathtaking Renaissance vinework, green and woven with golden sunshine—are you listening or aren't you?—where the hummingbirds and birds of paradise gleam with turquoises and rubies. Suppose Gauguin painted it. So what? The trouble with this production is that the proscenium is too large. Too tremendous. Too beautiful. Venice herself! Even Shakespeare is dwarfed in such a background. Now my new play..."

"Do you have the effrontery to mention your own play during a performance of Shakespeare?"

"...will have no scenery at all. Just two chairs and a table. Be suggestive! Be a poet! The imagination of the audience will conjure up the Himalayas, Niagara Falls, the Gobi Desert or the golden pagoda of Emperor Cho Chin—whatever you want. I won't even look at this farce any more. It isn't art—it's sacrilege on a business basis. A production of tourists for tourists! Are you staying? How typical of you. All right, I'll see you at the Florian."

Pognár weighed nearly two hundred pounds, and when he stood up the entire grandstand began to rattle. It was not easy to escape from the middle of the audience. The rattle of the grandstand was heard over the reverent hush, like the groans of a broken accordion, until he finally managed to worm his way out. The dinner jackets and the evening dresses heaved a sigh of relief when the open-shirted Balkan character finally disappeared.

Zia craned her neck toward the stage, storing up her attention for the rare moments that invited laughter. The dull gold sheen of her apple-green dress accentuated the luster of her eyes. Around her neck she wore a fabulous string of pearls, a present of a year ago on her eighteenth birthday. In the past few years her cane-blond hair had taken on a golden hue, until it was the color of ripening wheat. Fresh from the mechanical marvels of the hairdresser, it shone silkily. Her exquisitely rounded shoulders, in the lines of which there was still a certain childishness, glittered audaciously above her evening gown and seemed as white as the carnation in Count Dupi's buttonhole. Count Dupi's opinion was that the German actors wanted to delay the end of the play as long as they possibly could. Indeed, they defended their roles heroically, but finally had to give up the struggle when Gratiano was forced to declare that he would fear no other thing so sore as keeping safe Nerissa's ring, and the performance drew to an inescapable close. The departing sandals shook the stage for the last time. Polite applause, and then the grandstand stood up and merged its motley colors with the square. The freebooters, too, began to descend from the rooftops.

The dinner jackets and the evening gowns returned to their hotels, to meet a half hour later at the palazzo of Marchese Delfrate, who was giving an elaborate reception after the outdoor performance. Count Dupi knew the marchese from before the war. The latter had been a nobody at that time, but since then he had carved out a distinguished career for himself, and now everyone knew him to be one of the richest men not only in Italy but in all Europe. His wife was the daughter of a wealthy Jewish dynasty in Switzerland. The marchese stood close to Mussolini, and consequently the reception in the palazzo on the Grande Canale promised a brilliant quartet of wealth, politics, art and high estate.

The marchese sent his own gondolas to call for the more prominent guests, one each for Mr. Mellon, Lord Rothermere, Prince Olaf of Sweden, Chesterton, Reinhardt and István Dukay, who also figured in the top rank. Count Dupi and Zia boarded the wide black and gold vessel, propelled by crimson-sashed, white-shirted gondoliers. The wide sleeves of their shirts were fringed with lace. Noiselessly they drew the gondolas up before the Palazzo Delfrate, which bathed its forehead, bushy with wisps of balconies, in the sweet, rank water of the lagoon, golden-brown and gleaming. There was great commotion along the marble staircase, flanked on both sides by jet-black Moors in gaudy period costume and with halberds in hand, who seemed a sequel to the outdoor performance. The dinner jackets and evening gowns mutely mounted to the entrance, which was as luxurious as the interior of an Italian cathedral. Their ascent was very much like the climactic moment of a procession through the Heavenly Gates. It was incomprehensible that among the evening gowns and dinner jackets hastening into heaven there should be two figures in street clothes and open shirts: Imre Pognár and Paul Fogoly.

Zia did not realize that she was truly mounting to heaven. Upstairs in one of the salons was Filippo Maria Ozzolini, the young Prince of Perugia, a lieutenant in the First Italian Air Force.

At the entrance to the spacious ballroom the marchese and his wife greeted the guests. There was a French, English, Italian or German phrase for each guest, wrapped in the most captivating smiles of Europe. But the same phrase for everyone, of similar length and similar text. The guests filled the marble-lined halls, the art treasures of which were redolent with the paradisal atmosphere of the rocky cliffs of Cadore, the woodlands of Assisi and the quondam studios of Florence. The priceless, world-famous paintings were so illuminated by spotlights hidden behind curtains or suspended from above that they practically stepped out of their frames, and those that were life-size mingled amiably with the guests. Other paintings beckoned the visitors to enter their soft, pleasant tents of light. The rays of light glistened as they slid down the steep, pink-tinted marble walls and clung to the dark velvet hangings and Gobelins. In those halls Mr. Ryan—Mrs. Ryan's husband, of course—felt as if they had just accused him of forging counterfeit banknotes. Immediately after the war, when the purchasing power of the dollar stepped into the European arena with the muscles of a champion wrestler, he had furnished his Park Avenue home in Venetian style. He had a complete little palazzo dismantled on the Grande Canale, and the marble tiles, the doors and window frames carved of stone, the worm-eaten gilt rafters of the ceiling, the delicate viridescent locks, the door handles, the door-stops, the furnishings, paintings, tapestries and chandeliers were all packed separately and shipped to New York. Now he felt he had done a vain and futile thing. The chambers were wonderfully weightless here, due perhaps to the fact that the rafters seemed to have shifted slightly, slowly and imperceptibly, from their original position. One of the green marble pillars was definitely aslant, and the shapely lintel of a doorway was awry. In places the marble walls exhibited a gentle bulge of convexity, elsewhere they seemed dented and concave. Slender cracks whispered that for four hundred years the entire palace had been sinking, silently and in a manner befitting its dignity, no faster than Atlantis had done at one time, and this was unquestionably the work of the lagoons, which bent the staircases imperceptibly and tricked the Spavento rafters into ingratiating and elderly winks of the eye that not only violated the rigid Gothic geometry but also lent to their own sulky rusticity a surpassing and sublime beauty. Everything in the house on Park Avenue was straight and symmetrical, the stones and stuffs lost the delicate music of their dissolution, and what is more: lost that ceaselessly working, mysterious power that is known to weave exquisite stripes in Scotch pebbles.

The guests passed under the arched lighting of the pictures as if they wanted to introduce the old masters to the modern mutations of the white race. The Scandinavians were recognizable for their tall stature and their long heads, Englishwomen waved large bony hands in which tennis racquets were more at home than dainty fans, the gazelle-eyes of Spaniards flashed, while carrot-colored hair and a freckled arm loaded with diamonds betrayed a woman from Holland. Some of the Italian women wore their hair close to the skull, like a tight, shiny, black lacquer helmet. The Prussians could be recognized from behind, and by the close trim of hair over their ears, the Frenchmen by their poor posture and the lively movement of their heads. Occasionally a characteristically Jewish face bobbed up. The Austrians, Swiss, Poles and Danes mingled indistinguishably, like the pioneers of a united world, and the sole representative of oriental beauty was the Caucasian camel driver's nose of Count Dupi. In the plenitude of diamonds and pearls there were jaspers and chalcedonies as well, and many enormous tinted rings that shrieked of cheapness. All that was lacking were rings on the women's toes, but for the time being they simply exhibited blood-red toenails through the openings of their gold and silver sandals.

One heard remarks like this as the passing parade shuffled by the various pictures:

"Dürer achieved the ultimate in draftsmanship with the wings of one of his birds, but the gentle *motion* of *these* wings no one has ever surpassed!"

They stood before a Tintoretto. In general, the Italians held the floor:

"Veronese used saffron for the shades of orange, and dark scarlet for crimson. You think it sublime? I should hardly say so. Real art does not appeal to the imagination, but remains within the confines of humanity in the strictest sense. Think of Fra Angelico: he saw the earthly joys of Florentine maidens, who were not entirely moral, in the virgins trooping through heaven's gate."

Pognár and Fogoly, whom young Miss Ryan took to be detectives, stood by the wall and scrutinized the galaxy of guests as if the entire spectacle had been staged for their benefit.

Zia was just wondering how she could escape the interminable "Aw, that's *wonderful!*" of Miss Roberts when her restless eyes caught a glimpse of a slender young Italian officer who was in conversation with someone under a large Titian. They were obviously not discussing the painting. His pose was supercilious, one side facing her, in the corner of his mouth a black cigarette holder the rim of which was ornamented with tiny diamonds. Zia's glance swept by him at first and then returned to ascertain whether he was really alive, for he seemed to be one of the peripheral shapes in the huge Titian as he stood in the light. When her eyes returned to him for the third time she examined him more carefully. His was a broad-shouldered and athletic frame, but light and graceful nonetheless. He was slim, but not too tall. His profile was delicate, his lips dark red and full in the Italian fashion. His eyes were large Italian eyes, with long lashes. The ears were small, and might have been somewhat larger. His glossy, black, wavy hair gleamed silkily and was well suited to his dark skin, the original Italianate brown of which had been tanned the color of wild chestnuts by long months of sun-bathing. In all probability his entire body was similarly dark. His forehead would have benefited from the additional height of a fingers breadth. As it was, the forehead lent his face a look of passionate sensuality. Zia looked away. But a few seconds later the young officer attracted her scrutiny once again, although he showed no consciousness of the apple-green eyes. Was he a naval officer or an aviator? Zia could not tell from his dark blue, tunic-like jacket. In the stance of that jacket under the soft light there was something dreamlike and beguiling. Now, as Zia looked at him for the fifth time, she was aware of a mild nervous tremor. Is it possible that human bodies, too, are broadcasting stations, like butterflies that can transmit sexual messages over long distances by means of the microscopic wave lengths of their antennae? The Italian was no more than eight steps away from Zia. It may be that the tiny shock Zia felt in her nervous system was a message from his dark, sunshine-sated body. In the middle of a sentence the young officer glanced around the hall, and for an instant his compelling black Italian gaze brushed past the brilliance of Zia's apple-green eyes. But it did not falter. He continued his sentence, as if his shoulders had described a half circle in the meanwhile merely to lend emphasis to his words. To whom was he speaking? One could not see his companion, because no more than a shoulder of that dinner-jacketed shape was streaked by the beams of light, and otherwise he stood in shadow. Had he stood squarely in the brightest light, Zia would have seen no more of him.

"Yes, darling," she nodded to Miss Roberts, though she had no idea what the English girl at her side was babbling about.

She must meet that vision: this she had already determined. In fact—this was a Dukay trait—she had begun to think of the young man as belonging somehow to her.

The plum-blue face of the Argentine attaché joined the two men in conversation. Here was her opportunity. With a vague "Excuse me" she abandoned Miss Roberts and started toward Señor Calandra. Two outstretched hands carried her "Bon soir cher ami" like a chalice.

Then a strange thing happened. A feminine voice rang out near by: "Filippo!" —and the vision raised his arms and disappeared before noticing the approach of Zia. By the time Zia arrived there were only two of them, the Argentine and the other man, and of the latter only the fraction that the saber of light had spared, like a shoulder hanging from a butcher's meat hook, Señor Calandra was moved by the unusual warmth of Zia's greeting, for he had not been asked to the most recent Dukay banquet and this still piqued him a bit. Zia's appearance and the friendly ring of her voice seemed to indicate that his proposition, of which Elizabeth had been the intermediary, did not perhaps stand utterly rejected. He introduced the other dinner jacket, which stepped into the light and suddenly became a hippopotamus that wore a pince-nez and answered to the name of Chesterton.

Zia turned her head from side to side in vain; the vision had finally vanished from the crowded hall. Now she endeavored to free herself as soon as possible from Señor Calandra's interminable exclamations of "Ah, comme vous êtes ravissante!" She felt like a race horse with one hoof in quicksand.

"Have you ever asked yourself," Pognár, standing by the wall, inquired of Fogoly, "why it is that art really flourishes only in the periods when public life abounds with the most horrible crimes of bloodshed and brutality? I'm not thinking of the Renaissance alone. The Aztecs! Bloodthirsty and savage tribes have lived wherever the bewitchingly beautiful amphorae of decorative art are found. Look, here comes that little Dutch girl again. What a divine bottom she has! Gorgeous!"

A prominent right-wing member of the Hungarian Parliament recognized his compatriots and went over to them.

"Really, why aren't you two properly dressed? You're a disgrace to your country."

Pognár placed his hand on the politician's low shoulder:

"My dear man, while they're taking you to the gallows some years from now, you can comfort yourself with the thought that nothing happened to us when we telephoned the Marchese Delfrate and told him we were in traveling clothes. He insisted on our coming. In-sis-ted."

For a few moments the deputy studied Pognár's Adam's-apple, and then he glanced up at him mildly:

"Do you think they're going to hang me?"

"I'm absolutely certain of it," said Pognár, in the voice of a conductor announcing that the train would leave at seventeen minutes after eight. Paul Fogoly nodded his head in mute agreement with his friend's statement.

The politician was laughing heartily when he left them. He could not know, then, that the prophecy would come true.

An enviable task, the task of the invisible clairvoyant at large in the splendid halls of Marchese Delfrate's palace, for he is the only guest here who can see into the future. He can count four Italians and fifteen Germans, among them one Italian woman and two German ladies, whose lives will end on the gallows or before firing squads in a decade and a half. What a good humor Herr Willheim Schmidt is in, his tails marvelously well cut, the champagne glass suspended between two fingers, as he discusses Goethe's Italian correspondence with the Polish Ambassador Izvolsky without betraying that a few years later, as one of the leaders of Himmler's *Aktionsgruppe,* he alone is to slaughter seventeen thousand Poles. How moving, for instance, this sentence of his: "Oh ja, Excellenz! Goethes letzte Worte: *Mehr Licht!* verbinden uns alle Europäischen!" He employs the broadest and most beautifully North German *ay* in pronouncing the word *Ayropäischen.*

All Europe was assembled here in the midst of the many radiant Peruginos,

Borgognones, Tintorettos and Raphaels. The celebrities were celebrating themselves, and there was hardly any celebration left for the works of art that seemed to stand with hat in hand like mute beggars, their eyes pleading for the praise of the late centuries as if afraid that their immortality was nothing but an illusion. A tiny Lorenzo Lotto, which pictured a woman of Padua in a moment of obsessive passion, bid with tears in its eyes for the attention of the multitude to the brush-stroke of her silken dress. A Veronese offered the plumage of its iron-gray turkeys with the vehemence of a fishwife in the marketplace, and alongside Correggio voluptuously displayed the soft whiteness of a naked woman's body. But Schiaparelli and Molyneux provoked more discussion than Donatello or Leonardo. Still, there were some good-hearted people who took pity on the pleaders. Baron Kohlstein was in the process of explaining to an extravagantly blond Scandinavian beauty, whose eyeballs, caught in a stray beam of light, were as red as a white rat's, that Michelangelo was the master of drawing while the master of coloring was Titian. The skill of draftsmanship (he said) sweeps over the canvases of Michelangelo like the will of the wind over the waves of the ocean. Fortunately Pognár was not in the vicinity, for he would surely have noted that Ruskin had made this statement, though not in connection with Michelangelo but about Reynolds.

The tiny but exquisite Bellano bronze, declared Giraudoux at that moment, the statuette of Aurora in the corner was so fiery in inspiration that the entire *quattrocento* played in its flames, and its lines were fraught with the melody of Lombard skies. His face stern and officious, Count Dupi stepped up to a nut-brown stranger and announced that her neck was the most beautiful female neck he had ever seen. The lady was startled because she spoke no French, and for the past two years she had been living in constant fear that her husband, who made illicit deals in international exchange, would be arrested at any instant. Sir Evelyn, curator of minerals in the British Museum, asked Marchesa Delfratc to slip her emerald ring off for a moment. From the pocket of his dinner jacket he took a magnifying glass, and then returned the ring with the words: *Next to biggest!* He had determined that the stone was the second largest emerald in the world. During the examination the Marchesa did not take her black jackdaw-eyes from Sir Evelyn's hand for a moment, because she did not care for the gesture with which he reached into his pocket, and in her heart, even while she returned the ring to her finger, there was a certain anxiety lest the yellow-mustached old English gentle-man should have exchanged the emerald for another with an imperceptible and lightning-swift sleight-of-hand, for the Marchesa had long been the mistress of an Italian magician named Zuccarelli, and the master had taught her that nothing was impossible.

Now that they are all gathered here, the invisible clairvoyant is beset by a secret yearning to borrow the Voice of the Lord from the works of Madách and thunder forth, from the gilt rafters of the ceiling, the truth of what will happen to Europe in fifteen years. But no, let us not disturb them. Poor Pognár need not know that during a cross-examination in the former Harlecky Villa, which will become Gestapo headquarters, a German lieutenant will beat out one of his eyes with a bronze statuette, by mere chance a copy of Bellano's Aurora and more suitable for such a purpose than the original. Fifteen years? Things to come are much closer than they seem. Mr. Ryan would not chortle so joyously over the jokes Countess Innamorati is making about Reinhardt's potbelly if he knew what was going to happen to him two months from now on the New York Stock Exchange, for we are in September, 1929.

In another group they were discussing the first American talking picture, *The Jazz Singer,* which they had all seen. Count Karg observed that to him the talking picture was like a very beautiful but very stupid woman who makes the mistake of opening her mouth. They all agreed that there was no future for talking pictures. Roger Tollier, who was preparing for a record-breaking transatlantic flight, joined the group. This subject in turn occupied their attention. Alfred Kriegs, a shell manufacturer from Sweden, expressed the opinion that large passenger planes would never be able to overcome the storms and distances of the ocean. Generally their statements indicated how clearly they all foresaw the future. The future, to them, was nothing but the prearranged agenda for the stockholders' meeting of a large corporation.

The pell-mell currents of milling guests gradually coalesced in one direction, like the sonorous North wind above the unkempt sea when it finally decides which way to blow and begins to waft the waves southwestward. They started for the buffet table.

O Giorgione, Titian, Velasquez and Tintoretto, lend this hapless writer your brushes, so he may render an account of those buffet tables! Of the noble fish frozen in pale gold aspic, the roses and pinks of the cold meat, the colors of the star-shaped tartlets and the loud laughter of the fruit baskets. Stopping in front of a yard-and-a-half-long branzino, Baron Kohlstein informed the Scandinavian beauty, whose red eyeballs had since turned mauve, that a week ago he had caught a much larger branzino in the Bay of Pago with a relatively small hook—but his statement did not produce the desired effect.

In the space of minutes the beautiful buffet tables were turned into rubbish heaps. Spilt dark wines of Dalmatia spotted the gleaming whiteness of the tablecloths, stripped vertebrae of fish stared bleakly, while the discarded skins and seeds of Sicilian grapes disfigured the neighborhood of an untouched slice of red roast beef. Boots seemed to have trampled down the magnificent multistoried cakes, and the remnants of goose liver with truffles looked like nasty little nuisances on the plates. The battered cups of day-laborers and beggars never betray such evidence of man's cannibal nature after eating. Zia's eyes constantly sought her vision, but visions apparently do not take nourishment.

In the middle of the square inner courtyard of the Palazzo Delfrate there was a beautiful fountain. Above its marble curb was a fringe of wrought iron, like the tail feathers of the lyrebird. There were balconies on every floor of the palace, and now the audience stepped out on these balconies to listen to the crew from the yacht of Marchese Delfrate, especially summoned for the occasion. The swarthy sailors of Chiogga were dressed in sparkling white, with a dark blue sash around the waist of each. They settled on the curb of the fountain, and in the lap of one of them a mandolin began to play, as sweet as the fragrance of spring flowers in Piemonte or the pang of first love in the heart. The sunny baritones started to sing old Italian songs, and Pognár noted that Marchese Delfrate had outdone Reinhardt at his own game. Looking down at the narrow courtyard from above, down at the fountain in the moonlight, at the sailors composed in picturesque groups, listening to the sound of "O mia Fiamma bellissima" sung in four parts while a mandolin accompaniment sketched the basic harmonies with the tenderness of celestial light on Fra Angelico's silvery pink clouds—it was truly wonderful. Zia could not bear the beauty brimming in her heart. She turned to look for her vision. Her sudden movement overturned a champagne glass held by a deeply tanned masculine hand, the continuation of the hand being the vision himself. Ambassador Izvolsky of Poland, whom Zia knew well, stood beside him. The champagne spilled over the dark blue military jacket,

"Oh, I'm so terribly sorry," Zia murmured apologetically in English, perhaps because it was Miss Roberts with whom she had most recently been speaking.

"Never mind," the ebony cigarette holder said coolly, almost impolitely. Even now the holder, with its crown of four little diamonds, was stuck into the corner of the mouth, as if for the sole purpose of revealing to the world the white and damply glistening teeth behind the full, dark red lips. It cost Izvolsky only a wave of his hand to introduce them, but the names were too indistinct to be heard. The futility of the introduction was enhanced by the fact that Izvolsky said Eszterházy instead of Dukay, and although he immediately noticed his error he reconciled himself to it with a somewhat pained expression which was the height of his diplomacy. With her minuscule and scented handkerchief Zia began to soak up the incredibly tiny pearls of champagne that had settled on the dark-blue jacket near the region of the heart. Immobile, the ebony holder tolerated the careful, in fact excessively careful, ministrations of the handkerchief, and when the operation was finished he lifted his champagne glass, which was still half full, and spilled it on the same place. Turning his heart nearer to Zia he said only:

"Please."

It was well done. Well done, with a face carved of wood and humorless. Laughing, Zia once more began to sop up the liquid pearls. As a joke, Izvolsky lifted his full glass of champagne, threatening to pour it on Filippo's raven-black curls. But now a hissing of voices bade them be still. From the depths a new song mounted toward the moonlit sky. It was only proper for Zia to face toward the front. When she turned around a few moments later, the vision was gone again. Only Izvolsky remained. At least she could ask him who the champagne-drenched young man was. The title of *principe* made no impression on her, because at the family table she had learned that in Upper Italy everything that wore trousers was a prince.

The sailors were not inclined to stop their singing. Of all the guests Zia was the only one who found their concert too long. The audience was moved, and listened in silence. After each song applause drenched the courtyard like a warm cloudburst. But this, too, came to an end.

The music began in the ballroom and Señor Calandra, lying in wait like a black panther, snatched Zia away for a fox trot, in the course of which she discovered that the attaché's teeth were brownish-yellow and that his thick ears, though carefully trimmed, were still hairy. She was not surprised when her vision presented himself as her next partner, because she assumed that in the meanwhile the young man too had asked Izvolsky who she was. And at such times it did no harm to be a Dukay. The muscles of Filippo's upper arm were hard to the touch, like a column of wood covered with cloth, and while dancing the column of wood constantly sought the resilient softness of Zia's breasts. The virginal little breasts did not protest. It was the same below the hips, in the motion of the loins

366

and thighs, a contact that can always be pardonably attributed to the rhythms of the music and the dance. Had Pognár been there, he would once more have been impelled to maintain that the dance is nothing but stylized sexual intercourse. He would have been wrong. Zia's supple body became even more supple while dancing, but there was no sensuality in this. How did the unidentified dinner jacket phrase it? Even in the virgins trooping through Heaven's gate Fra Angelico perceived the earthly joys of Florentine maidens. The art treasures of Marchese Delfrate filled these halls with invisible rays of celestial beauty, and Zia too became a participant in the celebration. Best of all, they danced without speaking.

The black panther pounced again. Unfortunately it was necessary to pay for the extravagance of that "Bon soir cher ami." Then new partners followed. But their arms lacked the firmness of a certain column of wood. The colorless lips exuded tobacco fumes and sour breath, the heavy bodies lacked rhythm and, although panting asthmatically, they chattered without end and occasionally required an answer. More than an hour passed this way, and Zia felt that the vision had finally disappeared. The guests grew fewer. And then, behind her left ear, again unexpectedly, the ebony holder spoke up in French:

"Your father tells me this is your first trip to Venice. The moon is very beautiful. The palazzos are in a deep sleep by now. Would you care to take a gondola along the canals? I'm a Venetian, and I'd be glad to guide you."

Later, when Filippo was helping Zia into a gondola, she learned that his hand felt warm and dry, like the richest leather. It must have been about two hours after midnight. Count Dupi directed the gondola toward the hotel first. He claimed a greater familiarity with the lagoons than with the acacia-lined avenues of Ararat. He made this comparison by way of poetic license, whereas it was strictly true. In parting he remarked to Filippo:

"Don't forget to show my daughter the Palazzo Ferri."

Filippo issued directions to the gondoliers in a low voice. The tiny diamonds on the rim of the ebony cigarette holder sparkled in the moonlight, and his teeth shone white around the mouthpiece. They sat face to face on the velvet cushions. They had arrived in one of the narrowest canals, and the gondoliers took care to dip their long black paddles into the moonlit water noiselessly, lest they disturb the sleep of the elderly palaces. So closely did they skirt the houses, from time to time, that an outstretched hand could have touched the walls where peeling plaster had left large pockmarks and the reek of rats bespoke ultimate decay. All of this, at close quarters, was ugly and frightening. From afar, however, the black Renaissance rooftops sketched matchless patterns in moonlight against the silver sky. The two young people did not talk, and there was something heart-rending in the silence. It was as if all Venice were waiting in the night for the magical moment when an unexpected and frantic outcry of mermaids would shatter the silence, and with a great clattering and splashing the aged palaces, their moment come, would disappear beneath the murky water of the lagoons.

"Palazzo Dandolo," Filippo said discreetly. "Early Gothic. Eleventh century."

And the names of ten or twenty other palazzos followed at long intervals, telling Zia only that Filippo's voice was warm and pleasing. Palazzo Malipiero: even such a phrase could sound like *I love you.*

Suddenly she realized that the gondola had stopped at the entrance to her hotel. She looked at her wristwatch: it was half past three. They alighted. A strong masculine grip is in order when a fragile woman steps from a floating gondola to the firm bank. Once again Zia felt the similarity of Filippo's hand to fine and fragrant leather thongs.

"Would you like to have dinner with us tomorrow?"

"I'm sorry," Filippo replied, "tomorrow morning I must join any regiment."

He raised his hand to his cap with an easy gesture. Zia mutely extended hers, and to that sad little hand Filippo said:

"But two weeks from now I shall see you in Hungary. An Italian parliamentary commission is going to Budapest."

Once more he saluted, and once more the moist white teeth glistened behind the black mouthpiece.

Zia ran up the stairs as if pursued. When she reached her room she stood stock-still in the light of the chandelier. Her glance was riveted somewhere in mid-air, and she began to chew the nail on the middle finger of her left hand, which was not a customary gesture of hers. Her face was tearful. She had no one near by to hear what had happened to her.

Chapter Seven

I
T IS amazing how empty a city can become, how dull, even repulsive, in
the absence of the one who has laid our hearts captive, and Venice is no
exception. Next day Zia passed beneath the seductive splendor of the loggia
in the Palazzo Ducale as if it were nothing more than the public telephone booth
on the corner of Septemvir Utca. Poets and writers from Petrarch to Paul Fogoly
have represented the awakening of love as an apparition of the ideal. But they are
on the wrong track altogether. When we consider that Laura bore her husband
Hugh de Sade eleven children, something that could hardly have escaped the
attention of the Lombard poet, and that upon her death Petrarch persisted in
writing, with Vergilian accents: "They have buried her beautiful, *virginal* body
in the church of the Minorità…" then, suddenly, the ideal love of all literature
stands revealed as a complete fraud. It was no secret to Paul Fogoly, either, that
the *artiste* Kócsag was the mistress of a wine merchant from Miskolc, nor that
her exquisitely carved lips, which made music of Augier's or Pailleron's delicate
phrases even amid the clatter of Hungarian *es*, continued to ring with the same
French melody in the wine merchant's bed. The poet knew all this quite clearly,
and still he wrote, in *Songs for Eva:*

> *Light of the stars, Eva, O star-lit sheaf*
> *Threshed fine and gold on the floor of my belief…*

No, love has little to do with the ideal. Filippo was a handsome lad, but of a type
which can be found by the dozen, decked out in dinner jackets on the high stools
of cocktail bars, or in swimming trunks along the sands of fashionable seaside
resorts. We also know that gorgeous women occasionally evince an inexplicable
yearning for human chimpanzees, while living female skeletons attract the blind
passion of princely males. There is something else at work in love, something
besides which physical or spiritual beauty and sensuality itself seem incidental.
Nor is it true that the humors of love need birdsong, twilight, walks along
nameless little ancient streets, moonlit Venetian gondolas and other such props.
Awakening love pursues its victim even into the dentist's waiting-room, and does

369

not leave him alone in the bathroom either. In addition to pleasure and joy, terror and horror are principal constituents of love. Its ephemeral moods are often similar to the soft screaming *piu* of a bullet as it whistles past a soldier's ear on the battlefield, and resemble the terror attendant upon the unexpected stop of an elevator between floors, when we wonder whether it will hurtle to the bottom of the shaft. This is all comprehensible when we reflect that the blind impulses of love urge the soul on to a substantial sacrifice, a sacrifice of body and of heart, an outpouring of thought beyond all hindrance, an offering of honor, of life insurance policies, of health, of two little old chests of drawers, or of the rented mansion that is part of the dowry, but above all a sacrifice of time, the single treasure of our lives, the priceless work of art of which no copies exist because it is an artifact composed of birthdays, normal blood pressure and a rich harvest-home of spermatozoa. The evanescence of youth, some writers call this work of art. And still, we must make the considerable sacrifice; there is no escape; it is the destiny decreed for us in the subterranean molehills of our instincts.

"Wouldn't you like to step into the Basilica for a moment?"

Obediently Zia followed her father. Inside, she knelt on the cool stone.

Most tragic of all was the fact that the altar on which the sacrifice must be placed was not an immobile Renaissance or baroque creation but a living, moving person. Perhaps it was not true that Filippo had to join his regiment.

Two dreadful dangers threaten the victim of love. One danger is that the vision may vanish and, in vanishing, leave our lives barren; this is a poverty more painful than the rack, more hopeless than the grave. The other danger looms larger: when the object of our love becomes our own, having modestly accepted the sacrificial offering, we cannot know what is concealed in the dark depths of its character or of its diseased kidney: downy pillows or sharpened stakes? We are aware only of the downward plunge. What is love? At the age of thirteen Imre Pognár ended his first story with the words: "Love takes the place of everything, but nothing takes the place of love." Although it sounds like an advertisement for powdered eggs, there is not a poet who has made a more profound revelation of the ultimate secret of love.

"Let's go home, Papa," said Zia, after she too had succumbed to the allure of banality and photographed the pigeons on the Piazza San Marco.

"Wouldn't you like to go to Rome with me—since we've already come so far! Just for a few days."

Again Zia obediently gave in to her father's affectionate grumbling. It made such little difference—Rome or the lava fields of Thingvellir (for there was talk of a trip to Iceland that summer). The world had lost all meaning, and would only come alive with noise and light two weeks later.

"Papa, do you know anything about an Italian parliamentary commission that's supposed to go to Budapest in two weeks?"

"I've lost all interest in politics since Schurler was knighted. If we start now we'll be in Rome by nightfall. There's still time to have an ice at the Florian."

Yes, it was now the tenth year that this certain Schurler had been upsetting Count Dupi's stomach, like a heavy, undigestible celluloid dumpling. The elder Schurler had been his batman, but the count was forced to fire him long before the war because of his unabashed thievery. His son, Robert, was of the count's age, and had then been studying at the Sorbonne, at Oxford and the German universities. Robert Schurler appeared on the scene of Hungarian politics after the war. By now he was a member of the Upper House, and only a few weeks before had been raised to the nobility. In the Casino he was always the first to cry, "Hello, Dupi!" and one could hardly strike him down, for he was an apostle of legitimist, right-wing and Church politics. A talented rascal, he had appropriated Jesus Christ, Crown Prince Otto and the concept of Magyar racism as his own. He wore the national gala dress constantly, and had sprung a belly from avid feasting on the wounds of revisionism. A subdued aversion for Robert Schurler was beginning to flicker in the István Dukays and descendants of other families whose forefathers had been among the first settlers, but it went no further than one or two murmurs of this sort.

That night they arrived in Rome. In those days Rome was aglow with the light of eternal peace. The Italian papers carried elaborate reports, with photographs, of the British troops in their plaid kilts as they retired from the Rhineland to the skirl of Scottish bagpipes. Editorials made no secret of the fact that credit for the consolidation of peace in Europe belonged to one man alone. That man was Mussolini. There was a good deal of truth in this conclusion. The political power and popularity of the Duce were at their zenith.

Next morning Count Dupi and Zia were sitting on one of the terraces along the Via Umberto. They were desperately bored.

"Tell me, cricket, wouldn't you like to take a picture of *le monsieur noir?*"

The apple-green eyes flashed.

We should know that in those years it was not proper to pronounce Mussolini's name aloud in public places. The wonderful spaghetti houses, the sunlit terraces, the fish-frying taverns, the glass-enclosed Latin forums, the railway compartments and seaside beaches simply whispered it to one another: le monsieur noir—the man in black. It all sounded like the deep murmur of litanies in a cloister: Thou shalt not take the name of the Lord in vain.

Count Dupi stood up to go to the telephone.

"I don't know the bricklayer personally. But I have a friend on the Fascist Grand Council."

He stayed away for quite a while. When he returned there was a twinkle in the corner of his eye.

"Tomorrow morning at thirteen minutes after twelve! But you'll only have two minutes. At the Palazzo Venezia."

Zia wrinkled up her nose:

"Fine!"

The bells of the church of Santa Rita were chiming the noon hour when Zia, with a fairly weighty carrying case in hand, climbed the stairs of the Palazzo Venezia the next day. The case contained her finest camera, a collapsible aluminum tripod, a magnesium gun and several floodlights. Nobody stopped her. She might as well have had twenty pounds of dynamite or an infernal machine in her case. But in those days it was not necessary to watch over the person of the Duce, for he was guarded by the unseen angels of peace.

A bored, secretarial individual finally appeared to ask her name and the purpose of her visit. The secretary had been notified of the appointment, and he led Zia into a quiet marble-walled chamber which was furnished with hardly more than a large rug. In French, and in a tone which must have been current among the pagan worshipers in the ancient bowers of Remus, he repeated: "Thirteen minutes past twelve. And for two minutes only! Seulement deux minutes!" Then he left her alone, obviously with the intention of giving the lady an opportunity to offer up a prayer and compose herself in meditation.

The lighting of the chamber, Zia found, was excellent. She would have no need for floodlights. When she had decided where Mussolini would enter and where he would come to rest, she set up her camera. But suppose he would not stand there after all? for it was difficult to predict the vagaries of dictators. She-elected, in any case, to make use of her magnesium flashgun, with which she could even shoot the Duce through the head if the fancy seized her. This thought ran through her mind, for the figure of a tyrant betrays even the most gentle spirit into entertaining such ideas. As the moment of meeting approached, Zia felt no excitement. A Dukay, in the face of an encounter like this, remained unshaken. Rather she wondered how best to snap the Duce in a smiling, human pose, for the world was full of photographs in which he concealed his bony skull under a round steel helmet, thrust his tightly knit, enormous jaw forward and glared so savagely that the iris of his eyeballs swam with white, as if he intended by means of all this to strike terror, once and for all, into Hailie Selassie, Bartou, Hoover, Joseph Stalin and the little Italian miss who was offering him a bouquet of flowers. How was she to make a charming, smiling, unposed and unreserved picture of the Duce? The words of M. Mongés rang in her ear: the man, the man, the man beneath the skin!

She glanced at her watch. Thirteen minutes past twelve. Already the marble floor of the corridor resounded with a hurried, energetic tattoo of heels. About five people were coming.

The Duce and his escort stepped into the chamber. Mussolini gave the photographer a determined and dour nod, hastened to the center of the carpet and with a single sharp movement he folded his arms over his chest. He thrust his jaw further forward than ever, and his eyes became threatening black buttonholes in a field of white. Who could know what sentence had been interrupted at his cabinet meeting? His face writhed with savage wrath. Zia realized that the situation was completely hopeless. Now was the time to pronounce that eternal phrase of photographers: Smile, please. Under the circumstances, however, she felt that the invitation would sound like *Please be good enough to stand on your head* or something similar. A man of his stature could not be budged from a historic mood in a matter of seconds. And the seconds were fleeting ominously. Still, Zia did not lose her composure. The Duce wore a light summer suit of unbleached linen and a soft silk shirt with a yellow bow tie. His large skull had been carefully mowed with clippers and almost gleamed with whiteness. All this, like the wreath of flowers on the brows of Caligula, crowned him with cheerfulness. It would have been a wonderfully blithe portrait, had he not assumed his fierce, steel-helmeted expression. The folds of his jacket, however, needed adjustment; a thoroughbred photographer could not be denied this privilege. Calmly Zia advanced toward the motionless statue that was the Duce. She was not near-sighted but her eyes, like all apple-green eyes, were sensitive, and she had to squint when she wanted to see something closely. Below the yellow bow tie, at an opening of the silk shirt, she noticed a dusky wisp of feathers which, of course, must be plucked away. Forming a tweezer of her thumb and forefinger, narrowing her eyes even more, she clasped the feather, but the downy cluster slid from under her fingers. Once more she captured it and began to tug.

The Duce lowered his head to look. The movement wrinkled his lips, and his jowls grew larger. He spoke, so close that the warmth of his words touched Zia's hair:

"Don't disturb that—it's my private property."

And with a finger he thrust the feather into his shirt. It was a wisp of the hair on his chest. Zia fled back to her camera. A snort resounded in the chamber. The Duce could not restrain his laughter.

"S'il vous plaît!"

And the magnesium gun flashed. The Duce nodded, and started away.

"Encore une fois!" Zia ordered him back to his place with the voice of a circus dog-trainer directing his artfully clipped beasts.

Obediently the Duce lowered the foot he had dipped into the air, but his face immediately became as stern as of old.

"Merci, Excellence!"

Another unsmiling nod, and the ringing steps returned to the cabinet meeting.

Zia looked at her watch. The two minutes were still not quite up. Swiftly, fugitively she packed her instruments into the case and danced down the steps. That is to say that she merely attempted to dance, for the weight of her carrying case commanded a greater decorum. The second picture was not worth a penny, but the first…the thought of it excited her. She went into the nearest photographer's shop, introduced herself as a colleague, and the persuasiveness of her eloquence—and of her voluminous lira notes as well—pried open the door of the darkroom. She developed the plates herself, in the heat of eagerness. Excellent! Excellent, excellent. Arms folded over his chest, the Duce leaned forward slightly, a movement compelled by the muscles of his diaphragm as they shook with laughter, and the inclination of his body added a touch of humanity and confidence to the otherwise pitiably pompous posture of his outthrust chest. But no, no, this was not a toothy picture of laughter issuing from the dark cavern of an open mouth. An enchanting Latin smile swam on the closed lips, and the same smile brimmed at the corner of the eyes, which now shone with the gaiety of Father Philemon, free of mystery and implication. The smile was a door leading to the heart. The close-clipped, prominent bones of the skull smiled too, and the jaws smiled as they withdrew from the limelight to their proper place, like circus horses that have finished their turn. The little yellow bow tie was smiling, and the tips of the handkerchief in the breast pocket— Zia suddenly kissed the wet print. Before the afternoon was over she had visited an international news agency. They snatched the picture from her and passed it from hand to hand. Then she signed several contracts, after deleting a number of points and substituting others. She had learned all this from M. Mongés. She received an advance of two hundred dollars. It was the first money she had ever earned.

"Tell me, cricket, won't you buy me a bottle of champagne out of this wealth of yours?" Count Dupi asked during dinner, after he had heard the account of her adventures.

Zia shook her head in mute refusal. She was thinking of M. Mongés, and of the patched elbows on Madame Mongés's laboratory smock. A new secret had come into her ken, a secret horrible and at the same time beautiful.

Within a short time the first and only picture of a smiling Duce covered the front pages of pictorial newspapers from Melbourne to San Francisco, from Capetown to Stockholm. Paul Beylard based an editorial in the Paris *Demain* on the photograph, calling it "The Smile of Peace." He wrote: "The delightful monster has finally discarded his iron mask. Amazed, the world heaves a sigh of relief as it sees the smile of Pompilius and Marcus Aurelius course over his lips and his face. Let the little nations rejoice, let Albania and Abyssinia rejoice for the favor of history that has permitted them to sign an alliance of friendship with Italy. We all know the source of the Duce's smile: it is the sweetest well-spring of peace. Let mothers rejoice, for this smile protects the lives of their sons."

The world took him at his word and rejoiced. Zia knew little or nothing of this, for the principal advantage of the excursion to Rome was, in her eyes, that it consumed five days of the two weeks. They spent three days at Abbazia, but by the time they returned home there were still five days left. The message book by the telephone at home contained four entries of the same name: Calandra. The senor was still driven by the extravagance of Zia's "Bon soir cher ami," as if it were an unusual and powerful aphrodisiac which had greatly enhanced his sexual energies. There were several invitations, one to the British Embassy, one to a hunt at Uncle Andrew's, and one to Anci Vörös's new millinery shop in town; a number of those illegible postcards from abroad, the authorship of which one can never actually determine; and three letters—this was the mail that awaited her. Elizabeth wrote from Biarritz with alarming frankness of her new affair with a Canadian tennis champion. The second letter was from Kristina in Deauville, where the season was still in progress. "Really, Zia dear," wrote Kristina, "you might tell Papa to be a little more generous. He hasn't answered either of my last two letters, although by now I really need the little sum of money I asked for a while ago. I shall have to sell my necklace..." Zia knew about the little sum of money, for on the homeward trip Count Dupi had complained of Kristina's prodigality. Her most recent request had been for half a million francs, and Count Dupi suspected that she had fallen into the hands of "some clever fellow." The letters from Elizabeth and Kristina saddened Zia, and she was not particularly cheered by the Park Club invitation to a Hopla Hop party. But György's letter was more comforting. György was in the eighteenth month of a prolonged visit to America, and in March of the previous year he had accompanied a pilgrimage of Hungarians to the unveiling of the statue of Louis Kossuth in New York.

Zia sought refuge in her room from the impressions of the letters and of the past few days, for they disrupted her vision, as the presence of foxes and wolves disturbs the deer approaching a water hole. Filippo seemed as distant and improbable as the melancholy chimes of the church of SS. Giovanni e Paolo, or the mauve-shirted Paduan gentleman's curly locks in one of del Piombo's portraits, or the roof of the Palazzo Contarini as it loomed like black lace in the moonlight. She wanted to be alone with the iridescent glitter of tiny diamonds on an ebony holder, and everything else distracted her—Elizabeth's Canadian tennis champion, Anci Vörös's new millinery shop, the hairy chest of Mussolini and the statue of Kossuth in New York.

The next morning she walked to the cemetery, to Berili's grave. She had hoped for an answer of some sort, but neither the French text on the black marble tombstone nor the flowers spoke up. September breezes nudged the browning mulberry trees, impudently pushing their way to greet the approaching autumn. The silence of the cemetery, in any case, was shattered by the triumphant, malicious, earsplitting gratings and squeakings of trolleys in an adjacent roundhouse, and someone near by mounted a resolute assault on the inscriptions of *Requiescat in pace* with sharp belches of his broken-down motorcycle.

Prince Fini came to dinner that day. At this time Countess Menti had begun to invite him less and less frequently, though he was the favorite among her several brothers and sisters—which means that he was the only one of them with whom she was on speaking terms. For a number of years the prince had behaved in an intolerable fashion. The signs of senility began to manifest themselves in the increasing obscenity of his epigrams, almost as if this were a means of recalling the vanished privileges of the Schäyenheims to a forgetful mankind. Just as Zia accompanied him into the foyer the footman announced that Señor Calandra was on the telephone. Zia dismissed the call with a wave of her hand. Prince Fini, who always knew everything about everyone, diligently buttoned his raincoat:

"This Señor Calandra," he remarked, "wanders about in society like a male gorilla in the primeval forests, leaning on a long and heavy club. But this fellow leans on his own virility."

He offered his hand in farewell to Zia with an inimitable gesture:

"Grüss Gott mein Kind!"

Undeniably the good will and protective benevolence of an experienced uncle lurked in his remark.

"Primeval forest, yes: that's what it is," thought Zia as she went upstairs on the thick pea-green carpet that covered the ancient staircases of the palace in Buda. Uncle Fini was right, it was a primeval forest in which monkeys grinned, with packs of cards or the tools of their sex in their hands, bounding from tree to tree in Anci Vörös's latest hat, clutching breviaries and saucy French jokes, bombarding each other with collection plates and photographs of Otto. She was not being fair to her parental home, but children on the wing are never fair. The fledgling bird waits impatiently for that moment of first flight, the plumage on its crop and breast repelled by rot and refuse in the nest.

Now she could hear the chimes of the church of SS. Giovanni e Paolo quite clearly.

She demanded the newspapers impatiently each morning. She scanned them all carefully—something she had never done before—for reports of the arrival of an Italian parliamentary commission. But she was one of those unpracticed newspaper readers who can find everything but what they seek. The announcements were there, of course, and Zia simply failed to find them. Blindness of this sort is probably due to the fact that such readers invariably decide that the headline of a sought for article will begin with an O or a P, and let their restless eyes skip over anything else.

And yet the two weeks were past. Time, with great difficulty, had finally consumed them, as a wolfhound inconceivably engulfs the marrowbone that one could not at first believe his throat would contain. Slowly, inch by inch, the points of the snow-white fangs and the acid of the saliva work on the steely bone. One afternoon Zia set out on her customary walk. Carrying over her shoulder the leather-encased camera from which, like a gamekeeper and his rifle, she was never parted, she descended from the ancient fortress of Buda. She strolled along the gentle undulations of the northwestern ridges, along the suburban streets where stonemasons were industriously hammering out their hideous gargoyles on the gates of a villa destined for a newly rich bank president, a thread manufacturer or a successful playwright. She was on her way to the summit of the watchtower atop Józsefhegy, which suited her purpose for all that it was merely a knee-high stone parapet, since one could sit on its ledge. The city below spread eastward, flat and deep, rimmed by a veil of factory smoke behind which one sensed the plains stretching all the way to Asia. At this hour the sun shone from behind the western slopes, already aslant, breeding long black shadows which seemed to multiply after the light rain of noon. Zia loved this expansive panorama, the oriental and medieval aspect of occasional details on the fortressed hill of Buda, with the gleaming ribbon of the Danube in the depths below reaching northward among the green islets all the way to Vác and, to the south, disappearing for an instant or two behind the black mounds of the Gellérthegy and Sashegy, its color the gray of molten lead, as if the river sought to pour its entire mass into an ear of the rebellious Vata. Past Old Buda, where the stream ran into the city, wharves surrounded it like plain-clothes men around an assassin, and one by one the bridges snapped on their chains. In the spring, when this picture was framed in the pink and white blossoms of almond and peach trees, Señor Calandra had remarked in this very watchtower that the beauty of the scene was matched only by the Bosporus and at Rio de Janeiro.

Zia would have liked to live here, in a quiet little villa, away —but not too far away—from the castles on Septemvir Utca and at Ararat.

About five government cars labored up to the foot of the tower. This was a customary sight, for foreigners were invariably brought here to see the view. The black-coated shapes were already on the way up the steep steps, among them several in military uniform and—wearing black shirts! It could only be the members of the Italian parliamentary commission. Yes, there was the sound of Italian speech! Now they covered the summit of the watch-tower like

crows on the tip of a bald tree. But Filippo was not among them. The State
of Hungary, equipped with a frock coat and a limp knowledge of French,
guided the visitors. The State exhibited St. Margaret's Island and the suspension
bridge with becoming modesty, as if they were personal property and had been
inherited only last week from an aunt who died of heart failure. One pop-eyed
Italian deputy devoted his whole attention to Zia rather than the suspension
bridge. He had heard a great deal about the oriental hospitality for which the
Hungarians were renowned: a telegram of welcome and a bouquet of flowers
in the hotel room to greet the foreign guest, soda and bottles of brandy, jars of
exotic tobacco and bowls of fresh fruit on the night-table when it came time to
retire, and under the comforter an entrancing little naked wench whose body
had already lent a gentle warmth to the fresh, cool sheets. As Zia sat on the
parapet, her short skirt revealed the rounded pinkness of an updrawn knee in
its transparent silk stocking. The Italians heaved exclamations of *Molto bello* and
Meraviglissimo down at the precipitous and barbaric beauties of the city and
its bridges, somewhat patronizingly, as the Caesars of old used to throw a few
stalks of flowers to the blood-besmirched gladiators in the arena. Their eyes were
accustomed to the formidable antiquity of the Bello Sguardo basin, with the
black, taciturn cypresses of Florence punctuating the secretive olive-green mists
like exclamation points. The pop-eyed Fascist deputy pierced Zia with another
eloquent stare and then, visibly disappointed, took up the rear of the column
descending the steps.

Filippo was not among them. The fact struck Zia like a death notice. She
wandered homeward along the usual route as if tiny and invisible chops of her
blood were leaving a trail on the path. She decided to go to bed at once, without
any dinner. At the beginning of the fall season there were guests for dinner every
evening, the usual diplomats and aristocrats. Now every human face and phrase
promised to cause her pain. It was only out of habit that she glanced at the
marble table in the foyer, where place-cards stuck into a leather pad showed the
seating plan each evening. She stepped closer, and then a name flashed before her
narrowed eyes: Achile Ozzolini. But where was Filippo? Nowhere. She held the
leather pad close to her eyes and read the names with care once more. Filippo's
name was nowhere to be found. Who was this Achile? His brother, or a relative?
Now she would, indeed, have to appear at dinner. By the time she had changed
and entered the salon the Italians were there, mingling with the Hungarians.
It was apparent that the Italian party on the watchtower had been a second-

string crew, for she saw not a single familiar face. During the introductions their names, of course, were completely incomprehensible. But she remembered the place designated for Achile Ozzolini and kept turning her eyes in his direction during dinner. Achile was a gentleman of about fifty years, nearly bald, and with an expression that denied the possibility of a cure either for the world or for his own dyspepsia. He bore no resemblance at all to Filippo. Obviously they were similar in name only.

After dinner this certain Achile Ozzolini, among others, approached Zia. He asked her whether she liked Puccini; whether she had ever eaten pheasant *en casserole;* whether she had seen Pirandello's latest play; what she thought of the resignation of Chicherin; how she felt about Litvinov; had she ever gone skiing; and did she know Gömbös, the new Hungarian Minister of War, personally? He asked these questions with the tone of a prosecuting attorney who is not entirely convinced of the defendant's alleged culpability, and in the meantime he kept looking at his own hand, now at the palm, now at the back, turning it slowly as if he were carefully singeing a steak over a fire. He was not inimical. Throughout, it was on the tip of Zia's tongue to ask whether he knew Filippo Ozzolini, but she was afraid that the quaver of her voice would betray her. The heart shields its secret, at a time like this, in as gingerly a fashion as a hand will favor an open wound in its movement. If he knew Filippo, or if he had brought a message, he would say so anyway. But Achile, while he continued to toast the palm and the back of his hand, only rendered a not entirely favorable opinion of Byrd's expedition to the South Pole. Soon Zia slipped away from the whole company.

Count Dupi showed his Italian guests the chambers of his palace on Septemvir Utca, and explained that the house had been built in 1468, in the time of King Matthias Corvinus. It was in this house that Regiomontanus had made his plans for the Danubian Academy; of course there ensued much talk of Beatrice, and she emerged from the conversation as a lady who left her royal father in Naples and married King Matthias only to make the Italian parliamentary commission feel more at ease during its stay in Budapest.

The Septemvir Utca Palace was nothing to be ashamed of before the Italians. The works of Courbet, Delacroix, Renoir, Greco, Munkácsy, and especially the *Woman in Purple* of Corot stood out like the stone steeples of Benedictine monasteries, centuries past, in the swamps of Pannonia. Nor was the library to be despised. Count Dupi exhibited an eighteenth-century edition of Dante, bound in human skin, which he had bought in Paris. Signor Lampronti, director of the National Library in Rome, took the volume in hand, examined it carefully and then handed it back without comment. He had been relieved to find that the binding was not human skin but the skin of a fish. He was familiar with the type of bibliophile who can be persuaded to buy any old rag so long as the dealer accompanies it with a convincing story. Sad to say, Count Dupi belonged to this type. Twenty years ago he paid a modest fortune for three nicked billiard balls with which Napoleon was said to have played in his days as a lieutenant of artillery. Near the end of the Nineties, in Paris, they palmed a pale, long-nosed seamstress off on him one night with the tale that she was a niece of Andrée. The name of that ill-fated aeronaut was common currency throughout the world at the time.

Completely dressed, Zia lay outstretched on her bed, studying the ceiling with motionless eyes, like someone struck down by a sudden bolt of lightning.

Next morning, when Achile Ozzolini opened his eyes in the hotel on the bank of the Danube, he reached for the telephone and asked for a connection with Venice. Seconds later his number answered, and the conversation consisted of nothing more than this:

"Poi venire. You may come."

He put the receiver down and slept on. No fateful conversation between father and son could have been more concise—for we have begun to guess by now that Achile was the father of Filippo. A preliminary to this conversation had been Filippo's request, some days after the reception of Marchese Delfrate and the ride in the gondola, that his father take him along to Budapest. Why? asked Achile. A close bond of friendship prevailed between father and son. Filippo related his meeting with a young Hungarian countess who had made a deep impression on him. He had never been so deeply moved in the presence of a woman. A devout soul, he had prayed to St. Rita, who managed the affairs of the family, and in the quietude of the duomo at Milan the saint had given him encouragement. Achile Ozzolini heard him through attentively and with emotion, meanwhile roasting the palm and back of his hand over that invisible fire. Then he raised a forefinger in the air and shook it repeatedly:

"You mustn't come to Budapest just yet. I shall go ahead and look into the family."

Achile Ozzolini was devout too, but he did not care to rely on St. Rita for everything. Apparently the information he gathered on the spot concerning the Dukay family and the Dukay fortune impressed him favorably and resulted in his *Pot venire*. His paternal caution must not be taken amiss. Beneath the far-strewn wreckage of the Habsburg throne there occasionally were found young Hungarian aristocrats of ancient title who served as dancing partners in cosmopolitan dance halls, as well as women who had abandoned the confines of their native land and did not represent the noble Hungarian orders with fitting dignity.

✝

Budapest is one and a half hours from Venice by plane. Filippo arrived that very afternoon. And the receiver trembled in Zia's hand as she answered confusedly:

"Oui...non...come to dinner tonight!"

At the last moment Rere and Mr. Badar were sent into hiding. The leather pad remained empty; there was no need for a seating plan, since Filippo was the only guest.

Filippo, wearing a dinner jacket, was waiting in the grand salon when Zia entered. The tiny diamonds glittered on the rim of the ebony holder, and behind the mouthpiece Filippo's teeth glittered white and moist.

"That holder is in his mouth altogether too constantly," thought Zia, "I'll have to break him of the habit."

It is wonderful how swiftly the hopeless heart becomes carefree. This was Zia's mood when she sat down to dinner. Filippo sat at the right of Countess Menti, while Count Dupi was on her left and Zia faced her across the table. Thus everyone was beside everyone else, and it seemed, as they sat alone, that Filippo had become a member of the family without pause for ceremony. They spoke of the open-air performance, of Marchese Delfrate, of the development of the Italian aircraft industry, but their thoughts were elsewhere, like the hands of a magician while he makes eggs disappear. Countess Menti inquired whether the Azione Cattolica was active in Italy, and all the while she was thinking that the young man resembled an Italian teacher of her childhood.

Soon after dinner the parents retired, and the two of them were left alone in the little blue salon, under the light of a shaded Chinese lamp, swirling the brandy from time to time in their large, opaline snifters. Zia said things like this:

382

"I'm most impressed by what Palladio wrote about architecture, that it is really nothing more than the symmetry of the members of the human form. It's what the Greeks had already called eurythmics..."

Now she found the lessons of M. Mongés extremely opportune, for Filippo too was generously dispensing quotations from Vasari and Wölfflin.

One or two sentences, and then silence set in, and for a long time they looked at one another beseechingly. And just as the ardor of their bodies and their souls reached a point in the stillness where they were ready to fall on each other's lips with sharpened teeth, Filippo spoke. It was his turn to summon the ice-floes of the South Pole to his aid:

"In my opinion, the mistake of Nobile's expedition was that it did not begin by heading eastward..."

Then silence again, and once more the eyes began to plead mutely. In the meantime they studied each other, observed the most minute details, the shape of the nails, the pores of the skin, the line—always slightly oily—at the root of the nose, the resonance of the spoken word, in all of which they sought telltale fingerprints, for both of them felt they were on the scene of the deed itself, both of them knew that something had already happened, and it was necessary to establish nothing more than who they were and how many participants had been involved, for they shared as well the mutual knowledge that in themselves, as in all men, there lived various spirits and that these unidentified accomplices, concealing their faces and outward features, were also present at the inquiry. Zia discovered that Filippo's small ears nestled quite closely to his skull, that a long scar, probably a relic of childhood, ran along the back of his left hand and that he pronounced the French word *je* in Italian fashion, *ze*. Filippo discovered that Zia's teeth were brownish-gray and seemed somewhat soft, but her shoulders were beautiful and an ineffable sweetness emanated from her entire body and even from her voice.

Only so far did they surrender, once, to the temptations of privacy as to hold their hands, at the end of a lengthier silence, side by side in the air, in order to compare, finally, the remarkable difference in shade between the two. Zia's hand was lily-white, because a sensitive skin did not permit her to do any sunbathing and she still used the lotion purchased with Berili from Madame Goujon in the Rue Payenne. So are the dead immortalized by hand lotions. Filippo's hand, beside Zia's, looked like the black paw of an estimable puppy. Their mutual laughter at this was meaningful, as if at that moment their thoughts had dared to venture ahead, to the black and white nakedness of two bodies, the intertwining of which confronted the imagination so vividly that for an instant they were forced to close their eyes. Then came another one of those remarks:

"Do you suppose, if Briand fails, that Tardieu will become the new Prime Minister of France?"

Thus they discoursed. Filippo asserted that he would be demobilized in December, The tone of his voice was a reminder that they would hardly see each other until December came. In a further remark he gave as his opinion that Europe stood at the threshold of peaceful economic expansion, and that the future of passenger travel by air in Central Europe was unbelievably bright. In a few words only, he indicated his ambition to establish a large airline. He had even thought of a name, *Lucello Italiano,* but Achile found "bird" too light and poetical. He called his father nothing but Achile, and spoke of him as if he were a younger friend whose advice he was occasionally impelled to seek.

At two in the morning Filippo rose to leave, and in the doorway of the little blue salon the chestnut-hued Italian gaze and the apple-green Hungarian glance met and merged once more. It was the long, very long mute look that is full of pleading, encouragement, inquiry and answer, mingled with some tears and a little laughter—a look barely perceptible, but still it causes physical pain at the very summit of the heart and penetrates to the kidneys as well, a look from which the warmest arias of Puccini strike their flame, a look which represents the highest pinnacle of spiritual exaltation but precipitates, too, something of a mucous flow in certain parts of the body.

Once again Zia ran upstairs as she had done in the Venetian hotel, as if she were escaping from something, her two hands clutching the full, heavy folds of her long silk skirt, a gesture which made her seem the living incarnation of a rococo lady on one of the porcelain clocks. And once again she lay on the bed as if lightning-struck. She had only been seriously kissed once in her life, by Sigi, on the upper terrace of the Park Club a year ago. But how different, how much richer had this mute look been than that series of wet and cigarette-flavored kisses.

Next morning Count Dupi dropped into a chair in Zia's room:

"Tell me, cricket, is this Italian after something?"

The glowing apple-green eyes answered only with a mysterious smile.

Count Dupi gave the stump of his mustache several vigorous pokes with the crippled forefinger of his left hand and then departed, clearing his throat as he went. He retired to his room and sat down at the desk. A single motion of his right hand brought the desk closer. This was a Dukay gesture with him. He would not draw the chair nearer to the desk—rather preferred to move the two-hundred-pound desk. There was an element of ancestral wrath in this movement, directed against the writing desk and, generally, against every occasion that called for action. They say the Hungarian character is impulsive and quick of decision. It is merely impulsive. Quick to decide? This is asserted only by those who persist in confusing the Magyar character with the outer German crust it has put on. The Magyar brought from Asia his sense of *time enough,* a close cousin of the Russian *sichas* which means *right away* even though it often outstrips Einstein in the measure of its reference to the unbounded curve of time—coming through Mongolia, leaping the Bering Strait, then edging southward in Indian disguise and finally mingling with the blood of Cortez' Spaniards, it is a distant relative of the Mexican *mañana* and is there more cautiously phrased as *tomorrow,* whereas the concept of tomorrow is also known for its capacity to contain the infinite curve of time. Count Dupi did not like to decide and act. However, this was a matter which concerned Zia. At first he thought of asking Marchese Delfrate for information of the Ozzolinis, but the marquis loomed in his memories of old as the man who once maintained, at the Officers' Club in Vienna, that during a stag hunt in Bosnia he and his little mare had jumped an eighty-foot abyss. A man no more forgets something like this than he would forget a direct slap in the face. Count Dupi feared that the count might outleap himself again. Senator DeVoto in Rome? Absent-mindedly gnashing his teeth, he gave the name a thorough chewing but did not, finally, swallow it. He rang for his secretary. Angry by now, he threw the name of Achile Ozzolini at him, drawn in saber-shaped letters on a sheet of paper. Ozzolini was written with a single *z,* for the count dreaded double consonants in every language, even in Hungarian. He directed Mr. Gruber to obtain information about the Ozzolini family through some reliable Italian lawyer. Mr. Gruber took his leave with a low and fervent bow; his bow contained an acknowledgment of what was afoot.

What does a Gruber do in a case like this? He went to see one of his solicitor friends on Uri Utca, and there he picked the name of Arrigo Tandardini, an attorney in Venice, from an international record. Why Arrigo Tandardini in particular? Because the name sounded like the first seven bars of a certain Schubert lied, and Mr. Gruber was fond of playing the piano. He returned home, took a sheet of Dukay writing paper liberally engraved with the dark blue woodpecker crest and eleven-pointed coronet and, employing elaborate French salutations, notified the Venetian attorney of his commission.

What does an Arrigo Tandardini do when he receives such a commission? He rises from his desk, with its accumulation of pending briefs bound together by narrow black ribands and piled so high that they threaten to collapse and kill the two enormous cats sleeping outstretched on the blotter. Having telephoned Prince Ozzolini to ask for an immediate appointment, he painstakingly brushes his black overcoat, for he is a poor, lonely bachelor. Crossing the Ponte di Rialto, a cheery smile on his face welcomes the pleasure of a change, for he customarily specializes in slander suits. In Venice there was indeed a satisfactory amount of slander, if only mildly reminiscent of the days when the doges had bloodthirsty daggers at their disposal; nevertheless, after thirty years the constant concern with slander has become monotonous. He is thinking of the right words to inform the principe—of whose closefistedness he too has heard—that he expects a fee for his services.

Hardly a week passed before the information was on Count Dupi's desk, in excellent French, signed by Arrigo Tandardini but composed by Achile Ozzolini. It was accompanied by Signor Tandardini's modest bill for fifty thousand liras. And Count Dupi was already reading the report, holding the sheets far in front of his spectacles:

"The Ozzolini family stems from Lombardy, and its first appearance in history was recorded in the middle of the thirteenth century, when Matteo Ozzolini waged valiant warfare on the side of the Visconti and against the Delia Torre family for the possession of Milan. In the fourteenth century Bernabo Ozzolini married the daughter of the French king, John the Good, and was one of the foremost military men of his time. He conquered Pisa, Perugia and Bologna and founded the Certosa monastery at Padua. In 1376 Emperor Wenceslaus of Germany conferred the tide of Prince of Perugia on him and, had he not died of the plague, he would have received the bishopric of Milan the following year. His younger son, Giangaleazzo Bianca, bore arms against Venice in league with King Sigismund of Hungary. According to the family archives, it can be established beyond question that Raphael's *Portrait of a Young Nobleman* is a representation of Luchino Ozzolini, while Michelangelo used Liliana Ozzolini as the model for his figure of Dawn on the sarcophagus of the tomb of Lorenzo di Medici."

"Present members of the family are Prince Rodolfo Ozzolini, a retired general, eighty-three years old and bedridden; his cousin, Achile Ozzolini, who married Marchesa Orsola Ghezzi; and the children of the latter, Orsola Annunziata and twenty-five-year-old Filippo Maria. The Ozzolinis, though they have no considerable family fortune, are financially independent and able to live in a manner suitable to their station. Achile Ozzolini, one of the leading statesmen in Italy today, is a member of the Fascist Grand Council, president of the Cadore Glass Works and a director of the Misurina Federation for the Commercial Exploitation of Fish Scales."

It is evident from the above data that Achile Ozzolini had supplied a modest, reserved and factual dossier on himself. Count Dupi was especially consoled by the part which dealt with the Ozzolini's lack of a substantial family fortune, for that at least was credible. At the same time they were a polished, ancient Catholic family, and this, more than anything else, was of consequence. He made his way upstairs to Zia's room, and once again there was a twinkle in his eye. In his left hand he held Arrigo Tandardini's letter.

Should anyone care to accuse Count Dupi, or Mr. Gruber, or Arrigo Tandardini of superficiality and even irresponsibility in this matter, let him rest assured that Emperor Wenceslaus of the fourteenth century, no matter what his efforts, will not be the one to determine whether these two young people, having looked into each other's eyes, will lead a happy life or not.

The first few letters to Italy said *Mon cher ami,* but by November there was one which opened with *Mio caro Filippo!* Zia was studying Italian, Mr. Gruber having found an Italian instructor in the person of Signor Vallencic; wearing a tail coat and snapping his heels together, he appeared every morning at eleven o'clock, and under his arm was a remarkable Hungarian-Italian grammar which contained sentences like this: *The sister-in-law of my father's uncle eats bread. The sparrow has built a nest in the pear tree of the sister of my cousin's mother-in-law.*

Not pointlessly do we quote these grammatical marvels, in which the death rattle of an entire continent can be heard. The European population of five hundred million, divided into thirty-eight nations and heaven only knows how many nationalities, spoke seventy-nine languages within the bounds of a territory only slightly larger than the United States and not even half the size of the Soviet Union. People living at a stone's throw from each other were unable to understand one another's language. Books of grammar which enjoyed the widest circulation generally engaged in reciprocal trade of phrases and sentences that were like dead rats wrapped in genitives and packaged in cunning little wooden boxes. Only grain dealers, aristocrats, cocottes and diplomats dealt in the major living languages of Europe; the scholars were notoriously close-mouthed. But even these linguistic skills were of a limited nature. Stockbrokers learned to prevaricate with fluency only within the narrow confines of a professional jargon. Aristocrats were informed by Galsworthy himself that *Forsyte* is pronounced *Forsit* and not *Forsite,* but a word like *kalapácsnyél,* for example, stumped them at once. Cocottes familiarized themselves only with the names of certain products and with the terminologies proper to menus and sexual intercourse, while the diplomats exploited only the aspect of language that enabled them to deny in a subordinate clause what they had affirmed in the principal clause. Apart from the realm of drafts and proclamations, where they knew every screw and bolt as well as a locksmith knows his workbench—apart from that realm, and forced to take the knives and forks or walking sticks of language in hand, they suddenly became maladroit. It was in those years that the Hungarian Ministry of Foreign Affairs addressed a document to the Quai d'Orsay which gave La Maison d'Amour de Clothilde as the literal translation of the Clothilde Home for the Needy. Fortunately the benevolent Archduchess Clothilde herself never learned how it came to be known in French official circles that she had founded a house of ill-fame instead of a refuge for the indigent. Viewed from the comparative humanism of the Latinate middle ages, modern languages languished in isolation alongside each other and lay in self-imposed exile within themselves, like variegated carcasses of animals both large and small in which the maggots of rancorous nationalism cheerily whimpered and eagerly feasted—the carcasses to which politicians and the daily press, fattened on gangrenous livers, referred as patriotism and high principle. There were some who were frightened by all this. The Esperantists wrote letters to one another as feverishly as clandestine Protestants in the age of Calvin. Fiery businessmen hastened to manufacture linguaphones, only to go bankrupt a few months later. Radio stations introduced hours of language instruction into their programs and failed to realize that as soon as the dulcet phrases of *Die Familie Schuster* or *We are in the home of Mr. Brown* began, Europe speedily turned off the set and reached for the morning paper, in which the lead article was already expounding the view, clearly if cautiously, that certain races would have to be wiped out to the last man. Thus, at first with much circumspection but later with increasingly ardent yearning, Europe prepared for death. Only infrequently did the embattled languages bombard each other with nothing more lethal than the invisible little light-ray of *Mio caro Filippo!*

Filippo and Zia corresponded in French. The letter in Italian was only for display, like the first, misshapen sampler embroidered, for Mamma's birthday, with the picture of two turtledoves kissing each other—although, alas, the doves too often resemble crows. But the letters in French were transfused with pure poetry, such as the secret springs of literature provide even for carpenters' assistants and scullery maids in their full glory, if only on a short-term basis. Letters like these know the unfettered enhancement of passion; in their inchoate phrases, but especially in their lines of dots there lurks—shrieking and gesticulating—the ultimate tempest of ecstatic emotion, as in the verses of Villon or the symphonies of Beethoven.

To Septemvir Utca, in the first days of December, came the letter from Venice, crested with the rampant lion of Perugia, in which Prince Achile Ozzolini requested, on behalf of his son Prince Filippo Maria, the hand in marriage of Countess Terézia, youthful and charming daughter of Count István Dukay. The salutation of the letter read "Excellence!" and its tone was reminiscent of the letter Vittorio Emanuele sent on the occasion of their treaty of alliance to the dusky emperor of the Abyssinians, whom the king of Italy suspected of occasionally feasting on human flesh in the seclusion of his silken tent. However much of a Dukay a man may be, the West invariably conceives a Hungarian as the epitome of the East, carrying a leather shield and gulping great draughts of mare's milk—not, one may say, without reason. The woodpecker crest, with its eleven-pointed coronet, answered with more tenderness and emotion. Count Dupi himself composed the letter in French, but his attempt to emulate the crystal chill of the letter from Venice was only moderately successful. He tried and tried, but some sentimental Hungarian hug, some affectionate embrace kept sneaking into his sentences, and expressions like *votre charmante personalité* began to sound like *my dear brother...*

A few days later Filippo arrived, and on the 19th of December, which was Zia's nineteenth birthday, the engagement was announced to a close family circle. Only the Reverend Alajos Galovics, the chaplain, and Prince Fini were

389

invited, and before dinner Countess Menti summoned the latter to her room and made him promise to refrain from making smutty remarks. Of course Prince Fini kept his word, but throughout dinner he sat in silence and sadness, like a child whose toy is taken away as punishment. The ceremonial address was delivered by Reverend Lojzi, whose upswept bristly hair had been cropped for the occasion, and the scale-sized freckles on his ruddy forehead and on his turkey-neck seemed, too, to have been polished with especial care. His speech was beautiful, but too long. It mentioned—not by name—some mysteriously mere egg that disappeared, reappeared and generally fluttered in the dim future. Count Dupi and Zia looked at each other inquiringly for the third time. What sort of a mere egg was it? And why, in particular, mere? The look on Count Dupi's face showed that he took the mere egg of undetermined origin to be some oriental ornament, perhaps with a beard, bearing a marked resemblance to a Greek Orthodox archbishop. Zia conceded the beard, but saw the mere egg as a rabbi, for she knew that in his secret heart the Reverend Lojzi was a confirmed and unctuous anti-Semite who catered to his obsession with the persistence of an onanist.

As soon as the platinum rings were on the fingers of the engaged couple, the glasses rang and speech-making drew to an end.

After dinner Zia asked the Reverend Lojzi what he had meant by the mere egg that recurred so often in his speech. Reverend Lojzi was capable of writing an excellent Hungarian, as the presidential speeches of Countess Menti attested, but his pronunciation was extremely Slovakian.

"Well! What do you think? Mere egg! The mere egg of life!"

From the opposite corner of the room came the rumble of Count Dupi's voice, aglow with sudden illumination:

"*Mirage,* you monster! The *mirage* of life!"

He could permit himself the paternal tone, for he had taken Lojzi from an orphanage as a child and supported him during his education for the priesthood.

The Reverend Lojzi hastened to correct his error:

"Ah! Yes, mere age!"—this time transforming the fata morgana of the Hungarian plains into a simple matter of senescence. But this sort of thing would not prevent him or his copious cousins from becoming the leading canons, prelates and bishops of the Hungarian Church in a short time.

Filippo spent the Christmas holidays in Budapest too. The family council had decided that they would not own up to Rere as yet. But Zia mentioned the existence of a brother who was seriously ill. In the meantime the serious invalid took advantage of an unguarded moment in his remote room on the ground floor to consume a raw ham, filched from the well-stocked meat locker of the palace, in its entirety, using both tooth and nail.

In the little blue salon, on the silk shade of the Chinese lamp that was a fist carved of black *hu mu* wood, the almond-eyed, parasol-twirling *hsiu hua* beauties, as they strolled among sea serpents, globes of pearl and grains of rice, among ball-playing lions, wind-swept reeds, wild and cloud-fringed geese, among the flowers symbolic of longevity—the graceful almond-eyed beauties could have told quite a tale. It was as if their storybook embellishments and attitudes were intended to be eloquently expressive of all that took place on the beet-red brocaded settee just beyond the circle of the light they cast. They saw a great deal, but heard little except the occasional whirlwind, long and passionate, of indrawn air, the work of lungs after holding one's breath for an unconscionable length of time. Kissing was now a formal privilege of the engaged couple. The intermittent striking of a clock guarded their solitude in the hush of night, and so sentient was the stillness that one could almost hear the faint cackle of the wild geese as they skirted the distant clouds on the silken shade. But Zia stubbornly fended off every stray endeavor of Filippo's hands.

It was a bitter winter. The gamekeepers on the estates kept reporting the discovery of groups of two and three frozen deer carcasses, and after the exceptionally hard winter of the previous year it began to be rumored that all the partridge in the country had been wiped out. Above Old Buda, five-ton trucks crossed and recrossed the frozen surface of the Danube.

In the afternoons Zia set out on her customary walk toward the watchtower. The trees of the Buda hills and the mustaches of the policemen were trimmed with frost, and the Hungarian winter amazed even Filippo, for it bore no resemblance to the sunlit winter on the snowy ski slopes of Italy. Winter here was the wolfish breath of hibernal Russia.

Mr. Gruber announced that a villa on Fuga Utca was undergoing renovation and would be ready for occupancy by the first of May. They went to look at it but found little to see, since the villa was like a woman when she puts on a heavy sheepskin coat; one cannot tell whether she is pretty or not, for only her nose is visible and even that extremity is ruddy from the cold. The housetops were concealed under two feet of snow. They entered nevertheless, and inspected the villa from cellar to attic. Inside the un-plastered brick walls, both of them could already envision the velvet chaises longues where only dirty bags of cement now sprawled.

"Don't you think this wall should be knocked out, Filippo? And the dumb-waiter might as well be moved…" Both the dimensions and the internal arrangements of the villa were found satisfactory.

After New Years Filippo departed. During January and February the bills for long-distance phone calls mounted to dangerous heights in the palace on Septemvir Utca. In March there was talk of the possibility that Zia might spend a week in Venice, but of course the proposal had to be abandoned, for there was too much work to do, preparation, shopping and planning.

In the middle of April they moved to the castle at Ararat. Filippo telephoned around noon one day that he had arrived in Budapest and would soon be starting for the country. No, they should not hold dinner for him; no, they need not send a car, for even now he was darting around in a little automobile borrowed from the Italian Embassy. No, he would not get lost, the map was in his hand and he knew the way. Yes, yes, the first left turn off the highway after the roadside shrine. Yes, the *first* left.

It was the end of April, and the belated spring was flushed and warm, like a youngster who has run all the way to school lest he be punished. The meadows, forests and clouds raced to unleash their colors in the sage-scented sunshine.

Zia made frequent trips to peer out of the window, with a movement of her head and an expression that has been the common property of prospective brides since time immemorial. The wide, sandy drive was visible from the first-story window, as it curved from beneath the tent of chestnut trees and approached the main entrance of the castle. The road, before winding its way up the hill, stroked the bank of the large fishpool ever so lightly, as a hand will stroke a harp. Silvery-white pines and gently blossoming beeches gave the light stroke a dreamlike tone. The water wore a thick coat of water lilies, and only infrequently did the floating swans cut into the green mash, like scissors in heavy cloth, to disclose the metallic, nude gleam of the water beneath its gown. Some distance away, the black and cinnabar rooftop of the bathhouse, built in the shape of a Chinese pagoda, peeped from between the branches of the willows. The chestnut trees, oh, the chestnut trees! One can speak of them only with many, many oh's and ah's, now, when from one day to the next the cone-shaped little canopies of their flowers overspread the entire tree, from stump to summit, as if they had arrived in a surreptitious folk migration. They seem to have pillaged every native-born flower in the forests and the fields, to have snatched up all the white and yellow and pink hues they could find, and they are wearing them, every one, now. Zia left the window open so she might hear the familiar clamor which autos made as they passed the birchwood bridge and struggled up the rise.

It was already four in the afternoon. Filippo had still not arrived, though he might have been there by now. What had happened was, simply, something that has happened to every motorist in the world: after passing the roadside shrine he took not the first but the second turn to the left. At such times, in order to vex travelers, the first fork in the road regularly hid under a blinding patch of light or crouched beneath the black shadow of an elm. In fact, a little bug was under contract to settle on the nose of the driver at the very moment that the road and the automobile came into view of each other. When they hurled past one another, a single defensive wave of the driver's hand sufficed to conceal the road as it cowered flat against the ground. The bug would fly back to the bluebells along the first road to report gleefully that he had succeeded in leading the automobile astray. The second road, on the other hand, did everything possible to attract the attention of the yes-I-know-the-way driver. It was a wide and friendly road, and went so far in its deception as to wear the marks of automobile tires, garnered from just-leave-it-to-me guests who had been on the way to the castle. Actually it was nothing more than a common sheep-path, and led toward the sheep-folds. Led? Nonsense. It merely continued for a few hundred yards, growing narrower all the way, and then, especially in spring, turned into a series of slippery bogs— bogs which were facsimiles in little of the craftiest anti-tank traps ever devised.

That is what happened to Filippo. The resident shepherd and his family were well versed in such matters by now; from a distance their outstretched arms called the visitor's attention to the footpath leading toward the main entrance of the park, and young Sándor was already running for the team of oxen to rescue the beswamped automobile, while the shepherd's wife quickly made a bridge of wagon-planks lest the trousers of the bog-skipping gentleman be splashed.

393

Without further misfortune Filippo made his way to the large iron-grated gate of the park, and found it wide open. Poplars and bush basils greeted him. Then, when he reached the plateau after passing the red quadrangles of the tennis courts, the castle made the same impression on him that it had once made upon Madame Couteaux when she first caught sight of it: with countless windows, tiny in the distance, and with the ancient black tower of the chapel at its center, the castle was like a tremendous ocean liner that had dropped anchor here on the hilltop, above the hamlet of Ararat. Had the tower been belching smoke, like the smokestack of a ship, the illusion would have been complete.

Filippo was wearing a suit of unbleached linen which well became his dark complexion. Even now the ebony holder, aglitter with diamond droplets, was fixed between his teeth. He had left everything else in the car. Now he was at the point where the road touched the bank of the fishpool.

And then a dreadful thing happened.

A derby-pated shape leapt into sight from behind a hedge, barefooted and with striped trousers rolled knee-high to reveal hairy legs. The derby was profusely embellished with chicken, rooster and pheasant feathers; with claws bent, and grating its large yellow horse-teeth, the apparition clutched Filippo by the waist from behind before the latter could defend himself, whirled the victim over its head and tossed Filippo far into the fishpool.

Mr. Badar was already approaching at a breathless run, and with a single rabbit punch he laid the culprit low. The gardener came running, and footmen from the castle. Zia, who chanced to see the entire incident from her window, began to scream and succumbed to a crying fit. Two liveried footmen and Mr. Badar himself waded waist-high into the water to rescue the bridegroom, whose great presence of mind was evidenced by the ebony holder which he still gripped between his teeth. Otherwise he was unrecognizable; it was almost as if a beslavered, slimy green tablecloth had been thrown over him, and even when he reached the bank he still resembled a Mohammedan bride, with face heavily veiled. The swans had navigated into the neighborhood and were croaking in raucous celebration, as if they had been the instigators of the affair. Rere lay outstretched in the grass, his naked soles turned reproachfully up at the world. He had meant no harm, and was merely playing. They swiftly spirited him away, like a sack. A blanket was spread about Filippo's shoulders, and he was escorted to a bathroom.

Count Dupi's face was livid. The flash of his eye as he looked toward Countess Menti was a sight to see, but so were the ice-blue eyes which refused to acknowledge his message. "Call Mr. Badar at once." He was unable to come because his trousers were wet. "Tell him to come!"—came a gnashing of teeth. And Mr. Badar, his trousers dripping, was compelled to report to the count's room. He looked as if an artist had begun to paint him green all over, but grew bored with the task and abandoned it at Mr. Badar's waist. A roaring lion greeted him in the count's room. "Your Excellency, I must submit my resignation... I can't keep Count Rere in chains constantly!" The choking wrath began to subside: Well, then, what had happened? For days Count Rere had been reading Carl Mays *Vinetou,* and the Indian tales in that adventure story of the wild West had gone to his head like May wine. It was sheer chance that he had singled out the bridegroom for an antagonist.

A brief consultation with Countess Menti, and a half hour later the sentence was pronounced. Rere and Mr. Badar were exiled to a hunting lodge four miles from the castle. They were forbidden to approach the castle. An armed gamekeeper was posted as sentinel. They were to start at once. Rere, who had recovered consciousness in the meantime, reached into his pocket and continued reading *Vinetou* as if nothing had happened.

As a matter of fact, nothing of consequence had happened. Two experienced oxen had dragged the car from the bog long ago, Filippo's suitcase had been brought to him and he was already putting on a complete change of fresh clothes. The bug that had caused all the trouble was artlessly buzzing about the honeyed saucer of a bluebell. Zia was still weeping in her room. Filippo entered and took the unhappy betrothed in his arms. While dressing he had learned all about Rere, and by way of consolation he assured her that there was a half-wit in his family too, a female cousin, much more dangerous because she was an arsonist—and she had once attempted to kill him with a kitchen knife. It may be said to the credit of his chivalrous nature that not one word of the whole story was true, but his vivid account had the desired effect, since Zia stopped her fitful sobbing and tried to explain that Rere was not evil, fundamentally, but merely odd at times, and that he had many fine traits as well. She told of the presents with which he had consoled his brothers and sisters in childhood when a governess stood them in the corner for punishment, and Filippo joined her in laughter. She did not mention the derbies. There are things that seem great catastrophes at first, but then the element of danger quickly evaporates; the fright which they cause, in fact, leaves spirits refreshed. The most cheerful atmosphere prevailed throughout dinner.

After dinner Filippo had to be shown around the castle. He saw it all: the apartments of the parents on the ground floor, including Countess Menti's yellow-brocaded bedroom where Zia was born, the large dining hall which would comfortably seat sixty wedding guests, the medium-sized dining hall which served for smaller parties and the small twelve-passenger dining hall. He saw the great red salon, the orange salon, the green salon, the two smoking rooms, the library, the picture gallery, the billiard room, the endless corridors with their thick foliage of stag, roe and ibex antlers, the room in which Maria Theresa had slept on the mezzanine, the two adjoining rooms which Edward VII had occupied while still the Prince of Wales, and he saw the guest rooms, and whenever he and Zia were alone for a moment they fell into a tight embrace, clung to each other's neck and began kissing as vehemently as if this were their first and last opportunity. It was all quite wearing, but finally they dropped anchor in Zia's room. By then the entire castle was asleep. In view of the fact that the wedding was imminent and because he thought he deserved some compensation from Zia for the ducking administered by Rere, Filippo became insistent. He tumbled her onto the bed and twisted her arm behind her back. But Zia's supple body kept slipping out from under him. No, no, no!

The last Sunday in May was set for the date of the wedding.

Chapter Eight

THE ITALIAN guests arrived from Venice by special military aircraft two days before the wedding. Zia and Count Dupi were waiting for them at the airport. The zealous police officer on duty, recognizing Count Dupi at once, considered it no infraction of the bounds of respect to render a formal salute, for the well-known and popular count was a member of the legislative Upper House. The romantic adventures of István Dukay's career as a Hussar were often a topic of conversation at household tables when wine was passed, or during long nights of good talk in rural taverns. The stories grew, like the delightful Hindu Ramayana, and developed into a minor Hungarian saga; new details were added to the ribald pranks of the Lebovice Officers' Reading Union, until not only the home of Fanny Nathanovics herself but the entire Jewish Quarter was garlanded with lilies of the valley in the middle of a winter snowstorm, and Count Dupi was alleged to have superintended the scrubbing of the entire market place, and not merely the Caffée Kazmer, with French champagne. These incidents became the epic poems and the legendary songs which were a source of inspiration to obscure clerks struggling along on a fifty-florin salary and debt-ridden, billiard-playing law students. The police officer came to a halt just three steps away from Count Dupi, stiffened to attention, saluted and announced:

"Your Excellency, the Italian plane will be here in a few moments."

Count Dupi knew how to return such unexpected shows of courtesy with a complaisance in which there was not even a hint of condescension. Smiling, he walked up to the police officer and introduced himself:

"—Dukay."

And while he shook the officer's hand, his nut-brown eyes gazed as warmly and winningly into the eyes of that worthy as if he were an old friend, or even a close relation. This warmth of friendly familiarity—whether in count or commoner—is a Hungarian trait.

"Thank'ee for the kind attention."

Count Dupi addressed the familiar thou to anyone in uniform. He often called assistant secretaries of state, however, by their surnames alone, finding it difficult to keep in mind any civil-service rank below minister. He introduced the policeman to Zia too, but she, after having prevented the officer from kissing her gloved hand, was unwilling to enter into conversation and retired to a distance of a few feet. Count Dupi winked at the police officer and whispered from beside his cigar:

"She's waiting for the bridegroom."

Even her father was a burden to Zia right now. In the final moments of waiting the air seemed full of a mysterious rustling and whispering. Perhaps the wide expanse of the airfield was responsible for this, and the expanse of sky overhead, fresh and blue, against which tiny May clouds glistened in ceremonious stillness, holding their breath and facing toward the southwest and the expected plane.

Suddenly a microscopic gleam of silver appeared from that very direction, low on the horizon. Zia clasped a gloved hand to her throat, lest she cry out. She was on the point of weeping. At that moment the noonday chimes began to peal from some suburban steeple. Their metallic tones, sweetened by distances were already like a memory. Unexpectedly, unscheduled and unsolicited, like a surprise, the chimes rang a greeting to the incoming plane. It was the will of God that they should be ringing now, at this moment. The inventors of the airplane had no idea what vistas of loveliness they created for brides who wait for their bridegrooms to drop from the clouds. The motor was cut during the final circle of the plane around the field, and the plane came to earth noiselessly, on angelic wings. Filippo was the first to jump out. Zia catapulted toward him and the two fell into each other's arms as if they were angels themselves. Zia was a blue angel, with a light blue veil on her hat, while Filippo was a sandy-yellow angel. He flapped the wings of his trenchcoat as he flew toward Zia. The next angel to come to earth wore the uniform of an Italian general, and in his mundane existence he answered to the name of Lucio Paccapuzzi, commandant of the First Italian Air Force. He was a man of short stature who looked as if he were trying to emulate Vittorio Emanuele's dwarfish figure as a sign of fidelity to his monarch, but the attempt was not altogether successful. The black Italianate sheep's-eyes that sat in his puffy dark-skinned face bespoke more good nature than generalship. He was Filippo's immediate superior, and the bridegroom paid his respects to the Italian Army by asking General Paccapuzzi to be one of his witnesses. The prospective in-laws followed the general from the plane, and behind them came their daughter, Princess Orsola, with her laurel-shaped face. Finally a very elderly couple emerged, the closest kinsmen of the Ozzolinis,

Marchese Farriello Ghezzi and his wife, who seemed like poor relations in this assemblage. The marchese wore a stiff, winged collar of unusual height, and starched cuffs, obviously an indication that in the past thirty years he had steadfastly spurned every stupid onslaught of change in gentlemen's fashions. His wife was dressed in a manner which Countess Menti would not have tolerated even in the One-Eyed Regent. Filippo's parents, however, Prince Ozzolini and his wife, were formidably distinguished, not only in appearance but even in their tone of voice. With their very first words they sought to communicate the fact that they had descended not only from aerial heights—the plane flew at an altitude of fifteen thousand feet above the Alps—but from certain historical and spiritual heights as well, visitors come down from the land of the Roman emperor-deities and of Leonardo da Vinci. There was gentle forgiveness in the marchesa's voice as she spoke to Zia, forgiveness for Hungary's defeat on the side of the Central Powers in the World War. Occasionally her words broke off in half, because the high altitude had not improved her asthma. Zia noticed nothing of this. Resting her entire weight on one foot, she held Filippo's right arm with both hands—he had come to her on the wings of the bells. They turned toward the cars. Once again Count Dupi noted that the bridegroom's father bore a striking resemblance to a gypsy fiddler he had known while in the army, but whose name he had long forgotten. He sensed the atmospheric pressure that emanated from the Ozzolini couple, and imperceptibly modulated his voice, so full at first with the amicability which he had addressed to the police officer, into the mode of mild scorn and polite distrust that Sultan Semzanes, one of the chieftains of the Bactrian tribe, employed in welcoming foreigners who wandered into the salty Asiatic deserts of his country.

They dropped Filippo at his hotel, because the younger males of Hungarian aristocracy had arranged a bachelor dinner for him that night. The rest of the company went to Ararat.

Kristina, György and János met the Italian guests at the main entrance of the castle. Countess Menti was waiting in the great red salon. There are moments when mothers become more beautiful, and this was one of them. Standing in the center of the salon, her hands clasped before her and holding a dainty ivory fan, she seemed once more to be posing for Lenbach's life-size portrait, as she had done thirty years ago, soon after her marriage. She was fifty-five years old, but had scarcely changed at all. At the moment there was something in her posture of Frederick Barbarossa's resentment for the defeat his cavalry had suffered in the twelfth century at the hands of a rabble of *condottieri* from the dirty towns of the Lombard plain, and at the same time something of the expression of Emperor Frederick II, whose troops forced Pope Innocent IV to take refuge on French soil one hundred years later. What does a Schäyenheim princess, kin to the Habsburgs, say to the wife of a Prince of Perugia, whose mother was a born Strozzi and numbered the Medici among her ancestors? Naturally she spoke of the journey, and of the hour and a half spent on the aircraft. But the subject of their conversation was as nothing compared to the stiffness that prevailed. Their sentences passed each other like heavenly bodies, inexorably and without danger of collision. The constraint was considerably relieved by General Paccapuzzi, who took an active part in the conversation and spoke such a laughably bad French that he would surely have been a great success in a Parisian operetta. The elder Ozzolinis were lodged in the suite once occupied by Empress Maria Theresa and later, at the end of the previous century, by Edward VII, then Prince of Wales—a circumstance which Mr. Gruber, who escorted the guests, did not fail to mention, if only casually, while he threw open the doors of the nobly furnished suite:

"This white button rings for the chambermaid—Maria Theresa slept in that bed—this is the writing alcove—that desk was used by Edward VII…"

The bachelor dinner lasted until nine in the morning. Late the next afternoon Filippo arrived at the castle, somewhat green and with circles under his eyes, and he was just in time, for the town clerk Mr. Makkosh, wearing the national colors on wide, crisscrossed ribands, was already standing behind the table in the red salon, ready to run through the formality of a civil marriage ceremony. The town clerk was a slender, brown-complexioned Magyar with a small black mustache, one of those notaries who attend law school but cannot afford the expense of finishing. He did not make a fuss over the civil ceremony, did not seize the occasion to launch into a soulful harangue. A quality in his deep, full voice, however, suggested that he had matter enough to talk about if he would have wanted to speak. It seemed as if there were something that he already knew and the others present did not know, so he tactfully refrained from mentioning it. Following the formalities he too toasted the young couple, glass in hand, but shortly afterward he disappeared, like someone who understood quite clearly that it was not as Endre Makkosh that he had been invited to the nuptial dinner on the morrow, but as a town clerk whose name, incidentally, happened to be Endre Makkosh.

Meanwhile the automobiles kept arriving every minute of the day, and the eighty guest rooms of the castle began to fill with wedding guests. The last time the castle had held so many guests was in 1895, at the wedding of Count Dupi and Countess Menti.

It was the wish of Count Dupi that Zia's wedding be conducted on the basis of traditions preserved in the Dukay archives, in accordance with ancient Hungarian custom. His decision was not made without reason. He felt he owed this to his country. The bridegroom was an Italian, and Italy—an ally of the victorious powers in the World War—was making overtures of sincere friendship to the disfigured little land of Hungary. It was necessary, therefore, to show the Italians what it meant for a daughter of the Dukays to marry an Ozzolini. This was a characteristically oriental trait of the Magyar nobleman in him, to spare no sacrifice when there was occasion to display the pomp of his past, of his rank and of his treasures, especially before the eyes of the West. Five hundred years ago King Matthias did the same when he married Beatrice, the daughter of the King of Naples. The castle at Ararat was preparing, as it were, for a minor coronation. Let the Italians open their eyes in wonder! Mr. Graber was thoughtful enough to make sure that the Italian press would be represented at the wedding. And Signor Ghiringhetti the journalist did indeed arrive on time, accompanied by a photographer. Signor Ghiringhetti was a Neapolitan, a fact that was evident in the way the bristles sprang skyward from his temples, as if from a fountain of hair. He was lodged in the Garibaldi room of the castle, so called not because Garibaldi had ever been there, but in honor of the life-size portrait of the Italian liberator on the wall. Ghiringhetti had seized at the invitation, for at that time public opinion in Italy was in thorough sympathy with the Hungarian side of Italian foreign policy. Hitler was already making an excessive noise in Germany, and the Italians felt it would do no harm to place a geographical steel helmet on the head of Italia. The role of steel helmet was given to Hungary, the country that had taken arms to expel Charles IV—furthermore, the history of the Hungarian people was nothing but an unbroken series of defensive struggles against German oppression. In fact, Italy was now approaching the highest point in her history since Frederick Barbarossa. This was Signor Ghiringhetti's view of history, and it was with this spiritual outlook that he arrived at the castle, where he hoped to get to the bottom of an important story: how much was true of the rumors that the Magyars wanted to install one of the princes of the House of Savoy on the Hungarian throne. At such a time Mr. Gruber, in the company of the butler who acted as keeper of the keys, always guided guests to their rooms and threw open the doors and the various recesses. When he was alone with the journalist after leading him to his room, Mr. Gruber inquired after his expenses, but Ghiringhetti continued to shake a protesting hand in the air as he explained in bad French that he considered himself the representative of Italian public opinion—in fact, he launched into an oration on the subject of Italo-Hungarian amity. So overwhelmed was he with the heat of oratory that he lapsed into Italian. Mr. Gruber, although he understood not a single word of Italian, deemed it proper to reply, and he proceeded to deliver an expression of gratitude, in the name of the Hungarian nation, for the journalist's glowing words—in German, of course, a language of which Signor Ghiringhetti was completely ignorant. But this did not keep the two men from standing face to face in the middle of an empty room and haranguing each other for more than a half hour. Mr. Gruber was in the middle of his speech when one of the footmen, a look of urgency on his face and with the Italian photographer at his back, entered and mutely pointed at the key-ring in the hands of Mr. Gruber. Mr. Gruber did not interrupt the sentence he had begun:

"Wir wissen schon—" meanwhile he handed the keys to the footman "—wie wir die italienische ungarische Freundschaft pflegen sollen. Mit unseren Herzen! We know how we must nurture Italo-Hungarian friendship—with our hearts!"

But the Italian photographer was gone by the time Mr. Gruber came to the final phrase.

The advisory council of the general staff that had planned and prepared the strategy of the day included, besides Count Dupi, Prince Fini, as master of the revels, Count Peter Dukay, the estate agent Egry-Toth and Mr. Gruber the secretary. Count Peter was considered a learned historian, for he belonged to the Academy and his two-volume history of Hungarian metalcraft and architecture in the sixteenth and seventeenth centuries was held in high esteem even in professional circles. He had found most of his source material in the Dukay archives, and was therefore most qualified of all to superintend the revival of ancient and courtly wedding customs. The traditional customs had begun to die out in the past hundred years.

Count Peter decided that Zia's wedding would be patterned after the nuptials of

Katalin Dukay, who married Ferenc Illyesházy in 1632. The entire record of that wedding, even to the smallest expenditure, was intact in the Dukay archives.

This is the time, then, to look around the vast dining hall of Ararat castle and summon up the memory of Katalin's wedding, for it was in this very same hall that the great doings took place three hundred years ago; and the former wedding couple is present too, though spending the twilight of their lives in picture frames. The first life-size painting on the walls of the gallery of ancestral portraits is a representation of Katalin Dukay, her eyes rigid and glassy, her skirt more like a wine barrel than a skirt. Even experts might find it hard to determine whether the animal stretched at her feet is a chow dog or an Angora cat, but it is simple enough to see what she is, for her forehead and the Caucasian slant of her eyes betray the Dukay. In the painting alongside stands Ferenc Illyesházy, wearing a carnation-colored silk dolman and a leopard-skin cape over his shoulder, his head oval, his temples protuberant. He bears an uncanny resemblance to old Dome, who used to be one of the gardener's helpers in the park, and this resemblance can only be due to the fact that gentlemen of Ferenc's day had not yet forsworn an interest in pretty bondwomen—in fact, they still exercised the *ius pimae noctis.*

There along the wall of the dining hall, too, stand the six small mortars, ornamented in the manner of the Renaissance, which used to fire a salute to the wedding pair in olden times, but now serve only to trip the footmen occasionally. The family vaults still hold the wedding veil, bordered in gold, of all Dukay daughters, and the "kissing cup," the silver washstand and other paraphernalia of ancient brides.

The dining hall is seventy-five feet long and at least thirty feet wide. Balconies open from the mezzanine at both ends. At Katalin Dukay's wedding the resident musicians of the bride sat on one balcony and the house orchestra of the groom sat on the other. At Zia's wedding these balconies will serve at best to accommodate photographers, for the palace musicians once kept by noblemen have long been superseded by piano teachers, phonograph records and the radio.

At Katalin Dukay's wedding, according to exhaustive records in the archives, thirty-six oxen, seventeen buffalo, one hundred eighteen calves, and countless sheep, pigs, deer, rabbits, pheasant, capons, geese, eggs, salmon, trout, crabs and lobsters were consumed. Concerning the buffalo, we must note that the last buffalo in Hungary was shot in 1814, but at the time of Katalin Dukay's nuptials there was still an abundance of them in the forests of Nógrád and Hont, which were all part of the Dukay properties in those days. As for the salmon, we should mention that they were of the beautiful black-spotted variety common to the basins of the Black Sea and very plentiful in those days, particularly in the Straits, where hundred-pounders were often caught. At that time fish was already considered a food fit for the king's table. To continue: a quintal of black pepper, ginger, cloves, nuts, saffron and lemons and two and a half quintals of wild honey were brought to Katalin Dukay's wedding, shipped by wagon and four-horse team from Vienna, for in those days there were no grocery stores.

However substantial Count Dukay's fortune, there could be no question of such a feast in 1930. Nearly three thousand guests, and their five thousand horses, came to Katalin Dukay's wedding. At that time a force of this size often sufficed to win epoch-making battles. At Zia's wedding they expected twenty-five automobiles and prepared dinner for sixty guests. Sixty guests exactly, because there were sixty settings of the gold service. The plates and the serving dishes were of gold too, naturally. This gold service of sixty settings was as much a part of the national consciousness as the fact that the Danube is the largest river in Hungary. The service was made in 1816 for Christopher Dukay, and was the only one of such size in the entire country. In the days of Katalin custom demanded that guests bring their own eating utensils, a leather-cased knife stuck in the belt—with this knife they ate the buffalo-meat boiled in pepper, and with this knife they slashed out at each other when they got very drunk.

There were other aspects of a traditional wedding that could not be duplicated. It was no great problem to barbecue some oxen in the park for the peasantry, but to provide gold stirrups, expensive furs and even saddle horses as gifts for each of the guests—that munificence could no longer be duplicated, for there were no serfs any more, while in Katalin Dukay's day the serfs bore all the expenses and taxes of the wedding, including the usual errors in accounting. When a wedding was over in former times, the Dukay fortune was not only undiminished but somewhat increased.

Finally the great day dawned—the day of Zia's wedding.

At eight o'clock in the morning the Reverend Lojzi conducted a quiet Mass in the chapel of the castle at which Zia, Filippo and the other people in the house were present. All of them took Communion. Signor Ghiringhetti the journalist did not attend Mass, and while the service was going on he entered the following notes in his journal for a forthcoming series of articles:

A surprising thing happened after breakfast. Footmen came to my room and removed all the rugs. The same thing was done in all the other guest rooms; in fact, as I later discovered, the vast and priceless carpets in the corridors and the ground-floor salons were carried away too. I could see by the faces of the footmen that something unexpected and unpleasant had happened to disturb the opening hours of the wedding day. I saw gloomy, officious individuals moving about in the park, and could come to one conclusion alone: bailiffs had appeared in the Dukay Castle at the worst possible moment.

After Mass everyone went to make a change of clothes, even the servants. Tiring-women and bridesmaids helped Zia dress. Her wedding gown was the national costume worked in white silk, with an eighteen-foot train over which there was another train of similar length, made of Brabant lace. On her head she wore a tiara of thirty-six diamonds which had been set aside for her at birth from among the Dukay jewels. In accordance with time-honored custom, neither Filippo nor any of the male members of her family were allowed even to approach her room while she dressed. Zia's dressing did not proceed without tears. The tiring-women and chambermaids sobbed and sniffled too. According to the archives, her friends the bridesmaids should have wept as well, but none of them shed a tear except Vira, a bronze-haired young countess whose weeping was heartfelt, perhaps because she too was betrothed.

Finally it was only five minutes before ten o'clock, when they were to repair to the great red salon and go through the formality of the "summoning of the bride." The wedding bouquet was in her hand, and the breviary, and the gloves. Six little cousins, from four to eight years old, were assigned to their places, at the end or along the sides of the eighteen-foot train. Somehow, this matter of placement is never concluded without a clash. Six-year-old Baron Akos punched the nose of one of the ladies, seven-year-old Princess Olga, who promptly had a nosebleed and made a bloodstain about as large as a silver dollar on Zia's train. Cold water and soap, quickly! One of the tiring-women gave little Baron Akos such a vigorous pinch that throat-splitting yowls began to issue from the child, who was dressed in imitation of Crown Prince Otto's coronation costume. The lower age group, composed of four- and five-year-olds, immediately joined in the clamor. Some chocolate, quickly! At length, after considerable difficulty, order was restored, but blood and tears had already contaminated Zia's train. Three minutes left. Quietly, like heartbeats, the seconds passed. The chimes began to ring in the chapel. The procession started to move.

All the wedding guests were already assembled in the red salon. They formed a half circle about Countess Menti, who stood in the center of the room with the little lace-fringed ivory fan clasped in her hands, waiting to play her well-rehearsed role. Footmen threw open the double doors to the terrace and Count Lajos entered, proud and erect despite his seventy years, holding in his right hand the gilded staff that was the symbol of the groom's best man. He wore the Magyar gala in claret-colored velvet, and the Order of the Golden Fleece was about his neck. With a splendid rattle of spurs he clicked his heels before Countess Menti and tipped his egret-plumed cap.

"I come for the bride on behalf of Prince Filippo Ozzolini."

Countess Menti curtsied and replied in the voice of an amateur actress:

"My compliments to the Prince! I shall bring the bride at once."

She vanished behind one of the doors and reappeared a moment later, leading—Vira.

Count Lajos ceremoniously circled the bronze-haired girl, raising his patent-leather boots high as if to music. After he had thoroughly inspected his own granddaughter from the front and the back, he declared that she was not the bride.

Once again Countess Menti vanished through the door, and this time she led the One-Eyed Regent forward by the hand; the old woman's face was set in a grimace that made her look like the limestone bust of Queen Nofretete in the Berlin Museum. Spinsterish resentment at having been cast for such a part was in the lift of her nose. In the depths of her heart she would have liked to be the bride herself on such a day and in such company.

Count Lajos strutted like a rooster around the One-Eyed Regent too, and announced once more that this was not the bride. The fine silvery peals of Baroness René's laughter rang out from the throng of wedding guests.

The French doors swallowed Countess Menti anew and now she led forth Mistress Michael Döme, the seventy-three-year-old washerwoman. At this even Baron Adam's bass-pitched laughter began to boom.

While Count Lajos pranced around Mistress Döme, the little hunchbacked woman revolved with him and winked at him as broadly as a naughty Budapest flirt. But to no avail—again Count Lajos maintained that she was not the bride.

At that moment, just outside the door, the gypsy fiddler started to play, and the strings of his instrument well nigh melted with the strains of "Csak egy Kislány van a világon," which means that there is only one girl in the world for me.

Biting his nails, Count Peter apprehensively surveyed the course of the spectacle he had directed. When the music sounded, both wings of the French door opened wide, as if by themselves, and Zia glided into the salon with three little courtiers and three ladies-in-waiting carrying her train. The tiara on her head seemed to glow with fire. But the glow in her green eyes was even brighter, because they were swimming in tears.

Count Lajos started to circle Zia too, but the train obstructed him. He paused for an instant, perplexed. Count Peter gnawed his nails more fiercely: "The devil! I didn't think of the train." But Count Lajos had already solved the problem. Turning, he retraced the half circle and then informed Countess Menti that this was the bride indeed.

A casino-bred young aristocrat called out:

"Better take another look!"

This ended the ritual of "summoning the bride," exactly as it had taken place at Katalin Dukay's wedding. They moved into the courtyard of the castle.

The rich confusion of color produced by the oriental pomp of Magyar regalia was the same as it had so often been in past centuries, whenever a daughter of the Dukays was wed. Signor Ghiringhetti watched from one of the upstairs windows as the guests gathered in the courtyard. He hastily fumbled for his notebook and entered the following observation:

> This Hungarian nobility, when it assembles in national costume, is remarkably like a chicken farm. Without question the dress of the roosters is more elegant, with their swords sheathed in velvet scabbards, their eagle- or egret-feathered caps, their cloaks of blue, green, black or red satin. Some of them have lemon-yellow boots on. The plumage of the hens is not so colorful.

Prince Fini, whose green-painted staff designated him as master of the revels, assembled the procession, calling the names of the couples as they appeared on a written list. The couples obediently stepped forward when summoned and fell into line like recruits on a drill field. The Italian and German names gave him no trouble, but the tongue of Prince Fini tripped over the accursed Hungarian names.

Zia and Count Dupi were the first couple in the procession. Count Dupi was dressed in the ermine-trimmed dark green costume he had worn at the coronation. The second couple was composed of Princess Ozzolini and her son Filippo, the latter in the dark blue dress uniform of the Italian Air Force, with the wide red and white ribbon of an unidentified order of merit around his collar. They were succeeded by couples ranged in order of ascending rank, with those who were in closest consanguineous relationship to the wedding pair at the end of the procession. Countess Menti and Achile Ozzolini made the final couple. A twenty-piece gypsy band trailed the long line, and the Dukay colors were pinned in attractive little cockades on the black jackets of the gypsies. Prince Fini raised his green staff high in the air, and the procession began to move. The gypsies broke into the song called "Nincs cserepes tanyám." As they passed out of the fountain-studded courtyard, which was bounded on three sides by the U-shaped castle, a motion-picture camera set on top of a kitchen table began to buzz, as if to drench the marchers with a gentle rain of machine-gun fire. Newsreels were in the making. They did not go through the park but toward the West Gate, beyond which were the outskirts of the village. The church, about five hundred yards from the gate, was already crammed full of spectators, and an enormous mob milled outside. It would surely have been impossible to accommodate so many people in the chapel of the castle. They had hardly stepped out of the castle gate when, much to his surprise, Signor Ghiringhetti sighted the carpets from the castle, for they covered the road from the gate all the way to the church. The orgy of carpeting was Count Peter's idea, for this had been done at Katalin Dukay's wedding too. Lawyer Makkosh, who looked as if he were in a funeral procession, reflected that the rugs had been brought out to protect the cordovan boots and the silk slippers of the nobility from the dust of the earth, the hundreds of thousands of acres of earth that served to support the Dukays.

A mounted band flanked the carpeted path on both sides—peasants wearing collarless shirts, bell-bottomed pantaloons and crimson waistcoats edged with gold braid. On their heads were round plainsmen hats embellished with feather grass, and they carried hatchets in their hands. Among their mounts there were one or two eye-catching roans, but in the main they rode overworked draught horses. Feminine hands, however, had painstakingly woven colored ribbons into the manes, and the square-jointed nags now looked like their masters, who don their very best clothes only once in their lives and in honor of only a single occasion: a wedding feast. The peasants of the neighborhood thronged behind the riders, wearing their Sunday dress. The men were in bleak black, the girls in motley skirts with kerchiefs on their heads. They cheered, but the cheers were neither very loud nor heartfelt; they strewed the carpets liberally, however, with flowers supplied by the head gardener. Count Dupi's face was full of emotion as he led the procession with Zia on his arm. They walked alone, separated by the length of Zia's train from the rest of the marchers. Zia was pale with happiness and the grandeur of the moment.

Then a rather unpleasant thing happened to mar the beatific atmosphere. A drunken yokel astride a tub sighted Count Dupi at the head of the procession, pushed his peony-trimmed black hat to the nape of his neck and shouted at the top of his voice:

"Long live the great estate!"

The voice was not hostile. It had the quality of a heckler at a political rally. The unexpected shout brought a laugh from the people, and Count Dupi himself betrayed a smile. Two rooster-plumed gendarmes hastened to the peony-decked farmer, removed him from his tub and gently urged him to be quiet.

But the shout stabbed into Zia's heart. We are stabbed like this in dreams, by knives fashioned of mist, knives which have no edge, cause no pain but are still terrifying. Her heart was oversensitive now, and the shout seemed an emissary of the Copperplated Twilight.

Prince Fini ran ahead to halt the procession at the church entrance by raising his green staff. The gypsies subsided. They waited for Countess Menti, who now left the end of the line, came forward and entered the church alone. A wide aisle between the two rows of benches led to the altar. Countess Menti went all the way to the front of the little church, and came to a halt on the foremost stones, worn hollow by the press of boots over hundreds of years. She stood like a statue, ready to play her part. The benches were crowded and many people stood along the walls, among them some newspapermen, representatives of liberal dailies who had come without invitation.

Outside the church, meanwhile, Count Dupi released Zia's arm and Princess Ozzolini drew her white-gloved hand from Filippo's arm. The bridegroom offered his arm to the bride and as they entered the church the organ began to peal in the balcony, which was also packed with spectators. Schoolmaster Karika was playing Beethoven's Wedding Song.

When the young couple had passed the rows of benches, Countess Menti stepped forward and barred their way. Zia and Filippo came to a stop. The countess stripped the glove from her right hand slowly and with dignity, raised her hand and slapped Zia's face. Then she seized Zia by the shoulder and pushed her toward the altar. The slap did not resound and her shove was not violent; it was clear to everyone that this was a symbolic scene, part of the wedding ritual.

It happened at Katalin Dukay's wedding too. A crafty canonist had introduced the custom of the slap into the marriage ceremony at the end of the sixteenth century; if the marriage proved unhappy, it served to enable the bride to claim, in a divorce suit, that she had gone to the altar under parental duress. This goes to prove that the Church, while forging formidable manacles over the wrists of married couples, also provided keys to undo those manacles in case of dire necessity. Even the contracts men make with God are full of loopholes. Only the stamp of *nihil obstat* is important. And since Church authorities in previous centuries had not taken exception to this custom, Bishop Zsigmond raised no protest against Countess Menti's gentle slap when the plans for the wedding ceremony were brought to him for highest approval.

The exchange of vows was preceded by Mass, which His Eminence Bishop Zsigmond celebrated with the assistance of the Reverend Alajos Galovics.

In the meantime the gypsies retired into the shade of the trees outside the church. They had no business inside. They were the pagans of worldly life, and passed their collection plate at the end of frivolous and frenzied nights. While the tinkling bell bade the worshipers kneel inside the church, the bull-fiddler and the violist settled on the grass and began a game of "twenty-one" with a dirty pack of cards that was bloated like a waffle. Some of the others were tuning their fiddles.

The exchange of vows began. Bishop Zsigmond addressed a beautiful sermon to the young couple. He compared marriage to a vessel tossed on the stormy sea of life, but a holy vessel that the waves cannot pull under. He reminded them of their duties to their religion, their country, to society and to their parents. He made mention of the unfortunate royal family, who were present only in thought. This sentence was meant as a reference to the telegram which arrived with the signatures of Zita and Otto from Belgium that morning, the text of which Mr. Gruber had immediately communicated to the press.

The wedding ceremony over, Prince Fini raised his green staff once more and reassembled the procession outside the church.

Meanwhile the flowers strewn on the carpets had wilted in the sun, and the ranks of gaping onlookers had been greatly reduced too. The chimes were ringing noon. From time to time some of the emaciated work horses whinnied beneath the creaking saddles of the riders. They sent plaintive messages into the distance, to their faraway comrades. Mr. Makkosh, the town clerk, thought he could discern a certain similarity between their whinnies and the bawls of the peony-decked peasant.

The major-domo Herr Jordan waited at the main entrance of the castle, with the tiny ribbon of a military decoration in the lapel of his frock coat. He bowed deeply before Zia, much more deeply than ever before, and said in a somewhat affected manner:

"Je vous salue, *Madame* la princesse!"

He was the first to address her as *madame*. Her eyes filled with tears.

Dinner was to begin at one o'clock, so there was time enough for the guests to catch their breath, for the men in costume to adjust any neckpieces that were askew and for the women to recover, by means of rouge and powder, the freshness of countenance of which Bishop Zsigmond's long sermon had stripped them. Through the open windows of the first floor, in the vicinity of the guest rooms, came the sound of toilets groaning reproachfully at each other.

There was still time before dinner for the visitors to inspect the wedding gifts—*res paraphernales,* to use Count Peter's term, who was as addicted to such expressions as doctors are to the Latin names for disease. The gifts were on display in the wide billiard room. As far as items of value were concerned, a single table would have sufficed to hold them, but Count Dupi had decided that the gifts of the villagers and the staff should be displayed as well, and these occupied considerably more space, although the value they represented was considerably less. A card under each present bore the name of the donor.

One small gift sat all alone, almost lost on the vastness of a table covered with green velvet. It was a woman's prayer book, bound in ivory, *The Still of Night,* a volume which we already know to be the work of Bishop Zsigmond. Beneath the prayer book was a card: "Gift of the Rightful King." It was obvious that this present was the result of correspondence between the bishop and Otto, and that the crown prince had graciously agreed to this solution of the gift problem. They surrounded it and gazed at it with awe, although the little prayer book looked like a lump of ice in the middle of the table, and there was reason to fear that it might melt. The agent Egry-Toth, who alone was familiar with the expenditures of the Dukay estates, swiftly made a mental calculation and came to the conclusion that the little prayer book had been dearly purchased in terms of assistance extended so far by István Dukay to the exiled royal family.

Naturally the other presents did not merit separate tables. But these too were arranged by rank. On a suede cloth square in the center of the adjoining table stood a medieval painting in a frame, not very large, about thirty-five inches wide and fifteen inches high. The card below read: "Breughel: *The Birth of Eve.* Gift of Prince Achile Ozzolini." There was a crush around the table.

"Priceless..." someone whispered.

Count Joachim was the only one who made no remark. A single glance told him that this was indeed the work of Breughel; not of Pieter the elder, however, but of Jan. Had it been by Pieter, the painting would be worth at least forty thousand dollars, but in fact it was not even worth eight hundred. He did not say a word until a discussion over the proper pronunciation of Breughel's name arose behind him.

"*Brüchel*" he belched, introducing a hoarse Dutch intonation into his voice until it sounded like a mild case of laryngitis, and then he proceeded to the next table.

There on the next table was Count Lajos's witty token of his gift: a freshly lacquered license plate. The lemon-yellow little sedan to which it belonged stood in the park. The rest of the gifts were not so interesting. Silver trays, a blue fox stole, horn-handled sets of tableware, smaller jewelry, a woman's hunting rifle, a gilt icon effervescent with pearls (the gift of Uncle Dmitri), a camera, a tennis racket and other similar things. There was more calculation than heart in the presents.

Zia already wore the bridegroom's gift, a large solitaire, on her finger. The gift of her parents, the three-thousand-acre parcel of land that they had decided after long conferences to split from the estate at Duka, could not be placed on the tables, but everyone knew of it the day after the engagement was announced. Three thousand acres was not a great deal in relation to the total Dukay holdings of one hundred ten thousand acres, but we must note that the daughters of nobility are always slighted in the matter of inheritance. The groomsmen and the bridesmaids were presented with gold cigarette cases, gold-knobbed riding crops, smaller jewelry and expensive writing sets.

The billiard tables bore the gifts of the staff and the villagers. Here there was more to look at. On the very first table lay an ancient shepherd's crook, as if on display in a museum of folk art. According to the card, it was the "gift of Maté

Balog, Chief Shepherd of the Estate." In letters carved with a jackknife around the ornamented cherrywood ran the following verse: "Maté Balog made me. Long live my mistress lady." It was during the war that the chief shepherd had ventured into the park, where he had never gone before. He turned his heavy boots toward Zia, who was rolling a hoop. She was eight years old at the time. "Missy, couldn't you help me out, now? My boy, now, he's in the hospital at Lebovice, three times wounded. I want to bring him home."

Zia listened with fright in her face to the gruff voice that issued from beneath the mustachios which looked like crow's wings and held her attention like a delicate spiderweb. And then, without a word, she darted away. Maté Balog thought he had offended the young mistress by his intrusion. Actually he could not have found a better person to ask. All children take their first serious commission very much to heart. A few minutes later Zia was clinging to Count Dupi's neck, and the telegram was already winging toward the War Ministry in Vienna, and from there to General Pflanzer-Baltin, and from there to the hospital in Lebovice. This is why, twelve years later, the gift came from the pastures; Maté Balog had sent his staff, on which he had leaned for forty-three years.

And there was the double-humped bread baked by Mistress Hecsedi, large as a millstone, still full of the warmth of the oven, its rosy-red crust expressing gratitude for the fact that her son had been placed as a baggage handler with the railroad in the previous years. Old Mother Compo, despite failing sight, had embroidered six tiny handkerchiefs with her own hands, decorating the corners with leaves that lacked only the penetrating fragrance itself of patchouli. Then there were Mistress Domak's two jars of dog-rose jam; the tremendous wreath of wildflowers sent by the Catholic Girls' Club; a flask bound in pony-skin; a brand new cedar chest made by Berecki, the estate carpenter, with tulips painted all over the outside; a clothesbasket as large as a bathtub that Paul Bandi, the blind veteran in the village, had woven out of willow rods; and there were flower vases and ashtrays which pertly proclaimed: we know the genteel thing to do. And loud, chrome-plated trifles from the cooperative store which even the servants' rooms would not have contained. Beside them a fruit bowl made from the bottom of a siphon looked like a treasure of folk art. The estate blacksmith was represented by a picnic grill, and the estate locksmith by a decorative paperweight which bore the letters *Z-i-a* cleverly worked in wire of finger thickness. Yes, this was the people, the heart of the people and the gratitude of the people widespread on the tables. But Mr. Makkosh, the town clerk, as he looked at the gifts, thought to himself that something else was involved. He saw sinister betrayal in old Balog's crook, in Mistress Hecsedi's miracle of bread-making and in the tremendous wreath of wildflowers. They had sold themselves, the people of Ararat had sold themselves for the discharge of a soldier, for a medical examination, and particularly for letters of patronage which resulted in minor jobs at the railroad warehouse, at the revenue bureau, at the national foundry—letters which gave birth to grammar school teachers, customs guards, vizor-capped handy men in government offices, policemen, kindergarten supervisors, gave them birth and then abandoned them on the first step of the staircase of social advancement. "If His Excellency the Count would be gracious enough to speak to the Minister ..." "If His Excellency the Count would write a note to the Director..." And the coroneted, woodpecker-crested sheets of writing paper were not reluctant, especially since it was sufficient in most cases for the secretary Mr. Gruber to sign them. They sold themselves—Mr. Makkosh said to himself—in order to be among the elect, passengers on the Biblical bark when the great holocaust came. They have betrayed millions upon millions of their brothers, who were driven to America by the freehold with black bundles on their backs or are rotting at home, consumptive and hopelessly impoverished. The young town clerk was a man of revolutionary spirit.

It would be unkind to omit all mention of Rere's presents, although these gifts, for various reasons, did not figure among the objects on display. Rere, as is known, was still an exile in the hunting lodge where he had been sent after hurling the Prince of Perugia into the fishpool. Every morning since then he had asked Mr. Badar whether "Ziza's" wedding would be on the morrow. His gifts were modest, but they came from the heart. He sent an enormous stag beetle, its husk completely excavated by ants. He tied a tiny card to one of the legs of the beetle with this notation: "*For Pilipo.*" It spoke, this gift, with the faint voice of contrition and reconciliation. To Zia he sent a bouquet of wildflowers, unusual only in that the bouquet contained toadstools, molted pheasant plumes, desiccate thistles and a brush sodden with the green paint which the gamekeeper had recently applied to the window frames. Inexplicably, too, he sent a long lath, stripped from the chicken coop, which still bore its rusty nails. Mr. Badar, who had observed Rere's mounting state of excitement for days, made no protest, for he realized that the slightest remonstrance would elicit a fearful attack of rage. In his capacity as censor he also read the letter which Rere despatched to the bride. For well-nigh fifteen years of attendance upon Rere, Mr. Badar had spent his time in reading; he was the most assiduous reader of all who frequented the castle library; thus he had a degree of literary judgment. Rere's letter moved him deeply. Neither Sappho nor Villon nor young Cocteau, in his opinion, had ever expressed human sentiments more feelingly. Rere devoted hours to the composition of the letter, in the course of which he devastated a great quantity of paper, littering his room with crumpled balls of crested stationery. The letter read as follows:

My dear little Ziza: On this ocasion letme too take this ocasion Godbless Love Rere.

Not only his eyes but his brain, too, filled with tears as a result of the intensity of his emotion. Tristan Tzara, a modern poet who was in vogue at that time, deliberately strained his every sound wit to be nonsensical; in Rere's letter, however, the dark eagle-wings of a senseless spirit flapped frantically in an effort to achieve the most magnificent heights of sense.

It was only last night that Zia received the presents and the letter. And early this morning, before Mass, she took time to visit Rere. She bore, in her heart, the celestial mercies of forgiveness with which she meant to consecrate this day. Rere, when he sighted the approach of his sister's carriage, dashed indoors and tore the door of Mr. Badar's room open with an impetus that left the doorknob in his hand.

"Ziza's here!" he bellowed.

Zia came to a halt in front of him, took Rere's large horseface between her two tiny hands and gazed mutely into his eyes for several moments. Then she kissed his forehead. She patted his face in farewell and left without a word.

Rere retired to his room after her visit, and no sound was heard from him until noon. At about noon he broke into Mr. Badar's room again:

"Ziza was here!"

For some reason or other he found it necessary, after long reflection, to inform Mr. Badar anew of the great event, forgetting that Mr. Badar had been a compassionate witness to the meeting between brother and sister.

At one o'clock precisely Herr Jordan appeared in the large red salon and announced with a bow toward Countess Menti that dinner was served. The wedding guests moved toward the great dining hall, at the doors of which two footmen stood with the silver washbowls of yore. In a symbolic gesture, everyone who passed by dipped his fingers into the water. These bowls had been used at Katalin Dukay's wedding, but the washing of hands was of more immediate import then.

The long oval table, set for sixty people, shone with gold flatware, Meissen and Sèvres porcelain, crystal decanters and epergnes of flowers atop the white damask tablecloth. Footmen stood behind the sixteen seats of honor, ready to pull the chairs out for the guests as they approached the table. This distinction was accorded only sixteen guests, since there were but sixteen footmen. They too were ranged in order of rank: four chamberlains, four hussars, four chasseurs and four butlers—these were degrees within the hierarchy of footmanship. The chamberlains wore tail coats and black ties. The hussars, in thickly braided red pelisses, red trousers, and boots polished to mirror brightness, were reminiscent of the age of Maria Theresa. The chasseurs wore dark green uniforms with silver epaulettes, and their breeches bore a double stripe of dark green. The buttons of their costumes were made of horn. The flat silver buttons on the black jackets of the butlers were stamped with the Dukay crest. The high waistcoats below their white ties glittered with narrow stripes of the blue and red Dukay colors. All the footmen wore white cotton gloves.

The two adjoining chairs at the center of the table went to the bride and bridegroom. Count Dupi sat at Zia's right and Countess Menti at Filippo's left, and thus the Dukay parents seemed to flank the young couple with their protection. The opposite place of honor—*ecclesia praecedent*—was reserved for Bishop Zsigmond. Princess Ozzolini was at his right, and old Marchese Farriello at his left. Count Lajos, the best man, sat beside Princess Ozzolini, while Prince Ozzolini was at Countess Menti's side. The remaining places were ranged not in order of rank but of consanguinity. Makkosh the town clerk was at one end of the table, and Gruber at the other.

Two photographers were stationed in readiness on the balconies at either extremity of the long dining hall. The Italian who accompanied Signor Ghiringhetti from Rome was on one, and on the other was a photographer from *The Aristocratic World*, which planned to devote a special edition to this wedding of nobility.

Count Lajos raised the gold staff symbolic of his position as best man. Prince

Fini gave a similar signal with his green staff. Herr Jordan already knew that these signals would begin the wedding feast. At a gesture from him the rigid troop of black chamberlains, red hussars, silver-green chasseurs and striped butlers sprang into action. The serving of the meal began. The menus on the table listed the orders of events. Monsieur Cavaignac had outdone himself. But the menu holds little interest for those of us who know that seventeen buffalos and five hundred eighty peacocks were consumed at Katalin Dukay's wedding. We may compare this present feast to a ten-course dinner at the Hotel Royal Danieli or the Waldorf-Astoria. But not quite—for at the instigation of Count Peter, Monsieur Cavaignac had managed to recreate something at least of the delicacies served three hundred years earlier: roast peacock basted with raisins and almonds. And there was something else. The footmen held the platters so that the groomsmen were constrained to select the potato fritters especially prepared for them. These fritters contained shoestrings, lumps of pig bristles and large nails. Such practical jokes had been played on the gentlemen groomsmen at the wedding of Katalin Dukay too.

The photographer of *The Aristocratic World* covered himself with his black cloth and looked into the opaque viewfinder once more. He was enchanted by what he saw. A hawker of imitation jewelry must feel like this on a visit to the vaults of the Maharajah of Kapurthala. In terms of the carat-weight of historical name and estate, veritable man-Kohinoors were seated at the table, bald-pated, sharp-faced, fine-cut, and lady-emeralds (if with heart disease), and rubies (with high blood pressure), and the pale oriental pearls of youthful beauty.

They do not know, these strange and death-bound birds of the primeval forest, that they are thus foregathered for the last time, gathered to chirp and preen and twist their heads, parading before each other and the world the beauty of their plumage, of their hand-wrought swords in velvet scabbards, of their family jewels, of the sables and the dolmans of effulgent splendor and Tatar pomp in which the passage of centuries has clothed them, of their words and their tones of voice and the high culture that is surprisingly unreliable beyond a certain point, of their refined and compassionate opinions of the lower classes and their hardy persistence in averting their eyes from the affairs of the world.

Let us not forget that it is May of 1930, and all Europe is radiant with Maytime. The Lateran Accord with the Fascist government has already been signed in the Vatican. France has returned the confiscated wealth of the monastic orders, and Stalin has exiled Trotsky to Turkey. Yes, there is reason to hope that everything will be as before. Bishop Zsigmond has just told Princess Ozzolini in a whisper, as if it were a joyous secret, that heir apparent Otto recently received his first shotgun and was already popping pheasants in the game preserves of Belgium. He concealed the identity of the donor of the shotgun so artfully that Princess Ozzolini's keen perception readily knew the bishop himself to be the one.

Through the open door of the adjoining smoking-room came the sound of the gypsy band, playing the song that begins "The lake is dry..." playing it softly but with deep feeling. The primás held the throat of his fiddle fixed high in the air.

While they are dining is the moment, our last chance, to inquire after some of the guests we have not met so far.

We should know of Count Lajos, the best man, that he was a member of one of Franz Joseph's cabinets at the turn of the century, and received his Order of the Golden Fleece from the emperor at that time, when Edward VII of England visited the aged emperor in Vienna with the feelings an affectionate nephew dutifully entertains toward his wealthy and severe uncle. There is a difference, then, between this Fleece and the one at the neck of Count Dupi's green velvet cloak, however much they look alike, for the letters patent of the latter were signed in the palace at Gödöllö by Charles IV in the days of the revolution, some minutes after he had raised a jewelry dealer to the rank of baron. We learn all this from Countess Betty, Count Lajos's wife, who is seated opposite her husband between Achile Ozzolini and General Paccapuzzi. She has been explaining the difference between the two Orders of the Golden Fleece, merely for the sake of historical accuracy. She is a woman of sixty-five, very erect, the only woman here with a beautifully curved nose. She is the perfect example of a real Hungarian *grande dame,* and it is too bad that she did not become a queen. She detests the Germans. Only her doctor knows that she has an incipient cancer of the stomach.

Kristina sits beside Count Lajos, and beside Kristina is Count Aaron. He is ninety-four years old, and so deaf that he would not notice the detonation of the six little mortars at his back if they were all fired at once. But Rodin's mouth would water at the sight of Count Aaron's bald head. His gala dress is a braided, simple black cloak, of the sort worn in the last century by Hungary's great men. Count Aaron comes from Transylvania, which is noteworthy because the aristocrats of Transylvania are much, much poorer, much wiser, much longer-lived, much more Magyar in blood and thought than the Western counts and princes, whom they hold—somewhere in the depths of their souls—in a disdain that is liberally reciprocated. They are poorer because their ancestors fought the battles for liberation from the Habsburgs. They wear fewer Fleeces, too, because they are generally Protestants. They live longer because they bathe less often than the westerners. They have given Hungary some real artists and writers, while the westerners merely play at Maecenas—though gifts of this sort cannot be strictly scrutinized in every case. Judging from his countenance, one would think that Count Aaron is suffering from heart-rending homesickness, but it is merely regret for having forgotten to bring his yard-and-a-half long chibouk with him. Note how he beckons to one of the footmen for the third time; he eats and drinks as much as four men. He has shot thirty-five bears in the course of his life, and still has a handsome seat on a horse. According to a reliable witness, he successfully courted a cashier in Kolozsvár last year. There is no reason to doubt the evidence, since it was supplied by the cashier herself, Brunhilda, who spread the happy news all over the historic city on the following day. A young doctor interrogated the girl closely, and when Brunhilda swore that the ninety-four-year-old gentleman had made two distinct offerings on the altar of love within the space of twenty-seven minutes, the doctor wrote an article on the event for the *Wochenschrift für Untersuchungen über die Libido sexualis* of Munich, of course without mentioning the old man's name. When Brunhilda showed the article to Count Aaron he was dreadfully upset. His parchment-colored bald dome turned as red as a poppy:

"It's a rotten shame—why didn't they use my name?"

But his long life is not due to his enormous appetites so much as to the forty-year-long deafness which has given him thorough protection against Hungarian political addresses in the past decades.

His wife Countess Sarolta, seated at the right of Marchese Ghezzi, was eighty-nine years old this spring. This event was celebrated simultaneously with their seventieth anniversary of happy married life, on which occasion the National Casino invited one hundred guests to a dinner in their honor. Countess Sarolta unexpectedly raised her white eagle's-head at one point during the meal and began to speak:

"I should like to say just once more, and perhaps for the last time, that I am now the only woman alive who was kissed by Sándor Petőfi, our great national poet, who died eighty-one years ago. I can clearly recall the light brown texture of the poet's face, his narrow shoulders and his sparse little mustache. A long-stemmed, cup-shaped pipe was in his hand, and he wore a brown shirt that was the color of coffee. I can recall his voice too, slightly high-pitched and sharp. I was a girl of six, and the incident took place at five o'clock in the afternoon on the 2nd of October in 1847, when my late father and I were on a visit to Koltó, where the young poet and his bride were spending their honeymoon."

She said only that much, and sat down. Her narrative did not produce the effect she had imagined. Mention of Petőfi's name, especially in the neighborhood of Prince Andrew, was likely to evoke unpleasant remarks. To Prince Andrew, the word *poet* was synonymous with Communist.

At the right of Methuselah-like Count Aaron sits Princess Karola, craning her nervous yet attractive little mouse-head every which way. She persists in forgetting that Count Aaron is at her left, and her ceaseless conversational sallies rebound from the deafness of the busily champing nonagenarian like a rubber ball from a backboard.

Opposite Count Dupi, a little to the right and seated between two women as yet unidentified, is Prince Andrew himself, also with the Order of the Golden Fleece about his neck (Franz Joseph!). The prince seems to be about sixty and has long been afflicted with Addison's disease, an anemic condition caused by disturbances of the suprarenal glands and accompanied by deposits of dark pigment in the skin. As a consequence he is popularly known as the Black Prince, an appellation that is both unfair and inaccurate, for the face of Prince Andrew is more a mixture of ash and bronze, and it is a fact that this malady is often known as the bronze disease. Prince Andrew is the only Hungarian nobleman with blood of the House of Árpád in his veins, and the claim itself is elaborately circumstantial, based as it is on kinship with Otto Morva, who married Euphemia, daughter of King Béla I, in 1093. According to some historians, Euphemia's name was actually Buzilla. Another school of historians maintains that the ancestress's name was not Buzilla but Odola, who married Prince Magnus of Saxony. We need all this information in order to understand the constitution of the soul of Prince Andrew, who is said by economists to be the wealthiest man in Central Europe. Hungary has Prince Andrew to thank for its first successful rice crop, for the introduction of the Laocyn inoculation against pig fever, for the canal system on the Pónya River, and for the suicide of Mari Kádár, the most beautiful actress in Hungary at the turn of the century, whom the prince refused to marry despite his promise. The prince's manner is exceptionally winning. His voice is soft and almost apologetic.

He neither drinks nor gambles, but he does setting-up exercises in the nude every morning. He rides for an hour every afternoon. He acquired his enormous wealth not by inheritance alone, but by dint of an inexhaustible capacity for work, and is known as an experienced, skilled agriculturalist. He is one of the three men in Hungary to own a private airplane, but the plane is not a nobleman's hobby. He flies it himself, and regularly drops from the clouds onto his vast estates all over the country to inspect the tilling, the threshing, the irrigation, the feed, and to see whether the overseers spend their afternoons asleep. The prince has only one abiding obsession. Now medical knowledge has not yet discovered the fundamental source of obsessions. We must suppose that the human body (and soul) is a closed vessel full of albumen, salts, cells, fibers, bacilli, impulses and many other things. Somewhere in all this the obsessions are born, and later choose their careers. One becomes a chess player, another a fisherman, the third a nicotine addict, an alcoholic, a flower fancier, a nail-biter and so on. One such obsession in Prince Andrew's soul was preparing to be a surgeon, but long before finishing its studies it chose another career and became a painter. Let us not flaunt the observations of others; it was Count Joachim who made this discovery. Every morning, after his bath and breakfast, Prince Andrew paints a full-sized landscape. He paints his landscapes with teeth clenched, at incredible speed, his face pale with fury. According to his wife, the strong smell of turpentine in the paint excites him. It is his opinion that anyone can paint clouds and the sky; therefore it is the duty of his valet John to have the sky painted on each landscape by eight in the morning, at which time the prince himself enters his studio. It was he who gave Zia a tennis racket as a wedding present.

His wife Marie was born an Austrian countess and is seated between old Marchese Ghezzi and young Count János, wearing a choker of diamonds so large that they might be taken for imitations. The princess is ash-blond, and slightly snub-nosed, which is attractive withal, even beguiling. The roots of her eyelashes are often inflamed, as they are now, and thus her eyes are framed in a thin red ring, like those of certain Indian varieties of chicken. Her wrists are square, her hands bony and strong. Before dinner Count Dupi grasped her incredibly narrow waist once again, to see if he could still fit it within the span of his two hands. He failed. And he remarked mournfully: "It's no use, my fingers are beginning to grow shorter!" Princess Marie, known to the family by the name of Bibu, was the most famous horsewoman in the Monarchy before the war, and her waist is still wonderfully slim. When her four grown sons appear, people wonder how such tremendous young men ever issued from such a flyweight. However, there is no doubt about it, nor deception; she is really their mother. But whether Prince Andrew is really the father of the four boys is a matter of popular conjecture. Everyone likes Princess Marie. Her manner is simple and unreserved, her conversation gay and witty. Years ago one of her cousins, a broken-down Austrian baron, plagued her with his wish to become agent of the estates because Jéznák, the elderly agent, was seriously ill. At the old man's funeral the baron confronted his cousin once more and asked: "What do you think, can I take Jéznák's place now?" At which Princess Marie glanced at the bier and answered: "If the old man's family agrees, I have no objection."

Count Henrik, seated beside white-haired Countess Sarolta, is the twin brother of Count Joachim. In their youth the resemblance between them was deceptive, and particularly so in Vienna, where they were both volunteers in the Uhlans at the very same time. The similarity of uniform increased their resemblance until it was impossible to tell them apart. They moved in different circles, however. Joachim was an average billiard player, while Henrik was a veritable champion. One afternoon at the Café Leopold Joachim staked ten shillings on a hundred-point game, and allowed a handicap of twenty points. His regular partner, knowing Joachim's middling skill, took his friend to be temporarily stricken either with generosity or lunacy, and happily accepted the wager. He already had ninety-three points, while his opponent had no more than twenty-five. When Joachim's turn came up again, he laid his cue on the green felt and with the usual "Excuse me for a moment" he disappeared in the direction of the washroom, to be replaced a few minutes later by his brother Henrik, who took the cue in hand and did not put it down until he had won the game. The unfortunate partner failed to notice the substitution. Joachim was customarily shaved by a famous barber on the Kohlmarkt. One morning he told Herr Pfünzmeyer, a former court barber to Archduke Rudolf who reserved his personal services for the rank of colonel or higher: "I don't know what's wrong with your assistants, old man. My beard grows out a half hour after each shave they give me!" The white-haired master barber was offended: "Herr Graf, please—I'll shave you myself this morning, and if you're not still cleanshaven a half hour from now, why, I insist on giving you a free shave every morning as long as I live!" Joachim's face was as smooth as marble when he stepped from the chair, but a half hour later he returned—with a five-day growth of beard. In their youth they took pleasure in this game of mistaken identity, but later it grew wearisome and often inconvenient, which is why Joachim decided to wear a Henry IV beard and horn-rimmed spectacles. The twins were only outwardly alike. Count Henrik lived at the card table—it was not an obsession but a profession rather. He rose at three every morning, took a cold shower after his bath and spent a half hour lifting dumbbells. Bright and fresh, he appeared at the Casino at a time when the hair of all the players was hanging in their eyes and their eyes were hanging out and the boundless consumption of French brandy had had the usual effect. Count Henrik handled cards as a fencing champion handles his foil. It is truly a mystery how he managed nonetheless to lose twelve thousand acres of land in the course of the years. He did not go into society, and had renounced all worldly pleasures. In the afternoons he locked himself into his room, and the silence was disturbed only by the soft whirr of an experimental roulette wheel. Surrounded by mathematical treatises, he too was working on a foolproof method that would break the bank at Monte Carlo. He was as deeply engrossed in his studies as German scientists in atomic research, at which they were working feverishly by that time.

His wife, Baroness René, is the daughter of Baron Jakab, who received the title in 1912 for his services in the interest of increased Hungarian industry. Baroness René's attitude toward aristocratic society is that of a dog toward a rodent: he takes it in his mouth and rolls it around but will not swallow it. If low, pleasant and silvery laughter resounds from one end of the table occasionally, we have Baroness René to thank for it: she always enjoys herself in such company, and enlivens it with her wit.

For a moment we must return to the train-bearing youngsters, who are dining in another room. However incredible it may seem, there is a big-eared, crook-nosed little Jewish boy among them, who draws his eyebrows together at the center of his forehead whenever he speaks, pulls his shoulders back, turns the palms of his hands in and out and pitches his voice high. But the German SS men who invade Hungary will be surprised when they ask him his name, for the little boy is Count Herbert Hohenstauf-Maringen and he really cannot help the fact that he is the image of his grandfather Baron Jakab.

Count Charles the lion hunter, who is here with his wife Clara the politician, is presently dressed in the light blue pelisse of the former Nádasdy Hussars. By some egregious error, a black Turkish mustache has been pasted on a face that perfectly resembles Dante. We may recall that the Mödling school of philosophy distinguished two categories of human character, the tiller of the soil and the breeder of beasts; but in the latter category they included a special subdivision for hunters, who are more unmethodical than any of the others and have no patience even for breeding animals, but trust their fortune to their bows and arrows, spears, Cordike rifles with telescopic sights, their journeys of exploration, their stocks and bonds, their packs of cards, their three-act plays or their burglars tools. Count Charles was the prototypical hunter in the most literal sense, with the eyes of his falconer ancestors. Thus we can understand his aversion for politics and for the decadence of modern man. The stirrings of an African night on the Massawan Reserve, the shrieks of quarrelsome hyenas, the grunts of Impala bucks, the hoots of owls and squeaks of bats were more meaningful to him than all the noise that musicians, singers or orators can make. The sight of Count Charles in a bathing suit was enough to freeze one's blood. His right breast was ferociously clawed to the shoulder, and so was his left thigh. The ugly hollows of the wounds indicated that his body was short of flesh by several pounds. The accident took place twenty years ago in the vicinity of the Kapiti Plains camp, when he went into the brush after an insignificant little lioness that he had wounded. Since then he has learned that when chasing lions it is more important to load one's rifle with ammunition than to load oneself with cognac. For a long time the count has been impoverished. The sum of his debts, however, would be sufficient to amortize the Hungarian national debt. His motto was, "We live only so long as we keep paying off." What is amazing about the motto is that Count Charles does not pay off. The trophies in his apartment make it almost impossible to move. The walls are covered with the heads of buffalo, antlers of antelope, panther- and tiger-skins, and with ceiling-high elephant tusks. The ashtrays are made of crocodile eggs, the umbrella-and-cane stand in the hall is the sawed-off hoof of a hippopotamus, the coat hooks are made of various horns, and when Schütz the usurer makes his daily appearance he hangs his hat on the nose of a rhinoceros. Several times, in his excitement, he has made a hole in his hat.

Only one couple of any importance is left: Count Samu and his wife Baroness Leona. Both of them are from Transylvania. The count's gala is mallow-colored, and he wears a black bandage over his left eye. He lost one eye in a duel with a Rumanian attorney. He is a wind-burnt, slender, strapping character who seems capable of taking the handles of the plow in hand on his little estate in Marosmente. Possibly he does just that. He is a Protestant, an opponent of Otto, and one of his ancestors was ruler of Transylvania for a short time. His wife, Baroness Leona,—her name is familiar to all lovers of music—is a world-famous pianist, and her face is a frequent sight on the placards of Albert Hall in London or Carnegie Hall in New York. Zia insisted that they be invited, because she spent an unforgettable summer with them last year. It seemed to her that the sparrows were larger at Sebesd than at Ararat, but this was because the Sebesd "castle" was unbelievably small. It is one of the finest and oldest manors in Transylvania. The little rooms are so low that one can touch the beams of the ceiling with an outstretched hand, and it is hard to see how these tiny rooms sheltered the many centuries of resistance to the German and the Turk, so many that grooves have been worn in the thresholds. A blue brook flows through the grass-covered courtyard, and when a window is opened the black-rooted old pear trees immediately offer their boughs, heavy with fruit. Sophie, the count's daughter, is Zia's best friend.

The young people, the groomsmen and bridesmaids do not particularly interest us, for we have hardly heard of them. We already know flaxen-haired Elizabeth, who made Señor Calandra a gift of her virginity, and bronze-haired Vira, whom we shall meet again, and Sophie from Transylvania. As for the young men, let us rest our eyes for a moment on Baron Ubi, who will play a brief but important role in Zia's life. He is the one who galloped through the banquet hall dressed as a three-year-old infant during a dinner in honor of the manager of a tobacco plant. Right now he is constantly turning his head to look at the bride because, though but seventeen years old, he is madly in love with Zia.

Short-necked Count Ferenc will be married to Vira next month. We already know Sigi, and there is no one else of any interest to us among the youngsters.

But wait! For here is Miss Gwen Steele, the young lady whom Zia invited, together with her mother, at György's request, though György did not say why. And there sits Mrs. Steele at the right of Count Henrik. She is an exact replica of her daughter, but her rosy and youthful face is already framed in silver hair. Both of them are alive with the best qualities of North American beauty. They arrived in Europe with György, and this is their first visit to Hungary. Seated at the table, they look as if they were watching a bullfight in Spain.

Who is missing? First and foremost among the missing is Dr. Kliegl, whom Count Dupi would not invite under any circumstances, though it was the express desire of János. Missing too are Count Zoltán and his wife Rosamond, who could not come because they are in mourning for their second son. He lost his life last week in a plane crash. And these two would have impressed Mrs. Steele and her daughter, because Rosamond is an American too, of a family so important that we hesitate to reveal its name. It is in a class with the Astors, the Morgans or the Vanderbilts.

Signor Ghiringhetti has engaged little Countess Hannah at his side in a confidential discussion of politics. Hannah, an acquiescent little girl of sixteen, has no objection to the enthronement of a Prince of Savoy in Hungary. Ghiringhetti will take the news to Rome as the unanimous opinion of the most exalted Hungarian circles.

Among those in civilian clothes we recognize Mr. Gruber the secretary, Mr. Makkosh the town clerk, Alajos Galovics the chaplain, Bruckner the lord lieutenant and Hönig the county sheriff. The local parson looks like nothing more than a cassock, without a man inside. The estate agent, Egry-Toth, will also play a part in Zia's life several years from now. Down at the end of the table, they belong among the people whose names cause a disturbance when an invitation list is being composed, but they are finally retained on the roster with "Unfortunately we must invite them," human pebbles of the larger size. This is how they feel, too. They are talking to each other. The sheriff remarks to Egry-Toth:

"How much would you say, József?"

Gnawing on the kidney stew, the estate agent withholds his answer while he runs his eyes along the assembled company, stopping at each head for a second or two.

"Not entirely. But almost."

He too has estimated that about a million acres are seated at the table, of which Prince Andrew alone represents one hundred and forty thousand. If we include the *fundus instructus,* the mills, factories, town houses, art treasures, family jewels and foreign investments, it comes to little less than a billion dollars at the current rate of exchange.

"I don't understand," remarks Mr. Makkosh, "why, when an array like this can be assembled at one table, this little country of ours is always showing its wounds."

The tone of his voice is such that Egry-Toth does not answer.

"The estimate is not quite correct," says the lord lieutenant, "because we haven't subtracted Count Charles's debts from the total."

"On the other hand," replies Hönig, "we could safely add the American millions of Countess Rosamond. And Baron Jakab isn't small fry, is he? His entire fortune will be left to René."

This is intricate accounting, in which we cannot become engrossed right now, because Count Lajos has twice raised his gold staff again. And Prince Fini has echoed the count's signal by lifting his green staff into the air twice.

The gypsy music came to a stop and the rattle of tableware ceased. Count Lajos stood up, holding the four-hundred-year-old silver nuptial bowl which had been emptied in toasts to the newly-weds at so many Dukay weddings. And the toast offered by the best man had not changed much in the course of four centuries. With very little change, he said more or less the same thing that has been said by best men all over the world on such occasions. His voice showed that he felt somewhat out of place in this particular realm of oratory.

After the next course Prince Achile took the floor. He spoke in French, pronouncing the French *je* as *ze,* a characteristic of most Italians. He began his speech with a most unfortunate phrase:

"As the House of Ozzolini lifts this blossoming girl unto itself..."

This evoked a general exchange of glances at the table. The eyebrows on the rigid faces of the ladies moved with especial eloquence, mounting toward the middle of their foreheads as if by prearranged signal. *Who* was being lifted? And *who* was doing the lifting? This was the query of the eyebrows. The unsuspecting prince from Perugia did not realize that there were Huns at the table, and that a remark like his provoked, in the depths of their souls, the reply that Pope Leo once went on his knees before Attila to beg for peace. Count Dupi cleared his throat noisily, and it sounded like an interposed objection. No matter what the prince—who had the face of a gypsy fiddler—might have said from then on, no one would listen to him. The blood of the Ordonys and of Elizabeth Habsburg flowed in the veins of the "blossoming girl," so what was there to "lift"? This was the general feeling. Count Peter began to unburden himself of something that had long been on his mind. In a low voice, which disturbed the speaker nonetheless, he started to tell Baron Adam—who sat across the way—that according to his understanding it had not been Bernabo Ozzolini but Giangaleazzo Visconti who married Isabella, the daughter of King John the Good of France. This was clear to anyone with the slightest smattering of history. As far as the title of prince was concerned, it had not been granted to but rather purchased by the Ozzolinis, for Emperor Wenceslaus of Germany had been a lazy, drunken good-for-nothing who profited from his Italian possessions only by the corrupt practice of selling titles for a low price. In those days every draper became a prince.

Meanwhile Prince Ozzolini concluded his speech and sat down, looking very satisfied with his success. His satisfaction was principally due to the noisy flourish the gypsies played when he ended his remarks.

Now one speech followed another, to the accompaniment of a rattle of tableware that was discreet at first but gradually increased in volume. Prince Fini toasted the parents of the bride and groom, and Baron Adam toasted the witnesses—since he was in the uniform of a colonel of Uhlans, he thought it behooved him to greet the entire Italian Army in the person of General Paccapuzzi. The sheep-eyed general, who understood not a word of what was said, was as startled by the mention of his name as if he were waiting to be hanged. It was an unexpected surprise to hear his own name, and the speaker pronounced it with great emphasis, *Pac-ca-puz-zi,* lest he say Puzzapacci by accident. When the general's neighbor had explained what it was all about, the general too rose to speak. Using short, military phrases, he toasted the armed forces of Hungary, but his remarks seemed—particularly to those who did not know Italian—as if he were scolding the footmen for something or other. This was so because he did not look his audience in the face but let his eyes wander in an arc beyond the table, and put an exclamation mark after each word: *Armata! Gloriosa! Ungherese!*

"What's so glorious about it?" Count Charles asked audibly, for it was his opinion that the new Hungarian Army had no feats of valor to recommend it, not to mention the fact that it bred German-named generals like jack rabbits. In this company it was hardly felicitous to mention an army the leaders of which had fired on their own crowned sovereign.

"How strange," Princess Karola remarked to her neighbor, "in the mouth of a general the Italian language is like a rattling of chains." *Wattling* was the way she pronounced it.

The gypsies hardly began a tune before someone waved for silence because a new speaker had arisen. There were toasts to the bishop, the master of the revels, the bridesmaids, the groomsmen, but at about four o'clock the table finally broke up after the lord lieutenant had spoken.

The wide terrace, on its own initiative, invited dancing. But these dances were symbols merely, pale imitations of the reels and jigs of former days. Count Peter had planned to have the seven groomsmen dance around the bride with burning torches in their hands, in accordance with ancient custom. But Count Dupi vetoed this part of the program, saying: "That fool Ubi would set the bride on fire!"

Zia and Filippo danced first, for hardly more than a minute. Then Prince

Fini, as master of the revels, approached the bishop with a silver platter on which he bore a dark green silk scarf embroidered with gold, one of the oldest of the Dukay relics. Bishop Zsigmond, with the tip of the scarf in hand, stepped up to the bride, and Zia grasped its other end. The gypsies broke into the music of an old Hungarian dance—they had committed it to memory especially for this moment. Holding the ends of the scarf at a respectable distance between them, the bishop and the bride danced a few turns. This is how it was done at the wedding of Katalin Dukay too, three hundred years before. The scarf served the purpose of keeping the dancers apart, since clerics were not allowed to touch a woman's waist. In the audience Count Sigi, referring to the gossip that was current about the bishop, remarked that the scarf was really unnecessary. And Bishop Zsigmond's cadenced steps could hardly be called dancing.

"He trips around like a flustered little girl," Count Joachim commented.

Now it was the best man's turn. As a member of the laity, Count Lajos had a right to take a firm grip on the bride. And that is what the old gentleman did, with a sly twinkle in his eyes.

Then the seven groomsmen danced a ring around the bride. Count Peter had not allowed himself to be talked out of this event. But they brandished no flaming torches, of course, and there was no danger of setting the bride on fire. She was already on fire in any case. As she stood in the center of the circle, with her tiara and her tear-filled eyes, she looked like a great white flame.

Through the branches of the trees in the park, from the direction of the Klementina Meadow, came the sound of a brass band playing in the distance. It was like a summons from the primordial wilderness. The squeal of the horns was like the trumpeting that issues from the trunk of a bull elephant. They were playing "Ladi-ladi-lom." They scarcely knew any other number.

The nobility set out to take part in the festivities of the villagers. For the site of the public celebration, Count Peter had selected the two-acre clearing between the park and the game preserve known as the Klementina Meadow, because Countess Menti used to rest a moment or two there in the course of her afternoon walks. The Klementina was covered with great tents to keep the crowd of more than a thousand people dry in case of rain. All the villagers of Ararat, large and small, were there, and many had come from the neighboring hamlets. Everything was ready for the feast. The thirty-foot pole was up, trimmed smooth and thickly greased, with a basket at its tip which contained hams, sausages, a purse, a razor, a mustache curler, a jackknife, a pocket mirror and other mundane treasures. The basket would go to the first one who climbed the pole without slipping on the grease. The young bucks around the pole were already spitting on their palms experimentally. And the women were already baking the six-foot-wide fruit pie which would be placed on the grass and later surrounded by contestants, their hands tied at the back. There was a five-pengö piece in the center of the pie for the one who could dig his way to it with his teeth. It promised to be an uproarious sight, with the diabolic visages of the competitors, who would turn into tar-babies with jam on face and hair in the great pandemonium.

But the high point of the festivities would be the barbecue. Among the family records Count Peter had found a detailed account of the ox-roast at Katalin Dukay's wedding. Unfortunately they were unable at first to find a man for the job. Monsieur Cavaignac, who took part in the preliminary conferences, had declared that the whole thing was a myth: it was impossible to spit an ox and roast it in one piece. But the chef did not know the Magyars, for whom nothing is impossible where their stomachs are concerned. Finally, from a distant county, they secured old János Kigyó, who was so much a master of the rare art that he had been summoned to Budapest for the ox-roast on St. Stephen's Day a year ago. And Master Kigyó appeared, a short little wrinkle-faced man, so small that one wondered how he managed to contain so much knowledge. Brandishing his cherry-wood stick, he issued hoarse commands from beneath his gray walrus mustache. He supervised every step in person, tested everything. He took the knives in hand, and the platters, the spits, the crosspoles and the pokers, even tasting the cakes of lard and the salt. He dismissed each item to its task with a cry of, "Good enough—let 'er go!"

First he skinned the ox, after explaining that the head and the hoofs must be left in place. He slit the throat to make room for the spit, which was as thick as a telegraph pole and would come out at the tail after passing under the backbone. He cut a hole into the stomach of the ox, just large enough to receive a calf, which would replace the tripe, the stomach and the lungs. But the kidneys were left inside. When all this was done they produced a quail larded with bacon. Master Kigyó took it in his hand and looked it over.

"Did you salt it on the inside too, Julie?"

"Salt it, love—of course, I did! Don't ask so many questions!"

"Good enough—let 'er go!" and Master Kigyó handed the quail to one of the assistant butchers.

They placed the quail inside a plucked capon. Good enough—let 'er go! They put the capon in the stomach of a lamb, and the lamb was nestled inside a calf. Good enough—let 'er go! Now the calf was crammed into the stomach of the ox. The poor ox had never imagined it would sometime be so pregnant.

They drove the tremendous spit through the flayed beast. And now came the most difficult part. Kontyos, the estate blacksmith, came forward with five-foot-long iron spikes under his arm. They drove these through the backbone of the ox so that they penetrated the spit and came out of the belly. It was hard work that took expert skill. It was even harder to nail the legs of the ox to its shoulder blades so it would seem to be in a reclining position—for the ox would have to be served, in its entirety, from the center of the table. Finally it was secured. Twenty strong men were needed to lift the spitted ox onto the cross-poles. There a mechanism similar to that of a grindstone would turn the beast. Of course Csengös, the estate cartwright, had fashioned a wheel for the tail end of the spit, which was long enough so that the men turning the spit would be out of range of the blazing heat. They tried the wheel, and found it worked splendidly. Good enough—let 'er go! The two-thousand-pound ox began to turn.

"All right! Light the fire! Let's move! No loitering!" But Master Kigyó did not use the *ai* or *i* sounds. What he said was, "Oll rot! Lot the fair."

But first the wood had to be stacked, and that took considerable finesse. The logs were placed on both sides of the cross-poles, none of them longer than the ox itself, and far enough from the meat so that it would be enveloped in heat but not touched by the flame. If only there be no wind! for if a breeze should strike up, the whole arrangement would have to be moved to face it, and the whole business started from the beginning again. The horns and hoofs of the ox were wrapped in wet rags, lest they catch fire in the course of roasting. Just let the horn take fire, and then watch everyone run from the smell!

The women were melting the lard and boiling the salt in a large kettle. This mixture would be poured over the roasting ox. They were already tying saucepans to the ends of broom handles.

"Good enough! Let 'er go!"

They lit the bonfire. The sparks began to crackle, the dry oak logs popped angrily and the smoke whirled skyward just as it had done once upon a time in Asia, in the ancestral home. Slowly the ox began to revolve to the tune of

"Ladi-ladi-lom," for the arms of the turners unwittingly took on the rhythm of the music.

Kegs of beer and tuns of wine were tapped. Skirts flew, hands slapped at boots, and dancing began for all who were in condition to dance. The brass band outdid itself. True, they played nothing but "Ladi-ladi-lom," but we must acknowledge that this itself was a major accomplishment when we consider that the band was composed of lads like Laji Hal and Józsi Szunyog, one of them a bicycle-riding postman and the other a stable-boy. Neither was over fifteen years old.

It was past five o'clock when the varicolored troop of the nobility appeared on Klementina Meadow from beneath the branches of the park. With reckless determination the brass band launched into a new number; in the opinion of some people, it was the "Rákóczi March." Loud cheering broke out, and hats flew off.

Count Dupi distributed his handshakes generously, though he knew not one of his men by name. A whole ring of girls surrounded Zia. Filippo received his share of calloused handshakes too. Beer-fringed mustaches made speeches at him, and toothless old women fluttered behind, stroking him.

"How beautiful he is, dearie! —A prince, isn't he? That he is, a prince!—How is it he speaks no Hungarian? He speaks it well enough, he's just frightened!"

Count Dupi led the judge's wife into a dance. For the sake of variety, the brass band played "Ladi-ladi-lom." Gradually all the wedding guests were absorbed into the throng of peasants. Hands grown broad on the handles of hoes and scythes encircled the slender waists of countesses. They left their mark, too, on the light-hued silk.

Filippo and Zia succeeded in slipping away from the dancers. It was time for them to change into their traveling clothes.

Off to one side, Baron Adam and Princess Karola watched the dancing. They were joined by Prince Fini, who had just been whirling a pretty peasant maid on his arm.

"*Diese Bauerin*—" began his exposition "—these peasant women use their odor to ward off the attacks of gentlemen. In the old days this wasn't so at all. Our ancestors stank just as much as the peasants did."

"Couldn't you talk about something else?" asked Princess Karola.

Prince Fini pretended not to have heard her remark. The upturned tips of his Angevin spurs peeped out of the grass, and the heavy silver chain rattled on his chest when he adjusted the cruciform sword that dangled from the chain.

"The Creator burdened me with a particularly sensitive sense of smell. I almost fainted a while ago when dancing in this mob of peasants."

János Kigyó doffed his hat and clicked his heels together before Count Dupi.

"Beg to report to His Excellency the Count—tha ox us done!"

Three hundred years earlier a certain Andorjás Kucs made the same announcement, in the same tone of voice, to Lászlo Dukay— this was one of the fruits of Count Peter's research in the archives. But Andorjás Kucs used the *ai* and *i* sounds when he made his report.

"Tha ox" had been revolving over a tremendous heat for nearly four hours. Now it slowly came to a standstill. They put the fire out on both sides, and removed the kettles as well to make room for the carvers. From the horns and hoofs they removed the steaming wet rags that had been periodically dampened during the roasting. Master Lusztig, the estate painter, stood with his brush and cup in hand, ready to spread gold paint on the hoofs and horns. When this was done, Master Kigyó personally tied the Dukay seal, with its eleven-pointed coronet, between the two horns.

"Good enough—let 'er go!"

Five wagonshafts were poked under the ox, and ten strong-fisted men lifted the enormous roast from the cross-poles. They put it on a wide table that Master Berecki, the estate carpenter, had made for this very purpose. The ox lay quietly on the table, its legs drawn under, like any ox when it settled down to rest, with the difference that this one had settled down to roast. And how it had been roasted! Its crackling exterior was iridescent with the most beautiful hues of rose-red and deep brown, for it had been continuously drenched with fat while it was cooking. There lay a ton of ox, with the Dukay seal on its forehead between the tremendous, forked, golden horns, in Renaissance splendor. Count Peter was well satisfied with the masterpiece. Run and get Monsieur Cavaignac, let him see what Hungarians can do! A wonderful fragrance pervaded the Klementina Meadow.

The dancing was interrupted, and Laji Hal gave "Ladi-ladi-lom" a rest too. Someone shouted, as if at a political convention:

"Long live János Kigyó!"

Long may he live indeed. So much knowledge in such a little man. But his grandfather had been chief *rôtisseur* in the Grassalkovics house. Wisdom of this sort is handed down from father to son.

"Bring the knives!" commanded Master Kigyó. And the women brought their clothesbaskets full of kitchen knives. Now came the final embellishment:

hundreds upon hundreds of knives were driven into the ox. The multitude of black knife-handles made the ox look like some quilled beast of prehistory.

János Kigyó offered Count Dupi a long knife, and when he saw the count eye the ox indecisively he whispered into his ear:

"From tha brosket, Your Lordshop, from tha brosket. Thot's the best!"

Later, when the hungry knives began to slice the ox apart, the nobility retired to the castle.

The station master's red cap appeared from a hazel bush.

"Have Their Lordships gone?"

"They just left."

The station master called back into the bush:

"Then come along, Jolán, let's see what's going on here..."

And soon Schoolmaster Karika and his wife appeared in the same way, and the manager of the cooperative store, the warehouse supervisor, the kindergarten teacher—all those who had been ashamed to associate themselves with this gobbling mob in the sight of the nobility, for were they not gentlefolk? This was a mark of their middle-class pride, the pride which had just been ferociously attacked and overwhelmed by the fragrance of roast ox that carried for miles around.

In the meantime Filippo and Zia had changed their clothes. Now came the closing scene of the wedding. It was eight in the evening, and there was still light enough outside, but the naked sun had dipped halfway into the foliage of the chestnut trees, like the station master when he bathed in his great green tub at the end of the yard. The guests brought long shadows with them when they gathered in the salon.

The bride's farewell scene was at hand. Countess Menti and Count Dupi stood in the center of the wide carpet. Then Zia appeared, in traveling clothes, with a veiled hat and thick-soled sport shoes. She approached her parents slowly and knelt before them. The scene had a certain barbaric beauty. She repeated the same words that Katalin Dukay, kneeling on the same rug, had spoken to her parents:

"Thank you for bringing me up...for loving me...for giving me in marriage..."

434

She was unable to continue. She bowed her shoulders and gave way to muffled sobs, burying her face in her doeskin gloves.

Countess Menti did not move. Count Dupi was pale. He leaned toward his kneeling daughter, raised her up and took her in his arms. Tears were streaming down his face too.

It was only a matter of seconds for them to get under way.

They left in Count Lajos's present. The little yellow car flew out of the park like a canary freed from its cage.

The squeals of "Ladi-ladi-lom" were still audible from the Klementina Meadow. In the castle, too, the gypsies began to play, and the young people started to dance.

Bottles of champagne popped till dawn, but when the sun rose the last guest had left the castle, and until high noon it was as quiet there as if every vestige of life had died out.

Early the next afternoon Countess Menti sent a messenger to the hunting lodge to tell Mr. Badar and Rere that they might come home.

Toward evening a faint cannonade resounded in the park. They were beating the many carpets. Then the cannonade died down, with distant plaintive echoes. The estate was as still as a cemetery.

Twilight, and darkness fell.

Several foxes appeared on the Klementina Meadow and began to gnaw the discarded ox-bones.

A gentle breeze from the violet-hued cliffs of Dalmatia descended on the waters along the northeastern shores of the Adriatic. Flying fish leaped from the water like silver-brown sparrows, but only for seconds at a time. The ship was approaching the harbor.

Zia and Filippo had arrived in Mandria.

Chapter Nine

IN APRIL Mr. Gruber had been delegated to go to Mandria and see if he could find a villa both suitable and available for the newlyweds. He was to exert every effort, for the bride would be unhappy if she could not spend her honeymoon on Mandria. And so one evening at nightfall Mr. Gruber disembarked in the harbor of Mandria after a complicated journey. The little ship that made the rounds of East Adriatic ports left Fiume but once a week. No other vessel touched at Mandria. Anyone who had money enough was free to charter a motor launch; but no one with any money ever went to Mandria. This was apparent to the sharp eyes of Mr. Gruber as soon as he looked around the Piazza Vittorio Emanuele and saw the piles of refuse resting on the shallow bottom of the concrete lagoon that extended from the harbor. Signor Occhipinti, whose pharmacy was better supplied with scrub brushes and fishing tackle than aspirin or iodine, always stood at the doorway of his shop in the evening, and he was kind enough to inform Mr. Gruber that the Pension Zanzottera was the only place for him—there might possibly be a vacant room. If he did not mention the Albergo Varcaponti, we know it was because he was not on speaking terms with Signor Varcaponti. He soothed his conscience with the thought that the plumbing had still not been repaired at the Albergo Varcaponti. No such shortcoming embarrassed the proprietor of the Pension Zanzottera, since there had never been any plumbing in that hostel at all. Signora Zanzottera showed Mr. Gruber the available space. It behooves us to know that no other room in the pension was ever offered for rent. The little house consisted of two habitable rooms in all, and the widowed signora rented the more attractive of the two as a means of supplementing the meager insurance left by her late husband. The room was not unfriendly—it was high enough and wide enough, certainly, and its tiny terrace opened on a tiny garden crowded with orange trees and fig trees. The situation looked hopeless to Mr. Gruber. He had been commissioned to secure a vacant villa with at least three rooms and bath. The signora's inquisitive glances and her entire personality seemed to compensate for all the guests one would find in a large and populous pension. In those days the cost of living was incredibly low throughout Italy, and especially so in Mandria. Nevertheless, it was with misgivings that the signora revealed the daily rates: five liras a day with meals but without wine, and three liras a day with breakfast alone. Mr. Gruber took his revenge on the inquisitive looks that almost ripped the laces from his shoes, by finding the rates altogether too high. However, he reserved the room for two days, for his own use. Mandria was the last stop on the itinerary of his ship; after a day of rest it would set out on the return trip. He had one day, therefore, to solve his problem. It looked hopeless.

Why had Countess Zia chosen Mandria, of all places? Mr. Gruber could not know that the tinted prospectus which Zia fished out of the wastebasket while still a child had rooted a dream world and a fairyland in her heart and now, when her every dream seemed about to come true, she could not be unfaithful to Mandria. But it was not in Mr. Gruber's nature to look for reasons. That was why he was an ideal secretary. He had been given much fancier assignments in the past. Find out by six in the evening whether Hubermann played any Tschaikovsky after the first intermission of his concert in Brussels last year. Procure a narwhal tusk at least five feet long by eight o'clock Thursday morning. Buy, in your own name, the Domino Motion Picture Theater in Zurich. On Wednesday afternoon between five and six in the Café Meteor in Budapest, slap the face of a character known as Ervin Kugyec. A good secretary does not look for reasons but gets results.

What to do now, however? From the terrace of the Trattoria Marica he surveyed all of Mandria. A red-walled villa stood on the hillside. Around it was a square garden, with cypresses, magnolias, and grape arbors, all surrounded by a stone wall. Whose is that villa? It belongs to General Hasparics. How large is it? Four rooms. Is it for rent? Impossible. The retired general lives in one room, and as long ago as last year he promised to rent the other three rooms to a family for a period of six months. The family has already moved in, Gospodin Tomsics' family.

"Go and get the general at once. Tell him I'm from the former War Ministry in Vienna and have come to discuss his pension."

In less than ten minutes the general was limping toward the Trattoria Marica. He looked about sixty-five, wore civilian clothes and was trailed by his four dogs. At the rear was an overstuffed dachshund, in the van a large mutt of incredible ancestry, perhaps a combination of dachshund and St. Bernard; then there was a poodle whose sire had been a fox terrier, and a fox terrier whose dam had been a poodle. The dogs seemed to caricature the southern peoples of the sometime Monarchy as they had been swept ashore on the island

437

of Mandria: Italians, Austrians, Dalmatians, intermarried and commingled.

"—Gruber!" Introducing himself to the general, the secretary pronounced the name as if it were Hindenburg. There was fright on the general's face. Since the collapse of the Monarchy, military pensions had been in constant danger. A delicate network of veins, like photographs of lightning, was sketched in a blue that was almost black on the general's puffy red face and even on the bridge of his nose. He had a good command of German, Italian and Hungarian, speaking Hungarian with a German accent, German with an Italian accent and Italian with a Croatian accent, since Croatian was his mother tongue.

"Your pension is very small." Mr. Gruber opened the conversation.

"Well, yes, it is," General Hasparics said somewhat asthmatically.

"That can be remedied. Rent me your villa for a month."

The general did not know what to make of this unexpected turn of events.

"Unfortunately I can't do that. The villa…"

"I know. But the Tomsicses will leave."

"Have you talked to them?"

"I haven't talked to them, nor do I intend to."

"They won't leave—the devil they'll leave! They wouldn't dream of leaving."

"They'll leave," Mr. Gruber announced. "Listen to me. What did the villa cost you? I'll give you twice as much. And I only want the place for a month—from May 20th to June 20th. Then you can rent it again."

The general was deep in his own thoughts. Then he shook his head.

"The Tomsicses won't go. They're wealthy people. He's a rope manufacturer."

"They'll go!" Mr. Gruber nodded as if he knew a secret. He tapped the general's chest gently with his fist.

"A man's either a general or he's a son of a…"

Count Dupi would never have dared to address a general in such a tone of voice. Only the secretaries of the Count Dupis dare to speak like this. In this case the intimacy of the tone had no untoward consequences, since the general was in fact nothing but a lieutenant colonel. Mandrian public opinion had presented him with the rank of general, less out of consideration for Hasparics than for the prestige of the island, in order to raise the level of Mandrian society. The baker, Eligio Fanfoni, claimed to have it on good authority that Hasparics was not a lieutenant colonel either but a major, had never been to the front but limped because of rheumatism, and had built his villa out of funds filched while an officer in the Quartermaster Corps.

438

Gruber and the general had supper together. In fact, even the four dogs were the guests of Dukay hospitality. The next day Mr. Gruber wired Zia that the matter was well in hand but it would take several days to make final arrangements and he would have to wait a week for the next ship. Her telegraphed reply instructed him to stay and attend to everything. This pleased Mr. Gruber considerably, if only because he would have a week for recuperation. His duties in connection with the elaborate wedding had exhausted him utterly, although the preparations were then still in a preliminary stage. Marica knew how to make heavenly baked *orada* and *branzino,* in oil, with garlic and browned parsley. And what about cold *san-pietro* in pepper and vinegar? And *scampi,* baked over hot coals? And *brodetto,* sliced from the neck of a devilfish and served with young mussels? Monsieur Cavaignac was a great artist, true, but one cannot listen to Debussy from morning till night either, not for years at a time. Unquestionably, it is good to make an occasional change.

Two days later Mr. Gruber found that his eyes were no longer offended by the black and crimson hulks of clothing, the yellow halves of lemon, the silvery hollows of empty tin cans or the lacquered but leaky chamber pots at the bottom of the lagoon. In the late afternoon hours, moreover, when the fierce sunshine has dried out the human excrement deposited on the Piazza Vittorio Emanuele during the night, the fragrance of laurel in these parts is strong indeed, wafted down from the hills, and all Mandria bears what can be generally described as a touching air of candor. Candor, that is, so far as the world of nature and matter is concerned. The people themselves are astonishingly reckless liars, a characteristic which, however, serves to dispel the threat of boredom that attacks Mandria with greater violence than the mad North wind.

On the third day the Tomsics family began to pack, and on the morning of the fourth day they left on an especially chartered motor launch. Gesticulating heatedly, the rope manufacturer and the general continued their discussion even at the water-front. The general's gesticulations revealed his perplexity.

The motor launch had hardly putt-putted away with the unhappy Tomsics family when Mr. Gruber began to direct the re-decoration of the villa. He purchased druggist Occhipinti's entire supply of insect powder and extermination kits. He had new mosquito nettings stretched over the beds, for the old ones had holes so large that not only mosquitos but bats and even smaller eagles could have flown in and out with ease. Some pieces of furniture had to be replaced. The general's friends lent suitable replacements for a nominal consideration.

Again the general asked whether his dogs at least might not remain in the villa—because, you see, it will be difficult to board them out, the people of Mandria don't care for dogs particularly, nobody will take them in although these dogs are very engaging and obedient beasts that never utter a sound. They're as mute as fish. No, they might not stay! Although the villa was at quite a distance from the Pension Zanzottera, Mr. Gruber was unable to close his eyes all night because of the interminable four-part chorus of barking that emanated from the general's house, as if the seven plagues had struck somewhere in Dogland and the four criers wanted to broadcast the news of this dire catastrophe. Only the widow Frau Kunz was allowed to stay in the villa, a Viennese woman whom Mr. Gruber hired to keep house for the aristocratic tenants. She would run the bath, prepare breakfast, shine the shoes—a widow from Vienna would know what had to be done for a young couple on their honeymoon. Who were the aristocratic guests? After some reflection Mr. Gruber selected the name of Count Öszverfalvy. There were two reasons for this—first, because it was a name nobody in Mandria would be able to pronounce, and second, because it was customary to reduce the actual rank by one degree when choosing an incognito. Prince Ozzolini became Count Öszverfalvy. Under certain circumstances, and perhaps not without innuendo, Count Dupi used to go under the name of Baron Bullpoint.

Meanwhile the Tomsicses had arrived in Trieste. That very evening Gospodin Tomsics called on certain friends of his and communicated his suspicions. The Italians must have found out something about their secret Irridentist Society which stood for the annexation of Trieste by Jugoslavia. He suspected this was so because of the strange things that had happened to him in Mandria. There had been no trouble at all for the first two weeks. Then a monstrous stink invaded their dining room one afternoon. During the night or at dawn, he discovered, all the fish entrails that the Pescateria generally threw into the ocean had been placed under the window of that room. There was an entire mound, which began to rot in the sun as the hours went by. He called the general at once, found him similarly incensed, and together they went to complain to the podestà. Yes, but what was the name of the podestà? Felice Pascoli! A name so Italian that it fairly crackled! He received them with noticeable coolness, since the general was also Jugoslavian, and promised to take steps, but when they departed it was the opinion of General Hasparics too that the podestà would not so much as lift his little finger. He, Tomsics, had the pile of entrails carted away at his own expense. But next morning there was another pile in its place, so much larger that it must have included the lot of the previous day. Who were the hired workmen? Italians! Of course, Italians! Unfortunately it was impossible to hire any other laborers in Mandria. But that was just the beginning. Enormous rats began to infest the rooms the next evening, and Madame Tomsics found three live toads under her pillow. During the night a letter was sneaked into the foyer—it bore no text, only death's heads and exclamation marks. For two days they did not dare to eat, and subsisted on dried figs. At this point the general himself advised them to leave. It spoke for the nobility of his character that he returned three months' rent. Tomsics concluded his speech at the meeting of the secret Irridentist Society by declaring that Italian anti-Jugoslav sentiment was unquestionably strong in Mandria.

But the latent Italo-Jugoslav differences do not interest us at the moment, for if we should want to keep in mind all the frontier conflicts, Italo-French, Franco-German, German-Sudeten, German-Polish, Austro-Hungarian-Czech-Rumanian-Greek-Turkish-Bulgarian-Russian and God only knows what else, that began to trouble the sinews of Europe in the spring of 1930 like gout in damp weather, then we could not keep an eye on the painters in the Hasparics villa—where everything had to be ready before Mr. Gruber left. And it was done. By the time the next ship arrived, the general's villa was newly painted and speckless, waiting for its mysterious guests. Mr. Gruber took the general and his four dogs with him and placed them in a hotel in Fiume, lest they remain in the villa out of sheer absent-mindedness. He thought it quite natural that Occhipinti the druggist began calling him Herr Baron in the last days of his stay, and that Eligio Fanfoni even escorted him to the wharf on the day of departure and bowed low in farewell, saying: "Arrividerci, Excellence!"

It was after such preparations that Filippo and Zia sailed into the Mandrian harbor on the evening of the day after their wedding. It was Monday. Darkness was falling.

"Frau Kunz!" Zia called, following Mr. Gruber's instructions, and the Viennese widow simpered forward at once. And the company set out for the Hasparics villa, with a safari of black and almost naked Italian children carrying the luggage. There they go up the hillside, and the circular beam cast by a little flashlight is like the moon, come to earth and dancing with happiness as it leads the lovers to their nuptial bed.

Now let us leave them alone. It is not seemly even for us to disturb the young couple on their honeymoon. Nor should we follow when, leaving Mandria at the end of June, they continue into Switzerland, to the French resorts and later to Scotland. Let us leave them to themselves—in the fall we shall catch up with them in Budapest.

✝

We too must catch our breath after the ordeals of the wedding. Meanwhile there is time to look about the world a bit.

We should start with Spain. Kristina's letters from Spain inform us that the dictatorship of Primo de Rivera has ended and General Berenguer is the new Prime Minister. Kristina's latest letter tells of a sensational turn of history for which the American press associations would pay a goodly sum, but the letter strictly enjoins Countess Menti from mentioning it to a soul. The fact is that King Alfonso XIII of Spain has decided to abdicate, which means that Spain will shortly become a republic. It is easy to imagine what effect this news had on Countess Menti. The only consoling feature in Kristina's letter is the statement that Alfonso always calls her *cousine.* In view of the circumstance that Alfonso's mother was Archduchess Maria Kristina of Austria, while the Schäyenheims... in any case, there is sufficient ground for this form of address. The letter does not say how far Alfonso allowed himself to go on the basis of the relationship with Kristina. And sentences like, "When we got out of the car with the king and started for the secluded hunting lodge," or "The next morning we ate fresh strawberries for breakfast on the terrace of the lodge"—sentences like these do not explain whether they were alone or in the company of others. Kristina is already thirty-four, while Alfonso is forty-four. This alone tells us nothing, of course. Why does Alfonso want to abdicate? According to Kristina, he is of the opinion that if he does not abdicate soon he will be assassinated, for an attempt was made on his life as long ago as the day of his wedding, well before the World War, and since then the anarchists have been constantly at his heels. Communist demonstrations in Madrid these days were ominously frequent. As Kristina reported them, the king's exact words while eating strawberries on the terrace of the hunting lodge were: "Sais-tu ma chère cousine" (What's this, the familiar thou?) "do you know what it means to be king nowadays in a country with bullfighting as its national sport, where the spectators cheer only when the bull has ripped the horse's belly open until the entrails are dragging on the ground? And to be called Alfonso the Thirteenth in addition...I'd like nothing better

442

than to become a forest ranger somewhere in Canada as soon as possible."

Let us have a brief look at Budapest. It is the last day of June, and most of the theaters played their final performance tonight. Midnight is long past, and the café terraces are relatively deserted. These terraces are like sieves. By midnight the finer grain of the middle-class terrain has been strained through, has gone home to bed and by now only pebbles as large as hazelnuts or walnuts or even as large as a fist are left in the sieve, pebbles that are usually hidden underground in the daytime but are now sitting in groups of two and three, here and there on the meadow of tabletops, putting off the idea of going to bed. And they are right: the Budapest night turns even sweeter at this hour. The trolley cars have put their earsplitting screeches and squeaks to rest, as conscientious workmen do with the tools of their trade, and gentle, refreshing breezes from the Danube timidly cluster about the terraces. At such an hour the breezes seem like nude mermaids.

Four fist-sized pebbles are stuck in the sieve at one of the tables: Pognár, Paul Fogoly, Eva Kócsag and the wine merchant from Miskolc have been playing barkova. According to Paul Fogoly, this game resembled the falconry of the ancient Magyars—but he never explained the resemblance in detail. Perhaps he referred to the lightninglike and winged strokes of genius the game entailed, and the keen insight that is other and more than physical vision. The game was perfected during long Hungarian evenings in the course of these years, very much as the internationally known peach brandy of Hungary was brought to perfection in the vineyards of Kecskemét. One player left the room while the others chose a word for him to guess. If he guessed correctly within fifteen minutes, he won the twenty pengös on the table; otherwise he had to pay ten more. The odds were with the one who had to guess, and he deserved it for his complex and exhausting intellectual exertions. His rapid questions had to be answered by yes or no. The questions struck at the root of the riddle like hatchet blows, and the substance of the matter grew harder as they progressed. The search for the hidden word was a process of elimination. If it was not animal, then it could only be an object or an idea. If it was neither solid nor gaseous, then it had to be liquid. If it was not a man, then it was probably a woman. If it was neither white, nor green ... and so forth. Pognár was a famous barkovist; only a week ago he guessed the Gulf Stream in seven minutes and a crab louse took him only eight minutes. However, he foundered on the word *neighbor,* for a neighbor can be man or woman, old or young—he gave up the struggle, exhausted, after a half hour of cross-examination. The accursed problem, of course, had been set by Paul Fogoly.

"You go out, Imre," Eva said to Pognár.

Resting both hands on the table, Pognár raised his two hundred pounds from the chair.

"Do I have your artistic permission to use my absence for another purpose?"

"Go, go…" she urged. And when Pognár was gone, they put their heads together. The wine merchant suggested the term "acetic acid," which is produced when the fermentation of wine miscarries. Fogoly preferred the word *üvér*, generally known only to someone who is a linguist six times over. A white, vitreous substance, it is also called glaze and, erroneously, adobe. He painstakingly explained that the town of Vérhalom, which literally means "blood-hill," was originally named Üvérhalom, or "adobe-hill." Pognár was always bragging that he knew every word in the Hungarian language, wasn't he? But Miss Kócsag the *artiste* was ready with her own idea, and would not be shaken. She whispered it to the others. It met with a cold reception.

"He'll guess in a minute and a half," said Paul Fogoly, shaking his head. But they had to accept it, if only because the time allotted for consultation had expired and Pognár was approaching. The champion placed his ten pengös beside the wine merchant's twenty and Paul Fogoly, watch in hand, acted as starter.

Animal?—No. Vegetable?—No. Is there one on the table?—No. In Budapest?—No. In Germany?—Yes. Only one?—Yes. Larger than my finger?—No. Ugly?—Yes. Dark?—Yes. Very ugly?—Yes.

Pognár reached for the money.

"Hitler's mustache!"

Paul Fogoly threw the actress a scornful look and turned his back on her, chair and all. Eva Kócsag's close-plucked eyebrows flew up in amazement at the dizzy speed with which Pognár had solved the riddle. She had been convinced that it was insoluble. A few seconds later the wine merchant remarked, almost to himself:

"Acetic acid would have been better."

But it was a remarkable instinct of the one-track feminine mind to choose the mystery that filled the air, that was present in the imagination of every European: Hitler's mustache. Now, whether they wanted it or not, the discussion veered to politics. A newspaper that had been read into rags sprawled on one of the empty chairs, shouting the headline: "French Troops Retire From Ruhr Today."

Kócsag the *artiste* began to yawn. Political discussions invariably produced the effect of a sleeping pill in her drink.

"I wonder what Mussolini thinks of Hitler in private?" Pognár mused, half aloud.

"It's very simple," began Paul Fogoly. "Let's say you are Mussolini. And let's assume your play is a big success. A difficult assumption, but let's assume it. Now I enter—I'm Hitler. The first thing I do is to steal the basic plot of your play, rewrite it and have it produced with a much larger cast. And now comes something that will surprise you. My play is much more successful than yours. What do you say to that, Pognár-Mussolini?"

Pognár picked at a tooth with a broken match and nodded thoughtfully. The analogy, he considered, was not bad at all.

The wine merchant leaned closer to the table and declared that he had received important news from Poland. The Polish government was engaged in secret conversations with France, and the two nations had decided to launch a preventive war against Germany if Hitler were to seize power. In that case Italy would also participate in a preventive war. The Italian and German interests had never been reconcilable. But all this was *non putarem*; the September elections in Germany would wipe Hitler off the map.

The Jews in those years had a vast number of arguments, statistics and suppositions which must have been a source of consolation to them. Pognár did not take so bright a view of the Nazi activities in Germany. In connection with race theory, he began to speak of the mass instincts of men.

Someone called from the sidewalk:

"Kócsag! Are you going to rehearsal tomorrow? Because if you're not, then I won't go either."

Pognár, whose back was to the newcomer, now turned his chair to face him. His own play of that summer was in question. He shouted the answer to a query which would not have been made if the speaker had known that the playwright was present.

"She'll be at the morning rehearsal, and on time, and if you are as much as a half minute late you'll get out of the play. Scoundrel!"

As this insult was pronounced the actor Ludasi appeared on the terrace. He was an enormous figure of a man. His face dark, he stopped five steps from the table and asked threateningly:

"Was that remark addressed to me?"

Pognár pointed to the empty street:

"Do you doubt it, Romeo? Is there another scoundrel here besides you?"

The actor removed the evacuated Ruhr from the unoccupied chair and sat down. He pressed a hand to his heart, like a man who has just survived some great danger.

"You frightened me—I thought you meant someone else!"

Would it have been right to go home? To leave these fine Budapest nights half finished? The yawns disappeared from Kócsag's delicately arched lips, and the wine merchant ordered champagne.

But since the actress has already conjured up Hitler's mustache in our imagination, let us proceed to Germany and go straight to Munich, to an apartment on Maximilianstrasse where—after a hiatus of long years—we may renew our acquaintance with Dr. Otto Kliegl the tutor, together, of course, with young Count János. We no longer speak of them as teacher and pupil, for János has passed his twenty-fourth year. Now he addresses the tutor simply as Otto, and Otto calls him János rather than Your Excellency. Otto is engrossed in the writing of a book nowadays. He has dedicated the book to Adolf Hitler and given it the splendid title of "Dein Kampf." Hitler will have no possible objection to the title, for the book is full of adulation, one continuous vocative, so to speak, which is enough to give any author the right to address the familiar thou to the object of his homage. The naive readers of that book—Otto's friends and relations, principally—may be given the impression, however, that Otto was really on intimate terms with Hitler, no mean accomplishment in view of the fact that Hitler permitted only three men to use the thou of familiarity and evidently found even that number too great, for he soon dispatched one of them, Captain Roehm, to the realm of shades. "Dein Kampf" was composed of formidable profundity and thorough historical research. Only the final revisions were lacking. The book wielded the iron of logic to prove that the present catastrophic situation in Europe had been brought about by none other than Metternich, at the Congress of Vienna in 1815. In a dynamic world that was gravitating toward the principle of race supremacy, the concept of a status quo was *wie ein vereiterter Blindarm*—like an infected appendix (during the composition of the book Count János had been operated for appendicitis in a Munich sanatorium). A separate chapter was devoted to the endeavors of Austrian and Hungarian legitimists on behalf of Crown Prince Otto, and it contended that these activities were remarkably similar to a meaningless and repulsive custom observed by some patients: *den entfernten Blindarm im Spiritus aufzubewahren*—the custom of preserving the extracted appendix in alcohol.

Otto and János have become inseparable friends. Although four rooms were at their disposal in the apartment on Maximilianstrasse, including separate bedrooms, they generally slept in the same bed. It was all a result of the importance Otto attached to setting-up exercises every morning, which they performed in concert and unclothed. Later they exercised before retiring too. Otto had a handsome, white, feminine physique, albeit with a lupus the size of a hand above his left nipple, which he exposed to sun lamps, treated with unguents and dabbed with flesh-colored powder until it was practically invisible. The little toe of his left foot curled about its neighbor in a peculiar way, like a worm on a twig, and consequently his left shoes had to be built especially wide at that point. But these were the most infinitesimal of physical blemishes. One evening he unexpectedly kissed Count János on the mouth. This kiss led them into that dream world in which Otto assumed the name of Anne-Marie.

Of tutor and tutelage only this much remained, that as they strolled on the streets of Munich Otto still carried the conversation, and his tone of voice was as of old, but now it was not the artistic and historical shrines of the Bavarian city that held their interest. They crossed the beautiful Luitpold bridge without comment, and paid no heed to the statue of Count Rumford either.

They stopped in front of the former Sternecker Tavern.

"We're here," Otto said, and his hat was in his hand even before they entered. They retired to the small room at the back of the tavern, where they were the sole guests at this hour. Wearing a green apron, the single waiter placed the white steins of dark beer before them as respectfully and silently as a sexton handling the ancient Psalters in a Protestant church, for he had often seen this type of visitor. Carved, heavy chairs, some tin pitchers, several sets of deer antlers, a stuffed squirrel and a stuffed falcon decorated the room, as well as the yellowing, fly-specked, framed group photograph of one of the glee clubs of Munich. They raised their steins, looked at each other and drank.

"This is where it began," said Otto, after he had placed the beer stein on the table with utmost caution, lest he disturb the ecclesiastical silence. His reverent expression was not enhanced by the white mandarin mustache left below his nose by the thick foam of the beer, which he forgot to wipe away.

"It was in May of 1919," he continued, "when the commandant of the Second Infantry Division sent one of his men to attend a meeting of the German Workers Party and observe what went on. The soldier came, and stood beside that door."

Otto pointed toward the stuffed squirrel.

"He was unable to find a seat because there were already twenty people in the room. Gottfried Feder was lecturing. The soldier waited till the end of the long and boring lecture and then, thinking he had heard enough, was preparing to leave when the question period began and an elderly professorial gentleman with a monocle and a frock coat rose to speak. He tore Feder's analysis of the mainstream of German thought to ribbons, and countered with the surprising argument that Bavaria should secede from the German Empire. Austria would soon enter into union with her when she became an independent state. At that point the soldier asked for the floor, and told the monocle what he thought of him in no uncertain terms. When the meeting adjourned a man who looked like a laborer approached the soldier and took his name and address. Several days later the soldier received a postcard informing him that he had been accepted as a member of the German Workers Party. The soldier was amused and at the same time irritated by this method of recruiting members, but he went to the next meeting anyway, intending to announce that he did not want to belong to the party.

"Zahlen bitte schön!"

Otto paid their bill practically in the middle of a sentence and they left. He kept silent on the street. They went to Herrenstrasse and entered the Alte Rosenbad, one of the smallest and dirtiest restaurants in Munich. Again Otto ordered two beers. Then he turned to János:

"The party held its next meeting here in this restaurant. Five young men sat in the light of this old gas lamp at this very table, and one of them greeted the soldier effusively, as the newest member of the party, when he stepped through that door."

In Otto's voice, as he said all this, there was something of the tone of a Nazarene telling for perhaps the thousandth time the story of the birth of the Child, Who was born amid the beasts in a manger.

"The soldier did not make his announcement yet. He wanted to wait for the opening of the session. Herr Harrer, president of the "Imperial Federation," arrived. There were no others—just two presidents and four members. They constituted the entire party, and the soldier had come only to protest his involuntary enlistment."

Otto took a long pull at the mug of beer, and once again the white mandarin mustache remained under his nose.

"The minutes of the last meeting were read and approved. Then came the financial report. The assets of the club—they still called themselves a club at that time—were seven marks and fifty pfennigs. Five of them gave the treasurer a vote of confidence. Blushing and embarrassed, the young treasurer stood up and bowed. The soldier had still not said a word—he was merely watching and waiting. Excuse me for a minute."

Otto stood up, went to the plump proprietress and asked her where the washroom was. We are already familiar with the weakness of his *musculus constrictor vesicae.*

Left alone at the table, János gazed into his beer and wondered how Otto's mysterious soldier would fare. The young man parted his soft, bread-colored blond hair on the side, and his nose was the Schäyenheim nose, so straight that it was matched only on the statues of Polycletus, as Count Joachim once remarked. His narrow lips were taciturn, and there was a certain emptiness and coolness in his dark blue glance. He was twenty-four years old, but there was little more to know about him, for he seldom spoke.

Otto returned from the washroom, buttoning his trousers as he came, which is always a sign that an individual is extremely preoccupied with his thoughts. He sat down to his mug of beer and continued:

"Then Drexler, the presiding officer, read Herr Harrer's reply to several out-of-town communications, and these were unanimously approved. The soldier listened to the ridiculous proceedings of the club with a mixture of pity and irritation. They did not even have an official seal. When it was time to initiate him into membership, the soldier did not want to offend these well-intentioned young men, said he would think the matter over and requested a copy of their platform, which was a set of slogans typewritten on a sheet of paper. He returned to his small, bleak room in the barracks and amused himself, as he did every evening, by feeding crumbs to the mice. He liked these little beasts, for he too had experienced great misery in the course of his life. In the meantime he perused the party platform several times and came to the conclusion that the slogans were empty and meaningless. After two days of consideration he decided to join the German Workers Party and fill the void himself. He was issued temporary membership card number seven. Zahlen, bitte schön!"

While they waited for the proprietress, Otto added the following details to the history of the Alte Rosenbad:

"They distributed handwritten invitations to the next meeting among their friends, and the soldier himself accounted for eighty of these, but the result was disappointing. There were still only seven of them at the meeting. But then the membership rolls began to grow from fortnight to fortnight: twelve, thirteen, seventeen, twenty-three, thirty-four."

Otto stood up and adjusted the straps that crisscrossed his green shirt. Before leaving, János glanced about the low room once more with the look that tourists wear in limestone caverns, where the mysterious underground forces of nature have fashioned immortal statuary out of damply gleaming, burgeoning stone mushrooms.

Thus they proceeded to the cellar of the Hof bräuhaus, as they had once toured Paris, when Otto stood beneath a window in the Rue Rivoli and explained which room had witnessed the assassination of Admiral Colligny on St. Bartholomew's Eve in 1572. Then, as now, his facts were reliable, with the difference that the data committed to memory out of the *Guide Bleu* were forgotten the next day, while these particulars sprang from source material which had gone into the preparation of "Dein Kampf" and was deeply engraved, in capital letters, on Otto's heart.

In the cellar of the Hofbräuhaus he recounted the meeting which was attended by a hundred and eleven people. The soldier made his first public speech on that occasion, in the fall of 1919. His appeal for funds produced a total of three hundred marks from the enthusiastic audience.

They proceeded to the cellar of the Eberlbräu. The natives of Munich stared at the two green-shirted individuals, but some of them already knew that the green shirt was the uniform of the Hungarian Nazis, whose symbols were an arrow and a cross.

"There was an attendance of one hundred and thirty at the meeting in October. Two weeks later, here in the same place, there were one hundred and seventy in the audience!"

They continued to the Deutsches Reich. This was a larger establishment.

"The first meeting here attracted two hundred and three people, and the second drew a crowd of two hundred and seventy!"

Otto's voice grew increasingly shrill as he pronounced these figures. They continued their tour.

"On February 24th, 1920, the first mass meeting of the new movement was held in this hall. Two thousand people attended, beer mugs flew through the air, bloody fistfights interrupted the speeches and revolvers were fired at the platform. But the forty-five young men whom the party had delegated to maintain order fought like maddened wolves and finally expelled several hundred of the opposition from the hall."

Only the stadium remained to be inspected, where five thousand six hundred persons thronged the shell-shaped stands several months later. The soldier had doffed the worn, bluish-gray uniform of a noncommissioned officer in the Second Infantry Division, and was now the Führer, standing on the platform in a brown shirt over which he wore a Sam Browne belt and an armband. Enormous swastikas decked the platform, banners which were based on the design of a dentist from Starnberg. The dentist had drawn a swastika on a field of white, with bent tips, like the hooks of the pliers he used in pulling teeth. The original design was elaborated by the Führer himself, who was a skilled draftsman. They discussed the choice of colors for weeks. Black, black and red, black-red-gold, white and black, white and blue...and finally the Führer made the decision: the ground was to be red, a color which excited the masses. The white field symbolized German nationalism, while the black swastika represented the supremacy of the Aryan race, and the red ground stood for Socialism. According to the Führer, this served to attract the mass of German Socialists into the Party, but did not prevent Rosenberg, the first Party publicist, from labeling even Socrates as a dirty Socialist.

In the course of the next few days, Otto addressed a respectful application to Party Headquarters, which contained the request of Otto Kliegl and Count János Dukay of Hemlice and Duka for an audience with the Führer.

The application went unanswered for two weeks. Their second application met a similar fate. Otto imagined that the Party leaders did not think it worthwhile to pass the request on to the Führer— evidently the name of Dukay did not elicit the desired effect. Foreign politicians, particularly from the southeastern nations of Europe, were already storming for appointments with the Führer in those days. Most of them were possessed of immoderate but unsuccessful political ambitions, and wanted to beat their local opposition to death with the flagstaff of the swastika. In relation to the future of Europe, the Führer was the artillery barrage which precedes an attack. It was not easy to gain access to him.

Otto's third application was couched in more dignified and somewhat offended terms. He did not emphasize the Dukay name this time, rather the fact that as representatives of the Arrow Party of Hungary, which entertained ideals similar to those of National Socialism, they sought to deliver the thousand-year-old Hungarian nation into the Führer's camp, a nation the military prowess of which was historically demonstrable to be beyond question. Although Otto brought no such commission from Hungary, and the Arrow Party in turn had scarcely more than seven members at that time, the Party leaders in Munich looked with more favor on this application and submitted it to the Führer, and a few days later they were notified that an appointment had been arranged for five minutes after four on Thursday afternoon. The audience would last ten minutes.

"Ten minutes!" Otto waved his hand. "Once I get inside it will last an hour and a half!"

Tactfully, apologetically he informed Count János that they would have to sleep in separate rooms for a few days, since he intended to work at night. He made elaborate preparation for his statement to Hitler. Through the door Count János occasionally heard loud and heated declamations that sounded like an actor rehearsing his part.

On Thursday morning they summoned a barber, had their hair cut, were manicured and pedicured, and twice Otto returned his boots to Joseph the footman because they were not well enough polished.

At Party Headquarters armed guards wearing the insignia of the *Sturm Abteilung* demanded to see their passes. In the anteroom they took his briefcase away from Otto and inspected its contents. They smiled oddly at the sight of the title, "Dein Kampf," on the front cover of the typed manuscript, but they returned the briefcase. The two of them were led into a waiting-room.

Since they have fully an hour and a half to wait, let us leave them for a while. It is time for us, in any case, to dip into the past briefly.

It is the spring of 1906 and we are in Vienna, in the garden of the Dukay palace on Bösendorferstrasse. The events of the outer world leave this garden untouched. Who is interested in the Algeciras Conference? Who even remembers it any more? It was on this day, on April 7th, however, that the conference drew to a close. Belgium, France, Germany, England, Holland, Italy, Portugal, Russia, Sweden, the United States and the Austro-Hungarian Monarchy were represented. This was the conference where it first became clear that Germany had only a single friend in the world: the Monarchy. The other delegations were antagonized by the German manner of conducting a discussion. We should know something else about the international scene of the time, namely, that the tsarist government in Russia was carrying out mass executions in an effort to quell conspiracies and demonstrations. Otherwise Europe snoozed quietly in the arms of Peace and Tranquility.

There comes Countess Menti down the semicircular steps which curve into the garden. She is only thirty-one years old right now. Of her five children, János and Zia are not yet born, but János is already on the way. This is quite clearly revealed by the shape of the countess's figure, for she is in the seventh month of her pregnancy. From one of the upstairs windows come the sounds of a piano lesson: Kristina, ten years old, is practicing scales with her teacher. There is indignation on the countess's face. For days now two laborers have been at work in the garden, for Countess Menti herself drew the plan for the flower beds, and she insists on having her favorite flowers bloom on time. She has exhorted the workers to finish their task as soon as possible, since it is already a little late. The elder is busily at work, but the younger has retired to the end of the garden for a rest more than once. Right now he has been sitting on a rock for a whole hour. He thinks nobody notices him, but he does not know that the countess has been watching them from a window all day. Now he is in for it! The countess picks her way through the half-spaded flower beds toward the workman with a noisy rustle of skirts. The indolent workman has seen the approaching countess but does not stand, does not move, just sits there with his elbows on his knees. The indignant countess stops in front of him, but before she can say a word she notices that the grass at the workman's feet is bloodstained, obviously a sign that he has been vomiting blood.

"Sind Sie krank?"

"Ja."

"Tuberkulose?"

"Ja."

The young laborer seems still a child. His brown hair hangs over his forehead. His mustache has hardly begun to grow.

"Ah, mein Gott!"

The silk skirt rustles back to the palace, carrying the enormous belly cleverly concealed beneath the ample cut of an outer coat. She summons Mr. Gruber, whose figure is still dapper, his hair abundant. He wears a winged collar so high

453

that it would be the envy of a giraffe. And Mr. Gruber summons the young workman into his office.

"How old are you?"

"Seventeen."

He writes the address of a Viennese physician on a sheet of paper and directs the workman to visit the physician, who will give him a free examination and free counsel. At the same time he gives the workman two hundred crowns, a present from the countess.

We shall not pursue the story any further, partly because the rest is uninteresting and partly because the Führer's door is opening and a blue-shirted, cross-belted character has stepped out. Otto and Count János enter. The room is furnished with a matched suite of brown leather, a couch and two armchairs. The Führer was seated on the middle of the couch and he comes to his feet but does not advance to meet his guests. The first impression: his hair and mustache are brown, whereas they have seemed black on photographs. There are round pouches of equal size under his eyes. His hands are of the sort people call artistic—they look as if they would be at home on a piano or were accustomed to modeling in clay. The veins stand out like cords on the back of his hand and even at the tips of his fingers. His hair is clipped short at the back, and thus the bare skin gleams forth behind his ears and on the nape of his neck.

"Setzen Sie sich," the hoarse, deep voice says after introductions and handshakings are over—the voice that was already so familiar and so much at home in the apartments of every radio listener in the world. There are two other men in the room, both in brown shirts with Sam Browne belts and swastika armbands, their napes close-trimmed and their faces marked with the scars of Prussian school days. But they do not sit down; boots apart and hands clenched at the back, they stand behind the leather couch. An entire hour-and-a-half long oration is on the tip of Otto's tongue. And he proved to be right—the conference actually lasted one and a half hours, but the difference was that he got no further than a timid *bitt'schön* or two. The hoarse deep voice spoke continuously for the hour and a half, growing fiery from time to time, and the fist, which seemed to be bound in vein-strands, beat the table rhythmically. He began with the causes of national collapse, shifted to the international policies of the Party, scolded the Viennese for their racial impurity, which was the source of all corruption, discussed the false face of federalism, the problems of propaganda and organization, and found time to fling a *brave Soldaten* at the Hungarians while he considered the German policies of alliance and eastward expansion. There was room for a humorous observation now and again, which rightly called for laughter, and at such times the two figures behind the couch broke into a loud and resounding ha-ha-ha, like two synchronized laughing-machines. The Führer smiled too, a smile which completely distorted his features. His jaws opened like rubber, his large chin receded and the look on his face became the look of a good natured and delightful shark. The Führer's oratory was rhapsodical. His childhood years were mixed in with the subject of alliances, and the Jewish problem with Viennese dynasties. He said things like this:

"My father wanted me to become a civil servant. When I told him I wanted to be a painter he said I was crazy!"

"Ha-ha-ha," laughed the two attendants.

As for the Jewish problem:

"Physical cleanliness is alien to the Jews. Unfortunately this is apparent even when our eyes are closed!"

"Ha-ha-ha," said the laughing-machines, and Otto wriggled on his chair as if someone were tickling him.

An hour and a half later the Führer stood up. He turned to Count János:

"Which Dukay's son are you, Herr Graf?"

"István Dukay's."

"Do you own a palace in Vienna, on Bösendorferstrasse?"

"We still have it."

"Is your mother alive?"

"Yes."

"In good health?"

"Yes."

For a moment the Führer stared down at the carpet. He was thinking of the few days he had spent as a day-worker in the garden at the age of seventeen. Otto had been wrong. It was not the offer to sell Hungary that had made the interview possible, for the Hungary that boasted of a thousand years of military prowess had already been offered up for sale on a more substantial basis and in a more reliable manner by politicians who bore Magyarized names. In this case it was the name of Dukay that struck the Führer, and he was the only one who would ever know why, since Mr. Gruber had not asked the young tubercular workman his name. The Führer extended his hand to Count János and said:

"Remember me to your mother."

Otto's trembling fingers were fumbling in his briefcase. He produced a photograph of the Führer and asked him, amid stutters and blushes, to write a dedication. The Führer drew his eyebrows together and his mustache seemed to grow smaller:

"Ich bin keine Schauspielerin! I'm no actress!"

The refusal was almost rude, and so it seemed out of the question for Otto to read excerpts of *Dein Kampf* aloud. The two brown-shirted figures started for the door and almost swept the visitors with them. They were smiling at the word *Schauspielerin,* and a silver tooth appeared below the mustache of the shorter one as he opened his mouth. The mustache was trimmed exactly like the Führers, and its coloring ranged from whey to vermilion.

Otto and Count János walked along the street mutely for a long time, side by side. There was a reason for their silence. Otto was hurt by the rebuff he had received, and the fact that he had not managed to get a word in edgewise made him ridiculous in the eyes of János. He brushed a speck from his green shirt while walking, and said only:

"Never mind! Wait till *Dein Kampf* is published!"

János was wondering how best to convey the greeting to his mother, for Countess Menti was certain to object pointedly.

But let us leave the two green-shirted figures as they hasten along Maximilianstrasse—let us return to Hungary.

Zia and Filippo arrived at the end of September.

The house on Fuga Utca was warm and waiting, like the motor of an automobile. This is as much as to say that the freshly painted windows opened easily, the flower beds were already thickly furred with blossoms and the house had lost the rawness that is like the feel of new and as yet unlaundered shirts. The staff had been in the villa since May: the doorman, the chauffeur, the cook, the valet and Elizabeth the chambermaid, who had been in Paris with the Dukays. The entire staff had been recruited from the Dukay fold, so carefully chosen by Countess Menti and the One-Eyed Regent that none of them but came from a family which had served the Dukays for three generations. They were like the furnishings that had been selected, under similarly careful scrutiny, from camphor-sprinkled storage rooms in the attics of the Dukay mansions.

While they were still engaged Filippo and Zia had drawn detailed plans for the furnishing of each and every room. Filippo was indubitably the more inventive and resourceful at interior decoration, although Zia came a close second. Hungarian aristocracy possessed those simple secrets of taste which the wealthier middle classes were unable to make their own. As long ago as Christmastime Filippo had spent exhaustive hours poring over the blueprints with the architect. Despite Mr. Stendhall's raised eyebrows and dismay, he had the stucco ornamentation removed from the forehead of the villa, drew his pencil through the cement urns on the pillars of the gate and transfused the whole outward appearance of the house with the noble simplicity of his own taste. The Italians are masters of this art. In Beatrice's time, too, they were the ones who brought beautiful little palaces to Buda on the decks of their iron galleys.

Filippo and Zia arrived, as honeymooners usually do, without fanfare. Her parents and friends scrutinized Zia as if she were a patient just discharged from a sanatorium after a serious operation; as a matter of fact, the beginnings of marriage are indeed something like that. This has to do with change of climate, change of blood, the curative or poisonous effect of strange words and foreign phrases. Her family and friends were reassured: Zia seemed happy.

Not only the villa on Fuga Utca awaited Filippo, however, but the modern offices of Lucello Italiano as well, in midtown, with concave show-windows, neon lettering, circular green divans for the comfort of customers and convex booths enclosed in thick glass, above which glass placards hanging from silk ribands identified the information counter, the ticket window and the baggage department. The placard over a tobacco-colored curtain to the left bore the words: *Presidente, President,* and *Elnök,* which—of course—is Hungarian for president. Naturally, the president was Filippo. During the past four months, with untiring industry, the six employees of the firm had exhausted the entire stock of novels, from Walter Scott down, in the near-by lending library, for they had no work to do. The firm, financed by Count Dupi as principal stockholder, had run no risk of airplane crashes so far, for its fleet of passenger planes consisted of nothing more than the propellor in the front window. But this was not so important as the fact that the employees received their salaries punctually on the first of each month. The president himself had set the presidential salary, which was so generous that the bureau of internal revenue might well have attributed the ever-increasing hum of motors in the sky over Budapest to the activities of Lucello Italiano. But we must not suppose that the pistache-colored leather divan was entirely unfrequented. Every forenoon saw the appearance of Count Sigi, who claimed to have a formidable terror of air travel and braced his courage at each visit by consuming a half bottle of the French cognac that was dispensed at the baggage department. Whoever approached the ticket window and asked for passage to Bombay was served with excellent coffee, freshly roasted, while the information counter provided *vol-au-vent*. The doorman, dressed in a slate-blue uniform with *Lucello Italiano* embroidered on his cap, constantly flitted between the office and the neighboring Gerbeaud. He was the only one in the firm to fly a number of miles each day. Lucello Italiano became the meeting place of aristocratic society; Count Charles the lion hunter appeared at the counter almost every day to inquire when the first flight to Alaska would be scheduled, because he wanted to hunt grizzly bears; and Count Henrik the gambler came; and Baroness René; and even Prince Andrew, when he learned that the delicacies consumed at the counters of Lucello Italiano were free. Thus we can hardly be surprised that the first semiannual statement failed to show a profit. But a firm cannot be expected to show a profit at the very start. Count Dupi understood this quite well at his occasional business conferences with Filippo.

It was now 1931. What sort of a life did a young married couple lead in Europe?—if we may refer to Fuga Utca as Europe; and why not?—since the villa is occupied by an Ozzolini prince and a Dukay countess who are linked to all of Europe by a network of friends and relations. The network even encompasses the United States. Their bathroom is the same as the bathrooms in castles along the Loire, and their footmen move with the same formality as footmen in the castles of Scotland.

We shall start with breakfast. They awoke at ten, which is understandable when we consider that they rarely went to bed before two in the morning. In answer to the sleepy ring of a bell, the chambermaid and the valet brought the breakfasts of their master and mistress on those little collapsible trays which can be rested on the bed for the convenience and comfort of its occupants. Tea, toast, ham, boiled eggs, butter, jam and grapefruit—in those days grapefruit was inexpensive and available at the most modest fruit stores in Buda. In the way in which the tray was set—the quilted tea cozy that preserved the warmth of the silver teapot, the little slip covers that kept the eggs warm, the shape of the rosy slices of ham—in all this there were nuances of taste, but they are relatively unimportant at the moment.

Somewhat headachy and with rings under their eyes, they played a set of tennis on their own court after breakfasting and bathing, and then they discussed their plans for the day. By this time it was almost noon. Filippo sprang into the little yellow car (Count Lajos's wedding gift to Zia) and headed toward his presidential duties in the office where clients were impatiently awaiting him. Zia stayed at home, wrote letters, worked in her darkroom or went on the solitary walks of which she was so fond. At two o'clock they met for the midday meal, which of course bore no resemblance to the usual stomach-filling Hungarian dinner with its white tablecloths, napkins tied in rabbit's-ears around the neck, hot soups, greasy pork chops, heavy vegetables and boiled noodles for dessert. Following the foreign example, they ate a light lunch which was more a token meal than anything else. Afterward Filippo adjourned to a low-slung armchair, settled into the adjustable back and rested in a half-sleep for thirty minutes or so. Even now the corner of his mouth would not relinquish its grip on the ebony holder which glittered with tiny diamonds. Zia's efforts to break him of this habit had come to nothing. Zia regularly settled on the floor at Filippo's feet, resting her arms on his knees where they were like bathers atop an inflated rubber mattress on the gentle, motionless waves of the sea. The sleepy wheat-blond head nestled in Filippo's lap, her face near the region of his heart and often lower. The even breathing sent its mysterious warmth through the cloth to the masculine skin, and the feminine fingers often chanced to settle at a place where a young husband's flesh is most sensitive. These siestas usually ended in a daytime sequel to their nocturnal connubiality, for the Lombardy sunshine had blessed Filippo with incredible potency.

Cocktail parties occupied the afternoon hours, parties which were as alike as the mailboxes posted throughout the city, whether they took place in the vaulted palaces of Buda, in foreign embassies or in the neighborhood of fashionable Museum Utca. Concert, opera or theater in the evening; then to supper in a private home, with *scampi* already a little rank though flown in by plane, smoked trout from Jugoslavia, or grouse dripping with *haut goût* flown in baskets from the north of England. Or they had supper in one of two or three exclusive restaurants where the waiters could be counted on to know that Princess Marie drank cold water and abhorred mineral water, that Baron Adam did not like salt on his dilled lobster and that Count Joachim's Henry IV beard demanded *padlizsán* cooked according to the recipe that he had brought from Constantinople. The gypsies made secret note of everyone's favorite tune, lists which referred back over decades and were always on hand under the cimbalom, so that a mere glance enabled the primás to surprise Baron Adam by remembering his favorite song after a period of twelve years. One's eyes fill with tears at such a moment, when the fiddle begins the melancholy sweetness of "Cserebogár, Sárga Cserebogár"—it is a moment fraught with the mystery of unassuming fidelity, the most beautiful moment in the whole cruel world. An elderly lady dressed like the wife of a provincial mayor reigns over the adjacent powder room, amply supplied with handkerchief-sized cloth towels because she knows that certain of the guests prefer these to paper. After supper one had to spend "just a half hour" at the Blind Mouse, or the Monterey Bar, or perhaps at the Andalusia Club, where Zia could see Adelbert once again, Uncle Paul's little elephant of yore, only slightly grown and coated with gold paint from top to toe, with Señora Lidanda (known as Rose Liebschutz after working hours) of the flowing Lorelei tresses on his back, reciting the latest lyric composition of Erno Hiplic in a ringing voice for the benefit of blind drunk, glass-eating Levantine horse traders and for the money-changers who look like diplomats and wear, with their soft silk shirts, diamond studs and golden-slippered inviting mistresses—the daughters of retired generals or of Rákoscsaba shoemakers.

Sundays served to relieve the weekday monotony. Mass in the morning, then golf on the Svábhegy, or perhaps an all-day drive into the country, or a hunt, depending on the weather. There was occasionally time to read one or two of the shorter books, but the most determined act of will did not account for more than the opening chapters of Romain Rolland's *Jean Christophe* or Galsworthy's *Forsyte Saga.* They did, however, frequent Princess Karola's literary salon.

Princess Karola's literary salon did not lack for variety. Here one could meet the more notable writers, actors and creative artists, who seemed like unsuccessful imitations of aristocrats on the silken couches; but their range of conversation was like a limitless plain on which, like galloping horsemen, they took up the pursuit of *The Bridge of San Luis Rey* or of Golvonsky's latest concert or of any other quarry that leaped out of the bush at the instigation of the hostess. These intellectuals had an inexhaustible store of anecdotes of the theater or the literary world, stories which were considered wet gunpowder in their clubs decades ago but could still be counted on to explode in Princess Karola's salon. The salon was a meeting place of the lustrous lights of intellect, and an invitation conferred a special rank on its recipient, like membership in some secret academy, but from time to time someone like Erno Hiplic turned up too, to offend the habitués by his mere presence. His invitation was based on the rumor—which reached Princess Karola before anyone else—that one of the theaters had allegedly accepted his first libretto. Hiplic hastened to accost Count Joachim with a brotherly thou, and his second sentence was the declaration that he did not consider Bernard Shaw to be a writer. Occasionally and exceptionally the really great also put in an appearance, at the repeated insistence of telephone calls and telegrams in which Princess Karola threatened to take umbrage if they did not show up. They appeared, so to speak, under threat of prosecution. These rare beasts looked sad, as if they had lost their last illusion, and—already bundled in the taciturnity of their own statues—they seemed to be gazing back from another world. They often wore brown shoes with their unpadded tuxedos. These were the paths Zia and Filippo followed, somewhat monotonously, like the pendulum of a clock swinging in its established pattern. They celebrated their first wedding anniversary by staying quietly at home. But the next day it started all over again and continued.

✜

One afternoon in September Ferenc telephoned to ask whether they wanted to go to the theater. He and his wife had a box. What was playing? Oh—they'd forgotten to notice. It was an opening night, at any rate. Fourth, left, parterre. Ferenc had married Vira, the bronze-red beauty who was ten years his junior and had been Zia's maid of honor. The two young couples were almost like Count Dupi's famous four-in-hand team, so regularly did they venture into the Budapest night together.

Like a dutiful wife, Zia undertook to translate the play for Filippo as it progressed. But she made the mistake common to many a whispering interpreter in the boxes. Her rendering went like this: "Now a woman in a green dress comes in…now she pulls out a revolver and fires at the man…" Only infrequently did she spare a phrase or two for the dialogue: "The woman says that yesterday…" But she was unable to divulge what the woman had said, because the dialogue sped on and occupied her whole attention although she had already missed some of it. It kept her at a constant pitch of excitement, and occasionally she translated only such scraps: "Tomorrow afternoon…You, too?…Must be thwarted…No, must not be thwarted…Uh, thing, how do you say it?…" She bent her head and stabbed the forefinger of her right hand at the middle of her temple, but the right word did not come to mind. Meanwhile the dialogue on the stage had raced ahead, like the favorite at a horse race after his closest rival has loomed alongside. Zia could not possibly catch up with the sense and the story.

The first act ended amid applause. Count Ferenc began a discussion of the way opening nights are conducted in various countries, maintaining that the character of the various peoples was reflected in these differences. According to the tradition of the Comédie Française, the playwright's name does not even appear on the program. At the end of the performance the leading man steps forward, takes his wig off and says: "Mesdames et messieurs, the play we have just performed was written by Monsieur So-and-so." The audience may clap or whistle, but the playwright remains unseen. Of course the whole town knew months ago who it was that wrote the play, but the theater has preserved this fine old tradition of anonymity just as it has preserved the peculiar series of thumps which indicates that the performance is about to begin in a French theater. French actors take curtain calls between acts. The English do not. The applause rings out after each act, but the actors do not come forth to thank the audience until the play is over. An English playwright is present at the performance but does not go out on the stage. If his work is a great success, he acknowledges the applause with a short speech from his box. In New York the playwright's name appears on the program, but the playwright himself does not take curtain calls or make his presence known from a box. This, maintained Count Ferenc, was the right way. Other customs obtain in Vienna and Germany. They drag the playwright before the curtain after each act, and the audience views the unfortunate corpse with terror—because the playwright is, indeed, greener and grayer than a corpse. There are two reasons for this. First, the playwright is pale with excitement and anxiety. Second and more important, the actors who drag him forth are painted all shades of dark brown and mauve, so that the playwright, even if he happens not to be filled with anxiety, looks like a fly in a milk bucket beside them. Experienced playwrights remedy this difficulty by putting make-up on too. Backstage the playwright pretends that only the ultimate exertion of strength will make him yield when the time comes for him to be dragged from the wings by his arm, but in the great excitement he often forgets himself for a moment and shouts, stamping his feet: "Come and get me, for heaven's sake!" It is said that the composers of Viennese operettas popularized this struggle of might and main before the curtain, but on the Hungarian stage too, a whole circus takes place between acts. First comes the entire cast. Then a mere two-thirds of the cast. Then half. Then the two stars. Then the supporting players. Then each star alone. Then the playwright and the two-thirds cast, followed by the playwright with half the cast. Playwright and the leading lady together. Playwright and the two stars separately. Finally the playwright alone. With stop watch and notebook in hand, the manager stands by the curtain and keeps an official record of the number of curtain calls after the first act: how many for the company, how many for two-thirds, how many for half the company, how many for the stars and how many for the playwright. The curtain ringer works as feverishly as a hook-and-ladder company at one of the larger fires to contain the conflagration that has broken out in the audience. Up, down, up, down—the curtain behaves like an enormous pump that inhales the frenzy of the audience with one stroke and, by way of grateful compensation, expels the bowing actors and the playwright with the next. In the meantime the drapes of the curtain create a strong wind which blows an accumulation of dust from the stage into the near-by boxes and stalls, into the evening dresses and the coiffures of ladies fresh from the hairdresser. Vira asked Filippo whether Italian actors took curtain calls between acts. The empty ebony holder replied that between acts Italian actors turned cartwheels in front of the curtain.

"Author! Author!"

His two hundred pounds stuffed into an outgrown dinner jacket, Pognár now makes his third solitary appearance before the curtain. He is deathly pale, but we already know the reasons for his pallor. His wavy, dark hair is like a rich wreath above his white forehead. The curtain behind him pumps frantically. Then a dreadful thing happens. The playwright who stood before the curtain with abundant hair a moment ago is now as bald as a melon, because a tip of the descending curtain came close to his head and flipped his toupee off like a whip, with a winglike sweep, and the toupee flies away as if it were a great bat. Where does it fly? Into the box of the archduke. Fortunately the audience hardly notices any of this, for Pognár suddenly covers his billiard-ball dome with two hands and disappears behind the curtain. He runs to the curtain ringer and gnashes his teeth: "—villain! where did you put my hair?" He would willingly slap the face of the curtain ringer, but both hands are pressed to his skull and he does not dare take them away. The curtain ringer still has no idea what is going on. Meanwhile the stage manager has dashed up into the royal box and goes on hands and knees to fish the toupee forth from between the chairs, at the same time answering Archduke Richensa's queries with the statement that the overwrought playwright has cast his toupee at the feet of His Highness as a mark of homage.

Other kinds of excitement are under way along the corridors backstage. Stagehands, reporters, relatives, photographers and wardrobe mistresses dash about and collide. The tailor has still not delivered the dress of one of the actresses who will appear in the second act. The actress stands in the middle of the dressing room and shrieks at the top of her lungs; she would tear her hair too, but cannot do so because her mother is holding one arm and her fiancé the other, lest she go quite mad. In the meantime the curtain has pumped all the applause out of the audience, and the playgoers retire to smoke cigarettes, and only the lovelorn students in the third balcony are still shouting: "—Kócsag! Kócsag!"

But the curtain has come to rest. Kócsag the *artiste,* wearing a green gown, goes out before the curtain no more; but she is standing behind the curtain at the peephole. She alone knows whom she seeks in the audience. At most we can merely surmise that it is not the wine merchant from Miskolc. Meanwhile the hairdresser has glued Pognár's flying toupee together, Pognár, with an exhausted look on his face, is receiving his friends, who offer either mute handshakes or voluble outpourings from which it is hard to know precisely what they mean to say. "Imre, old man! You've never in your life written anything like this!" Such a sentence fails to indicate whether they mean anything as good or anything as bad. As for the silent handclasps, they might well be a form of consolation, something like "It's all right, you'll write a better play some day." But Pognár's spirit, somehow, is still soaring in uncertain clouds of hope. A myriad problems and tasks are burning in his brain like fiery steel. There are final instructions for the actors, the lighting technicians, the scene shifters (don't put the piano too close to the armchair again), but his strength has given out. If the Viennese producer in the audience takes an option on the play, he thinks, and if the play becomes a world-wide success, then he'll be able to buy that villa on Sashegy and, despite everything, he'll marry Eva Kócsag. This inner reverie brings tears to his eyes. Suddenly leaping up and bowling all the well-wishers over, he darts to the community dressing room on the second floor and screams at an actor in the livery of a footman who, with the calm resignation of all bit players, is reading a detective story: "You moron, you said Councilor Reznovsky again! It's Greznovsky, Grez-nov-sky, you idiot!" And he hurtles toward another dressing room.

In the meantime Pognár's widowed sister, in the role of spy and eavesdropper as always, is mingling with the audience out front and listening to their remarks. She cannot understand how, after such a thrilling first act, people can discuss tomorrow's picnic, the resignation of the Minister of Public Welfare or the importation of textiles. Disguised in the obscurity of her own identity, however, she manages to overhear some phrases of the conversation between several agents and the Viennese producer, all of whom, in a group apart, are already weighing the possible Hollywood sale. One of them remarks:

"The first act is excellent."

"That's the trouble!" replies a horn-rimmed eyeglass. "Hungarian authors have not learned the French secret of play-writing, which is to write a wonderful third act, a mediocre second and a dreadful first."

The second act is about to begin. Filippo returns to his seat as if it were a dentist's chair, and Zia resumes her role of interpreter. The audience is not yet aware of the impending catastrophe on the stage: in the heat of excitement one of the stagehands has forgotten to remove the folding ladder from which he was repairing the chandelier. The actors, as they enter, are surprised to encounter this new if silent member of the cast. It prevents them from moving about properly, for every step has been carefully charted. Pognár is in the wings, his face buried in his hands, his forehead pressed against the wall. All is lost! Conferring in whispered agitation, the stage manager and the director are trying to cook up some lightning-stroke of genius that will whisk the ladder off the stage, for it is stuck in the play's throat like a tremendous and potentially fatal fishbone. The actor Ludasi unexpectedly saves the situation. Dressed in a dinner jacket and holding a top hat in his hand, he is supposed to address the following lines to his wife:

"Good-bye, dear, I've got to hurry away to a conference with the Secretary of State."

He says, instead:

"Good-bye, dear, I've got to hurry along to a conference with the Secretary of State—he's a very high personage, you know."

And he exits with the ladder on his shoulder.

A hurricane of laughter and great applause from the audience. Baroness René's silvery trill resounds from a box on the right. Count Ferenc and Vira come to Zia's assistance, and when Filippo finally understands that a Hungarian Secretary of State is an exalted personage who cannot be reached except by means of a ladder, he breaks into a whinnying guffaw also. The Regent's rigid countenance is gradually softened by a smile, and he too joins in the clapping, but only as if he were demonstrating the art of applause in slow motion. The clapping of his hands has a precise echo in the archduke's box across the way. Someone remarks that this was the first witty stroke so far in the play. Jaundiced wolves of the theater nod at each other in appreciation. Hearing the waves of applause, Pognár presses his forehead even closer to the wall—as he will do again, years later, during the bombings—for he supposes the final catastrophe has come. The truth is that the ladder scene has bridged the gap of dullness in the first half of the second act. Then he too learns what happened, and abandons his secret resolve to shoot the miscreant stagehand after the performance. But he still shouts at Ludasi, whom the producer and the others are lionizing in the wings: "What do you mean by improvising in my play?" When the act is over the circus begins again, with the difference that this time Pognár, as he takes his bows, holds the toupee on his head with the middle finger of his right hand. It looks as if he were saluting the audience. He thinks nobody notices this gesture.

The four-in-hand escaped before the beginning of the third act. They went to the usual place for supper, that excellent little midtown restaurant where the gypsy looked into his secret book as they entered and began playing the favorite tunes of Count Ferenc, Zia and Vira, one after the other. He knew that Count Ferenc's favorite was the English song which began "Tomorrow evening…" Almost every table was occupied by their acquaintances—but not with their spouses, generally. Princess Marie sat with a tall, bony-handed individual in dinner jacket, and they were conversing in French. Elizabeth sat with an unknown man in a tuxedo, and Count Charles the lion hunter with a well known actress. Princess Karola was accompanied by her entire literary retinue. At a lonely little table by the wall sat two representatives of marital fidelity, Count Peter and his wife Margaret, who was known as Red Cross Margie because of her activities in connection with that organization. After midnight—it was almost one o'clock, in fact—Count Ferenc made his usual suggestion:

"Let's go down to the Blind Mouse for a little while."

The little yellow sedan obediently trailed in the wake of Count Ferenc's dark blue roadster.

Sigi was already at the Blind Mouse, blind drunk and in the middle of a speech. When he sighted Filippo he launched into a discussion of the importance of Italo-Hungarian amity. His speech was necessarily fragmentary because, out of deference to the distinguished ladies present in the night club, he pronounced improper words in a voice so low that it was audible only to the members of his party, but they had ample reason to rock with laughter. And he had to cut his speech in half when an adagio team began its act on the dance floor.

Another party arrived at two in the morning: Pognár, Paul Fogoly, Ludasi (the hero of the ladder scene), and Eva Kócsag, at whose side the place of the wine merchant from Miskolc was occupied by a police officer. Pognár and Paul Fogoly greeted Count Ferenc with a casual, "Hello, Ferenc!"—a greeting which we mention only because it would have been inconceivable a hundred years ago. In his letters to the Count de Keszthely, both the vast body and the equally vast spirit of the writer Daniel Berzsenyi writhed in repulsive self-abasement. The theatrical party was given a place alongside Zia's table, and conversation flowed between the two groups. Vira and Zia had met Pognár and Paul Fogoly briefly at Princess Karola's salon, but of course they had forgotten the names of the writers. The writers, on the other hand, were completely aware of the countesses' names. The police officer also looked familiar to Zia. The ladies had not met Kócsag the *artiste* before. After the second bottle of champagne Count Ferenc called out, "Let's push 'em together," which was his invitation to push the two tables together. This was done, and the two parties merged into one. As the introductions were being made Eva Kócsag, who knew that Filippo did not speak Hungarian, offered him her hand and said:

"Good-bye!"

Her knowledge of languages was weak, but she wanted to show that she knew the right thing to say. Only in German was she fluent enough to make herself understood by foreigners. The police officer turned to Zia:

"Perhaps you don't remember me, Princess. I was on duty at the airfield when you were waiting for your fiancé."

The two groups soon warmed to each other. The only trouble was that Pognár, surmising that the "push 'em together" was coming, had warned Eva against making her usual smutty remarks before the countesses, who were very sensitive. Consequently Eva assumed the tone and gestures of Lady Windermere, a role she had played on the stage last season. The countesses did not know very much about the actress, who had only recently come into the limelight and was still considered somewhat second-rate. But Count Ferenc was not sparing of praise for her performance that evening. Pognár particularly wanted to know what they thought of the third act. His question rather benumbed the two aristocratic couples, but Count Ferenc's presence of mind came to the rescue:

"I was completely charmed. The last scene between the man and the woman was positively formidable."

He thought it safe to suppose that every play must have a final scene between the leading lady and the leading man. Pognár nodded thoughtfully.

"How did you like the scene where the husband takes the manicuring scissors from the drawer?"

"Perfect!"

When they explained to him that Pognár was the author of the play he had just seen, Filippo congratulated him warmly on the ladder episode, which he considered a stroke of literary genius. At that point Ludasi cleared his throat quite audibly, but he had enough of a sense of honor among thieves to refrain from betraying his secret in front of the posh company. The eyes of Vira and Zia kept straying toward Eva. They studied the thin hairline of her eyebrows, plucked and newly drawn, and her fine-cut lips, her wealth of brown hair, her indolent, velvety but still provocative glance; they scrutinized the nostrils of her pliant, slightly large nose, and the almost over-lush whiteness of her skin, and the badly shaped and scarlet fingertips of her cushioned hand; they contemplated her whole body, which verged on stoutness. They eyed her as if she were some baffling, bizarre beast, whose habits of feeding and reproduction, whose entire mode of life was not fully known to zoology as yet. Paul Fogoly, on the other hand, kept his eyes on Zia, on the golden sheen of her wheat-blond hair, the apple-green glow of her glance, the odd, eager little line in the set of her lips that had reminded Count Joachim of fledging birds, the well-formed, unpainted conch of the fingernails of her beautifully shaped and clever little hands, the wonderful pliancy of her shoulders, her slightly brownish-gray and somewhat soft teeth, her nose—which was just the slightest bit off center—and her nostrils, around which there was the faintest hint of shine. He stared at her so because he was seeking a model for the heroine of his new novel. Ludasi's gaze, however, was centered on Vira. He was visibly attracted by the bronze-red beauty.

They danced, everyone with everyone else. Only Pognár and his two hundred pounds remained seated, declaring: "I've no talent for dancing!"

"Nor for anything else," remarked Paul Fogoly.

It was five in the morning when they finally broke up. The little yellow car galloped along the empty streets in the early dawn at seventy miles an hour, and here and there a policeman reached for his notebook. The police already knew

468

that in the early morning hours it was not gasoline but champagne that moved these cars.

Of the play and of the whole evening only one image stayed with Zia: the picture of Vira's profuse bronze-red hair resting on Filippo's shoulder as they danced. She clung to him with such abandon that her face was completely hidden as they swayed to the music of a fox trot. Zia knew how the muscles of Filippo's arm groped for the softness of a bosom, and she knew the mute eloquence of Filippo's thighs. True, that was how she had danced with Ludasi, but she had been thinking of Filippo at the time. Was Filippo thinking of her, however, while the bronze-gold torrent clung to his shoulder? Jealousy penetrated her heart for the first time, like the mysterious ache of an unfamiliar and fatal disease.

Chapter Ten

PERHAPS six weeks had passed. It was the end of October, and autumn was displaying her splendor once again. The forests on the surrounding hills of Buda seemed to glow with crimson in the autumnal sunshine, and the hazels in the Buda gardens cast a purple light. Zia stood on the terrace in her red dressing gown, on the wonderful terrace that gave a view of the entire city. In the little lemon-yellow car Filippo was coasting down the steep incline of Fuga Utca, noiselessly, for he had not started the motor. The ebony holder was in his mouth, as always, when he looked back from the corner and stretched his hand high through the open window to wave good-bye. On the terrace Zia replied with a similar gesture, hardly thinking that this stiff salute did not belong to her as much as to the Roman legionaries whom Mussolini had brought back from the tomb in Italy. She simply copied Filippo's gesture, as she unconsciously copied so much from him—for example, the funny way he had of scratching the top of his head with an outstretched, vertical forefinger when deep in thought. And she occasionally caught herself saying *ze* in imitation of Filippo's Italian mispronunciation of the word *je*, and even substituted an *oo* for the ü-sound, saying *ze sooy* or turning *lugubre* into *loogoobre*. This inclination came from the wellspring of her desire and was the pliancy of a woman in love, a melting with her eyes closed.

On the terrace the upraised hand was held aloft for some time, like a red semaphore. Zia's eyes followed Filippo's car as it bobbed along beneath the branches of the suburban streets in Buda, disappeared and then popped up again like a yellow thrush flitting about an orchard. Finally it vanished in the direction of the Margaret Bridge. Not until then did she lower her arm. Her hand dropped to her side with a gesture of sadness and anxiety. A near-by church was ringing noon, and the chimes resounded in the pearly mist of autumn very much as they had once pealed forth at the airfield. Filippo would not leave the office of the president at Lucello Italiano until after two o'clock. She would not see him again for two whole hours.

The ringing of a telephone reached the terrace, uncertainly, almost as if it came from the neighboring villa. Zia flew to the telephone; perhaps Filippo was

470

calling. At first he had often called immediately upon arrival at his office, only to ask "Comment vas-tu?" There was little reason for such a "How are you," for they had taken leave of each other only a few minutes earlier. But who looks for reason in love, in the cooing tones of a young married couple?—tones which are all brazen and scarcely veiled passion even when they say merely, "Remember to pay the gas bill," or "Don't forget to bring a package of aspirin with you." Such queries of "Comment vas-tu?" were reminders of what had passed between them in the night, continuations of something that never surfeited.

A woman's voice cowered in the telephone. Cowered, because the first "hello" was followed by that certain pause which reveals that the caller had hoped to speak with someone else.

"Is His Grace the Prince at home?"

"He left a little while ago. Who is calling?"

A momentary silence.

"Thank you. I'll call back in the afternoon."

The voice put down the receiver. It was Vira's voice—Zia had recognized it at once. Vira's "nearsighted" voice, for narrowed eyes make one's voice squint a little too. It was impossible that she had not recognized Zia's voice. She must have recognized it—that was why she hung up without giving her name. What did she want with Filippo? Was there something going on between them? For a long time Zia stood beside the phone, biting her lip and staring at the phone fixedly until her eyeballs grew weary with the rigidity of her look. Then she tore her eyes away, gave her head a little shake, closed the eyelids over her sensitive eyes by way of repose and then opened them again to stare anew at the telephone. How stubborn, how dark, how threatening the silence of a telephone can be! Of all lifeless objects it is the only one that has turned into a mechanical nervous system for mankind and is capable, unlike a water tap or a doorknob, of maintaining an eloquent silence. She ought to call Vira, tell her she had answered the phone, ask her what she wanted. Perhaps she was imagining things—perhaps it was some unimportant and innocent matter, after all. Perhaps Vira had been half asleep in bed when she telephoned, drowsy after a gay night somewhere. Or perhaps she should call Filippo and tell him to ring Vira, tell him Vira wanted to speak to him. Perhaps Filippo's voice would reassure her. But Dukay discipline told her not to reach for the telephone. The face and figure of Vira appeared in her imagination as she had last seen her at the Blind Mouse, her abundant, bronze-red hair hiding Filippo's broad shoulder while they danced. Strange that she had not

471

seen Vira since then. They had always gone out together before, they had been the four-in-hand. Why had they stayed away? Perhaps this, too, was significant. So sharply did the phone call conjure up the vision of Vira's bronzed head as she clung to Filippo's broad shoulder that it was almost as if the electric current of the wires had detonated the image in Zia's imagination, like an infernal machine concealed about the house in the guise of an ashtray or a bonbonnière. And the explosion served to pull down walls, to reveal hidden matters and mechanisms. It was only about three weeks ago that she had happened upon Filippo and Vira in a midtown *espresso* one day. It was nothing, really, and meant nothing more than that tiny throb in the heart that she had felt at the Blind Mouse and that every young bride feels when she sees her husband with another woman. But now the images and memories suddenly took on meaning.

Filippo was having an affair with Vira. It began not long ago; the very moment of its inception could be precisely determined. All the things that had been carelessly strewn in Zia's mind began to move. They moved, to rush at each other, to coalesce and form a dim verity. It was ten days since Filippo had touched her last. Yes, ten days exactly; there was the last mark on her calendar, a week ago last Wednesday. Not since their wedding night had she forgotten to note on the calendar something she did not know by name in any language, not even in French, for it was the only word Berili had concealed from her. The marks were small red dots, just the slightest touch of a pencil's point, and no one but Zia herself could know what the little red dots meant. Behind the red dots lurked something that she thought of in terms of a name she herself had given to it but never pronounced aloud, *Päckhaus,* a word associated with the vivid memory of the metamorphosis from maidenhood into womanhood that took place on a night when the Fiume Express had stopped somewhere in lower Austria and the young bride pulled the curtain of her sleeping compartment aside slightly to look out. This was the first word out of the reality of a life from which she had been a star's distance apart, and all the teeth-rattling terrors and wonderful giddiness of great distances came to an end with the sudden jolt of the train, and the distances disappeared, and through the curtains of a compartment that had just been hurtling in interstellar space peered the mundane reality of life with a single word: PÄCKHAUS—a sign on one of the doors in the Austrian railroad station, a sign which read GEPÄCKHAUS in its entirety, a sign that monotonously performed the duties of a sign and did not know that a telegraph post had blocked out the first syllable, did not know that the cloudy feminine eyes behind the curtains of a sleeping compartment would seize upon this mutilated fragment as a symbol for something with which the sign had nothing to do, something with which the sign was implicated in all innocence. The sign simply said GEPÄCKHAUS, drily and rationally, with paint beginning to peel from its edges and rust forming on its wrought-iron letters. *Päckhaus* took its place beside the Copperplated Twilight in Zia's soul, somewhere in the depths of her heart, like secret documents of decisive importance hidden in the innermost recess of an armored vault.

The little red dots that meant *Päckhaus* regularly appeared on each day of the calendar; sometimes there were two, and sometimes three. Each month was marked with three- or four-day omissions which had their natural causes. And then in February there was a lapse of eight days, when Filippo had influenza and was in bed with fever. There was no explanation for the present hiatus of ten days, and so far Zia had not sought an explanation. But now the explanation had appeared, unexpectedly and full of foreboding, like some shapeless beast rearing on its two hind legs, bloodthirsty and ready to spring.

Vira. Her heavy bronze-red hair nestles against Filippo's shoulder, and now the music of the fox trot fills the room. The sleepy whine of a silvery trumpet can be heard quite clearly, and then the musician's face comes into view, his swollen eyelids half closed as he blows the horn; but the image barely circles the room as a bat will fly through an open window on a summer night, circle around once or twice and then disappear as it came.

Vira. Her nails are large and a little spongy, and there is a certain vulgar and brutal strength in the whole woman. In her movements—the way she can draw her broad shoulders together, can almost hide them. The way those shoulders move and bend in the air when she starts to walk. Her nearsightedness—there is something menacing in the narrowed eyes with which she looks at everyone and everything. Vira—beautiful? Her waist is incredibly supple, remarkably slender in proportion to her wide shoulders. In the clear colors of her skin and the natural richness of her hair there is, perhaps, a sort of magnetism that affects men only. Her mouth is large and ugly. It is a hungry mouth. Her clothes exceed the limit that befits a countess. That beet-red dress she wore to the Blind Mouse! she looked like a cocotte. Of course Uncle Fini maintains that cocottes and countesses dress entirely alike these days, the simple explanation of which phenomenon is that cocottes want to be countesses and countesses cocottes, and both sometimes succeed. Vira is a cocotte through and through. She undoubtedly deceives Ferenc. They tell each other everything, true; but this is one thing Vira doesn't talk about. Not everyone is like Elizabeth. Someone—someone not very reliable, it is true—said that on her honeymoon Vira even experimented with the Negro doorman at her hotel, not out of perversity but simply out of curiosity, by way of sheer research, just as Uncle Charles once tasted jellied human flesh cooked in a dirty earthenware pot on the Polynesian Islands.

Three days ago Filippo phoned to say he would not be home for dinner because he had to go to a business conference. The directors of the Aviation Corporation of Rome were in Budapest, true, and he did have dinner with them. But Filippo came home at six in the morning. Where was he until dawn? Just now, when he left, he called back from the door to say that he would be home for lunch but had a conference again in the evening.

Zia felt so weak that she could hardly stand. She stretched out on the sofa and gazed with unmoving eyes at the ceiling for a long while. Her breathing was like the breathing of someone seriously sick. Then she jumped up, dressed, ran an enormous violet-colored comb through her hair once or twice before the mirror and started out on her morning walk. Automatically she hung the leather case of her little camera about her shoulder. She was going somewhere, but did not quite know where. She had walked a long way when she came to a sudden stop. Then she turned back. She knew where she wanted to go.

In the neighborhood of Sas Utca, on one of the side streets of the shopping district downtown, there was a sign which read: "Grünberger and Company, Egg Exporters." Several workmen in front of the relatively shabby shop were unloading crates of eggs from a two-horse freight wagon. The work was under the supervision of a young man in a brown smock that might once have been a dressing gown. Writing pad in hand, he kept a tally of the crates, but when the tempo of unloading demanded it he stuck the pad and pencil in a pocket of the former dressing gown and helped carry the crates inside, a task which required the caution of an expert since it involved eggs. The young fellow was a powerful, broad-shouldered type with thick wrists and silky blond hair dangling over his forehead—just as blond as the manes and tails of the two heavy-hammed Mecklenburg horses hitched to the wagon. The young man hardly seemed twenty years old. His forehead was dotted with tiny red pimples, as if someone had long been using it for a pincushion. Inside the establishment, in a glass cage marked "Office," Grünberger himself was attending to the more intellectual aspects of the business, surrounded by stacks of blue and red bills of lading. He called through the door:

"Come in here for a moment, Baron."

Yes, this young man was Baron Ubi, whom we last saw among the groomsmen at Zia's wedding, dressed in Magyar regalia with a sword at his side.

"I'm-m com-m-ming, right away," replied Baron Ubi, with the slight bow in the direction of the summons that was a relic of his upbringing. He stuttered slightly, but only on the letter m, and he always held his head a little to one side. A year ago Ubi won a silver cup at the motorcycle races in Vienna. When he was sixteen he turned such a somersault with his machine that he was bedridden for five months. Since then he has held his head a little to one side and stuttered slightly, but only on the letter m.

It was he who dressed up as a three-year-old boy some years ago and made the mistake of galloping into a testimonial dinner for the manager of a tobacco plant. Ubi spent his evenings faultlessly attired in dinner jacket, dancing at the Park Club in the company of the most aristocratic of aristocrats. This aristocratic egg dealer was a kind of transitional mutation in the world of social change, like the Australian lungfish, or like Eohippus, the little horse found in the Eocene epoch which, though scarcely larger than a cat, was still a horse. Ubi was already an egg dealer, but at the very beginning of his development. Compared to him, Grünberger was a veritable Mecklenburg of egg dealers. Roux, who made such strides in the study of the secrets of personality individuation among the lower orders at the end of the past century, would have rejoiced over the pimply young baron if he had been able to encompass mankind within the range of his microscope and of his theory. Behind the word Company on the sign outside the door lurked Baron Ubul Lerche-Friis. In those years aristocratic names were altogether too modest to figure on industrial signboards. Since they had sufficient resources to start a partnership—which means that Grünberger had some money and the young baron had useful connections at the Ministry of Commerce—Grünberger took the son of the former Danish Ambassador under his wing and covered him with the word Company as a setting hen will cover her chick. We might make the incidental but not entirely superfluous observation that ten years later, when persecutions of the Jews had begun in Hungary, the sign over the establishment was altered to read "Baron Lerche-Friis and Company." We need hardly say that it was Grünberger who lurked behind the word Company by then, and this was not an easy assignment, not only because Grünberger weighed more than two hundred and twenty pounds, but particularly because he blustered and blundered too much, like the fat and excited boy at hide-and-seek who crawls under the bed but lets his whole bottom protrude. He deludes himself into thinking that no one will find him.

The name of Baron Ubul Lerche-Friis gave everybody the impression that someone had posed a Magyar leopard-skin cape on the shoulder of a Danish diplomat's dinner jacket. The explanation of the ancient Hungarian name of Ubul was that the young baron's mother had been Countess Irma Dukay, who chose this means of endowing her son with a constant reminder that he stemmed from the Ordony clan on his maternal side. After applying himself with quiet perseverance and incredible tenacity to the dissipation of every last cent of both his own and his wife's fortune on horse racing, the Danish Ambassador—like someone whose life's work has been accomplished—proceeded to shoot himself through the head, leaving his widow and child in extremely straitened financial circumstances. Nature and bitter experience, however, had toughened the widow. No misfortune could deprive her of her boundless ebullience. People who are constantly good-humored are grateful to fate for whatever it brings them and consider themselves wealthy in situations which might drive others to suicide. Irma Dukay was not grateful to fate without reason. Her marriage had been completely happy. Baron Carl Lerche-Friis surrounded her with the tenderness and adulation of which only a guilty conscience is capable. The true, thoroughbred, large-scale gambler makes the best husband. When he wins he buys his wife a present because he has won, and when he loses he goes home with a stack of presents lest his wife suspect that he has lost. Such moments become the lifelong property of the recipient, and neither the pawnbrokers nor the bailiffs can take them from her. With an extremely happy marriage behind her, the eternally good-humored widow was replete with good will and love of mankind. A first cousin of Count Dupi, she spent ten years as a common cook in the home of a lawyer in suburban Jozsefváros where, at her own request, everyone called her Irma. They were most discreet with her, did not notice or discuss the fact that she was born a countess, since, like an ugly cancer of the skin, it was something she could not be blamed for. The wealthy lawyer and his family were enlightened folk. They did not flaunt their cook's mistake of birth before their guests. When they had company they did not ring for her on one pretext or other, as some people would surely have done, to give their visitors the opportunity of seeing an actual Dukay countess face to face while they asked, "What are we having for supper tonight, Irma?"—they did not put her on display as if she were a Bearded Lady. How was it possible for this to happen to a first cousin of Count Dupi? There were two reasons. First, the aristocracy is unacquainted with the institution of familial solidarity which is considered natural and self-explanatory, for example, among Jewish families. It is not that they have hearts of stone—they simply do not practice this custom. They do not know the rules of the game, they do not even play the game, just as they play cricket rather than bowls. The other reason is that misfortunate aristocrats retain their pride even in poverty. A well-mannered person does not eat the bread of charity; he prefers to starve. We cannot speak for Austria; but in all Hungary Irma Dukay was the only cook in those years who spent her free Sunday afternoons on St. Margaret's Island and was a regular competitor in the clay-pigeon tourneys, where she won more than one prize. She did not take part in the tourneys in order to mingle with her aristocratic relations. On the contrary, she was generally haughty and aloof with them.

Her son Ubul, who was known in society as Ubi, had gone to business school because he could not afford the university. This is how he became an egg dealer. The relationship between him and the fat Grünberger, who was Ubi's senior by ten years, could hardly be called tender, but they liked and esteemed each other as much as two business partners could possibly do. They were both industrious and honorable men, fundamentally, and it was this that held them together over a lifetime. At the age of nineteen, Ubi was the only consanguineous descendant of the Ordony clan who not only earned his own living but was slowly beginning to accumulate a fortune of sorts. He had furnished a small apartment for his mother; the relationship between mother and son was touching and beautiful. It was as if they had preserved, out of an aristocratic past, only their inborn taste and the delicate instrumentalities of good breeding.

Zia touched Ubi's shoulder. He turned, and when he saw Zia the mass of pimples on his forehead vanished. He blushed so thoroughly that the redness of his blush completely effaced his red pimples. We have already mentioned that Ubi was desperately in love with Zia. The hopelessness of his love gave it true flavor and purity. Ubi did everything to hide his feeling from Zia, but this was as impossible as it would be for a native of Nyam-Nyam to conceal the blackness of his skin. Women have a remarkable tendency to err in the wrong direction when evaluating such matters, but it is a fact that not even the slightest vibration of the masculine soul escapes them. Zia sometimes patted Ubi's cheek, and her hand once slid to Ubi's neck and Ubi, who held his head to one side anyway, took her hand captive and held it pressed between his shoulder and cheek for a few seconds, very much as one holds a warm little bird between two palms. It was all that had ever passed between them, and this had happened two years ago, when Zia was still unmarried and Ubi was seventeen.

"I'd like to talk to you. Do you have a minute or two?"

Ubi turned toward the suspicious glass cage.

"M-Mr. Grünberger—I'll be with you in a m-moment!"

Swiftly he stripped the brown smock from his broad shoulders, as if he wanted to tear it to shreds in his vehemence. He combed his hair with five widespread fingers and turned to Zia with a slight bow:

"I'm at your service."

They went into the street. Zia seemed quite calm.

"I want to ask a great favor."

"I'm at your service."

Meanwhile Ubi had recovered his presence of mind, as a result of which the tiny red pimples again appeared on his forehead, like those little red insects that bask in the sun on tree stumps in the forest.

"What are you doing this evening? I may need you all night."

Ubi spread out his two hands, which were quite dirty from the crates he had been carrying. His mute gesture asked: What else is there for me to do when there is a chance to help you? But he said only:

"I'm at your service."

They walked slowly along. Zia lit a cigarette, which was a fairly unusual thing to do, for in those days women did not smoke on the street.

"Do you know the little park at the corner of Fuga Utca? Be there with your motorcycle tonight at six. Watch for Flippo to leave the house. You may have to wait for some time. You know the car—the little yellow sedan. When you see him, go after him but don't let him see you. Stay on his trail and phone me from time to time. Will you do it?"

Ubi nodded vigorously, twice in succession, and as a consequence his soft, straw-yellow hair fell into his face. Once again he had to comb it with five fingers.

"You mustn't tell anyone about this. Promise?"

Ubi nodded again, which called for another combing. Zia stopped and stretched out her hand to him. The hand was extended stiffly, in a masculine gesture, for a farewell that was also a seal of agreement. Ubi seized her hand and shook it awkwardly, leaving the mark of his palm on the fresh, clean doeskin glove. The handclasp, for all its awkwardness, came from his heart, where the most beautiful impulses of knightly service and self-sacrifice and honor are located. Before she turned the next corner Zia looked back and raised her hand in the air, waggling her fingers at Ubi in French fashion.

✝

She hastened homeward, somewhat relieved. She crossed the suspension bridge on foot and was so occupied with her thoughts that she failed to turn her head when several persons tipped their hats to her. She knew that the ultimate key to the mystery was now in her hand, for Filippo would not be able to escape Ubi's motorcycle. There were two Zias going homeward side by side now, two Zias who had never met this way before. One Zia was a betrayed, terrified and sniveling-hearted unhappy little woman, while the other was a hard, proud Dukay daughter capable of taking action and exacting revenge, a Zia whose ancestresses had occasionally given the wheel of history a smart turn in bygone centuries. She felt a profound and warm pity for Filippo. Poor Filippo was nohow to blame, he had simply fallen into Vira's clutches. Calmly Zia contemplated what she would do when the proof was in her hands. She would say nothing to Filippo. Poor Filippo need know nothing of all this. She would seek out Vira, and during tea she would say in an unconcerned voice, as if talking of the Dog Show:

"I know everything. I'll give you three days to go abroad for a year. You may come back a year from now, but you must never see Filippo again as long as you live."

She would open her pocketbook and, with the gesture of producing her compact, she would take out a little revolver, saying:

"If you won't do what I ask I shall kill you."

Two things might happen. Vira would most likely laugh and say: Agreed! Vira was familiar with the rules of the game and she knew the Dukays. Being a clever woman, she would keep her word. The other possibility was that she would not be frightened by the threat. Three days later, in that case, Zia would open her pocketbook again and fire all six rounds into Vira, whether on the street or at the French Ambassador's banquet.

"Grüss Gott, Zia!" Somebody took her by the arm. It was Ferenc. But he skipped away from her a few seconds later because the cable car to Buda had just pulled in.

✝

Filippo came home for lunch at two in the afternoon, as usual. He seemed preoccupied and out of sorts. They lunched out on the terrace, which was already in shadow by that hour. There was still sunshine on the left tip of the terrace, but the sun withdrew from there too while they ate. The golden train of the sun seemed to catch on every thorny bush within the iron grating of the terrace, as it drew noiselessly, cautiously away.

"Has Ascarelli left?" asked Zia, as she dipped a thick, chilled asparagus tip into its green sauce. She was very careful to seem completely calm.

"Of course not," Filippo said in a headachy voice. "I told you this morning that we're going to continue our conferences tonight."

"Oh, of course," was the somewhat absent-minded and apologetic answer of Zia, who had gone to the hotel along the Danube after seeing Ubi and learned from the doorman that Signor Ascarelli, director of the Aviation Corporation of Rome, had left on the morning of the previous day. During lunch Filippo touched on the difficulties of the current conferences in a few of his brief remarks. These statements, which dealt with capital investments, airline routes or the negotiation of contracts, made no sense and had no consequence; as sounds, they differed from the tinkle of the tableware only insofar as they were made by a human voice. The pauses between remarks were that much heavier and more oppressive. Zia exerted all her strength to melt the ice-cold manacles of the long silence with a smile or two, and she asked questions like this:

"Are you planning to have separate flights to Bucharest?"

"Mm…" nodded Filippo as he ate, but it was impossible to know where his thoughts were straying. As she furtively regarded Filippo's narrow little black mustache and his full, dark, red Italian cheeks, as she felt that the tang of the air on the terrace and the movements of the footman were exactly what they had been the day before, Zia was seized with uncertainty. She felt that her appeal to Ubi had been too hasty. What if she was only imagining things? What if Vira had really not recognized her voice, had mistaken her for the chambermaid? But why did the doorman say that Signor Ascarelli had checked out? The doorman

480

might have been wrong. The ten-day lapse was a much greater question mark. But Zia found an explanation for that as well. So far, if not always, she had been the one to take the initiative, only with incredibly faint little words, it is true, which were as far as *Päckhaus* from their true import and only represented eager little chirpings in the bird-language of love. For ten days she had not approached Filippo. Now she thought, with a twinge of apprehension, that Ubi must already be disassembling his motorcycle, oiling it lest some motor trouble hamper the evening hunt. There were moments, especially during the strawberries, when Filippo's expression seemed so innocent that Zia would have liked to nestle in his lap and ask his forgiveness while she wept.

After lunch, as usual, they went to Filippo's room for coffee and cigarettes. When they were alone, Zia knelt on the ground before Filippo, which was her customary move at that hour. And when they had finished their cigarettes, she buried her head in his lap. She feigned a light sleep. But her sleeping breath burned through Filippo's clothing. The breath called to him, reminded him, urged him. At these times Filippo's hand would grow heavy on Zia's head, and then on her neck. But now his hand did not even move. Instead of the hand, expected beyond all expectation, Filippo's knees moved, politely, almost apologetically, indicating that he wanted to stand up. And Filippo stood up, stretched, cracked his joints and started toward the bathroom. On the way he began to whistle softy, but this whistle was only intended to alleviate the embarrassment of the rebuff, the embarrassment that stayed in the air like a cool, almost discernible, palpable draft.

Zia did not move. She remained on the ground, sitting like a supporting member of a statue, abandoned by the principal shape and thus bereft of all meaning. Her position was ridiculous and degrading. Attentively she began to wind the fringed edging of the armchair with two fingers. She did not stand up until the bathroom door had closed. Now there was no doubt in her mind that Filippo was deceiving her. She left the room and strayed aimlessly into the garden. She tried to read, taking along a half-finished book that Berili had once discovered in the library: Racine's *Iphigénie*. Why must she suffer so? Why did she deserve this dreadful fate? Iphigenia's father had offended the goddess by killing the sacred hart. And only the blood of Iphigenia would appease the vengeful goddess. Zia felt herself to be Iphigenia, immersed in a fateful tragedy, but without particularly fancying herself in such a role. She was simply aware of vengeful powers at work, sometimes known as the goddess Artemis, sometimes as Vira, sometimes called an illness or an airplane accident; and these vengeful powers picked their victims from the ranks of the innocent. How dreadful life was! It was so still in the garden that one could hear the delicate rustle of the falling leaves as they fluttered to earth. Suddenly Zia turned her attention toward Filippo's room. Through the open window upstairs came a peculiar noise, and Zia knew it by its rhythm but had never heard the noise like this, in the open and from a distance. The noise was composed of deep, scraping sounds like the sound of a broom slowly, lazily sweeping over frozen terrain. They were the sounds Filippo made when he snored. The book in her lap, Zia listened to Filippo's long, even snores for some time. She was unable to understand how a guilty conscience could sleep so sweetly.

All through the afternoon hours, wandering from room to room, she struggled with the shades of loneliness and of a hitherto unknown bereavement. She tried to work in her darkroom. The negatives she developed were spoiled, and the ominously tomblike light of the green lamp did not improve her spirits. She went out to sit on the terrace at about six o'clock. The October twilight had the coloring of a blue fox, and the air was soft to the touch. Down below, the city was preparing for the adventures of the evening: the great yellow expanse of the twilight sky was the city's mirror as it put on an evening gown. Now the Danube drew diamond bracelets on the city's wrist: the illuminated bridges.

Around seven Filippo appeared on the terrace, a soft black hat pulled low over his forehead. No one could be more dashing in a dinner jacket than Filippo. Had such an article of clothing not existed, it would have been necessary to invent it for Filippo's sake. The trouble with the dinner jacket, as with most black clothes, is that it generally gives men's faces a pasty color. Filippo's brown Italian skin counteracted this whitening effect of the funereal garb. Another trouble with the dinner jacket is that it gives men a solemn look that is always a little ludicrous. Filippo looked as natural in a dinner jacket as in a well-worn, waterproof hunting coat, perhaps because he always wore soft shirts of the finest linen, and the bow of his tie was always loosely knotted. His hair was black too, and his little narrow mustache. Just the right amount of black in each place. His cigarette holder was black, except for the tiny diamonds that glittered around its rim.

"Au revoir, chérie."

Zia mutely offered her forehead for a kiss. There are kisses that remain lifelong memories, like a deep scar. But time alone gives them this quality. When they are given or received, they go unnoticed and seem as nothing. This was such a kiss.

Leaning on the balustrade of the terrace, Zia watched Filippo as he took the car from the chauffeur, who had driven it out of the garage. She called down:

"When will you be home?"

"Very late, I'm afraid."

He raised his hand and disappeared into the car.

Zia also waved farewell with a Fascist lift of the arm. Her eyes followed the little yellow car as it rolled unsuspectingly down the incline of Fuga Utca. It had hardly passed the tiny park on the corner when a motorcycle leaped out of the bushes in its wake. It was getting dark, but Zia still saw this clearly. Her heart began to beat tearfully. Somewhat farther away the car reappeared among the trees once again, and behind it the pursuing motorcycle. Then the darkness and the distance swallowed them.

Almost a quarter of an hour later the telephone rang. The bell shrilled as if every nerve of the city's millions were atingle. Ubi was making his first report.

"He went to the National Theater."

"Alone?"

"Alone."

"What are they playing?"

"*Bánk Bán.*"

"Where are you?"

"In a public phone booth."

"Wait for me at the entrance of Corvin's. I'll be right there."

Zia ordered a cab and quickly started to dress. Before leaving she hesitated for some time over a choice of opera glasses. Lion hunters pick their rifle-bored weapons as painstakingly as this before they proceed into the jungle.

It was easy to find Ubi. Poised on his motorcycle in front of the entrance of Corvin's, he looked like a subdued bull that threatens to break loose at any moment. There among the cars parked near the statue of Tinódi was Filippo's car too, invisibly tethered to Ubi's motorcycle. They began to confer in whispers.

"Go and get me an upstairs box."

The ticket window was still open, and Ubi soon returned with the ticket in his hand.

"Stay here," Zia whispered, "keep your eye on the car. Maybe he'll leave during the performance."

"Where will you be then?"

Zia looked around and pointed to the Runcsík Restaurant near by.

"There, in that restaurant. As near the telephone as possible."

"Good. I'll ask for you by the name of Teréz Hemli."

"Hemli?"

"Hemli. You can't forget it. Terézia Dukay of Duka and Hemlice—that is, the first two syllables of your name, and the last two but one."

No one could beat Ubi at devising such ideas.

Zia waggled her fingers at him in French fashion and disappeared into the main entrance of the theater. As she walked inside it struck her that Filippo did not understand a word of Hungarian, and so it was hard to imagine that *Bánk Bán,* the classic of Hungarian historical drama, had much attraction for him. Probably he had arranged to meet Vira in the orchestra or in the depths of one of the boxes. Zia's box was on the third tier. The theater was already dark, and only the stage was alight. Cautiously Zia approached the edge of her box. She had never before seen a theater from such a height. From there on high the orchestra looked like a huge cauldron, so deep that it was almost menacing. The ceiling had grown to astounding dimensions, while the tremendous stage shrank into a square no larger than the plate-glass window of a café. The actors looked like the tiny figures of a puppet show. Right now, according to the stage directions, Queen Gertrudis was supposed to be whispering, but her whisper was a veritable shriek, for the praiseworthy and communal purpose of enabling the gallery, despite the dramatist's injunction, to hear what the queen was saying. But Zia was not concerned with the stage. Her opera glasses vainly sought for familiar figures in the audience. Everything blurred together in the dark depths of the cauldron; the light of the stage illuminated only the first few rows. At most she could differentiate between the heads of men and women, but their backs were turned to her. Judging by the shape of their heads, at least twenty black figures could have been Filippo. It was in vain, too, that she scanned the boxes which were within range of her own.

Finally the curtain fell and the great chandelier overhead lit up. It was as if they had snatched a dark veil from the audience, which is sometimes called a thousand-headed hydra. The veil once removed, Zia's opera glasses saw the ominous and awesome monster to be composed of members of the Casino, inoffensive mothers with their broods, young married couples or sweethearts holding hands.

Filippo! There he sat in the third row! But there were men to the right and left of him. The opera glasses excitedly pried into the audience as it moved toward the exits. Vira! She was finally found! She had just stood up at the left of the orchestra, wearing a grass-green dress with a gold Roman buckle. Zia knew the dress well. But there was her husband Ferenc beside her. His close-cropped, almost neckless head loomed like a bubble in the crowd. Meanwhile Filippo had stood up too; they were meeting, and exchanging greetings. They chatted for a few moments, and then started for the exit together. What did this mean? Why was her husband there? This was typical of Vira's strategy; she did not want to make an appearance in public with Filippo alone. Would the three of them have supper together? How would Vira get rid of her husband? For it was certain that the two of them would sneak away somewhere. What reason had Filippo given Ferenc for Zia's failure to go to the theater with them? Oh, how ignominious it was!

The audience returned, the theater grew dark, and the second act began. What did the second and the third acts portend? What would the denouement of the drama be? Not of the drama on the stage—who cared about that?—but of the one unfolding here in the audience, of which God was the author. Zia tried, or at least pretended, to watch the stage. She did not hear a single word the actors were saying. She was playing in her own tragedy, repeating her part to herself, like the actors who stood behind the flats in plumed medieval casques and curled sandals and mentally rehearsed the ancient iambs of their roles, even when the assistant stage manager's outstretched hand was already on their shoulders, ready to nudge them at the right moment, as if they were great electric buzzers, and to release them toward the stage with ringing steps or leaping motions, whichever were appropriate.

The play was in five acts. After each curtain Filippo, Vira and Ferenc continued to meet for a few puffs of a cigarette, for the short intermissions lasted no longer than a third of a cigarette. This is why five-act plays were preferred by the ragged, grotesque figures lurking about the exits, the cigarette-butt vultures. The shorter the intermissions, the longer the butts. There are, however, people so mean that they spit on the tip of their half-smoked cigarette when the bell rings, rub the hard black edge of ash off on the wall, surreptitiously slip the remnant of the cigarette in their pocket and light up again during the next intermission. These characters are a disgrace to the middle class, and deserve no more than a scornful glance from beneath the ragged rim of the hats on the vultures leaning against the wall. And when a two-act play is scheduled for performance, the vultures—blessed with an exceptionally well developed sense of dramaturgy—do not appear on the battlefield at all.

The acts never seemed to end. The play did not want to draw to a close. The actors recited and recited and recited. Zia was unable to understand how the audience stood it, why some one did not leap up like a giant and demand with a shake of his fist that the performance end at once. Bánk snatched a dagger and stabbed it into the queen's heart. Swords rattled in air, the colors of medieval costumes clashed, the attendant knights secured the assassin. While all this happened Zia's face looked as if dull and interminable setting-up exercises were being performed on the stage.

Finally the curtain fell, and the impulsive rush of the spectators indicated that they were heading for the cloakrooms. Only a rear guard of enthusiasts stayed for the curtain calls—twenty or twenty-five people whose exaltation was so fervent that they thronged toward the stage from the back rows, applauding with hands held high, calling the names of the actors. It was their way of expressing gratitude for free tickets—without exception the clamoring, enthusiasts were poor relations of the actors. Cousins and uncles who deserved a better fate kept the curtain ringer at work. One of these free tickets meant a minor financial catastrophe for such poor relations, since trolley fares, cloakroom tips and fees for the concierge were involved, which wrought havoc with meager pensions; but the sacrifice had to be made, the familial applause rendered to produce the "howling success," for in some little street of Buda or near the Zugló it meant something when Matilde, in the grocery shop, asked: "Is it true that you're related to Miss Csókás the actress?" Along that street it was a sign of rank.

The company of enthusiastic relations diminished, and the curtain ringer grew weary of his work. The actors themselves were pumping the curtains now, and came out for bows less and less frequently; Biberach, who was in a hurry to get to Runcsík's, had already taken his make-up off.

The ushers appeared in the empty orchestra and began collecting the programs and the discarded candy wrappers between the rows of seats. They rattled and rustled in the sea of waste paper like mice in a deserted attic. And they were mice indeed, the mice of this great cathedral, little gray old women whose eyes and hands were unbelievably practiced at searching for wallets or even diamond rings among the seats where the dinner jackets and the evening gowns had been, although such a find had happened about once in every twenty years of the theater's history. But it was hope that made those bent backs so indefatigably industrious. And hope springs eternal, like Buddha, who was fifty-eight times a king, forty-eight times a tree spirit and six times an elephant, not to mention his other incarnations. Last week the ushers at the Opera found a monocle in the orchestra, and a single gray glove, and a woman's bloodstained handkerchief.

Zia was still hidden by the wall of her box. Only her face ventured out, and even her face was covered by the opera glasses. It was impossible to see her up there from down below.

And now a strange thing happened—a strange scene in a strange play. The decisive scene, that veritably whirls the drama in a new direction with a swoop. The turning point that enters like a wild current of air, to upset everything and seize the spectator by the throat. Something that no one could have expected, as often happens in plays about criminal cases, when truth like a monster suddenly leaps on the stage, the truth that it was not the janitor's wife who murdered the old millionairess but the magistrate himself.

What happened was that after the ranks of enthusiasts had dwindled away a single dinner jacket remained near the prompter's box, with hands raised high in solitary applause. And only a single figure kept coming before the curtain again and again, bowing deeply to the "exultant audience": Queen Gertrudis. Now, beneath the waves of the towering crimson wig, beneath the cherry-tinted queenly robes, Zia's trembling opera glasses recognized the features of Eva Kócsag.

Besides the mice there were only two persons in the huge, empty red and gold auditorium: Filippo and Eva Kócsag. They were playing their own scene now, putting the splendor of Thalia's temple to a reckless and sacrilegious use. The golden cherubim on the pillars that supported the boxes, whose rigid faces had viewed so many generations of comedies and tragedies without a smile, had never witnessed so brazen a love scene. Perhaps, at certain moments, inanimate objects can live and reason too; at least it seemed as if the immobile faces of the cherubim were watching this mutual declaration of love with bated breath, for it was a scene that had definite style and novelty, and perhaps the cherubim knew as well that this drama had a third actor, a twenty-one-year-old countess in a box on the third tier, whose hand had dropped the opera glasses and whose head leaned against the wall of the box as she watched the scene from her darkness. It was only minutes ago that the maddened Bánk had twisted the dagger in Queen Gertrudis's heart. Now, with a reversal of situation, the queen, resurrected from the dead, was back and bowing, and her every single bow was a dagger stroke in the heart of an unhappy little wife who was foolish enough to believe blindly in

487

the vow that the young Prince of Perugia had made in the presence of Bishop Zsigmond hardly a year and a half ago. The cherubim observed it all. The mice paid no attention. The bent backs went from row to row, like the people said by a Chinese legend to be burdened with a weighty curse for all their lives. They were searching for wallets and rings, and once again there were none. Up in the balcony the mice rustled the empty peanut shells, for fountain pens and prophylactics still intact were occasionally to be found there.

The chandelier overhead was suddenly extinguished. Darkness engulfed the players. Only with the help of the meager light that came through the windows from the street lamps was Zia able to feel her way downstairs. She made the alarming discovery that all the exits of the theater were locked. Steps resounded somewhere in the distance. She did not dare to shout, but began beating on a door with her fists. And then the uniformed watchman came with his ring of keys. He took a long look at Zia before he would let her out.

"What are you doing in here so late?" he asked suspiciously.

"I lost something," said Zia, almost gasping the words.

The ill-humored watchman was evidently satisfied with the explanation, because he opened the door, but asked in the meanwhile:

"Did you find it?"

Instead of answering, Zia pressed a banknote in his hand, from which the watchman concluded that the little lady had lost something very precious but had fortunately found it again.

Zia succeeded in flitting unnoticed across the square to the entrance of Corvin's, where Ubi was waiting for her in the shadow of the wall and did not even move his head when Zia joined him. He was like a springer spaniel pointing at the prey. They began to whisper.

"We'll have to wait. While she takes her make-up off."

Ubi did not ask who was going to take her make-up off. Only after a few moments did he start to say something, but he broke off after the first syllable because Filippo suddenly appeared on the empty square, a cigarette smoking in his black holder. Slowly he approached the car that glistened in yellow solitude near the statue. Zia grasped Ubi's arm; only the sound of her breathing could be heard. Ubi found it unnecessary even to breathe, although they were perfectly safe. They were a considerable distance away, and in any case they stood in a spot that was completely hidden in shadow. Filippo leaned his elbow on the top of the little car and shoved his hat to the back of his head. He stood like that for several minutes. Then he began to walk alongside the car, clasping his hands behind his back. When he grew tired of this, he went back to lean on the car. From time to time he lit a cigarette, smoking one after the other greedily. At such times the glow of the lighter illumined his face momentarily. Zia could clearly see the flat little gold lighter in his hand, although it was actually not visible at that distance; but it was a lighter she had bought for Filippo on his last birthday. She looked at Filippo now as if he were some unearthly shape who did not stem from reality. And her hand tightened on Ubi's clublike arm as if she wanted to crush it. Neither of them ceased looking at Filippo. Once again Zia noticed how light his walk was, almost as if she were seeing him for the first time in her life. Or for the last time, as if this were her farewell glance at a living man who was condemned to death for some reason but did not know it yet. She studied the design of him: how incredibly and inimitably smart his movements were as he leaned an elbow against the top of the car, placing one foot on the running board, holding the cigarette holder negligently in the hand on which his chin rested—for his teeth would not relinquish the holder for an instant. The minutes passed heavily.

With whatever nervous urgency and unprintable expressions one scolds a tiring-woman, it takes more than a minute or two for a medieval queen to divest herself of her silk cocoon. Let us use this interval, then, to devote a few words to the fourth actor in this strange play, who is having supper with her husband in a quiet midtown restaurant at this very moment. Not a word is true of the allegation that Vira had affairs with anyone while she was still a girl. There is even less truth in the story of the Negro doorman. And it was not she but her cousin who played an important part in the love life of the French Minister of Aviation. Vira was as virginal when she went to the altar as Zia had been. If marital fidelity still existed in the white man's world at this time, then Vira was the paragon of womanly virtue. Not even in her thoughts did she deceive her close-cropped, neckless Ferenc. And nothing was further from her mind than to seduce the husband of her dearest friend. But there are women whose very presence stimulates the fantasies of men. Such provocations operate in animals too. Dogs attack only those who fear them, for their remarkable olfactory sense can smell the scent of fear when it is manifest in the invisible dampness despatched to the surface of the skin by the nervous system. It is these hidden impulses and irritations, too, that make human life so frightening, so incomprehensible and at the same time so dazzling. There are women whose shade of hair, whose movements, whose piercing glances or whose modulations of voice, perhaps, awaken desire. And further, respectable women are always surrounded by the envy of their less respectable friends. A woman of good repute forgives the waywardnesses of her friends, but the wayward friends never forgive her virtue. And respectable women are surrounded by something more: the wrath of rejected lovers. When a man successfully courts a woman he does not speak of his success, for men are generally gallant and find their satisfaction in the achievement itself. But when they have courted unsuccessfully, they make every effort to give the outside world the impression that they are intimate with the lady, for they owe this to outraged vanity. This is how legends involving Negro doormen grow up about the Viras, while women who have relations with their chauffeur are accorded the respect usually reserved for abbesses. Men's fantasies, for some reason, do not take hold of women of the latter sort, and gossip will not attach to them, very much as iron will not hold plaster. It was not Vira who telephoned this morning, but Eva Kócsag. But where telephone receivers are concerned it is often one's complete conviction that decides to hear the voice which imagination first brought to mind, and from that instant on the voice does not issue from the telephone but from an endless store of voices recorded and revolving in our brain. It was sheer coincidence that Vira and Ferenc happened to be at the theater tonight.

But there was no room for Vira in Zia's thoughts right now. At most she reflected that her preparation had been to do battle with Vira, and this had not seemed hopeless because she knew her opponent. Vira was not only a woman but a countess too, of the same age and breeding as Zia. One could anticipate her offensive or defensive moves. One could predict the direction and dimension of her forward or backward leaps. This knowledge furnished a basis on which to choose weapons of suitable caliber and ammunition of adequate penetrating power. But what is there to know about an actress? This was an animal Zia had never encountered. Right now she felt like a hunter who enters the jungle after a panther and is faced instead by an unknown monster rising from the brush, the very sight of which is unnerving, for it is like a dreadful, sharp-clawed, tiger-toothed Mesozoic reptile, like a Queen Gertrudis, or like the daughter of a suburban janitor; and the movements of this tyrannosaurus, the dimensions of its leaps, are completely unknown, wherefore the choice of caliber and the penetrating power of ammunition remain uncertain, because one cannot know

490

the thickness of its skin, whether it has either heart or brain at all, and where it can best be wounded. There is nothing one can know about an Eva Kócsag. To Vira, Filippo would have been merely a twenty-six-year old male. Vira was wealthy. But to Eva Kócsag Filippo was not only a Prince of Perugia but a car, jewelry, a palace. Who knew what leaps and strokes this actress-reptile had at her command, rising from the primeval swamp of poverty and deprivation?

And there was Eva Kócsag, coming from the theater entrance. She minced on high-heeled slippers, and her short, narrow skirt hindered her progress as well. Her brown hair was bushy beneath a little green hat, and now she bore no resemblance at all to Queen Gertrudis. Zia summoned up her memory of that face as she had seen it when they had been together at the Blind Mouse. The indolent, velvet-smooth and yet provocative eyes, made provocative perhaps by the pliant nostrils of her slightly bent, slightly large nose. Her taut, cushioned skin, too white, almost nauseatingly white, a whiteness that made her body seem to verge on obesity. There was something antique about her personality, an eroticism that had outlived a fashion. The women in the harem of Mussafar-din must have been like this. Strange that this remark had come from Filippo, when they were homeward bound from the Blind Mouse in the early morning and discussing the various members of the group. Perhaps the disparaging comment was already meant to be misleading.

Zia sank her nails into Ubi's arm, and the youth imagined he could hear the beat of her heart. In lieu of greeting, Filippo seized Eva Kócsag's arm and led her toward the car. They disappeared into the low-slung little car as if they were burrowing into the ground through a comparatively small opening.

"Mmhaa..." Some sort of gasp like this came from Zia, similar to the sound that issues from the throat, despite whatever anaesthetic, at the moment when a multi-rooted molar is pulled. But this was a moment that called for action. Ubi shook the tightening grip of Zia's fingers from his arm and quickly started his machine. He mounted the seat and took hold of the handles. Motor and muscle awaited the simultaneous moment of departure. The motorcycle trembled, quietly but with the speed of a tuning fork, and it shook the leather saddle too. It is amazing how some objects and machines have learned to assimilate and express the trembling of human nerves at certain times. But Filippo's car did not depart. It stood as motionlessly as a half hour before, when it was empty. This pause meant something that the best will in the world could not suppose to be simple conversation or idle inaction. Filippo's movement as he started toward

Eva Kócsag, the movement with which he had seized her arm and almost carried her to the car, suggested other conclusions.

And finally the car began to move, almost unexpectedly, in fits and starts. Hardly had it turned toward the Elizabeth bridge when the motorcycle darted after it like an arrow stealthily shot from the cover of a bush. The chase had begun, a pursuit of motors and hearts, between which, in the final analysis, there is hardly any structural difference.

It was around eleven o'clock. The statue, in its solitude, and the square, in its emptiness, seemed meaningless. Here and there in the windows of the Rókus Hospital a yellow light still glowed. People were dying there. To the left, on the ground floor, the frosted glass window of the operating room gave off a blue light. Work went on there all night long. They cut stomachs open, or threw human limbs into a blood-filled bucket. At the entrance of the Corvin Department Store, leaning against the wall with one hand, stood a woman, born a Dukay, beautiful, young, healthy. At this point it would have been difficult to determine, in the measure of human misery, where the axe blows of suffering struck most deeply, whether in the desiccate cambial rings of human apathy and renunciation or beneath the tender boughs of youth and wealth and their uncompromising demand for happiness.

After some hesitation Zia crossed over to the Runcsík Restaurant, where the mild scent of dishwater in the air was perfumed with other smells, the smell of beer, the aroma of coffee, the fragrance of cheap perfume and the sour stench of the cigar butts in the ashtrays. This was all strange to her. What can a young Dukay countess order in a place like this, when she is not hungry and is so unfamiliar with spirits that she can hardly tell the difference between the taste of beer and peach brandy?

"Bring me a glass of Vichy, please."

The young waiter turned to look backward, somewhere into space. This is a waiter's glance when he is waiting for an order to take final shape. Since nothing followed, he turned back.

"What would you like, please?"

"A glass of Vichy."

"Nothing else?"

"Thank you, no."

The waiter left, but not to fetch the Vichy. He went to the headwaiter, said something and pointed somewhat conspicuously in Zia's direction. He refused to assume sole responsibility for the unusual order. The headwaiter waddled toward Zia's table and when he reached it he adjusted two corners of the tablecloth. Every waiter from Hong Kong to Acapulco does this when he wants an excuse for approaching a guest's table.

"Have you ordered?"

"Yes, a glass of Vichy."

Old headwaiters learn more about a customer in a moment than the customer's relatives could discover in a lifetime. The leather case of the opera glasses on the table, the quality of the gloves, the shape of the woman's hands, the fragrance of her perfume and particularly the slightly apologetic modulation of her voice instantly told the headwaiter that he was dealing with something entirely different from a glass of Vichy.

"Right away!" he said, almost gently.

Leaning against a pillar, the younger man awaited the master's decision.

"Wait on that lady! And mind your manners!"

The waiter brought Zia's glass of Vichy on a little silver tray. There were few customers in the restaurant. At one of the tables, as always, actors were drinking beer. They were the ones whose names usually appear at the bottom of theater programs and whose artistic stature scarcely differs from that of scene shifters. Therefore they were peaceable, jolly people, familiar with the virtue of fraternal solidarity and the quiet joys of a glass of beer. These pleasures gave them patience to hear the same stories told over and over again for decades, night after night. Perhaps once in the course of twenty or thirty years each of them had had the opportunity to replace an ailing principal and soar, if only temporarily, to the heavenly heights at the top of the program. This had happened perhaps once in the course of twenty or thirty years, but around the table they spoke of these roles as if they had always played them.

The telephone boy crossed the restaurant and began to call:

"Telephone for Miss Teréz Hemli!"

He passed Zia's table twice, but Zia had long forgotten that she herself was Teréz Hemli at this moment. The singsong voice, moreover, was like that of a newspaper vendor or a candy butcher at a railroad station. Her face motionless, Zia sat behind the glass of Vichy, which was untouched and had already lost its effervescent pearls.

The telephone boy stopped at the actors' table too, and sang out:

"Telephone for Miss Teréz Hemli!"

"For who?" An old comedian rudely cupped a hairy ear toward the boy, whose call had interrupted the story he was telling for the second time.

"Miss Teréz Hemli."

"That's me." The old master of comedy made as if to rise from his chair, and drew a chorus of guffaws from the mugs of beer. But he sat down again, and this time shouted at the boy:

"You idiot, can't you see that only men are sitting here? Go to hell!"

The boy glanced over his shoulder and tittered as he ambled away. He looked around the restaurant, and then went straight to Zia's table, for she was the only feminine figure in the place. He did not sing out this time, but simply asked:

"Miss Teréz Hemli?"

Zia came to her senses. Anyone else in her frame of mind would have overturned chairs in a dash to the booth. She stood up calmly and walked to the booth even more slowly than was necessary. This was Dukay discipline. The receiver buzzed with Ubi's voice:

"They went to the wom-m-man's apartm-m-ment at Fourteen M-menta Utca. You won't forget the address?"

"No, no..."

"Take a cab. The driver'll know where it is. It's on Rózsahegy, in Buda."

"What are they doing there?"

The question had little meaning right now, but there was a weepy strain in the voice that asked it. It was the question of a frightened child, inquiring into mysterious and terrifying adult matters. Ubi had an answer.

"They're having dinner. On the way they stopped at the Hungaria and the doorm-m-man put a basket in the car. They m-must have ordered the dinner ahead of time."

"Are there any other people there?"

Ubi did not reply at once, because her tone told him she was grasping at the last straw of hope.

"No. They're alone."

"I'll be right there."

"Wait a minute!" Ubi shouted, fearing that Zia would hang up. "Repeat the street and house number!"

There was no answer. Zia had already forgotten the name of the street.

"You see! You're upset. Write it down—I'll dictate."

"I won't forget!"

"Write it down!"

"How can I write it down? I'm in a dark booth...I don't have a pencil...oh, my God!"

"Think of your mother."

"Why should I think of my mother?"

"Your m-mother is called M-m-menti. The name of the street is M-menta. That way you won't forget it. Repeat it, now."

"Menta...I know."

Only an egg dealer could be so practical. A life of business and bills of lading gives birth to these sly ways of jogging the memory.

"Fourteen. Think of a horse, because a horse has four hoofs, and then add ten, because it's a round number."

Ubi himself realized that this explanation would be much harder to keep in mind than the number fourteen itself. His voice issued from the darkness with a new notion:

"You know what? It wouldn't be very smart to drive right up to the house. Stop at Number One—you can't forget, that."

"All right, all right...I'm going. Number One Menta Utca—I'm on the way."

Zia stepped from the booth and, as usually happens under such circumstances, she took a few steps in the wrong direction.

"I'd like a taxi, and my bill, please," she told the headwaiter.

"I'll order it right away," the old man said, and went outside to raise a forefinger in the air. The cab stand was directly in front of the restaurant. Returning, he announced grandly, as if he had roused the president of the Amalgamated Hack Association from a deep sleep:

"Your cab is waiting."

He made out her bill—for ten fillers—and was not surprised when the lady refused change for a twenty-pengő note. He hastened to the door, held it open for the customer, then bounced out on the street like a rubber ball and opened the door of the taxicab too. His bow was so deep as he closed the door on Zia that his forehead almost hit the running board. It was not for the twenty pengős. He had had hundred-pengő tips from drunken financiers, fat high-booted country squires and morphine-laden ladies of pleasure. He did not know who this customer was, but he was sensitive to the rare phenomenon of thoroughbred beauty, as an elephant mahout will lose himself in admiration of an azure-winged butterfly during a pause in the day's run.

✝

Ubi was out in the middle of the street to corral the approaching cab. Menta Utca was one of the streets on the hills of Buda that had metamorphosed out of goat pastures after the war. The trees along the border of the sidewalk were young, hardly ten years old, like the villas themselves, both small and large, private and rented, as evidence that the great war, not here alone but everywhere else in the world, had girdled the earth like a heavy May downpour, in the wake of which the symptoms of middle-class well-being burgeoned forth in the suburbs, whether of Brussels or Belgrade, as large as prize-winning cabbages at a country fair. The symptoms were present on the villas along Menta Utca too, brick-red awnings over the terraces, and luxurious flower beds brocaded with the silver of tiny rock gardens, and doghouses, and terra cotta friezes built into the walls, imitations of Luca della Robbia's *Madonna* which were manufactured in such great quantities to deck the God-fearing world that they might have been nothing more than razor blades. The foundations of the villas along Menta Utca were built on the Treaties of Trianon and Versailles, the Locarno Alliance and the Kellogg Pact. Some years later it became necessary to supplement the villas with garages that violated the quiet symmetry of the original design, elbowed their way into already narrow gardens and generally behaved in an increasingly insolent fashion. The sweet, wind-stilly October evenings, full of the smell of wilting leaves and the half moon's glow, and the peaceful rattle of lowered window blinds, the occasional and altogether unwarranted bark of a dog, the gasp of a distant motor struggling uphill and homeward bound—these evenings rocked the villas along Menta Utca in the bosom of Elysian calm and security, as if the hero of the Golden Age of Irish legend were still reigning on earth, O'Donoghue, who rises from the emerald-green depths of Lake Killarney amid a host of shining fairies and gallops in dazzling splendor over the mirror of the water on his snow-white steed. This is what Budapest evenings were like in those years. The villas on Menta Utca could not have had the slightest inkling of the fact that in another ten years the vengeful goats would return to claim their pastures.

Ubi took Zia's arm and led her under the branches of the trees toward No. 14, like an elderly relative escorting the widow just returned from abroad to the grave of her dear departed husband, newly dead. His motorcycle leaned against the fence of the house opposite, its handlebars turned outward and its cruel wire-glass eyes riveted on the little yellow car. The motorcycle gave the impression of being on the alert to hurtle after the little car if it dared to move from No. 14.

They were concealed by the boughs of the trees. Ubi pointed to the first floor of the house across the way, where a light glowed in one of the windows. The adjacent window showed only the token illumination of a tiny decorative lamp.

"They're up there," he whispered in a low voice, because the windows were open. "How do you know?"

"I asked the concierge. The wo-m-man is called Eva Kócsag," he added, as if Zia did not know this. Then he started to explain:

"Don't worry—I did it all very carefully and they don t suspect a thing. I rang the bell and told the concierge I was looking for Dr. Fuchs."

"Who's Dr. Fuchs?"

"I don't know. Just a name. The concierge said: 'There's no Dr. Fuchs living here.' 'Of course there is,' I replied, 'He lives on the first floor.' 'No sir,' said the concierge, 'M-miss Eva Kócsag the actress lives on the first floor.' 'I can't understand it,' I said, 'this is the address they gave m-m-me. Perhaps the actress is having a party, and Dr. Fuchs is there.' 'I'm afraid you're m-mistaken,' he said somewhat rudely, 'there's no party at M-m-miss Kócsag's.' And that's how I found out."

So Talmudic a manner of reasoning could not have originated with a Baron Ubul Lerche-Friis. The spirit of Grünberger sat ensconced in the young baron's mind to handle cases like this; for the business partnership had not failed to leave its mark. It was a reciprocal arrangement: Grünberger was not only instructor but was instructed as well. He learned from Ubi that only waiters wore a black tie with tails, that the word *intelligence* was not pronounced "intelligents," that *detective* was not "detective," that it was not necessary to insist on kissing the hand of a young woman, and that Primo de Rivera was not an Italian egg dealer but the former head of the Spanish Republic. In his own circle, Grünberger made as much use of his newly acquired knowledge as Ubi did of the many thousands of years' experience that the Jewish spirit provided for dealing with delicate and difficult moments in life. In the final analysis, it was Ubi who made the better bargain.

Zia and Ubi sat on the stone wall of the villa across the way and watched the two illuminated windows, shining high above the branches. It was past midnight, and there was no sign of life in the neighboring villas. It was not hard to discover that the brighter of the two windows opened on the dining room where they were having supper. The rattle of plates could be heard, the opening of doors and even the sound of voices, although the width of the street made it impossible to understand what was said. What language were they speaking? German, the language they had used at the Blind Mouse too. A great deal can be expressed with a small vocabulary. The more dimly lit room was evidently the bedroom. From time to time Zia perked up her ears at the distant purr of a car. She was still hoping against hope that a fleet of cars would suddenly invade Menta Utca, with Vira and Ferenc and ten, twenty others; and sometimes she felt an urge to telephone home in case Filippo's message was already waiting: "Come on down to Fourteen Menta Utca, we're all having a grand time at Eva Kócsag's."

But the purring motor was swallowed up in the night every time. Perhaps an hour passed this way. Suddenly the yellow light went out, and Zia gripped Ubi's arm. A few seconds later a black shape appeared in the dim square of the bedroom window. It was like a silhouette in a frame. Quite clearly this was Filippo, seated on the window sill. Even his black holder was discernible as it slanted from his mouth.

Ubi had no idea what they were waiting for, what was to follow and what his assignment would be. He had brought his revolver along, in any case. If Zia, whose grip on his arm grew ever fiercer, had whispered at that moment: "Go upstairs and kill them both!"—he would have done it without a moment's thought. As his motionless eyes studied Filippo's silhouette he reflected that the latter's head made an excellent target. Nor would it be hard to find the heart of the silhouette from this vantage point. Ubi was a noted marksman, having inherited this talent from his mother. He felt that the "favor" Zia mentioned in the forenoon had not yet come to light in what had happened so far. Ubi was a Dukay too and he knew that the Dukays expressed most complex things in the simplest words. When Zia became engaged to Filippo her kinsmen had discussed his person thoroughly, and his origins as well, and Ubi knew that one of his ancestors had been Lucrezia, the sister of Cesare Borgia, and that the walls of Florentine palazzos still dripped with the blood of countless family murders. In a café last spring Grünberger slapped the face of a certain Zilzer, who had made advances to his wife. This was a middle-class riposte. But Filippo's silhouette in the window frame, here in the night, summoned up the ways of the sixteenth century with particular force, because someone who has become an egg dealer soars to even greater heights when there is occasion to obey the dictates of Dukay ancestry, and especially when that someone is only nineteen years old.

Filippo's silhouette vanished from the window. The window was closed, and then the Venetian blinds cascaded down like a farewell burst of machine-gun fire aimed at the outside world. The only remaining light came from a faraway street lamp. Ubi and Zia stood up. And some moments later the silence was broken once again by the sound that seemed to come from a dentist's chair of pain, but this time it did not break off. It was Zia's sobbing, her choked moans as she bit her lips, a frightening, hysterical weeping fit the like of which Ubi had never heard. He took Zia in his arms. Her whole body was trembling, and he could feel her helplessly biting into his shoulder. Her weeping had an improbable sound, lustful and dreadful, like the caterwauls sometimes heard on rooftops.

"Someone's co-m-ming," Ubi whispered, so close that his lips touched the lobe of Zia's ear.

Zia subsided. She hung like a corpse in Ubi's arms. A policeman was approaching. The slow click of his boots on the sidewalk was like the tick of a human metronome measuring out the time in its own peculiar way. The policeman passed without stopping, and only glanced at them out of the corner of his eye. Clenched like that in each other's arms, unwilling to release their grip even when someone passed, a boy and a girl would not have any burglar's tools. At such times another kind of burglary was going on. They were timeless shades of the lukewarm night; their motionlessness, the policeman well knew, was like that of heavenly bodies, of the stars and the moon.

When the policeman's clicking strides were far in the distance, Ubi made Zia sit down on the stone wall.

Zia sniffed, and her whimpering voice soon said:

"Do you have a handkerchief?"

Ubi snatched at his pockets with both hands, as if a live rat were running beneath his clothes. But he found no handkerchief. He only carried handkerchiefs in his dinner jacket. Zia held the back of her hand under her nose with a gesture that urgently demanded a handkerchief. Ubi reached under his vest, pulled out his shirt and tore a handkerchief-sized piece off with a loud rip.

"At your service."

The solution was not practical merely; he meant to make Zia laugh. Zia took the unusual handkerchief and blew her nose vigorously. Then, holding the handkerchief at her nose, she began to laugh, in empty, cold trills and rising crescendos, demented and dreadful sounds which made Ubi tremble with the apprehension that she had lost her mind. Her odd laughter had no relation to reason, it was like the blue flame that sometimes springs from a burning body and flies into the air of its own accord. And then she suddenly stopped laughing. She gave the handkerchief to Ubi with a natural gesture and lit a cigarette. She calmly puffed the cigarette, and all at once she made a surprising remark in a simple, objective voice, almost to herself:

"God damn it to hell."

She had not completely recovered her poise, but was past the danger of abnegation. It is not altogether easy to tread the path from the shores of madness back to the clarity that is known to us by the vague name of reason. What could the word *God* signify to Zia's soul right now? Nothing but the moments of the wedding, there in the church, and Bishop Zsigmond's well-shaped hand as he drew the ring on kneeling Filippo's finger, and the "until death do us part" of the marriage vow that once rang as clearly as an eternal truth and here, in the darkness, behind the lowered blinds, had become the pair of discarded socks which Filippo, carelessly enough, used to strew around the bed.

Zia spoke up once again:

"Do you know a garage somewhere? I want to take the car away. I have my own key. Anyway, the car is mine, all the papers are in my name."

This cold conclusion greatly surprised Ubi. He found it amazing that even at such a moment the sense of property should occur to the mind first of all. But he was glad to see how rational she was. At the same time he felt a certain disillusion. The strange evening, which his imagination had begun to make into a dashing Renaissance tale, was turning into the insignificance of a wife's vengeance: they were snatching the car from under Filippo. But Zia had something else in mind. She needed the car as conclusive evidence.

"You can use the courtyard in our warehouse. There are three em-m-pty garages there."

Zia had already started toward the car. For the first time Ubi was close enough to take a good look at the automobile, for during the pursuit it had wavered ahead of him like a yellow spot. While Zia groped for her key he looked the vehicle over with the eyes of a man who has only a motorcycle. He decided that the machine was a little marvel.

"Follow me," Zia whispered from behind the wheel. The policeman was not in sight, fortunately, for otherwise he would have nabbed the car thieves. Here, too, the street sloped somewhat. Noiselessly they rolled away from Menta Utca.

Ubi had a key to the rear entrance of the courtyard and to the garage as well; thus equipped, they whisked the car inside without being seen.

"Now call a cab," Zia said.

"We don't need a cab. Sit behind me and hold onto my neck."

He made this suggestion not because he was grasping but because he wanted to be grasped. Zia agreed to the proposal. Ubi drove slowly and with care, if only to prolong the trip, to prolong his contact with the gentle weight of the passenger at his back, with the softness of her small breasts and the hands clasped around his neck. There was a certain childlike sadness about the clasp of her hands. There is no feeling in life more beautiful than to support, protect, succor someone. The lonely motorcycle huffed and puffed through the deserted night. This time the policemen did not reach for their notebooks as they watched from the doorways.

The gardener opened the gate. The arc lamp came on over the entrance, and its bright glow put an end to the magic of the strange night.

Zia extended her hand to Ubi.

"Thank you," she said simply. And before she vanished through the iron grating of the gate she raised her hand once more and fluttered her fingers at Ubi in French fashion.

✢

It was about three o'clock in the morning.

At about five o'clock Filippo left the house on Menta Utca. It was still dark. When he failed to find the car in its place, he stood stock-still and pushed his hat back on his head. He put his hands on his hips. The black holder clasped between his teeth quickly traveled back and forth from one corner of his mouth to the other, as if it had divined the situation too. The gate was locked. Filippo had to ring for the concierge. And the concierge spoke nothing but Hungarian. Filippo's hands asked where his car had gone. Instead of replying, the concierge merely stared at him with sleepy eyes.

"Toot-toot," Filippo explained, and started to press an imaginary horn in the air. It would have been simpler to say auto, which is the word for auto in every language, but this did not occur to him now. In any case, he did not consider Hungarian a tongue fit for humans. The concierge began to understand what was going on. He stepped out on the street, looked around, raised his palms, shrugged and answered in the same tongue:

"Toot-toot...nincs toot-toot."

This was not much help, for so much Filippo already knew. They stood for some moments in bewilderment. Filippo rejected the idea of returning to the actress, who had been dreaming her sweetest dreams when he left the bed. What was he to do? There was no way to tell the brutishly stupid concierge to phone for a cab. He waved the man inside and started to walk down Menta Utca alone.

His fists were clenched, as if carrying two heavy suitcases. Had the black holder not been made of hard ebony, he would have crushed it with his teeth at this moment. He was an Italian, and could hardly control his rages. The disappearance of the car was even more awkward because, while lying in bed between passionate embraces, he had presented the car to Eva. It was a somewhat reckless if truly noble gesture, brought about by his inability to evade her innuendoes. He merely stipulated that she have the car painted, because everyone knew whom the lemon-yellow little automobile belonged to. This much, at least, he owed his wife. Eva had learned to drive on this car—that was how it all started—and it is well known that everyone falls in love with the first car he drives. This mysterious relationship between motor and master, man and machine, has not yet been completely clarified. Without a doubt, however, there is something like the first surrender of love in the initial acquiescence of the machine to one's hands and feet. Filippo's idea was that Eva did not ask for the car simply because she wanted to own a car—for she was, after all, a truly modest and refined soul. She wanted *that* particular car, and this was understandable. Jewelry was something else. She demanded jewelry in order to own jewels; certainly, under such circumstances, such a woman is entitled to a jewel of some dimension. It is true that at least a quarter of the capital funds of Lucello Italiano had been devoted to this purpose; but everything in the world takes money. It was even worse that Filippo had no idea where he was going. At first he turned from one street to the other on the downhill slope, thinking that the downgrade would finally lead to a larger square, but this supposition led him into a gully where there were even fewer houses on the streets and from which all the streets ran uphill. He began to be afraid. He had already seen one suspicious character approaching, and had crossed to the other side of the street. He had had an adventure like this once, going through a park one night in Nice. Two men dressed like sailors tried to rob him, and one had a knife in his hand. Fortunately policemen mounted on bicycles came wheeling through the park at that very moment. On that occasion, too, he had been wearing his dinner jacket. Dinner jackets were well suited for theaters or indoor wear, but not for suburban streets on a dark morning in a strange town

502

where he did not know the native tongue. Furthermore, it was beginning to rain. To rain? It was a veritable downpour. If he could have put his hand on the car thief at the moment, Filippo would undoubtedly have throttled him. Always, everywhere, taxis cringe from the rain. Cabs go underground when it rains. But perhaps this is only an optical illusion. In any case, it was about seven o'clock when Filippo staggered home, muddy and drenched, in full daylight.

He slept until three in the afternoon without a break, and breakfasted in bed oblivious of the hour. He bathed and dressed, in order to be at the Casino in time for his afternoon poker game. While bathing he remembered the car. He should report the theft to the police, but if he did this he would have to say where it occurred, and the incident might get in the papers. He was trapped; he had trapped himself. Nothing so enrages a man as to be balked by something of his own, to catch the pocket of his jacket on a doorknob or close the door on the trailing sash of his dressing gown. While washing his hair Filippo became so angry and rubbed his scalp so viciously that he almost set fire to it with his finger tips.

Later, when he was ready to leave, he met Zia in the salon. Approaching her with a smile, he said lightly:

"Imagine what a stupid thing happened to me last night—my car was stolen."

Zia stood in the center of the room, as erect as a candlestick. Erect and pale.

"I took the car away. At night, from Eva Kócsag's house."

Filippo's hand froze in air. So surprised was he by his exposure that for a few moments he was unable to speak and only his face altered, fearfully and strangely. His chestnut-colored glance, which could fill with such pleading, was now cold, and cast an unknown light. He stepped close to Zia and his voice was something she had never heard before. There was choked anger in his rasp:

"Comment as-tu osé? How did you dare?"

"The car is mine," Zia answered quietly and coolly, raising her chin a shade higher. Bestial wrath flared in Filippo's eyes. His upper lip curled back repulsively as he struck Zia in the face with the full force of his fist. Zia went down and lay on the floor like a discarded garment She was unconscious for some moments, and only recovered at the gunshot of the door as Filippo slammed it after him.

She slowly rose from the floor, with a dreamlike motion. She felt as if she had no jaw. It was an odd, frightening feeling, very much like the feeling she once had at the dentist when the whole side of her face vanished after an injection. This occupied all her thoughts for a few moments. Then she began to scream. It was a marrow-shaking scream. But her scream was one word, clearly syllabified:

"Beri-liii!"

The long, drawn-out *i*-sound, sharpened into a scream, carried as far as the voice can possibly carry when a human being screams for help in a moment of great danger. Frightened by her own scream, she shivered and ran, with teeth chattering, into the bathroom. Had someone heard her scream? Filippo was already on the street, but in any case he would have heard nothing but the mutterings of his own wrath. It was even less likely to have been heard by the one whose aid it beseeched.

The scream meant that there was nobody for Zia to turn to. Her mother? Countess Menti's opinion would have been that under such circumstances a countess pretends to notice nothing, and under no circumstances may she scream. Her father? Count Dupi would have rumbled and grumbled, taken her in his lap and consoled her like a weeping child with a thorn in her foot or a cut on her finger. At most he would have said: Nonsense.

Zia rang an hour later, Elizabeth stepped in, the chambermaid who had been with her since childhood. She must have been quite close to come so quickly.

"Call the chauffeur and the footman."

Zia did not care whether the mark of the blow still showed on her cheek. She gave orders calmly. To the footman:

"Phone the station. Reserve a compartment for tonight on the Trieste Express. Then come and help me pack."

To Elizabeth and the chauffeur:

"Bring me all my trunks."

She rejected two suitcases, two ancient pigskin bags that had come from her parent's home and bore the eleven-pointed coronet and the blue and red Dukay stripes. First she dismantled her photographic equipment. All her lamps, papier-mâché trays, cameras and accessories were packed in a flat trunk, carefully so they would not break. This was work enough for the chauffeur and the footman. Another large trunk was filled with books. Then Elizabeth helped Zia pack her clothes. Traveling, and packing too, requires a high cultural perspective. Middle-class women, facing shorter journeys in much calmer states of mind, are beset with uncertainty as they survey the open suitcases. For unknown reasons they insist on packing vast flower vases, and at the same time forget to take their toothbrushes.

504

Here the problem of packing was handled with the efficiency of doctors at a major operation, where assistants hand the instruments, where objects and the hands of men work with a marvelous coordination, unhaltingly, unhesitatingly. This packing was like a major operation in another respect as well. Blood flowed here, too, but invisibly, and the odd extremities of life were severed from the flesh. Inventory book in hand, Zia calmly directed the packing. Separate pages in this inventory were devoted to overcoats, dresses, underclothes, shoes, stockings, belts, buckles, toilet articles, parasols, gloves, mysterious feminine things, prayer books, family photographs. Each item had its own number and its own place in the drawers and on the shelves. By the time the two cabs arrived, every trunk was closed and already on the way downstairs. One taxi took the footman and the luggage. Zia entered the other cab.

Before leaving, she gave the chauffeur two letters to be delivered that very evening. One of them was addressed to Septemvir Utca, to her father:

Dear Papa, I should like to spare myself and all of you the recital of what has happened. The details aren't important anyway. Don't fret, don't worry about me. I am going away for a rest; more, more than anything else, I must have solitude. Zia.

The other letter was a large, fat envelope addressed to His Excellency Baron Ubul Lerche-Friis. This letter said:

Ubi, Enclosed are the necessary papers and the letter of transfer. The car is yours. Zia.

She did not look back, either at the room or at the house. She told no one where she was going.

Chapter Eleven

THE SHIP that left Fiume once a week to tramp the eastern coasts of the Adriatic arrived in the harbor of Mandria at eight o'clock in the evening. Six natives of the island disembarked. First and friskiest was Ettore Domeneghetti the barber, frisky because he carried only a few bars of soap and some bottles of hair tonic in his barber's kit. Ettore Domeneghetti never wore a hat; instead he wore the mark of his trade on his head by way of advertisement. The advertisement took the form of his own coiffure, for his hair was parted on the side and arrayed across his pate in enormous waves the like of which only the morning breeze known as the *tramontana* could whip up in the tresses of the awakening sea. Now, as always, three good-sized combs in parallel line clasped this walking advertisement in place. Behind him the butcher Aldo Faggiani proceeded with more difficulty, because the blood-stained canvas sack on his back contained a side of veal. This half of a calf constituted the meat supply of Mandria for one whole week, for only the intelligentsia ate meat, and they only infrequently. Today as always Faggiani had voyaged to the market in Lussinpiccolo on Pietro Torriti's rickety motorboat and, as always, he had chosen this somewhat safer means of returning home with his precious cargo. The butcher's long nose, dipping over his mouth, and the rounded muscles that cushioned his body gave him the look of a tapir thoroughly domesticated and trained to do various clever stunts. The third passenger was a fat, dark woman, Amalia, the wife of Niccolini the grocer, and she too had been to Lussinpiccolo for supplies. She panted under the weight of a suitcase, made of fiberboard and fastened with string. The fourth passenger was Eulalia, with hair parted in the middle and handsome black eyes and two front teeth missing. She was the manager of the dairy. Her bundles did not overburden her, for she brought only a little cheese and some curds and butter. Behind her on the narrow gangplank came Parson Muzmics and Nyinyin the bell ringer, back from an official visit to the Episcopate. The elderly parson had a wide, good-natured peasant face and a saddle- shaped Slav nose, and instead of hair his crimson skull had a thick covering of tiny whitish-yellow bristles, like barley buds blossoming in a basement. The parson had the chest of a turkey cock. The bell ringer Nyinyin looked the wiser of the two, but perhaps only because he wore spectacles. One of the earpieces of his spectacles was broken, and black thread held it in its socket, a makeshift device. According to druggist Occhipinti, who was renowned for his pithy sayings, Nyinyin wore glasses to help him with his bell ringing. The glasses and their owner recently sat for two months in the prison at Fiume for smuggling, but this, in the opinion of Parson Muzmics, had already been forgiven by the Good Lord. The parson must have enjoyed a goodly share of divine forgiveness too, for he did not scorn smuggling either. By now it is safe for us to reveal that the parson, whose yellow fingernails betrayed a consummate addiction to the pleasures of nicotine, sported a chest like a turkey cock because one thousand gold-tipped Jugoslav cigarettes were hidden beneath his soutane. These were the six Mandrian travelers.

The seventh passenger was a young woman who arrived with a vast amount of luggage. During the crossing the Mandrians had already discussed her presence, but could come to no satisfactory conclusion. There had been nineteen vacationists in Mandria during the summer, but they had all gone home long ago. Obviously, since Mandria was the last stop, the young woman was coming to Mandria. Finally Parson Muzmics solved the riddle. The woman was tubercular. In the past forty years he himself had escorted seventeen tuberculars down the final road to the cemetery in Mandria, all of them outsiders who came to the island because the ocean air was their only hope. The Mandrians, in a group apart on the deck, had nodded in agreement with the aged parson's words. The young lady sat all by herself on the opposite, side of the deck and stared into the air for hours, as if her apple-green eyes were already exploring the afterworld. Aldo Faggiani, the butcher, gave her only a few months more to live. The estimate of Nyinyin the bell ringer was prejudiced by the number of strokes he would have to ring at the funeral, and he wondered whether there would be any money to cover burial expenses, for indeed the blond young man from Linz who died the year before last had left only two handkerchiefs behind him. Nyinyin was comforted by the sight of the woman's huge trunks. The Mandrians disembarked from the ship with the conviction that their island would soon be richer by one corpse.

It was by no means simple to take that luggage ashore. One large trunk almost tore the arms off the half-naked youngsters who were idling about the wharf. That one was full of books. The second, a large, fiat trunk, contained the cameras and photographic accessories. The third, packed with dresses and miscellaneous clothing, was the lightest. Where could she find a room? Occhipinti the druggist obliged with an answer:

"Only the Pension Zanzottera can come into consideration."

They secured some handcarts and the caravan set out for the Pension Zanzottera. Darkness had fallen, and this time too they felt their way up the improbably narrow street with the help of a flashlight, but for Zia the light shone otherwise than it had a year and a half ago when they were climbing toward the Hasparics villa. The smell of fish frying in oil greeted them as they entered the hallway. Was there a room to be had? Was there a room—of course there was, the signora replied excitedly, wiping oil from her shiny chin. With each of her smiles two narrow rows of contracted teeth sprang to the forefront of her mouth. Zia inspected the room that Mr. Gruber had once occupied, and looked at the terrace as well. She found it satisfactory. In the space of seconds her eyes refurnished the room, which was wide enough to permit installation of a darkroom in one corner. How much was the room? The signora gave her chin a final wipe with the handkerchief before she answered, and her answer was a question: For how long? Zia gazed into the air, as if called upon to decide in two seconds the most important question of her life—how long before Filippo would come for her. That he would come for her was certain, but it was difficult to know when he would come. During their honeymoon, seated once on the terrace of the Hasparics villa and looking down at the wonderful quietude of the bay, Zia had told Filippo:

"This is where I shall come if I'm ever in trouble."

Tears came to the corners of her eyes as she said this, for the sweetest moments of happiness are always ready to tempt sorrow. Filippo noticed her tears and tried to make a joke of the whole thing. He took out his notebook with great seriousness:

"Wait a moment—I'll write it down before I forget it"

And he wrote: *If Zia gets into trouble—address, Mandria.* But there was no need to write it down. In the course of a lifetime there are some sentences that stay in the memory as long as teeth last in the tomb. If Filippo wanted to find her he would know where to look. But when would he come? Waiting patiently, the signora leaned down to adjust the tip of a rug.

"It's not definite yet. But I would take the room for a month."

The answer satisfied the signora. Although there was no more oil on her chin, she began to wipe it again.

508

"Thirty-five liras daily for room and board."

Zia understood foreign exchange, unlike her family and friends. Still, she could hardly believe that the rate was so low. She turned her head toward the signora, and the latter took fright from this movement

"Let's say thirty-two," she amended hastily, and her narrow dentures came shooting out twice like the tongue of a snake. Zia nodded, lest the signora reduce the rate even more.

"Frau Kunz?"

"She's no longer in Mandria. She's not likely to come back, either, because she had a quarrel last year with Giuseppina, the butcher's wife."

This reassured Zia. Frau Kunz was the only one who might have recognized her. During their four-week stay here, she and Filippo had hardly moved out of the Hasparics villa, and they had worn dark sunglasses on their few excursions to the Piazza Vittorio Emanuele. Before her departure from Fuga Utca, she had taken care not to pack a single garment that she had worn on her previous trip.

"Has the lady been to Mandria before?" inquired the precipitate dentures.

"Once, a long time ago; but I merely passed through."

The porters—whose number had grown to more than twenty on the way— brought the trunks in. The oldest could not have been more than fifteen years old. When the signora sighted the large and fashionable trunks she stuck her teeth out in a smile that dripped with vinegar. There was mighty regret in her heart for the three liras she had conceded on the daily rate. She opened the register for Zia. Unhesitatingly Zia wrote down the identity she had decided upon during the voyage: *Teréz Hemli*. Occupation: *Photographer.*

"Would you like some supper?"

"No, thank you. I ate on the ship."

"Can I help you unpack?"

"Thank you, no."

The signora spread clean sheets on the wide studio couch and then left the tired-looking guest to herself. The long trip had really worn Zia out. Here in Mandria she felt as far removed from Budapest as if the Pension Zanzottera were not even on the face of the earth. She took nothing more than a mallow-colored silk nightgown from her trunk; unpacking could wait till tomorrow. She placed her tiny red slippers beside the couch. Hardly had she put them down when the sight of the little red slippers suddenly struck a pain in her heart. The two little slippers lacked substance and led nowhere now; they looked terrifying, like two

509

bleeding feet chopped off at the ankle. At home those two little slippers had always led to the great French bed. And then to Filippo. She sat on the edge of the couch and began to whimper. It was a solitary sort of weeping, when the tears flow freely along the face and sometimes the tongue collects the salty tears around the mouth because they have grown ticklish; the hand has not enough strength left to reach for a handkerchief. Zia got into bed. She lay on her back, with both hands stretched along her thighs. Gradually the tears in the corners of her eyes cooled, and grew as cold as soothing eye-drops. Weariness soon put her to sleep.

Next morning the signora knocked and brought a breakfast tray, with a boiled egg, coffee, toast and a little jam. Might she sit down for a moment? Signor Occhipinti the druggist had a spare radio and would be glad to lend it to the lady if she would undertake the cost of repairs. "No, thank you." The signora kept returning to the subject of Occhipinti the druggist, and Zia surmised that there was something between them. The signora was a woman of about forty. Black, darting eyes, a small, sharp nose and a sloping forehead gave evidence of former beauty.

Zia did not want to acknowledge the existence of an outside world. The radio did not interest her, nor had she ordered any newspapers sent after her. No one knew she was in Mandria; only Filippo's little notebook knew. Her impulse now was to become a real Princess Oasika, who once built, with the help of elephants and tigers and with no other materials than her memories, a crimson citadel with yellow towers on the Hill of Oranges.

The dead say that the first day in the grave is the hardest. Decomposition sets in, the gristles come loose and the collarbones release their grip to let decay suffuse the cavities of the body freely. On that first day Zia warded off the onslaughts of her mind and her memory by occupying herself with work. After breakfast she went down to grocer Niccolini's shop on the Piazza Vittorio Emanuele, where cloth was sold too, of course. He had only three different patterns of calico, true; but Zia found a green and brown flowered pattern that she thought would do and, much to the surprise of the incredibly long-necked Niccolini, she bought the entire bolt. Two little Niccolinis carried the vast quantity of calico home for her. The Italian lessons with Signor Vallencic two years ago stood Zia in good stead now; and a lot of Filippo's Italian had stayed with her too. At the Pension she borrowed the signora's sewing machine and set to work. She recalled, now, how the One-Eyed Regent had reproached Berili for teaching her to sew at the age of thirteen. Zia's room, in addition to the large studio couch, contained two armchairs, a wicker chair, a smallish table that served as a writing desk, a larger table for meals and two rather charming old cherry-wood wardrobes. Then there was an old-fashioned marble washstand and beside it the bidet, hidden from view by a screen. The colors of the slip-covers on the couch and the armchairs clashed raucously with the tablecloth and the screen, however, destroying the atmosphere of a room that was otherwise pleasant enough. But noblewomen know the simple and serene secrets of furnishing a room, and Zia knew that if she covered the multitude of conflicting colors with a charming, unpretentious, uniform pattern, the mood of the room would at once be changed. But there must be no sparing of material. The sewing machine hummed in her room till late in the evening. The tape measure flew in her hands, and the large shears snapped. The signora herself, when she came in, was surprised to see what a warm little nest the room had become. There were ruffles on all the slip covers, and the same pattern replaced the ugly burgundy curtain. The same material covered the dressing table on which the silver-framed mirror that Zia always took on trips abroad was already preening. Her tortoise-shell toilet set, the wedding present of Princess Marie, was arrayed before the mirror. She had but to discuss the darkroom with the signora. It needed only some shelves, a few plateholders and a carpenter. The outside of the darkroom would be covered with the very same material.

By the afternoon of the next day the darkroom stood ready, and by evening it was covered. The wardrobes were filled, and the empty trunks went up to the attic. The sweet, slightly nauseating smell of fresh calico pervaded the room. Her feverish efforts carried Zia through the first two days.

On the morning of the third day she entered the church of San Simeone, where she had visited with Filippo now and again. This time she was alone, kneeling near the altar. Parson Muzmics and bell ringer Nyinyin came out of the sacristy and walked down the aisle of empty benches. They stopped to crane their necks for a moment at the tubercular woman, the certain prey of death, but they did not speak of this right now.

Autumn was here. The ship from Fiume changed its schedule and now docked at Mandria only once every two weeks, at four in the afternoon. The days were still warm, and the children gaily splashed in the sea. Nothing so poignantly expresses the death of summer as an abandoned bathhouse. The music of gramophones, the shrieks of children and the slaps of their mammas are painfully absent from the empty cabins; and from the green water the dignified breaststroke of the elderly is missing, and the dolphin capers of the young; and the tanned bodies, sprawled out like seals, are missing from the sandy beaches. The sun still shines fiercely in the noon hours, but the ever-shortening days along the unpopulated beaches mark the obsequies of summer.

Twice each day Zia covered the length of the water-front. She passed the bagno and only turned back at the stone bridge, which spanned the deep but dry riverbed that ran down from the hilltop. The arid stone bottom, which reached in an irregular and constantly narrowing white stripe into the heights of the dark and distant hills, looked as if fire rather than water had once rushed over its surface and burned the stones to whiteness. At this time of year, in truth, the golden fire of autumn poured like a flood from the hills into the riverbed, Zia would sit on the stone railing of the bridge to rest. To walk to this point took fully three quarters of an hour. Thus she walked for an hour and a half each morning and each afternoon. It was these three hours of daily walking that kept the spirit alive in her. Nobody else ever ventured this far. The rubber-soled shoes made her own footsteps inaudible, and this greatly augmented the sense of stillness and solitude. Now she was Princess Oasika indeed, who built herself a crimson citadel with yellow towers, aided by tigers and elephants, without materials except her own memories. She sat on the stone railing of the bridge just as she had once sat on the parapet of the watch-tower in Buda, with one leg drawn up, showing the pink bend of a silk-sheathed knee beneath her short skirt to an eagle wheeling in wide circles so high in the air that it looked scarcely bigger than a sparrow. She was watching the progress of the construction, and her thoughts were similar to those of the thread salesman who once sat on an overturned plaster-barrow and watched the construction of his villa on Fuga Utca. The Brahman elephants moved great beams with their trunks, and these beams bore a resemblance to the gilt Spavento rafters that decked the ceiling of Marchese Delfrate's salons. The yellow-striped tigers carried white-fleshed Correggio nudes up the hill with their teeth, and the parched, stony riverbed sang "O mia Fiamma bellissima." From the violet-hued Dalmatian cliffs came the distant sound of mandolins. Her eyes strayed to a near-by magnolia tree that slowly came to resemble the door of Filippo's bathroom. She opened the door and there was Filippo, naked beside the tub, resting one foot on the little rush chair and carving his toenails with manicure scissors. The hard little nail clippings scattered like buckshot. Even now the white teeth at the left corner of his mouth gripped the little ebony holder, and the diamonds glittered around its rim.

The ship would arrive at four o'clock on Thursday afternoon. There were still three days to go. Had she already been here for eleven days? She did not know. Nor did she know the date of her departure from home. She had to count back into the past to recall that she had left on the twenty-eighth and arrived in Mandria on the thirtieth. She took it for granted that Filippo would be on the Thursday boat. It was better that the whole thing had happened like this, that Filippo had struck her. When Filippo stomped out after their scene, he walked down Fuga Utca, and must have gone on foot to the nearest taxi stand. What was in his heart when he left? Such blows always hurt the one who strikes more than the stricken. Then, like a brief but alarming attack of high fever, the fury leaves the body. Because, yes, such fury is the work of the body, of the nerves. Filippo took a cab. Where might he have gone? He probably went to the Casino to sit in on one of the games of bridge. Now she could clearly see the movement of Filippo's hands as he held the cards. The brown thumb, with its rather short nail, curved arc-wise back. Then what happened? Did he see Eva Kócsag that evening? It was unlikely. Filippo went home, perhaps without any supper. At home he walked up and down the rooms, around the big beet-red brocade settee in the salon, into the dining room, and all the way to the bookcase, in his own room, which was the itinerary he had always followed while pondering the plans for the establishment of Lucello Italiano. He walked like this for hours, until midnight was long past. Sometimes he stopped, raised his right hand and began to scratch his skull with a stiff forefinger. This was a sign that his spiritual travails were beginning to abate. But his mood changed from moment to moment. Sometimes he threw himself into the big beet-red settee which had accompanied them from the palace on Septemvir Utca; they had taken it along because it had shared the most beautiful hours of their engagement, in the light of the shaded Chinese lamp. There sat Filippo on the beet-red settee, and suddenly he buried his face in his two hands. Yes, Filippo wept. He had to weep because of what he had done. Zia pictured it all perfectly.

Now the elephants and tigers turned about on the hilltop and came down the empty riverbed to fetch new materials. The elephants carried large buckets of Filippo's tears up the hill with their trunks. The tigers, unable to lift them with their teeth, dragged the shapeless, dark buffalo and rhinoceros carcasses along the sharp stones: Filippo's sorrow and his pangs of conscience. The cloud-skirting wild geese on the Chinese lampshade broke into a loud and terror-stricken cackle.

Filippo would arrive on Thursday. He would stand at the prow of the ship, and the wings of his sandy colored trenchcoat would wave in the wind. On his head would be a black Basque beret, pulled over one ear, and the black line of the holder at the corner of his mouth would stick out of his face.

Eleven days. What had happened at home in the meantime? She had despatched brief notes only to her father and Ubi at the time of her departure. Why had she not written to her mother? Although she was not aware of it, there was an element of mute revenge in this—because, during the final moments of the wedding, when she broke into tears as she knelt before her parents, the white-gloved hand of Countess Menti, which knew how to hold the little ivory fan with such majesty, had not moved. It was Count Dupi who had leaned over and taken her in his arms. That moment summed up everything that had passed between Zia and her parents since her birth. Now she suddenly wondered whether her father was still alive. Since Berili's unexpected death in the sleeping compartment, and since Uncle Paul's death of a heart attack in the space of minutes, she had often thought of her father's face as it looked when the monotonous hum of the motor put him to sleep in the car on the way to Venice. The sleeping face had discarded its mask, betraying the secret marks of approaching death.

On Thursday afternoon she was in the harbor a full half hour before the ship was scheduled to leave the yonder shore. Up and down she walked, between the customs inspector's booth and the stubby iron bollard around which the hawsers of the ship would be bound. The customs inspector, Guido Castelli, stepped out of his booth, for he attributed the young woman's pacing to the irresistible power of his own masculine beauty, to which any woman in Mandria would fall a victim if he wanted her. In this young woman's appearance, however, there was a certain disdain and dismissal, and at the same time a certain attractive charm. Guido Castelli, who was a stoutish, dark Italian, suddenly noticed that his smile was not working, and some inexplicable embarrassment kept him from addressing the little lady. But finally the yellow teeth flashed between his puffy, dark red lips and when the woman passed by he asked encouragingly, "Are you waiting for someone?" But he hardly recognized his own voice. There was a purple stripe along his dove-gray trousers, and the shape of his hat was like the one which the whole world had already seen in photographs of the squat king of Italy. Because he had somewhat outgrown the dove-gray trousers they gave prominence to the outline of his private organs, especially to his substantial pendant. It was Guido Castelli's custom to put his coat on only after the ship had docked. Right now he wore braces over his sweaty shirt, which described a large X on his back and were tied in knots at the front because the elastic had lost its resiliency. Undeniably there was something reminiscent of Filippo in his face, in the color of his hair and of his dark skin. But he was taller and fatter than Filippo, and considerably dirtier, to be sure. Seen from the back, the buttocks curving below the capital X were large enough even to suffice for two men. "My breeding bull" was what Occhipinti the druggist, well known for his pithy sayings, used to call Guido Castelli the customs inspector, whose question, "Are you waiting for someone?" sounded like an introduction as well. All Mandria knew of the conquests of the customs inspector, and also knew that he was unable to squirm out of the affair he was carrying on with Eulalia, the dairy manager, who was approaching forty, wore her black hair with a part in the middle and lacked two front teeth. Understandably enough, this affair did not content Guido Castelli. Eulalia, on the other hand, was constantly threatening to kill him if he deceived her. Guido Castelli had often complained of this to Niccolini the grocer, who was his intimate friend. There was fiery lust in the dark chestnut-colored eyes of the customs inspector as he stood, with some embarrassment, before Zia: "Are you waiting for someone?"

"Yes," Zia said after a little thought, and then she turned on her heel and left the dove-gray trousers in the lurch.

The smoke of the ship appeared in a northwesterly direction, as mysterious and threatening as the first smoky wisps of a forest fire that seems insignificant and harmless until it covers the entire forest with flame.

The billows of smoke from the approaching ship grew larger. The large X over the dove-gray trousers, having passed Zia for the third time with its hands clasped at the back, did not realize that at this moment it was farther from hope of conquest than any man had ever been.

The ship neared swiftly. Now it was possible to make out some figures on deck. But the prow of the ship was deserted. Still, there...yes, there beside the smokestack stood the sandy colored trenchcoat! The billowing smoke intermittently hid the ship from view, and then, as the vessel turned, the glare of the sun blinded the eyes of the sole spectator. Finally it was made fast alongside

515

the pier. Only one passenger disembarked, the butcher Aldo Faggiani, with the side of veal in its canvas sack on his back.

It was this sack that Zia had mistaken for the sandy colored trenchcoat.

She went home, and as she sat in the armchair by the window a terrible fear seized her. The next day was Friday. How would she struggle through the day? Why was this Friday so menacing? There was no particular reason, except that people do have such inexplicable forebodings. We dread the morrow, but only the morrow, for the day after tomorrow will be simpler. What does the morrow threaten? Nothing. It is this very nothing that is dreadful.

On the morning of the following day Signor Occhipinti the druggist came to pay his respects to Zia. He declared that his twenty-fifth wedding anniversary was coming, and he wished a photograph of himself and his wife for that occasion. He inquired about prices. Zia said she would gladly make the photograph, but could not accept any money because she did not have an Italian commercial permit. This was something Occhipinti could understand, and the next day he appeared with his wife Rina who, for all that she was very fat, did not seem happy. Two days later the picture was ready, and it made the rounds of the natives of Mandria. Occhipinti presented Zia with a tube of hand cream of his own manufacture, but she found that it smelled unbearably of fish. It proved to be useful for oiling the knobs of her photographic tripod and the hinges of squeaky doors. One morning Aldo Faggiani the butcher came to her door and announced that one of his brothers lived in Canada, they hadn't seen each other for twelve years, and he would like to be photographed together with his family. He inquired about prices. Zia explained that she could not accept money because she had no Italian commercial permit. The photograph was taken for nothing, and turned out to be a great success.

Faggiani sent Zia two pounds of veal that already had a somewhat strong smell. Zia presented the meat to the signora, who was very pleased. The following day Niccolini the grocer appeared and related that his sister, whom he hadn't seen for eight years, lived in Cairo. He inquired about prices. Zia informed him that...The Niccolini photograph brought a gift of a musty carton of biscuits. And so it went. All Mandria came. Tattered fishermen appeared, one marvelous character after another, to inquire about prices, since they already knew that the photographer lady did not charge anything. But they did not remain in her debt; they brought gifts of fresh fish or lobster. All this eased the signoras housekeeping expenses considerably, and for the time being she abandoned the idea of raising her guest's monthly rate. The free photographs created a warm bond of friendship between Zia and the inhabitants of Mandria. The rush of business was due to the fact that a rumor, based on Parson Muzmics's considered opinion, had spread throughout all Mandria, to the effect that the lady photographer was tubercular and had not long to live. Thus they all hastened to take advantage of the free pictures before it was too late. Between themselves, the Mandrians began to call Zia nothing but *la fotografa morta,* the dead photographer lady. It afforded the Mandrians considerable amusement to see a living corpse walk among them with a camera hanging from a strap, wearing white tennis shoes and simple but fine little dresses. The corpse became a familiar visitor in Demetrio Niccolini's grocery, where she purchased large quantities of sweets for distribution to the little Mandrian children. Every day she bought six quarts of milk at Eulalia's dairy and carried these up the hillside herself in a little basket, to several poverty-stricken households, among them the orphaned children of Egislo. Two years ago the squalls of the bora had sent one of the bragozzas to the bottom, and Egislo with it.

The next two weeks passed in this way. Thus, for the second time, the smoke of the ship appeared over the empty horizon on Thursday afternoon, and for the second time only Aldo Faggiani the butcher came ashore with the side of veal on his back in a canvas sack.

The last days of November were here, the children bathed less and less often in the sea, the flavor of the sunshine grew increasingly tart and one night Zia woke to the sound of muffled cannon-fire. The bora, that wild North wind, had assaulted Mandria. The arching waves beat their brains out on the reefs, so wrathfully did they storm the steep shores. Dark clouds hid the sky during the day too, and cold blasts hurtled against the rooftops. The bragozzas took refuge in the innermost corner of the shallow lagoon, with orange-yellow sails tightly furled. Their wide black frames completely covered the lagoon, and covered as well the motley aquarium at its bottom. But here too, in the shallow lagoon, they danced and stretched, rubbing their large, ungainly, pitch-smeared bodies together, clinking the tips of their masts. Sometimes such a rush of surf came from the sea that the water overflowed the lagoon, forced its way into the church and Niccolini's grocery and scrubbed the brick floors with hissing foam. But this was no novelty in Mandria. The salty foam even did the dirty old bricks a lot of good. One could hardly move out of the room. Zia ventured out nevertheless, to observe the rare display of the sea. But from the window of his booth Guido Castelli warned her not to go out on the promenade, for some years ago in just such a storm an unexpected wave had lifted a Klagenfurt shopkeeper off the Corso Mussolini and swept him into the sea. The bora itself was occasionally capable of tossing people into the air at such a time. Zia accepted his good advice and went home.

The blusterings of the bora lasted two whole weeks, and Zia reached the fourth volume of *Jean Christophe*. She could not go for walks. Even the elephants and the tigers in the riverbed suspended their construction.

✠

While the bora rages over Mandria, let us return to Budapest and see what has happened in the meantime. Filippo did not spend the evening of their estrangement exactly as Zia had imagined. Her version was accurate only insofar as Filippo did indeed walk down Fuga Utca on foot until he came to the nearest taxi stand. The cab, however, did not take him to the Casino, but rather to Eva Kócsag. Only with difficulty did Eva comprehend what had taken place, because their conversations were conducted in German, a language in which both of them were very weak. Moreover, Filippo's account of the scene was nervous and muddled, and he suppressed the fact that he had struck Zia. All that was clear of the entire incident was that Zia had stolen the little yellow car from the front of the house, and this incensed the *artiste* to a considerable degree. During supper they made their plans. They decided to go abroad together within a few days' time. Filippo went home in the early morning, but the following day he appeared in the offices of Lucello Italiano at ten o'clock. It was the first time this had ever happened. He summoned Mr. Hardt the cashier and gave him a presidential authorization to withdraw the entire capital of the firm from the bank at once. At the bank a big surprise awaited Mr. Hardt. There was an obstacle, the director informed him, in the way of further withdrawals. Mr. Hardt rushed back to Filippo, who immediately telephoned the director and learned that his father-in-law had called right after the bank opened to stop all payments. By what right? In the first place, because he was the principal stockholder. The firm, moreover, did not have an independent account; so far all incoming drafts had been charged

518

against the Dukay account. "Thank you," said Filippo, both to the telephone and to Mr. Hardt, whose face was pale as he stood beside the wide presidential desk. Filippo himself was pale too. Pale, not with excitement but with fury. Fury manifests itself in various shades of green on such dark skins as his.

There was something Signor Tandardini the attorney had neglected to do at the time he was commissioned to collect data on the Ozzolini family. Had he made inquiries among the head-waiters in the restaurants and cafés on the Piazza di San Marco, he could have been abundantly enlightened on the subject of Filippo Ozzolini. They would have told him that the young prince was the most frivolous member of Venetian aristocratic society; that he had an extraordinarily ugly temper, furthermore, and that there were few public places in Venice where he had not been embroiled in scandalous fights. In almost every case the fights were with women. The responsibility for the latest instance did not devolve upon the Ozzolini parents, who were generally held in public esteem. When Filippo told his father of his intention to marry, Achile—who had already suffered much bitterness because of Filippo—had long, soul-searching talks with his son and warned him to change his ways. Filippo swore by heaven and earth that he would do this, and made every promise. The boy was not corrupt by nature, in the opinion of Achile Ozzolini, but was still in the throes of adolescent exuberance.

An affair between an Eva Kócsag and a Prince Ozzolini could not be kept a secret in Budapest for even half a day, for the *artiste* herself hastened to spread the whispered rumors. In the past few weeks the precise details of the matter had come to the knowledge of Prince Fini, Señor Calandra, the flaxen-haired Elizabeth and, generally, all the midtown beauty salons. Everybody except Zia knew all about it. Count Dupi knew about it too, because they told him at the Casino. He was not pleased, but considered the matter a temporary annoyance. At any rate, he could hardly set himself up as an arbiter of morals. Zia had left at nine o'clock in the evening on the day of their estrangement. A half hour later the chambermaid Elizabeth was already in the Septemvir Utca Palace, urgently requesting an audience with Countess Menti. Elizabeth adored Zia and had the remarkable ability of the Hungarian peasant to conceal such things. Elizabeth was of the same age as Zia and, as a youngster who belonged to the staff, had grown up with her in the park at Ararat. This aspect of Countess Menti's method of raising her children was decidedly to her credit. She did not keep them apart from the peasant children of Ararat; in fact, it was her express wish that her sons and daughters be in constant company with village youngsters of their own age. In this she was at variance with her sister Stefi and her brother-in-law Paul, who strictly forbade the children of the peasants to so much as set foot in the park of their estate. Several barefooted, pigtailed little peasant girls, among them Elizabeth, were always at home in Zia's childhood rooms. She was a good-hearted child, and shared her playthings, her sweets and oranges with her fellows. Later Elizabeth went to Fuga Utca as a chambermaid. She was forever at Zia's side, not only in thought but physically as well, ready to ward off any unexpected danger. Zia's state of mind had not escaped her on the day of the estrangement, and she knew that something would happen that very day. She did not eavesdrop; she was simply in the vicinity when the heated scene took place. Standing at the door of the salon, she heard the growing violence of the exchange in French, she heard Filippo slam the door behind him, and in particular she heard Zia's heartbreaking outcry when her mistress shouted Berili's name a few moments later. Then she noted the mark of the blow on Zia's face. From the evidence of the hasty packing and the sudden departure, it was not difficult to guess what had happened.

The One-Eyed Regent heard Elizabeth's story through patiently and deemed the matter serious enough to submit the girl's request for an audience to Her Excellency the Countess. And it took place when the countess retired to her room after supper to play patience. Countess Menti's face, while she heard the report, looked as if she were listening to routine business of the Catholic Women's Union or the Anti-Tuberculosis Institute. But, after dismissing Elizabeth with a nod of her head, she judged it important enough to go to her husband's room, in itself an unusual departure from custom. Count Dupi was already in bed, reading a saucy French novel. For a long time after hearing the story he said nothing, but merely jabbed at the root of his mustache with the crippled forefinger of his left hand. Then he suddenly leapt from the bed. There was, however, little significance to his leap, for after painstakingly slipping his feet into his slippers he went to the window and adjusted the curtain pull, which happened to be completely unnecessary at that moment. Then he went back to bed without comment. Countess Menti left him to himself.

Two days later Filippo and Eva Kócsag stole away secretly. The actress, who took sudden "sick leave" and even forfeited her salary, departed like someone who leaves all the taps running in a great wine cellar. The story now current was that Zia and the *artiste* had engaged in a hair-pulling fray, but different versions placed the battle in different places. Finally Mr. Runcsík, the proprietor of the restaurant where Zia ordered a glass of Vichy while waiting for Ubi's phone call, came forward with his testimony. Mr. Runcsík confessed to the editor of a little weekly paper that the scandal had taken place in his dining room. What exactly had happened was that the young Princess Ozzolini appeared at the restaurant around midnight in an obviously liquored state and ordered a bottle of cognac. About a half hour later Eva Kócsag and the Italian prince entered. They sat down at a table without noticing the wedded wife, who was musing in solitude. Hardly were they seated when the princess sprang up, dashed to their table and struck the *artiste* on the head, twice, with her parasol. The prince jumped to his feet and pinioned his wife's arms, while the *artiste* threw the salt shaker at the princess, striking her on the forehead. The prince escorted his wife to the street, where he slapped her roundly. The restaurateur even showed the journalist the broken parasol, but without revealing that this parasol had been found on the battlefield after a clash between a prostitute and a drunken horse salesman.

"But please, szerkesztö ur," Mr. Runcsík whispered, "you know I only tell you about it because you're an old customer of ours, and I don't expect anything for the information, but as long as fate has decreed that this unfortunate affair should happen to take place here, I'd like to ask you to be good enough to say a few kind words about our little restaurant when you write your article."

Zia's instinct had been right when she left without making any arrangement to receive news from home. In those days the scandal created a greater sensation in the Hungarian capital than the Japanese invasion of Manchuria, against which United States Secretary of State Stimson, considering it a violation of agreements embodied in the Pact of Paris, registered a sharp protest. Stimson urged Britain and France to take similar action, but they had no inclination to wage war against Japan and entrusted the Manchurian conflict to the League of Nations, which had proved to be an admirable recourse when leading powers wanted to evade their responsibilities. At that time, in November of 1931, no one suspected yet that the seeds of the destruction of Hiroshima and Nagasaki were contained in Stimson's protest.

After attending to her daily shopping and gossiping at Niccolini's grocery one morning in the early days of December, the signora returned to the Pension Zanzottera, and as she was crossing the hall she heard the rumble of a masculine voice in the lady-photographer's room. She stopped to listen at the door. At first she thought that General Hasparics had come to call on Zia, but she soon discovered that the rumbling voice was foreign and spoke a language that contained a great many e-sounds.

Count Dupi was smoking a cigar as he straddled one of the wicker chairs. Some salty drops of the sea still glittered on his nose and face. In the harbor an enormous motor launch rolled on the waves. There were many gapers on the wharf, for so large a launch had not moored at Mandria within the memory of man.

"How did you find out where I was, Papa?"

"I asked Scotland Yard to track you down."

"But really!"

"Simple logic."

Zia knew that in such cases simple logic meant Mr. Gruber.

"And how did you know I was at the Zanzottera?"

Zia was afraid her father had revealed her incognito when he made inquiries.

"It was much simpler than you imagine. The launch had not quite pulled into the dock when someone shouted from the shore, 'Are you looking for the photographer lady?' At first I didn't know what he meant by the photographer lady, but then I realized it could only be you."

Count Dupi looked around the room.

"How long do you expect to stay in this cell?"

"As long as I'm happy here."

Zia began to ask about her mother and her brothers and sister. They talked for an hour without any mention of Filippo's name by either of them. Count Dupi reached into his waistcoat pocket for the thin gold watch that had accompanied him since the days when he was a lieutenant of Dragoons, and then he asked where they should go for dinner. Zia showed him her album before they left and, leaning on her father's shoulder, began to identify the various faces. The album was quite full by now. It began with Occhipinti the druggist and his unhappy fat wife, and ended with the fifteen-year-old daughter of Luigi the fisherman, Domenica, who stood alongside the drying tunny nets with an amphora balanced on her head, against a background of the angry sea and the distant violet-colored cliffs of Dalmatia. A strong wind fluttered the tips of the nets, fluttered Domenica's long hair and whipped the light dress against the supple, virginal shape of the girl, almost tearing her clothes off. This was the picture Count Dupi studied longest.

On the way to dinner Zia related how her camera had helped her to make the acquaintance and win the friendship of Mandrian society.

"You know, Papa, I've discovered something here in Mandria that I'd never known till now. Security, I mean. Do you know what I mean?"

Count Dupi nodded. He was thinking of the slanderous gossip circulating about his daughter, and of the sensation-seeking article in a certain weekly paper. He did not suspect that Zia knew nothing of these things. He imagined that she was in close correspondence with all her friends and had been precisely informed by them of every detail.

They went a little way without talking.

"Don't think," said Zia, "that nothing happens here in Mandria. Every day I'm told exactly what there was for dinner at the druggist's house, and why Eligio Fanfoni the baker slapped his wife's face outside the fishmarket last Wednesday, and how far young Ettore, the barber's son, has managed to get with the youngest daughter of Eulalia. Two weeks ago Luigi caught a tremendous shark that got into the fishing nets. Something like that happens about once every two years. A reward of six hundred and fifty-one liras was due him because that's how many pounds the shark weighed. But he had only managed to subdue the creature by firing five bullets into it. Since he didn't have a shooting license, they fined him exactly six hundred and fifty-one liras. It's what Sigi used to call tit for tat."

There was no one on the terrace of the Trattoria Marica. The crew of the motor launch were just settling down to a table at the other end. Zia ordered *orada*, fried in oil, with garlic and browned parsley.

"What do you hear from the royal family in Belgium?"

"Ask Schurler," rumbled Count Dupi. "Since that scoundrel staked out a claim to the whole thing, I've lost interest in it."

Zia knew that her father judged all Hungarian politics by the person of Robert Schurler, whose photographs constantly appeared in the right-wing Christian and legitimist press, wearing the national costume with a sword or an imperial cape as he unveiled new heroic monuments or opened livestock expositions.

"We're all idiots, and I've told them so in the Casino. We've put considerable sums of money into the support of legitimist and Christian Catholic policies. We support a press that's good for nothing but editorials in praise of Schurler every Sunday. You can't control the newspapers any longer. Excellent!"

This "excellent" was not intended for Schurler but for the fried fish, which was still crackling in oil when Marica set the frying pan before them. Later they topped the meal with a little fruit. Count Dupi lit a cigar.

A question fluttered at the tip of Zia's heart: "What is Filippo doing?"

Instead of asking her question, she merely gathered the crumbs on the tablecloth into little piles. Every hair on her head was saturated with those words—why not say them? Was it self-discipline, or shame, or fear? Rather the latter. She was afraid her question would be followed by an answer like "—dead. Shot himself." Or, "He's married that actress." Or, "He's gone mad, and been put in an asylum." Such answers must have been lurking in the smoke of the paternal cigar. And then everything would be over, the kneeling solitary prayers on the stone floor of the church of San Simeone would lose their meaning, the smoke of the approaching ship over the horizon of the sea would lose its meaning and would no longer be a black banner of hope, the side of veal in the canvas sack on the back of Aldo Faggiani would become meaningless, its slow approach would bring no more long, sharp, sweet, painful aching to her heart.

Their attention was engaged by a woman who stood a few steps away on the wharf. Two smallish children clutched her skirt. Zia knew her—she was Tonia, the wife of Luigi the fisherman. And there came Luigi's black bragozza, struggling with the waves at the entrance of the harbor, its orange-yellow sail half set. Tonia's glance was riveted to the boat, but it was still too far away to see her husband's face. Her own thin, dry face was stiff with patience, self-denial and suffering. Luigi appeared at the bow of the bragozza and his eyes caught the eyes of his wife. Almost imperceptibly Tonia lifted her chin with a movement that could not be misunderstood. It was a question: What did you catch? Luigi's two empty palms, as he turned them outward, were like fish when they turn their flanks for a moment and display the silver secrets of their bodies. With that gesture, Luigi turned his head away. Tonia sniffed, and smoothed her apron. The bragozza pulled in at the wharf, but the flat, open-topped wooden crates which usually held scampi, squids, asinellos, san-pietros and club-headed redfish —the crates, carefully stacked one on top of the other, stood empty on the deck. Luigi came ashore with a single polyp dangling from his forefinger, and that polyp was like a soaking, tattered, repulsive dishcloth. The children, as they turned to follow him home, did not speak to each other but quietly disappeared along the narrow little alley that clutched the side of the hill by the Salumeria.

Count Dupi had also observed the scene through the thick smoke of his Havana, but the expression on his face did not reveal how much of it he had understood. Zia's face and eyes mirrored the whole mute little drama, the significance of which was increased, perhaps, by the background: the sullen sea that almost swept the bragozza into port. The wide-bellied black fishing smack had a cambered, copperplated prow that preserved the handsome lines of the vessels of the ancient Romans, and its inner fittings had hardly changed in the course of two thousand years, but now the boat rocked lifelessly at the end of a rope, as if without purpose or place in the world. Yes, in these winter months the blue sea hid its silver, black, red piscine treasures from the nets of the bragozzas, and the daily bread of the fisherfolk, even the *polenta* kneaded of ground corn meal, was in hazard. It was the mute outcry of this dread that had appeared on Tonia's rigid face and in her black eyes. The Italian press of those days was constantly wailing that the fish reserves of the Adriatic had declined dangerously. Luigi's bragozza in front of the Trattoria Marica had cast the same social problem ashore, but simply and more comprehensibly. There was more dramatic power in the speechless meeting of Luigi and Tonia than in the open-air performance of *The Merchant of Venice*. The rising smoke of the fat Havana seemed out of place on the terrace of the Trattoria Marica, for the terrace was accustomed to the exceptionally rank cigarettes and pipes of the Mandrian natives. The blue cigar smoke slowly danced its seductive veil dance above the table and thought of the new Hungarian Prime Minister, a count and a man of immense wealth, who forbade the use of government automobiles after assuming office and exemplified the virtues of thrift by riding on trolleys himself under the happy illusion that he could conceal a hundred thousand acres of land behind a trolley ticket. Yes, there was something in this world, a certain implacable demand for an accounting, that had been unknown in the age of Franz Joseph. To be a wealthy man in those days had been a virtuous state, and to spend one's money a virtuous act. Now it was a sin, a social offense. The blue cigar smoke thought of the good days in Lebovice, of the naked female bodies that served for candlesticks in the Officers' Reading Union; of the cavalry charge in the Lemberg café; of the wholesale purchase of the Lower Market Place, when screaming pigs, fish both dead and alive, shoes, boots and remnant linens flew through the air; and then of Paris, the Paris of "Le charmant comte Dupi," and of everything in life that was wonderful and mad. It seemed the world was really dying. This approach of death was reflected in the rigid face and black glance of the beggarly Italian woman. The cigar smoke sensed this too. Reproaches against rich men on the face of a sick earth were breaking out like ugly tumors. It was not the masses that wanted change, unrest, revolution. The poor still liked to receive big tips, and the masses

525

liked nothing better than to snatch kicking pigs, and chickens, and boots, and round cheeses from the air. The unrest was the work of political adventurers, and it was about time to clip their wings. The people were insane to believe that a better fate would follow if they wiped out the world of the wealthy around them. The wealthy man takes no more into the grave than the most wretched beggar. The wealth remains, a comfort to more than the ones who manipulate the taps of the barrels of gold. And certainly no rational man can maintain that people are equal and are born to enjoy equal rights.

These were the thoughts of the blue cigar smoke as it lifted its veils in the air over the terrace of the Trattoria Marica with the movement of a prissy dowager trying to free herself from a muddy marsh. Alberto, the renting agent of the bagno, and Ettore Domeneghetti, the barber with combs stuck in his wavy mane, had settled at a neighboring table on which they were now noisily slapping soiled cards.

The crumbs under Zia's fingers, forming first a ring and then a cross, thought otherwise than the cigar smoke. They discerned the Copperplated Twilight in the black glance and rigid countenance of Tonia, and they saw that Tonia was Lucien Veyrac's mother, who churned butter from the milk of her breast to keep her several children from dying of hunger while partridge and truffles was served on silver platters in the castle of Marquis Raverney.

Count Dupi found that the terrace of the Trattoria Marica accommodated an altogether too indiscriminate company, especially when ragged fishermen began to settle at the lame little tables around him.

"Pagare!" he called to Marica. When the check came he gave Zia, and then Marica, a long look. He was not accustomed to such modest figures. Before leaving he slipped a thousand-lire note as large as a bedsheet beneath the plate. Zia took the large banknote from under the plate.

"No, Papa, things like this attract attention here, and they don't help me either. Marica is in no trouble, business is very good in her restaurant. I'll find some other use for this."

They left. All the shopkeepers along the Piazza Vittoria Emanuele stood in their doorways, for the arrival of the motor launch had excited the fancy of the Mandrians. Occhipinti the druggist, Niccolini the grocer, Eligio Fanfoni the baker, Eulalia the dairy manager, Aldo Faggiani the butcher—all of them were standing in front of their shops where they looked as if they had paid a special admission for the privilege of seeing the photographer lady with her mysterious elderly cavalier. Even Guido Castelli, the customs inspector, stepped from his booth to stare at the tall, lithe, fashionable old gentleman as he disappeared in the direction of the Pension Zanzottera with Zia at his side.

A few minutes later the electric grill filled the room with the good fragrance of strong coffee. But there was hardly anything left for them to talk about.

"Do you intend to spend the holidays here?" asked Count Dupi, watching Zia's back as she prepared the coffee. His heart at that moment was much taken with his unhappy daughter. Zia nodded absent-mindedly. Through the open window the sound of the surf breaking on the reefs grew louder.

"Don't you need some money?"

"Thank you, no; I have everything I need."

"What do you spend here?"

Zia made a swift estimate and named a sum that Count Dupi found very reasonable. However, when Zia told him that the sum represented not her daily but her monthly expenses, he began to guffaw aloud. Then he drew the flat gold watch from his waistcoat pocket and stood up to say good-bye and leave. He put his two hands on Zia's shoulders, and then kissed her forehead. He would not release her at once. For several minutes they gazed into each other's eyes mutely. Two lines that Zia had never seen before appeared beside Count Dupi's mustache. And his gaze, too, was strange. Then he took his hands from Zia's shoulders and started toward the door. They walked speechlessly to the motor launch. Count Dupi climbed in and turned with a twinkle in his eye:

"This filthy sea is going to lead us a merry dance."

He looked out to sea. The launch dropped her cable and cut into the gray waves with a furious roar of motors. Count Dupi stood in the bow and waggled the fingers of a gloved hand at Zia. Zia replied with a similar waggle of her fingers. Both of them liked this French salutation. And they waggled their fingers at each other until the distant waves hid the swift launch.

There was nobody near by, fortunately, and thus no one could see Zia's face. No one could see her agitated, frantic dash to the end of the wharf when the launch was only barely visible. No one could see the gesture with which she caught her two hands to her face. It was as if she had made a funnel of her two hands and was sending a frantic, heart-rending cry in the wake of the launch:

"Pap-a-a-a! What about Filippo?"

The launch that had taken her secret away reached Fiume in the late hours of the evening after barely managing to wrestle through the stormy seas. Count

Dupi spent the night at the hotel where Oscar, his fat chauffeur who bore an unaccountable resemblance to a Persian rug dealer, was anxiously waiting for him. The following morning they left for home. In Vienna Count Dupi stopped the car before a hardware store on Maria Hilfer-Strasse and went inside.

He returned to the car with two bunches of keys threaded on rings. He was bringing them home as a present for Rere, because he felt that of all the Dukay family Rere was the only one who had shown a particle of sense by throwing the Prince of Perugia into the fishpool.

Zia entered the church of San Simeone at the very moment that Parson Muzmics and Nyinyin the bell ringer were leaving. They greeted each other with nods, as is customary in the presence of the Lord. The two servants of the Church turned back at the doorway to watch the photographer lady as she knelt near the altar. The expression on the young woman's face had not escaped their notice. They looked at each other, and their glances said that the condition of the patient had grown worse—it was only a matter of weeks. As they disappeared in the direction of the Piazza Vittorio Emanuele, Parson Muzmics was already making a mental note of the grave for the photographer lady, in the left corner of the cemetery, between two other graves, in one of which rested butcher Faggiani's first wife, who died of childbirth, and in the other old Giuseppe Fanfoni, who quietly mounted to the bosom of the Lord at the age of eighty-five.

Chapter Twelve

M R. GRUBER placed a new calendar on Count Dupi's desk and vehemently seized the old one, intending to tear it in two and cast the scraps in the wastebasket. But the old calendar would not give way; its paper backing was apparently too stiff. Mr. Gruber, after a long struggle, finally threw the calendar away as it was, untorn. It was almost as if the year 1931 were clinging to life frantically, unwilling to surrender itself so cheaply. It seemed to know that the days and months of the new year were approaching with sinister bundles on their back, and that these bundles contained infernal machines which were to be placed beside the pillars of Europe.

Yes, this year of 1932 brought a great many things. There was, first of all, the case of Briand, who shook the hand of Stresemann so warmly in the Locarno Hall of the British Ministry of Foreign Affairs, where they made a solemn vow, before the eyes of the entire world, that France and Germany would never take arms against each other again. Briand wriggled out of his promise. He wriggled a good long way, where no living man can catch up with him, after yielding his place to Laval of the sooty countenance. In the early months of spring the Germans returned Hindenburg to the presidency, but the entire world seemed to know that the square-headed, mustachioed veteran was no longer anything but a deaf old grand-daddy in an armchair who still managed to wave the fly-swatter to and fro, but with a wrist so weak that he could not even kill a single fly.

Let us agree, at the very start, that the wine merchant from Miskolc had been wrong. The German elections, instead of wiping Hitler off the map, gave him two hundred and thirty seats in the Reichstag, at which point Otto Kliegl jumped up from beside the radio which announced the result and said to Count János, with a single wave of his hand: "I told you so!"

Not everyone took this unqualified view of the matter. Consider Imre Pognár, for example. After reading *Mein Kampf* twice with great care, he came to the conclusion that the book was written by a madman. Not only did he come to this conclusion, but he said as much in one of his articles. In those years the liberal Hungarian press, Jewish and Christian, showed well-nigh incredible courage in attacking Hitler. The right-wing press slowly turned toward German

Nazism, only tentatively at the beginning, and then they too were sucked in by the Führer, like scraps of paper in the face of a whirling propeller. This is how it went throughout all of Central Europe, generally.

According to Paul Fogoly, Pognár's article was not objective—*Mein Kampf* could not be condemned on the simple premise that it was written by a madman. Undeniably, Pognár had sought to preserve a semblance of objectivity, and even produced statistics. He counted the number of times the following terms appeared in the four hundred and seventy-six pages of *Mein Kampf: scoundrel, blood, hanging, extermination* and *legislative louse.* He devoted a separate bracket to the phrase *if only because,* which occurred fifty-three times in the book. He quoted these words from Page 14 of *Mein Kampf,* where the author was discussing his career as a painter: "I admired everything that had to do with warfare or with warriors."

In Pognár's opinion, a more clear-cut certification of lunacy than this book had never been written.

The following week Paul Fogoly wrote an answer to Pognár, with the judiciousness proper to controversial articles that appear in the same newspaper. Paul Fogoly took the tenets of Freud's *Massenpsychologie und Ichanalyse* as his starting point. It was his opinion that the *libido,* the sexual urge that thirsts for love, idled aimlessly in the souls of most people, and that this latent urge contained tremendous energies. In public this repressed and unsatisfied libido assumed the trappings of some form of ideology. In Hitler's case it took the shape of racial theory. The libido latent in the mass soul thronged to the *manifest* libido. Paul Fogoly found the mode of manifestation, or *publicity,* extremely important. He maintained that not only in the days of Demosthenes but just ten years ago Hitler's behavior would have been ineffective because the radio had not yet come into its own. Paul Fogoly maintained that there was sexual magic in the voice of Hitler. He agreed with Hitler that a printed text could never compete with the magic of the spoken word. Radio not only magnified that magic but made it accessible to the masses in quantities hitherto unequaled in the history of the human spirit. Mussolini would not have been able to take the Italian people by the throat, either, without radio. Paul Fogoly deplored Pognár's use of the expression *madman,* saying that it was similar to the tone Hitler employed toward the Jews.

The evening after the publication of this article Pognár stopped at Paul Fogoly's desk in the editorial room, saying:

"Hello, Fürst! How's your libido?"

His remark referred to the fact that the Teutonic trumpets blown at Nürnberg tended to bring everyone's German origins back to life.

Pognár, who learned to speak German fluently during the two years he spent in Vienna after the death of Franz Joseph, conceived the idea of taking a trip to Braunau, Hitler's birthplace. At that time the inns in the little Austrian village on the Bavarian border were already occupied by a number of foreign and even overseas correspondents whose mother tongue had once been German. In order to make the local inhabitants think they were nothing but innocent vacationists, the correspondents stuck porcelain pipes in their mouths. They made haste to collect everything pertaining to Hitler's childhood past, for at that time the traces had not yet been entirely eradicated. Pognár, too, stuck a porcelain pipe in his mouth, by which the inhabitants of the village instantly knew him for a foreign newspaperman. He also exposed himself industriously to the beer served in the Braunau inns, with the result that in two weeks he gained eight pounds. In the meantime, almost parenthetically, he began an affair with a widow named Elsie whose cheeks were as red as a Jonathan apple. Pognár returned from his voyage of discovery with sensational facts. He had ascertained that Hitler was Jewish on his father's side. He learned in Braunau that Hitler's father had married three times, his third wife being his second wife's little servant girl. This scullery maid gave birth to Adolf. It was a matter of common knowledge that the elder Hitler was much addicted to alcohol. Beer weighs a man down, whisky bowls him over, but wine makes him brutal. The elder Hitler drank nothing but wine. According to Pognár's argument, there was evidence for this in *Mein Kampf* itself. Although Hitler's recollections of his father were full of praise, a few pages later—on Page 31—he was already writing of the way most children were subjected to scenes of domestic discord and brutality verging on violence, scenes which were usually the result of paternal intemperance, and according to Hitler's own words he had often witnessed such scenes himself. Like all writers, he naively betrayed himself between the lines. The Braunau inns had a good deal to say about the way Hitler's mother often had to borrow small sums of money from a local wood dealer, a Jew. This wood dealer always treated the unfortunate little woman with the greatest tenderness. No one could know what passed between them, of course—no one had held a candle to the man's window. But Pognár set out on the track of logic, and it was not difficult to recognize the techniques of barkova in his train of thought. From his philosophical studies he recalled the inductive and deductive processes of inference, and in the case of Hitler he chose to employ the inductive process. This means that the *universal* must be inferred from the *particulars*. Pognár established the following *particulars* in connection with Hitler: the color of his hair was dark; he had an incredible sense for propaganda; his gestures were generally vapid, and his hand, when he rendered the Nazi salute, hung from his wrist like an empty glove; he was exceptionally sensitive and often broke into tears. All these were Jewish traits. According to Pognár, extreme anti-Semitism was also a Jewish trait. He cited the example of Otto Weininger, the Viennese philosopher who met an early death before the war; he wrote a fanatically anti-Semitic book despite his own Jewish origin. On this basis Pognár classified Jesus Christ as an anti-Semite. He went even further. He suggested the thesis that the most avid anti-Semites were those about whose origins there was some uncertainty. Thus his theory introduced the steel helmet of the Roman soldier into the room of beautiful sixteen-year-old Miriam of Nazareth, and brought the wood dealer of Braunau closer to Hitler's mother.

"That mustache! That mustache, my friend!" Pognár thumped the table at the Press Club. "He wants to hide something under that mustache! It's all a matter of the unconscious!"

For the first time in the history of the liberal newspaper for which he worked, the editor refused to accept Pognár's series of articles. He found the conclusions altogether too reckless and the evidence too weak. Such statements could not be made on the basis of tavern hearsay. Pognár did not give up the struggle. He sent his articles to England, but was again turned down. His endeavors, at any rate, netted him the privilege of appearing among the first few names on the secret list of those who were to be executed when the time was ripe.

People were no longer talking about Eva Kócsag's erotic adventure with the Italian prince. The earth of some foreign land had swallowed them. Lucello Italiano was now a real *espresso,* and the change necessitated little more than a new sign over the door: AIRLINE ESPRESSO. Miss Piroska still served black coffee where the ticket window had stood. Cunning sandwiches, fish spreads and tomato salads still coquetted invitingly where the sign had read BAGGAGE, but they were no longer free. The idea had been Piroska's, and Count Dupi took her at her word. The employees fared well, and Lucello Italiano began to make a tidy profit for its principal stockholder.

The concept of a Greater Germany and the blaring trumpetry that accompanied the soaring exaltations of race theory could be heard in the Septemvir Utca

Palace from the open windows of neighboring homes, when Hitler's hoarse, fiery voice poured like lava into the quiet street. But only from neighboring windows, because Countess Menti strictly forbade the palace servants to listen to the radio. We already know of the addiction to anti-Semitism that lurked behind the unctuous phrases of the Reverend Alajos Galovics. Mr. Gruber, who was German in name only and not completely clear on the subject of his own origins, only wrinkled his brows as he paced up and down in the solitude of his room. The libido of everyone worked in different ways. Count Dupi greeted the tide of events in Germany with a quiet, obscure hatred. Countess Menti, who also chanced to glance into *Mein Kampf,* flung the book away with revulsion when she reached the pages that calumniated the Habsburg Dynasty. György despatched an occasional letter from Chicago, but only infrequently. He disclosed that, in the estimation of a number of Americans of German descent, forty million Germans were living in the United States. According to György, they arrived at this figure by considering Roosevelt, for example, to be German. It was his opinion that the German spirit was already stirring in thousands of Americans. It would be hard to say in what part of the world Kristina was wandering. János and Otto Kliegl were often seen in the streets of Budapest and Munich. Relations between Count János and his parents had broken down so thoroughly by now that he went to a hotel when he was in Budapest. And Otto Kliegl had been forbidden the palace long ago. The Dukay children were strewn about the world, and only Rere remained with his parents.

One evening Count Dupi stomped home from the Casino and swore he would never go there again. His Excellency Robert Schurler had begun to explain that Hitler was right in a number of respects.

Occasionally old Sándor, in the porter's lodge, became involved in conversation with Bogó, the attendant in the near-by Ministry of the Interior. Both of them came from Ararat. When they had thoroughly thrashed out the latest developments, the old man would twirl his splendid, dense, silvery mustache thoughtfully and express his entire opinion thus:

"Clever, those Germans."

The case of Jozefin was more interesting. She had come from Germany during the war and entered the service of the palace as second chambermaid to Countess Menti. Jozefin's fiancé was a German Communist, a fugitive Spartacus, and it is easy to understand why Jozefin despised Hitler. Countess Menti took cognizance of her chambermaid's anti-Nazi sentiments with satisfaction, especially since she did not know about the Communist fiancé. One afternoon she set out for a meeting of the Catholic Women's Union and had reached the street before realizing that she had left the text of her speech in a drawer of the writing table. In the great tumult, Jozefin did not notice the return of her mistress. The radio was blasting at full volume. Jozefin sat on the floor in a veritable state of collapse, listening to Hitler's speech. The hoarse, sensual voice had beaten her to the ground. She was beaten to the ground by the libido that had already shown the way to millions upon millions of people. Two weeks later Countess Menti released Jozefin from her duties for accidentally breaking a bathroom glass.

On the 12th of August Hindenburg received Hitler for the first time. Everyone felt that this marked a beginning of something, but no one quite knew what it was. The skies over Europe were not black as yet, but bolts of lightning flashed on the horizon. They shot Doumer, President of the French Republic. They murdered Inokai, the Premier of Japan. In Hungary a young man of unusually charming manner dynamited the largest viaduct in the country and the shreds of the Night Express from Vienna hurtled into the depths. The culprit was not punished because the medical examiner declared him insane. Historians of the future will be able to claim, with complete conviction, that beginning with these years insanity was not only the most reliable safe-conduct in Europe but also the best means to success.

What happened in Mandria meanwhile? We last saw Zia in December of 1931, as she entered the church of San Simeone after the departure of Count Dupi—roughly speaking, that was about a year ago. We may recall that Parson Muzmics and Nyinyin the bell ringer stepped out of the church at that very moment, and glanced at the face of the lady photographer. At that time the face said that the lady had only a few weeks left to go, and in his thoughts Parson Muzmics had already reserved a grave for Zia between the grave of Aldo Faggiani's first wife and the grave of old Giuseppe Fanfoni, who died in the Lord at the age of eighty-five. Nyinyin had begun to estimate how much he would get for tolling the bells.

In the following months nothing of note happened in Mandria beyond the fact that the photographer lady failed to die; in fact she even paid one of Niccolini's youngsters fifty liras for a puppy-dog in February, with the thought of raising it herself. This in itself betrayed her intention to remain alive for many more months. In the eyes of the servants of the Church, this very nearly constituted an offense. Not since the beginning of the world had anyone given money for a puppydog in Mandria, since nearly all of them were thrown into the sea; therefore the payment of fifty Bras seemed an unusual thing, almost like the establishment of a trust fund. As a consequence, the day after the news of the puppydog purchase spread throughout the island the signora appeared in Zia's room and, lamenting her rising costs, raised the daily rate from thirty-two liras to thirty-five. Zia gave in after a token show of resistance. The following day Eligio Fanfoni the baker stopped her on the street and ducked his rat-face up and down in deep apologetic bows while he explained that there was a bill outstanding since November for sixteen liras which she had forgotten to pay, Zia gave him the sixteen liras, although she had never purchased anything in Master Fanfoni's shop. When she reached home around noon she was met by old Jacopo Torriti the locksmith, who suffered from a rupture. He gave her a bill of twenty-two liras, stating that Zia had ordered a new key for her door in August but said she did not have the money at the time and told him to bill her after the New Year. But he had been unable to come at New Year's because his rupture kept him in bed. Zia told old Jacopo that she had not even been in Mandria in August; and she did not pay the bill. She felt that all this was a consequence of the puppydog, and decided to refrain from similar prodigalities that might attract attention to herself in the future.

The puppy was only a few weeks old. She christened it Fifi. A psychologist may easily claim that the name was linked with something else, that she bought the dog only to be able to repeat its name over and over again in the course of the day and even to shout it on the Corso Mussolini along the ocean-front: Fifi! True, she had never used this pet name for Filippo. But the syllable *fi* was a fragment of something, like the broken-tipped and completely rusty hook among the quantities of string, cigar butts, nails and crusts of bread that Earless Mungu unaccountably carried in the pocket of his unbelievably ragged trousers.

The obstinate persistence of the photographer lady's life was a quiet but constant sensation in Mandria. Many people, and druggist Occhipinti first of all, were finally reconciled to the inevitable fact of her survival. Sitting on the seashore one evening, the signora explained this unusual development to Parson Muzmics with the statement that the photographer lady possessed a secret and miraculous drug against tuberculosis. It was called *Anlesitina*. She saw the name

535

of the drug on the label of a little bottle while cleaning the room one day, and had even written it down for herself.

It was true that Zia actually used those little yellow-gray pills, if not with any regularity. The name of the drug, however, was not Anlesitina but Entalisina. It was not for tuberculosis, but had a beneficial effect on the bowel movements, particularly for people exposed to a change of climate and diet for long periods of time. The drug was of Mexican origin, and had been recommended to Kristina by one of her Spanish friends. Kristina, of whom we know that she was sickly as a child, carried a portable drugstore in one of her suitcases on her travels. A year ago, when she was last in Budapest, she gave Zia two bottles of Entalisina. Zia brought the pills along on her Mandrian exile, because there was one thing she feared: appendicitis. The ship called at the island only once in a fortnight; in case of emergency there was Pietro Torriti's motorboat, but he had constant trouble with the spark plugs and when the seas were heavy the boat would not start at all. It was possible, therefore, that an attack of appendicitis would put Zia in grave danger. Appendicitis ran in the Dukay family. All the other members had already had their appendixes out, even Rere, and János recently underwent an appendectomy in Munich. Zia was the only one who still carried this baleful and wormlike vestigial organ. Although Entalisina had no connection with the appendix, it still gave her peace of mind, and this, after all, was the most important thing.

Fifi the puppydog did not take Entalisina and was therefore constantly subject to intestinal disorders. This was a source of serious concern to Zia. She remembered the night when they were carousing with the actors and the playwrights at the Blind Mouse, the fateful night when Filippo met Eva Kócsag, and she remembered what a hit the *artiste* made, particularly with Filippo, when she remarked that her dog was completely streetbroken. By this she meant that the dog refused to do its duty on the street and devoted its exclusive attention to the carpets indoors. When the remark was translated to him, Filippo found it uproariously funny. In this respect Fifi too was completely streetbroken, and probably she had particular cause to recoil from the Piazza Vittorio Emanuele and the Corso Mussolini. But these motherly worries and minor exasperations gave new color to Zia's life. As for the rest, Fifi was a combination of poodle, dachshund, fox terrier, and St. Bernard, like most Mandrian dogs, and it could hardly be said that this distinguished family tree worked to the advantage of her physical appearance. Her soft-boned dachshund legs were white, a color which accentuated their crookedness. The large, degenerate St. Bernard head almost reached to the ground because the poodle neck was unable to support it. Of the fox terrier there remained only the crookedly clipped stump of a tail that Mungu's tailor shears had spared at the request of the Niccolini youngster, for in his spare time Mungu was a tailor. Fifi required baskets, cushions, drinking bowls, eating bowls, leashes, combs, brushes, bone-shaped rubber balls, delousing preparations and many other things, and all this somehow brought life to the lonely room in the Pension Zanzottera. Somewhere beyond the outermost limits of reality, amid the sweet and sorrowful echoes of solitude, Fifi answered to the name of Prince Achile Zia Ozzolini di Perugia, and was a marvelously handsome human baby. Childless women squander the orphaned treasures of their maternal instinct thus, on dogs, cats or canaries.

In these days, now that the furious bora came less frequently, Zia resumed her daily walks. The walks still extended to the stone bridge, where the empty riverbed twinkled whitely as it ran down the hillside. The tigers and elephants made a fresh start on the construction of the citadel; sometimes, however, when Zia sat on the railing of the stone bridge and gazed blankly before her, they were nowhere to be seen. Fifi did not approve of these walks. Oftentimes she sat down, and sometimes behaved so stubbornly that it was necessary to drag her, and on these occasions she slid several yards on her belly. She was generally of the opinion that it was the better part of wisdom to lie on the warm stones of the harbor with paws and pink belly exposed to the sun.

At the end of February the bougainvillea blossomed on the wall of the Albergo Varcaponti that faced the courtyard, and the Niccolini children ventured to dip themselves in the sea.

With two younger partners who were not from Mandria, Luigi the fisherman set out on a three-day voyage on March 6th. Mungu accompanied them in another bragozza. They always left in pairs, and the orange-yellow sails of the two bragozzas bellied into veritable balloons as the vessels disappeared on the white-fringed, blue waves in the direction of the violet-hued Dalmatian cliffs. It was a beautiful spring, day. The next day the bora returned, with a vehemence that seemed to boil with wild rancor for having been routed by the spring. The sky became a dark, leaden mass that threatened to descend on the hills of

Mandria and crush them with its gigantic weight. The raging wind blew with such strength that it tore the customs booth off the wharf and knocked the chimney off the Trattoria Marica. The waves inundated the cement lagoon and swept over the entire Piazza Vittorio Emanuele as if exasperated with its layers of filth. Most of these they carried into Niccolini's grocery shop, which was at the lowest edge of the square, and left them there by way of a crude joke. The hissing waves flowed under the old benches of the church of San Simeone and spread all the way to the altar, something that had not happened in the past ten years. The wind was so furious that nobody dared to go outside. The following day brought an abatement of the weather, and the people stood in little groups as they looked out over the sea, which rocked the great swollen waves in its lap unconcernedly but with a cruel countenance. Everyone was in a state of anxiety for the two bragozzas. Tonia, Luigi's wife, stood in one of the groups, her face cradled between the thumb and fore-finger of her left hand, and there were deep lines around the black Italian eyes that filled with deathlike sadness as she stared out to sea speechlessly. The baker, Eligio Fanfoni, gave vent to the opinion that the two bragozzas would not return. Saturday passed, and they should have been back on Saturday. On Sunday the weather was quite clear, and just before noon one of Nyinyin's children dashed up the Corso Mussolini shrieking with all his might the news that the bragozzas were coming. All Mandria rushed to the harbor. And truly, there to the north the orange-yellow sail of one of the bragozzas was quivering in the mild breeze. But only Earless Mungu had returned, and they could hardly get a word from him when he stepped ashore. The storm had caught them in the neighborhood of Punta Dura, at about two in the morning. The sea swallowed Luigi's bragozza—all three men were lost. Tonia stood in the crowd and listened to his recital, resting her face on the thumb and forefinger of her left hand. Her face did not move—it was as if the black eyes surrounded by deep lines could be no muter or more sorrowful. The crowd slowly broke up. The catastrophe occasioned no particular disturbance in Mandria. According to the unwritten law of these shores, the sea generally claimed one bragozza every three years.

In the ensuing weeks it became a customary sight to see Tonia standing in the harbor, supporting her face on her left hand with its cracked fingernails, watching the sea. Occhipinti the druggist, who had been to America in his youth and was known for the profundity of his wit, remarked that Tonia stood in the harbor of Mandria like the Statue of Liberty outside of New York. There was

538

some truth in this cruel and rather unworthy observation. The figure of Tonia, in fact, standing on the shore with three infants clutching at her skirt, expressed something more and something mightier than a mere fisherman's tragedy, for the unwavering glance of the black Italian eyes in their deeply lined sockets contained the desperate sadness of the entire poverty-stricken world.

The tragedy of want, the bitter struggle for a mere existence touched Zia more closely here than it had ever done on Septemvir Utca or at Ararat. She watched Tonia in secret as the woman hopelessly, almost half-wittedly, waited for the murderous sea to give Luigi back to her. Did her own eyes, Zia wondered, fill with such heart-rending sadness as she watched each fortnight for Filippo to arrive on the incoming ship?

Late one afternoon in March the signora and General Hasparics were sitting on a bench along the seashore. Zia, in a vermilion bathing cap, swam by before them. She always went swimming at this hour, when the sun had disappeared over the horizon, because her sensitive white skin did not take kindly to sunburn.

The general spoke up after a long silence, in a voice that crackled as if he were cracking walnuts:

"I'd give two thousand liras for that little red hat."

The signora glanced sideways at the general's broad, tremulous nose, with its hairline-thin and delicate network of blue-black veins. There was a sneer in her smile as she crossed her thin arms over her bony chest. In the past seven years, since the general's retirement to Mandria, they had consummated several deals of this sort.

"Ridiculous," the signora said after a moment or two, and for the sake of greater emphasis she stuck her narrow dentures out between her thin lips. The general's blue eyes swam in a cloud of greedy and lustful light when he turned to the signora:

"How much?"

The signora did not reply at once. It was not the first time they had sat on this bench and discussed the lady photographer. Connoisseurs both, they had spoken with the highest appreciation of the young photographer's beautifully rounded shoulders, of her firm little breasts, of her incredibly supple waist and the fine lines of her legs, the thoroughbred ease and elegance of her movements.

But this was the first time the general had made an actual offer. In the previous year he paid the signora two thousand liras for Fräulein Wissmann. The signora launched into a lengthy harangue. How did the general imagine that this Parisian photographer could be mentioned in the same breath, or even on the same day, with Fräulein Wissmann, who—the signora was now prepared to admit—was not really an attorney's wife but only the governess in an attorney's home in Klagenfurt. How could he compare Klagenfurt to Paris? No, no, better drop the whole thing, there could be no discussion on that basis. For a long time the signora mutely shook her narrow outthrust dentures.

The little red cap swam by for the third time, well out to sea and hardly larger than a good-sized apple. This seemed to excite the general, for he resumed the discussion. Actually he had long considered as his own the lady photographer who often passed by him in the course of her walks, her fine little shape clothed in a simple but perfectly tailored linen suit that was always speckless and freshly ironed, and she left a light and healthy feminine fragrance in the air. It was strange how the four dogs, sprawled at the general's feet, would also turn their heads to watch her when she had passed, something they did not do with anyone else. The lady photographer's narrow tennis shoes always looked brand new, and the leather-cased camera slung over her shoulder on a strap lent her appearance a certain elegance. She always gave the dogs a friendly glance, but never deigned to notice the general himself. Sitting alone in his room over the third quart of after-dinner *vino rosso* amid a variety of heavy odors, the general had for weeks been walking the nude photographer lady up and down in his imagination, and at such times his wine-clouded eyes glowed with an eager, sensual fire. But he had often purchased horses on behalf of the army, and he knew the ins and outs of shrewd bargaining. He began to make unfavorable remarks about the lady photographer to counterbalance his earlier encomiums. The woman was too thin. Her legs, and especially at the ankles, were not entirely unexceptionable. Her appearance lacked middle-class dependability, and this suggested the risk of venereal disease. The signora answered each of these remarks with a short and belittling "Poof," and she turned her face all of one hundred and eighty degrees away each time. Finally they agreed on five thousand liras.

After supper that evening the signora knocked on Zia's door. Zia was already in bed, smoking a cigarette with a pillow under her elbow as she read Ferrero's book on the fall of Rome. The signora burst into the room with her sweetest smile, and behind the smile her teeth seemed narrower than ever. Zia pulled the light piqué cover up to her neck, for she was naked on the large studio couch. Asking whether she was disturbing Zia, the signora did not wait for an answer but brought a chair and settled down. This was unusual enough in itself, for Zia had broken the signora of the habit of entering her room without invitation. After confiding somewhat inconsequentially that the leather warehouse in Piccolo had caught fire the previous night and that the podestà's son had sprained his left arm, the signora veered to the subject of the general. She recited the names of several villages where the general had waged victorious battles: Lirini, Mantin, Godanza …these names suddenly came to mind from her childhood, and the fact that never in the history of the world had any battles been fought in those places did not disturb the signora in the least. Finally, as if it were the best news of all, she revealed that the general wanted to have his picture taken and had requested that she appear at six the next afternoon in the red-roofed villa. The signora explained how to find the general's villa on the hillside, not suspecting that Zia had spent an entire month there two years previously. Zia, whose imagination was not readily susceptible to bawdry, still did not see through the signora's confused smiles, and said merely:

"I'm sorry, I can't do it. I don't have an Italian permit."

"The general is very rich! He'll pay three thousand liras for the photographs!"

And when Zia continued to shake her head, the signora suddenly cocked her head to one side and her dentures popped all the way out of her mouth as she regarded Zia with mute meaningfulness for a few moments, and then she playfully jabbed Zia's side with a forefinger and said:

"You won't have to take any photographs!"

She crossed her two arms over her chest, leaned all the way back and announced:

"You can have the three thousand liras anyway!"

The outthrust dentures now made quite clear to Zia what was afoot. She stretched out her arm and carefully pressed the cigarette into the ashtray. Both of her naked shoulders peeped out from beneath the cover with this gesture. These were the beautifully rounded shoulders for which even the general's stuttering tongue had found fitting words. For several moments Zia's steady eyes held the signora's hideously cloying glance. Her first impulse was to chase the woman out of the room at once. The thought of becoming, for three thousand liras, the mistress of that dirty, drunken old man in the very rooms where she had enjoyed the felicities of her honeymoon with Filippo—this thought filled her with horror.

She almost moaned aloud at the sight of this bottomless pit of life, deep and dark, in the signora's slyly sweet smile. At the same time she would have liked to laugh out loud. She decided on a third course. Coolly, she said only this:

"Please tell the general that I don't have a permit for that sort of thing either."

The gesture with which she reached for her book and began reading gave the signora to understand that she was dismissed. The signora sprang from her chair, hardly knowing how to dispose of the words that were on the tip of her tongue. Four thousand liras! But she did not dare say them, because in the neighborhood of the lady photographer she always lost the disdainful assurance that she had felt toward other feminine boarders in the Pension. Before leaving the room she threw a terse "Tsk!" toward Zia, which was meant to sum up her offense at the rebuff, clear her from any suspicion of having entertained indecent thoughts and especially to express the exasperation she felt at the loss of what seemed a certain profit.

Next day the general noticed that the lady photographer, when she passed his bench on the seashore toward nightfall, neglected for the first time to give even his dogs a glance, and he concluded from this that the signora's negotiations were not meeting with spectacular success.

Zia was not surprised by such conquests, for Mandria really offered no rival in this field. On the other hand it may truthfully be said that the conquests did not make her happy. Some days previously she had discovered something unusual in druggist Occhipinti's eyes too; and Eligio Fanfoni also kept turning his rat-face in her direction after it became known that, as a result of some miraculous drug, *la fotografa morta* was not going to die at all. As for Guido Castelli the customs inspector, he made himself positively ridiculous by the vehement looks with which he embraced Zia whenever he saw her. Guido's large sheep's-eyes were exactly like those of General Paccapuzzi. As he sometimes paced the Piazza Vittoria Emanuele, with hands behind his back, shirt sleeves rolled up, cap pushed to the nape of his neck and his back crisscrossed by braces, Guido seemed to be engaged in a parade of his masculine appurtenances before the ladies of Mandria. When he came face to face with Zia he stood in her way, his eyes bulged out even more and his entire neck turned red:

"It's warmer than it was yesterday…"

He grunted forth sentences like that. And his sentences abounded with carnal lust.

"Yes, indeed," Zia would answer amiably, then turn on her heel and leave him gaping. Eulalia often stuck her head out of the dairy to keep her eye on her lover. Like a cuckoo in a broken cuckoo clock, she popped out well enough but failed to cuckoo. When her black glance swept over the Piazza Vittorio Emanuele, one could really believe that she would murder the customs inspector if he deceived her.

In the beginning of June the summer guests began to straggle in. Since the memory of man, the number of summer guests at Mandria had hovered between fifteen and twenty, though the individuals themselves were constantly changing, since no one who had once been to Mandria ever came back. That summer, however, there was an exception. At the end of June the twenty-first guest arrived, Erich Pringsheim, a Viennese physician and neurologist who returned after an absence of nine years and went straight to the Pension Zanzottera. The doctors tubercular wife had died in the room where Zia was now living, and Pringsheim came to visit her grave. For his sake the signora gave up her own room, something she would not have done for anyone else, and set up a cot in the kitchen. Dr. Pringsheim planned to stay for two weeks. He was approaching his seventies, and exuded the atmosphere of Vienna in the past century. The color of his side whiskers was like that of old family flatware, coruscating with black and silver. There were gold spots in the iris of his watery gray eyes. His neck was confined in a hard, stiff, starched collar and at the end of his shirt sleeves he wore detachable pipe-shaped cuffs that sometimes rattled. However great the heat, he refused to part with his gray cotton gloves and his gray umbrella. Zia met him on the first day of his visit, and after that they were often together. Like castaways on a desert island, they discovered the European in each other. After supper they sat in the garden, on the red bench under the old fig tree, in the light of the terrace lamp. Pringsheim held his hands over his abdomen, with fingers tightly locked as if concealing something between his two palms, but while talking he occasionally displayed the two empty palms of a sudden to show that there was nothing hidden there. He spoke with the soft and delicate Viennese accent that Zia had grown accustomed to hear among her relations. Dr. Pringsheim talked of old Vienna and the collapse of the Monarchy with quiet regret. But he saw the matter from a medical point of view, and since an accumulation of sluggish protoplasmic molecules in the cells inevitably produced a senility of the organs, the end result—he maintained—had been inescapable. Like all physicians, he made the mistake of taking for granted that his listener knew what protoplasmic molecules were.

The radio blared from the Albergo Varcaponti, and from time to time the cadenced howls of an enormous audience at the Sportpalast punctuated Hitler's speech.

The conversation turned to politics, and Pringsheim characterized the activities of Mussolini and Hitler as dangerous congestions of blood in the senile brain of Europe. After a few moments of silence Zia spoke up:

"I'd very much like to have you examine me before you go. Not that there's anything really wrong; but just because I'm lucky enough to have you here on this desert island now."

"I can't do it—I don't have an Italian permit." Pringsheim echoed Zia's words, for Zia had given him an account of her photographic adventures during their walks along the seashore, and without omitting the general's offer, at which Pringsheim guffawed with amusement for a long time.

The examination took place the next afternoon. Zia had never undergone such an examination before, and her sense of modesty was dealt a little blow when Pringsheim began by telling her to strip to the skin. So far only Filippo had seen her without any clothes on. Pringsheim examined her lungs, her heart, her stomach—"Lie on your back...Lie on your stomach...Take a deep breath." He did all this with a touch of boredom, occasionally repressing a yawn that persisted after his midday nap. His first glance at the naked body told him there was nothing seriously wrong. Then came the questions: cigarettes, liquor, sleeping pills, diet, habits, sleep, coughing, rheumatic pains, parents' and brothers' and sisters' health. In the meantime Pringsheim took Zia's temperature and blood pressure and tested her reflexes, after which he said with an almost imperceptible yawn: "Put your clothes on." When he had carefully packed the instruments into his little black bag, he asked:

"As a matter of fact, what do you feel is wrong with you?"

Zia knotted the sash of her bathrobe about her narrow waist tightly. She did not answer at once. She sat down and rested her chin on her hand, as if she were talking out loud to herself about these things for the first time:

"I'm restless. I don't know...nervous, in an odd way. And that bothers me a great deal sometimes. I remember Aunt Stefi, who used to gnash her teeth at night...she wore the enamel off, and the doctor made a rubber mouthpiece for her to wear at night. I don't gnash my teeth, but—how shall I put it…"

She closed her eyes and pressed her two fists together with a shiver:

"Sometimes I feel that my whole body is gnashing. I don't know whether I can make it clear…"

Pringsheim simply let the words struggle forth of themselves without saying anything. There were forty-five years of experience behind him. He was as familiar with Aunt Stefi's gnashing teeth as another man might be with the key to his apartment. Once he surreptitiously throttled a faint yawn.

"I'm restless," said Zia, casting about for words. "I toss in bed… sometimes I bite my own arm…there's something inside of me that I want to get rid of. But it's not like anything…in other words, I don't know."

"How old are you?"

"Twenty-one."

"Married?"

"Divorced."

Pringsheim looked at the window. According to his forty-five years of experience, this word generally defined the loose women, the kept women, the better class of cocottes. Besides, on the day of his arrival the signora had blurted out a story about an elderly, rich gentleman who was the photographer lady's lover.

"What sort of a sexual life do you have?"

It was the first time Zia had ever heard these words, phrased as they were now. It is probable that they occurred in books she read, but she had not noticed them. The meaning was clear, however, and she understood it at once. The little pout of her lower lip, which was a bitter and embarrassed smile, said soundlessly but quite unmistakably: None.

"Are you a Lesbian?" asked Pringsheim. His lips pursed up meanwhile and it was apparent from the quiver of his nostrils that he was repressing another tiny yawn. Physicians put questions like this to people from whom they do not intend to accept money for their services. That was the meaning of his slight yawns as well.

This was a term with which Zia was more familiar. In fact, she had even had an adventure. Some years past, when she was still a girl, a large group of guests came to the castle at Ararat one summer. The beautiful young wife of a foreign diplomat kept looking at her all day in a peculiar way, and in the evening she unexpectedly came to Zia's room, to chat, as she said, because she could not sleep. At first the lovely dark Gido sat on the edge of the bed and started to talk somewhat restlessly about an English historical novel, but later she stretched out on the bed and turned the light off. What happened between them was wholly unusual but not at all unpleasant. Gido began to kiss her, first her eyes, her ears, her mouth, and then her kisses ranged over the girl's body. Then Gido, suddenly exhausted and panting, rested her jasmine-scented black head on her loins for a long while. This was Zia's only adventure of this sort. It took place in the dark and seemed almost a dream, for Gido left the next day and she never saw her again. Later it was the flaxen-haired Elizabeth who described the details of this kind of love-making; Elizabeth had often done it and proposed that the two of them make a start, but Zia declined this offer just as she had refused Calandra's. She was in a position, therefore, to answer Pringsheim's question with a clear conscience:

"No, not at all."

"How long is it that you've not lived a regular sexual life?"

"About a year," Zia said after a little reflection.

"Tell me in detail about your sexual life so far."

Something in the tone of voice with which the question was put suggested boredom even before the answer was uttered. The silver-black side whiskers were more like an instrument than the appurtenance of a living man. Zia raised her left hand in the air and, holding her forefinger vertically stiff, began to scratch her scalp. She had borrowed this comic gesture of perplexity from Filippo. It was hard to make a proper beginning, but Pringsheim helped her constantly with leading questions which suggested that the elderly Viennese physician knew much more precisely than she the most minute detail of what had taken place between her and Filippo. Zia looked at the floor and only intermittently glanced into Pringsheim's tired eyes as she exposed the secrets of her unhappy little body. After a momentary pause Pringsheim asked:

"Do you know what an orgasm is?"

Zia had never heard this word. She thought Pringsheim was trying to change the subject, for the term suggested two words to her mind: organ and chasm. Pringsheim immediately recognized this familiar type of feminine ignorance on Zia's face, and he began a detailed and thorough explanation in the course of which he displayed his two empty palms more than once to show that there was nothing concealed between them. The tone of his voice was exactly that of an elderly history professor who has recited the details of the counter-Reformation of the Synod of Trent—who knows how often in the course of forty-five years?—

with this difference, that his sentences were full of words like *coitus, vagina, clitoris, climax, consummation,* but he pronounced these words in a tone that hardly differentiated them from *confederation of states, parliament, ratification* or *insurrection.* Zia felt that Pringsheim's gray phrases turned the secretive and seething matter of *Päckhaus* to ashes. She followed his lecture with rounded eyes and bated breath, for she was beginning to see that beyond *Päckhaus* there was something medical knowledge called an orgasm, an unfamiliar and wonderful fulfillment of a woman's life from which Filippo had barred her, and this intelligence struck her so explosively that her knees even began to tremble a little.

Pringsheim stood up, went to the window slowly and looked out into the garden. There was a pause, which made him seem to be consulting with the old fig tree about this present case. He turned away from the window and took his instrument bag in hand, but he did not start to leave yet.

"Ja, mein Kind! That's what the trouble is with this modern, nervous world. That's why there are so many divorces. The men, and especially the young men, are selfish. They are in too much of a hurry, and think only of their own satisfaction. They excite a woman, but they do not satisfy her. We doctors call this a *rhythm deficiency*."

Zia put the middle finger of her left hand in her mouth and began to chew the nail, something she very rarely did. Pringsheim stared into space and nodded mutely; his nod was of the rare and unusual variety that indicates denial rather than assent.

"Now you expect me to give you some sort of prescription. I could prescribe one of several drugs to calm your nerves, or I could tell you to take a cold water cure, go on long walks, swim and row as much as possible, but all this would be like telling a starving man to read the collected works of Tolstoy or to play the piano for eight hours a day. Ja, mein Kind!"

Pushing aside the breast of his jacket, he quietly began to scratch his back at the buckle of the waistcoat, saying meanwhile:

"There are many kinds of poverty in the world. One of the greatest is sexual poverty, about which—stupidly enough—very little is ever said."

From her chair Zia looked up uncertainly at the rather tall physician, who caught her glance and understood its meaning. He put his hand on Zia's shoulder.

"You're twenty-one years old, child. You're perfectly healthy and very beautiful. Advice? I can't give you any advice. I can't even tell you to turn to the signora, though I imagine that in this particular field of human misery the signora is a veritable benefactress."

Enunciated with his pleasant Viennese accent, the last words, *eine wirkliche Wohltätigkeitsdame,* emerged from his silver-black side whiskers like a Mozartian roulade on the candlelight-splashed keys of a piano.

Laughing, Pringsheim started for the door. Zia stopped him and asked what his fee was for the examination. Pringsheim wrinkled his brows:

"I'm sorry, I have no Italian permit!"—and again he laughed good-naturedly.

Once more Zia asked him to wait, while she hurried to her writing table and took an enlarged, mounted photograph from the drawer. She gave it to him without a word. Pringsheim looked at the picture, and then, with a start, held it far away and averted his head. It was almost as if he were offering the picture to one of the wardrobes, asking that it be taken from him. For several moments there was a queer and clear silence in the room. Pringsheim turned back, and stuck a thumb under his spectacles to wipe the tears from both his eyes. Then he looked at the picture once again.

"Beautiful. Beautiful!" he whispered feelingly.

The picture was truly beautiful. Zia had exercised great stealth and cunning to make this photograph. Pringsheim stood at his wife's grave in the Mandrian cemetery. His expression and his stance were completely noncommittal. He held his hat in his right hand, and the gray umbrella hung from his left arm. In the background to the right, however, deep black but blurred to obscurity, there stood a tall cypress which expressed all that was missing from Pringsheim's face. Far in the depths was the sea, with the outlines—as light as a human breath—of the violet-hued Dalmatian hills. But the sky was most marvelous of all. The sky shone with a clear and resounding felicity which—this being a photograph— was naturally the result of a fortunate concatenation of clouds. The sky looked like a frozen patch of ground after a wicker broom has swept the snow away, when only the stripes of powdered snow are left in sight. This was how the *ponente* had swept the sparkling white and fleecy clouds across the Mandrian sky, and the felicity of the sky said that all sorrow had been swept from the world. Dangerously close as it was to poster art, the simple photograph reflected a pure and wonderful tranquility.

Pringsheim drew Zia's head close with one of his hands, kissed her forehead and quickly went out without a word.

He left the next day.

✝

The other twenty guests who remained were unpretentious Italians, Austrians and Jugoslavs. The Italians were generally fatter than the Austrians and the Jugoslavs better humored than the Italians. Of all the vacationists perhaps only the name of Herr Stern is worth mentioning. He was an insurance agent from Fiume, with a round double chin, numerous rings on his fingers and a saffron-colored mustache beneath his nostrils which he clipped so close in Hitler fashion that at a distance of several feet it seemed to be a reddish-yellow fluid running from his nostrils. By way of slight exaggeration, Herr Stern registered as *von* Stern in the guest book of the Albergo Varcaponti, and consequently the baker, Eligio Fanfoni, addressed him as Herr Baron on the following day.

As soon as the vacationists were on hand in full force, the bells began to ring in Mandria. In the belfry tower of the church of San Simeone were five bells: in order of name, two gaffer bells, one widow bell and two infant bells. The gaffers boomed, the widow wailed heart-rendingly, and the infants shrieked maliciously. That is to say, only one of them shrieked, for the other was cracked and made a sound like a broken kettle every time the clapper struck. Nyinyin and his four children marched into the belfry at four in the morning, and from that moment until nine o'clock the bells hummed and shrilled without respite, sometimes all five at once, sometimes only three of them and sometimes the cracked childish voice alone, persistent in its solitude. For days the summer guests staggered about Mandria with half-closed eyelids, splitting headaches and swollen eardrums. Why were the bells incessantly ringing? No one knew, or would provide, the answer to this question. There was no escape from the bells. Occasionally they pretended to make an end of the ringing, only to begin the frantic din anew a moment later. They clanged and rattled and it sometimes seemed that they had come to blows. Occhipinti told Baron Stern, who threatened to leave at once and send a letter of protest to the *Corriera della Sera,* that they rang so many bells in Mandria because of an ancient custom whereby old women who had bad dreams went to Nyinyin with a piece of fish or some money and had him ring away the revenant. But this custom only obtained in the ancient past. It was not the bad dreams but the fish and the money that had decreased in Mandria.

The summer guests occasionally convened in a menacing group on the Piazza Vittorio Emanuele and cast despairing stares up at the belfry tower, where they could see the working of the ropes and the green rims of the bells as they fluttered in lunatic pandemonium.

Under the leadership of Baron Stern, the summer guests went to lodge a complaint with the podestà, but the latter merely shrugged and said he would not interfere with the affairs of the Church. This happened on the fourth day after Parson Muzmics left Mandria on a trip. Finally one of the guests came to the rescue with a bright idea. They entered into secret negotiations with the bell ringer himself. This diplomatic measure proved to be spectacularly successful. In return for a relatively modest fee, Nyinyin indicated his willingness to refrain from any and all bell ringing. The summer guests collected the money in a matter of moments.

From then on life was different in Mandria. Silence, wonderful, celestial silence descended on the Piazza Vittorio Emanuele and the Corso Mussolini. On occasion it was possible to hear the faint music of the breeze known as the *tramontana* and the gentle song of the waves. The nerves of the summer guests began to return to normal. Nyinyin sat on the terrace of the Trattoria Marica all day, in the company of a half bottle of *vino rosso*. His four sons fished in the harbor, which was also an activity pursued to best advantage in silence.

But one afternoon, unexpectedly, the bells began to rave again. The slender stone tower almost rocked with their raging. Nyinyin and his four sons were tugging at the bell ropes for dear life. No one knew what had happened, and everybody feared a catastrophe, an earthquake, a forest fire or a tidal wave. But only the summer guests were seized by panic; the native Mandrians showed no concern. Occhipinti was a picture of indifference as he stood in the doorway of his drugstore and picked his teeth. On the terrace of the Trattoria Marica, Aldo Faggiani the butcher and Ettore Domeneghetti the barber continued to slam their soiled cards on the table. Finally Baron Stern learned from Marica that Nyinyin had drunk his very last cent that morning.

The vacationists congregated below the belfry. They waved bathing suits and pajamas in surrender. There were some who held up silver coins.

Nyinyin looked down from the belfry and saw the coins, at which the bells of the Lord lost their voice once more.

Zia struck up an acquaintance with only one of the summer guests, Helen Gieseler, a teacher from Innsbruck. This happened on the Corso Mussolini one evening when Helen confronted Zia, clapped her heels together, rendered a mock salute and introduced herself. She wore a rustic Tyrolean dress with a divided skirt, and there were wildflowers in her straw-blond hair. The porcelain blue of her eyes was even bluer than the eyes of the Schäyenheims. Her neck and her calves were bright red from sudden exposure to the Mandrian sunshine. She asked permission to accompany Zia for a while. She seemed a friendly and amusing soul. On the seashore the next day Zia suddenly noticed that a group of bathers was listening to a speech and guffawing loudly. The speaker was Hitler, who wore a Tyrolean skirt from the waist down and had sunburnt calves. Helen had made a Hitler wig out of a piece of dark flannel, pasted a Hitler mustache on her upper lip and donned Baron Stern's raincoat. It is evident from all this that life in Mandria was not altogether uneventful.

The ship entered the harbor every week at seven o'clock on Thursday evening, and Zia was always the first to watch for it on the wharf. She walked up and down, from the customs inspector's booth to the iron bollard around which the hawsers of the ship would be bound. Guido Castelli always left his booth when he saw Zia, and was always inexplicably embarrassed. As if struck dumb with excitement, he never got beyond "Are you waiting for someone?" or "It's a warm day again, isn't it?" The ship pulled in and the sandy-yellow shape beside the mast that looked like Filippo from a distance always turned out to be the bloodstained sack in which Aldo Faggiani the butcher carried his side of veal.

Helen spent more and more time with Zia. Now she often came to the garden of the Pension Zanzottera after dinner and, sitting on the red seat under the old fig tree, she would hum Tyrolean folk songs and would even yodel with some skill. Her friendliness was rather a burden to Zia because of the high-powered temperament that blazed in the girl. One evening they were still seated in the garden after the signora had retired. Helen asked Zia to show her the photographs of a seashore fishing excursion that had taken place the week before. She was enchanted by the photographs, chattered interminably and with noticeable excitement, and she paid no heed to Zia's hints at the lateness of the hour. Finally Zia, yawning, told her she wanted to go to bed. "Schön," said Helen, seating herself at the side of the bed, and with a perfect imitation of the facial expression of an old Tyrolese peasant she began to sing ancient German lullabies, so softly and so charmingly that Zia did not have the heart to send her away. As she closed her eyes, she enjoyed the clear simplicity of the melodies. But at the end of one of the songs Helen unexpectedly threw herself at Zia and began to kiss her. Zia had to push her away with outstretched hands. And when Helen left she was seized with boundless sadness and disgust. She recalled Pringsheim's

551

words, that an alarming sexual poverty prevailed in the world. This was now her perspective toward Mandria and the world at large. Guido Castelli was becoming increasingly impudent. That very afternoon he had seated himself on her bench along the water-front, but his excitement was so great that he had been unable to say a word. His large black eyes bulged with such prominence that they almost cracked apart. His eyes were infernally ugly, but there was something in them that reminded her of Filippo. She was no longer able to walk past the drugstore in peace, for Occhipinti's eyes flared ever more brightly and when she had passed him she could feel the druggist's gaze tangle about her ankles, her legs and her skirt like a tendril in the wilderness. There was Eligio Fanfoni, too, and the way his lust invaded his rat-face whenever he saw her, not to mention General Hasparics, on whose tremulous nose the network of blue-black veins that was like a tracery of lightning bolts began to flash, and his fuddled glance became even cloudier, when she walked by the bench where he sat with his four dogs. It seemed that the Mandrian air gave especial strength to the passions. She found this was true of herself as well, for when she lay naked in the confines of her room during the hours of afternoon heat she could not fight free of memories of *Päckhaus,* her restlessness grew from day to day, she could feel Gido's jasmine-scented black hair on her loins, and at such times her listlessly writhing body was a single vain importunity for the mysterious and strange orgasm and the complete fulfillment that Pringsheim had talked about. Yes, one could not be twenty-one years old and healthy in all innocence, especially when burdened with a legacy of heightened sensuality, the bequeathal of an overbred stock that inhabited her overcultivated body.

Otherwise the days passed quietly in Mandria, apart from the continuous clamor of shrieking children that resounded from the bagno. After the lullabies Zia broke her friendship with Helen. The comparative calm was disrupted about once each week by the blast of bells which came like a fire alarm from the belfry tower. But the summer guests knew the rules of the game by now, and quickly put the fire out with several hundred liras.

By the end of September the very last visitor had left Mandria. Small seaside resorts turn desperately sad for a few days at a time like this, until they can reconcile themselves to the vacant approach of fall. The slow exodus of the summer guests and the gradual disappearance of the varicolored swimming suits they hung out to dry—all this was like the falling of the leaves, and at noon the vacant stillness on the terrace of the Trattoria Marica also spoke of decay. On such autumn days the passing years tell the human heart in whispers that they are going away and will never return.

Zia ate *brodetto* at noon one day, an Italian fish soup that the signora prepared to perfection. The following day her stomach was mildly upset and, as always when this happened, she decided to take two Entalisina pills. She was terrified to discover only one pill left in the bottle; moreover, although two bottles were listed on the inventory, the other bottle was nowhere to be found. Then she remembered having given one of them to Elizabeth. This discovery completely dispirited her. In her present Mandrian existence, Entalisina played the part of the talisman around the neck of a seasoned sailor or the rosary around a nun's waist, without which their lives are lost. Zia felt that the exhaustion of Entalisina unlocked a door previously closed to her and laid the way open for the arbitrary entrance of death. The arrival of autumn and the sudden onset of solitude combined to aggravate her despair. And there was the matter of Fifi. It was the third week since the dog had run away. Unaccountably Fifi had attached herself to the smallest of the Nyinyin progeny, the spectacled Moco. It must have been a case of blind passion, for as far as nourishment was concerned she certainly fared worse in Nyinyin's house. So complete was her faithlessness that she even turned her muzzle away when she saw Zia on the Piazza Vittorio Emanuele. Zia would stop and scold her roundly. She told her what a shameful thing it was to leave one's loving foster mother, and she began to negotiate on the score of forgiveness and homecoming. Fifi kept turning slightly under the influence of the long moral lecture until it was finally her tail that faced Zia. Pieces of cheese purchased at Niccolini's store did not serve the purpose either. Triumphing over temptation, Fifi would suddenly fly away, bobbing her outsized head and leaving the cheese behind. In all this there was something laughable, but at the same time it was sad and frightening. Zia was deserted by everyone and everything.

She spent the 30th of October in her room. It was the first anniversary of her life in Mandria. She went to church in the early morning, and the thought of confession crossed her mind. For reasons unknown even to her, she did not like Parson Muzmics' glances. She preferred to converse with God in solitude, and was making two daily visits to the church of San Simeone nowadays, in the morning and at nightfall, when she was alone with the fragrance of withering floral bouquets and smoking votive candles at the foot of the pictures of Mary, with the peculiar light streaming through the stained-glass windows and the hush of solitude so characteristic of such little Italian churches, like special products that are available only in certain department stores and nowhere else.

Zia had suffered a great deal in the past weeks. She was tortured by nervousness, restlessness, headaches, especially during her most recent monthly malaise. The discussion with Pringsheim had upset her spiritual equilibrium, and there were hours she spent sitting naked before her silver-framed mirror, shielding her breasts and shoulders with her arms, contemplating her body and the desires that coursed through this supple, youthful flesh as if they were some serious medical problem. The flesh complained, implored, asking for sustenance like the cracked lips of a feverish patient.

On November 10th something important happened to her. As always, she appeared on the wharf a half hour before the arrival of the ship. Lukewarm breezes were playing over the sea and the shore, and their path could be seen with the naked eye, for they dodged above the water like animals in tall grass. One could not actually see them, but the ribbon of a wave showed where they ran. They filled the air with an odd vivacity. Occasionally they collided, and at these times they vanished with a faint, ecstatic cry. And sometimes they met in front of Zia's face and suddenly whispered incomprehensible things in her ear. There was a pile of boards waiting for the ship beyond the iron bollard. The flighty breezes were presently occupied with spreading the strong, resinous fragrance of the freshly cut boards over the harbor and the sea. Guido Castelli, the customs inspector, stepped from his booth in dove-gray trousers supported by the large X of the braces on his back, and as he passed Zia he chokingly informed her that autumn was on the way. The carnal glow in his chestnut-colored eyes was stronger than it had ever been.

The ship was not yet visible, but its horn blared forth from behind the twilight fog bank. At this point the foghorn sounded like an unearthly and improbable howl that was remarkably human. It mingled the exaltation of a cry for help with a shiver of fascination. The warm breezes began to dance with wild excitement and the sea, too, suddenly bristled with waves.

Something in the air gave Zia to know, with complete conviction, that Filippo would arrive and was already close by, at most a mile and a half away in the fog bank.

The ship disengaged herself from the mist. The yellow and red rosebuds of several lamps blossomed on the ponderous, dark, rolling mass, and the blossoms filled the trough of the waves with orange and red petals.

Slowly the ship approached the wharf. The sandy-yellow patch was already visible beside one of the masts. Zia's heart began to beat wildly, for she clearly knew that for once this sandy-yellow shape was not a side of veal in the sack of Aldo Faggiani the butcher—it was Filippo's trenchcoat. This was her thirteenth month in Mandria, and this was the forty-seventh appearance of the ship. She had never felt so certain of Filippo's arrival. It was all so bewildering, so horrible and beautiful that Zia was unable to stand on her legs any longer. Exhausted, she sat down on the stubby iron bollard.

The ship pulled into the wharf and the sandy-yellow shape started down the gangplank. It was not Filippo, but only Aldo Faggiani once more. He walked by Zia. Drops of blood fell on the large, white, wave-washed cobblestones.

In a matter of moments the harbor was deserted again. Zia remained seated on the little bollard, and her eyes studied the tiny drops of blood with a rigid stare. As certain as she had been a quarter hour before of Filippo's arrival, so she was now assured that Filippo would never come, and the knowledge filled her body with a terrible emptiness. It was slowly beginning to grow dark.

When she stood up to go home Guido Castelli the customs inspector fell into step with her and confided that the warm days would only last a little while longer, after which the days would start to get cool. And this was the first time that Zia held the customs inspector's gaze with her eyes, held it for an unconscionable length of time, at which Guido Castelli almost began to tremble but did not know what to say. Suddenly Zia turned on her heel and started homeward. She did not look back, but she sensed that the dove-gray trousers were following her.

The signora was not at home. Like a sleepwalker, Zia crossed the hall but left the door open. When she reached her room she began to undress and, as was her custom, she stretched out naked on the wide studio couch, softly humming "O mia Fiamma bellissima" in the meanwhile, the melody of which returned to her memory now with crystal clarity. But Pringsheim's ear would probably have found something unusual in her humming, something that resembled an intoxication of the spirit and was near insanity without being insanity. Zia did not usually hum. She was doing it for the first time. It was almost as if a certain madness had possessed her now, a rebellion the blind forces of which stormed about the world and were known to Pringsheim, forces which hurled the transcendental clangor of orgasm over the earth, into jasmine-scented black tresses, into wildflowers woven through straw-blond hair, into the glances of Occhipinti the druggist and all the men of Mandria. The room was almost dark, but one bald branch of the old fig tree outside the window let in a little light. The sound of timorous steps came from the hall. She suddenly stopped humming and closed her eyes, like one who is ready to yield to the dire commandment of life. She clenched her teeth to keep them from chattering. She heard the customs inspector step into the room, and she heard the quick turn of the key in the lock. Then she felt Guido Castelli's hot breath on her forehead. Later, by the time she was alone again, the room was completely dark, and in the window the black outline of a dry branch on the old fig tree had also faded. She sprang up, lit the little shaded lamp and with muffled whimpers of terror issuing from her throat she ran behind the screen, almost knocking it down. When she unwound the rubber tube of the shower-spray with trembling hands, it squirmed like a live red snake. She began to wash in wild haste, using large quantities of every sort of scented water and disinfectant. Sitting on the bidet, her legs spread wide apart, she moaned softly, like a wounded child. Fortunately the signora was not at home, for otherwise she would surely have heard this odd, quiet plaint. Then she dressed from top to toe, put on her traveling coat and carefully adjusted a dark red Basque cap on her head. She sat on the edge of the bed and tried to think, but she could not comprehend this thing that had happened to her. She was dazed, as if struck down by lightning. When she heard the signora enter the house she swiftly put out the light. She had no idea how long she sat in the dark. Fully clothed as she was, she stretched out on the bed and it was past midnight when she awoke. She lit the lamp again. This time she was able to concentrate. For a moment there was no doubt in her mind that she would have to leave Mandria as soon as possible. The island and her isolation were now a sinister menace. If she had allowed this thing to happen tonight, she would not be able to resist becoming the mistress of the gibbous-eyed customs inspector, from beneath whose armpits a warm, sour smell steamed forth. And all this out of wild pursuit of something that, for her, would never be realized, perhaps, for even now her flesh had been flooded with nothing but a loathsome fever that left only filth behind, spiritual and physical filth. She stood up and began to pack, cautiously, lest she make a noise and rouse the signora. She crossed and recrossed the room with dreamlike movements, and once, when she glanced at the window, the black outline of the withered branch on the old fig tree was clearly visible. By the time she snapped off the lamp it was totally light outside. She went to bed, exhausted, and slept till noon. But she still did not move from the room. She told the signora she was ailing, and indicated that she did not want to be disturbed. She asked that her empty trunks be brought to her room on the following day, because she was leaving. Where was she going? the signora asked apprehensively. To Paris. Yes, she had decided to go to Paris. She felt she had nobody in the world except Monsieur Mongés.

✝

But nothing came of her trip. Life, which occasionally intervenes with unexpected brutality, solved her problem. Three days later an event took place that stirred not only Mandria but caused the banner headlines of the entire Italian press to quiver like reeds for days. Between Sunday night and Monday morning Eulalia—manager of the dairy and wife of Alberto, renting agent of the bagno, the woman with two front teeth missing and black hair parted in the middle, whom everyone in Mandria knew to be the mistress of Guido Castelli the customs inspector—Eulalia shot her faithless lover to death at five o'clock in the morning on the Piazza Vittorio Emanuele, having lain in wait for him while the customs inspector spent the night in the bed of the barber's wife. Ettore Domeneghetti, the barber, was not in Mandria. When Guido Castelli stepped out of the barber's house in the crepuscular light of dawn at five o'clock in the morning, Eulalia attacked him and a noisy quarrel broke out between the two of them. The customs inspector was unable to shake her off, and when they reached Niccolini's grocery—which was shuttered behind an iron grating at that hour—he struck his forsaken sweetheart. A scuffle began, and Eulalia succeeded in snatching the customs inspector's revolver from the back pocket of his dove-gray trousers. She fired once and then, smoking pistol in hand, she ran back to the barber's house and fired five shots through the window. The last five shots, fortunately, hit no one, although one of the bullets penetrated the pillow of the barber's youngest daughter. By this time people were pouring from their homes, and they secured the raging, deranged Eulalia.

When Zia set out for church in the early morning she knew nothing of all this. Eligio Fanfoni the baker rushed by, grabbed her arm and dragged her toward Niccolini's grocery, where a great mob had formed. The baker forced his way through the throng, pulling Zia with him. Zia still did not know what had

557

happened—she imagined someone had caught a shark, or a moonfish, or a giant polyp, which was always an occasion for excitement and tumult. The customs inspector's body lay on the stone pavement, covered with a bloodstained canvas similar to the sack in which Aldo Faggiani the butcher usually carried his side of veal. Eligio Fanfoni leaned over and politely uncovered the corpse for Zia to see. Guido Castelli's dove-gray trousers were dripping with blood. He had received a stomach wound, and must have died in great agony, for his tongue, purplish-black and bitten through, dangled from the right corner of his mouth, where little green flies were already roosting. Deep, bloody scratches of feminine fingernails were clearly visible on his left cheek. Zia turned her head away and almost fainted. She was staggering when she reached the church of San Simeone, where she threw herself on her knees before the altar. Only then did her mind begin to grasp what had happened, and what might also have happened to her. She saw a supernal omen in the unforeseen but terrible solution: she was meant to stay in Mandria.

The customary smile was missing from Eulalia's face right now, and consequently the gap of her two front teeth was not in evidence. Her heart-shaped face, in its frame of black hair parted in the middle, was a desolate image of tragic splendor at this moment.

The inquisitive crowd and the children saw the murderess only. Had Pringsheim been among them, he would have taken another view of the manacled Italian woman. He would have discerned the black specter of the blind forces that were storming about the world, a victim of the sexual poverty that lurked in churches, pulpits, political movements and high principles. This is what he would have seen in Eulalia, the manager of the dairy in Mandria.

Chapter Thirteen

A YOUNG day-laborer laid down his spade one day in the spring of 1906 in Vienna and retired to vomit blood in the garden of the Dukay Palace on Bösendorferstrasse, and twenty-seven years later, on the 30th of January in 1933, this young man, whose life Countess Menti saved with her gift of two hundred crowns, became the Imperial Chancellor of Germany.

Thereupon events in Germany followed in rocketlike succession until the whole world was dazed. After Hitler's accession to power the German Communists tried to persuade the Social Democrats and the Christian trade unions to join in a communal workers' strike against Hindenburg's choice of Hitler for Chancellor, but it was no longer possible to realize this united front of German labor. At the end of February the Nazis set fire to the imperial assembly hall and blamed the conflagration on the Communists. The Reichstag's pillars of smoke and flame were needed to muster the unanimous consent of German public opinion for the extirpation of the Communist Party. In the first days of spring the Nazi Parliament at Potsdam invested its unlimited authority in Hitler, and with this power in his hand he promptly stripped the governments of separate German states of their independence. On the 14th of July he prohibited the formation of any sort of party in Germany.

On that day, at four o'clock in the afternoon, Mandria had still not arisen from the peculiar hush and immobility induced by the afternoon heat. These are the enchanted hours of the Mediterranean shores, when all human life is at a standstill. This is what the afternoon hours in the dog days of July must have been like in the time of the Roman emperor-gods two thousand years ago, the hours of the *siesta,* when the togaed plebes slept through the heat in their low-ceilinged, mosaicked rooms. All movement ceased, and only the sand in the hourglasses continued to fall silently.

At this time no human soul appeared on the Piazza Vittorio Emanuele either. The calm was almost frightening, as if the universe were no longer breathing. The sea glittered like freshly poured lead in the dazzling sunshine, as smooth as if it had hardened into solid metal. The hot air was compact gold, in which the light wings of the gulls moved only with difficulty. At these times the gulls perched on little islands dappled with their own droppings and awaited the resurrection of the universe. The only sign of life in an empty sky was the two almost imperceptible arcs of the wings of a high-flown windhover which began to flap with some rapidity from time to time, apparently for the purpose of storing up new strength toward a further immobility, as if commissioned by the laurel forests of the distant, widespread mountains to watch over their afternoon sleep. The same enchanted hush and immobility reigned about the concrete lagoon of the harbor, which generally echoed with a Latin din. The fisherfolk slept at the foot of the houses in the narrow ultramarine stripes of shade that the blinding sunshine, with grudging condescension, had spared from the flood of light. They slept on the bare stone, with the palms of their hands as the only pillows, and most of them were so motionless that they seemed like pell-mell casualties on a battlefield. They were undisturbed by the proximity to their faces of discarded fish-guts.

It was during these enchanted hours that the shallow, honey-yellow waters of the lagoon were invaded by eight- to ten-pound branzinos in schools of four and five, a noble fare for long silver platters, the wariest fish of the Mediterranean. But they were apparently capable of succumbing to curiosity too, for they turned on their flanks to examine the yellowing lemon peels, and here and there the silver sheen of a discarded tin can, and the decaying rags of red and black that grew to great size under water, like flies under a magnifying glass. When these big fish, turning on their flanks, suddenly flashed the solid, glittering silver of their delicate frames, it was as if they became realities for only a fleeting second or two and then reverted to dreamlike, weightless, blue-brown shades. The appearance of the majestic fish in what were, for them, dangerous waters was like an ascent to the summit of Mont Blanc by fashionable tourists at the risk of their lives, or like the descent of foreign and fastidious millionaires to the most lurid Apache haunts in Montmartre, there to sample the hot spices of life. As they slowly advanced above the refuse on the show-window bottom of the lagoon, their translucent fins gripped the water with a lightness that was the ultimate in quiescence and ease. There was something both breathtaking and baffling in their movements, poised as they were at every turn to escape headlong into the dark-blue depths of the sea, to whisk their immeasurably muscular bodies into flight with a lightning motion, like arrows shot from a bow, if a shadow were seen or a noise heard at the edge of the lagoon, for incessant terror was inscribed in their nerves. And their terror was not groundless at the moment, for there in the transparent shade of the sail of one of the barks at the upper corner of the lagoon sat Earless Mungu, dangling his black feet in the yellow water and holding the handle of a harpoon in his upraised hand. Dark and glistening like oil, the muscles of his half-naked body were strained with the tension of an explosive and at the same time petrified posture. Mungu relaxed and lowered his arm, not suspecting that the rare prize was only a few yards away. Of course the big branzinos noiselessly swept away at his gesture, and when Mungu lifted his harpoon to a stiff immobility once again, when he scanned the lagoon bottom with the look of his primordial ancestors in his eyes, he was only shaking a stick at empty water.

Beside the fishmarket an emaciated kitten with lusterless fur stared at a mousehole, its pupils dilated, its soft body as packed with the repressed power of readiness for a leap as only felines can be when they are motionless. A spider-web stretched between the rusty iron teeth on the upper edge of the stone wall around the Albergo Varcaponti, and the spider crouched invisibly in a crack of the stone, its nerves taut, like a revolver. And up on high the wonderfully keen eyes of the windhover sentiently scrutinized the most minute detail of the landscape below. Murderous intent skulked everywhere in the cheerfulness of Elysian tranquility and repose. It was in this hour that one of the heads of cabbage in Niccolini's grocery store embarked on its ultimate decay. This smell now pervaded the Piazza Vittorio Emanuele, overwhelming even the sweet and incessant stench of the fishmarket. According to experts, one rotting head of cabbage has a greater odoriferous potential than ten human corpses in an advanced stage of dissolution.

What has happened to the dead photographer lady in the meantime? All signs indicate that *la fotografa morta* is still alive, for in the garden of the Pension Zanzottera, stretched between an orange tree and the old fig tree, there is a clothesline, and hanging on the clothesline to dry are silk stockings as fragile as cobwebs and feminine lingerie as light as the stuff of dreams.

The steeple clock struck four, signaling that the end of the classical siesta was close at hand. Its deep tones sank into the silence like sheets of metal into water. The prevalent silence signified, at the same time, that this season too the liras of the summer guests had subdued the raging of Nyinyin's bells. In the customs booth, in place of Guido Castelli, there sat a new inspector, Fabrizio Scorzi, who was completely unlike Guido in appearance. Fabrizio Scorzi slept at the desk in his booth, his forehead resting on his wrist. He started at the striking of the clock, and broke the even rhythm of his snoring, like an accordion player when someone pushes his elbow, but the music resumed its monotone in two-four time: Bruu-hraa…bruu-hraa…All Mandria was still asleep.

As always at this hour, Zia was lying on the studio couch in her darkened room, completely naked, which was the general and obligatory attire for this period of the day in Mandria. She lay outstretched with arms folded beneath the pillow and with open eyes, sleeplessly, for she did not know the joys of daytime dreams. The little red slippers were all she had on. Her eyes stared into space. The human soul always assumes something of the atmosphere of its environment. Zia's thoughts were cloudy as she rested on the couch; she too was waiting for the moment of resurrection in Mandria, which was not far away. At about half past four the Piazza Vittorio Emanuele began to fill with yawning, stretching people. Occhipinti, the druggist, appeared in the door of his shop, paring his nails with a penknife. Domenica, Tonia's oldest daughter, pulled up the shutter of the dairy with a great clatter. Since Eulalia was led away in handcuffs, Tonia had been managing the dairy.

The two silent actors of the drama last fall—Alberto the renting agent and Ettore Domeneghetti the barber, with combs fastened in his wavy hair—settled on the terrace of the Trattoria Marica and began to slap the table with their soiled playing cards. Eulalia had been sentenced to four years in prison. When she returned, life would take up where it had been before, since Mandria was not familiar with the institution of divorce.

The clamor of the Niccolini children resounded from the bagno. The baker, Eligio Fanfoni, mounted the bicycle that leaned against the door of his shop and rode away.

The emaciated kitten with lusterless fur, its mousehunt apparently unsuccessful, now squinted on the warm stone in the strong sunshine and gnawed a rotting fish-head, sinking its tiny needle-sharp teeth daintily into the food.

As she lay outstretched on the wide couch in her darkened room, memories swam soundlessly in Zia's mind, like the branzinos in the shallow lagoon, brushing the motley remnants of bygone minutes and hours with their fins. Zia's consciousness floated somewhere on high, like the wings of the windhover, and her sensuality, like sharp little cat-teeth, daintily gnawed on a decaying recollection or two. The air touched the most sensitive points of her nude body with velvety lightness: the arch of her abdomen, her loins, her breasts, and the soft curves of her shoulders.

✚

The doorbell rang above the gaudy windowpanes in the hall, transforming the whole sleeping house into a headachy reality. Some long moments later one could hear the signora's door opening, and the sound was definitely ill-humored at this time. Then the second creak of a door, and the sound of four feet on the cocoanut carpet. Two of the feet approached Zia's room, and the signora knocked:

"Signora! Vi cerca un signore!"

Zia leapt up so vehemently that one of her red slippers flew off, and she had to fish it forth from beneath one of the wardrobes. Crouching on the floor, reaching under the wardrobe with her forearm, she called toward the door in a muffled voice:

"Un momento! Vengo subito."

Quickly she slipped into her light, ankle-length wine-red negligee and fastened it about her improbably slim waist with trembling hands. Her knees shook, and there was hardly strength in her legs to support the light weight of her body. Now, all at once, the oppressive and giddying stillness that had pervaded her nerves and brain and body burst into flame, like a sultry hayrick when it suddenly takes fire in the heat of summer. A thought struck her with painful and piercing splendor: Filippo was here, he had finally come! How? On a rented motor launch, probably. The role she had intended to play at this moment, waiting for the incoming ship on the lonely edge of the wharf in the twilight, the words, the expression, the gestures, the very dress—all this turned to nothing now. She felt cheated, like an actress summoned to play Juliet, not in a white silk toga and a Latin headdress on the balcony, but with a wrinkled and unpainted face in the shabby hall of the Pension Zanzottera, called upon to blurt out a confused and stupid part instead of Shakespeare's "Ay, pilgrim, lips that they must use in prayer." She flung herself into the chair before the silver-framed mirror to put herself to rights, but the mirror looked so compassionately at her ash-gray aspect that she buried her face in her hands in desperation, knowing that she inexplicably turned ugly during the days of her periodical malaise or in moments of nervousness and anxiety. Her heart beat madly in her throat, and she was on the verge of fainting with pain and ecstasy. But this lasted only for a few seconds; new strength suddenly came into her dominion. She hurried to the door and threw it open, somewhat theatrically.

A stranger stood in the hallway where a landscape was hanging, studying the painting with the preoccupation of a man kept waiting. He wore nothing but sandals and bathing trunks, a costume entirely suitable for paying calls in Mandria. It would have been surprising, indeed, had he been more fully dressed at this hour. Several articles of clothing were folded over his left arm. At the sound of the opening door he turned.

Zia recognized him at once as the summer guest whom she had named the Forehead. It was with names like this that she generally distinguished the vacationists about whom she knew nothing. Among the bathers this season were Shortlegs, Longneck, Belly, Rolypoly, Striped-trousers and Carrot-top. This one was the Forehead, who always carried books and notes wherever he went, whether on the beach, on a bench along the Corso Mussolini or on the terrace of the Trattoria Marica.

There was sincere apology in the eyes of the Forehead.

"I'm Dr. Mihály Ursi. I heard in the restaurant that you are Hungarian, and a professional photographer. I've lost my passport, and I need some passport photographs urgently."

Zia's stance as she stood in the open doorway was the one she had meant to greet Filippo with, her right hand outstretched and gripping the door knob, dramatically expressive of an animation both painful and joyous, replete with deep-felt reproach and exalted forgiveness. It is amazing how many things the same attitude can express under different inspiration. At the moment this attitude bore a great resemblance to the forbidding appearance of a solitary and retiring woman whose afternoon nap has been disturbed.

Ursi felt something of this in her expression, and hastened to add:

"I know an urgent order will involve some inconvenience, so I wouldn't want you to do it at your regular rates."

Something in the caller's face now betrayed the realization that he should not have come in bathing trunks to visit this woman whose haughty manner commanded respect without inspiring antagonism.

"I don't have an Italian permit," Zia said, "and the Italian authorities are very strict about that sort of thing right now."

The caller's five widespread fingers disappeared into his soft, burnished brown hair, which started high on his forehead. In the meantime the look on his face was that of someone who has just received an unwelcome telegram.

"The fact is," he said with an abstract air, gazing at the floor, "the fact is that it will take at least ten days to get another passport. My vacation will soon be over. If I have to wait for the next boat because of the photographs, I'll lose four days. The motor launch happens to be leaving tomorrow, and it could take my application."

After he had debated the matter thoroughly with one of the mosaic blocks on the floor, scratching his head and studying his feet, he said with an importunate smile and an ingratiating tone in his voice:

"Couldn't you help me out?"

And then he added: "Just because we're compatriots."

His last words left Zia cold. She recognized neither their substance nor their sympathy. This was an unwitting result of her training, of the Dukays' magic circle which involuntarily barred them from contact with inferior classes simply by reason of historical origin and financial position. Moments like this were evidence that by traveling on their own exclusive thoroughfares they had become cosmopolites, citizens of a world where a Marchese Delfrate or an Earl Hamson was much more their compatriot than a Dr. Ursi or any what's-his-name. The first appeal made greater headway with Zia: "Couldn't you help me out?" And so did the embarrassed, beseeching little smile that accompanied it, with its air of friendly complicity. It was Berili who had planted the deeper significance of the word *help* in Zia. And the heart of a child absorbs these simple words more completely than all the lessons of religion, which sometimes look as bare in their textbooks as the questions and answers on an income-tax form. Fundamentally, too, Zia belonged to the type of women in whom it is a sheer instinct to lend assistance. Assistance: their gluttonous hearts cannot withstand the sweetness of the word.

"Come in," she said, releasing the doorknob.

Ursi stepped inside with circumspection. At such moments the atmosphere of a photographic studio dangerously resembles that of a doctor's office. But in this instance a different atmosphere greeted him. The cover of the wide studio couch still bore the faint impression of Zia's body, like a drawing on smooth sand, betraying something of the intimate mystery of a feminine room. With a few swift motions Zia straightened the cover and the marks disappeared, fled from the visitor's scrutiny, like inhabitants of another world suddenly roused from their sleep. Zia brought forward the white canvas screen that she used for portrait photography. A few moments later the camera stood ready on its flamingo-legs, and the powerful floodlights were aglow. Zia pushed one of the little mushroom-shaped stools before the canvas screen.

"Please sit down."

Her voice was calm and businesslike. She studied her victim with the eyes of a surgeon preparing for a major operation. She would have to amputate this patient's body from the abdomen down, since a passport photograph had to show the head and shoulders alone.

"Don't you want to put your clothes on?"

"Yes," Ursi said, "I've got them right here."

And he started to slip into the short-sleeved shirt and the light linen jacket that he had brought on his arm.

"I didn't bring any trousers with me."

Hardly had he said it when he realized how odd the statement sounded in the fragrant solitude of this feminine room—a gentleman telling a lady at their first meeting that he had not brought his trousers along. Zia herself, who stood waiting by her camera, broke into a smile. Ursi noticed her smile and was embarrassed. Meanwhile he had finished dressing, if this process could be called dressing. The shirt covered his bathing trunks, but his thighs showed below the shirt, and the large humps of his knees, and his muscular calves, and all this suddenly gave an impression of immodesty. Having put his clothes on, he seemed to have undressed instead. Ursi himself sensed the incongruity of the situation, which he had not foreseen in his haste and excitement. His embarrassment was further increased by having come for passport photographs to a professional photographer and finding a young woman instead, a young woman in whose personality there was a bewitching, delicate melancholy, a refined sense of withdrawal and at the same time a goodly portion of natural feminity and forthrightness, that was manifest, all at once, in her smile. These were his thoughts as he seated himself on the mushroom-shaped stool, dressed like a summer dandy from the waist up and looking like a naked savage below. The stool proved too low for a man of his height. He endeavored to assume an expression that would make a reassuring impression on the suspicious customs officers of Europe.

Standing by her camera, Zia narrowed her eyes slightly as she studied the subject to be photographed. A good head. The broad, high forehead disappears with a graceful line beneath the soft brown hair. The face is just a bit Mongoloid, a characteristic particularly evident in the smile, when the otherwise unobtrusive cheekbones are elevated into prominence and the openings of the eyes are drawn aslant. The mouth: large. The colorless lips: soft. There is a narrow silver band at the base of the right eyetooth, indicative of a false tooth, the masterpiece of some inexpensive or institutional dentist. A deep cleft runs down the middle of the strong-boned jaw. Two similarly deep lines appear on the face, at both sides of the nose, revealing the softness of the skin. These lines add a severity and a manliness to an otherwise youthful face, and clothe it with intellectual dignity. This heightened, vigilant; intellectuality was the man's most striking and most characteristic feature. Zia had never encountered a face like this before. There was good will in the brown eyes, and a constant, deep preoccupation. Zia, who had learned a good deal about the analysis of faces from Monsieur Mongés in Paris, was reminded at this moment of Ady's large, intoxicated, explosive eyeballs, or of the inner horizons of Eleonora Duse's enormous, introspective eyes, a dark velvet veil that cloaked her entire soul. There was nothing like that about this man's eyes. His glance turned outward rather than inward. Zia knew this glance; she had discovered it in several of the members of her family. Count Joachim once painted Peter Dukay in the costume of a falconer, with a hooded falcon on his fist. Uncle Himi called it the Asiatic look, and there was something of this in the countenance of the man sitting on the low stool. Compact muscles ran from the broad neck into the shoulders, which were strong and bony but far from athletic in appearance. The flat belly, the inarticulate, long, smooth muscles of the arms, the thighs, the shoulders, bespoke some less arduous sport, hunting or golf. The powerful wrists were somewhat rectangular, and the hands broad but well formed. The hard nails at the tips of the fingers tapered almost to the point of delicacy, which is always characteristic of the intellectual.

"Are you a physician?" Zia asked, after looking into the camera.

"No. I'm an astrophysicist."

On the outer flank of the astrophysicist's left thigh there was a finger-length scar, of the type so liberally distributed during the World War. From this it was possible to estimate that he was at least thirty-three years old.

"You're too serious. Couldn't you smile a little?" asked Zia, whose fingers already gripped the rubber bulb of the shutter.

A wide smile appeared on the astrophysicist's face and suddenly lit up the attractive Asiatic features. The smile was natural and cheerful, and was apparently occasioned more by the peculiarity of the situation, his trouserless state, than by the command from behind the camera. But before Zia could press the shutter the smile on the astronomer's face froze into the strained expression to which most human faces fall victim at the moment of being photographed, the artificial grimace which is responsible for the fact that most passport photographs convey an impression of mild idiocy. Ursi started to get up, but Zia ordered him back.

"Wait a moment, I want to make another one. Try not to think of anything."

In the present situation her bidding seemed impossible of accomplishment, especially in the case of such a thought-crammed forehead and glance. And the natural countenance of a man who had been thinking about his lost passport all morning could hardly be other than thought-crammed. He relaxed his facial muscles, with the result that his face took on the look of a man condemned to death.

The camera snapped, and Zia pulled her lips to one side.

"The pictures won't be anything to be especially proud of—but good enough for a passport, perhaps," she said, while she detached the camera from the tripod and collapsed the aluminum supports.

Ursi quickly dressed, which in his case meant that he quickly slipped off his clothes. Only when he had stripped to bathing trunks again, with his clothing over his arm, did he really look like a completely clothed Mandrian summer guest, dressed in his own sunburnt, brown-red skin.

"How much do I owe you?"

"I told you I can't accept any money."

A good-humored Samoyed smile appeared on the astronomer's face.

"Are you afraid I'm an *agent provocateur?* A secret agent of the Italian Economic Council, perhaps?"

Her eyes half closed, Zia looked the astronomer up and down cruelly.

"Perhaps."

"When will the picture be ready?"

Zia did not reply at once. She was busily putting the canvas screen back beside the wall. There was some hesitation in her mind between artistic vanity and the unfamiliarity that stood between her and the astrophysicist. Finally the former won out.

"It's already done," she said without turning.

Ursi looked at her with a narrow and suspicious smile, like a child who knows that something is being put over on him but is willing to participate. Zia opened her photograph album and turned to a picture. The enlargement showed the astronomer seated in the garden of the Albergo Varcaponti, manicuring his nails on a white towel stretched over the garden table. The thumb of his left hand was at a right angle to his chest as he cautiously trimmed the cuticle, and at the same time his nose was twisted sharply, almost improbably, to the left, and his lips and the out thrust tip of his tongue as well followed the path of the sundered cuticle with the greatest concentration. The photograph was so human, and so laughable, that Zia herself counted it among her most successful efforts, and she could already hear Monsieur Mongés's praise when she showed it to him. Only rarely can one succeed in laying under contribution these most intimate lines on the face of human seclusion. The picture had been taken in secret, from behind the grapevine-covered iron grating of the fence that surrounded the Albergo Varcaponti.

Ursi fixed an astonished glance on the photograph, and the handsome, broad Samoyed smile slowly crept over his features. He studied the picture for a long time and then said softy, almost to himself and without any trace of mere politeness:

"Wonderful."

He could hardly tear his eyes from the picture. As he leaned over the album and scanned the photograph, Ursi's brown and naked shoulder came close to Zia, who thus discovered that the skin of the astronomer had a pleasant fragrance. "May I?" Ursi asked, and he began to scrutinize the rest of the photographs. There was the emaciated kitten with lusterless fur, daintily sinking its needle-sharp teeth into a rotting fish-head. There was a dog named Fifi, who turned tail to the world with profound contempt. The horse feasting on melon rinds outside Niccolini's grocery store. The Mending of The Nets, The Easter Procession and finally the Incoming Ship in a number of poses, none of which offered any proof to future generations whether the ship was actually arriving or departing.

Ursi wore the look of an expert as he studied the ship in the misty veil of the quiet sea; the streaming curtain of smoke did not seem to come from the ship, rather the ship seemed to have sprung from the clouds of smoke, as the seeds of heavenly bodies are born of fiery gases. Ursi could not know what electrical storms of hope and sadness the arrival of that ship produced in the heart of the young woman who stood at his side, whose body and wine-red negligee breathed forth a light fragrance of lilies of the valley. Ursi turned to Zia and looked into the sensitive green eyes that always swam with an odd and slightly moist poignancy—looked into them as if he were acknowledging, for the first time, the lady photographer's earthly existence. He held her glance for a long time, and then said drily:

"You have a lot of talent."

"Thank you," Zia retorted shortly, and a swift, sarcastic and bitter little pout appeared on her lower lip that did not advantage her looks but was as much a part of her essence as someone else's misshapen fingernail or a scar awkwardly placed. As she glanced at the picture again there was something in her pout that accepted but rather disparaged the acknowledgment of the unknown onlooker, if only because of what the ship meant to her.

"May I ask what your name is?"

"Teréz Hemli," Zia answered, her mind elsewhere as she lit a cigarette without offering one to Ursi.

"Hemli—" Ursi repeated the name to himself, and then added:

"It sounds like a Swiss name."

"I'm Hungarian," Zia said, blowing the first puff toward the ceiling, with an almost involuntary reticence in her voice and an imperceptible shade of hauteur as she thought at the moment of the pioneering Ordony clan—about which a Dukay, in the very depths of the soul, never forgot.

"Do you have a studio in Budapest?"

Zia answered with a negative shake of her head, holding the cigarette in the corner of her mouth and squinting one eye because of the smoke, a habit that remained with her from Paris. She carefully closed the album and returned it to its place.

"I worked in Paris, in Mongés's studio."

She pronounced the name of Mongés with the reverence professional people use when mentioning the names of the masters in their profession. This time she turned her head toward Ursi.

"I gather you know something about photography."

"I'm a photographer myself. But I photograph mists and stars."

Once again the Samoyed smile spread beneath the high forehead, and now it was somewhat inquisitive. "What is your native language?"

Zia could not help laughing. "Do I speak Hungarian so badly?"

"You use the French *r*."

Zia did not reply. There was something in her silence that signaled the end of the conversation. Ursi spoke up.

"In view of the fact that I can't use that marvelous manicuring photograph in my passport, since the Italian customs officers would think I was sticking my tongue out at the Duce, I have to ask once more when the pictures will be ready."

Zia swept back, the ample sleeve of her negligee, revealing her white wrist as if it were some hidden work of art with the wonders of which she wanted to stun her visitor. She glanced at her watch.

"Come back at six o'clock."

And she added: "Perhaps you'll find your passport in the meantime."

"No hope of that," Ursi said gloomily. "I rowed out to sea in my boat early this morning. When the sun came up I took my jacket off, and as I put it down the passport sprang from my inside pocket like a prisoner and jumped headlong into the sea. I could see it swimming toward the bottom with swift strokes."

"A very strange way for a passport to behave," said Zia, and offered her hand with a smile.

Ursi bowed, just as deeply as his attire demanded, for in bathing trunks a man salutes a lady otherwise than in a dinner jacket.

When Zia was alone she set to work with a will. The appearance of the astronomer had been an event in the monotony of her days. And the Samoyed smile, when it occasionally lit up the severe but unusually intelligent face, was like the momentary flash of exquisite silvery secrets when fish turn their flanks. There was something in the smile that Zia had never before seen on a human face.

The double door of the signora's room was always open a finger's breadth, enabling the signora to see what went on in the hall without herself being visible through the aperture. When she answered the doorbell with a sleepy headache and admitted the stranger who was inquiring for the photographer lady, her persistently one-track mind concluded that Zia had probably met the man on the beach, where they had arranged this rendezvous. That was what her female lodgers had been doing for decades. The visits always took place at an unusual hour, when hardly a living soul was abroad in Mandria. The hour of high heat and blazing sunshine passed, from the viewpoint of discretion, for the dark of night. The signora knew of old the short, tentative little rings behind which there always stood a man in bathing trunks. Not for a moment did she suppose that photographs were being made inside. A man might want to be photographed in bathing trunks, but only on the beach. Thus, when the door closed behind them, the signora noted with a complacent quiver of delight that the life of her seclusive lodger had finally started down the right road. The photographer lady had been in residence for a year and a half but, apart from the gruff-voiced, rich and elderly friend who had visited her three times so far, this was the first man behind whom the door of her room had closed. The signora pricked up her ears while she resumed her knitting and listened for the occasional muffled sounds that issued from the adjoining room. In her view, the fact that they were both speaking a foreign tongue bore out the accuracy of her original hypothesis. They were fellow countrymen, and had known each other in the past. Perhaps Bathing-trunks, who had just come to Mandria, was the inevitable young lover with whom the laws of nature and an orderly sex-life complemented the presence of the monied old man in the life of a seclusive and beautiful young woman. The knitting needles cheerfully took on speed in the signora's hands. Understandably enough, her thoughts of the photographer lady's chaste existence were always rather resentful, since it had cost her a considerable financial loss. In a short time now, perhaps, she would be able to bring up General Hasparics's offer again. She knew from experience that once a lodger in the Pension Zanzottera opened the door of her room, even after refusing the landlady's offers, it was never one man alone who gained admittance. Now, after Ursi's departure, the signora glanced up at the clock on the wall and noted that the visit had lasted for thirty-six minutes. It was not long, but long enough for one quick rush of life.

The doorbell rang again at six o'clock. Bathing-trunks was at the door, but this time he was fully clothed. He wore a freshly pressed but obviously oft-laundered dark blue linen jacket, shiny where the iron had passed over the seams. His gray flannel trousers looked new, and the signora surmised from the carefully polished brown shoes that he had polished them himself, for shoes were never polished quite so brightly in Mandria. In his left hand he carried a lattice-lathed basket of fruit full of Mediterranean specialties, clusters of giant grapes, large purple-green figs and Sicilian oranges. The very shape of the basket revealed that it all came from Niccolini's grocery store. The visitor made a mute gesture in the direction of the photographer's room. The signora suddenly bared her narrow dentures, and there was a mysterious little smile gleaming on her wet lips which was meant to indicate that she was entirely aware of the situation.

After knocking, Ursi entered the room and placed his basket on the table.

"Since you won't take any money, at least you'll accept a little fruit," he said, and a childlike and attractive confusion flooded his face.

"Oh-h-h," exclaimed Zia, and her apple-green eyes began to smile with the drawn-out *oh* while she snipped off a large grape and put it in her mouth.

"Are the pictures ready?"

"Only the first one. The smiling one."

Ursi inspected the pictures:

"Am I as beautiful as this?"

He held the six little prints at a distance, fanwise, like a hand of cards.

"What happened to the second picture?"

"It didn't come out," Zia said with deadly seriousness, but at that moment she turned her head away and broke into irrepressible laughter, laughter of the sort that collides with a wall of restraint and increases in strength for that very reason, as if subject to the physical laws that govern explosives. As she turned away, her head disappeared between her updrawn and rounded shoulders, and she covered her face with her hands while her whole body shook with mirth, the contagion of which gradually seized Ursi as well. He was beginning to suspect what her hilarity was about. Without waiting for permission, he picked up the six prints that were lying face down on the table. When he had glanced at them he too began to guffaw. Apparently Zia had surreptitiously exchanged lenses between exposures, and thus the second photograph was not a portrait bust but rather a full-length snapshot. It was an extremely successful picture. The upper part of his body fully clothed, but with his thighs and legs bare, the astrophysicist sat on the mushroom-shaped stool that was too low for him with the desperately sad expression of a child on a chamber pot when its parents have administered a reprimand.

"May I have some copies of this one too?" asked Ursi, after catching his breath.

"Help yourself," Zia said simply, wiping tears of merriment from the corners of her eyes with the back of her hand.

The astronomer took his leave with a friendly handshake.

When Zia was alone again she was seized with an inexplicable melancholy. The soul sometimes behaves like this after heartfelt laughter. Such great and excessive hilarity is like a fluid that runs from the soul as blood runs from the body. A desperate bleakness sometimes follows mirth of this sort. Zia's glance strayed to the basket of fruit. The wide eyes of the grapes had suddenly filled with sadness too.

✠

The next day there was a change in the weather. Sometimes the bora visited Mandria during the most violent heat wave. Somewhere in the north the cold masses of air wearied of eternal shivering and succeeded in escaping from their snow-capped prison guards. They swooped with glad outcries from the Austrian Alps to the Adriatic for a few days' vacation. They blotted out the sky with the dark duffel bags in which they brought the rain and the wind. They blew the sun-bathing, chocolate-brown human seals off the terraces of the bagno, stormed the cliffy shores in cold, steel-gray waves and gave the Piazza Vittorio Emanuele a thorough airing. The aspect of Mandria changed completely at such a time. Bathing-suited visitors donned winter clothes and were unrecognizable.

In the afternoon of the fourth day the bora subsided, and around six o'clock the sun came out of the crevasses of the vast retreating mass of clouds, looking like a woman's hat after an automobile has run over it. The bora's three-day flood of oxygen had bathed human lungs and nerves as well as the trees and bushes and flowers, and the outlines of everything became clearer when liberated from the fog. The dirty sails of the bragozzas seemed cleaner too, the steeple of San Simeone had put on a clean shirt, and the tile roof of the Hasparics villa looked as if it had just left the barbershop. At six o'clock the water-front was crowded with strollers. One after another they appeared, Short-legs, Longneck, Belly, Rolypoly, Striped-trousers and Carrot-top, as Zia had named them. General Hasparics's four dogs romped wildly, mad with fresh air and the holiday joy of liberation, leaping over benches and babies. The sun spread its warmth over the calm like a stove in a tiny room, while the mufflers and overcoats crept back into their chests of drawers. In a matter of minutes Mandria recovered its bright flush of bathing suits.

Zia too slung her leather-cased camera over her shoulder and set out hunting in the sudden burst of sunlight. On her way home she discovered the astronomer on the terrace of the Trattoria Marica, his imitation Panama resting on a chair beside him. Books were spread on the table in front of him and, as always, he was at work. Zia's rubber-soled shoes did not betray her approach, and for a few moments she silently regarded the high forehead leaning over a manuscript; then she spoke up, in that soft little tone which, without intending to beguile, strikes to the heart nevertheless—a tone the inexpressibly delicate shades of which only the most aloof women manage to achieve:

"What are you doing?"

Ursi raised his head. He looked up with the glance of a man immersed in his work, momentarily oblivious to his surroundings and the person confronting him. Then surprise and pleasure mounted to his face. He dropped the pencil on his pad and did not reply at once, as if concocting a suitable answer to a difficult and complex question. His voice, when he answered, was that of someone who has made an intellectual effort and arrived at a satisfactory solution:

"I'm working."

Zia's expression showed that she was formulating a further query, for there are moments in life when a good deal depends on every single letter in the phrasing of a question. Her second query, after much premeditation, went as follows:

"What are you working on?"

"I'm writing a book."

Rather than ask further questions, Zia stretched out her gloved hand and examined the title page of one of the open books. A gesture like this hardly differs from the intimacy of straightening a man's necktie or brushing the hair back from his eyes. There are women who manipulate such gestures as violin virtuosos do the most delicate, tenderest intonations of their instrument. *The History of Serfdom.* A wry, laughable little grimace appeared on Zia's face, the expression of a child when he opens a tempting box in his nursery and finds a live green frog instead of the expected chocolates. She looked at the tide page of another book: *Hungarian Aristocratic Life in the Angevin Age.* She was struck by the name of the author; it was fairly unexpected thus to see the Dukay name in print. She knew of this book by Uncle Peter, but had never read it. She closed the cover and looked at Ursi, as if to make sure she had not betrayed something about herself.

"You said you were an astronomer," she remarked in a somewhat disillusioned tone.

"Right now I'm on a terrestrial trip, but only exceptionally," said the Samoyed smile which appeared from time to time on his face, not as a racial characteristic so much as a speck of an unknown element seen on a distant asteroid through the delicate prisms of a spectroscope.

Zia took a flat ivory case from the tiny pocket of her linen coat and lit a cigarette with the easy and practiced movement that only women know how to perform, whether with cooking utensils, sewing kits, cosmetic tools or cigarette lighters in their hands. She offered one to Ursi with an absent-minded gesture.

"Thanks, I don't smoke."

The finely made, flat ivory case with a handful of Egyptian cigarettes inside, obviously not of Mandrian origin, told Ursi something, as when a faint meaning begins to gleam from the obscurity of Assyrian hieroglyphs. For a moment

Zia stared at the smoke, lost in her own thoughts. This little silence also had a meaning of its own.

"Would you like to walk a bit?"

"Very much."

Ursi collected his manuscripts and books, slapped them under his arm student-fashion, and they set out.

"Why are you reading a history of serfdom?"

"Source material. I'm writing my book about our own contemporary problem of land tenure."

"So you play politics too," was the rather reproachful comment of the apple-green glance, which was now moving along in the air without turning to either side.

"If you like. I don't belong to any political party and I have no political ambitions."

"Did you get the passport?"

"I expect it to arrive tomorrow. I've only five more days left on Mandria."

Walking thus side by side, they would have liked to know all about one another by now. But their curiosity did not extend to inquiries. Zia thought she discerned the upper middle-class background of the astronomer, his father a physician or a professor, his mother wearing a somewhat old-fashioned dark purple dress with a tiny gold crucifix at her throat. On the other hand, Ursi decided that the impression the photographer made upon him was completely the opposite of what had been contained in the gossip of the woman from Zagreb. There was a dreamlike weightlessness about the appearance of Teréz Hemli, In her freshly pressed pea-green linen jacket and snow-white tennis shoes she looked somewhat smaller than while taking photographs in a dressing gown that reached to the floor and covered even her throat. There are young women of boyish build whose very boyishness endows them with an exceptional feminity. The woman whom Zia called Rolypoly was walking ahead of them on the Corso Mussolini. Rolypoly, in pursuit of the latest fashion, wore masculine flannel slacks, with the result that her physical contour, especially when viewed like this from behind, was that of a single round buttock to which extremities were attached like spider-legs.

Zia and Ursi reached the arid riverbed, and Zia mounted the railing of the stone bridge for a smoke and a rest. In the clear stillness the radio in one of the waterfront houses could be heard delivering a speech of Goebbels, with occasional interruptions of cadenced bellowing or of stormy applause from the crowd. The house itself was hidden from sight, and so it seemed as if the universe were shouting for the strollers' exclusive entertainment. Zia smoked her cigarette thoughtfully, while Ursi placed his hat on the stone railing and surrendered his forehead to the evening breeze. Earless Mungu approached from the direction of the bay, looking like a Venetian painter's conception of Biblical fishermen, barefoot, with broad soles, in heavy, dark trousers rolled to the knees and the shirt open over the chest. In his left hand he bore a dirty rush basket, and a long fishpole bobbed on his shoulder in rhythm with his steps. Unexpectedly, passionately, Goebbels' voice rang out, and for a moment it sounded as if he were threatening Mungu, who quickened his steps noticeably like someone struck by a sudden gust of wind.

"Do you know exactly what is going on in the world?" Zia asked, still gazing into the cigarette smoke.

"We don't know anything exactly," said Ursi, while his eyes followed the diligent capers of two dolphins as they sprang forth like two enormous and supple brownish-green bottles, in perfect simultaneity, and then disappeared in the kindly waves.

"I'm afraid I'm very ignorant," said Zia, straightening her skirt to conceal one of her kneecaps which, sheathed in flimsy silk, was flaunting its charms like a rose, independent of its owner's will.

"Your fear is not unfounded," Ursi remarked, still staring at the dolphins. It was the sort of conversation that two people usually conduct without looking at each other; they put their questions to the world, and their replies as well.

"Modern man is dreadfully ignorant," Ursi continued, "and what he does know sprawls inside him like the parts of a disassembled motorcycle. When the time comes to put it all together, he stands bewildered in the mess he has made. In any case it would be a hopeless task, because a number of parts are missing, and many of those he has are of the wrong size."

"Are you ignorant too?" Zia glanced at Ursi with narrowed eyes.

"I'm an exception. But I can tell you in confidence that the learning which we exceptions—scientists, writers and a few others—have accumulated consists of nothing more than a knowledge of the way to handle certain keys. We can quickly find the answer to something we don't know. We've learned our way around the fairly simple labyrinths of the libraries."

"I've a suggestion to make. You say you have five more days in Mandria.

Well, give me five lessons in history, in the late afternoons like this, when you're not working anyway. I'd like to get a clear idea of the basic outlines. The next time we come out here I'd like to understand, for example, what Goebbels is shouting about."

"I can't guarantee that, for even Goebbels doesn't really know; I have it on fairly reliable authority that Hitler and Goering and Hess are on different paths altogether, and despise one another."

"What holds them together then?"

"They don't want to lose the power they have right now."

Zia liked his quick, spontaneous reply.

"How shall I pay for these five lessons?"

Ursi looked into the air with narrowed eyes. "Give me five Mandrian photographs from your album, one for each hour."

"Agreed. You can pick them out yourself."

The little gloved hand disappeared into Ursi's broad palm for a moment. They sealed the bargain with a handshake.

The next morning the *tramontana,* the morning breeze of the Adriatic, folded its light golden-green wings at an early hour, like a listless peacock, and breathless heat prevailed in Mandria once again. The human pelts stretched on the decks of the bagno roasted in the hot sunshine like *orada* in the bubbling oil of Marica's frying pan. The unmannerly odors of the Piazza Vittorio Emanuele had taken flight before the onslaughts of the bora, but now they ventured out again from the direction of the Pescateria and from the piles of refuse heaped in front of the houses.

At five in the afternoon, as they had agreed, Ursi entered the garden of the Pension Zanzottera and, standing by the old fig tree, called up to the open window of Zia's room:

"Teréz!"

This was the mode of address he had found, after some consideration, to be the most suitable. Zia's unkempt head appeared at the window:

"I'll be right down!" she said in a somewhat muffled voice, the tone of which suggested a conspiratorial rendezvous.

Seated under the fig tree on the cinnabar-red bench, Ursi felt that life was beautiful, a feeling that comes to a man only rarely with such crystal clarity. He did not have long to wait. Zia suddenly spoke up at his side; approaching noiselessly on rubber-soled shoes, she seemed to have dropped from the branches of the fig tree.

"Let's go."

She was wearing a brick-red linen suit now, under which there could have been nothing more than an improbably flimsy silk slip, but even this was only conjecture. The strap of her tiny aromatic leather camera case was slung over her shoulder, and the strap itself gave off the rich aroma of leather. In her right hand she carried the net bag that held her bathing suit. Good-humored and childish excitement was evident in her features..

"In today's lesson—" as they set out, Ursi intentionally exaggerated the professorial tone "—we shall consider the beginnings of the world and the origin of man. Pay close attention, please, and interrupt if there is something you don't understand."

"All right."

"We'll begin at the beginning. The void of the universe, space, in which our Earth is a mere grain of sand, is largely empty, for there are vast distances between celestial bodies. What do we mean by a fixed star?"

"A star that is stationary."

"Not at all!" Ursi cried vehemently.

Zia pulled in her neck with fright.

"Fixed stars," Ursi continued, "are characterized by the fact that they move in space. Which only goes to show that even the language of science is full of ambiguous expressions. Fixed stars, however, move so slowly that it takes thousands of years to observe their courses."

They came face to face with the two summer guests known as Carrot-top and Striped-trousers, who were discussing certain problems of the lumber industry in the Laibach dialect of the German language.

"Sometimes," Ursi continued, "people forget their constant participation in the tremendous and various mobilities of the universe. But let's get back to the point: the beginnings of the world."

There are scientists who show a deep emotional involvement when they talk about a subject dear to their hearts. Their words are like volcanoes, whose smoke and lava merely betoken the nature of the seas of fire with which they are in association. One could question such scholars continuously, but they would not reach an end of all they have to say, not in an entire lifetime. Zia listened attentively as he explained, in concise, orderly sentences, that the sun blazed with much greater heat at the earth when life first began, that there were terrific tempests and vast earthquakes, that the tides rose to a greater height because the moon was then much closer to the earth. He explained that life, according to modern biology, first began in steaming swamps, a beginning which had left no traces because the first living things were extremely tiny and soft.

"By the time we reach the bagno," Ursi said, "we shall have finished with two billion years, because there are only five terms for you to learn. The first refers to the earliest period in the geological history of the earth, which was also the longest—it lasted for eight hundred million years. We call it the Azoic, which means, literally, the Lifeless Era. But as a matter of fact there probably was some life during that era."

"What do you people mean when you say 'probably?'"

"That's a very good question. When history or politics says 'this is the truth' of something, the statement generally is not even probable. When natural science says 'probably,' then we are, to some extent at least, in the realm of fact. Red and black iron oxide often occurs in the most ancient sedimentary rocks, which leads one to assume the existence of living things. What is the name of the earliest geological era?"

"Azio…"

"Az-o-ic."

"Azoic!"

"The second era, which has left traces of protozoa and medusoids in the raw mud, is known as the Proterozoic."

"Oh, oh, oh!"

"Don't let it scare you. It merely means the Beginning of Life. Say it after me: Pro-ter-o-zo-ic."

The Proterozoic Era served at least to give Ursi an opportunity to take the girl by the arm for a few moments, as if to help her over an abyss.

"Proterozoic."

Her merry sigh indicated that she was out of danger. Zia now began to roll the word before her, playfully and with increasing speed; "Proterozoic, Proterozoic, Proterozoic…"

"Excellent. The next time you meet the word in a magazine or a book, you'll be able to greet it like an old, charming, white-bearded friend. And if you should happen to be in the company of scientists who discover that you don't think Proterozoic is a suntan cream, they'll break into tears with emotion, like a savage from the Congo when a white man in the middle of New York addresses him in his mother tongue. After the Proterozoic came the much shorter era of invertebrates, which lasted approximately three hundred million years. Science acknowledges, however, that when it says something like 'a hundred million years,' it might well mean only ten million. This third era is called Paleozoic. Pa-le-o-zo-ic."

"Paleozoic."

"This era teemed with scorpions three yards long. The name of the fourth era is much easier to remember: Mesozoic—think of mezzosoprano. It is the Middle Ages of geology, the age of monstrous, large-bellied and generally weak-kneed reptiles. You've probably seen a picture of a dinosaur. This era lasted one hundred forty million years in all. The name of the fifth era is still easier: Cenozoic. The first mammals began to appear on the grassy steppes and in the forests of *terra firma*. I told you that space is largely empty. Well, time is equally empty, for in those hundreds and hundreds of millions of years the development of life made hardly any progress. And then it burst into flame, for what follows is only a half million years before the birth of Christ. And the time to which vast libraries of historical books refer—the time we generally call the epoch of civilization—is scarcely more than six thousand years old."

They had arrived at the stone bridge. With her usual movement, Zia mounted the stone railing and lit a cigarette. Ursi put his hat on the railing and did not speak until long moments had passed:

"When I think of Prince Eszterházy, I am always reminded that for the several hundred million years of the Paleozoic Era his Grace the Prince, like me, was a triploblastic crustacean."

The name Eszterházy was almost as if Ursi had said Dukay. Zia gave him an unobserved glance, almost suspecting that he had guessed something. But the astronomer's face showed quite clearly the depth of his immersion in the past.

"Now I shall give you a brief recapitulation," Ursi said, as they started homeward, "of the history of those half million years which concern the origin of man. You probably know of Darwinism. Many people are still alive who were contemporaries of Darwin—it is as if those great controversies raged only yesterday. Nothing is more characteristic of our intellectual infancy than the fact that several decades ago the English universities were still violently opposed to Darwin. Wells cites an account of a debate between Bishop Wilberforce and Huxley, the champion of Darwinism. The bishop, whose imagination was unwilling to relinquish the picture of an Eve with long, wavy tresses and a fig leaf, sarcastically asked the scientist whether it was on his maternal or paternal side that he considered himself a monkey. Huxley retorted in an impassioned voice, something to the effect that he would be much more ashamed to number among his ancestors a man who sought to hide the truth with empty oratory, rhetorical evasions and the clever use of superstition. One of the religious women in the audience passed out cold."

At this point Zia recalled a summer in the distant past, when Bishop Zsigmond and Peter Dukay once quarreled vigorously after dinner in the red salon at Ararat. The subject of their quarrel was something of this sort, but she had been unable to comprehend the burden of the exchange, and it was rather the high temperature of the words than their meaning that stuck in her memory.

"It need not be supposed," Ursi continued, "that our ancestors were gorillas or chimpanzees. You might say that they are simply relatives on a collateral line, like the Hottentots, for instance, but more removed."

By the time they reached the neighborhood of the village Ursi had explained how the first remains of primitive man had been found in a sand pit outside of Heidelberg, in the Neander Valley near Düsseldorf and on the island of Java—the skeletal remains of the earliest man, who was tall of figure, broad of face, had a protruding nose and an incredibly well-developed brain. And the endocranial cavity of one of the female skulls was larger than the brain of the average man today.

"That skull was bashed in with a single blow—which goes to show that domestic differences are not exactly of recent origin."

The memory of Filippo's face suddenly flashed through Zia's mind, a picture of the two of them standing face to face in the room of the villa on Fuga Utca: the chestnut-hued glance, which could fill with such pleading, had suddenly glowed with a fearful and foreign light on that occasion. His upper lip twisted into a sneer of disgust when he struck her cheek with the full force of his fist.

Ursi stopped and pointed to the sea:

"Ten thousand, or perhaps thirty thousand years ago, this sea bottom was still a human habitation. The Mediterranean Sea was then a group of lakes, linked at most by rivers. During the last Ice Age this sea bottom consisted of a series of slopes with a moderate climate, and the black-haired white man of the Neolithic Age made himself at home among them. The water level of those beautiful lakes was much lower than that of the oceans, like the Dead Sea or the Caspian Sea today. Then came the catastrophe. With a roar the ocean broke into this inclosed basin from the direction of Gibraltar, overwhelming the inhabitants and their animals and their gardens and their pile-dwellings. This is the catastrophe commemorated as the Flood in the Old Testament, when Noah's ark escaped the raging waves with a few chosen people aboard, and was cast ashore on Mount Ararat in Asia Minor..."

(Again a word that shook Zia.)

"The development of primitive thought," continued Ursi, "the role of fear and wish-fulfillment in primitive religion, the comprehension of the stars and the seasons, the inception and ramification of human languages and races, the history of the early civilizations—it would take too long to outline all this now, and in any case I'm not a reliable authority on these fields. If you like, I can recommend a few good books that deal with those subjects."

"When you return to Budapest you might assemble a library of, say, fifteen or twenty books that you think would serve to patch up my ignorance. Will you do it?"

"How long are you going to stay in Mandria?"

Zia shrugged her shoulders, as if to say that she did not know. The gesture was also an indication that she did not care to answer the question.

"I'm going in for a swim," she announced simply and irrelevantly. She looked around, and vanished behind a tree to undress.

At moments like this, when we are aware of the presence of a beautiful and naked woman, there is always a peculiar tension in the air, even if we do not see her. It is as if an invisible bird were flying past. Actually, she undressed in a matter of seconds. A bathing suit took the place of the brick-red linen skirt and jacket. She held her net bag out to Ursi.

"You might watch my things in the meantime."

"I'm going to fetch my rowboat. I want to row a bit."

Ursi returned to the wharf and quietly rowed back. Zia's clothing sprawled on the seat opposite. The tiny tip of a silk slip peeped from under the carefully folded linen suit. The white tennis shoes and the items of clothing were redolent with femininity. Meanwhile Zia swam far out, so far that Ursi could hardly locate her little red bathing cap in the graying waves. He rowed toward her. By this time he was also dressed for swimming.

"You've come too far. Sometimes there are sharks in the sea."

583

"I don't bother the sharks."

"Stop your nonsense—climb in."

He released his oars and began to hoist Zia in. The emerging body, weightless a moment ago, gradually recovered the hundred-odd pounds of which the heavy, salty sea water had deprived her. Meanwhile the cool, wet, rounded arms entwined around Ursi's neck, and at the height of her emergence the resilient little breasts pressed firmly against his chest.

That evening they dined together on the terrace of the Trattoria Marica.

History lessons were resumed the next day. Up to the stone bridge, the second hour dealt with the nomads, the Sumerians, the Assyrians, the Chaldeans—the history of ancient Egypt, India and China in simplest and most cursory form. The first gods, kings and priests made their appearance on the way back from the stone bridge, and beyond the bagno the first slaves bobbed into view, and then the caste system of India and the mandarin orders of China. The third hour considered Holy Writ and the age of the prophets, the prehistoric role of the Aryan peoples, the Greeks and the Persians, Alexander the Great and the learning of Alexandria, the origins of Buddhism, and then the Roman emperors, in purple robes, who settled between the immense Asiatic wastes and the western seas. Ursi enjoyed and was skillful at presenting clear pictures. He guarded against overburdening his pupil's brain with unnecessary details and dates. The fact that he did not have every historical detail in mind made this all the more easy to do. But it is certain that he paced the paths of those ancient millenia with as much assurance as he did the Corso Mussolini, where it would have been truly difficult for anyone to go astray. The fourth hour dealt with Judea, with the coming of Christ, the Great Völkerwanderung, Mohammed and Islam, and then the decline of the Roman Empire, the Merovingians and Charlemagne, the separation of the French and Germans, the Crusades and the ranks of the great popes: from the stone bridge homeward he covered Genghis Khan, the rebirth of Western civilization and the opening of the great ocean routes.

"Note," said Ursi, during the fifth and final stroll, "that the closer we come to the present, the fewer centuries we can digest at one sitting. You remember how we trampled two billion years underfoot from the pension to the bagno during the first lesson. This illustrates, better than anything else, the architecture of our historical knowledge, which is shaped like a perfect pyramid."

"What's the shape of astronomy?" asked Zia.

"Hyperbola," Ursi replied after a little reflection.

"And politics—?"

"—is the shape of an extremely dim-witted man shouting angrily."

Interpolations like this spiced the age of sovereigns, parliaments and great powers during their last walk, and the emergence of democracy in France and America, the career of Napoleon, through the "visionary" nineteenth century and up to the World War, until they reached the clear causes of the catastrophe of modern imperialism. It was growing dark when they returned, and a radio speech of Mussolini was shaking the trees in the garden of the Albergo Varcaponti.

Near the church of San Simeone they sat on a bench which was still warm from the heat of the sun.

"What would the state of the world be today, I wonder, if Hitler and Mussolini had fallen somewhere on the battlefields of Flanders or Isonzo?" Zia mused, almost to herself.

"We've no way of knowing," Ursi said after a few minutes of silence. "There are two schools of thought on this point. According to one school, conditions would be exactly the same, with the difference that Mussolini would be known as Vassolini or Dalconi, and Hitler as Himmler or Hess or Priemel—because history is not shaped by individuals but by the will of the masses, who can be said to elevate, or even to catapult, leaders from their midst. A light bulb wouldn't give light, a telephone wouldn't ring if the electric current were not at work in the walls and the underground conduits."

"And the other school of thought?"

"According to the opposite school, the mass in this sense is a nonexistent entity. The mass has neither will, nor intellect, nor determination. One must think of the mass as a vast hollow cave which simply echoes the slogans someone else calls out. Let's imagine for a moment that Germany is a great forest. Can a forest catch on fire by itself? Not likely. And if it's damp, or green—impossible. It's also impossible, in that case, to set the forest on fire. If Germany were damp or green—that is, if things were going well for Germany—Hitler's efforts to set fire to it would be in vain. But the country is dry and brittle; the World War dried it out, and the conditions of the Versailles Treaty made it brittle—combustible, like tinder. But this alone doesn't mean that a fire will break out. There've been many forests in the history of the world which were fire hazards but never caught on fire—blossomed, rather, and came to fruition gradually. Think of China, for example, in the days when the ruling houses of the North held sway. Or the Maurian Age in India."

Zia leaned forward as she listened to Ursi's explanation, the fundamental significance of which she did not completely grasp.

"So you think…"

"I think—" Ursi stepped into the breach of her hesitant question "—those two formidable characters are like dangerous pyromaniacs in the 'dry' forests of Germany and Italy. Had Mussolini and Hitler been killed in combat, as you suggest, the world would not now be threatened with fire."

"You think there'll be a war?"

"I don't know. The masses are inflammable, and at the same time amazingly stupid. People in general hope for some sort of miracle, hope that the German comet, approaching the earth at terrifying speed amid a spectacular display of light and sound, will not strike the rooftops of Europe but will suddenly stop somewhere, at skyscraper height, and become an entertaining and edifying celestial body, a sight worth rushing into the streets for, worth showing the children."

Mussolini's voice no longer blared from the direction of the Albergo Varcaponti. The radio was playing soft English dance music, and the fragrance of the laurel groves came floating down the hillside as if it had been waiting for this very invitation to the dance.

They had supper together on the terrace of the Trattoria Marica.

"Are you leaving tomorrow?" Zia asked during supper.

"Yes. My ship leaves at ten in the morning."

During the moments of his departure the next morning Ursi vainly scanned the narrow little street that skirted the church of San Simeone and led to the Pension Zanzottera, and along which he expected to see Teréz; but she did not come to the wharf to take leave of him once more. Among the memories of the photographer that stayed with him was the moment of lifting her into the rowboat when her cool, wet arms entwined around his neck; and her inquisitive, wondering, attentive, dismayed or gaily flashing apple-green glance; the almost inaudible whisper of her tiny tennis shoes—all these recollections were like certain gleams of light that are visible in the neighborhood of Andromeda and the Great Bear but whose presence has not yet been satisfactorily explained.

Chapter Fourteen

EARLY in November there was a so-called "little supper" in the Septemvir Utca Palace. The Dukay family came up from Ararat a few days earlier; even Kristina had spent the summer there for once, if only because Count Dukay was holding a tighter rein on her expenditures abroad. In the recent past Kristina had become one of the regulars in the gaming rooms of Monte Carlo and Deauville. She had been idling at Ararat since May with an air of profound injury, like a leading lady whose role is taken away because of a quarrel with the director.

There were eleven persons at table for the "little supper" of this evening. In addition to the members of the household, the guests included the authoress Princess Karola with her husband, Baron Adam; Peter Dukay and his wife; Count Joachim and his wife; Count Sigi—the sometime popular night-club orator, now grown sober, married and embarked on a diplomatic career—and his wife Sophie, the Transylvanian countess who was Zia's closest friend. Retiring to the salon after supper, Count Sigi turned on the radio and tuned in a broadcast of gypsy music. One of the melodies stirred a controversy between Count Dupi and Countess Ilona, one maintaining that it was the tune of "Kiöntött a Tisza vize" while the other held that it was the music to "Korcsmárosné, jön a pandur." This led to a wager, with a two-year-old filly as the stake. The wager was won by Countess Ilona, the wife of Count Joachim, who spoke Hungarian with the flavorsome dialect of the Upper Tisza. She spoke French and German with the same intonation. Apart from the charm of her pronunciation she brought little else from her parental home than the ice-cold aristocratic arrogance with which she attempted to compensate for the fact that her family was not of the nobility for all that it was one of the most ancient and distinguished Hungarian lines, with a genealogy that extended back to the thirteenth century. The countess was typical of the higher gentry, with a walnut-brown complexion and a figure that also bore a resemblance, unfortunately, to a walnut—for this stock has a tendency to stoutness after the age of thirty. They have, in fact, few other tendencies than that, except an inclination to label as a dangerous Communist and gallows bird anyone they cannot understand or who does not think exactly as they do in politics, literature, science, art and music. It was apparent from the first that Countess Ilona would win the wager, since her familiarity with Magyar songs, if with nothing else, was encyclopedic.

Count Sigi, who was manipulating the dials, began to search for news from abroad and tuned in a German voice just as it announced the withdrawal of Germany from the League of Nations. This momentous development precipitated a heated discussion. Baron Adam—who viewed the world with alarm through steel-blue eyes and a red and white complexion inherited from a Swedish razor-blade factory on his maternal side, and who enjoyed excellent connections in Sweden—Baron Adam expressed the opinion that the condition of German economy resembled an overheated locomotive which would surely explode in a short while. Count Joachim was of another opinion altogether. He based his view on information gained from the British Fascists. According to him, war was inevitable, and in this next war England, Germany and the United States would oppose Italy, France and the Soviet Union. The people who occupied the capacious brocaded armchairs in the Dukay salon had access to the most reliable sources of information through their familial or financial connections, yet their opinions turned out to be entirely contradictory. According to Count Peter, England would first incite Germany against the Soviet Union, and then would disdainfully dispatch the two bloodstained antagonists. They debated like this until midnight without convincing either themselves or one another. Countess Menti spoke up but once, inquiring in a timid and anxious voice what the role of Otto Habsburg would be in the New Europe. Her query was followed by a long, mute pause, more eloquent than any reply could have been. No one moved during the silence, hands did not reach for a glass, ashes maintained a rigid immobility at the tips of cigars and cigarettes, and this motionless hush greatly resembled the two minutes of silence with which it had become fashionable to commemorate the victims of the first World War. When it was evident that the prolonged silence constituted a discourtesy toward Countess Menti, Princess Karola turned her little mouse-head toward her hostess and began to inquire after Countess Menti's children. Countess Menti disclosed in an aloof tone that her son György was still in America, while János was living in Germany.

"And Zia?"

"My daughter Zia is staying with one of her friends in Italy, and travels a good deal."

Princess Karola did not pursue the subject, since membership in the Park

Club afforded her precise intelligence on the activities of Zia. Rumor had it that more than one person had seen Zia in Rome, in the company of the Prince of Aosta, a relationship which required no further explanation.

It is obvious from all this that there were two Zia's in the world: one was the silhouette which lived in the imagination of society after the great wedding and was ever given new roles to play in that imagination, and then there was the other, the real Zia, who—on this windy November night, while the footmen were noiselessly distributing the large, bulging brandy snifters in the grand salon of the Septemvir Utca Palace, while the cherry-wood logs were blazing in the fireplace—who was, yes, riding the black waves of the Adriatic in the single and unventilated cabin of Earless Mungu's bragozza on this November night, in the vicinity of Punta Dura, where the year before the raging bora had sent Luigi's bragozza to the bottom of the sea.

What was Zia doing in Earless Mungu's bragozza on the perilous seas at this hour? After Ursi's departure, and in the ensuing days, when the last summer guest had taken his leave, the autumnal solitude that descended on Mandria was bleaker than Zia had ever known it to be. She decided that if Filippo did not arrive on the last ship of the season she would set out with Earless Mungu in his bragozza on the day of the first great bora. It was not a maudlin thought of flirting with suicide that informed her decision; still, she committed herself to the dangers of the excursion with the feeling that she might not return. There was something in this of the bravado of the Dukays, and of the vague death-wish that had seized her. The old forms of her life at Ararat, on Septemvir Utca, in the Park Club, repelled rather than attracted her. The sharp-edged and bloodstained shards of that existence littered Zia's heart—shattered by Filippo when he struck her. Mandria, on the threshold of her third autumn, seemed as meaningless, hopeless and painful as old Torriti's irreducible rupture of the abdominal wall, or Mungu's ear, which a gasoline explosion had burnt off, or the door of the Pension Zanzottera, on which the antique paint was blistered and peeling, as if the door suffered from a serious disease of the skin—there are things that willfully and insolently display their repulsive absurdity when the soul is in a certain state. Nor had the five history lessons served Zia well. The Copperplated Twilight took visible and palpable shape in her consciousness when Ursi exposed the constellations of human history to her view, the wretchedness of man in the multitude, a mean condition that sometimes rears like the sea during a bora and attacks the shore with arching waves, blackly glistening, which shake the chimney from the Trattoria Marica, overturn the customs booth, foam with hate as they invade Niccolini's grocery store to scatter every kind of refuse among the barrels of salt herring and dried figs, and force their way to the altar in the church of San Simeone. No one in Mandria ever spoke to her of poverty and want, no one ever complained. The cheerful scent of laurel, the vigorous, salty, life-giving air and ample sunshine pervaded the island—and poverty and want unfolded of themselves in Mandria, mutely, involuntarily, when pain misted Tonia's eyes as she sometimes contemplated the sea that was of a velvety softness to the bathing suits of the summer guests but was a black-throated murderous inferno to her; or when old Torriti writhed on the ground outside the Albergo Varcaponti with the pain of his irreducible rupture. The history lessons had taken root inside of her, and she now knew clearly that her upbringing and her society had revealed life's meaning in a curiously refracted light, in distorted and artificially tinted beams among which the shape of Berili, clad in lace-fringed, knee-length drawers, danced so fitfully nowadays that her laughably ugly, knobby legs simply trampled the inflexible and oblique beams underfoot, for Madame Couteaux could not redirect those rays of light without first shattering them. It took the advent of the astrophysicist to lift the heavy, refractory glass plate from her mode of thought and let the unbroken beams shoot into the depths of her like the pangs of a hitherto unknown pain.

And so one afternoon Zia appeared on Mungu's bragozza, which she had only seen from the wharf before. A trap door between the two masts led into the dark depths of the vessel, a trap door so narrow that there was room for but one person to descend at a time. Through this larynx one could slide into the belly of the boat without a ladder, simply by an exercise of acrobatics. There was room to move about below, but only if one bent double. The darkness was suffused with a corrosive smell of pitch and a sweetish stench of fish, since the mucus of fish and mollusks had for generations been dripping through the cracks in the deck and into the "net pit." Zia looked about her and came to the conclusion that no human workshop could be less pretentious, more pitiful or closer to death. Beneath the opening of the trap door was a fireplace. The embers were in an iron kettle that sat on two bricks imbedded in sand, and the opening above served as a chimney. This hovel of human habitation between decks was decorated with a cheap picture of the Virgin Mary, no bigger than Mungu's hand; wreathed in faded flowers, the little colored print seemed larger and more significant than Rubens' marvelous *Madonna with Garlands*. A votive candle burned in a nicked glass beneath the little picture, its minute flame flickering in the darkness like strange, giant bat's wings. Alongside the dark, greasy paneling there stood three earthenware pitchers, the primitive grace of their shapes reminiscent of immortality, of the cults of Isis and Serapis in Alexandria. One of the pitchers contained drinking water, drawn from some Mandrian cistern in which live eels, selected for domestication, devoured the watery rubbish. The black-stained pitcher should have contained *vino rosso,* but had been empty for who knows how long. The smallest pitcher exuded the smell of rancid oil. Of the two sooty tin frying pans against the wall one, as disclosed by the traces of food, was for frying fish, while the other served for the preparation of *polenta* from coarse-ground corn meal. The only bed was the bare boarding of the floor, and the linen consisted of several nondescript rags, trousers with split seams, vests, jackets, and even women's skirts. This constituted the entire furniture. This, then, was what Luigi's and so many other Adriatic fishermen's living tombs had been like. The rest of this between-decks partition was a storeroom for ropes, and was stuffed with dented, rusty pails, with empty tin cans preserved as articles of especial value, with crooked nails and used corks, and contained as well a triangular sliver of a mirror and a razor-thin, oval, tiny, dirty mass which must once have been a bar of soap. Dry twigs and pine cones for the fire were stacked in a corner.

Some days before they sailed Zia took part in the Saint's Day procession. It was not the first time she had done this. The sea and the concrete lagoon on the Piazza Vittorio Emanuele were linked by a narrow channel, and a bridge was erected over this channel on the occasion of a procession. Not even rowboats could navigate between the inner lagoon and outer bay at these times. All Mandria took part in the processions, with the sole difference that the rich people and gentlefolk—or those who were accounted rich and gentle in Mandria—wore holiday dress, while the poor wore white embroidered shifts that reached to their knees. The peasants in these Italian regions have their shrouds sewn long in advance of death, and wear them in every procession. When she first saw the poor of Mandria in these white, funereal shifts, Zia had a heartrending vision of

591

what Ursi called the upward striving of social classes and the tragic motivations of the human world. The barber, Ettore Domeneghetti, and the butcher, Aldo Faggiani, stalked in dark blue suits somewhere near the center of the procession, but their parents, the elderly Domeneghettis and Faggianis, still wore the white shifts of the afterworld in the presence of the Lord. The procession—with the white shifts in the van and the dark suits in the rear, where the person of General Hasparics represented the summit of social rank in Mandria—clearly showed that a certain quiet, persistent and passionate migration was continually taking place in the lives of the people, from the white shifts of Earless Mungu or Tonia to the somewhat outgrown overcoat of Demetrio Niccolini and the dark blue, double-breasted jacket of Signor Occhipinti the druggist.

Public opinion almost required Zia, as a permanent resident, to take part in the procession. Occhipinti, who organized the event, placed the lady photographer somewhere in the middle of the line beside Marica—who, as a representative of the tourist trade, had naturally risen from the low degree of her parents and no longer wore a white shift. She minced at Zia's side in a black silk dress that was redolent with cheap perfume and a decided aroma of garlic. In the name of Mandrian patriotism, and perhaps for other reasons as well, we cannot take it ill of druggist Occhipinti that he considered the signora to be of higher social rank and placed her in a more auspicious position than the lady photographer, whose past and person were still somewhat vague in the view of the Mandrians. After all, Occhipinti knew all there was to know about the signora. Zia was in a simple black and green afternoon gown that she had last worn, in her past life, at a garden party given by the French Ambassador. Only a few days ago had been the second anniversary of her arrival in Mandria after the scene in the villa on Fuga Utca, and on that anniversary her mind was as alive with thought as Occhipinti's house had been alive with the bailiffs and hyena-like auctioneers who came some weeks ago to rummage in his clothes, his furniture and his few articles of value, for Occhipinti had been reckless enough to become involved in some sort of speculation on the stock market. Zia chanced to see the arrival of the officials who came to carry out Occhipinti's financial execution. Disembarking from their motor launch, they carried briefcases like headsmen's hatchets under their arms. Occhipinti's Mandrian friends had agreed not to let his worldly goods be sold out for trifles—they undertook to buy everything themselves and then to return the goods to the druggist bit by bit. But there was no need of all this conspiracy, as it turned out, for Niccolini the grocer saved the situation all by himself. Occhipinti, a broken man, sat on the corner of his couch and wiped his tears with an invariably scented polka-dot handkerchief.

This happened on the same day that Ursi's package arrived, twenty carefully selected books. Historical studies, and books that dealt with literature, art, music, the social and natural sciences, in Hungarian, German, French and English. A cool, brief note from Ursi apologized for the delay on the ground that several of the volumes were out of print and had to be located in second-hand bookstores. The cool, brief note indicated Ursi's recognition of the fact that the photographer, who had not even gone to the wharf to say good-bye at his departure, did not care to continue their friendship. Zia searched in vain for the bill she had requested, but there was no bill.

She answered his note that very day. She hesitated over the salutation for a moment, for she had never called Ursi by his Christian name of Mihály, but had brought into play that especially remarkable talent of aristocrats which enables them to avoid, even for weeks of continual companionship, the more intimate forms of address—a talent that keeps acquaintances or friends of lower rank dancing in circles like a hollow caoutchouc ball atop the spray of a fountain, neither discarding them nor letting them come close. The astronomer must have had a higher specific gravity than the general run of middle-class caoutchouc balls, for on the occasion of their first history lesson he called toward the window from beneath the old fig tree: *Teréz!* And on that very first day his full, warm masculine voice was the simple voice of intimate friendship. The voice sounded like an awakening and a summons, a serious note of warning that did not, however, lack tenderness and cheer, as if it wanted to continue: *Wake up, wake up, it's time for school!* And thereafter for five days his *Teréz* resounded from beneath the old fig tree like the chimes of the church of San Simeone.

Zia opened her tiny featherweight typewriter, the wedding present of Uncle Himi, and began to write swiftly. Swiftly, because women are much quicker at composing such letters than men.

Dear Mihály:—The books have come, and they fill my room like long-awaited guests.

She stopped a moment at this point. The first sentence did not please her; it had the attractive but somewhat stilted sound of a countess's style. Still, she continued without throwing it away:

593

Grazie! Grazie! I've peeped into them, one after another, and I somehow felt that you wrote them all. Don't you think that when someone strongly reccomends (or is it recommends) a book to a friend, he assumes its authorship to some extent? Apropos: friendship! I must confess I greatly miss your afternoon summons to school. I promise to study hard and when next (?) we meet, to pass all the exams. Please, think of your isolated friend and grateful pupil sometimes. Where is the bill? What do I owe for the books? Cordially…

P.S. By way of a fee for the history lessons, I enclose the enlargements of the five Mandrian pictures—I've just finished them.

Zia read through the letter and was particularly pleased with the parenthetical question mark after the word "next." And indeed, only women know how to strike to the heart of the secrets of destiny with such incalculable glimmers of solitary punctuation marks.

The title of the first photograph was "International Affairs." It showed Aldo Faggiani the butcher and Ettore Domeneghetti the barber on the terrace of the Trattoria Marica at the moment when the latter threw his cards away and, springing from his chair with bloodshot eyes, struggled to snatch a disputed banknote from under the butcher's shovel-sized hand. One of the chairs was on the point of tumbling over. In the background, with gaping mouth and arms raised to heaven, came Marica. The second photograph was called "The General at the Head of His Troops as They Set Out to Occupy the Corso Mussolini." It represented General Hasparics and his four hounds, snapped from behind. The third photograph: "The Fly." Torriti, who ran the motor launch, was sleeping on the warm stone of the wharf. Roused from his dreams, he angrily scratched the tip of his ear. Behind him, unobserved, crouched Fanfoni the baker with a straw in his hand, choking back his laughter. The fourth photograph: "Lust." The summer guest known as Striped-trousers was looking back over his pince-nez at the arching bottom of the woman called Rolypoly, who had just passed him in her masculine flannel slacks. The fifth photograph: "No Return." It showed Tonia standing on the water-front, resting her face on the crack-nailed forefinger of her left hand and staring into the distance. Her expression, once again, was an expression that could not have shown more ashen sorrow and resignation. Zia added a subtitle to this picture: "This represents me a little bit too."

In these few words Zia was deliberately trying to say something about the mystery of her long stay in Mandria. A typewritten note is always too much like printing and deprives a letter, particularly a woman's letter, of the sudden dash and excitement of the handwriting itself, which speaks more plainly than a facial expression. Zia, before signing the note, made a trial of penmanship. She covered an entire sheet of paper with the word *Teréz*. She was writing the name for the first time, and as a consequence the paper was quickly covered with pert Terézes, sorrowful Terézes, humorous Terézes, Terézes of grandmother's time, enthusiastic or timidly bashful, bored, ice-cold or wanton come-hither Terézes. Finally she found a Teréz that started with a capital *T* made of two bold strokes and was simple, serious, warm and friendly—she could almost hear Ursi's voice as he called to her window from the fig tree each afternoon. She practiced this *Teréz* once or twice more, as she had practiced a new scale during piano lessons, and then she sent it sprawling at the bottom of the typewritten letter. When she contemplated this Teréz, she felt for the first time that she had really become Teréz Hemli the photographer. And this new Teréz, dressed in a dark green and somewhat golden gown, still glistening moistly from the fountain pen, was setting out to go somewhere, apprehensively and eloquently.

At the Salumeria the procession turned into a narrow street that struggled uphill toward the Calvary. The colors of the old silk banners gently melted into the late October sunshine, and so did the crimson and white tints of Parson Muzmics' cope as he hastened beneath the baldachin. Many different qualities of voice mounted to heaven in holy song, sensitive feminine voices in a soprano transfigured with weeping and cries for help, deep male voices that seemed to break forth from throats overgrown with hair. When the procession passed the Hasparics villa the four dogs in the garden began to howl, pitifully, angrily, maliciously and aggrievedly, each in the way best suited to his character, and the contrapuntal harmony of howling dogs combined with the holy hymns. In the midst of the song, between two verses, Occhipinti remarked to Niccolini at his side that the dogs were howling because the general had not once put his fine uniform on in the course of his ten years in Mandria.

The path climbed steeply toward the top of the cliff, and it seemed as if the procession, led by a shrouded contingent, could no longer set foot on earth but hovered somewhere between the sea and the marvelously blue autumn sky. It was as if the whiteness of the otherworldly shifts had reared into the heights while the rest of the procession, where the dark suits were grouped, was dragging along the ground like a dark and dismal train. Zia would have liked to be hovering on high with the white shifts. She endeavored to sing. Her timid, soft voice grasped the dense, metallic alto of Marica at her side like the thin hand of a child holding her mother's skirt.

The first bora came some days later. Zia sought out Mungu in the harbor and told him that she would like to spend several days at sea in his bragozza, taking pictures of the stormy waters. Mungu sat on the ground and fondled the gray, spongy toenails on his black feet. He looked suspiciously at *la fotografa morta,* and told himself that she was completely mad. Imagine someone wanting to sail the seas at a time like this if she did not have to go! Then he began to fondle his toenails again, as if to discuss the matter with them. Finally he announced that he would not take anyone free. He asked five liras a day, fifteen liras for the three days' sail, payable in advance. Zia explained to him at great length that newspapers would pay for the pictures she made on his bragozza, and because she did not want him to be a loser by the deal she would pay twenty liras a day— and she produced the sixty liras. As Mungu took the money his face reflected concern at the thought of what might happen if the photographer lady should decline into permanent lunacy during the trip.

They left at dawn the next day. Mungu's assistant was Enrico, his sixteen-year-old son, and old Antonio sailed the second bragozza with his son-in-law. Zia took a sleeping bag, foodstuffs and a thermos bottle along. Before their departure she noted that the pitchers had multiplied to five under the effect of the sixty liras.

The three-day journey was a disappointment to Zia. She had thought to catch sight of the ultimate in poverty-stricken misery, as if it were some apparition, and to hear the transcendental organ music of danger and death in the storm. Instead she was constantly seasick, despite the pills she had taken along. She did not know that the prosaic considerations of the flesh always disperse the most magnificent phenomena of the spirit. And when she felt better, she discovered that Mungu and Enrico, under the influence of the *vino rosso,* were incessantly whistling, singing and guffawing loudly. Not until the evening of the second day, in the vicinity of Punta Dura, did they close the trap door over the three of them with the expression of men lowering the lid of a coffin. And this same look was on their faces as they stretched out flat, for the suddenly infuriated storm had begun to toss the bragozza wildly and the vessel performed contortions which seemed indicative of a desire to descend into the bottomless pit of death. But the resilient water always caught her with a frightening splash as she fell. As they lay outstretched, they sometimes rolled over each other and Zia and the others were ridiculously entangled, but this brought a smile neither to the face of Mungu nor of Enrico. During those hours their faces were like rigid masks, like the shamans of a primitive people, who look as if they knew something of ultimate mysteries. One could sense that the little picture of the Virgin Mary and the weak, leaping flame of the tiny votive candle beneath assumed their mute role in these hours of extremity as even the human voice, ringing with commands, could not do.

The sea was completely still by morning, but all the abundant contents of the basket of foodstuffs from Niccolini's grocery store went to the fishermen, since Zia wanted to try a diet of nothing but *polenta* for the remaining time despite the ravenous appetite that suddenly seized her on the calm sea. She discovered that she had eaten pastry much worse than *polenta* in expensive London restaurants, and when she tasted the tiny squids fried in oil that evening she could not find any difference between Mungu's frying pan and the famous *frutta di mare* served at the tables of Venetian hotels. When the vessel was heaving violently, Mungu and Enrico performed their physical functions while squatting on one of the rusty pails, but this seemed to them the most natural thing in the world and they continued their merry banter with Zia in the meantime, the brittle Italian melody of which was occasionally slowed down or interrupted by a grunt. At these moments Zia felt that this degree of poverty and human civilization was very similar to sickness, for in her world only serious invalids were permitted to do such things in the presence of their doctors or nurses. As a result of the three-day excursion, she felt that the ultimate shores of poverty and death were not only barren and inconsequential but particularly unventilated and malodorous.

Ursi replied with a longer letter this time, and asked permission to charge the cost of the books against further photographs of Mandria, saying that he was known to be a better business man than an astrophysicist. His letter was good-humored, and thenceforth there was a regular if not frequent correspondence between them.

At the end of November Count Dupi wrote that he was ailing somewhat. He complained of his heart and declared that this year his Christmas visit would have to be canceled. In fact, he even threatened never to visit Zia in Mandria again.

I hope this will entice the cricket from her hole, for there really is no sense to this insane exile any more.

Zia read the words *there really is no sense* to mean that Septemvir Utca finally had definite news of some sort about Filippo. After this letter Zia hovered about Mandria like an object at that theoretical point in space where the gravitational pull of the moon and the earth annul each other.

She set about reading the books, which did not affect her as she had imagined at first that they would, since there were so many of them. Sometimes she fancied she could hear Ursi's full and yet soft voice, and this helped her over the more difficult and duller passages. Books devour the days quickly, and Zia soon found that Christmas was upon her.

It is unfortunate that by this time the view Europe took of contractual alliances of friendship, ceremoniously undersigned, was that of a retired old magician faced with the sleight-of-hand of his young and untalented colleagues, for otherwise everyone would of necessity have felt that the year of 1934 was beginning well: in January Germany and Poland signed a nonaggression pact. In February, during the days when the cannon were rumbling in Vienna, Mandria was treated to Occhipinti's ill-boding analyses. According to the druggist, it was Hitler who had stacked the cards for civil war between the Heimwehr and the Socialist workers, because he was laying the groundwork for Nazism in Austria. The air was cloudy with smoke for a while, but when spring came the first of the summer guests began to arrive in Mandria.

On the 26th of April, Zia was hurrying homeward on the Corso Mussolini at about seven o'clock in the evening when she stopped to chat with Tonia in the harbor. The ship was just coming in at the time, and merely out of habit Zia waited for it to tie up at the wharf. It pulled into port exactly as it had done for the past two and a half years, dragging a fluttering train of smoke behind, and there beside the mast as always was the sandy-yellow patch that invariably turned out to be Aldo Faggiani with the bloodstained canvas sack of his side of veal.

And it was on this evening that the miracle happened. It happened simply, like an afterthought. This time the sandy-yellow patch was really Filippo's trenchcoat. Filippo saw Zia at once, for there were only a few people on the wharf. He hastened toward Zia with a smile, holding out his two hands. But the intended embrace ran into the wall of Zia's eyes. Zia, as she chatted with Tonia, was watching the ship over her shoulder and now, as Filippo approached, she did not turn around. She could not have seemed more apathetic had it been Aldo Faggiani who bounded from the ship. She watched Filippo over her shoulder as he drew near; by now only his right hand was outstretched, and he said softly, with a somewhat embarrassed smile:

"Bon soir, chérie."

The look that flashed into Zia's glance was a look of recognition, which is the way one looks when an approaching stranger turns out to be a friend. She swung around too, and extended her hand to Filippo good-naturedly, while her lips opened in the smile that patrician women employ with such warmth and urbanity and assurance when greeting distant relatives or acquaintances at cocktail parties or big receptions. And this quality was in her voice as well:

"Bon soir, Prince Filippo!"

The word "Prince" cut into Filippo's countenance like a thorn. Filippo knew the argot of social intercourse in high society, knew there was neither jest nor sarcasm in the use of the title with his Christian name, knew that at this moment the usage meant there was no hope for him. He had not thought the meeting would be like this. He had prepared for an emotional scene behind closed doors at the moment of meeting, for he really did not expect to find Zia at the wharf after two and a half years. He had imagined he would lock her in his arms violently, force her lips open with his lips and then fall on his knees before her, embracing her knees with remorseful sobs that begged for forgiveness while the room filled with outbursts of misery and joy; and then, cheek pressed to cheek, they would achieve a tearful repose on the mysterious ground of soulful solitude. The wharf was too large a stage for the meeting Filippo had worked out in detail and the effect he had sought to create. The "Bon soir, Prince Filippo" was full of atmosphere and friendliness and complaisance and, for that very reason, full of a fatal disdain that made all explanation and apology unnecessary. Zia was the first to speak again after the greeting:

"Excusez-moi..." And, turning back to Tonia, she walked a few steps away to finish what she had been saying. Filippo was left hanging in mid-air for those few moments, and he felt like someone called upon in the midst of a dangerous trapeze act to recite the touching little verses he once had learned for the occasion of his grandmother's birthday. His situation was desperate right now, for his economic future depended to an alarming extent on the reconciliation with Zia.

Zia returned, and for a moment or so the scrutiny of her glance rested on Filippo's face, where the little ebony holder with tiny glittering diamonds around its rim was missing from the left corner of the mouth, and its absence made his face look as if a tooth had been knocked out. It occurred to Zia that Kócsag the *artiste* had proved her strength of character by breaking Filippo of his holder, and at the same time she noticed a slight wound on the iris of his right eye and two almost imperceptible marks below the eye. Zia thought of Eva Kócsag's plump and cushioned hand at this moment, of the image of that hand with sharp, triangular-tipped nails as it stayed in her memory of the time they had spent together at the Blind Mouse.

"Avez-vous retenu une chambre? Have you reserved a room?"

"Not yet," said Filippo, forced to realize from her polite and obliging words that it was Zia's decided intention not to spend the night in the same room with him. Zia helpfully attended to the disposition of Filippo's luggage, and when the youngsters had taken the two suitcases in hand she said: "Albergo Varcaponti."

They were past Niccolini's grocery store before Filippo broke the long silence: "Pourrais-tu me pardonner?" he asked softly. "Can you forgive me?"

In a voice devoid of feeling, but looking Filippo straight in the face, Zia said simply:

"Mais je n'ai plus de rancune envers vous, Prince Filippo! But I'm not angry with you any longer!"

Filippo felt that Zia was brandishing the word "Prince" like a cocked pistol in her hand. No further words passed between them until they reached the Albergo Varcaponti.

"I hope you'll find a room here," Zia said, giving him her hand. And she added: "I imagine you want to speak with me. I'll walk outside here while you get ready."

Filippo realized it was not an opportune moment for any sort of expostulation, for they were surrounded by the ragamuffins who carried his bags. He nodded, and hurried into the Albergo Varcaponti. Zia began to stroll slowly between the dairy and the bakery. The meeting had moved her deeply, keyed her up and filled her with happiness. But not the meeting with Filippo—rather, the meeting with herself. For she had met an entirely new version of herself—a version hitherto unimaginable. This was how a serious invalid might contemplate his recovered self after convalescence. Or a prisoner might feel this way long years after his release on meeting, in some congenial company, the judge who condemned him. Zia found it extremely interesting to note that the dairy and the bakery still stood exactly where they had been before her meeting with Filippo. She felt only subdued pity and strange disgust for Filippo, with no desire for revenge and satisfaction.

Filippo appeared at her side unexpectedly. This was another Filippo, one who was beginning to resemble the youthful Prince of Perugia. His tactics had changed as well, for he no longer used the pronouns of intimacy, but in the formality of his address there lurked a little smile which meant that all this was nothing more than a sly little game, a preparation for something further.

"Where shall we have supper?"

"We can go to Marica's."

When they were seated on the terrace of the Trattoria Marica and had ordered their meal, Filippo put his hand on Zia's hand, leaned closer to her and said in the voice of an elderly, understanding friend:

"What has happened to you since then?"

Zia looked at him, her head to one side.

"A lot. But let's agree not to ask each other questions about the past. Let's get to the point."

She drew her hand from beneath Filippo's, not with aloofness but only to smooth some wisps of hair under the dark red Basque cap with pert little motions. Her expression was preoccupied, as if she were regarding herself in a mirror.

"I should like you to start divorce proceedings as soon as possible. Let's get the stupid formalities over with."

"That's out of the question!" Filippo said heatedly. "Why, I don't want to divorce you!"

Zia was still busily straightening her hair around the edge of her cap, apparently paying more attention to this task than to her words:

"It won't be as simple as that. My tiara and my pearls are missing from my jewel box. My father had the strongbox opened in the presence of official witnesses."

She stopped speaking and looked mildly at Filippo.

"Are you trying to blackmail me?" Filippo asked, and something in the flash of his eyes reminded Zia of the way he had looked when he struck her.

Almost sadly, with a slow shake of her head, she said: "No. I don't want to blackmail you. But if you want to fight, then..." She grew silent. Then she turned toward Filippo with an odd little smile at the corner of her mouth:

"I don't recommend it."

She leaned closer: "What do you want of me? We have nothing in common any more, Filippo."

Filippo struck with a fencer's vigilance at the spot where the "Prince" was missing. "You despise me," he said swiftly and painfully.

Zia projected her lips into a bitter, odd little pout.

"I don't despise you," she said to the empty air, as drily as if pronouncing a series of numbers. Her glance was fixed in space at that moment. She was recalling what Pringsheim had said about the boundless sexual poverty that ruled the world. And she remembered—it was something she did not want to think about—how she too had fallen victim to this poverty in the person of a customs inspector named Guido Castelli. She sought no distinction between herself and Filippo in this slough of misery. Her voice filled with deep sincerity and sadness as she repeated:

"I don't despise you."

Marica approached them like a corpulent cherub in a cloud of garlic. The smell of food spirited them back to the checkered table-cloth from which they had strayed. They ate their supper without talking. Filippo had been prepared for mention of the jewelry, and had brought an explanation as long as a legal brief with him. Naturally, he intended to suppress the fact that he had presented the priceless jewels to Eva Kócsag during their journey; and that, later, Eva had pawned them without his knowledge while they were in difficult straits in South America, setting off a series of formidable quarrels. At the end of their adventure the actress barely managed to struggle back to Budapest from Rio de Janeiro by selling the lesser jewelry that the Miskolc wine merchant had given her. It is evident from all this that the entire adventure had proceeded according to pattern, exactly as her beer-drinking colleagues at the Runcsík Restaurant predicted, and when Eva Kócsag unexpectedly turned up at a rehearsal one afternoon, Ludasi greeted her as she passed him in the corridor:

"Hello there, Kócsag—I haven't seen you for weeks. What was wrong, did you have the grippe?"

As a matter of fact, the only unusual thing about their escapade was that it lasted for more than two years. Filippo had little appetite as he wielded his fork above the plate; he was afraid there was no longer any need for the explanation he had concocted in connection with the jewels. But he did not abandon all hope as yet. He placed his trust in the night. The fact that Zia had waited for him outside the Albergo Varcaponti and then had brought him to the populous terrace of the Trattoria Marica was, he surmised, a weapon of weak women, who defend themselves by restricting maneuvers to public places. Filippo industriously kept Zia's glass filled with *vino rosso*.

After supper they set out for a walk—this, at least, was what Filippo thought. But at the corner of the nameless and narrow little street that led to the Pension Zanzottera Zia stretched out her hand in farewell.

"Tomorrow?" asked Filippo.

"I'm sorry—I have an appointment tomorrow."

And without hesitation, but a little wearily and with evident ennui, she said: "Good-bye, Prince Filippo."

And this time the "Prince" struck fear into Filippo, for at this moment of parting it had an air of unshakable finality, perhaps for the very reason of its feathery lightness and lack of innuendo. Words pronounced as if through a barely repressed yawn can have an annihilating effect on men whose strength lies in their physical attraction.

Zia had already turned the corner, and Filippo's "Au revoir" fluttered in mid-air aimlessly. He cast a fixed glare into the black throat of the narrow street that had swallowed Zia.

"She's got someone," he thought, and imagined the man already lying in bed, smoking cigarettes impatiently as he waited for Zia. He threw himself impulsively at the darkness in the direction where Zia had disappeared. He rang a doorbell at random it happened to be the doorbell of the Pension Zanzottera, for there were no lights on anywhere else. The signora was talking with someone when she opened the door of the lighted hallway, Filippo recognized Zia's voice and he saw her as she quickly vanished through the doorway opposite. Brushing past the signora without so much as a glance, he hastened inside but found that door locked. He knocked.

"Darling, I want to talk to you!"

He said this in English because the signora was watching apprehensively from the open doorway of the hall.

"I'm sorry, I'm very tired." There was indifference and dismissal in Zia's voice.

"I must talk to you!" Filippo shouted passionately. "I must, do you understand?"

"I've already told you I'm tired!"

"Open the door!"

"I won't!"

Mad with fury, Filippo began to shake the knob as if to tear it off. At this the signora flitted from the hall into the dark street. Meeting with no success at the knob of the door, Filippo tried to break down the door itself with his shoulder. He was a muscular lad, but the door would not readily give way. And then it surrendered with a vigorous crash. Zia's room was dark, and he could hardly find the light switch. He looked around with the light on: the room was empty. The open door to the terrace disclosed the avenue of her escape. Rapid steps could be heard in the hall: Aldo Faggiani the butcher was the first to appear, with Domeneghetti the barber, Fanfoni the baker and an immense, unidentified, barefooted portside character behind him. The expressions of them all were arrayed in knightly armor. Behind them the signora's black eyes fluttered in her pale face.

It is unfortunate that linguists were not present with stop watches in hand during the moments that followed, to time the dizzying velocity of which the Italian language is capable. When it seemed that nothing could possibly overtake the accelerated expostulations of the five men, the signora unexpectedly threw herself into the race at record speed. Their subject was not so much a lady's honor as the proper recompense for the damaged door. When Filippo was escorted back to the Albergo Varcaponti he was surrounded by so many people that he could hardly move. They were all shouting at once, with equal vehemence and equal velocity.

Zia spent that night on a chair in the kitchen of Tonia's house. Tonia vainly offered her own bed to the visitor; Zia would not accept, and her reticence is understandable for a number of reasons. Calm and watchful, she sat with folded arms all night. The cavaliers of Mandria decreed that Filippo should not be allowed to wait for the departure of the ship on the following day; he was required to leave Mandria in Torriti's motor launch at dawn. His departure was effected under the supervision of Aldo Faggiani the butcher, in his youth the wrestling champion of the Fiume Athletic Club, and he politely asked Filippo— who had registered as Filippo Fuga at the Albergo Varcaponti—not to entertain any thoughts of revisiting Mandria in the future.

Ursi's most recent letter announced his arrival at the end of June. Slowly the summer guests appeared, exactly nineteen in all, and all new faces, as if Mandria were some wonderful new machine for testing the laws of probability. Each year there occurred eighteen or at most twenty-one inhabitants of the earth who decided, for reasons unknown, to spend the summer in Mandria. This season a married couple from Calcutta and a spinster from Philadelphia were among the precipitation of people.

On that certain fourth day of the week, on a Thursday at the end of June, the ship from Fiume arrived with Mihály Ursi on board. Zia was waiting for him on the wharf.

Only their diaries can give an accurate account of their life in the two months that followed. It must be admitted, however, that neither Zia nor Ursi kept a diary of those days. Still, there are periods in our lives when our memories operate with greater sensitivity, carve out a deeper record of things that we shall later live over and over again in moments of solitude. At these times the spirit and the flesh instinctively learn every impression by heart, so they may know the correct answer at a given moment. After retiring and snapping off the light, we conscientiously rehearse the words, gestures, glances of the day like a table of square roots, commit to memory the differentials of our feelings and the recondite physical laws of our heart-beat. Years and sometimes decades pass in which we do not fuss with these matters so much as at a period like this, a period of but a few weeks. Only at such times do people live the life of a higher order; otherwise they vegetate like plants.

The diary which follows is written in cigarette smoke, with Zia lying in bed before she turns off the light. It is a diary nonetheless, for she formerly did not light a cigarette before settling down for the night. And a diary is diligently kept in the Albergo Varcaponti too, not in cigarette smoke—for Ursi does not smoke but on the broad, red, lobster-patterned carpet that sprawls before the armchair. The astronomer sits in the armchair, till dawn sometimes, patiently twisting the soft brown strands of hair above his temple with the forefinger of his right hand—which is, with him, an indication of the deepest concentration.

Here, then, are excerpts from the unwritten diaries:

URSI: "I arrived in Mandria on the 28th of June. When we were still far from shore I noticed that *T* was waiting on the wharf, although it was still almost impossible to make out the figures of the people. Evidently some sixth sense is at work at such times. I identified a vague, motionless green patch, which might just as well have been a bush, as Teréz. Those moments of our approach were wonderful, as *T* was gradually born of a tiny green cloud as the whiteness of

605

her face appeared, and the dark red cap above it, and the white tennis shoes on her feet. She recognized me from a distance and raised one of her arms. When we were quite close she waggled her fingers at me—it is a greeting I've only seen Parisian women use. When she gave me her hand she merely said: Good evening. But her strange green eyes, which are always moistly asparkle with poignancy even when there is no cause for it—her strange green eyes looked at me for a fraction of a second as if I were the one for whom she had been waiting all her life. I must be careful not to delude myself with vain imaginings. I'm afraid I've inclined toward that sort of thing since meeting *T*. I must finish my book by Christmas."

ZIA: "The ship was still far away, but I could see the sandy-yellow patch beside the mast. It no longer set me afire—it was good to know that the patch was nothing but Faggiani's sack. It is good to be free of something that has had such an unconditional power over me. I once read somewhere that freedom depends not on others but on ourselves—for the first time I felt the truth of this. It was good to be waiting for the ship. I am beginning to realize the value of something that is, I think, the most important thing in life: *dependability*."

URSI: "This is my second day in Mandria. At dusk I walked along the waterfront with Teréz. A simile that came to my mind was not very original, I fear: The heart is like fruit. It takes time to ripen. And it needs sunshine, the sunshine of the mind and memory. She too, I think has thought as often about me since we last saw each other. Both of us were constantly thinking of each other, and something ripened inside us until we are now full of sweetness toward one another. It was wise of us not to permit any sentimental sighs of love to creep into our letters. The sweetness would have flowed from us as from fruit split prematurely. Anyone might have heard what we talked about on our walk. She told me what had happened in Mandria during the past ten months. She mentioned names behind which I could see no features, and the incidents were not very interesting either. I tried to explain the political situation to her. It was my feeling, when I mentioned Daladier or Suvich, that the names meant no more to her than when she mentioned Occhipinti or Niccolini. Now I know that a declaration of love cannot be couched in terms more beautiful than, 'Doumergue wants to mitigate the wild career of French parliamentarism with constitutional reform.' As I glanced at her I felt she knew what I wanted to say."

ZIA: "Yesterday I had supper with *M* on the terrace of the Trattoria Marica.

He doesn't yet know, but I do, how the two of us seem in the eyes of Mandrian society. When Fanfoni, Domeneghetti and Faggiani occasionally brought their heads together at the next table, I sensed quite clearly that they had already solved our puzzle. This is something *M* and I have not been able to do yet. It would be hard to give an account of my state of mind. When I was with Filippo I was always afraid of something; I know this for certain now. *M* seems to be somewhere far beyond my world, and yet he is wonderfully close sometimes. This can only mean that I have gone far away too, but I don't know where yet. Perhaps this sort of distance has no name. While we were having supper I looked at *M*'s hand—it has something of the quality of a simple but perfect instrument. Mongés once said that an orchid can be disgustingly ugly, and at the same time a cork or a hammer can be beautiful. The tips of Filippo's fingers were a little crooked, and his hands trembled ever so slightly. I would not have dared to admit this to myself before. In the company of *M* I am alarmed to think what a low forehead my brother János has, and what a human parasite Uncle Fini is."

URSI: "After supper *T* and I both listened to the radio in the garden of the Alb. Varc. All Mandria was there—the events have upset everyone. I tried to think things through, but it didn't work. Very bad night."

ZIA: "I despise the radio—I don't want to know anything about the world. All I want is this crazy, dirty, beautiful little island of Mandria, just as it is. Last night the radio slapped us in the face like a fire-hose in the face of peaceful pedestrians. But it was spitting blood. On a wonderful June night like that, every radio in the world was blaring out that Hitler had beaten down the Roehm putsch and allegedly shot Captain Roehm with his own hand. They murdered General Schleicher and his wife in Berlin, and a lot of others as well. Occhipinti said that war was a matter of days—Mussolini was bound to declare war on Germany. *M* took a different view of the situation. According to him, the caliber of international affairs has degenerated to an alarming extent with the mass murders of the Germans; but he thinks Occhipinti's opinion is nonsense, for it is only two weeks since Hitler and Mussolini first met in Venice. He says he cannot imagine that those two insane public enemies chatted about nothing but fishing and the Milan football game while they were in Stra."

URSI: "*T* still likes to go for a long swim at nightfall. I follow her on the shore, or row at her side. I don't let her go out too far. I have no idea what she looks like to anyone else, but I think she is beautiful. And I think she is the sort of woman who would never deceive me. If she were to fall in love with someone she'd tell me first, like a child—'I'm hurt.'"

ZIA: "Occhipinti's loud prophecy of war has not come true, thank God. The atmosphere in Mandria is peaceful again. The days are beautiful. *M* works on his book in the mornings, and we are together in the afternoons. At five o'clock every afternoon he appears beside the old fig tree in the pension garden and calls up at my window: Teréz! His voice seems to wake me from a long, deep sleep, the sleep I have been sleeping since I was born. I see myself turning into someone called Teréz, and my Zia-eyes can observe the movements and words and thoughts of this person called Teréz. I like this Teréz."

URSI: "During supper last night it was on the tip of my tongue to suggest that we tell each other the story of our lives. Mine isn't interesting. Hers is, I think. Yesterday I discovered from something she said that she is divorced. She didn't say so, but I know her marriage was very unhappy. The tone of her voice tells me she doesn't want to talk about the past. I shall try to imagine what the man was like: A Frenchman—I think—thin, nervous, a painter or a musician in a beret, an older man, well known and with a good income, with an English pipe in his mouth and a vast flood of words. A gift of gab—the moral insanity of an artist, probably. *T* never talks of her parents or her family. Her behavior, her manner, her movement, her urbane assurance, the simple elegance of her dress indicate that she grew up in good circumstances. If *T* doesn't talk about her past by herself, I shan't ever ask her."

ZIA: "The signora takes a dim view of my friendship with *M,* as if it were a violation of the higher morality over which she alone stands guard in Mandria. The real reason is that she feels herself cheated, and one can hardly blame her for that. Her birthday is next week—I'll give her my little diamond ring. So far she's only been muttering to herself. Yesterday I had supper in the garden with *M*—we made fish soup over an open fire. The signora pulled a sour face when she lent us her kettle, and sarcastically asked us not to set the house on fire. *M* loves to cook. I watched him as he made the fire. This takes especial skill. When the fire was burning well, he picked up one or two large coals that had rolled away and put them back with a calm, slow gesture. I've only seen the peasants at Ararat handle live coals like that before, and Uncle Charles at a chicken roast in the woods once—he camped in the open a good deal while hunting in Africa. *M* is an odd mixture of a savage and an armchair intellectual. It's wonderful for one man to know so much at once about the habits of fish, the chemical components of fire, the stars, disease, history, art, and the mechanism of the signora's sewing machine, which he repaired yesterday. Frankly, I didn't care for the fish soup at all, but of course I was ecstatic over it."

URSI: "*T* and I talked about love for the first time. We discussed love in the same tone with which we would talk about the counter-Reformation, or the Second Ice Age, or the influenza epidemic after the war. We decided that love has nothing to do with character, friendship or happiness. Love springs from the body's sexual longing, carefully clothed in the veils of poetry, or in the well-worn slippers of marriage, because it would be altogether too bestial if unadorned. Love can—must—be present in the lifetime association of two people, like good health, a strong stomach, firm teeth, and it does no harm to take one's marital tenderness to the dentist every once in a while. But communion—that is rarely present in love. After dwelling on love for more than an hour, every time we walked a few steps without speaking we felt that the silent hills, the waves, the rippling breeze on the Corso Mussolini and the mercilessly screaming children in the bagno were shouting that we were in love with each other, and this made us inexpressibly happy. We did not show it; when one quotes Kant or Nietzsche or Galton in conversation and strikes a few notes of Chopin and even blows a few blasts on Wagner, as if on a tremendous horn, it is unsuitable to be childishly happy, for this would compromise the dignity of those world-famous worthies of the intellect, who—if the truth were known—seem like gibbering idiots compared to what we feel at a time like this. I should finally like to kiss *T* once. To kiss her closed eyes."

ZIA: "There is a peculiar, vague terror inside of me. Yesterday I dreamt again that my mother, her throat slit, was being dragged along the downstairs corridor of Ararat Castle by the hair, and her body left a long, red stripe on the marble floor. Hitler wrapped my mother's hair around his wrist as he dragged her along. And I have another such dread—of being in an automobile accident. Strange, that I'm not afraid of airplanes but shrink from cars. And I'm not afraid of horses either, although I've had some stiff falls, and I sprained my left arm when I was twelve and Boby threw me. I'm only at ease in a car when my father's chauffeur, Oscar, is driving. In my dream last night I sat alone in father's car. The big machine began to tear along the open road at hair-raising speed, although it was impossible to see ahead for more than twenty yards. I asked Oscar to drive more slowly and when he turned around his face was the face of Mussolini. Yesterday

I gave the signora my diamond ring. Now she apparently shares my happiness. I think the men of Mandria have finally given me up for lost. The baker Fanfoni no longer turns his wrinkled little rat-face at me, and the eloquent fire has gone out in Occhipinti's eyes. Now, when I walk by, he calmly stands in the door of his drugstore and continues paring his nails. Formerly he used to hide the penknife when he saw me coming. Today is three weeks since *M* arrived."

URSI: "During the winter months *T* absorbed the books I sent to an extent far beyond my expectations. Now she sometimes sees important connections with surprising clarity, and she feels that the great truths which rule mankind (and which politics and religion, by main strength, have rendered excessively complex) are simple and beautiful. So simple that they brook neither argument nor contradiction, like certain laws of natural science. I take great pleasure in seeing how *T* receives these simple truths and how her intelligence is taking shape, throwing out its branches, blossoming, ripening. Yesterday, while we were seated on a bench along the Corso Mussolini, she suddenly broke into tears, although up to that point her attention had not wavered from what I was saying, which happened to be about some remote sociological problem. It is mystifying to see how such storms of emotion sometimes break out in a woman's soul. In this respect they are different from men. Her weeping was beautiful—mysterious human tears, welling up from the depths. As she wept I put my arm around her and tried to calm her, but she did not seem to notice. When she had cried herself out she sniffled and blew her nose, looked down at her shoelaces and said: 'I bought these shoes for eighty francs in Paris.' She can be a child, a woman and a superhuman being all at once. I love her so much by now that it sometimes hurts."

ZIA: "Yesterday, for the first time, *M* talked about the book he is writing, which occupies him from early morning until late in the afternoon. Last year he mentioned in passing that he was writing a book of some sort about the theory of land ownership. Now I know that the book deals with the problem of agrarian policy in Hungary, and more specifically with the Hungarian system of land tenure. As he explained the historical background of the subject, and listed the mammoth estates in Hungary, he mentioned the name of Dukay. It was not the first time I heard my name mentioned as if from a distance and as an abstraction, for it appeared in my school books, and Dukay Utca in Budapest or in Sopron didn't mean much to me. But it was so unexpected to hear the Dukay name on *M*'s lips that I suddenly blushed a little and my heart began to beat furiously.

He has a severely critical opinion of the great estates in Hungary. This doesn't surprise me, for there are people in our own circle who think otherwise than my father. I remember, when I was still engaged, walking in the park at Ararat once with Uncle Peter, when he analyzed the reasons why the Hungarian system of land tenure was intolerable. In this respect, he said, we were the last buffalo in all of Europe. But he asked me not to mention this talk of ours to my parents or my brothers and sisters, for they wouldn't understand anyway. What will happen when *M* finds out who I am? I should like him never to know."

URSI: "*T* was happy all day today. She told me proudly that an American picture agency had paid her two hundred forty dollars for two of her photographs, 'The Fly' and 'Heavenly Love.' The latter shows two gulls clasped in mid-air. As I study her way of life here, I can see that such a sum would support her in Mandria for half a year at least. But I still can't understand what has tied her to the place for years."

ZIA: "It all happened so simply and so wonderfully. We were sitting on the Corso Mussolini, on the bench which *M*—after ceremoniously asking my permission—once christened the Teréz bench. It was growing dark. General Hasparics and his four dogs had already marched past, on their way home. We were alone, and to me it was as if we were the only ones in the whole wide world. Suddenly I was attacked by a sense of sadness because I was so very much alone in life. My mother? My brothers and sisters? They are like distant relatives. In any case, my mother was never more than a governess wearing a crown and seated on a throne. Papa is my only family, but I feel that in his life too I figure only as a pleasant adventure under the heading of fatherly love. I apologize for having offended him with this thought of mine.

"We were sitting on the bench and simply listening, because we had run out of things to say. All at once I took *M*'s hand, which was resting on his knee, opened it and stuffed my clenched fist into his palm, as if my fist were looking for a nest, or as if it were cold. One by one I closed his fingers over my fist and then, carefully wrapped in his hand, I put it back on his knee, like an object entirely independent of me, a poor little object that deserved a better fate. We looked at each other and smiled a smile that was almost like weeping. I never felt so soft, so much a woman, before. He put his arm around me and said: 'I should like to kiss your eyes.' Coming from his lips, these words were as surprising as if the signora were suddenly to speak up and recite the Gay-Lussac Law or some such recondite formulation of physics. I almost broke out laughing. I put my arms around his neck and quietly kissed his mouth. I crept close to him and we kissed for a long time without saying a word. It was quite dark when we went home. As we reached the lights that glowed at the wharf we seemed like two strangers returning to reality from an improbable world."

URSI: "Why wasn't I happy yesterday, when I parted from *T* after supper? Some of my premonitions are amazing. I've completely lost touch with world affairs. At this moment I have no idea whether I might not be called to Budapest tomorrow to join the army."

ZIA: "That damned radio has assaulted Mandria again. Now everything is topsy-turvy. Yesterday the Nazi putschists assassinated the Austrian Chancellor in his office. I remember him well, he once had supper with us on Bösendorferstrasse. Poor little Dollfuss, with his great round child's eyes! Sitting at the table he looked so like a little boy that one wanted to pick him up in one's lap. What is going to happen in this awful world? Mussolini is mobilizing his garrisons in North Italy, and has moved troops up to the Brenner Pass and the Carinthian border. Could Occhipinti be right after all? People gather in groups on the Piazza— the men are speechless, and the women dash around moaning that war has broken out."

URSI: "The Italian mobilization is an extremely serious matter. I expect my telegram from Budapest at any moment. Thank God I misjudged Mussolini. Evidently Hitler was unable to bend Mussolini's back during their meeting at Stra; the Duce is playing up to his historical role right now. He will be the greatest single man of this age. It's about time for the Latin, Anglo-Saxon and Soviet peoples to take the wind out of the German sails."

ZIA: "The world is boiling, and even the sea seemed to take on a new color tonight. I felt that the hills were moving with me, as if they wanted to spread their wings. We're all flying somewhere, the whole world. Mihály hardly said a word all day. I can't decide whether his face was strangely transfigured, or merely preoccupied. Dinnertime was long past, and as we walked side by side along the dark waterfront, where the starlight merely suggested the outline of the dark massive seaside cliffs, Mihály unexpectedly spoke out in a profoundly preoccupied, whispering tone:

> 'It was a strange, strange summer even:
> An angry angel beat a drum in heaven.'

"I recognized the quotation, for Kristina had often recited this famous poem of Ady's even after the war. The two lines had taken root in Papa's memory as well, and he sometimes quoted them of a sudden, in his rumbling voice, when deep in thought.

"As I silently accompanied Mihály through the warm, fetid Italian evening, it truly seemed as if the angry angel were madly beating a drum in heaven once more. Mihály's taciturnity seemed to tell me that he too was listening to that mysterious and mighty drumbeat. As we approached the harbor the sweet little sounds of a mandolin issued from the darkness. Marica's terrace was deserted by then. Even during supper I seemed to know that something would happen between us tonight. But nothing happened. Except inside of me. I have made up my mind to let *M* have me. I want to bear his child."

URSI: "I can see things more clearly now. I too was misled by an illusion, if not quite so much as that loud-mouthed druggist. Not the fact that the threat of war is past but the *manner* of its passing is conclusive proof, to me, that the German and Italian dictatorships are gravitating toward one another. With irresistible force, I fear. For days *T* has been like a frightened child. I wish I could snatch her up in my arms and run away with her, anywhere out of this rotten human world."

ZIA: "This, too, happened so simply and beautifully, like our first kiss on the Corso Mussolini. We had supper at Marica's, and walked along the harbor, and then I told *M* neither of us could go to sleep anyhow, so let's go to my place, I'll make some fresh black coffee and there's a half bottle of maraschino brandy too. *M* left me just before dawn, when it was still dark. What time is it now? It will soon be noon. I don't have the strength to get up. I am still half in a dream, in the arms of a wonderfully sweet drunkenness that has nothing to do with liquor, for we only drank a glass or two apiece. The curtains aren't drawn, the room is in semi-darkness and it is as if Pringsheim were sitting in the armchair. I can see his silvery-black side whiskers quite clearly, and I can hear his soft, delicate Viennese voice. And I, my eyes closed, not speaking at all—I keep telling him over and over again about perfect rhythm and that other word, I don't remember it any more."

URSI: "I shall marry *T*. We didn't say a word about it, but both of us felt that it was bound to be."

ZIA: "The days pass as swiftly as if we were really flying somewhere, and it doesn't seem to matter that the world might vanish away in the meantime."

URSI: "When my book appears, the Prosecutor General will get orders from above to institute an action against me for 'intent to overthrow the established order of society'...that much is almost certain. I can expect a long term in prison. If there is any talk of marriage, *T* must be told about this. Will she be disheartened? I don't think so. She'll understand that I can't let anything stand in the way of the book's publication."

ZIA: "Every promise life ever made has been fulfilled."

URSI: "I am happy, happy to an extent I had not thought possible. My head is clear when I start work on my book each morning, and the work goes wonderfully well. Then, in the afternoon..."

ZIA: "I was eight years old, and I recall how the glass paperweight on Papa's desk cast an iridescent shadow on the blotter as the sun shone on it from the window. I was looking for a red pencil on Papa's desk, although this was forbidden ground. I couldn't find a pencil, and so I began to search for foreign stamps in the wastebasket, there were always some foreign stamps in it for my collection. That was when I happened upon the Mandrian prospectus. I ran away when I heard someone coming. I examined the prospectus in secret, as if it were a picture-book for grownups only. I kept it for years, and Mandria took shape in my heart like some miraculous vision of the future, the trump of judgment, the epitaph of fate. Now I feel that the road ahead will be long, humble, perhaps hard, but beautiful. I shall embroider a shroud for myself and travel long distances to take part in the Mandrian procession. Only the humility of death can repay the happiness Mandria has given me."

At this point, on August 31st, 1934, the unwritten diaries come to an end. They come to an end on this day because a senseless, cruel storm made rubble of Princess Oasika's crimson citadel of yellow towers, built with such effort and industry on the Hill of Oranges by tigers and elephants. Life would not long tolerate such a fairy-tale citadel, and neither would Mandria. What happened?

Did the radio break loose again? No, neither war nor the cataclysms of history can overthrow such citadels as this.

Something else happened. The ship from Fiume was idling in the harbor on its day of rest. Ursi was to have left on the ship the next morning because his vacation was over. But he wrote the National Astronomical Institute that he would be a week late. He was saving all the momentous things he wanted to tell Teréz for this final week.

And then, on August 31st, everything fell apart. In the morning, as usual, he worked in a cool arbor of the Varcaponti garden, where one could see—if one wanted to—the Piazza Vittorio Emanuele through the branches. At about eleven o'clock he saw Teréz walk past Niccolini's grocery store, on the other side of the concrete lagoon, in the company of a tall, white-uniformed naval officer. It was only a fleeting, momentary glimpse. Teréz came, unexpectedly, at noon. She asked him perfunctorily not to visit her that afternoon because she would be busy. That was all; she vanished without waiting for an answer. At the gate she turned back and waggled her fingers in farewell. She was in a great hurry. Ursi turned back to his work, but never finished the sentence he had begun, as if the strength had suddenly flown from his poised arm. What did she mean by "I'm going to be busy"? What was going to keep her busy? Developing photographs? Unlikely. It was in itself unusual that she had come to him at this time; she had never done this before, out of tacit respect for his working hours. And the way she had swept into view, uttering her words hurriedly! "I'm going to be busy this afternoon..." And then she vanished, with the obvious intention of forestalling any further questions. Recently their afternoon meetings had not begun with Ursi calling to Zia's window from the garden; he went straight to her room, most often with a short, faint knock on the door, and entered without waiting for an answer, like one who has a lifetime pass. There must have been some special reason for the postponement of his afternoon visit. The acute state of happiness in love is always extremely susceptible to jealousy, as an open wound invites infection. Pencil in hand, Ursi stared at his manuscript with rigid eyes, although it was now wholly devoid of meaning for him, and the view he took of Teréz was a view immortalized since the beginning of time: she was mysterious and unpredictable. This is a conception that men frequently and gladly forget.

Now he recalled that last year, when he still knew the lady photographer only by sight and spent several evenings walking with the blond woman from Zagreb out of sheer boredom, Ljubica had constantly gossiped about all the summer guests but most vehemently and most persistently about the photographer. She maintained that the supercilious and disdainful Parisian photographer was a dangerous nymphomaniac and even had an affair with the customs inspector who was murdered in the previous year—the inspector had bragged about it to Domeneghetti the barber on the day before his death. All Mandria knew she was having concurrent affairs with Occhipinti and Fanfoni the baker at that very moment. Ursi did not pay much attention to her chatter, since Ljubica slandered all the prettier summer guests in the same way, and it was not difficult to see that she was obsessed by the fear of a man-hungry woman lest they steal her chosen prey. Her behavior was so transparent that Ursi began to avoid all contact with her after a few days. But now her words returned. It was almost as if a disembodied snake had slithered from the shadows of the arbor and curled itself over the manuscript on the table. "I'm going to be busy this afternoon." Who was this Teréz? Actually he knew nothing about her, and women sometimes have truly dreadful and alarming surprises in store for men. Melanie—an old wound began to mount inside of him, like bubbles on a quagmire. When he was still a university student he had fallen in love with a girl whom he wanted to marry, and whom he thought the chastest angel in the world until he discovered, quite by chance, that she was a constant visitor at a private bordello. Teréz. Who was Teréz?—aside, that is, from the fact that she was a Paris-trained photographer. Aside from the fact that she was full of charm, delicacy, warmth and wonder —who was she? A host of surprises were probably lurking behind those qualities. The mystery in which she shrouded herself indicated as much. And another thing, about which Ormai, the young physician, had once spoken on the terrace of the Gugger Café in Budapest: women, once they take a man after not thinking of men for years, launch a number of affairs at once, their appetite growing with the first indulgence. From the waist down a body can differ greatly with the views of an apple-green glance. This aspect of life could be more menacing and repulsive even than the assassination of Dollfuss at his desk.

Ursi wrestled with these thoughts, as if gasping for air, until seven o'clock at night. Then he could stand it no longer, and set out for the Pension Zanzottera. Jealousy is always fully prepared when it enters a room at such a time, with a briefcase of documents under its arm like a combative lawyer entering a courtroom, but in its heart is a desire to withdraw the suit if possible, to reach an agreement. Nor was Ursi full of conviction when he hastened toward the Pension Zanzottera, accumulating counterarguments as he progressed and, with them, hope. Perhaps he would find Teréz at her papier-mâché trays, bathing her photographs, the sleeves of her smock rolled to the elbows—perhaps she was preparing the photographs as a surprise for him! Or he might find her in deep discussion with an elderly woman. It was not certain, after all, that he had seen Teréz pass Niccolini's grocery store with the naval officer, for the image had flashed by in a moment, and since then even the memory of the two vine leaves that blocked his view had engraved itself on his brain. But such counter-arguments only serve to make disappointment even more explosive. The signora answered his ring. She exposed her smile on the instant, but it was only a mechanical smile this time, and it did not escape Ursi's attention that her fleeting black glance darted from Teréz' door to his face not once but twice, flashing with surprise and confusion, as if she too knew that Ursi's visit at this hour was not prearranged. Ursi stepped straight to the door of Teréz' room and knocked, a knock that hovered between his usual short, faint knock and the official knock of a process server. He walked in without waiting for an answer, his heart in his throat and the tortured smile of hope on his lips, prepared to find his suspicions groundless, to confess his state of mind with contrition.

The photographic darkroom was in the right corner of the room. As he opened the door, the door of the darkroom closed, simultaneously, as if activated by the same mechanism. For an instant, through the crack in the darkroom door as it closed, he could clearly see the disappearing figure of the white-uniformed naval officer. Teréz stood in the center of the room, cut off in the middle of a gesture as if on a broken strip of film. One could surmise from her attitude that she sprang from her chair in the preceding moment, and the arm poised in air revealed that she had pointed out the only way of escape to the naval officer—one could almost see the muffled words of alarm in the air as they had issued from her mouth. Her face was barely visible, for she stood with her back to the light, framed in the blue rectangle of the darkening window with the dry branch of the old fig tree in the background, as in a tragic dream. In the bluish glow of twilight the tropical naval cap of the unknown visitor glistened whitely, with black and gold braid, on the table, announcing the complete fiasco of the sudden concealment, for at this moment the cap itself was more eloquent than the presence of the officer himself would have been. There was an alien cloud of tobacco smoke in the room, its aroma readily apparent to a man who did not smoke. Two brandy glasses stood beside the cap on the table. And there stood the bottle of maraschino brandy, which now took the shape of a peculiar key to a dreadful secret.

"Oh—excuse me," Ursi said, and the door closed behind him almost without having paused in its swing.

A few minutes later he found himself on the Corso Mussolini where, resting his elbows on the stone wall, he looked as if he were fatally wounded and bleeding to death. A woman with a big water pitcher on her head passed him in the dimness, like the walking ghost of a bygone Latin age. She looked back at him twice, and the heavy amphora on her head necessitated a deliberate turn of her body. The dusk turned to darkness, the laurel forests on the hilltop dropped their veils of wind and the sea began to breathe heavily. On a dark purple tablecloth of cloud in the eastern sky the moon was already glistening whitely, like a tropical naval cap.

Ursi began to walk back toward the harbor quietly. It must have been about half past eight. The wharf was deserted, and the yellow glow of several harbor lights rocked damply in the water. It was no more than a few minutes that he stood there before Teréz suddenly appeared, arm-in-arm with the white-uniformed sailor. They did not see Ursi, for he was standing in the shadow. But they walked on into the light, and all at once Ursi recognized the tall, slender naval officer. The discovery struck him like lightning: István Dukay! Certainly he recognized him—that face was as familiar to almost everyone in Hungary as the suspension bridge or the cupola of the Royal Palace. And suddenly everything he had heard about the legendary count swept into his mind. Everything—his mistresses, his harems. All at once the mystery was clear: Teréz was the mistress of old István Dukay. Standing motionless in the shadows, he was unable to take his eyes from István Dukay, whom he had seen more than once at close range in the corridors of Parliament, a two-legged great estate with a rumbling voice wrapped in the smoke of a Havana. The large motor launch was preparing to pull out. The blinding glare of its spotlights swept the terrace of the Trattoria Marica on the opposite side of the lagoon. The walls of the houses, the chimneys loomed white against the black background. The count took Teréz in his arms and kissed her. It was no longer difficult to discern the insignia of the Balaton Yacht Club on his naval cap. The motor launch started with a machine-gun burst, and the white figure of the count stood erect at the prow; he did not take his eyes off Teréz, who raised her hand high and waggled her fingers at the vanishing visitor. There was a sense of deep regret at parting in her gesture. Ursi turned and disappeared into the darkness. Zia made her way to the Albergo Varcaponti and when she did not find him there she sought him on the terrace of the Trattoria Marica, leaving a message to the effect that she was waiting for him at the pension.

The next morning she again appeared in the Albergo Varcaponti, where she learned that the Signor Professor had unexpectedly left on the morning ship.

Thus the Mandrian romance came to nothing. The astronomer vanished in the whirlwind of his own blind jealousy. Zia had no idea that Ursi recognized her father, but she realized that his departure without a word of farewell was the result of a fatal misunderstanding. She felt she was caught in her own trap, for it was a misunderstanding that could not be corrected without complication. Women are generally flattered by masculine jealousy, and what is pain to a man, at a time like this, is pleasure of a certain sort to a woman. But when a woman's soul is in a state of complete surrender, it is wounded, saddened by jealousy. This, or something like this, was what happened to Zia.

Mandria suddenly turned to ashes for her, lost all its meaning and mysterious inner magic. For some days she wandered aimlessly along the Corso Mussolini, waiting for a telegram or some sign of life. But the days passed in emptiness. Bitterness and rebellion seized her. Apparently everything was in vain. And she suddenly felt homesick, which was something she had never felt before. This homesickness was a longing for the ease of her former life. For three years she had been washing herself like a cat, bathing in the collapsible bathtub she had brought with her. Now she longed for the large, sunken marble tubs and the ample water from the taps of the Septemvir Utca Palace and Ararat Castle. Her wrist longed for the tennis racket, her hand for the reins, her thighs and her waist for the slow rhythm of a canter and the delicate music, the fine fragrance of a saddle. Hemmed in by the furniture of the Pension Zanzottera, she longed to return to the grave splendor of the rooms at home, the deep, warm, glowing, subdued hues of the great oaks. Her stomach yearned for Monsieur Cavaignac's masterpieces, her ear grew thirsty for the tenor chimes of the belfry in the chapel at Ararat, which seemed to call her back to her childhood. The skin on her head, her every single hair began to tingle with longing for the understanding hands of Mr. Kudera, the cosmopolitan hairdresser, ached to get under the large, tubular nickel helmet. Anci Vörös's millinery store beckoned with French veils and feathers from the wilds of Brazil. Like Venus from the waves, the nakedness of her shoulders yearned to emerge from the silk stuff of the latest evening gown. Her tongue and teeth longed for the idiom of her home and her society. Her olfactory senses longed for the strong smell of a cleanser called Holbok which used to fill the stairways at home in the mornings, and for the sweet tart fragrance that sprang from the water-lily clad fishpool in this September season, sprang from the branches of the great trees as they waved in farewell. The wound that Ursi's sudden departure had inflicted on her pride now longed for the low bows of the footmen. All this constituted her homesickness. Her disillusioned spirit avidly anticipated Uncle Fini's frivolous witticisms, and she wanted to laugh long and heartily once more at the foolish fun of the Park Club. The soul that in the course of three years had so often embraced the malicious vision of a sandy-yellow patch which always proved to be the canvas sack of a side of veal on the back of Aldo Faggiani—this soul longed for refreshment. The jocund filth on the Piazza Vittorio Emanuele, the somber message of the deep sea, the incomprehensible, obscene adventure with the murdered customs inspector, then the dawn and daybreak of world problems at Ursi's side, the hitherto unknown savor of love—all this would be left behind in the Mandrian cemetery, in the invisible sepulcher of Teréz Hemli.

She began to pack on the fifth day, surreptitiously, so that even the signora would not take notice. She announced her departure as a surprise, explaining that she had had good news of her family from abroad. She left the materials with which she had covered the furniture in her room, and she made the signora a parting present of the handbag which she had never carried in Mandria. She left but one letter behind, addressed to Parson Muzmics. When she went over her accounts, she discovered that she had spent not quite seventy-two thousand liras during the three years in Mandria. She converted this sum into francs, and was reminded that the gold-trimmed green evening dress she had worn at Marchese Delfrate's reception had cost considerably more than that. She enclosed a check for two hundred thousand liras in her letter to Parson Muzmics, with the request that he divide this sum among the poor of Mandria. She also included a list of potential recipients, for she knew everyone, and the fortune of everyone, in Mandria. She estimated that if she had lived abroad modestly but in keeping with her rank, she would have spent about this much more.

She left on the next ship. Standing on the deck, she gazed back at Mandria. The shore was slowly dissolving in the obscurity of twilight. For a long time the cemetery on the hillside stayed in sight, with its white headstones and the large black cypress that appeared on the photograph she had secretly made of Pringsheim. Zia reflected that Teréz Hemli was already at rest there, somewhere close to the wife of the Viennese physician.

Slowly Mandria disappeared into nothingness on the horizon. The Mandrian climate is susceptible to legends. In time, perhaps, a legend of *la fotografa morta* will be born among the poor of Mandria, who march at the head of the procession in their white shrouds.

✝

The aristocratic young woman who disembarked at Fiume with her boundless luggage, and impatiently called for porters, was Zia Dukay once more. More than ever Zia Dukay, perhaps, for on the occasion of such a restoration the soul clothes itself even more carefully than is needful, having lost its assurance somewhere and to some extent, like a heart that moves from the deep valleys to a mountainous climate.

It is an unwritten law of those mountainous heights to greet the newcomer without surprise, or amazement, without intrusive questions or even significant silences. Countess Menti's "Good morning, Zia" and her cool kiss were truly the somewhat exaggerated condescension of a distant and distinguished kinswoman. The staff found it natural for the countess—they no longer addressed her as princess—to reoccupy her childhood apartments. Of her brothers and sister, only Kristina and Rere were at Ararat. Visitors came at the end of the week; flaxen-haired Elizabeth arrived, who was evidently living in marital bliss with Señor Calandra, and Sigi and Ubi arrived, and it must be confessed that they behaved wonderfully. Their greetings reduced the three Mandrian years to an absence of three weeks. In their discretion, however, Zia felt how quickly they would forget her if she were to die.

It was only a matter of days before she blossomed out on her native soil. She spent the following two weeks on a visit to Sigi's castle, where she found the entire membership of the Park Club, all married and most of them divorced.

Sigi rounded up some gypsies for Sunday evening. Two gendarmes brought them from the next county in an overcrowded peasant wagon. This was necessary because the band had not wanted to come, which is to say that they wanted to come, of course, but had been hired to play for the manager of the mill, who was celebrating his name day that evening. Sigi called out the primás, and a hectic exchange of messages began, but the mill manager was not willing to renounce his rights in favor of the count. In any case, he was on the outs with the estate because of something that had to do with the milling of wheat, as a consequence of which he was said to be a dangerous partisan of the Left. The local town clerk was among the guests, and under Sigi's direction he ordered the gendarmes to load the gypsies on the wagon with force if necessary. In those years there were still some counties in Hungary where administrative authority served the count rather than the law. The gypsies looked as if they were being led to the gallows as long as the manager of the mill could see them, but they complied without any show of resistance, and they all began to babble as soon as the wagon was out of the village. There is a difference, after all, between playing for a mill manager and playing for a count.

A great carousal began in the castle. The fever pitch of their mood is indicated by the fact that it was eleven o'clock in the morning before the party began to break up. As the guests departed, Sigi volunteered to deliver Zia to her door. There were four people in the little roadster; Sigi was at the wheel, with Señor Calandra beside him, and Zia sat in the back with flaxen-haired Elizabeth, who was pregnant. The Calandras were on their way to Ararat for a few days. Señor Calandra was so drunk that he fell asleep at once after climbing into the narrow little car. His face, blue and cleanshaven in the evening but now shaded with bristle, dropped to his chest. Sometimes, his wife confided, he shaved three times a day. Sigi was at the most hectic height of daredevil humor. He shouted orders to himself, choking with laughter the meanwhile. Elizabeth chided him constantly for using expressions inappropriate to the presence of ladies. Zia rested her head on the back of the seat and closed her eyes. She had been drinking heavily for the first time in her life, and was beginning to feel the after-effects. A crooked smile of intoxication was on her lips, and a bitter little pout in the left corner of her mouth as her muddled, careening thoughts retreated from reality. The bitter little pout stiffened and stayed in place. She did not open her eyes even when Elizabeth cried out with fright because Sigi shot the car out of the park with such a burst of speed that the stone pillar at the gate tore the left fender from the car with a great screech. "Hopla-hop!" was Sigi's shrill farewell to the fender as he sped on.

A few seconds later the car was bounding like a rubber ball on the Balaton Causeway, which was as straight as an arrow. The rush of September air sang a dignified if monotonous hymn in their ears. The deep alto of a woman issued from the car radio, singing to jazz accompaniment: *"This is a beautiful day— pam— pam—This is the only, only way—pam—pam—to get ahead!"*

Hurtling at a speed well over seventy, Sigi lifted his hands in the air from time to time, like an orchestra conductor: pam—pam...

No one knew what happened. There was a sharp snap, and the car rose so high in the air that it turned two complete somersaults, first on its lengthwise and then on its breadthwise axis, and then it stopped in the ditch, turning its belly to the sky, showing the gray intestines of its axles and the dark oil of its blood.

A hoarse moan came from beneath the car, from Señor Calandra's chest. No sound came from Sigi or Elizabeth or Zia. A few minutes later Señor Calandra's moans subsided.

Only the radio kept playing. From beneath the overturned car, where shattered human bodies were buried, came the woman's deep alto, somewhat fainter than before but clear in the sudden silence, singing: *"This is a beautiful day—pam —pam..."*

Judging from the warmth of her voice, the singer was a Negress.

Chapter Fifteen

I T WAS the 14th of March, 1935. The Buda hills still wore their caps of snow, but these caps were in rags by now. At the ears of the round-pated hills, and often at the very tips of their heads, tufts of hair peeped from the torn headgear. The woods were beginning to bud, and the cloudy sky hinted here and there at the picture it would exhibit on the first spring day. The first snipe had swept through the purple twilight above the trees of the villas along Fuga Utca, but the air was still damp with the scent of snow.

At around seven o'clock Ursi entered the Gugger Café. Four men were seated at his *Stammtisch,* deep in discussion. Ursi put his heavy briefcase on an empty chair and joined them. He ordered coffee and three eggs in a cup—this was to be his supper.

Now there were five of them at the table: Hámor, Futó, Ormai and Endre Makkosh, the town clerk from Ararat. But there were days when they numbered twenty, and several tables had to be combined. Such groups clubbed together not only in the Gugger Café but elsewhere, with no knowledge of each other, as if in ostentatious display of the Magyar's every instinct for clubbishness and affiliation. These were real Magyars indeed, and anyone observing them closely in that Budapest café—the clientele of which differed not at all from the heterogenous clientele of cafés in Vienna, Prague or Paris—would have seen the splendid traces of Kirghiz, Tatar, Ostyak or Turkish lineaments on their faces, refined with time like pebbles in a brook. But in a period when race theories were common currency, they joined forces for the very purpose of giving race theory the lie, and there were Jewish intellectuals among them, even Hungarians with German surnames. They joined battle over ideologies as if, laying all cudgels aside, they were sitting down to play correspondence chess with opponents who were masters of the game. The greatest fault of their play was that, despite the excellence of (for example) a combination leading to the seventeenth move, they had neither the patience nor the endurance for the intervening steps. There were teachers among them, and artists, country priests and town clerks, scientists and businessmen, even high-booted peasants, who brought their flavorsome idiom and the astonishing freshness of their spirit to the *Stammtisch* like flowers of the field. They were conquerors without more than a university student or two to conquer. They sometimes started audacious little magazines in which every sentence was like the point of a steel bit, magazines with unbelievably small circulation and no life expectancy at all. The intellectual life of officialdom, the literary societies were, in their view, impotent dotards; they considered writers' and newspapermen's clubs to be a slavery to penmanship or the frivolity of irrelevance, and not entirely without reason. Only in men such as these did a religious devotion to human rights still survive; if any ideal of intellect, if any acuteness of instinct was manifest in Hungary during these years, here was where it appeared. There was a certain caution in their lack of organization, for they knew that if they organized openly the right-wing press would cut them to bits, not with its articles—these would not frighten them—but with impressment into the Germanophile army that supported reaction, and with other, even more effective means. At the same time the liberal press—in the hands of wealthy Jews, principally—did not regard them with equanimity either, since they did not consider Jews to be newborn lambs marked for slaughter. In the final analysis, these men were not true revolutionaries; they waved the flag of purest idealism with one hand, but with the other hand they pushed baby carriages, and it was not unknown for their harassed wives, beset with the problem of making both ends meet, to take a voice in their high ideals. Sometimes, to be sure, they tended to incur serious risks.

The Gugger habitués called themselves the "Jánoses," because the majority of their principals were named János: János Hámor, János Futó, János Ormai... They magnanimously forgave the Endres, Mihálys and Ferences who joined the group later for their deficiency in this regard. János Hámor, a teacher in one of the model *gymnasiums* of Budapest, was far above the average intelligence of secondary school teachers. János Futó was accounted an expert in agronomics, and specialized in matters dealing with farm cooperatives. János Ormai devoted his spare time to the practice of gynecology and, apart from the wonderful stories he told about the noblewomen who happened into his office, there was no one more thoroughly versed in the foreign literature of modern sociology.

They were discussing one of the new cabinet ministers, a personal acquaintance of Hámor; he claimed the man was radical in his convictions. Endre—nicknamed Bandi—Makkosh shook his head in disparagement:

"The way he felt five or ten years ago doesn't count! When a man turns minister he no longer thinks with his head but with his bottom, which glues him to the velvet cushion of his seat. I'll bet they'll institute proceedings against him!"

At the word "proceedings" Ursi glanced at Makkosh but said nothing. Everyone knew that proceedings in connection with Ursi's book would involve Makkosh, for if there was any trouble an investigation would easily discover that he had supplied most of the material concerning the Dukay estates. Hámor looked at the bulging briefcase:

"Galley proofs?"

Ursi merely nodded as he sipped the hot, creamy coffee.

"Are you mad at us?" asked Futó, who should have resembled a greyhound, if one could judge by a name that meant "racer"; but he had a great oval head, like all Magyars from Kunság. "We haven't seen you for five whole weeks."

"I've been working."

This was evident on his face, too. His taciturnity and slow movements, were eloquent with weariness. But of all his friends only Hämor knew that there was a reason other than exhaustion for Ursi's state of mind.

"When will the book be out?"

"Thursday."

Futé reached for the briefcase, opened it and took the proofs out. They passed them from hand to hand, examining the sheets as ballistics experts might examine detonators, familiar with the mechanism but not sure of the explosive potential. They made no remarks, Ursi put the proof's back in the briefcase. He was a little ill at ease at the *Stammtisch* right now. He had missed five weeks of their discussions, and felt like a supporting pillar of a house under construction, set in place but unaccountably bypassed when the roof was put on. Large-scale construction is always going on at such restaurant and café tables everywhere in the world, somewhat like the building operations of Princess Oasika, if only in that here too they proceed without materials, pouring a foundation of sheer thought, raising the walls out of temperament, framing a roof of conjecture and inclination—it was like this in the cafés of Paris once, where Mirabeau met with his cronies, or in the Pilvax in Budapest, or in the Swiss café where Lenin's bald head leaned over the chessboard, or in the Steinecker Tavern in Munich, where a soldier of the Second Infantry Division once stood to the left of the door, beneath the stuffed squirrel. There was as yet no way of knowing what roots of history would spring from the nicked marble tabletop in the Gugger Café, but it was indubitable that saber-toothed tigers and behemoths were doing the building here, as in the Brahmanic tale. Here too, perhaps, the edifice would soon collapse,

626

or one fine day the walls and pillars might simply turn offended backs on each other and walk away in different directions, retire behind the baby carriage in a two-room apartment or wander off and start building elsewhere. For the freshly joined walls were already beginning to crack. Only the foundation held them together, the hope of regeneration, the emergence of the Magyar people—but the walls higher up, the walls of the Jewish question, of territorial revision and of foreign policy no longer stood firm, which is why there were cracks at the corners. The four men were now debating the Rome Protocols, but without Ursi, who was absent-mindedly looking out the window. In a little meat market across the way the evening rush for smoked, boiled pig's-ears had begun. Ursi's glance was in that direction, but his thoughts were clearly elsewhere.

Mussolini and Laval had signed the Rome Protocols in January: they denounced Germany's increasing armaments as a treaty violation, and agreed to take the independence of Austria under their joint protection. In the interest of amicable relations with Mussolini, France favored Italy with minor territorial adjustments in Tripoli and Somaliland. Some weeks later Laval and Flandin proceeded to London, where they secured British endorsement of the Rome Protocols and guaranteed the integrity of Austria once again. It seemed certain that the Latin an Anglo-Saxon worlds, under the leadership of Mussolini, had joined forces in firm opposition to the growing clamor of Hitler; and business in the meat market across the street from the Gugger Café was, for the moment at least, in no danger. Hitler had attacked the Soviet Union with undisguised fury in *Mein Kampf,* had made it clear that German expansion was possible only at the expense of the Russians; consequently all doors were closed to him on that side. Now that London had accepted the Rome Protocols, another side of Hitler's plans for an Anglo-British alliance to finish off first the Russians and then the French went up in smoke. What would he do, alone against the whole world? He would shout a little longer, then pull in his tail gradually. This, at least, was the general opinion of the *stammtisch* in the Gugger Café, where the discussions did not lack sober judgement. The group began the break up as the members started for home. Only Ursi and Hámor were left, with neither supper nor family to go home to.

"Have you finished the forward?" Hámor asked, as he wiped his spectacles with his handkerchief. Without spectacles, his face looked as if a mask had been stripped from it, leaving nothing but pale, lifeless human skin. When he put his eyeglasses on, the face reverted to life and filled with wisdom again.

Ursi nodded.

Hámor reached for the briefcase. "May I?"

He took the proofs out and began to read:

The reader will be amazed to see an astrophysicist, after producing a few scientific works of modest dimension, suddenly fling himself at the deepest problems of Hungarian domestic policy. This does not depart in any sense from the wholly cosmic perspective of the author. Let me take a few words to explain what I mean by a cosmic perspective. Neither man nor beast could have come into being without the vegetable world. Only plant are capable of converting mineral substances into comestible matter; indirectly, even carnivorous beasts may be said to live in plants. The gazelle springs from the plant, and the plant from the mineral. Man, lion, cricket, bacillus—in the final analysis, all are *consumers of minerals.* However odd it may sound: we all subsist on celestial bodies. The plant, to convert minerals into food, needs light—which must be sunlight. Unquestionably, our lives depend on the sun. I shall not digress at this point to a discussion of the effect of sunspots, *faculae,* eruptions and prominences of the sun on our appetites, nervous systems, political preferences and many other human characteristics; I merely want to indicate that the known effects of the sun and moon—besides being the source of light and heat, they control the ebb and tide, day and night, the chance and change of centuries—these known effects do not exhaust the influence of the cosmos on terrestrial life. By now everyone has heard of cosmic rays, only recently identified by science. These rays, of wave lengths much shorter than light, represent vast energies that are constantly drenching the earth, penetrating our bones and tissues, like winter winds in the bare branches of the trees. They come from all directions of space; they easily penetrate a layer of lead thirty feet thick; and, according to our present understanding, they can spring from nothing but the endless annihilation of matter at the limitless limits of the universe. This is to say that matter becomes energy; in other words, there are always tremendous explosions taking place in the universe. Stars disintegrate, and we call these stars, which have burst in part or in entirety, *novas* or *supernovas.* Today, in 1935, we know a great deal about the constitution of an atom, but I share the view of nuclear physicists that the atom will not, cannot be split by artificial means, by human agencies, in the foreseeable future.

(Ursi did not know that in the past year, in 1934, a young Italian physicist named Enrico Fermi had already split the first atom in the laboratory of the University of Rome. And how should he have known, when even Enrico Fermi himself did not know what he had done? Had he known, the atom bomb would have fallen into the hands of Mussolini. And what would the Duce have done with it? There is no doubt but that the Mussolini of 1934, who was already composing the Rome Protocols in order to join with the British and the French in curbing Nazi Germany, would have turned toward Hitler first of all with an atom bomb in his hand. The invisible clairvoyant, who has the gift of prescience, is now in a position to disclose his secret to all: it did not happen this way. But why disturb Hámor, who is reading the foreword with his elbows on the table?—while Ursi stares out of the window toward the meat market. We know full well that he does not see the intermittent, watery snow twisting earthward in the light of the street-lamps, but is thinking of the Mandrian photographer, who vanished from his life in a train of fireworks like that of Nova Tycho—the only supernova observed by astronomers up to this point—which was visible in broad daylight when it left the Milky Way.)

When he lays down his complicated instruments, bolometers, actino-meters, pyrheliometers, photometers, his prismatic, grated spectroscopes, knowing that the hundred billion stars of the Milky Way represent but an infinitesimal fraction of the cosmos, the astronomer—when he says farewell to his laboratory, to the clouds of Magellan Major and Magellan Minor, to the constellation of Andromeda, to the clusters of spheres hurtling through space at a distance of hundreds and hundreds of millions of light years; when he sits down to supper with the evening paper in hand—the astronomer cannot help himself if his eyes, his brain and his whole frame of reference regard the tax bill submitted by the Finance Minister, the burglary-cum-murder on Dob Utca, regard even the price of kale in the column of market prices from the viewpoint of the universe as a whole.

This is what I call my cosmic perspective, my cosmic mode of thought. The difference is that only mental powers are at work when I meditate with pyrheliometer or spectroscope in hand, while my contemplation of the destiny of the world, of Europe, of the Hungarian people is mingled with emotional factors, because I survey this destiny not with the brain alone but with my heart as well. Even I, an astronomer, do not have too high an opinion of the human intellect. I cannot, therefore, underrate human impulses that are governed by sheer emotion. At this point I must disclose that I come of peasant stock, and my parents were farm folk. And I must also explain that when I made my first trip to the United States in 1929 I wanted not only to see the Mt. Wilson reflector, which is two and a half meters thick, and the Yerkes telescope, with its one-hundred-and-two centimeter lens, but I also wanted to see my mother. For one of my parents was driven to death and the other into emigration by the oppressive, homicidal system of land tenure in Hungary. My father was a hired hand at first, and then a miner. A man of deep-seated Socialist sentiments, he welcomed the revolution that followed the national collapse. After the failure of the revolution, the new government threw him in prison. One of his fellow miners undertook to liberate him. He was a man famous for his strength; but it is no simple matter to break down a prison gate. Not only were two gendarmes killed as a consequence, but in the struggle and the shooting the very man he wanted to liberate was killed. The miner himself escaped with a bullet in his arm. My mother fled with him into exile in Vienna, where they later learned of my father's death. Thence they went to Texas a few years later, as man and wife. I mention this detail of my personal history only to cast some light on the emotional aspects of my book. Others will regard as prejudice what is, to me, emotion. Perhaps they are right. But if we are to call the emotions prejudicial, then it is prejudice that makes men decide to marry, to put each other in prison, or to write books. To acknowledge this prejudice in myself is not a virtue, but simply the objectivity of an astronomer who is trained to make a conscientious record of every phenomenon that comes to light in the course of investigation with a photometer or a spectroscope.

The fact that, as an astronomer, I submit a book on domestic policy is mainly the work of chance. In the spring of 1933 a book called *Looking Forward* came to hand. It told how the scientists of New York State divided their state into small squares and determined, for each square, its geochemical composition, the nature of its substratum, the behavior of the winds and clouds above the square, how many people inhabited its several square miles, what their occupations were, what they grew, when they settled there, their average life expectancy, their ethnic origins, their birth rate—they examined fifty thousand square miles in this way, square by square. The investigation took fifteen years but was well worthwhile, for this became the only state in the entire world which could claim to know what all other states had failed to discover: itself. Only after finishing the book did I look at the name of its author: Franklin Delano Roosevelt. Since then I have read *Looking Forward* three times through, and I still read it as I used to read the works of Flammarion in my student days. There were other reasons for the interest it held. The population of New York State is twelve million in all. The population of postwar, truncated Hungary is eleven and a half million. I said to myself: instead of letting Hitler's agents employ our jobless university graduates and college students for political demonstrations at a daily fee of one pengö, why should we not apply the Roosevelt method to the territory of truncated Hungary, investigate and define it in exactly the same way? Articles of mine on this subject struck no responsive chord in the government. Undoubtedly, the Magyar aristocracy and the great landowners had every reason to shrink from the thought of letting some American system of squares pry into their secrets.

I have borrowed the title of my book, *The Great Fallow,* from Count István Széchényi, the noble and tragic thinker of our past century whose intellect and whose struggle for reform remind me of no one so much as Franklin Delano Roosevelt. It speaks well for Hungarian aristocracy that I draw my inspiration for an attack on that aristocracy from its own blood, so to speak, although what passed for reform in 1835 naturally sounds completely different today.

The Hungarian fallow: the great Magyar lowlands, all of truncated Hungary. The astronomer in me, who is not entirely unfamiliar with meteorology and geophysics either, knows exactly how much of the two hundred thirty billion horsepower of energy which the sun beams toward the earth is directed at this fallow. Thus, he knows the secret of the world renown enjoyed by Hungarian wheat, Hungarian peach brandy and Tokay wine. He knows the dazzling storehouses beneath the fallow topsoil which that flood of energy upon us has filled, in the course of millions of years, with power in the form of oil, natural gas and boiling water. He knows that this miserable little country paid Italy twenty-one million gold

631

pengös last year for out-of-season produce, for green peppers, for Brussel sprouts or roses from the Riviera, whereas this sum could be applied to the development of the greenhouse industry in Hungary, and every winter we could supply all Europe with out-of-season flowers and produce at one quarter the present cost, for the depths of the earth would provide free heat for these greenhouses, free irrigation, and neither the produce of Italy nor of the French seashore could compete with the flavor and fragrance of the products of our soil. Four million Hungarian peasants on the timberless fallow accumulate dried cow-dung and heat their stoves with this stinking stuff, and in winter they do not dare to open their windows lest the meager heat escape. Result: statistics show that the incidence of tuberculosis in Hungary is the highest in the world. We are sitting on a treasure chest, ten million beggars—we are condemned to die, although thirty million people could live in prosperity on this fallow. It is the Dukays who have pocketed the key to this treasure chest, for a Franklin Delano Roosevelt is a dirty Communist in their eyes. I do not view the Dukays and the ecclesiastical freehold as the murderers of my father; I consider them the murderers of an entire nation.

I have said that the Hungarian fallow is all of truncated Hungary. This must be amended. The Hungarian fallow is the entire world. It is not the great estates of Hungary alone that shrink from a settling of accounts. I have followed, with the liveliest of interest, the activities of American technocrats, who estimate that the industrial power at our disposal in the present state of technological development could assure four billion people a standard of living equal to a monthly income of fifteen hundred dollars at current prices—if only profits were eliminated. I do not wonder that they locked the founder of the technocratic movement, Howard Smith, in a mental institution, I do wonder, however, where mankind will end under the vaunted sanity of its present leaders.

I fear this book will get into the hands not only of those for whom it is intended, those who can still think and dare to think; but it will also reach, much sooner than that, men who will call for the police before they have even finished the book. Following the birth of the French and American democracies, Hungarian thought in the past century was perhaps the brightest of all the little nations of the world; today, one hundred years later, Hungarian thought has been completely straitjacketed by a German corporal who presides, in the form of a journalist, perhaps, or an industrialist, a university professor, a general or a minister, over seventy per cent of our national community; who made a point of attacking our middle classes during the very years when they were weary from loss of blood in a struggle for liberation. An influential segment of our middle classes—influential not only in numbers but in intellectual potency, sobriety, industry, culture and purposefulness—is the German and Swabian element, which sweeps the Magyars along, in most cases, as a minority group; but this is no excuse for the Magyars, merely the medical certification of history. We talk of minority problems, but refuse to recognize this ultimate minority problem of our middle classes. Understandably enough, the spiritual regeneration of Hungary is no interest of this middle class, which is driving its country into the arms of Hitler with such wild fervor. In the eyes of the New Germany, lunatic with race doctrine and a desire for world conquest, we are simply a "racial drawback," and we know by now what prescriptions Berlin has reserved for racial drawbacks. If the feudal freehold of the Church joins forces with this German middle class in Hungarian disguise to wrest the new-hoisted flag of Kossuth from the hands of the Hungarian people once again, then Hungary is lost. Lost, whether at the side of a victorious or a vanquished Germany.

—Budapest: March 15, 1935

Hámor folded the galley proofs, took his spectacles off and proceeded to wipe them carefully with his handkerchief. He did not say anything, but nodded mutely. Every author knows when his work is understood, and Ursi's eyes noted Hámor's nod. He knew what the nod meant, because he knew his friend did not resort to words to express his opinions and emotions at such a time. This was clearly a Japanese trait in Hámor, whose face had a slightly Japanese cast; there is no suitable word in the abundant vocabulary of the Japanese language for a common Western term—love. According to the Japanese, this word never need be pronounced, for when one person loves another the other always knows it. And if it is pronounced, then it is not true. Now they were both staring out the window. The meat market was closed by now. After a long silence Hámor said:

"Three years, I think. Three years in the penitentiary. But for the foreword alone."

Ursi smiled quietly, almost in satisfaction. "Finally I'll have time to write my study of the Great Coal Sack."

"What kind of a coal sack?"

"The Great Coal Sack—that's what astronomers call one of the darkest of the nebulae in the constellation of Cygnus."

They started homeward together, and walked silently side by side. They did not speak even when they shook hands in farewell at the street corner. As always before entering the hallway of his apartment, Ursi groped for the light switch and turned on the light, lest his muddy shoes tread on the mail which the postman might have slipped through the brass slot during the day. Not always was there mail waiting for him. This time there was some. The latest issue of a periodical called *Stars* was lying on the floor, and beneath it was an express letter which he picked up with astonishment. It was in a little square envelope, like envelopes in England, of the richest paper. On its back was engraved a dark blue seal encircled with gilt lettering, and an eleven-pointed coronet above the seal. There are letters which are momentous even in outward appearance. He opened it there in the hallway, hat still on his head.

> *Dear Dr. Ursi:*
>
> *I should be very pleased if you would come for tea tomorrow afternoon, Wednesday, at five o'clock. Teréz Hemli will be here too, who wants to talk to you about a very important matter. Until tomorrow, then.*
>
> *Cordially yours,*
> *Zia Dukay.*

Ursi's knees were so weak that he could hardly reach his room. Once there, he sat on a chair, winter overcoat, hat and all, and read the letter over again. Then he read it for a third time, and then a fourth time. He repeatedly examined the envelope as well to see whether it was really meant for him, since there was an engineer called Sándor Ursi in the adjacent building whose mail was sometimes delivered here by mistake. He examined the date, and the dark blue seal: No. I Septemvir Utca. And he inspected two words over and over again: Teréz Hemli. Then he turned from the letter and stared into the air.

What could this mean? Was it possible that István Dukay had been informed of the attack in preparation for him? If this was so, then the connection was obvious. His mistress, the photographer, had told him she knew the author of the book. And this was István Dukay's method of getting in touch with him. But who was Zia Dukay? The count's sister, or his daughter, or a relative only? The handwriting, gracefully curved from an English pen, seemed youthful. But how had news of the forthcoming book reached the ear of the count? Ursi's suspicions centered on Futó for a moment. But no, Futó could not be that low. Someone at the printshop? One of the typesetters? Lame Jancer, perhaps, who might choose this way to make some money. Poverty is often the greatest traitor.

He threw the letter on the table. The lightning bolt of Teréz Hemli's name had subsided, and only the thunder still echoed in his nerves and his understanding. He could almost hear the photographer's words: "Don't argue, Mihály. Don't be a fool." And perhaps she herself would disclose the sum that the count would be willing to pay for the suppression of the book. In his nerves, in his mind, the thunder mounted. He waited until he was quieter inside, and then went out to the hall, where he hung up his hat and took off his winter overcoat, slowly formulating his reply in the meantime. He returned to his room and sat down at the desk.

My dear Countess: Thank you very much for your kind invitation, which the pressure of other engagements, I regret to say, makes it impossible for me to accept.

Very truly yours,
Mihály Ursi.

He sealed the envelope, addressed it, and retired for the night. He opened his copy of *Stars* and began to read an article on astrometeorology. Later he turned off the reading lamp. But he was unable to sleep much that night. Observing his own symptoms from a meteorological point of view, he noted the incessant alternation of surd lightning and sinister thunder in his nerves and mind.

When he entered his office at the Institute the next morning he rang for the elderly attendant:

"Take this letter to Septemvir Utca. There won't be any answer."

The attendant left, and Ursi, resting his forearm against the wall, closed his eyes. The lightning struck with such dazzling violence at that moment that he leaped to the door and called down the staircase:

"Bring that letter back here, will you? I just remembered something I have to correct in it. No, don't wait, I'll attend to the delivery myself."

Alone once more, he set to work with a calmer and clearer mind. A man is weak only so long as he wavers; only in irresolution does he suffer from his weakness. He had decided to face up to the meeting. An exponent of self-analysis, he did not delude himself about his decision. He lacked the strength to stay away; knowing this, he also knew there was no point in fighting the knowledge. But if a proposition were put to him, he would have the strength to make a fitting reply. His strength for this would derive from what he had called his cosmic perspective. And it would extend to the meeting itself. Teréz Hemli had not made nor exacted a promise of fidelity. The gift of her love in the Pension Zanzottera had been a regal dispensation. She asked nothing in return, not even what stupid little women demand with such concern: eternal faithfulness. No, Teréz was of a much higher order. He might have known that she did not live on her photography, that the ivory cigarette case, the sumptuous luggage, the silver mirror, the clothes and perfumes were not a bequest from some deceased aunt or other. Ordinary photographers do not wear such linen, or have such apple-green eyes, such shoulders, such a captivating fragrance. And then, when the brutal truth came to light unexpectedly, neither the person of Occhipinti the druggist nor even General Hasparics could have caused so much dismay as István Dukay had done. In any event, Teréz was an emancipated woman, and if someone cannot reconcile himself to the concept of emancipated women, then his cosmic outlook is not worth a snap of the fingers. Those few weeks had been beautiful, had been wonderful—blessed be the memory of Mandria and the Pension Zanzottera.

When he entered the gate of the palace on Septemvir Utca at five o'clock, there was neither anger nor sorrow in his heart nothing but the strength of his determination to refuse any proposition they might make. Old Sándor, the doorman with the abundant silver beard, knew of his coming. A footman awaited him at the foot of the stairs, in crimson Hussar livery, with bright black boots and the yellow-braided cape of Maria Theresa's time about his shoulders.

The man's fine, Magyar, mustachioed peasant face hardened Ursi's heart even further. Without a word the Hussar led him up the four-hundred-year-old staircase, which was covered with thick pea-green carpeting. He opened one of the wide oaken doors on the mezzanine and admitted the visitor.

Teréz Hemli, the photographer, stood with arms crossed in the middle of the great salon. This was perhaps the only gesture she had inherited from Countess Menti. She wore a long grass-green evening dress, trimmed with dull gold and with a slight train, the same dress she had worn at Marchese Delfrate's reception. Perhaps she was in evening dress because company was expected for dinner and she did not want to shorten their meeting by the time it would take to change. And perhaps this was only a pretext of hers, for she knew the effect that dress could have.

Ursi stopped in the doorway and bowed slightly. His expression was cordial and friendly, if calm and serious. Possibly a little more serious than he meant it to be. The manner of their meeting had not surprised him. He had been prepared to be greeted by Teréz rather than Zia Dukay, of course, since she was to pave the way for what was to follow. But her face! It seemed only half as large as when he last saw her. And how chalk-white she was!

Thus they gazed at each other mutely for several moments. Then Zia took him by the hand, led him to a chair and sat down beside him herself. Again they regarded each other for a few seconds, and then Ursi spoke, without recrimination in his calm, friendly voice.

"Why haven't I heard from you for so very long?"

"I've been ill," Zia said softly.

"What happened?"

"An automobile accident. There were four of us in the car, the others were killed. My back was broken, and I was in a cast for four months. It was a miracle that I survived at all. I left the sanatorium yesterday morning."

Ursi recalled reading about an automobile accident in connection with the name of Dukay in the papers last fall. Perhaps Teréz had been in that car. He smiled encouragingly at the chalk-white face:

"Thank God there doesn't seem to be anything wrong now."

The eyelids in the pale, emaciated little face closed halfway, and when a quiet, painful smile appeared on her lips a formidable bolt of lightning shivered Ursi's heart, for compassion can sometimes be more fervid even than love. And then he made a grave mistake. But he could not help it—evidently the human soul is truly governed by meteorological laws. A steady pounding of thunder began in his nerves and his brain, and he impulsively blurted out the question that had been on the tip of his tongue for six long months, on his tongue and in his very sinews, the unasked question that had grown inside of him and now broke from his brain, his nerves, his lips without the accord of his intellect:

"What is your lover doing?"

Zia's head snapped up, but only for an instant. This was her first intimation of the fact that Ursi had seen the figure fleeing into her darkroom. What else was there for him to think?

"Which one of the many?" she asked, jokingly but provocatively.

"István Dukay! I happened to be there when his launch left. I recognized him!"

"István Dukay is not my lover," said Zia simply.

The thunder was still uproarious.

"He's only a patron of the arts, perhaps?"

"More than that."

Zia reached for her ivory case. She lit a cigarette, and only after exhaling the first deep puff did she turn back to Ursi.

"István Dukay is my father."

Ursi's face did not move, but grew even more rigid. Slowly, almost imperceptibly, he drew his eyebrows together.

"Are you an illegitimate daughter of the count?"

His question provoked a short laugh from Zia, a mere burst of breath. But the question was well founded. Public opinion took cognizance of István Dukay's illegitimate children—the children themselves saw to that. The lawful Dukay children, and especially Zia, were the only ones who did not know about his illegitimate offspring. Zia placed her hand on Ursi's hand.

"No, Mihály. There's no reason to conceal it from you any longer. I'm not Teréz Hemli, but Zia Dukay. You can understand why I didn't use this name in Mandria. But I had other reasons. I was married to an Italian who deceived me shamefully. I was hurt and ashamed when I went into hiding in the Pension Zanzottera. I wanted to forget everything connected with my former husband. At the same time I waited for him desperately, and suffered a great deal."

Ursi's eyes met Zia's glance for an instant. What she had said, and the necessity of believing it without reservation, was simple and logical.

Zia lit another cigarette. It was evident that these gestures were meant to collect her strength.

"I have returned from very far away," she continued quietly. "I may still seem weak after such a desperate illness. But I am very strong in spirit."

As she paused, and faltered over her words, as she brought the cigarette to her lips with trembling fingers from time to time—all this was in direct contradiction with what she said.

"What, exactly, do you mean?" Ursi asked softy.

"Only once in my life was I ever in love—with my husband. But I know, now, that this was rather impatience and curiosity, as in most young girls. But it no longer matters. That's how I see it today. What I feel for you is entirely different."

Zia realized that she had blundered into a banality. Her own words told her so. She shifted her body as if to flee from the constraint of her phrases, like a swimmer with a cramp in his leg.

"My dear astronomer, don't forget that it is not a photographer who faces you now, but a veritable countess."

This tone, too, was unsuccessful. Zia had strayed too far from the point she wanted to make. This, at least, was what Ursi's face showed. He offered no answer, simply gazed at the rug. For a moment Zia felt bereft of all courage. But this apprehension itself, as it shook her voice, gave her back a humanity that is only rarely made manifest. She raised the back of her hand and studied it.

"This paleness, which is a sign of death, will soon vanish from my hand and from my face. But never, never from inside of me. I want to be happy. And I asked myself: how can I accomplish that?'

Ursi sensed the struggle in her voice, the difficulty of what she wanted to express. And now he interpolated quickly, courageously, simply:

"You want to marry me?"

By way of reply Zia leaned back in her chair, as if in surrender to exhaustion, but with an air of liberation and happiness, grateful for not having had to say those words herself.

Ursi regarded her with consternation. Then he said: "It's completely impossible."

"Why?" Zia asked almost inaudibly.

Ursi raised his hands in bewilderment: "My book!"

"The one you talked about in Mandria? That has nothing to do with the question."

"You don't know what's in my book."

"Whatever may be in your book—an attack on my father—it doesn't matter.

This isn't to say that I underrate your book. But you must understand, once and for all, that I have broken with that world entirely."

Right now the lighting of the room was such that Corot's *Woman in Purple* looked directly at them from the wall. Directly at Zia, that is to say, and with a reproachful glance. A similar reproach was expressed in the four-hundred-year-old pale green tapestries, in the Venetian chandelier, in all the furnishings of the room. It was Zia who spoke again:

"You said you recognized my father when his launch left Mandria. But I don't believe you know any more about him than his face, his mustache, or his figure. I don't mean to defend him by saying this to you."

"My book is not a personal attack on him."

"Don't forget that people in our circle are not especially sensitive to political attack. They've had time to grow accustomed to such things. I had a long talk with my father yesterday. He brought me home from the sanatorium. When we were alone together for a few moments before leaving, he put his hand on my shoulder and said: 'God has given you back your life. I can tell you that the doctors had given you up. Ask me for anything you like—there isn't a thing in the world I wouldn't do for you.'"

"You mean to say that your father will think that way after the publication of my book?"

"That is absolutely certain."

Ursi looked toward the windows.

"Besides myself, there is someone else whose every nerve is set against this marriage." And he added, with a nod: "Someone sitting in the Gugger Café,"

All at once he leaned closer to Zia, as if he wanted to pour his entire soul into an explanation.

"I am that someone. My book will come out tomorrow. It will create a storm of protest. It's absolutely certain that I shall be dragged into court. One of my friends says I'll get three years. I expect it, and I'm prepared for it. Defendants in such political lawsuits are granted an amnesty, sooner or later. I imagine I'll get out, say, in two years."

His eyes froze the words on Zia's lips.

"I go free, and I marry you. The daughter of István Dukay. And I betray the three million impoverished peasants for whom the book was written. That fact can't be explained away. I wouldn't be able to account for it to myself either. There is no doubt but that it would make me completely unhappy.

640

And an unhappy man would be no good to you. Not to mention the fact that the prison gates are waiting for me. It's not impossible that I'll get five years, either."

It was Zia's turn to gaze toward the windows, and she seemed lost in thought. There was a long silence. Zia was the first to speak.

"I have a good income from my photographs. I didn't want to tell you in Mandria—but all the pictures signed Zia Photos are mine. I was afraid I would give myself away if I told you."

Again she was silent, and then she spoke after a few moments:

"Let's go to America. To your mother. I'll wait until you are set free."

Ursi's expression did not change. The quiet little words filled his heart. Finally a skeptical smile appeared on his lips.

"Do you think we could keep it a secret?"

"I imagine so. But suppose we can't? I understand your problem, but its not quite clear whether your conscience belongs to you or to other people!"

Smiling, Ursi raised his eyes to Zia.

"That's not a bad point at all! Let's think about it."

He locked his hands over one of his knees:

"Would we have a conscience if there were no human society about us, calling us to account for certain things? I'm afraid we would not. This leads me to believe that our conscience is not in our own but in others' custody. Someone in the Gugger Café, I said, is completely opposed to this marriage, and that someone is myself. I didn't express it quite clearly. It is not only myself, but my friends, too, sitting at that nicked marble tabletop. And, behind them, the public opinion which would take note of such a marriage. *This* is the voice we call our own conscience. Man is a social creature, and cannot see himself but through the eyes of his friends and of public opinion, for his courage is smaller by far than his vanity. I can hear the voices of my friends quite clearly, and I can see their expressions. Their voices are sarcastic, and their expressions are disillusioned. There's an element of cheap romance in the prospect of this marriage—a spawn of peasants marrying a Dukay countess. There: I had to say it, if only to get it off my chest. Now that it's said, I've regained the courage to see myself with my own eyes, independently."

Zia did not follow the sense of Ursi's words to any appreciable extent. She kept her eyes on the windows while he talked, and her little white face seemed sad. Women are always disconsolate when even a single thought separates them from what they were born for, written as it is in the shape of their bodies and the craving of their souls. She turned back to him and asked:

"What shall we do?"

It took Ursi a few seconds to answer:

"We're going to think."

Then he stood up. Zia stood, too, and gave him her hand.

"When shall I see you?"

"Tomorrow."

"Will you come to my place?"

Zia nodded wordlessly.

"In the afternoon. I'll expect you at five. You know where I live—we used to write to each other, after all."

Ursi started toward the door. Zia accompanied him, and her right hand rested on Ursi's shoulder for that little way. At the door they looked in one another's eyes once more.

Ursi met no one as he descended the green-carpeted old stone stairs. The invisible doorman pressed a button and the heavy gate swung open for him of itself. All this had the quality of a fairy tale right now. A cold wind was blowing in the street. It was about half past seven. He walked, with no idea where he was going. Soon he found himself in front of the Gugger Café. There were at least ten people seated at the *Stammtisch* tonight. Ursi pulled up a chair at Bandi Makkosh's side. The argument was heated, and, as it had done for weeks now, dealt with the Rome Protocols. With the help of ingenious if involved reasoning, they fenced Germany in with Stalin from the east, with Chamberlain from the west, Flandin from the north and Mussolini from the south. When the encirclement was complete, when the ring was closed, they pounced on Hitler and tied a noose on him with a few short phrases. Let him get out of that if he could! There was nothing at all wrong with their reasoning—except that it was logical reasoning. Then they foresaw the dominion of Latin thought in Europe, which would not tolerate the return of the Habsburgs under any circumstances. All this promised an encouraging Hungarian future, and eyes shone brightly. The soaring discourse was interspersed with humorous asides now and then, or an occasional story. When someone set out to prove that the fatuous foreign policy of Hungary was still forging a Berlin-Warsaw-Budapest-Rome axis, Futó remarked:

"Have you heard the latest about Mussolini...?"

Futó leaned toward the center of the table, and the others did too, lest the women playing cards at a neighboring table hear his earthy tale.

They broke out in stormy laughter of varying timbre. The several men contributed laughter of differing pitch, intensity and duration to the storm, which had already subsided in the main when Bandi Makkosh was still gasping for breath. Ursi was the only one who did not laugh, but no one noticed. At the moment he was able to see nothing in the world but Corot's *Woman in Purple,* diffuse in the background, and in the foreground a dress as green as grass, with trimming of dull gold, and a face strangely white, and white shoulders, grown somewhat thin, as they rose from the dress. He put his hand on Makkosh's shoulder.

"Come here for a minute."

They withdrew to another table.

"Do you know Zia Dukay?"

"Of course. I performed the civil ceremony at her wedding. Why?"

"Something to do with my book. But that isn't important now. What do you know about her?"

"She married an Italian prince, about...wait a minute...four years ago. But she divorced him long since. She was in a serious automobile accident last fall. I think she's still in a sanatorium."

This was Ursi's first definite information about Zia's husband. He did not continue the conversation because Futó joined them, thinking they were discussing *The Great Fallow.* Shortly afterward Ursi said farewell and left for home. Why had he called Makkosh aside? What did he want Makkosh to tell him about Zia? Nothing. But he had to find someone to whom he could say her name. He had to say it, for he was bursting with it. Had he not uttered her name his temples would have split open. He took Corot's *Woman in Purple* home with him, like the gleam of a flashlight in the foreground of which was the dull gold trimming of the grass-green dress and the pale little face. The next morning, when he went to his office, this same picture was before him even in daylight.

Zia rang a few minutes after five. She wore heavy-soled sport shoes, on which the mud showed that she had walked all the way. Her face was not as deadly white as it had been the day before. The keen wind had stung her cheeks during the long walk. Ursi took her in his arms and kissed her. He held her thus for a long time. Zia entered his room and looked around. The room was exactly as she had pictured it, yet somehow different. A large globe, at least a yard in diameter, stood before the bookshelves, and the bookshelves covered an entire wall. Those shelves of books said something to her; the yellow-backed French novels were missing, and only a glance was needed to see that this was a technical library. There was a desk beside the window, with several small, obscure instruments. The room contained but one armchair, always a sign of solitude. Zia peeped into the adjacent little bedroom too. We study the rooms, the furniture of those we love with exactly the same searching scrutiny we devote to their families on first meeting. In these two rooms, amid this furniture, these objects, Zia's impression was the same one she had had on the first walk along the water-front with Ursi. She felt the omnipresence of his spirit, and was given a comforting sense of security thereby. Crowded rooms sometimes seem empty, and empty rooms are often crowded. She thought of Filippo's overstuffed room on Fuga Utca. She sat down beside the table.

"Have you been thinking?" she asked, without looking at Ursi.

"I have been thinking," Ursi said a few moments later, as he busied himself with a canister of tea. His lips were strained toward the side on which he was endeavoring to pry open the tin. "But wait, I'll make some tea first."

He plugged in the electric burner. The tone with which he said "I have been thinking" signified that his thinking had led nowhere.

The first copy of *The Great Fallow* was there on the table. Zia took it in her hands and began to turn the pages. Meanwhile Ursi quietly walked about the room, produced cups from a little cupboard, and the spoons tinkled against the china. These little noises—the delicate creaking of the cupboard door, and then the murmur of the boiling water—filled the silence with an incredible sense of life.

Zia glimpsed a chapter entitled "The Dukay Estates" in the table of contents. She opened to that chapter and began to read the section that dealt with the Terézia Domain, for this was her farm, the three thousand acres given to her as dowry. The domain had been named for her when she was born, in accordance with the custom of christening a parcel of land after the newborn child for whom it was destined. While the water murmured in the kettle, Zia read the section devoted to the Terézia Domain:

This domain used to be called Woe Hill, although there is no hill anywhere in the neighborhood. It is a property that lies in the third county of the Ararat range. Its name is of symbolic significance: the woes of its inhabitants have grown to mountain height. I found many such old names connected with the various estates of the great freeholds: Carrion Trough, Pain Dale, Clout Farm, Graveyard Plateau. The proprietors gradually named these Klementina Meadow, Kristina Domain or István Gardens. This is a sort of amelioration by euphemism, as if medical science were to call cancer or tuberculosis Twilight Glow or Rose Petal and let it go at that. The overseer of the Terézia Domain told me proudly that a small house rents for fifteen pengös a year there. This seems in itself to be truly informed by concern for social welfare. But we must not forget that such a mud hut, with its thatched roof, hardly costs more than three or four hundred pengös. And the lessee must contribute twenty-one days of socage, or free labor in addition to the rent. However low the daily wage we take as a standard, this constitutes an annual income of at least twenty per cent on the original investment. And when the Dukays hunt these fields, the two or three hundred ragged beaters do not rattle the cornstalks out of sheer good humor. They are not paid for their services, and they are paying their rent the meanwhile. Furthermore, these tenants may be evicted without notice. I talked with an old peasant who wept as he complained of having been thrown out into the open air with his whole family because they could not pay the excessive rent, although his father and his grandfather had lived there and paid the value of that rickety mud hut at least five times over in the course of seventy years. There was not a single zither or mouth organ in those houses. There was not a single smile, not even on the faces of the children. Consumption, bleak poverty and the smell of death everywhere. And dire curses in every peasant's heart.

Zia was pale and speechless when she put the book down; Ursi had already set out the cups. He was about to speak, intending to say that he had pondered all night without being able to reconcile himself to the thought of emigration to America—for even his mother dreamed of returning home eventually. That was what he meant to say, but before he could begin to speak the teapot in his hand came to a sudden standstill in mid-air, for he saw that Zia was crying. Tears glittered beneath her closed eyelids, and her lips were bent with weeping.

This lent an ugliness to her little face, already marred by illness; the wind-blown flush had disappeared, and her countenance was once more as white as chalk. Ursi did not know what to think of this sudden change in mood. He could not suppose anything but that the few pages she read, leafing through the book, had wounded her after all. For she was a Dukay too. There was no way for him to know that these tears were the divestiture of a human soul.

That very instant Zia arrived at a solution.

But not even Ursi was told of her solution that afternoon.

Chapter Sixteen

"FOR THE doctrine that threatens the world from the East, the doctrine that held sway in our midst for a brief but bloody period, in 1919—... after the downfall of the Monarchy and, with it, of Hungary—this doctrine has not been entirely uprooted from our land. It is nothing less than monstrous, in our view, that a book like The Great Fallow is allowed to appear on the Hungarian market today, in 1935, at a time when truncated Hungary cannot look for an amelioration of her fortunes anywhere but at the side of Hitler Germany. Burglars who are prepared to commit murder if their purposes demand it do not wear a sign saying, 'I Am A Burglar!' And so Mihály Ursi comes in the guise of an insurance salesman, ringing doorbells on the pretext that he wants to insure the lives of the impoverished Magyar peasantry at preferential rates. We are familiar with this hypocritical artlessness of Moscow agents; we have learned to see through the false Kossuth beards that they paste on their chins. These agents, these terrorists, these dynamiters who seek to blow up the edifice of a thousand-year-old nation, to sap the foundations of Christianity and undermine European civilization—these hirelings are equipped with false credentials and forged character references which they can display if the police should sight them as they skulk in the shadows. One of the counterfeit letters of credit in the foreword of Mihály Ursi's book is signed by the man who is currently President of the United States. At the moment it is not within our power to determine the nature of sociographical surveys carried out under his gubernatorial supervision, but this would not interest us in any case, for we are in possession of documents which prove conclusively that both Franklin Delano Roosevelt and his wife are of Jewish origin. The First Lady, born Rebeka Friedenstein, is the daughter of an immigrant horse trader from Volhynia. This book demonstrates just one thing: the solidarity of international Jewry in its opposition to the world order of Christianity. It is an extraordinary and unparalleled audacity on the part of this addle-pated astronomer to refer as he does to the German Empire, with the clear intent of diverting the mounting tide of righteous anti-Jewish hatred and directing it against our German nationals and against Hungarians of German extraction. We too have often expressed our opinion of Hungary's aristocracy and the feudal estates in these columns, which are dedicated to the morality of Europe and the destiny of Hungary. But Mihály Ursi's book is not objective analysis or socio-political comment; it is the fiery wheel of Jewish Communist ideology. And we shall not stand for it. The Hungarian people will not stand for it. It is our hope that the Hungarian Government will not stand for it either, but will finally realize the consequences of its shilly-shallying in matters such as this. The sneaking spirit of defeatism, which occasionally ventures out in open assault, must be uprooted and exterminated. We have had enough! The time has come to act! Videant consules!"

"Absolutely right!" Prince Andrew pounded the table in the lounge of the National Casino as His Excellency Robert Schurler concluded his emphatic rendition of the editorial, which he read as if addressing a crowded political convention, albeit only a few elderly aristocrats constituted his audience. A few minutes later bald heads were bent over ornate sheets of writing paper in the adjacent writing room. The editorial itself was the work of Paul Fogoly, who had recently slipped cable and rowed over to the other side, abandoning his liberal paper and at the same time his lifelong friendship with Imre Pognár; under the potent influence of the editorial the bald heads were all writing letters of congratulation and encouragement to Managing Editor Donáthy-Drexler, under whose orders the unsigned article had been written. Others who remained in the lounge went further. They decided to approach the Regent that very evening and demand a thorough investigation.

The entire right-wing press formed a firing line to greet *The Great Fallow.* The *New Nation* went so far as to assert that Ursi, formerly known as Ungerleider, was the son of an Orthodox rabbi. In the ideological conflicts of those years the word *Jew* was already a formidable cudgel. The upper brackets of the Hungarian middle class had been glad to take this cudgel in hand, ever since the official program of pro-Christian preference began; as popular in recent times as the golf club on the Svábhegy links, it proved easier for them to handle than this latter instrument, and could be used to emboss their own escutcheons of nobility. The members of these upper brackets, who wore discreet little brushes of snipe feathers on their hats and emulated the aristocracy to the point of perfection, considered that they were serving the cause of humanity when, amid protestations of "I'm a liberal, if you please," they came to the defense of their black-nailed Jewish moneylenders or, in the best case, their family physicians. Meanwhile they closed their eyes and swung the cudgel above their heads. The English novelist Galsworthy, who came to Hungary as president of the PEN Club, got his comeuppance too. A club to which the fashionable gentry belonged discreetly finessed the honor of his visit with a confidential communiqué to the effect that the club, to its greatest regret, was unable to receive Jews. Pognár had sufficient sense of humor to pass the announcement on to Galsworthy, who roared with laughter and slapped his knees when he read it. This was easy for him, since he was English and had a return-trip ticket to London in his pocket. Probably the Roosevelts would not have taken it to heart either if a copy of Managing Editor Donathy-Drexler's newspaper had fallen into their hands. But there were those in Hungarian public life who felt the full force of this cudgel on their heads, and if they did not drop dead at once it at least left a mark—even at the *Stammtisch* in the Gugger Café there was someone who asked, apologetically but with a hint of disillusion, whether it was true that Ursi had changed his name from Ungerleider. Human nature is credulous and susceptible to suspicion, wherefore the marks of the cudgel were to become ominous brands in later years.

The liberal press, whose wealthy Jewish proprietors and well-paid editors were beginning to live in fear of a government ban, acknowledged the appearance of *The Great Fallow* with doorway reviews—Aha, there's shooting going on, let's hide in the doorway. These papers, with vast circulation, demonstrated their implacable courage in phrases like this: "The tax policy of the government threatens the interests of domestic industry and commerce..." "We must spare no expense in the drive to wipe out tuberculosis..." "Charlie Chaplin is marrying for the fourth time..." They resembled the caftaned Jew whose only weapon was a broad smile when a burglar approached him and his family with a kitchen knife in hand, and who supplemented his broad smile with the statement: "Well, well, my dear Mr. Burglar, and how are you today?"

Newton had no idea that his law of gravitation would apply to the public press: the circulation of a newspaper varies in direct ratio with the square of its cautiousness. Only the papers called *Frontier, Pillar* and *Accusation* dared to take a stand on Ursi's side. And the trouble with these papers was that they exaggerated the affair. Their hearty and muscular handclasp always left its recipient out of breath and shaking his fingers ruefully. *The Great Fallow* raised a considerable dust, but this dust did not rise from the great fallow itself; at best, it came from tables in castles, casinos, editorial offices and cafés, and these are known to be relatively dustless in the main. Adalbert, the gold-painted little elephant in the Andalusia Club, took no cognizance of Ursi's book, nor did the peasant carts creaking in the mud show an awareness of its existence as they carried manure into the Asiatic air of the Hungarian puszta for spring ploughing.

A telegram from the Ministry of Culture, suspending him from his position, did not surprise Ursi. He was so certain it would come that he had taken clothesbrush, towel and soap home from the office on the previous day, for beyond these items there is hardly anything else that binds civil servants to their government bureaus. It seemed that the visit of the National Casino to the Regent was beginning to bear fruit, for Ursi's book was banned three days after publication and the Prosecutor General, urged on by the furor of the press, instituted proceedings against the author. In the course of those days Ursi met Zia only around eveningtime, when they had supper together in little restaurants. He would not allow her to go to his apartment, for he expected eventual searches, and it would not have been pleasant for either of them if detectives found Zia on the premises. His doorbell rang all day long. Friends came, all those who frequented the *Stammtisch* in the Gugger Café, some of whom returned from the country to attend the trial, and they entered his hallway as if it were a hospital where they were visiting a relative who had been hit by a trolley. And unknown, fantastic characters appeared, bearing fat manuscripts which showed evident signs of having been thrown, together with their authors, out of countless editorial offices in the past ten years. Elderly women of peculiar demeanor came, practitioners of astrology who carried foolproof prescriptions for the redemption of the world in their midwife's satchels. An overseer, fired from one of the great estates, offered to furnish supplementary evidence against his former employer.

It usually takes months for such political cases to pass through police interrogations and magistrate's court and arrive at the date set for trial. In this case, however, it was obvious that proceedings were accelerated on orders from above. They wanted to remove all traces of *The Great Fallow* from public view as soon as possible, as if it were a hissing, dangerous bomb. Only a few days after a police interrogation Ursi was already in the chambers of the public prosecutor for preliminary inquiry. If there was any satisfaction for Ursi up to this point of the affair, then the public prosecutor himself provided it, a dry, taciturn man who hammered out his questions as if dealing with an opium smuggler or a bicycle thief, but somewhere in the background of his words there was a faint glimmer that said: We're brothers, you and I. The more concealed such an intimation is, the more beautiful its meaning. Political defendants in suits

650

of this nature did not always have reason to fear the members of lower courts.

The trial was set for the middle of April. Apart from the reporters, there were hardly more than thirty people on the benches of the little courtroom on that rainy spring morning. There were several young men who looked like university students of the more penurious sort. Imre Pognár sat among the journalists. He nudged his neighbor, old Halászi.

"What's the name of the defendant?"

"Don't you even know that much? Mihály Ursi."

Pognár shook his head. "He's not the defendant!"

"Then who is?"

"The President of the United States."

He leaned back on the bench, stretched out his legs and plunged his fists in his pockets.

"I'm curious to see how the Hungarian courts will dispose of the ideals that dominate this twentieth century."

At the end of the front bench, somewhat apart from the rest of the spectators, sat two elderly, well fed, sun-tanned gentlemen, whispering behind their palms. They were the emissaries of the agricultural associations, sent to represent the great estates at the hanging. A young woman wearing dark glasses sat on the fourth bench: a university student, judging from her clothes, or a newspaperwoman. No one would have recognized her as Zia. On the defendant's bench, cool and calm, sat Mihály Ursi. Press photographers were unable to attend, partly because a new Minister of the Interior was being sworn into office and partly because the christening of a film star's first-born child kept them away. The atmosphere of the half-empty little courtroom, the rain dripping blackly beyond the windows—these were clear indications that the ideals harnessed by the "addle-pated astronomer" lay outstretched on the muddy pavement, like a fallen hack horse.

Everyone was speculating on the probable severity of the sentence. Behind their palms the two whispering mouths agreed on five years. The reporters and the members of the *Stammtisch* wavered between two and three years. Old Halászi, for forty years a court reporter, considered it a pointless discussion, for the final decision in this suit would surely rest with the higher courts. Pognár offered to wager that the defendant would be acquitted. Old Halászi excitedly reached for his wallet, which was bloated with passes and pawn tickets. He peeled off a ten-pengö piece folded with geometrical precision and placed it on the bench as on a baccarat table. His gesture was an acknowledgment that no one would sit down to play with him except for ready cash. Pognár rather hoped to lose the wager, for by this time his play, *Children Grow Up*, had achieved considerable success in Vienna too.

The Court filed in. The prosecutor and the counsel for the defense took their places on the tribunal. A correspondent for one of the liberal papers, fat Bajomi, who had not taken part in the preceding discussions, sat with an expression which seemed to indicate that he knew something in advance, and this was not entirely impossible, for he was the brother-in-law of the prosecutor. The presiding justice opened the proceedings, his resolute voice cautioning the spectators that he would clear the court if they indulged in any demonstrations of approval or disapproval. It was as if he were warning the hack horse outstretched on the muddy pavement neither to break into a gallop nor to run over the approaching trolley. The only sound from the public benches was the half-swallowed yawn of fat Bajomi.

The trial took barely an hour. The preliminary personal data were quickly taken in evidence, not without the presiding justice's reproof of the accused: Take your hand out of your pocket! Experience shows that it is generally the defendants with clear consciences who put their left hands into the side pocket of their jackets. Murderers stand at rigid attention before the bar. After such a magisterial reproof, a grown man feels as if he had been ordered back into his childhood. Ursi obediently carried out the presiding justice's unfriendly command, but there was a certain sadness about the movement of his hand when it issued from the pocket and fell to the side of his jacket, as if the hand had been shamed into disgrace by the punishment. All this was reflected in the dark glasses of the woman on the fourth bench. For an instant Ursi thought of his book entitled *Cosmobiology*, which had appeared in England too and was said by the *Times* to be one of the most distinguished works of modern astronomy.

The prosecutor took the floor to deliver the indictment. He seemed a young man, a brown, Magyar individual, but prematurely bald. His thin face was practically a signed testimonial to the difficulties of an attorney with three small children in managing on a wretchedly meager government salary. He did not prolong his remarks, but snapped them forth, hard and dry, in terse sentences. By dint of considerable exertions Hungary, battered by the World War, had achieved a nationwide state of peace and security, which was also a guaranty of tranquil progress. The Government had no holier responsibility than to defend this propitious condition of the commonweal, won at the cost of much sacrifice, against all attempts at subversion. The book in question was prejudicial to the interest of national foreign policy, adopting an offensive tone toward the German Empire, a supporter of Hungary's revisionist aspirations with whom the nation was on the friendliest terms. The State asked that the accused be severely punished.

Kadar, a member of the Gugger Café *Stammtisch* acting as counsel for the defense, was a short man of about forty, with pince-nez, whose aspect and voice faithfully preserved the jurisprudential atmosphere of a past century which he had absorbed, out of sheer respect, from the formerly famous chief justice he had served. There are men completely modern in thought who, for reasons known only to themselves, persist in wearing gaiters. Kadar carved his words out with care and his *r*'s crackled as crisply as if, in his oratorical gesticulations, he were manipulating an invisible little nutcracker. His pleasant, deep voice lacked neither vehemence nor ardent devotion to the matter at hand; the only trouble was that he occasionally wandered far afield, and when, in depicting the condition of the poverty-stricken Hungarian peasantry, there was occasion to refer to the hardships of gaining an education, he expressed such a concept as the mid-term report card thus: The testimonial letter which bears witness to the educational achievements garnered in the course of the first half of the scholastic year. The language of Hungarian jurisprudence was capable of incredible accomplishments in this vein, for the academic texts themselves were couched in such terminology. It was considered a capital crime to express things simply, briefly and understandably.

The Court retired to consider a verdict. Conjecture began again along the benches of spectators. The young woman with dark glasses on the fourth bench heard talk of three years, two years, and, ominously, of five years if the case went before the higher courts. The possibility was mentioned that the accused might be placed under provisional arrest at once. She tried to imagine what these years would be like. The two of them, she and Mihály, had given this prospect a great deal of discussion, like moribund invalids in the contemplation of death. These two, three or five years seemed like a sample cut from an endless bolt of black cloth. She had spent three years in Mandria, and now, as she looked back, they did not seem so very long. She already knew that prisoners were permitted to see visitors once a week. And the political situation might change, too. She had one thought which she did not tell Mihály: she envisioned her father in the Regent's room, requesting an amnesty for Ursi.

The Court filed in once more and took its place on the tribunal. A great stillness filled the room, as it does at a gambling table when the stakes are high, just before the dealer turns over the last card. The presiding justice rattled off long paragraphs to which no one paid attention. Finally he came to a phrase which suddenly filled the room like an explosion:

"One year in prison!"

There was a buzz of voices. About twenty or twenty-five throats called out:

"Long live the Hungarian courts!"

The presiding justice's pencil rapped with exasperation, and once more he threatened to clear the courtroom of spectators, as if the voices had shouted: Down with the courts! And his threat was rendered even more meaningless by the fact that the performance was over, and almost everyone was starting toward the doors. The owners of the two whispering hands cast disdainful smiles at the cheering optimists, as if to say: Just wait till we hear what the higher court has to say! Meanwhile the presiding justice proceeded to the confirmation of the sentence. The murmur of voices continued.

"Are you satisfied with the verdict of this court?" the presiding justice asked the defendant.

Ursi glanced toward the counsel for the defense, as they had agreed, and the latter nodded vigorously.

"I am satisfied."

The presiding justice turned toward the public prosecutor and old Halászi, who could almost hear the prosecutor's mechanical response, "I appeal the sentence of this court for want of commensurate severity—" old Halászi had already risen from his seat and was left hanging in air, for the prosecutor stood up and said briefly:

"I am satisfied."

The members of the Court, and even the counsel for the defense, turned to look at the prosecutor, as if they had misunderstood him. But the prosecutor was already gathering his documents. Again a buzz broke out among the spectators. The presiding justice spoke the two words that closed the case and retired, in the company of his associate justices. Everyone in the audience sprang up again, but nobody moved from the courtroom. Only fat Bajomi disappeared on the instant, as if in fear that his fellow journalists, who knew he was related to the public prosecutor, would storm him with questions.

The spectators began to congregate in groups before the tribunal. For a few moments Zia was left alone among the benches and, lest she be conspicuous, she walked through the barrier and stood behind the debaters. The loud, agitated discussion told her only that the public prosecutor had done something unusual by resting his case, contrary to orders from above, in the face of so light a sentence. When both the State and the defendant expressed their acquiescence, the verdict became final; therefore the prosecution's acquiescence had snatched the case out of the hands of the higher courts. There was every likelihood that Ursi would have come up before Justice Surányi, formerly known as Schurler, a younger brother of Robert Schurler. He was a fearful jurist, who despised any vestige of left-wing sentiment. Ursi would hardly have escaped with less than five years under his jurisdiction.

The two hands had fallen from the whispering lips. Speechless and stricken, the two emissaries of the great estate stood apart from the arguing groups. To them, it was quite clear what had happened: the State's artillery had missed fire. It was a clear and ominous sign that the mechanism of social order was out of joint.

The reporters and lawyers were discussing the probable consequences. Old Halászi declared that there had only been one such case in all his experience, in 1898, when Bánffy, the Minister, instituted a libel suit against a newspaperman of the opposition. What would happen now? Disciplinary action would be taken against the prosecutor—that much was certain. But no, even that was not certain, for an investigation would bring to light the underhanded instructions from above, and this revelation would only impair public confidence in the alleged impartiality and independence of the courts. What would happen to the defendant? The Minister of Justice could order a retrial, but this would be in contradiction to the original purpose, which was to clear all traces of the case from public view as soon as possible. The left-wing reporters freely engaged the right-wingers in controversy, for in those years their differences in international outlook had not yet disturbed their friendships, either on their official rounds or at the card tables. Finally they came to the conclusion that the case would have no aftermath. Pognár began to shout:

"No aftermath? Are you crazy? This trial is going on all over the world!"

Zia and Ursi had agreed not to meet in the courtroom. Before she left the chamber they exchanged a little smile. Standing before the tribunal, Ursi was still deep in conversation with the defense counselor.

The press scarcely noted the Ursi affair. Interest in the question suddenly

655

subsided, for much more interesting discussions were under way at the conference tables of Europe. It was in these days that England and France, at the instigation of Mussolini, convened at the second Stresa Conference. The conferees sharply condemned Germany's abrogation of those clauses of the Versailles Treaty which limited the German armed establishment. Momentarily this gave pause to the Germanophile press in Hungary, which was dependent, after all, on the government. And the government was beginning to cast its eyes toward England. As a result, Goering, the Commissioner for Prussia, hastily journeyed to Hungary, and his efforts to bedazzle the statesmen of Hungary with a glittering display of uniforms were not entirely without result. At that time he was already a passionate collector of the highest German military ranks and titles, some of which he created for his own use, and he ordered a uniform of distinctive color and cut for each and every capacity. At breakfast, decked in the green and silver uniform of the Chief Forester of the German Empire, he discoursed on Czechoslovakia, which had just entered into a military alliance with the Soviet Union, and a half hour later, wearing the brown and crimson appurtenances of a Field Marshal of the German Empire, he explained how, under his direction, the German Air Force had been expanded to such a degree of striking power that it could blow England off the face of the earth in a matter of days.

The twists and turns of international affairs provoked complete confusion in the minds of men. By now it was entirely impossible to know what was afoot and what was to follow. England, in June, signed a naval agreement with Germany, which fostered an increase in the German battle fleet. At the same time the British Foreign Secretary, hoping to bring about a settlement of the Abyssinian conflict, offered Italy a plan for territorial adjustment which Mussolini refused with the statement that he was not in the habit of accumulating deserts because he had no warehouses in which to dispose them. In August the United States passed the Neutrality Act. Occasionally, and for weeks at a time, the white man's world seemed to be a fixed star, for all that it was hurtling toward destruction; and even the wariest industrialists entered into long-term contracts. No historiographer will ever be able to determine in what mysterious ways Laval's Italophilous policy, for example, or the resignation of the MacDonald Cabinet, or the state of the Hungarian Prime Minister's health, may have influenced such a matter as the Ursi case. The fact is that Ursi, together with a number of other political prisoners, was unexpectedly granted an amnesty at the end of September, although he had barely begun his study of the Great Coal Sack, which is one of the darkest nebulae in the constellation of Cygnus. Zia visited him once a week during his more than four months of imprisonment.

✦

A few days after his release Ursi received the following letter on the stately letterhead of *The Central Administrative Office of the Dukay Estates:*

My dear Sir:—

On behalf of His Excellency Count István Dukay I write to request the honor of your presence on Thursday, the 11th inst., at six o'clock in Ararat Castle. Your train will arrive at precisely ten minutes after five. I shall be waiting for you at the station with a carriage. The train to Budapest will leave at two minutes after nine on the following morning. Accommodations will be ready for you in the Castle, and His Excellency will be pleased to have your company at supper. I am, Sir,—

Respectfully yours,
Dr. Joseph Egry-Toth
King's Councilor,
Estate Agent

And on the appointed day, with a dustcoat over his arm, a gentleman of about sixty in a light gray suit walked up and down in front of the tiny Ararat railroad station which, with its window boxes of hollyhocks and petunias, stood beside the rails as if it were of a piece with the castle itself. The station had been built by the estate, obviously, for it bore no resemblance whatever to the depressingly bleak installations of the National Hungarian Railways which mirrored the chagrin of building contractors because they were unable to exact sufficient graft on government construction. The charming little station at Ararat was a whistle-stop which had given the castle-dwellers abundant service in the past century; but since Mr. Daimler's invention of the automobile the station had been relegated to the servants, like an out-of-fashion water pitcher. Nowadays it served, besides the staff, only the visitors who did not own automobiles, generally the ones whose duties alone brought them to the castle. Here it was that Mr. Husnik, the barber from Buda, arrived every two weeks during the summer months to

657

apply the tools of his trade to Count Dupi's hair. He always alighted from the train with a little black bag in hand, like a prominent medical practitioner. Here the tradesmen made their appearance, the tailors and bootiers summoned from Budapest, and the book salesmen who, dressed as aristocrats, were ready to climb the high stone wall around the park if need be to gain access to the castle, and it was always Mr. Gruber who successfully repulsed such attacks, for the castle abhorred modern Hungarian literature. Train-borne visitors were met at the station by the Lipica four-in-hand, harnessed to a coach that looked like an historical treasure—the very same coach, in the days when railroad lines were still at a considerable distance from Ararat, used to speed its passengers toward the capital, but nowadays it only served to bridge the two miles between the station and the castle.

The elderly gentleman who was waiting at the station opened the gold watch at the end of his heavy watch chain and noted that the train should already have arrived, but the attendant said it was ten minutes late. He continued his monotonous stroll, while the thoughts flitted over his face as if they had settled below the skin. Occasionally his eyebrows twitched, and his lips moved as if he were engaged in a debate with himself. It is not difficult to recognize him for Joseph Egry-Toth, the estate agent of the Dukay holdings. He had the handsome masculine bearing of well-to-do Hungarians, although his figure was somewhat lumpy by now as a result of overeating. In stockbreeders' terms, one might have called him "blooded," insofar as he retained the pleasant, oriental brownness of the Magyar race, the substantially hooked nose and the strong lines of the mouth. It was only by way of atavism that he occasionally twirled his mustache, for he wore that adornment in English style. At such times the lentil-sized diamond ring on his little finger glittered, in a setting of crescent hairs. And the large, extravagantly large sky-blue seal ring came into view, betraying a certain insistence that the world should not forget, even for a single moment, that the gentleman agent stemmed from the Egry-Toths of Tótfalu and might have become a chamberlain of the imperial court, which rank stands above any mere baronetcy, had his maternal grandfather not happened to be a tanner in Debrecen. Egry-Toth belonged somewhere in the middle ranks of Hungarian gentry. Among the Egry-Toths there was a renowned painter, all color and flame, and a general, famous in farflung lands for his stupidity, and several minor government officials who wore their brains and their moral stature on their seal rings, in miniature. He himself was a member of the board of directors of the Commonwealth Casino, and this position was an exact definition of his standing in Hungarian society. The National Casino was the stamping ground of counts, an amalgamation of the interests of the large landholders and a train trailing from the royal throne. The Commonwealth Casino was a retreat for the nostalgia of those who were unable to gain admittance to the National Casino. For want of a community of interests, the members bobbed and bowed before the aristocracy, viewed inferior social classes with aristocratic disdain, maintained an air of unreserved charm among family and friends, behaved with arrogance and rudeness in their barracks and offices, and considered the very existence of their subordinates to be a personal insult. In general, they abhorred all work and every sort of intellectual exertion. The rare exceptions served only to point up the historical quagmire of their origin, which belched forth sword-rattling officers, loud-throated pseudo-patriots and minor titularies who waxed fat on the feudal traditions of communal life in Hungary. During these years there was hardly another human type in all Europe which lurked in so sycophantic a fashion on the fringes of economic well-being and social rank; the Polish nobility was perhaps its single competitor, and it was no accident that such fellows in fate donned each other's clothes. The ankle-length, tight-waisted suede overcoats that were known as "Polish coats" became a familiar sight in the streets of the capital after the war. Polish noblemen wore this same coat, but called it a *bekecs,* after a magyar potentate of the age of Báthory; this, at least, was the explanation offered by Izvolsky, the Polish Ambassador, at one of the Dukay dinners.

The estate agent, too, had such an overcoat, and—exceptionally—he had an eighteen-hundred-acre farm, splendidly equipped, to go with the coat. If Joseph Egry-Toth's eyebrows twitched and his lips moved as he strolled up and down, it was because he had that farm in mind at this very moment. When Count Dupi issued the order for Ursi's invitation, he violated no confidence in telling the estate agent, who was privy to the innermost secrets of the family, that his daughter Zia wanted to marry the astronomer. And that was all he said. But after twenty-six years of service the count's taciturn face was like an open book to Egry-Toth.

While waiting for the train, Egry-Toth tried to picture the meeting between István Dukay and Ursi, a meeting which he too—for reasons as yet unknown— had been ordered to attend. But the prime reason was not altogether unknown, after all: he would play the part of a witness. The astronomical adventurer would be paid off and booted out. It was not the first time a noblewoman had been seized

659

by such an idea, which usually ended as another expense for the estate coffers. In his imagination, Egry-Toth could almost hear the precise words by means of which Count Dupi—politely, quietly, delicately, but with deadly hauteur—would break the jailbird astronomer on the wheel. This was something, surely, at which István Dukay was eminently skillful.

The minutes passed, and Egry-Toth awaited the train with increasing stage fright. It promised to be an awkward meeting from the very first moment. This man had made especial mention of the estate agent's person in *The Great Fallow,* posing the query: How had Joseph Egry-Toth, formerly an impoverished prefectural assistant, put his hands on an eighteen-hundred-acre farm? Egry-Toth knew the passage in question by heart, for his brain, afire with fright and fury, had photographed the printed letters at first sight, together with all punctuation marks and interlinear space. And since the appearance of the book he had recited this passage to himself daily, whether seated in the tub or squatting on the W.C., before falling asleep or even while working in his office, where he often turned tail on callers and retired to his room to repeat the passage half aloud, always with the blind hope of finding a word which would change its entire meaning, so incredible did he deem it that these lines had come to light. The passage went like this, word for word:

If Egry-Toth purchased this eighteen-hundred-acre farm out of his salary as estate agent—always supposing that he set his salary aside annually for this very purpose—then he must have been in service for no less than one hundred thirty-five years so far; but this is unlikely, for according to the Agricultural Almanach the gentleman is only sixty-two years old, and has served the Dukay estates for no more than twenty-six years. There is no evidence that this remarkable estate agent ever inherited a fortune or won first prize in a lottery. His personal life is of the highest repute, he neither drinks nor gambles; therefore he could not have won the wherewithal at cards. How did he acquire his eighteen-hundred-acre farm? This is a problem that has troubled His Excellency the Count least of all, for it is common knowledge that he has no sense of proportion in financial matters. Possibly the count himself, in a good-humored moment, made a gift of this farm to his favorite estate agent—this is something that only István Dukay could confirm or deny. And if it was not a gift, then the origins of this considerable property are somewhat obscure, to say the least—not even in Hungary do eighteen hundred acres fall from the sky. We mention all this—the vast demands of a stillborn legitimist press, the industrious activities of various members of the family at gaming tables abroad, and the ridiculously brazen, light-fingered gropings of socially glorified thieves, whose hands are not altogether clean—we mention all this merely by way of parenthesis, to show how the Dukay resources were dissipated at the same time that, according to statistics gathered in the two decades before the war, eight hundred twelve Hungarian peasants within the Dukay domains took their walking sticks in hand and shouldered their dismal bundles and emigrated abroad, family and all, saying a final farewell to the land which their fathers once occupied under Ordony leadership, the land for the defense of which they gave their blood over a period of centuries, shielding it against Tatar and Turk and Teuton. All this may be taken to demonstrate how inequitably the Hungarian fatherland distributes its favors among the children of a thousand years.

After the appearance of the book Egry-Toth had sought the advice of the foremost libel lawyer, in the evening hours, lest someone see him in the waiting room. He discussed his problem in the tone that an elderly, distinguished family man might use in consulting a physician about incipient venereal disease. The lawyer, after hearing the facts, advised him not to file suit, explaining that in such cases Hungarian civil procedure generally made defendants of the plaintiffs. That very evening Egry-Toth entered a sanatorium, not entirely without reason, for the lines cited above caused this one-hundred-ninety-pound worthy, who was extremely sensitive to matters of Casino honor, constant attacks of high blood pressure. While in the sanatorium, Egry-Toth had his gallstone taken out, and since then he carried the gallstone, as large as a pigeon's egg, inside his waistcoat pocket in tissue paper, and showed it to anyone who would look. This was his way, perhaps unconsciously, of trying to create sympathy for a sick old man who was subjected to such a brutal attack in the twilight of an honorable lifetime. And marks of illness were actually manifest on his face, for he often started up from the depths of sleep, wondering whether István Dukay would, after all, begin to think about the origin of the eighteen-hundred-acre farm. But he reassured himself, remembering a scene before the war when Count Dupi, at the end of a lavish hunt supper, offered ten florins to the famous gypsy primás who had been hired, together with his band of twenty, from Budapest. The primás began to mutter, explaining that their travel expenses alone had come to forty-two florins. Count Dupi nodded in agreement, produced the little key that dangled from his then fashionable long, thin gold chain, opened the Wertheim cabinet and gave the primás, uncounted, a bundle of more than forty thousand florins. He did all this with complete sobriety, without the flicker of an eye, and his gesture had the simplicity which alone is capable of creating legends. No, the count was without sense of proportion in matters of finance, although in the past few years he had begun to be decidedly closefisted, and Egry-Toth had even seen him perform the elaborate operations of addition with saber-shaped columns of figures in the estate accounts, something he had never done before. And there was a further threat in view. Count Dupi was sixty-seven years old and it was suspected that his heart was ailing; there was no way of knowing what sort of views Count György, heir to the entail, would bring home from America, where there were said to be adding machines which took into account even the congenital weakness of Hungarian aristocracy at arithmetic.

The mild, sunlit autumnal breeze of afternoon wafted a fragrance of hay from the direction of the meadows, and the diligent puffing of the estate tractor could be heard from behind a more distant acacia grove. The train was in sight, but as yet it seemed like a matchbox on the straightaway, at the vanishing point of the rails that flamed with sunlight as they fled into infinity.

Egry-Toth endeavored to prepare his expression for the encounter. Ursi himself had admitted, in the foreword of his book, that he came of peasant stock. And Egry-Toth belonged to the type of peasant-haters who handled the peasant as if he were a primitive brute whose latent irascibility, whose physical and moral abominations had to be taken into account. Egry-Toth knew that a well-timed slap, properly administered, was of more value in dealing with a peasant than any argument or explanation, and he had availed himself of this knowledge more than once, unaware of the unrestrained wrath and strength with which these casual head-splitting slaps would strike back, at a historically opportune moment, after centuries of silence; for Egry-Toth, like so many of his fellow men in Europe who deserved a better fate, was still unfamiliar with the laws of cause and effect. In social intercourse Egry-Toth was a pliable, soft-spoken and—as some people asserted—almost cloyingly sweet-mannered individual, and this, according to the observations of certain psychologists, always bespeaks the inner rages and rudenesses of a repressed soul.

The train came to a halt and a single passenger dismounted, who could be no other than the astronomer. He arrived in a simple dark gray suit, with a wide-rimmed black hat on his head, an overcoat on his arm and a tiny overnight case in his hand. Egry-Toth had not anticipated so lithe a figure, with such broad shoulders and high temples. He had expected a bull-necked, round-headed, bespectacled spawn of peasantry, with a spyglass or a scroll under his arm—for countesses were, after all, incalculable in their choices. Countess Ella, too, had thrown herself away on such an impossible character, if only for a short time, when she married the attorney in Temesvár.

They started toward each other simultaneously, and introduced themselves. Egry-Toth's experienced eye ascertained that the visitor's suitcase was too small to contain a dinner jacket, albeit a dinner jacket was *de rigueur* at Dukay suppers, even when they ate by themselves. Egry-Toth took cognizance of the missing dinner jacket with quiet, malicious glee. In the interest of historical accuracy we must remark that Ursi's sense of social refinement was really deficient on this score, for it was the first time in his life that he was expected for supper at a count's table.

"Did you have a good trip, Professor?"

Egry-Toth had decided on this form of address while waiting for the train, if only because it was the title applied to every tennis coach, riding master or language teacher who came to the castle, and to Mr. Badar as well. The four-in-hand carriage stood ready for them outside the station, and the fleshy, apple-gray Lipica horses, their coats gleaming, were impatiently rattling the silver bridles. On the perch sat a stiff-backed Hungarian coachman with long mustachios, wearing a heavily braided blue and red dolman, but instead of a ceremonial ostrich-plumed black coachman's hat, decorated with wide, flowing ribbons at the back, he wore a round plainsman's hat trimmed with feathergrass, the prescribed headgear for all Dukay coachmen. The carriage flew toward the castle noiselessly, and the only sound was the beat of hoofs, like the patter of rain.

"I am exceedingly sorry," Egry-Toth began the conversation, "that I've had no opportunity as yet to read your well-known book, Professor. Unfortunately we farming folk live at a great remove from literature. Have you never been to Ararat before?"

"Not in the castle," said Ursi, thinking of his stay in Bandi Makkosh's house four years previously, when with notebook in hand he explored the surrounding countryside, incautiously enough to arouse the suspicion of the gendarmerie, who allowed him to proceed only upon learning that he was a guest of the town clerk.

The spectacle that came into view upon their entrance into the park, like a vast operatic backdrop projected into space, never left even those visitors unmoved who were accustomed to the sight. The wrought-iron gates standing open at the end of a row of ancient lime trees; the gilt spearheads mounted atop the wall; the gatekeeper in livery that harked back to the age of Maria Theresa; the cathedral-like canopy of branches in the park itself, and beneath it the carefully trimmed English lawn, so sleek that the rare dry, black faggot or the occasional brown leaf which it sometimes wore seemed to be placed with an eye to aesthetic effect; and the rolling roads, smooth with yellow sand; the birch-railed bridges over the brook, and then the wide, cream-green, waterlilied expanse of the fishpool; the Chinese pagoda, the weeping willows and the hazels, the long-armed Methuselah chestnut trees, resting their branches against the ground like giant gorillas; and then, suddenly, the castle, its ill-omened dimensions outspread on the open plateau, a strange ocean liner run aground on Mount Ararat, truly reminiscent of Biblical scenes. Without glancing at his companion's face, Egry-Toth took secret satisfaction in the feeling which must have pervaded the peasant-sprung astronomer-revolutionist, for he had heard even foreign royalties exclaim with amazement at this moment of arrival.

Several liveried footmen ran down the wide steps of the castle to receive the carriage. From behind one of the trees a frock-coated, derby-hatted shape advanced toward the carriage with narrowed eyes, a mop over his shoulder, but he stopped at a respectable distance. This apparition was no surprise to Ursi, for Zia had given him an accurate account of all the members of her family.

"The footman will take you to your room, Professor," said Egry-Toth, and added with the expression of an executioner: "But I must ask you to be good enough to present yourself in the study of His Excellency the Count at exactly six o'clock."

This bloodcurdling statement was in no way matched by the short but eloquent feminine cry that plunged precipitously from one of the first-floor windows:

"Mihály!"

Zia was leaning out of the window, but there was only time enough for them to wave at each other. Egry-Toth pretended not to notice. No matter, he thought to himself, that's what countesses are like; and he feasted his thoughts anew on the prospective meeting between the count and the astronomer, which the range of his reading cast in the terms of an Indian maharajah's court, where, for the entertainment of the guests, hunting dogs are thrown before the majestic tiger as he pads from his cage.

It was only a few minutes to six. A footman led Ursi to Count Dupi's study, for he would otherwise have lost his way in the labyrinthine castle. It seemed as if Mr. Gruber had intentionally given Ursi a guest room from which he would have to run a veritable cross-country marathon through the long corridors, past the fowling pieces, and then the collections of porcelain, and the stuffed birds in glass cases, along two smaller staircases that were flanked by gilt Empire banisters gently curving with the marble steps, through the vestibule which housed the great statue of Diana and was large enough to serve as a university quadrangle, past the open doors that gave onto the cavernous depths of the tremendous dining hall with its two balconies, where Zia's wedding dinner had taken place, past further doors that drew the eyes toward the two-story-high cupola of the library towering above a magnificent mosaic floor, and toward the several salons resplendent with the coloring of autumnal forests in their haughty seclusion. Only two kinds of paintings were in evidence in the course of the marathon: the vast ancestral portraits inside the salons, with leopard-skin capes and redingotes indicative of the slowly passing centuries, and the innumerable English landscapes everywhere throughout the corridors, so many that Ursi's eyes were dazzled by the multitude of idealized horses, small-headed, with necks bent and tails cropped, by the inevitable red-coated hunters and their bustling packs of hounds, by the improbably thick-necked stags that frothed with blood.

He found Egry-Toth in the count's study, his face set in the solemnity suitable to the surroundings, and the estate agent greeted him with a handshake that one might accord a distant acquaintance whose identity is somewhat vague after long years of separation.

The furnishings of the room resembled the count himself. A splendid bearded bustard stood on a table by the wall, its beak half open in the impetus of amorous fervor and its wings bent double for the attack. On the red leather surface of the writing desk lay a pocket watch as wide as a man's hat. It pointed to six o'clock precisely. The other pieces of furniture, too, were extravagant in dimension, especially the soft doeskin armchairs which were set so close to the ground that the occupants felt themselves to be in the ornate, cushioned galley of an Egyptian pharaoh of yore. Similarly exaggerated in size were the ashtrays and humidors, ornamented with boar tusks and filled with Havanas as large as bowling pins, and the thick tapers that served as cigar lighters. Even the matches were half a foot long, with bean-sized heads, and to complete the illusion a magnum of cognac as tall as a five-year-old child stood on a low, lacquered Chinese table. This Gulliver magnum served as a relic of the bygone Parisian years of "le charmant comte Dupi" and was analogous to a violet pressed between the pages of Countess Menti's prayer book, a symbol of some innocent, ethereal memory. The furnishings included two tiger skins hanging on opposite walls, trophies of the count's trips to India in the Nineties of the past century.

The count kept his visitors waiting. A sweet, tart autumnal scent of falling leaves penetrated the windows that gave on the park, and from time to time the voluptuous, throaty screech of some birds of prey was heard. Egry-Toth remained silent, as the moments passed, perhaps with the intention of intensifying the solemnity of the occasion.

István Dukay appeared unexpectedly, almost soundlessly, through a door at the farther depths of the study, which was separated by a heavy curtain from the adjoining room. The two men heard only the rattle of the curtain rings, and when they looked up Count Dupi was already standing with his back toward them, carefully adjusting the rings as he drew the curtain back into place. Men whose lives are repulsive with disorder will often take incredible pains in arranging the pattern of the pencils on their desks, or in regulating the distance between such curtain rings to within a millimeter of exactitude on the pole. But the back that was turned toward them also suggested that the arrangement of the curtain rings was more important to the count than either the persons in the room or their purposes. Egry-Toth and Ursi had already come to their feet. Egry-Toth's face stiffened, and his eyes turned to fish-eyes. In the course of twenty-six years he had several opportunities to experience this enormous, strange man's violent outbreaks of unbridled rage. Now he sensed that something of this sort was brewing. Perhaps there would be questioning on the subject of the eighteen-hundred-acre farm. Under his breath, with lightning speed, he recited the relevant passage from Ursi's book. A merry little Samoyed smile appeared on Ursi's lips as he contemplated Count Dupi's back during the moments that the latter was busy with the curtain. The performance seemed to please him. Lacking eyewitness accounts, we cannot say for certain but only as a probability that the enigmatic smiles and narrowed eyes of Chinese and other oriental gentlemen must have been something like this in very ancient times, when they faced each other, their bodies naked and sharp scimitars in hand, in deadly duels.

When the count turned, Egry-Toth met him with a deep bow.

"Good evening, sir," Count Dupi's voice rumbled cheerfully as he stretched out his hand toward the estate agent. There was neither innuendo nor sarcasm in his "sir." It was a natural, generally accepted form of address which landed lords used toward their stewards, for whom in former days they obtained or purchased the title of King's Councilor—or, more recently, Councilor to the Chief of State—as readily as they equipped their footmen with livery. And however naturally such a "Good evening, sir" may have sounded, there was always something about it that bore a dangerous resemblance to the tone of voice which Count Dupi employed toward Herr Jordan, his major-domo.

Egry-Toth proceeded to give the count a report of some sort in connection with the affairs of the estates, having to do with a lawsuit currently before the Curia, and Count Dupi listened with arms akimbo and hands thrust under his waistcoat, the large, smoking Havana stuck in the corner of his mouth as he showed his yellowing, blunt teeth. Egry-Toth did not render his report at this particular moment without an ulterior motive. He held the count in conversation thus—let the astronomer dangle for a while, let him sway in the wind a bit like the gallows bird that he was. And he succeeded in his design, for Count Dupi, while listening to the report, did not look around the room or make any acknowledgment of Ursi's presence. And then, unexpectedly and inexplicably, the situation changed. Without waiting to hear the end of one of the sentences István Dukay turned directly toward Ursi, stretched out his two hands and greeted his guest, while shaking his hand repeatedly, with these words, spoken in a quiet, heartfelt voice:

"I'm very glad to see you."

Egry-Toth's eyebrows jumped. Had he heard correctly?

Count Dupi placed his hands on Ursi's shoulders and looked warmly into his eyes for a long while.

"So you're the one!"

His voice was not devoid of paternal emotion. But Egry-Toth's ear caught only so much as was necessary to ascertain beyond a doubt that the count had addressed Ursi with the thou of friendship, and at once he felt like an executioner who was being haled to the gallows. His hand shook as he buttoned and unbuttoned his jacket, certain now that the eighteen-hundred-acre farm would enter into the discussion.

Count Dupi pressed Ursi into one of the large armchairs:

"Have a seat in this bathtub. My brother-in-law Fini claims I had these chairs

667

made so large in order to make visitors feel small when they sit down."

And he laughed at this, an odd, dry, rattling, throaty laugh.

"Cigar?"

Count Dupi reached for one of the humidors, which was only slightly smaller than the suitcase which Ursi had brought with him.

"Thanks, I don't smoke."

The strange little smile had vanished from Ursi's face by now, and his expression did not take on the mood of Count Dupi's cheerful voice, as if he were harboring a mental reservation without which it would have been impossible for him to agree to this meeting.

Meanwhile Egry-Toth, at a wave from his master, poured abundant splashes of cognac from the oversized magnum, looking like a maladroit weight-lifter as he tilted the bottle and placed it back on the table. Count Dupi raised his glass toward Ursi first of all, with a tiny, amiable twinkle in his eyes which appeared there only in the most profound moments of friendship. He raised his glass toward Egry-Toth as if offering a lump of sugar to his riding horse. After the glasses had been carefully replaced on the lacquered and unduly low-slung Chinese table, the count began to peer at Ursi with deliberation.

"Have I met you somewhere before?"

"No," Ursi replied quietly. "But I know you by sight, of course."

Egry-Toth's eyebrows again flew skyward, as if pricked by a needle. The younger man had returned the count's thou of friendship, and in a tone as natural and self-possessed as only a child or a dull-headed peasant could use. Count Dupi turned to Egry-Toth:

"I asked you, sir, to attend this meeting because—" meanwhile he rekindled the badly lit cigar with one of the six-inch-long matches. This took some time, and in the interim of silence Egry-Toth's heart began to beat faster.

"—at the time of my daughter Zia's first marriage," continued Count Dupi, "I did not transfer the deed of the Terézia Domain to her name. Right now it would be hard to say whether this was mere oversight or a presentiment on my part. Now that she is going to marry for the second time—"

He did not stop, he continued speaking, but those few words, "Now that she is going to marry for the second time," were decisive, without question, without either explanation or further elaboration, and as they hovered in the air they seemed to touch on raw uncovered nerves, producing a different effect on the two men; at the same time the words, pronounced unemphatically and without pause to breathe, gave the impression of being truly able to convey a burden of human destiny.

"—now that she is going to marry for the second time, I consider it essential that the deed be transferred to her name as soon as possible."

"As you wish, Your Excellency," said Egry-Toth, bowing slightly as he spoke, an act which his obesity and the depth of the armchair rendered somewhat comical.

"How does Countess Zia's suit for divorce stand?" asked Count Dupi, with narrowed eyes and an expression indicative of his dislike for the subject.

"The civil courts granted the divorce last year. Annulment by the Holy See is still delayed, although His Grace Prince Achile Ozzolini has lent the matter his most considerate support, through the good offices of Cardinal Fieri, whose cousin is incessantly pressing the petition and has already had an audience with His Holiness the Pope."

Count Dupi puffed a smoke-ring from either side of his mouth and fixed his gaze on the smoke as it rose in the air. He recalled how vigorously he had opposed Count Peter's idea of incorporating the incident of the slap, modeled on traditional usage, in the rituals at Zia's wedding ceremony. At this moment he could see Countess Menti as she advanced along the nave of the church, blocked the path of Zia and Filippo, drew the glove from her hand with a dignified mien and gently slapped the face of her altar-bound daughter. This archaic scene was now paying ample dividends in the suit before the Holy See, as material evidence of the fact that Zia's vows had been entered into under parental duress. As for the elder Ozzolinis, his recollection of Filippo's parents remained extremely sympathetic. He was in friendly correspondence with them, and on his last trip to Mandria he had visited them in Venice, but without telling Zia. The two elderly people, of delicate and distinguished spirit, were horrified and heartbroken by Filippo's escapade, and the father had severed all relations with his son.

Count Dupi turned toward Egry-Toth with a slight nod:

"Thank you kindly."

Egry-Toth sprang to his feet as swiftly as the low-slung armchair and his one hundred ninety pounds would permit, for he knew that this "Thank you kindly" signaled his dismissal. He departed with a low bow. In his room he clenched his hands behind him as he stood in front of the enormous oil-green baroque stove and began to ponder, although his brain worked only haltingly in his present state of mind. It was certain that the worst was over. The count had not inquired into the matter of the farm, the question had probably never occurred to him. The estate agent found it more difficult to recover from the shock of learning not only that István Dukay consented to his daughter's marriage but that he took this particular view of the problem. It was impossible for the agent to comprehend all this. There were two things Egry-Toth did not take into consideration. The first was that István Dukay, nearing seventy and growing ever more familiar with the prospect of death, felt true affection for but one human being in the world: his youngest child, Zia. Nor could Egry-Toth know that István Dukay, when he visited Zia in the sanatorium, had placed his hand on her emaciated little shoulder and said: "God worked a miracle in giving you back to me. There is nothing you can ask, as long as I live, that I won't do for you." Had Egry-Toth known this, he would still not have approved the count's decision, for this was not a simple family matter but the clash, historically portentous, of two irreconcilable opposites. It was not his daughter that István Dukay surrendered to a dangerous revolutionary this afternoon—for, in the final analysis, the defection of one scatter-brained countess more or less did not matter—but he surrendered the whole of Hungarian aristocracy, the ideological bastions of a system of land tenure which was already under attack from other quarters. Yes, the ideological bastions—a good expression, he would use it in the Casino when they were debating this scandalous affair. István Dukay surrendered these ideological bastions to a terrorist just out of prison, and thereby lent this scoundrel not only the support of his own senility but of the weighty name of Dukay as well, took a stand at his side in the most monstrous abdication of right that a Hungarian nobleman had ever committed. In the eyes of the entire world he acknowledged the vile accusations which an obscene book had directed not only against his own person but against every great estate, and it was not impossible, in an unstable world, that he himself would start the avalanche. Only moral paralysis could explain this action. Many people knew that the count had suffered seriously from syphilis as a youth. It was possible that this avalanche would sweep away all properties over a thousand acres in extent; there had been talk to this effect. The count was too dim-witted to reckon with these consequences. Had the count given his daughter to a circus wrestler, or to a depraved adagio dancer white with the ravages of cocaine—well, at most it would have been another affair like that of Louisa, the princess royal who fell in love with a handsome gypsy primás called Jancsi Rigó and followed him around like a trained seal. But this was something completely different. Egry-Toth, slapper of peasants, saw the glint of millions upon millions of straightened scythes rising behind Ursi. What would Prince Andrew say, and the entire National Casino? How would the left-wing press greet the news of this marriage?

The estate agent cracked the knuckles of his fingers, one by one. Then he thought sadly of his own fate, the awkwardness of his position in society. As a reserve officer in the Hussars, he had been on intimate terms with Peter Dukay, had called him by the brotherly thou when they served as volunteers in the same regiment. And so with a host of other aristocrats. But he had to call István Dukay "Your Excellency," and the count occasionally spoke to him as if he were a coachman. Fini, the count's brother-in-law, despite the fact that he was a mediatized prince, was on terms of familiarity with filthy newspapermen, but referred to Egry-Toth as Herr von "Estate Agent." István Dukay stood like the wall of a steep cliff before him, and tossed him back into the depths of eternal servitude with unremitting persistence, although the Egry-Toth lineage was hardly less ancient than that of the Dukays and, viewed in a certain light, derived through an Irday ancestress from the Kürt clan and colonization. Now, as an afterthought, it occurred to him that he should have given Ursi the thou of familiarity at the first moment of their meeting. There would be time for this at supper. While his thoughts, like infected teeth, chewed on all this in gingerly fashion, he set about the chore of changing into a dinner jacket, for it was the meager consolation of the entire afternoon that Ursi would be the only one to wear street clothes at supper, and his clothes at least would put him in his place.

Meanwhile Zia entered the room where her father was in quiet conversation with Ursi. They were talking of astronomy, a science with which Count Dupi was not entirely unfamiliar. He explained that he had once bought an elaborate telescope in London, and subscribed to a British astronomical journal, but finally wearied of the hobby. The telescope stood in the library, where sometimes the guests and even the servants peered through it when they had nothing else to do.

During these warm fall days the castle was not, of course, without its guests. While Zia guided Ursi to his room she told him that, in addition to her parents, Kristina would be present at supper, and the other representatives of the family would be Bishop Zsigmond, Prince Fini, and Count Peter and his wife. They had been informed of everything, though not officially as yet; therefore he should not be surprised at being treated simply as another guest when introductions were made. Besides, these guests, two diplomats, a Belgian and a Turk, would be present at supper with their wives. The company would not stay up late, for there was to be hunting on the morrow, and thus the two of them would have ample opportunity to talk till midnight.

"What do you think of Papa?" Zia asked, after they had entered Ursi's room.

"He was completely charming," Ursi replied. He strolled up and down the room quietly, and a little smile twinkled at the corners of his mouth. Zia observed that little smile with anticipation, for it clearly had more to say. They were already fond of analyzing things out between them.

"I felt," Ursi spoke again, "that he loves you very much."

Zia blinked twice, for her eyes had become imperceptibly misty. This happened whenever she thought of her father nowadays.

"The presence of the estate agent," Ursi continued objectively, without glancing at Zia, "was necessary for two reasons. First, to acquaint me through him, as if by telegram, of your father's decision, and to let me know, without addressing me directly, that he intends to transfer the Terézia Domain to your name. The agent was also required to demonstrate how a gentleman of such stature bows and scrapes before your father."

Zia began to laugh.

"Yes, that's Papa!"

"Behind his decision I can discern not only his love for you but the political finesse of your sort of people. He thought the matter over and came, I think, to the correct conclusion: that nothing would compromise the tenets of land reform more thoroughly than for a man like me to marry his daughter."

Ursi paused for a moment, then leaned against one of the tables and gazed into the air:

"And this is where he will be very much surprised. For the system of land ownership in this feudal country of ours must and will be overhauled, even at the cost of a bloody revolution. No matter whom I marry."

Zia did not reply. She too was preoccupied as she stared at the floor. Then she glanced at her watch:

"I must go and change."

At exactly eight o'clock a gong rang, and a footman led Ursi to the little yellow salon adjoining the intermediate dining hall, where the guests congregated for an aperitif before going in to supper.

There were only seven people in the salon when Ursi entered: Countess Menti, the Belgian couple, Count Peter and his wife, Egry-Toth and Zia. Countess Menti stood before the white fireplace, holding the dainty ivory fan in her two lowered hands exactly as if she were still posing for Lenbach's full-length portrait of her. Past sixty, the lines of her neck and her queenly carriage might still have attracted mute adulation. The Belgian diplomat wore a white dinner jacket, and his wife stood at his side as if she had just stepped from the show-window of a great Parisian department store, where the wax mannequins nowadays were faithful reproductions, designed with consummate artistry, of live women, with the difference that women of such great beauty did not exist. Madame Pinkers, however, was precisely that beautiful. One's blood ran cold at the sight of this stiff, soulless Flamand beauty, for she gave the impression that her bosom, her belly and her thighs were of immaculate wax, without human heat.

Zia introduced Ursi to her mother. Countess Menti gave him her hand with the consummate grace, tailored for such "little suppers," which she had learned to perfection in the course of forty years before the same fireplace. Every letter was articulated in her somewhat drawn-out, syllabified "Good eve-ning." As the introductions proceeded, Egry-Toth noted with scornful delight that Ursi attempted to kiss the hand of the wax doll from Belgium, an attempt which the waxen hand resisted vigorously. Naturally the peasant did not know that this custom of hand-licking obtained in middle class circles only, and only in the rural districts of Hungary at that. The ill-fated obeisance looked, to Egry-Toth, as if Ursi had tripped on the rug. After the introductions Ursi turned up at the side of Countess Menti, who gave him to understand that there was a very "in-ter-es-ting" telescope in the castle library, where he could have a look at it after supper if he wished. She expressed the opinion that astronomy was a very beautiful science, as distinguished from that "fun-ny" astrology which was, in fact, under Church interdiction, although her "daugh-ter Kris-tina" was unfortunately an ardent devotee of that black art. Prince Fini entered the room, bringing new color to the salon with his tomato-red dinner jacket, of simple linen but perfectly cut. To flaunt his thorough familiarity with the Hungarian language, he greeted Ursi with a loud "Gud ivning" and a handshake, assuming from his dark gray street suit that the astronomer understood not a word of German. Ursi at once recognized the prince's comical, good-natured bat-face, from Zia's exact description of him. Kristina appeared in a great rustle of silk, making straight for Ursi, and the rapid flutter of her eyebrows up and down was her confirmation of the family secret they had in common. Bishop Zsigmond marched in too, and gave Ursi a profoundly suspicious look when they were introduced, but the fleeting gesture with which his left hand touched the back of Ursi's hand as they exchanged handshakes signified, if somewhat sadly, that he knew all and, since there was nothing else to do, gave this peculiar affair his blessing, for that very afternoon he had held Countess Menti in long conversation on the theme that Zia's marriage could not be taken as so cataclysmic a blow, since the Habsburg archdukes were marrying commoners one after the other. In any case, the circumstance that the bridegroom was an astronomer eased the situation considerably, and it would certainly not be difficult to obtain a membership in the Academy for "this lad." He did not mention *The Great Fallow,* which he had twice read from cover to cover with studious care, for his instinct told him—and correctly—that Countess Menti had not read the book. Dupi, too, probably knew the book only from a synopsis prepared by his secretary, so what purpose could be served by bringing up a painful subject?

The Turkish couple dashed into the room with a guilty sense of their tardiness. The fumes of domestic misunderstanding had not completely left their faces; the squabble between them had probably arisen because the Rose of the Bosporus found it impossible to keep an eye on the clock while dressing. The lady had a long waist and short legs, but her eyes were of the most beautiful dark velvet, with fire in their depths, as beautiful as anything the human frame could devise of moistures and membranes and inner light. A footman quickly pressed the aperitif glasses into their hands.

Now a tall, slender man of about sixty approached Ursi, who had missed his name when they were introduced. He resembled Count Dupi, but the lines of his face were gentler and less pronounced.

"We've met before—" and when Ursi looked at him with surprise he added: "You referred to one of my works in your book."

He was Peter Dukay. His voice was a solace to Ursi in all the great strangeness, for he felt as if he were standing completely naked in a Röntgen laboratory with the opaque glass over his chest. Although Bishop Zsigmond stood conversing with the white-jacketed Belgian in the opposite corner of the room, his eyes constantly studied Ursi. From another direction Kristina, too, scrutinized him in the same way. The two glances fixed him as a surveyor's transit holds a landmark in triangulation. Last to appear was the master of the house, obviously fresh-shaven.

The doors of the dining hall suddenly swung open. Herr Jordan's black-vested frock coat bowed toward Countess Menti, and the guests started toward the flower-decked, candlelit table which seemed altogether lost in the spacious room. While filing through the door the guests glanced at the cards on a leather chart that displayed the seating plan.

Bishop Zsigmond—*ecclesia praecedent*—sat at the right of the mistress of the house, and at her left sat the Belgian Ambassador, which was odd in itself, for the Belgian was an extremely young man, at least fifteen years younger than his Turkish colleague. Furthermore, in terms of area and international significance, the former empire of Suleiman was still larger than Belgium; consequently there must have been an especial reason for the violation of protocol. There was such a reason, and God help Mr. Gruber if he ever made a mistake in the seating plan. The Belgian Ambassador had assumed his duties in Hungary three months earlier than his fellow diplomat, and it was this that determined the order of precedence at table. That afternoon Mr. Gruber had held two overtime long-distance conversations with the Ministry of Foreign Affairs to determine the respective seniority of the two ambassadors. Zia hastily told Ursi all this when they were seated, in a low voice and with the appearance of leading him along the cages of some exotic zoo, betraying secrets about the civet cats and the crested hedgehogs of which only their keepers could possibly be aware.

Ursi was placed between the two Dukay daughters. Kristina's friendliness seeped through an invisible glass wall. Ursi found that she did not resemble Zia at all. There was an air of withered, cold beauty about her which seemed to emanate rather from the beauty of aristocracy itself than from her own person. There are types of beauty which do not belong to those who display them. At the opposite end of the table, with the Belgian wax doll on his right and the Turkish velvet on his left, sat Count Dupi, enthroned between them like King David, who surrounded the autumn of his flesh with young virgins.

Out of deference for the foreign diplomats, the conversation flowed in French and English alternately, which brought the silent sulks to Egry-Toth's face, for besides Hungarian he spoke only German. At the same time he was surprised to discover that Ursi handled both languages as fluently as his mother tongue, and this resulted in a sudden reversal of situation. Now it was the estate agent who wore street clothes to the supper table, and he was forced to admit that in this company the knowledge of languages was a more useful attire than the sleekest dinner jacket.

The conversation veered to the illness of King George V of England, and mention was made of the crown prince's love affair, of which the Belgian Ambassador knew the precise details, although the story was as yet unknown to the public at large. His recital did not enhance the dignity of sovereign princes, and Bishop Zsigmond, his neck red, remarked in a voice that was, for him, unusually sharp.

"Cette histoire est cousue de fil blanc! That story is concocted of whole cloth," which, in his ornate French, meant that it was a malicious fabrication.

Countess Menti, to dispel the awkwardness of the momentary lull that followed, turned to the Turkish Ambassador and asked whether he was familiar with an association of Japanese officers known as the Black Dragon. The ambassador, whose previous post had been in Japan, declared that he could hardly be familiar with it, since it was a secret society. What were its purposes? To put respectable politicians out of the way. For what reason? Because this was the purpose of all secret societies formed by army officers. Army officers all over the world were preparing for war with the enthusiasm of a master cabinetmaker turning out ornamental table-legs. They wanted, said the ambassador, to make a show of their talents. Prince Fini, in recent years an advocate of German warmongering, took his revenge by twice asking the Turk to repeat this rather florid phrase, and even cupped his hand about his little bat's-ear, simply to parade the Turk's halting, stumbling English up and down the table. Count Peter, sitting between the Belgian wax doll and Egry-Toth, looked at Prince Fini with slightly narrowed eyes. Kristina gazed absently at the tablecloth beside her plate, one eyebrow somewhat raised as she strayed from the bypaths of conversation to wonder how she had managed to make a muddle of the thing eleven years ago, at the celebration of the thirtieth birthday of the Prince of Wales in 1924, when she had been alone with him three times and felt certain that her charms were succeeding. Not to mention the fact that the British ruling house did not surround marriage with stupid, strict regulations, as did the Habsburgs.

After supper they adjourned to the great red salon, the proportions of which veritably engulfed this handful of people, especially when Count Dupi, Prince Fini, the Turkish Ambassador and the Belgian wax doll vanished as if the earth had swallowed them. They were playing bridge in the next room. The conversation took a new turn in the salon, as if in keeping with the atmosphere of the room. Egry-Toth dragged his involuntary silence about with him like the rusty iron ball and chain with which slaves were shackled in the days of ancient Turkey. And during supper, when he gathered that they were discussing the

British ruling house, he would have been happy indeed to explain, modestly and incidentally, that the grandmother of Queen Mary of England was the beautiful Countess Julia Rhedey, who married Prince Teck, and that it had been a Rhedey who married Amalia Egry-Toth at the beginning of the past century. This line of collateral kinship did indeed exist at one time, although the Rhedey family had died out since then, and, according to letters from members of the Magyar gentry in the files of the secretariat at Buckingham Palace, the Queen of England had more than two thousand first cousins in Hungary. Egry-Toth carried the records of this connection with him just as he carried visiting cards, to the text and typography of which he devoted considerable thought.

The Belgian Ambassador essayed a few French stories which were piquant to an extent that this company not only permitted but actually demanded, like the *haut goût* of grouse and pheasant. Seated beside Countess Menti, with whom he had little more to talk about, the bishop's eyes continued to peer through the subdued light at Ursi, whose physical appearance had not made a bad impression on him at all. He would have liked to summon this strange astronomer to his side and ask him for an opinion on the future of the Church lands. He was armed with arguments on this score which, like all good weapons, were always eager to do battle. But now it was Count Peter who settled at Ursi's side, having been abandoned by the velvet-eyed wife of the Turkish Ambassador when she left him and joined Egry-Toth in the interest of sociability.

"We have a lot to talk about," Peter Dukay said to Ursi, "but right now I merely want to say that your book made an unusual impression on me. There are some parts with which I don't entirely see eye to eye, but that's not important. I have facts, on the other hand, which I couldn't include in my own book simply because I'm a Dukay myself. There is a two-thousand-acre game preserve adjoining the park, for instance—don't forget to have a look at it. A six-foot stone wall, eleven miles in length, encloses the game preserve. I estimated that this wall consumed nearly twenty million bricks—all the details of the construction are in the family archives. It was built by socage service at the beginning of the last century, and took more than ten years. But that's not the most interesting aspect of the wall. The Dukay serfs were required to provide fresh eggs by the kettleful, and these were broken into the plaster barrows by the millions in the course of the years, for Baumeister Karg was obsessed with the idea that fresh eggs made the best binder. Yes..." added Count Peter, and offered no further explanation as he stared into the air. His face at the moment resembled that of a physician who has diagnosed his own cancer and calmly observes the spread of the deadly growth that has taken root in his body, making notes of clinical interest the meanwhile. All this demanded a certain praiseworthy spiritual strength and moral awareness that was, in fact, not lacking in some members of Hungarian aristocracy. Although they were speaking softly, Egry-Toth's ear caught the sound of Hungarian words, and he slowly drew near, like a thirsty ox ambling to the trough. Count Peter stopped in the middle of a sentence, which Ursi felt to be the sign of a secret and far-reaching alliance between himself and Peter Dukay. Egry-Toth's approach was intended, principally, as a demonstration—for Ursi's benefit—of the fact that the agent addressed the count with the thou of familiarity. After several of his remarks, with neither pretext nor purpose, had encountered the barrier of Count Peter's preoccupied and almost repugnant silence, Egry-Toth beat a retreat with a slight bow, like a trapeze artist familiar with the effect of his performance. He went into the next room and settled down to kibitz at Count Dupi's side, although he was completely unacquainted with bridge. But he was capable of camping beside Count Dupi for hours this way, as if in the shade of a large oak tree.

Ursi's glance occasionally sought out Zia, who was sitting at a distance with the Belgian Ambassador, and this time the astronomer was surprised to see that the Belgian's white dinner jacket had turned tomato-red. What had happened was that Prince Fini had simply yielded his place at bridge to the Belgian. Now Kristina joined them, and Ursi felt that they were discussing him, informing Zia of the impression he had made on them, as insincerely as connoisseurs praising the painting or the piano playing of an amateur kinswoman. Similarly, Zia watched to see who sat with Ursi, and a similarly sensitive instinct divined the content of conversations which were, after all, inaudible to her.

On the premise that Mohammed must go to the mountain if the mountain would not go to Mohammed, Bishop Zsigmond's gold pectoral cross unexpectedly bobbed toward Ursi and Count Peter. Ursi stood up to relinquish his armchair to the bishop, and he himself sat on the footstool. While settling into the chair, the bishop grasped his soutane as if he were preparing to open a meeting of the Eucharistic Congress. In these late evening hours the traces of bluish-green paint on his eyelids and of brick-red paint on his cheeks, so oddly incongruous with the large Renaissance frame, were clearly in evidence. His face fell within the circle of light cast by a shaded lamp.

"I've read your book, Professor," the bishop began, and once more Ursi was struck by the disproportionate thinness of the voice that issued from so large a diaphragm.

"Naturally I don't agree with a single point," Bishop Zsigmond continued, with consummate courtesy and a melancholy little smile on his lips, "but you probably know that the greatest strength of the Church lies in its patience. Allow me to ask: are you a believer?"

"Yes."

"That does not surprise me; in fact, I find it entirely natural. Nowadays the great modern natural scientists—to mention only Carrel—are joining the ranks of the faithful with forces which—I must confess—we, the servants of the Church, could hardly command by ourselves in the present materialistic world. Are you a Catholic, Professor?"

"Yes," Ursi answered patiently, and then he added: "I was baptized in the Catholic faith."

"Then you are not a Catholic after all."

"As you like," said Ursi, with an apologetic little smile.

The bishop leaned forward in his chair before putting the next question. Count Peter followed the exchange without interruption.

"I should like to know what inner objections you have to Catholicism. Don't answer, please, if you don't care to." The bishop raised his fine, ringed hand and then returned it to the arm of the chair.

"I agree with Wells."

Bishop Zsigmond smiled.

"I should prefer you to be in agreement with Merejkovski, Claude Farrèrre, Papini or Chesterton. Well, let's hear what Wells has to say. I'm sorry to say I gave him up after the Martians."

"Wells says it was St. Paul who led the magnificent teachings of Christ up a blind alley, when he superimposed dogma and organization upon them."

"Oh, oh—" Bishop Zsigmond pursed his lips. "Blind alley? C'est cousu de fil blanc, je crois," he said to Count Peter, forgetting that he had already employed this expression during supper, and forgetting as well that Ursi spoke French fluently. It was as if he meant to exclude Ursi from the conversation for a moment, an unconscious verbal tic which he and his kind exhibited when they mechanically tossed French phrases back and forth in the presence of a footman or a chambermaid, even when there was nothing secret in what they said.

This was what Ursi took the bishop's French remark to be, and he did not deem it necessary to continue in French. Count Peter did not raise his eyes, thereby fending off the remark.

"Well—St. Paul!" Bishop Zsigmond pressed Ursi for an answer.

"St. Paul, first and foremost. Don't misunderstand me, Your Excellency. I have every respect for his superhuman abilities, but I can't help being reminded by his life's work of a beautiful medieval legend that the greatest writer in the world might make into a shooting script for Hollywood, as a result of which the film will have a truly phenomenal success."

Count Peter broke into loud laughter.

"Excellent!" he cried.

The bishop did not find it worth his while to favor this comparison with a comment. Ursi himself would have given a great deal to recall his words. But the French interpolation of a moment ago had left him with a certain rancor.

After a pause of several moments the bishop narrowed his eyes and pointed his forefinger at Ursi like a revolver.

"The blind alley!"

"I withdraw the blind alley," Ursi said somewhat apologetically. "Actually, it is difficult to find an appropriate expression for the present state, or rather the dramatic disjunction, of the Church. In prison I read a Hungarian novel which appeared recently. I happen to know that one of the dialogues between the protagonist and a French priest actually took place here in Budapest between the author and a well-known Jesuit father."

"What did Bangha say?" asked the bishop, quick to know who was meant.

"I believe the question is more important than the answer. It went like this: Now, when everyone senses that the world is heading toward catastrophe, when the anti-Semitic Nürnberg Laws and the open secret of sterilization in Poland have shown us that the latent sadism of humanity, in ideological disguise, is prepared to make its first real attempt to crush, once and for all, the teachings of Christ— why doesn't the Church spring to its feet and take action? All the churches! Why don't the bells of every church ring out in this hour of the greatest danger that has ever threatened the Church? Why isn't that remarkable administrative machinery at work, organizing its countless millions of adherents for spiritual battle all over the world? This leads certain critical minds to believe that after two thousand years the Church has finally admitted that its skill at administrative detail functions to perfection only when collecting the ecclesiastical tithes. Now—let the Church unfurl its processional banners now! That would be the truly Christian triumph! Will anyone be able to doubt that the prayer books and toothless hymns of little old women can sweep away the machine-guns of the dictators if martyrs appear in multitudes, and especially from the ranks of the clergy?"

"The faith cannot ask its followers to become martyrs," Bishop Zsigmond said without looking up, while he adjusted the folds of his soutane with an effeminate gesture.

"That depends upon the faith. My father was a Nazarene. And when they discovered, at the front, that he refused to fire his rifle at all, his company commander summarily sentenced him to death. When they led him away to be shot, the squad leader told him in a whisper to fall down after the first round of firing, for they would fire over his head. Not a single member of the firing squad was a Nazarene, and there was hardly time for them to agree on such a plan, yet every bullet was fired into the air. All this demonstrates that the Christian idea is stronger than all the armaments of war, if—if it dares to show its strength in the face of death."

The bishop was silent for a while, and then, looking in another direction, he asked once more:

"What did Bangha say?"

Ursi replied only after lifting his two hands in perplexity:

"He also answered with this gesture—the weakest point of Christian doctrine."

Bishop Zsigmond nodded, and it was he, instead of Ursi, who pronounced the words:

"Render unto Caesar the things which are Caesar's, and unto God the things that are God's."

"Yes. And that's what is impossible. The moment may come—it may already have come—when Caesar simply says: Kill the Lord! In such a circumstance, how should the humble servant of Christ perform the impossible task of bowing in two directions at once? There is no doubt that one of the fundamental aims of Hitlerism is the total extermination of certain peoples. We Hungarians, too, figure on his list as 'racial drawbacks.' Hitler's favorite word, *vernichten,* is a dagger in the heart of God. Perhaps Hitler will win. If he does win, his victory will be a result of the elimination of all compromise from his mind. His doctrine is: Render unto Caesar the things which are Caesar's—period!"

The bishop shook his head mildly.

"Hitler will not win."

"I wouldn't dare to say that with such assurance. Those who survive all this may be able to say that Hitler did not win. Unfortunately those who have already perished in concentration camps and those who are going to perish have an entirely different opinion on this score. Or does Your Excellency think that the opinions of the dead do not count? Shall we leave them to Kingdom Come?"

Now Count Peter turned his head away as he spoke. This characteristic movement was apparently common to all the Dukays when they had something important to say.

"We cannot know what the tenants of mass graves think of the ill-fashioned monuments we erect in their honor."

"As far as the statement that 'the Church views the course of events passively' is concerned," declared the bishop, "it is a groundless accusation. The Pope has addressed an appeal for peace to the world. The most recent pastoral letter of the Prince Primate..."

Ursi did not wait for the sentence to end.

"Your Excellency, a majority of the clergy turned a deaf ear to the Pope's appeal for peace. The letter of the Prince Primate? I myself saw it on the table of a friend of mine, a country priest, and the Prince Primate's letter was folded between the pages of a catalogue that offered motorcycles for sale. Surely nothing is further from the good fellow's mind than the purchase of a motorcycle."

"The pastoral letter was read in our every pulpit."

"That is so. But a shaving cream still enjoys wider publicity. Your Excellency probably knows as well as I do that among the lower orders of the clergy, whether Catholic or Protestant, there is a goodly number who are not only anti-Semites but who actively put their shoulder to Hitler's wheel, with all the avidity of inner conviction."

The bridge game came to an end, and the four players entered the salon. Bishop Zsigmond touched Count Peter's knee with a light sigh as he rose to his feet. The guests began to make their adieux. Kristina confronted Ursi with a little notebook in hand.

"I've just heard that you're leaving tomorrow morning. You must tell me the day and hour of your birth."

Ursi provided the information in the compliant tone which an astrophysicist generally adopts toward an astrologer-countess. By now Zia stood at their side.

"I'd like to take a little walk in the park with you before going to bed," she said quite openly.

✠

It was eleven o'clock at night. Ursi and Zia entered the park and headed straight for the West Gate, which led to the village. The village lay in black somnolence; the only light shone in the town clerk's window.

Makkosh was waiting for them impatiently. His wife and children had already gone to bed. Upon entering, Ursi let Makkosh know with a single nod that everything was in order. They sat down and began to confer in whispers. Makkosh said that his wife had been packing all day—they would leave in a few days. He was exchanging posts with the town clerk in Duka, who had eagerly jumped at the opportunity. The Terézia Domain was on the border of the Duka parish, in Bihar County, from which the Dukays once took their name. The three thousand acres of the Terézia Domain were but a remnant of the ancestral holdings at the time of the original conquest. Zia revealed that they intended to have the civil wedding as soon as possible, very quietly, in a matter of weeks at the most. Not a word was said of Zia's "solution," which was making the marriage possible for Ursi.

The next morning Zia accompanied Ursi to Budapest. There was still a good deal to be done in their apartment before the wedding. She had found a five-room studio apartment on Andrássy Ut, the two largest rooms of which were to be her workshop. She did not keep the furniture from the villa on Fuga Utca; she sold, or exchanged, every single piece.

Society knew nothing of the imminent wedding, which took place without fanfare in the beginning of November at the district magistrate's office. János Hámor was Ursi's witness, and Peter Dukay was Zia's. But they did not let Count Peter into the secret of Zia's "plan."

After the wedding they traveled directly to the Terézia Domain, where not only Makkosh but the entire membership of the Gugger Café *stammtisch* was waiting for them. Everything was in readiness. About three hundred selected people had been summoned to a meeting after church on Sunday morning, to be held in the courtyard of the Duka Town Hall.

Ursi attended the meeting, but Zia remained in the town clerk's apartment, where they were lodged. When the people—mostly men, both young and old, of the poorest class—had assembled, János Futó was the first to address them. He outlined the aims and advantages of cooperative farming. His speech was short and clear, and its chief drawback was the low tone of voice in which he spoke; some of his listeners, especially in the rearmost ranks, were constantly calling "Louder." But Futó's voice had no great volume at best. The audience seemed to recover its sense of hearing when Bandi Makkosh's full, brown voice sounded from the pillared portico of the Town Hall. After some preliminary remarks he began to read from a document in his hand:

"The Terézia Domain of the Duka Parish, consisting of three thousand acres of arable land and all the agricultural implements pertaining thereto, has been divided into parcels of eight to fifteen acres by its proprietor Countess Terézia Dukay, who is conferring these parcels of land on the inhabitants of Duka here present. The parcels have been allocated in accordance with the size of each family, and the Countess has already made over the deeds of registry to the new proprietors. The complete effects of the Domain, including the power plant, the distillery and the dairy, together with all the installations which are essential to community farming, become the property of the cooperative association. In the interest of uninterrupted production, the overseers and other employees of the Domain will continue at their posts. János Futó has been named manager of the Duka Agricultural Cooperative. Terézia Dukay wishes to emphasize that the beneficiaries of this partition of land must not regard the bestowal as an act of generosity, for it is her conviction that the persons here present have already paid the price of their parcels by the forced labor of their fathers in past centuries, the low wage scales of more recent times and the inequitable rents set for farm dwellings by the estate.

Subscribed in Duka, 10 November 1935."

Makkosh expected the assembled peasants to break into spirited cheers and hoist the visitors to their shoulders. But nothing of this sort happened. The faces of the men remained passive, and some of the women adjusted the kerchiefs about their heads with a quiet little smile. The meeting began to disperse without further ado. Had they misunderstood the essence of the settlement? Did they think it too little—or had it impressed them as so much of gift that they did not believe it? There was no way of knowing. But there was something in the silence with which they received the announcement that was almost threatening.

Still, this was Zia's solution, which had frightened Ursi when she first told him of her intention, for he could see his own influence on the entire project quite clearly and he felt that he had been instrumental in her decision. It had an unpleasant savor, not only because of public opinion—it was obvious to him that her decision would have wide political repercussions—but in personal terms as well. He did not care, at first, to see himself in the role of *spiritus rector*. This had been the subject of their weekly talks when Zia visited him in prison. Gradually he became convinced that her decision did not spring from his personal views. Often there was something in her eyes, when she gazed into space, that he perceived only dimly. And he could not have seen it otherwise, for Zia never spoke of an inner apprehension that was perhaps beyond the reach of words. While the meeting was going on in the courtyard of the Town Hall, the absent Zia bore no resemblance to the emancipated countess in the imagination of a young *Accusation* reporter who was present. A thick muffler around her neck, she lay on the couch in the town clerk's apartment, suffering from a severe cold which she had caught while traveling in the windy, damp November weather. Her temperature was high, and in the course of those feverish hours she felt something that she would have been unable to put into words even to herself. She felt the bitter-sweet giddiness of liberation and recovery, she saw Berili's long knitting needles as they flashed, slowly and whitely, in the darkening room on Septemvir Utca, and the metal buttons glittering on Grandfather Veyrac's dove-blue cape. When she shut her eyes she could see Marie Antoinette and the Raverney family in the low-ceilinged room of the town clerk's apartment, the marquis in his poison-green waistcoat, the blond marquise with a tiny mouth below her long nose, and she could hear Countess Menti's impassioned voice behind the closed door, berating Aunt Stefi and Uncle Paul about a matter of roast goose, and in a pitch of fever she seemed to see Tonia listening to the quarrel, resting her face in the wedge of her right thumb and forefinger as she stood on the Mandrian wharf amid the din of the gray waves, and Uncle Dmitri appeared at the moment of interrupting a story about Russia. This all mingled kaleidoscopically inside of her, like the dumb suffering of the world's poverty, which occasionally explodes into frightening accusations. This much is certain: it was in the moments of sipping Mrs. Makkosh's herb tea that the Copperplated Twilight drew its bloodstained witching claws from Zia's heart.

They waited for the storm of newspaper comment in Budapest to subside. The papers, of course, considered the affair in terms of their political allegiances, briefly or at great length, but the majority took a sarcastic and suspicious tone of derision. One of the right-wing dailies asserted that the Terézia Domain had long been overburdened with debts and was, in any case, completely unfit for cultivation. The newspaper of Managing Editor Donáthy-Drexler revealed that the unfortunate countess had spent a long period of time in a mental institution some years ago, and that her person and her activities were consequently of no interest. He called attention to the Communist astronomer who stood behind her and with whom she was living in adultery. But the tempestuous sensation did not last long, for much greater tempests were brewing on the horizons of Europe. It was in those days that economic sanctions against Italy were put into effect as a result of the Abyssinian campaign, threatening to alienate Mussolini from the Western powers and drive him into the arms of Hitler. This question introduced a note of gloomy antagonism into newspapers throughout the world, and by the time Ursi and Zia returned to Budapest they noted with relief that neither of them was any longer in the public eye.

The apartment on Andrássy Ut stood ready. The glass plate, reading ZIA PHOTOS in letters of black and gold, stood ready and had only to be posted by its proprietor. The poster frames were ready at the entrance and in the courtyard for carefully selected enlargements, which of course included the famous smiling photograph of the Duce. The latter seemed somewhat atavistic by now, when all smiles had vanished from Mussolini's lips, but the picture still served the business interests of Zia's firm, though it was impossible to know how long it would continue to do so.

Upon their arrival Zia spent an entire morning hanging out her shingle and installing the photographs. When everything was in place she walked as far as the Opera and then turned back. Upon reaching the apartment house she glanced idly at the sign as if she were a casual passer-by, and when she found that its effect was satisfactory she returned to view it with the eyes of some unknown society woman. Walking now in the opposite direction, her manner was a perfect imitation of Countess Ilona's mincing pace. She stopped in astonishment when she reached the plate: Ah, *Zia Photos!* So that's where it is! Thus she tried to see her future self through the eyes of strangers and acquaintances.

In the early hours of the afternoon she set out for Septemvir Utca. She contemplated this encounter with feelings of anxiety. She was unable to imagine what the scene with her father would be like, but she did not share Mihály's apprehensions. She did agree with Mihály that it had been best not to let anyone in her family know about her plan beforehand, least of all her father.

It was Zia who insisted on the phrases which declared that the partitioned lands had long been paid for by forced labor and other hardships. Now, as she entered the gate, she felt certain of softening her father's heart with a few words, even if she found him in a bad humor. For he had forgiven Kristina's large gambling debts, although their total far exceeded the value of the Terézia Domain. Tears began to gather in her throat as she mounted the pea-green carpet on the old stone stairs.

The secretary's office led to Count Dupi's study. Mr. Gruber jumped up in alarm when Zia entered.

"Papa?" asked Zia in her usual way, as she headed for the door of her father's room without hesitation. But a pale Mr. Gruber barred her path.

"Please be good enough to wait a moment while I announce Your Excellency."

Zia hardly had time to level a cold stare at Mr. Gruber for his unaccustomed tone. His large brown shoes had already disappeared through the closing door. And Zia had not recovered herself before Mr. Gruber confronted her once more, fixing one of his eyes in space strangely as he told her, with a transfigured expression and in a voice which one might use to inform a close relation of some dreadful accident:

"His Excellency the Count regrets he is unable to receive the Countess."

For a moment Zia wore a confused smile as she looked into Mr. Gruber's disjointed glance, and then she suddenly turned on her heel and left the room without a word.

She almost staggered while descending the stairs. She had met her father, during these moments, for the first time. Now, for the first time in her life, she had encountered the true character of that strange human being. Mr. Gruber had been inside for only a second or two: István Dukay needed only a single negative nod to cast her aside. All at once the warm, rumbling paternal voice turned to nothing, and the little twinkle of friendship in the corner of his left eye, and the oft-heard "Look here, cricket" of childhood, and the comradely hours of his visits to Mandria, and the hands resting on her shoulders in the sanatorium—the man turned to nothing and only Mr. Gruber's eye remained, fixed in air in so peculiar a fashion as he intoned: "His Excellency the Count..."

István Dukay would have forgiven his daughter anything else. But what she had done—*this* he could not forgive.

Zia had reached the street by now. As she turned and looked back for a moment, the earth seemed to swallow the Septemvir Utca Palace.

687

But she was a Dukay too, and all trace of tears vanished from her throat. Only her face was somewhat paler than usual when she hailed a passing cab, for the November drizzle had begun again.

Chapter Seventeen

THE AUTHOR himself realizes that it is an indulgence in wearisome repetition to close this section of his story, too, with the death of a monarch. The nineteenth century declined to its grave with Franz Joseph, as the euphemistic pen of a historian might say. The coffin of Charles IV embraced the last of the Habsburg rulers, and now we must take our leave of a third monarch—who, although he wore no crown, was still king of his own domains. In the annals of mankind there are countless examples of lesser men who were called kings.

By now the reader knows that we are bidding farewell to Count Dupi. István Dukay died at the age of seventy-one, in 1939, and his death represented still another steep turn of the stairs which led to the deep cellar where the destiny of the Dukays was finally fulfilled.

But meanwhile we are in debt to the extent of four momentous years, for we last saw Zia in November of 1935 as she issued from the gate of the palace on Septemvir Utca, where the passers-by who saw her and recognized her had no way of knowing that the young countess would never cross that threshold again.

The year of 1936 had important events in store for the Dukay chronicles.

We may recall that two American ladies, Mrs. Steele and her daughter Gwen, were present at Zia's great wedding six years previously. Only Zia knew the real reason for their presence; the others merely guessed at it. Familiar with the hidden reasons for the inroads of European aristocrats upon America, we might suppose that Mr. Julian K. Steele belonged to the "sixty families" and boasted a fortune of more than a billion dollars, with less than which no Viennese librettist would be content to endow any marriage. We must, alas, eschew this particular road to romance. Mr. Steele was a butcher. But we also deserve to know that this appellation originated in part with Countess Isabella and in part with Otto Kliegl. Countess Isabella at least had a certain justification for her somewhat slighting appraisal of Mr. Steele's occupation, since she had marked György for her own daughter Elly, and had even settled the matter conclusively with Countess Menti ten years ago. Actually Mr. Steele was the manager of a world-famous packing house in Chicago, and it was a pleasantry on the part of Countess Isabella to maintain that he stood behind a counter in a blood-specked apron and sliced liverwurst for workingmen. On the contrary: Mr. Steele directed the affairs of an international industry from behind the enormous desk in his paneled office. A bouquet of fresh roses graced his desk at all times, and two substantial silver-framed photographs stood to his right and his left. One was a photograph of his wife Peggy as a bride, while the other represented his two children, Austin at the age of two and Gwen at the age of one. But this was many years ago, for the children's photographs were generally replaced on the average of every two years, as they grew up, although the picture of their mamma stubbornly stayed in its frame, probably with the fond thought that she would grow no larger than she had been as a bride. Mr. Steele's annual income was comparatively modest, about forty thousand dollars a year. His financial stature was dwarfed by the wealth which György Dukay would inherit, even if we consider the handsome, spacious red brick house which Mr. Steele owned in one of the suburbs of Chicago; nor had Peggy been entirely empty-handed when she married him.

An intention to study the meat-packing industry, with thoughts of building a modern slaughterhouse on the estate at Ararat, brought György to Chicago. There, as a graduate economist, he found employment in Mr. Steele's organization and, through his contact with the latter, was introduced—if only casually, for his employer was wary of European aristocrats—to Mrs. Steele and Gwen. Both mother and daughter were active members of the Chicago Society of Friends.

It was fortunate that Mamma Peggy had suffered from rheumatism for the past ten years, for her physician mentioned the famous thermal baths of Budapest among a number of various therapeutic resorts, and this was why Mrs. Steele and her daughter found themselves in Budapest in the spring of 1930. György knew of their prospective trip, although he no longer worked for the firm. Thus, when he returned home for Zia's wedding, there was nothing unusual in the fact that he traveled in the company of Mrs. Steele and her daughter, nor in his offer to act as their guide in Budapest, nor in the invitation he extended to his sister's wedding.

What Mrs. Steele and her daughter saw in the course of their day at Ararat left them both breathless.

György did not return to the United States until the following year, but the friendship deepened into regular correspondence. After his daughter's return Mr. Steele made no objection to the idea of inviting György to their home, but when

Peggy mused in private about possible romantic developments he protested vigorously against the prospect of a marriage. Mr. Steele, ensconced behind the roses on his desk, was a realistic American businessman who took a dim view of Europe by that time.

But the romantic developments did materialize, and serious obstacles loomed before György, too. These did not involve sentiment, for by then the affection between the young count and Gwen was serious and profound; but György Dukay III, who founded the entailment and with whose death in 1829 the ducal line became extinct, had stipulated in the letters patent that the heir to the entail must marry a consort with at least sixteen members of the nobility among her maternal and paternal ancestors, ten of whom had to be of the highest degree. Subsequent heirs to the estate had observed the letter of this stipulation with the utmost strictness. We may recall that Count Dupi, before meeting Princess Klementina Schäyenheim-Elkburg in London, was in love with a Hungarian countess from Transylvania and would have married the dark, blue-eyed Hannah if her ancestry had not, unfortunately, lacked two of the requisite noble titularies of the first rank, for the Transylvania aristocracy was wont to mix with the old Magyar families of the lesser nobility. A magnifying glass would not have detected a single tide of lesser rank on Countess Menti's family tree, which could be traced back for centuries, whereas Miss Steele's family tree would have thrown this same magnifying glass into utter confusion.

The laws of entailment remained in effect in Hungary after the king's death, and when György's engagement to Gwen became known, Otto Kliegl, in the name of his favorite spiritual offspring, Count János, armed himself with lawyers of the most formidable caliber and joined battle. Count János did not have to be incited to combat; the deadly and despicable conflicts which have surrounded monarchical succession since the beginning of history have also and always obtained between the first-born and the younger sons in the matter of entailed inheritance.

The patrimony had been fairly unkind to the other children: Zia and Kristina received only three thousand acres from the freehold, and János only five thousand. At the same time György would inherit one hundred thousand acres, as well as the entire Dukay fortune, or, more precisely, the income from that fortune. The result of such disposition, in general, was that the younger son ran his own lands into debt or dissipated them—one more reason for him to hate the heir.

There were weighty political considerations in the battle between György and János. If the Steele marriage disqualified György from his inheritance, János would become the heir, and the vast fortune would be enlisted in the service of the Nazis. This was to nobody's interest, not even the Hungarian government's interest, in those years. The lawyers who backed János's claim were, of course, big guns in the Nazi Party. The Dukay fortune began to assume the role of Austria, or of the Sudetenland in Czechoslovakia: would the Germans occupy it? Fortunately the relevant passage in the letters patent of the entail began as follows: "It is my express wish that the consort of the heir..." An express wish, however, is not necessarily a command. Furthermore, it was successfully established that György Dukay III granted his son Kaiman Dukay "exceptional" permission to wed Baroness Melanie Alacsy, who could scrape together only eight ancestors of the high nobility from among her forebears. The question was this: Would György Dukay remain the heir to the entail if he married Miss Steele? And the question was not so simple as it sounds, especially in view of the fact that counsel for both sides regarded the controversy as a milch cow waiting to be tapped. And such a controversy is even more compliant than the gentlest milch cow, for the courts are in no hurry to hand down a final decision. This is why the engagement of György and Miss Steele lasted for four full years, until the courts finally declarer that György Dukay's marriage would not affect his right of inheritance.

The wedding was held at Ararat in April of 1936, and Mr. Steele was present too. János and Zia were absent, and the wedding itself was on a modest scale. Instead of renting a house of their own, the young couple occupied a suite in the Septemvir Utca Palace and in the castle at Ararat, for by that time György was already managing the affairs of the estate.

The events of these years did not improve the condition of Count Dupi's heart. He never spoke of Zia to anyone, forbade the mention of her name in his presence, and those about him wondered at his spiritual fortitude, for everyone knew he loved Zia best of all his children. He naturally took György's side in the suit between György and János; the abhorrence he had conceived for "the German puppy" increased when that young man became one of the leaders of the green-shirted Arrow and Cross Party of Hungary. But the count's hair turned gray as a consequence of the lawsuit; people do not like to hear their own funeral orations recited while they are still alive, and the legal briefs simply buzzed with such tender statements as, "We must unfortunately take account of

István Dukay's impending death...in the event of the early demise of the head of the family..."

Every morning at eight Mr. Johnson, the English stablemaster, led Count Dupi's saddle horse to the main entrance of the castle. One morning Count Dupi already had his foot in the stirrup when he thought better of it and informed Mr. Johnson that he would not ride that day. He held his hand on his heart while he said this; as if to endorse his words with a solemn vow. Evidently the movement of placing his foot in the stirrup had struck a sudden and savage pain in his heart. Mr. Johnson noted that the count's face had turned ash-gray, and when his master slowly walked back into the castle Mr. Johnson could no longer recognize the pride which had once graced the carriage of the count's head and shoulders.

In September of 1936 Zia gave birth to a healthy girl-child who was christened Terézia at Ursi's insistence. Zia Photos was progressing profitably. Members of high society who had not been invited either to the Septemvir Utca Palace or Ararat Castle for decades appeared with their families to have their pictures taken, in the course of which they addressed Zia as if she were a grocery clerk. Aristocrats came, mainly out of curiosity, and they regarded Zia with the secret jealousy which six-month-old infants show toward the year-and-a-half-old sister who has accomplished the miracle of standing on her own feet. Of her brothers and sisters, Kristina was an infrequent caller, but György and Gwen had dinner at Zia's house fairly often. There was a real sincerity about their familial affection and friendship, although György and Mihály held opposing views on several points. György contended that socialization of the great estates should start not from the bottom but from the top, and he outlined his plans with fervor while the two women, Zia and Gwen, sewed under the light of a standing lamp in the adjoining room and debated the ponderous problems of child-raising. Gwen was already expecting her first child. Mihály held his own in argument with György, but never became deeply immersed in their discussions. Recently he had absented himself from the *Stammtisch* in the Gugger Café, too, and had gone into retreat behind his stars, a withdrawal of some distance. He was hard at work on his book about the Great Coal Sack, which is—as we know—the darkest nebula in the constellation of Cygnus. He made no attempt to retrieve his government post, for he grew increasingly less inclined to serve the current administration. His astronomical articles were widely published in American, English, Swedish and Swiss periodicals, and he was invited to lecture at a number of foreign universities.

Countess Menti called on Zia about once every quarter year. On these occasions she sat in the exact middle of the sofa with her hat on her head, holding her parasol in a gloved hand with an inimitable gesture, and her back was as straight as a reed—this' was how she used to appear in the modest homes of Ararat schoolteachers whose wives were hopelessly afflicted with kidney trouble. Countess Menti paid appreciative attention to Zia's latest photographs when she examined them through her lorgnette, but she considered the entire profession of photography a peculiar and incurable disease to which her daughter had fallen victim. On each and every visit she informed Mihály about the telescope in the library of the castle at Ararat, and expressed the opinion that astronomy was a very beautiful science, unlike that "fun-ny" art of astrology, but otherwise she found little more to say to her son-in-law. In the recent past Countess Menti's whole being had begun to fill with a mild and mournful spirituality. Sometimes she dropped a hint of a "great plan" in Zia's presence, but she never revealed what her plan was. "Sie werden das sehen, Zia—you'll see," she would say mysteriously, addressing Zia with the formal pronoun which she used toward all her children.

In January of that year King George V of England died, in March the Germans occupied the demilitarized Rhineland, and in December Edward VIII abdicated the throne of England. Romance donned royal robes to parade before the people in what was to be its farewell appearance for a long time to come, possibly intending a final display of power over all the insignificant and evanescent things which sententious historians call a "new age," or "the changing forms of life," or "the dynamics of class society."

Nothing emptier or duller can be imagined than the year that followed, 1937. One need hardly render an account of something like the treaty of Italo-Jugoslav alliance which Premier Stojadinovic of Jugoslavia and Count Ciano signed in Belgrade, for it was little more than cabaret comedy.

Another event, much more important, demands our attention: a conversation between two men seated on the deserted terrace of a café along the Danube Corso, reveling in the first warm days of spring. One of them is called Paul Fürst, and the other is known as Otto Kiràly. As we draw near we recognize Paul Fogoly and Otto Kliegl. One feels, in connection with their recent change of names, that Paul Fogoly's justification was the more honorable, when he decided to reassume the original name of his grandfather in open and courageous advertisement of repentant adherence to the great German Idea after a variety of feckless excursions into the realms of liberalism and Hungarian nationalism. In the case of Otto Kliegl the intent was not quite so clear. We must suppose that he assumed a Hungarian name simply to worm his way into the confidence of certain strata of Hungarian society with greater facility, for there were some who would be taken in by such devices. However much Paul Fürst and Otto Király differed in this regard, they were in complete accord on the tenet that a momentous hour had struck in the history of the German race, and that in the interest of the Idea the extermination first of the Jews in the German community and then of the backward peoples represented nothing more than the care with which a gentleman brushes his overcoat before leaving the house.

Speaking of Paul Fogoly, we should also devote a few words to his formerly inseparable friend, Imre Pognár, who married Eva Kócsag in October of last year after ten years of unavailing adoration. Nor must we be too hasty in offering our condolences to Pognár, who might seem to have deserved a better fate, for life offers countless examples of women like Kócsag the *artiste* and even stormier courtesans who became the most perfect, the most faithful wives. Daughters of Protestant ministers, of estimable town councilors, however, who approach the altar clad in the virginal myrtle of the purest middle-class virtues, who uphold the puritan ideals of society in their married state, who are considered by public opinion to be matrimonial paragons—such women embitter the lives of their husbands with matters like an unconquerable aversion to the smell of onions; or hinder their hurrying, frantic, office-bound mate at the front door with the demand that he replace his brown-striped shirt with a blue-striped shirt; or, for reasons unknown, harbor a passionate hatred for the wife of their husband's employer. Although the convention of their society does not countenance separation, they are incessantly threatening to leave their unhappy spouse. Women like Eva Kócsag, on the other hand, exhaust themselves of this sort of shrewishness before entering into marriage. Their frenzies are dissipated on the stage, at rehearsals, and their fantasies in their lovers' beds, and thus their weariness becomes humility, their disillusion becomes marital fidelity, and their tempestuous financial misadventures turn them into women of canny conscience and worldly wisdom who, in their skill at balancing income and expenditure, might well be the envy of gray-bearded accountants.

News of Filippo, too, reached Budapest from time to time. In recent years he had completely abandoned his wastrel existence, and participated in the Abyssinian campaign as a pilot officer. He was awarded a high decoration by the

Duce for bravery in action, which meant that he had flown low over an Abyssinian village and machine-gunned a group of gaping, naked native children.

Countess Menti's "great plan" finally came to light one afternoon when she entered her husband's study (we already know that her rare visitations of this sort were always of major significance) and told him, in the tone she might have used in discussing one of Monsieur Cavaignac's proposed menus, that she was retiring to Almaskö, together with her secretary, her companion, her senior chambermaid, two footmen, a chauffeur and the Reverend Alajos Galovics. There were two reasons why Count Dupi could not possibly oppose her plan: first, because he himself had banished the word *opposition* from their household; and second, because the two-thousand-acre country seat at Almaskö was the part of the vast Schäyenheim lands, north of the Danube and extending along the new Czechoslovakian border, which belonged to Countess Menti herself by right of personal inheritance. Except for the caretaker, the thirty-room hunting lodge stood empty.

At the age of sixty-three, Countess Menti was not retiring to this God-forsaken place purely for the purposes of repose. A week after she and her forces invaded Almaskö a strange company assembled in the lodge. There was among them a young pediatrician, three child supervisors and a progressive educator, to all of whom Countess Menti outlined her plan. She began with the assertion that mankind was very unhappy. She was not, sad to say, in a position to bring happiness to the more than two billion people in the world; the task was too large; but everyone had to share in that task to the best of his ability. She had decided, therefore, to raise one hundred infants at Almaskö, fifty boys and fifty girls, in keeping with the most modern principles of hygiene and education. She spoke in German, for it was her native tongue, and kept glancing at her notes through the lorgnette. She dealt in detail with the faults of current methods of child training. Children were constantly threatened, and frightened, and generally raised in an environment of fear. She mentioned an interesting experiment conducted by an American psychologist who made a study of the spiritual development of two infants. One of them was brought up in the ancient and erroneous atmosphere of terror, while in an adjacent room they released snakes and rats and saw the second child in gleeful play with the animals from morning till night. She quoted a psychoanalyst's monograph to the effect that children should not be beaten when they tie a cat in a bag and club it to death, or when they gouge out the eyes of goslings with their thumbs. The Creator gave man the nature of an animal, with dreadful sadistic tendencies. Therefore children must be encouraged to express their budding passions in childhood. The horror of their deeds should be explained to them with solicitude, not with threats and beatings, otherwise their repressed sadism would sink into their *Unbewust* and later, when they became army officers or statesmen, would manifest itself in frightful form. Countess Menti's lecture revealed that the edifice of her ideas was based not on reading alone but on other things as well. She turned to the topic of elementary instruction. The childish soul, in her opinion, was nourished on homicide and mass murder from the very first hour in school. She contended that children should be given textbooks of religion and history in which Cain did not kill Abel and Christ was not crucified, in which the Trojan War and other frightfulnesses of mankind were discreetly bypassed. At this point she commented on the problem of nutrition, too, and expressed the view that as long as men remained carnivorous, as long as they continued to murder and devour animals with such repulsive cruelty, they could not be expected to refrain from developing the desire to kill their fellow men. The hundred youngsters, therefore, would be raised as vegetarians. In conclusion, she dwelt on the subject of sex education and with the problems of sex in general. The substance of her remarks was that children should be freed from an inane and unnecessary sense of modesty; that girls should marry at the time of their first menstruation, to protect boys from the excesses of adolescence. Her voice was somewhat uncertain as she pronounced terms like "sexual intercourse" and "self-abuse," and her lovely neck was suffused with blushes. But she bravely said what she had to say without falling into a faint.

Recruitment of the children began shortly thereafter. Overburdened wives of workingmen and wayward peasant girls brought their babies, from among whom a medical examiner selected only the healthiest. The original plan was modified to the extent that twenty instead of a hundred applicants were accepted, for careful estimates disclosed that the available funds would support no more than this number. Administrative expenses accounted for the greater part of the budget. But Countess Menti and her staff hoped that their movement would eventually be nationalized; in the opinion of the Reverend Lojzi, in fact, it would swell to international proportions.

697

Countess Menti named her institution the "Glass House." Immediately after her arrival she gave the command that no one was allowed to refer to her any longer either as "Her Excellency the Countess" or, as some people mistakenly called her, "Her Grace the Princess." Instead, each and every inhabitant and employee of the Glass House was given the name of a bird. These were chosen by a special Committee on Names. From the very start, in general, there was a vast variety of committees. Among others, there was the Firewood Committee, the Committee on Conciliation, the Towel Committee and the Committee on Nature Worship. Countess Menti, in her new incarnation, was named Ibis, while the Reverend Alajos Galovics was rechristened Bustard. When Countess Menti met the gardener in the course of a morning stroll, the greetings went as follows:

"Good morning, Ibis!"

To which Countess Menti gave a dignified reply, rolling her *r*'s delicately:

"Good morning, Sparrow!"

During dinner Dr. Köhler, the progressive educator, occasionally called to the footman:

"A little more gravy, Ouzel."

And the footman was already on the way with the gravy boat, saying:

"At your service, Flamingo."

There was a number of honorary non-resident members of the Glass House, selected with extreme care by the Committee on Admissions. The non-resident members were also given bird names, and these were not devoid of a certain light humor. In view of her literary aspirations Kristina, for example, was named Lyrebird. Because of his short neck, György was called Barn Owl, while Gwen, who had a habit of whistling absent-mindedly, was Yellowthroat.

Among the twenty children there was a gypsy, two Jews, and even—which is almost unbelievable—three Protestants. We could hardly expect greater concessions of Countess Menti and the Revernd Lojzi, both of whom were members of the Governing Committee.

All this goes to show that there was, in the intellectual composition of the Glass House, something of the noble humanitarian heritage of the American Quakers, the seeds of which reached Countess Menti's receptive soul through Gwen. We must not look askance at the form which the splendid concepts, the gospels of William Penn, founder of Pennsylvania, took when they were adapted to the use of a hunting lodge in Almaskö. Great ideals wander about the world easefully, at a snail's pace, and sometimes assume entirely novel shape at different places. In the "vegetarian" theories of child-raising we can readily discern the influence of György's reminiscences of the dreadful carnage in the Chicago slaughterhouse. Apart from these lesser derivations, we can see that the Glass House was the sad, ineffectual withdrawal of a sensitive feminine soul from the world which Europe represented in 1938.

The first annual report showed that the budget was overdrawn. The number of children in training had to be cut in half, regrettably, while at the same time the administrative staff was increased by an assistant gardener, a chauffeur, a music teacher and an accountant.

We hardly need say that Count Dupi considered the Glass House "a lot of nonsense," birds and all. Although the Committee on Admissions elected him an honorary member too, if only by a bare majority, he refused to have anything to do with the Glass House. And this was fortunate, in the final analysis, for if the footman known as Ouzel had addressed a jolly "Good morning, Ostrich!" to Count Dupi, he would certainly have slapped Ouzel's face, thereby gravely compromising the principles which governed the Glass House.

The Glass House represented something entirely different to Count Dupi. Countess Menti had chosen this time to desert him, when it would have been so good to sit with her in the great, silent salons and talk over bygone days. She had deserted him at a time of illness and old age, when he was truly in need of the conjugal tenderness which reconciliation might have brought. He sensed a certain revenge in Countess Menti's departure, revenge for the early years of their marriage, when he had constantly, perfidiously, publicly betrayed her. The "gute Menti" had stored up those sorrows as carefully as she kept letters or noted the dates of acquisition of additions to her porcelain collection, and now, at the very brink of the grave, she was giving them back. If there was really something like this at work in Countess Menti's actions, it could only have been in the depths of her subconscious mind; thoughts such as these sprang, rather, from Count Dupi's guilty conscience.

Recently the lonely, white-haired count had begun to appear every morning in a little tobacconist shop which stood in the neighborhood of Septemvir Utca. Miss Dora, the proprietress, wore large, amber-hued combs in her ash-gray hair, stood straight and tall, and served her customers with a well-shaped wrist; her figure preserved its fresh, youthful lines for all that she was an old maid of forty. She had been granted a commercial license after the death of her pensioned mother, and the beneficence of the government was understandable in view of the fact that her father, an erstwhile state councilor, had once performed valuable services for his country. Count Dupi took his time about selecting his cigars every morning, and asked meanwhile: "How are you, Dora dear? Is there anything you need, Dora dear?" He bought flowers and bonbons for the not entirely youthful Dora dear. He even sat down to smoke his first cigar of the day in the tobacconist shop, thereby causing a serious traffic jam in the narrow little place. None of this, of course, escaped the notice of the Buda populace and, since humanity is always amused at the sight of a seventy-year-old grandfather in the throes of love, there was a vast increase in Dora dear's cigar and cigarette business during the morning hours, for the report spread throughout Buda that old, imbecilic Count Dukay was divorcing his wife and intended to marry the proprietress of a cigar store. The gossip, as always, was groundless. There was something that Dora dear herself did not know, something that only Count Dupi knew. Dora was his natural child. There are those who may have been surprised at the unusual benevolence shown by the government toward the orphan of a prominent and valuable civil servant—they will be relieved to know that it was Count Dupi, remaining discreetly in the background, who obtained a tobacconist's license for Dora after her mother's death. Sitting in wreaths of smoke of a morning, it was not Dora he saw in the movements of her delicate wrists, in the kind, somewhat sorrowful and already lusterless violet eyes—it was her mother, whose only and tragic love he had been, although that beautiful woman was no more than a passing fancy of the count. There was, in Count Dupi's frequent trips to the tobacconist shop, in his flowers and bonbons, a certain belated contrition, and perhaps the orphanhood of a paternal heart as well. He was seeking restitution for the loss of Zia.

Of the count's countless illegitimate children, Dora belonged among the "secret" ones. But he also had so-called "public" natural children, including two countesses, a titular bishop, a leader of industry, and Herendy, the popular film star whose mother, Rose Herendy, had been a well-known essayist in the Nineties. It was because of his mother that Herendy was unfortunately accounted a full-blooded Jew by the second Jewish Law; thereafter he always offered his left hand to acquaintances and when they asked: "What's wrong, Zoli, does your right hand hurt?" he answered: "Yes, my right hand hurts because it's Jewish, but my left hand is a descendant of the Ordony clan."

In the fall of the same year Count Dupi received an even greater blow than the Glass House had been. His Excellency Robert Schurler died. Count Dupi should have been ineffably happy, for he despised no one so much as the son of the thieving batman he had once booted out, that loud-mouthed, insolent pseudo-patriot who, after the favor of the Regent had made him an Excellency, never failed to shout "Hello, Dupi!" in the National Casino when he sighted the count from afar, and this had to be borne because he was a legitimist (and later set his sails for Hitler's haven, of course). Robert Schurler died in the spring and his memory soon seemed to be completely lost in the stream of eventful historical crises which followed. But when Count Dupi returned to the city from Ararat in October, the street sign on his house caught his eye as he stepped from his car. Over the handsome baroque gate, in place of the melodious eighteenth-century patina of Septemvir Utca, a freshly painted street sign glittered with the words: "Robert Schurler Utca." Pale with passion, the count raised his walking stick and would probably have thumped the silver-mustachioed doorman on the head if Sándor had not skipped aside. A stack of accumulated mail awaited him in his study, all addressed to "His Excellency Count István Dukay, Robert Schurler Utca No. 1, Budapest."

He ripped open all the drawers of his desk until he finally found some writing paper—which was in its usual place, of course—and began to write at white heat, choking with fury as he formed the tall, saber-shaped letters:

Mr. Mayor—I protest against this defamation of my home and my person...I shall have the new street signs removed at once and, if necessary, shall answer force with force...

These were among the milder passages in his letter, which was despatched by special messenger. The mayor answered promptly.

Your Excellency: Thank you for the kindness of your gracious letter, which I do not quite understand. If you have already had the street signs removed, why do you use the address of Robert Schurler Utca on your own stationery?

Count Dupi's face blanched. He had not noticed, when he sealed the letter, that the resplendent Dukay stationery, embellished with the woodpecker crest and engraved in red and gold, already bore the new address, Robert Schurler Utca No. 1, which was a result of Mr. Gruber's attentive and unflagging devotion to duty. Mr. Gruber had heard many, many war whoops issue from that study, but this was the first time the count ever threatened him with a chair.

And this was when Count Dupi had his first serious heart attack. From that point on he viewed developments with lackluster eyes. The optimism of his son György, who held that Hungary at least would remain neutral in the unlikely event of a second World War, was all in vain—István Dukay was beyond consolation. First Franz Joseph, then the Monarchy, and then Charles IV...and, in his own family, Zia, and then the Glass House, not to mention Rere, Kristina, János, and Robert Schurler Utca—all these had been the signs of an approaching death, like the gradual frigidity which invades one limb after another of a dying man. Then there was György: a serious, good lad—but, with his short neck, very much like a provincial mill manager. Where was the ancient Turkish charm of the Dukays, the verve, the dash? His blood was Zoskay blood, true, but the Zoskays had been a middling breed of Ostyaks. And there were all his plans, some sort of American hodgepodge. Prince Andrew and Egry-Toth were right peasants must be held in check. And the way György worked from morning till night, like a hard-pressed banker of ill repute, was almost indecent.

Only Rere, of all the members of the family, remained at his fathers side. After supper, when Count Dupi clenched his hands behind his back and stalked up and down the deserted, silent salon, Rere would sit in the depths of a large settee beside the Chinese lamp, indefatigably reading Cervantes's *Novelas ejemplares* in the original Spanish and laughing out loud from time to time, although he understood not a word of Spanish. This did not disturb Count Dupi's gloomy stride, and once he even stopped beside Rere to remark: "You're right, Rere. You're the only one who's right..." He patted his son's shoulder and resumed his pent-up pacing. Rere's eyebrows twitched like those of someone who dislikes to be disturbed while reading.

This was perhaps the first time in Count Dupi's life that he had spent the hot days of August in the Septemvir Utca Palace. In recent weeks he had read *The Great Fallow* for the third time, in secret, feeling as he had felt at the age of ten when he read his first books of pornography in remote corners of the palace or hidden behind a bush in the park at Ararat. The book struck him like a condemnation from which there was no appeal.

And for the first time in his life, during these days of meditation, he tried to take stock of his entire existence, of the youthful escapades, the love affairs, the luxury of his palaces, his income and expenditures—in fine, of the way he had invested his monies and his morals. He tried to answer the accusations, but without success, for he did not feel himself guilty and the charges themselves seemed to be couched in a language that was entirely foreign to him. It was as if someone were to confront him with a bill of particulars which demanded to know how he had dared to hunt tigers in India in 1894, or why he used aromatic salts in his morning bath. Behind these seemingly absurd accusations, nevertheless, he sensed a certain mysterious and menacing challenge to account for himself.

The major-domo Herr Jordan, whose room had been moved next to Count Dupi's bedroom to make him available at any time, used to wake at night to hear the count shouting in his sleep.

Count Dupi, too, knew of the passages in the family archives which described how the eleven-mile-long brick wall had been built around the game preserve at Ararat a century ago, and how the serfs were required to bring kettlefuls of fresh eggs, eggs by the million to bind the plaster. Once he dreamt that the eggs hatched in the wall and a multitude of little yellow chicks came climbing out of the peeling plaster, suddenly grown to large black birds with fearful claws and beaks; and they circled like vultures about Ararat Castle.

Count Dupi lived in terror of the outbreak of another war. He knew by now that another war would once again be followed by revolution, and he surmised that this revolution would not subside as simply as the events that followed the first World War had done, when nothing more momentous had happened than that Comrade Ibrik, who regularly took his afternoon naps on one of the sofas of Ararat Castle during the short-lived summer season of the Commune, left an ugly, greasy, sickle-shaped spot on the head-rest of the noble silk upholstery. No, something else, something terrible was in store.

Sometimes, late at night, he stopped and pricked up his ears at the sound of shouting outside. He could clearly hear a newsboy dashing through the street with one of the Budapest dailies under his arm, calling: "Extra! War breaks out!"

He would hasten to the window, pull the heavy silk draperies aside and lean out, terror on his face. Only when he saw that it was a street urchin who had been shouting something or other was he reassured.

And sometimes a fierce longing for Zia possessed him. Once his hand was already poised on the bell, to summon the car and dash over to see the "cricket." He seemed to sense that Zia, too, in the privacy of her apartment on Andrássy Ut, sometimes shed tears of longing for her father. But nothing ever came of the visit, for at the last moment the inflexible Dukay always came to the fore in Count Dupi.

✝

And then came the 31st of August, in 1939. Count Dupi was listening to the radio in the salon after dinner. This was when the knell of the second World War began to ring throughout the world. It was ten o'clock on a Thursday evening. The German ultimatum…mobilization in Poland…

While he paced fretfully between the great oaken door and the open window, his hands clasped behind his back, and while Corot's *Woman in Purple* and a shepherdess gathering mushrooms in the forest of one of the Gobelins watched his monotonous steps with anxiety on their faces, Count Dupi sought to bring his agonized thoughts into some sort of order. This was no simple task, for Count Dupi, according to the Schmidt-Kopper school of philosophy, belonged to the human type known as the breeder of beasts, who is unacquainted with the methodology of systematic thought, whose thoughts, like his beasts, range freely and along irregular paths. Lacking the capacity for objective thought, Count Dupi was able to conceive of the events of recent years only in terms of personalities. Not only the influential and reflective minds among the aristocracy, but members of the diplomatic corps and widely traveled, important personages from abroad as well, often—and with increasing frequency in the last few years—put in an appearance at the so-called "little suppers" in Ararat Castle and even more at those in the palace on Septemvir Utca. Therefore it was as natural for Count Dupi to let this society attend to his contemplation of the fate of the world as to permit Herr Jordan to decide which suit the master would wear each morning, to yield to Monsieur Cavaignac's authority in the matter of partridge with puréed lentils and to allow Mr. Gruber to handle his correspondence. When Count Dupi cogitated on the world he saw human lineaments before him rather than maps, nations, peoples, forms of government or abstract ideas. The thought of Germany, for example, brought only the image of Prince Fini to the count's mind, an image of the prince settling comfortably into a large armchair, carefully

704

interlacing the ten widespread fingertips of his two hands and delivering, in a tone of incontrovertible assurance, a detailed exposition of the certainty of the final triumph of Hitlerism, while the parchment of his somewhat batlike ears and the delicate wrinkles of his aging face turned red with inner conviction. Prince Fini was the sole representative, in the family, of unconditional Hitler-worship—that is, if we no longer consider Count János, whom Fini encountered only secretly by now, as a member of the family.

Italy, in Count Dupi's eyes, was Achile Ozzolini, whose official missions as a member of the Fascist Grand Council brought him more and more frequently to Budapest, on which occasions he always stayed at Septemvir Utca. He and his wife were often entertained, too, at Ararat Castle, where they would spend weeks at a time without mentioning the names of the children who had flown so far from under the protection of parental wings.

Representing England was Count Peter the historian, who had been educated at Cambridge and made more vehement defense of English interests when a controversy arose than Hewlitt, the newly appointed English Ambassador who studied the tips of his shoes attentively at social gatherings or cast his eyes at the ceiling with an unexpected throw of his head and maintained, generally, a cautious silence.

The mediary of France was Gaston de Ferreyolles, First Secretary at the French Embassy and a distant relative of the Dukays as well, for—as we know—it was the Marquis de Ferreyolles, son of General Bonaparte, who married Suzanne Dukay. Gaston was a diminutive, bespectacled figure with something of the complexion of a gypsy, and, unlike the English Ambassador, he did a great deal of talking, in the course of which he whirled his short arms like the sails of a windmill; he was the champion of the world, in Kristina's opinion, at lisping.

The Sphinx of Russia was present in this circle of family and friends in the person of Count Dmitri who, after his escape through Poland from the Lenin Revolution of nearly twenty years ago, had finally settled in Hungary and, aided by the remarkable Russian gift for languages, had learned to speak Hungarian perfectly. An expert horseman, he became a prosperous trader in horses, in addition to which he also capitalized on his knowledge of the Russian tongue in the studios of the Hungarian radio network. Spiritually, too, he underwent a prodigious transformation, and was forever defending the Soviet position in discussions. This did not mean that he became a Communist, but he did regard Russia as his true homeland. "One's country," he used to say, "is like a tooth. You take cognizance of it only when it begins to give you pain."

Nor was the United States unrepresented. György's wife Gwen, whose brother served in the Department of State, assured the constant presence of American and Rooseveltian policies in the house, and this sometimes provoked Prince Fini to exceptionally heated rebuttal. György's quiet "Please, darling" or Countess Menti's "Aber Fini!" vainly sought to still the outspoken exchange of words, and it happened not infrequently that Gwen stopped in the middle of a sentence, rose to her feet and left the room. At such times her mute departure and the lines of her well-shaped back gave almost audible expression to her opinion of Prince Fini: "*You idiot!*"

The day before yesterday, on that Wednesday evening when Hitler expressed a demand for Danzig in his reply to England, and yesterday, when Poland began to mobilize her forces, Princess Karola too was seated here beside the radio—the authoress Princess Karola, daughter of the Prince Wieromiej who first appeared in Hungary during the Nineties on a secret and important diplomatic mission but lost four and a half million florins in a single night at the Casino and was able to pay no more than three millions of his debt. It was only three years later, unfortunately, that Prince Wieromiej learned, at the Hungarian Press Club, the most important rule of card players, that "gambling debts, unless they are paid within forty-eight hours, become null and void." Princess Karola no longer spoke a word of Polish, but in her heart of hearts she was as much a Pole as Count Dmitri was a Russian. Perhaps the first and only time her darting, delicate little mouse-head froze to immobility was when the radio broadcast the tragic fate of her native land, Poland.

No one could have better represented the neutral nations of Northern Europe, chief among them Sweden, than Princess Karola's husband Baron Adam, with his reddish-blond, glistening mustache and the red-and-white complexion which he had inherited from his mother, the daughter of a Swedish razor-blade manufacturer.

Not nations and peoples alone, decked in smoking jackets or tails, appeared in this room, but the dominant ideologies of the world as well. The Church, for example, was naturally represented by Bishop Zsigmond's thin voice and querulously raised eyebrows, and another figure frequently seen at the "little suppers" was Prince Andrew, the "Black Prince" who was truly a statue of Feudalism cast in bronze, for his complexion reflected his Addison's disease ever more faithfully. Occasionally the statue did unusual things: it moved its arms, took nourishment, and even broke into speech from time to time.

It was with the mind of these human beings that Count Dupi, as he paced up and down in the salon, was now thinking. Midnight was already past: silence and darkness came flooding through the open window. On other such summer nights the silence of the city had been full of warm, soft stirrings, secretive and sexual sounds. Struggling up the hillsides, taxicabs had carried giddy wives and mothers to clandestine appointments in bachelor flats, and through the distance the strain of motors was hardly louder than the purr of a cat. The gypsy music on the terraces of cafés along the Danube and in the chestnut-bowered courtyards of taverns on the Buda slopes was never quite audible here, but somehow it always had seemed to fill the silence, very much as the fragrance of flowers in faraway fields filled the warm summer darkness. Now, however, the silence seemed lifeless, as if the evening blast of the radio had stilled every other latent, lurking sound.

Human shapes came to occupy the empty chairs in the great salon. There they all sat in the silken armchairs, Bishop Zsigmond, Princes Fini and Andrew and Achile, Counts Peter and Lajos and Dmitri, Baron Adam and Gaston de Ferrreyolles, Princess Karola, Kristina, György and Gwen, for these had constituted Dupi's family in the last years—Countess Menti was in the Glass House, János was who knows where, and Zia...ah yes, Zia. It was four years, more or less, since he had last seen Zia.

The familiar society with which his imagination now peopled the great salon seemed to have convened, this evening, for a final, fateful conference. They encompassed all of Europe, nay, the entire world, for Count Charles the lion hunter spoke intermittently of Africa and India too. There they all sat, gesticulating feverishly, working their lips at a great rate—but they had no voices, as if they were truly phantoms.

Someone was missing.

Count Dupi came to a standstill in his quiet pacing, like a man who happens to recall something long forgotten. For a moment or two he thoughtfully rubbed the bristles of his mustache with the crippled forefinger of his left hand. Then he stepped to the telephone and sought out—awkwardly, like someone unversed at such things—a name in the directory: Mihály Ursi. To Count Dupi this name, at this moment, meant not Zia alone, but meant the rearing, vengeful, sinister mass of Magyar peasantry somewhere in the darkness at the end of the telephone wires, meant mute Revolution, whose course in space the astronomer had charted as carefully as the parabolic course of an approaching comet. He dialed the number.

Zia and Mihály must come to Septemvir Utca at once. There was need to talk about…what? No matter what, there was need to talk. What time was it? They were not asleep yet, no one in the whole wide world was asleep now. They must discuss, immediately, a departure on the morrow. Departure to the seaside, or to the shores of the Balaton, with the two children. Zia already had two children, a girl of three and a boy of two, the age at which children were sweetest. And he had not even seen his grandchildren. But what else was there left in life? He was seventy-one years old, and his heart…yes, his heart. Now was the time to go away, anywhere, amid the valedictions of summer with the two children on his knee, to talk everything over and to forgive everything. No, not to forgive everything. But there were things that had lately taken on new meaning. That photographic studio—Zia Photos—was not a bad idea, for example. Who knew what the morrow would bring, when Ararat, Septemvir Utca, the Maginot Line, Hong Kong, the whole world had started into motion and set out somewhere like a leaf in a storm.

The telephone did not answer. They were probably not at home. Count Dupi resumed his monotonous pacing anew, with even quieter steps. Loneliness suffused him, and with it a cold fear the like of which he had never known before, a fear which now took the form of tiny little stabs at his heart.

But he was not alone. There was someone else in the room, sitting half-hidden in shadow beside the shaded Chinese lamp, speechless and motionless, with his gentle horse-head drooping somewhat and a witless smirk frozen on his face. For hours Count Dupi had been so occupied with his thoughts that he had not noticed Rere sitting in the salon as he sat each evening, sitting as quietly as a dog will lie at the feet of his master. It was by his stubborn and mute presence alone that Rere had lately expressed his devotion to the father in whom he sensed both loneliness and the approach of death. As he sat there motionlessly his nose, like a water tap in disrepair, dripped at thirty-second intervals, because Rere had been suffering from a cold for days. All of a sudden he twisted his lower jaw to one side, so far that the whitish gums showed above his large horse-teeth, and then he screwed up his nose as far as the skin would go, and then his whole face was distorted into a frightful grimace and grew rigid as he sneezed with the full lung-power of a town crier of yore, so loudly that the Chinese lamp tottered back and forth with the impact while the wild geese on the lampshade dispersed amid frantic cackling. Two green frog's-legs appeared on Rere's mustache, and one of them, in fact, was already stretching out its toes, exploring the depths to discover whether it was safe to jump. Rere fumbled for his handkerchief and, when he finally succeeded in snatching the damp dumpling-shaped cloth from his pocket, a completely chewed-off pheasant drumstick, one end of which was wrapped in tinfoil, fell out on the carpet too. Rere swiftly gathered it up and stuffed it out of sight, while with his other hand he endeavored to remove the unpleasant consequences of a cold from his mustache.

Count Dupi looked up in alarm at the sound of the detonation and whirled toward the Chinese lamp, almost as if someone had fired at him. Then, with a silent wave of his hand, he bade Rere leave the salon. Rere carried out the order obediently, but did not close the great oaken door completely. Nor did he retire to his room, but flattened himself against the wall of the corridor. He felt that extraordinary things would happen that night, for the nervous systems of idiots have something primitive about them and are as sensitive as the instincts of animals.

Left finally alone, Count Dupi made a last effort to comprehend the state of affairs, to seek out the connecting links and then stand before Corot's *Woman in Purple* and explain to her that what was taking place in the world would not affect the furnishings of the palace on Septemvir Utca—for that lady was now breaking the silence for the second time, announcing in a clearly, ghostly voice that brooked no denial: "There is no escape…no escape." He had to reassure her, as he had sometimes reassured Countess Menti at difficult moments.

And what indeed was taking place in the world? Prince Fini, Achile, Count Peter, Gaston de Ferreyolles and the rest—let them answer.

In the fall of 1935—or was it still in 1934?—Fini returned home with a stock of confidential information from Berlin. The use of gliders and the production of passenger vehicles had grown to fantastic proportions in Germany. Hitler had not violated the peace treaties as yet, but everything was in readiness for the break.

In the fall of the following year Count Peter returned home from London with the news that there was no need to fear for England, for the English had put two new, wonderful planes—the Hurricane and the Spitfire—into production. Possibly the Germans had a greater number of planes, yes; but wait till they saw these two. The new English planes were veritable hawks. At that point it was again Fini's turn to boast. They were like children bragging about their fathers' wealth. The German shipyards were already working in secret on the *Bismarck* and the *Tirpitz,* both of them incredibly large, one hundred twenty thousand tons apiece. Fini's figures were never reliable, but Gaston and Baron

Adam too already knew that smoke from factory chimneys was hovering over all of Germany, troops were drilling in the courtyard of every kindergarten and giant, mysterious canvas-covered trucks, driven at hitherto unattained speeds, were regularly overtaking tourist automobiles on the highways—some sort of great surprise was in preparation in Germany. Adam returned from Stockholm at about the time when Sweden was vigorously protesting the German program for compulsory military training. But England kept her peace, and even entered into a naval accord with the Germans. "It doesn't mean a thing," Count Peter remarked, "German naval strength can't be more than a third of the British!" Fini countered with the statement that the third was sufficient to assure German domination of the Baltic waters.

One evening last summer a curious humming had filled the skies over Ararat. The family was at dinner, but they all went out into the park. A giant Zeppelin, like a flying palace with its windows aglow, was passing beneath a faint, crescent moon. The dirigible was on a leisurely flight over Hungary, with a complement of newspapermen aboard who would write page-long accounts of the miraculous German machine. Kristina, of course, was one of the passengers. György estimated that the German Zeppelin was fifteen yards longer than the buildings of Parliament. Villagers who kept an early bedtime sprang from the depths of sleep at the rhythmic hum of the motors, with the result that millions upon millions of craners and gapers developed an acute pain in the neck that evening. Germany was beginning to flex her rippling muscles in public, like a professional wrestler in the ring of a provincial circus.

Hitler's mounting course began to draw even the anti-German milords of the Casino toward Germany. Schurler might well have been one of Hitler's paid agents, so loquacious did he suddenly become. Why did England fail to take action? Because if there was one chance in a hundred of endangering the peace by a move on her part, she would refuse to make it: this was Count Peter's paraphrase of Baldwin's words. When the Rhineland was occupied Flandin called for mobilization, but Downing Street turned him down. England did not take action because she was too, too decadent: this was Prince Fini's paraphrase of Hitler's words. Germany flapped her wings with a fearful noise and soared, soared, soared ever higher. Her rearmament program had long been a violation of the Treaty of Versailles; she had secured air superiority over England; she had built the Siegfried Line; she had gained an ally in Mussolini as a consequence of the Abyssinian War; she had engulfed Austria and Countess Menti's chambermaid

Jozefin, who used to fling herself on her knees before the radio in abjection; and then, disregarding Count Lajos as he shook his head in bewilderment, she had swallowed all of Czechoslovakia, including the Skoda Works—and it was incomprehensible that England still made no move. They discarded Eden, who urgently advocated armament on a nationwide scale, while Chamberlain waved his long arms at the world in reassurance and sought at all costs to be on good terms with the dictators.

Meanwhile new baby giraffes were born every day. It was one of Mr. Gruber's duties to peruse the humorous weeklies and to frequent the cafés, too, in search of good stories which would not take to printer's ink; each morning he reported to Count Dupi, as if to a chief censor or a cabinet minister, with a resumé of accumulated material. The giraffe story was current when the Jews had more than enough reason to be uneasy, and it told of two Jews who stood before the giraffes' cage in the zoo and silently regarded a newborn giraffe, long-necked and spotted. After a prolonged pause one Jew turned to the other: "What do you think—will this help us at all?"

Will this help us at all? What would help us? Following the Munich Pact, Gaston appeared with the whispered tale that Chamberlain, when he was left alone with the Führer, had remarked: "Look, now that we've reached an agreement, let's discuss the subject that is of utmost importance to us both—how we can best combine our strength to sweep the Soviet Order from the face of the earth." "Excellent!" said Hitler, and the discussion began. But a dictaphone was concealed under the table, and next day Hitler sent a recording of the proceedings to Stalin. Then, when the Anglo-French Commission, led by Admiral Drax and General Doumenc, reached Moscow to engage in conversations it was Dmitri who related this sequel—the Soviet experts who faced them over the conference table were unshaven and tieless and spoke fluent German among themselves. One evening the Russians unexpectedly broke off negotiations, and the next day Ribbentrop and his staff arrived to take lodgings at the very hotel where the Anglo-French Commission was staying. Crossing the hall on the following morning, Admiral Drax and General Doumenc turned pale with astonishment when they recognized, in the German generals chatting with Ribbentrop, the tieless and unshaven Soviet experts. The Russians had delegated German General Staff officers in mufti to confer with the French and the English and to discover their military secrets. Stalin had paid Chamberlain back for the secret recording. Impossible to know how much of this was true, for Dmitri too liked to stretch a point; but the results, at any rate, were plain to see.

Everything was so meaningless and agonizing. Now and then Count Dupi threw himself into an armchair and sat without moving for a long time, letting his hands hang over the arms of the chair like the statue of Lincoln. Then he resumed his monotonous strides. After a while he raised the telephone receiver again. One would have thought, from his expression, that he was summoning a physician. But it was Zia's apartment that he dialed. The prolonged rings at the other end of the line impinged upon the silence like dark wooden batons of uniform length marching in single file. Once more the number yielded no response. Count Dupi replaced the receiver with the gesture of a man who had abandoned all hope.

And now even the shepherdess looked up from her mushrooms and broke the silence, whispering something incomprehensible. Marie Antoinette said nothing, although she too stood there in a background of vaulted palace windows, her silks glittering in the peculiar twilight glow of copperplate. The queen said nothing, but her very silence was more eloquent than any words could have been when Count Dupi faltered for a moment in the course of his pacing.

His steps began again, but by now it was as if the weight of the body they had to bear was increasing minute upon minute. This time Count Dupi came to a halt before the open window, his widespread, upraised arms resting against the window-frames. He listened to the heavy, dark silence.

> It was a strange, strange summer even:
> An angry angel beat a drum in heaven.

He did not say the words aloud; the lines of the dead poet merely flowed down his memory, like cold perspiration on his forehead.

For a long time he stood by the window and clearly heard the angry angel's drumming in heaven. The hollow drumbeat was like the pounding of the gavel at an immense auction. "Corot's *Woman in Purple*...what am I bid?"..."A two-year-old thoroughbred filly from the Gere stud...what am I bid?"..."Photograph of King Charles, signed by his own hand...what am I bid?"..."Niece of André, the renowned aeronaut, with the merest physical blemish, for one night's use...what am I bid?"..."A rare edition of Dante, bound in human skin...Archduchess K.'s come-hither smile...Napoleon's billiard balls...what am I bid?" Rere was still standing outside the door, motionless and mute. He was listening to the gentle, uniform tread of his father's steps on the rag. Then, suddenly, he noted that these noises had come to an abrupt stop. He heard the scrape of a chair, and then the surrender of soft flesh as it seemed to collapse on the carpet. Then came a plaintive, gasping sound.

At that point he entered the salon. Count Dupi was outstretched on the carpeting, his face ashen-gray, and one of his hands was gripping the leg of an overturned chair. Rere ran to his side, raised his unconscious father in his gorilla-like arms and hastened toward the corridor. He stood at the foot of the stairs, cradling his burden, and began to emit long, drawn-out howls. At the sound of this strange bellowing the great brown oaken doors swung open on all sides, as if the heavy, sleep-laden eyelids of the slumbering palace were opening in fright. In a matter of moments the situation was clear to everyone. Bare-legged, pajama-clad shapes dashed upstairs and down, vaulting four or five steps at a time as if in flight. Bells began to ring, someone tripped over the telephone wires, lights went on in the courtyard and outside the gate; the whole household was awake by now, and the automobile growled in drowsy irritation as the chauffeur hurriedly started the motor. Meanwhile Rere cautiously descended the old pea-green carpeted stairs, still bearing the burden which he would relinquish to no one, which he himself placed in the waiting car. The long limousine roared into the night toward the sanatorium.

The news did not reach Countess Menti in the Glass House until the next morning, while she was presiding at a session of the Entertainment Committee. By early afternoon she was at her husband's bedside. The members of the family spent the following night in the sanatorium. János and Zia were not in Budapest.

The next morning the Reverend Lojzi administered extreme unction to Count Dupi. Countess Menti's poise wavered not for a single moment; with the utmost spiritual fortitude and practical circumspection she saw to it that everything was in place for the sacrament: the little table with its white cloth, the crucifix between two burning candles, the bowl of water for the Reverend Lojzi to wash his hands, the little spoon beside the bowl, saucers of salt, bread crumbs, and cotton to wipe the oil from the organs of the dying man. The Reverend Lojzi dipped a palm leaf in holy water and sprinkled the room.

"Pax huic domui et omnibus habitantibus in ea..."

He knelt in prayer, and then sprinkled the sickbed and Count Dupi with holy water:

"Asperges me Domini hissopo et mundabor...Anoint me, O Lord, with chrism and I shall be cleansed...In the name of Father and Son and Holy Spirit, I invoke the Blessed Angels, the Archangels, the Patriarchs, the Prophets, the Apostles, the Martyrs, the Confessors, the Virgins and all Saints to repel and cast out all powers of the ancient Enemy from thee. Amen."

There was a certain marked emphasis in the intonation of the Reverend Lojzi, as if he meant to console the dying man with the fact that the punctilio of precedence in rank and degree obtained in heaven too, in the strictly prescribed orders of Blessed Angels, Archangels, Patriarchs and the rest.

Count Dupi's eyes were fixed on the ceiling throughout the invocation, and then he suddenly exclaimed at the top of his powerful voice:

"Cavallerie!...Rechter Flügel!...Links um!"

He was obviously delirious. It is probable, too, that the nightmare of war brought these old Uhlan commands to his lips.

The Reverend Lojzi dutifully continued the administration of the sacrament. He anointed Count Dupi's eyes, ears, lips and hands with oil, in that order, in absolution of Count Dupi's every sin of sight, sound, smell, taste or touch. Finally he reached under the blanket and uncovered Count Dupi's feet.

"...through this anointing of thee and through its most pious mercy, be forgiven thy sins of trespass and carnal lust!"

Countess Menti's face turned a shade more rigid, if it were possible at that uttermost limit of rigidity, at the sound of these words.

The Reverend Lojzi's voice rose to exaltation:

"By authority of the Apostolic See, I now endow thee with the Apostolic Blessing which is an apprehension of final farewell. Dost thou rest content in the holy will of the Lord? However He judge thee, let His will be done."

Armchairs, covered in red, had been placed about a little table at the wider end of the semicircular corridor outside. They were for visitors. Prince Andrew, Count Lajos and others were already sitting there, about ten in all, most of them also at the brink of the grave. They leaned heavily on their canes as they stepped from their cars outside the sanatorium, coming to bid farewell to their oldest friend. But they were not permitted to enter the sickroom, through the door of which a white-coated physician had just stepped into the hall. As he passed by he answered the

714

query in their eyes with a wave of his hand, to indicate that the end was a matter of minutes.

Egry-Toth, Mr. Gruber, Mr. Badar, Herr Jordan and the One-Eyed Regent stood silently at the opposite end of the corridor, all of them filled with profound self-pity, for it was uncertain whether Count György would retain them in his service.

The assembled friends made their adieux to Count Dupi in subdued conversation. Prince Andrew, who had served with him in the Lebovice Uhlans, recalled the Officers' Reading Union, the wholesale purchase of the Lower Market Place in Lemberg, and the serenade to Fanny Nathanovics. Yes, that was all of fifty years ago. Was there another such cavalier, so munificent to the point of prodigality, so courteous, so charming, left in the world today?

Count Charles told how he and Dupi, at the invitation of the Emir, left for a hippopotamus hunt in 1902; Dupi traveled with sixteen large trunks. The Emir took fright, thinking that his guest intended to stay forever. The trunks were filled with costumes of every sort, and Dupi, as the Emir's yacht carried them up the Nile, donned a different costume each morning. He exhibited himself to the natives in the guise of a Hussar, a Magyar plainsman, a postman, a chieftain of the age of Arpád, a chimneysweep, and even as King Lear; nor did he fail to provide a demonstration of national dances.

They agreed that he had been the foremost steeplechaser in the Monarchy, and that the Prince of Wales himself must have envied Dupi's elegance in dress. They praised his lofty conservatism, and Prince Fini recalled that Dupi was extremely upset when women began to cut their hair short, for long hair afforded him the greatest sensual pleasure. One evening, when this newfangled fashion was the principal topic in the Casino, he had declared with the customary twinkle in his left eye: "I've found a way to get around those wenches. I had my barber make me a long-haired woman's wig, and nailed it to the bedpost" (in his secret bachelor flat, of course). "I turn out all the lights and clutch the wig with both hands when I'm with a woman. For all I care they can start shaving their heads…"

Count Joachim drew a veritable little character sketch of his cousin, dubbing him the model of a Magyar nobleman. Count Dupi had been loyal to his emperor, but his backbone yielded to no one. When the Swabians on the town council of the capital began to vie with each other in naming every square, bridge and hilltop of Budapest after the imperial pair, after archdukes and archduchesses, Dupi—as a youthful member of the Opposition in Parliament—proposed that the twenty-five square miles of sky above Budapest be named Franz Joseph Skyway. This was in the course of his first and last speech during his thirty-year incumbency in Parliament.

So they conversed, without realizing that they were taking leave not of a man but of an entire epoch.

A hospital attendant placed the early morning papers on the table before them. All at once the conversation ceased. The bald heads silently bent over the banner headlines.

The shrill cry of a newsboy was heard from the street:

"War breaks out!...Shooting starts in Poland!"

The dying man in the hospital room gazed at the door and asked in a weak but impatient voice:

"Still not here?"

Kristina answered softly:

"In a little while—any moment now."

Count Dupi closed his eyes, like someone reconciled not so much to death as to expectancy.

The door opened and Count János stepped in, black-booted, green-shirted. His father's blear eyes showed disappointment as the newcomer came into sight. Count János, who was not on speaking terms with a single member of the family, stood by the window with the expression of a material witness at a murder trial, convinced at least of his own innocence. But this did not detract from the fact that he had contributed materially to his father's illness.

Count Dupi cast his eyes around the members of his family as they gathered about his bed with solemn faces. He stretched out his hand and shook his fingers at each of them in turn as his voice finally recovered strength:

"There is no escape...there is no escape for any of you..." Eyes closed, he spoke with a somewhat melancholy malice. These were his last words.

When the door swung open anew and Zia rushed in with a convulsed face, he had only strength enough to stretch his hand toward her. Zia seized the hand and fell to her knees beside the bed. There was a faint little smile on Count Dupi's face when he died.

They all knelt. Countess Menti began to pray aloud:

"Vater unser..."

And the somewhat faded voice of Count János took up the prayer:

"Der Du bist im Himmel..."

Suddenly, unexpectedly, the voice of kneeling György Dukay, who had become the head of the Dukay family at that very moment, rumbled forth in a tone that was an incontrovertible order. He started the Lord's Prayer from the beginning, in Hungarian:

"Miatyânk Isten, ki vagy a mennyekben…"

Zia's high-pitched voice, choking with sobs, echoed him first, and then Kristina's, and then the voices of the rest of the kneeling company. Once again, at the deathbed of István Dukay, the spirit of Emperor Otto the Great and of an Ordony chieftain had met in conflict.

While the prayer proceeded, Rere traced mysterious letters on the floor with his forefinger. There was no way of knowing what was going on in his simple, indifferent mind.

From the Memoirs

The King continued to be delighted with the princess, who fully merited his affection by her extraordinary precociousness, her charm, intelligence, and response to his advances. He determined to lose no time after her twelfth birthday, which fell on 7 December, a Saturday, before celebrating the wedding. He let it be known that he would like the Court to be resplendent and himself ordered some fine clothes, although for years past he had dressed with the utmost simplicity. That was enough for everyone, excepting priests and lawyers, to disregard their purses, or even their rank. There was hot competition in splendour and originality, with scarcely enough gold and silver lace to go round and the merchants' booths emptied in a very few days; in a word, unbridled extravagance reigned throughout the Court and Paris, for crowds went to watch the great spectacle.[1] The thing was carried to such a pitch that the King regretted ever having made the suggestion, saying that he failed to understand how husbands could be so foolish as to ruin themselves for their wives' clothes, or, he might have added, for their own. But he had slackened the reins; there was no time to remedy matters, and I almost believe that he was glad of it, for he loved rich materials and ingenious craftsmanship, and greatly enjoyed seeing all the fine clothes, praising the most magnificent and the best contrived. He had made his little protest on principle, but was enchanted to find that no one had heeded him.

---

1. Versailles was open to the public on State occasions; anyone could attend the King's parties and eat his refreshments, provided he had a sword and a dress coat, or, if a woman, a court-dress. You left your sword with the officer at the top of the stairs.

This was not the last time that he so acted. He passionately loved to see every kind of splendour at his Court, especially on State occasions, and anyone who had listened to his protests would have found themselves sadly out of favour. Indeed, amidst so much folly there was no chance for prudence; many different costumes were needed, and Mme de Saint-Simon and I spent twenty thousand livres between us. There was a dearth of tailors and dressmakers to make up the fine garments. Mme la Duchesse took it into her head to send archers[2] to kidnap those working for the Duc de Rohan, but the King learned of it and was not pleased; he made her return them immediately. It is worth noting that the Duc de Rohan was a man whom he actively disliked and never scrupled to pretend otherwise. He did something else that was particularly chivalrous, and showed how much he wished everyone to be smart. He personally selected a design for some embroidery to give to the princess. The embroiderer said that he would put everything else on one side so as to finish it. The King would not allow that; he told him most explicitly to finish all that he had on hand, and only then work on his order, and he added that if it were not finished in time the princess would do without it.

It had been announced that the rejoicings should last until Christmas, but be restricted to two balls, one opera, and a display of fireworks, and there were no more balls during the rest of that winter. In order to save argument and quarrels the King reduced the ceremonial to the bare minimum, ruling that there should be no betrothal in his study but only in the chapel before the wedding, so as to avoid having royal train-bearers, for in the chapel her train would be carried as usual by the captain of her bodyguard. He also ruled that Mgr le Duc de Bourgogne alone should take her by the hand to lead her to and from the chapel, and that M. le Prince alone of all the princes should sign the curé's book. That, we concluded, was for the sake of the bastards, who might have felt humiliated at not signing, whereas the princes might have objected to their doing so. Mme de Verneuil was invited to the wedding and was given the lowest seat at the State banquet, as had happened at the marriages of the Ducs de Chartres and du Maine; but she was sent back to Paris immediately after. The Duchesse d'Angoulême, widow of Charles IX's bastard, was not asked because she did not rank as a princess.

2. Hoquetons: archers or yeomen. They wore smocks like workmen, and so, one supposes, would look as innocent as removal men, which in this case they were.

EXCERPT FROM...MEMOIRS OF DUC DE SAINT-SIMON

On the morning of Saturday, 7 December, the entire Court went early to the apartments of Mgr le Duc de Bourgogne and followed him to those of the princess. She was already dressed, attended by only a few of her ladies, most of whom were gone to the tribunes and stands erected for spectators in the chapel. The royal family had visited her earlier and were waiting in the King's study, where the bridal pair presented themselves shortly after noon. The King then led the way to the chapel. The procession and everything else was just as it had been for the marriage of the Duc de Chartres, except that Cardinal de Coislin officiated at the betrothal and everyone knelt between that service and the marriage.

It was on the whole rather a boring day. At seven in the evening the King and Queen of England arrived to supper; the queen was seated between the two kings. On leaving the table everyone went to put the bride to bed, men being rigidly excluded by order of the King. All the ladies remained, and the Queen of England gave her the nightgown, which was presented to her by the Duchesse du Lude. Mgr le Duc de Bourgogne undressed seated on a folding stool in the ante-room, attended by the King and all the princes. The King of England gave him the nightshirt, which was presented by the Duc de Beauvilliers.

As soon as Mme la Duchesse de Bourgogne was in bed Mgr le Duc de Bourgogne entered and climbed into bed on her right side in the presence of the King and the entire Court. The King and Queen of England then left, the King retired to his coucher, and everyone else left the room, except Monseigneur, the princess's ladies, the Duc de Beauvilliers who stayed beside his pupil, and the Duchesse du Lude who stood at the other side. Monseigneur remained chatting for a quarter of an hour, after which he told his son to get out of bed, ordering him to kiss the princess, despite the Duchesse du Lude's protests. It turned out that she had the right of it, for the King took it much amiss, saying that he would not have his grandson kiss so much as the tip of her little finger until it was time for them to live together as man and wife. Because of the cold Mgr le Duc de Bourgogne dressed again in the ante-room and then went to sleep in his own room as usual. That naughty little rogue the Duc de Berry thought his brother far too meek; he said that he never would have left her bed.

The Legendary Memoirs of Duc de Saint-Simon
Edited and translated by Lucy Norton

Memoirs of Duc de Saint-Simon 1691-1709: Presented to the King

*With a passionate eye for detail, brilliant character sketches and devastating wit,
Saint-Simon, a duke and a peer during the reign of the Sun King Louis XIV, paints
a dramatic portrait of his early years at the French court. Known for its treacherous
conspiracies, pompous rituals and ribald debauchery, it remains one of the most
famous royal courts in history. In Saint-Simon's first-hand account we meet the
legendary Sun King, his powerful mistresses and bastards, his decadent nephew –
and Saint-Simon's confidant – Duc d'Orléans, and a broad cast of characters
worthy of the most imaginative novels.*

Memoirs of Duc de Saint-Simon 1710-1715: The Bastards Triumphant

*The Sun King, Louis XIV is dying, and the French court is erupting in a frenzy
of twisted alliances and dark schemes in the struggle for power. As if we are
eavesdropping in the chambers and hallways of Versailles, eyewitness Saint-Simon
details the plots and counter plots, his own involvement, and his close relationships
with some of most fascinating and vividly sketched characters in history.*

Memoirs of Duc de Saint-Simon 1715-1723: Fatal Weakness

*Now that the King is dead, intrigue and espionage run rampant at a royal court
where indulgence and excess are the norm. Saint-Simon now has close ties to
the most powerful man in France, the Regent Duc d'Orléans, but he also has
enemies stronger than ever before. Both high drama and frivolous escapades reach
new heights as he takes us breathlessly into his final days at the French court,
and the conclusion of the Memoirs.*

1500Books.com